Esrahaddon

MICHAEL J. SULLIVAN

Limited edition cover design by Sarah Sullivan
Limited edition end sheet illustration by Marc Simonetti
Regular hardcover illustration by Marc Simonetti
Regular hardcover cover layout by Shawn T. King (STK • Kreations)

Limited edition: 978-1-943363-47-6
Regular hardcover: 978-1-943363-60-5

Published in the United States by Riyria Enterprises, LLC
Learn more about Michael's writings at michaelsullivan-author.com
To contact Michael, email him at michael@michael-j-sullivan.com

2 4 6 8 9 7 5 3 1

First Edition

Printed in China

RIYRIA
ENTERPRISES

This book is dedicated to Patrick Brunett and Cheryl Skynar.

To my knowledge, they are my only high school

friends who have read any of my published stories.

Works by Michael J. Sullivan

THE LEGENDS OF THE FIRST EMPIRE

Age of Myth • *Age of Swords* • *Age of War*

Age of Legend • *Age of Death* • *Age of Empyre*

THE RISE AND FALL TRILOGY

Nolyn • *Farilane* • *Esrahaddon*

THE RIYRIA CHRONICLES

The Crown Tower • *The Rose and the Thorn*

The Death of Dulgath • *The Disappearance of Winter's Daughter*

Drumindor (release date pending)

THE RIYRIA REVELATIONS

Theft of Swords (*The Crown Conspiracy* • *Avempartha*)

Rise of Empire (*Nyphron Rising* • *The Emerald Storm*)

Heir of Novron (*Wintertide* • *Percepliquis*)

STANDALONE NOVEL

Hollow World (Sci-fi Thriller)

SHORT STORIES IN ANTHOLOGIES

When Swords Fall Silent: "May Luck Be With You" (Riyria Chronicles)

Heroes Wanted: "The Ashmoore Affair" (Riyria Chronicles)

Blackguards: "Professional Integrity" (Riyria Chronicles)

Unfettered: "The Jester" (Riyria Chronicles)

Unbound: "The Game" (Fantasy: LitRPG)

Unfettered II: "Little Wren and the Big Forest" (Legends of the First Empire)

The End: Visions of the Apocalypse: "Burning Alexandria" (Dystopian Sci-fi)

Triumph Over Tragedy: "Traditions" (Fantasy: Tales from Elan)

The Fantasy Faction Anthology: "Autumn Mist" (Fantasy: Contemporary)

Help Fund My Robot Army: "Be Careful What You Wish For" (Fantasy)

STANDALONE SHORT STORIES

"Pile of Bones" (Fantasy: The Legends of the First Empire)

About the Book

A HERO TO SOME. A VILLAIN TO MANY. THE TRUTH FOREVER BURIED.

The man who became known as Esrahaddon is reported to have destroyed the world's greatest empire—but there are those who believe he saved it. Few individuals are as divisive, but all agree on three facts: He was exiled to the wilderness, hunted by a goblin priestess, and sentenced to death by a god—all before the age of eight. How he managed to survive and why people continued to fear his name a thousand years later has always been a mystery . . . until now.

From the three-time *New York Times* best-selling author Michael J. Sullivan, *Esrahaddon* is the final novel in The Rise and Fall trilogy. This latest set of stories sits snugly between the Legends of the First Empire books and the Riyria tales (Revelations and Chronicles). With this novel, Michael continues his tradition of unlikely heroes who must rise to the call when history knocks, demanding to be let in. This is the nineteenth full-length novel in a body of work that started in 2008 and spans four series.

Online version: bit.ly/3w9L6wP

ERIVANIA
ESTRAMNADON
UBER
MARN
Arkum
Gan
BARAN
ARCHIPELAGO
Green Sea
Strait of Hyphus
Shahabad
SaBar
Aoz Hilus
CALYNIA
ERBON FOREST
ROLANDUE
WESBADEN
URLINEUS
RaMar
Estee River
GUR EM
Dur Guron

Contents

Contents

Contents

Author's Note

After I published my first novel, *The Crown Conspiracy*, a critic wrote that my book was without merit and, in ten years, both it and I would be long forgotten. It has now been sixteen years, and by reading this, you're proving that fellow wrong.

Esrahaddon officially marks the publication of my twentieth novel. Such a thing naturally evokes a certain degree of nostalgia. Looking back reveals a pattern that managed to weave its way into my novels: the idea of the unlikely success story. In an era of artistic and cultural pessimism, my books are sometimes accused of being too optimistic. The common assertion is that life is misery, and great novels should reflect that reality, even if they are set in a fantasy world. The idea of Good triumphing over Evil has been relegated to a childish yesteryear of fairy tales. They say such a notion never existed in the past and certainly has no place in the future.

Except it has, and it still does.

I began writing stories around the age of twelve and had completed three full-length, typewritten novels by the time I was seventeen. Still, I never thought of being a writer because such an idea was beyond absurd. I didn't know the first thing about grammar, and my spelling was atrocious. While I didn't know much, I was pretty sure writers needed to master such things. So when I graduated from high school, I set my sights on becoming an illustrator. I won a scholarship, which paid for my first year at a prestigious art school: The Center for Creative Studies in Detroit. If not for the financial assistance, I wouldn't have attended college at all because of a lack of funds.

Like many Irish of the early twentieth century, my father worked at a steel mill. He also served in World War II. He died when I was nine, leaving behind four children and a wife whose only work experience had been filling in, Rosie the Riveter style, during the war. As a result, we lived on social security and veterans' benefits. This meant my clothes were a hodgepodge of hand-me-downs from cousins, as all our income went to food, housing, and utilities.

I wasn't good at much in school. I could draw and had a comic strip in the school newspaper, though I wasn't an official member of the paper's staff. I only had one creative writing course, the highlight of which was when the teacher picked my story to present to the class. She chose two other shorts that day, one written by another boy and the other by a girl named Megan. Having the girl selected was no surprise. She was the best in the class—likely the entire school—a bookworm who would achieve unexpected fame in her senior year as the high school musical star. The boy was an athletic sort, whose name I can't recall, and whose story was, not surprisingly, about sports. To my regret, I don't remember what Megan's story was about, but I found it to be well-written.

The assignment had been to create a short story of no more than three pages about a photograph that was shown to the class and then passed around. The picture was of a single flower—a daisy, I think. I felt my story was pathetic. Given such a limited prompt, I came up with an absurd concept. A boy who had lived his whole life in a bunker after some apocalyptic event is sent to the surface to look for signs of life. He wanders for a few hours through a hellscape until he stumbles upon the flower. Having no idea what it is, he plucks it from the ground and studies the daisy before discarding it and uttering the only line of dialogue: "Whatever you are, you have no place in such a brutal world."

I remember cringing as the teacher read my story. Afterward, I was surprised when no one laughed or made fun of it. They didn't applaud, either. After all, we were a class of sixteen- and seventeen-year-olds. But what did happen has stayed with me all these years. Megan, the leading wordsmith of my eleventh-grade creative writing class, looked flabbergasted and asked incredulously, "A boy wrote that?"

I took it as a compliment—my first ever.

After high school, one of my friends entered the US Air Force. The rest went to four-year colleges—paid for or subsidized by their parents. I worked as a dishwasher, then in a miserable job at a podiatrist's lab. The pay was the same, but "laboratory technician" sounded better. Few knew I was just pouring plaster into molds and standing for hours at a utility sink being splashed by frigid water while I shaped foot castings. When contemplating my future, I thought I *might* save enough money to afford a tiny mobile home where I would live alone, or if I were lucky, I might have a dog. Marriage wasn't in my cards because no one would want a guy who wasn't confident about his ability to support a pet. At the age of eighteen, I was ready to call it quits. My life consisted of working long, crushing hours at a terrible place, eating fast food, and never sleeping enough hours. Still, I was convinced this was the high point of my life. Things would only worsen as age brought aches, pains, and medical bills.

Then just like in a fantasy story—one I wrote, at least—everything changed.

I met someone, or perhaps it is more accurate to say I noticed someone I hadn't before. Nearly a year younger and still in high school, she was a waitress who sometimes played that new and somewhat infamous game, Dungeons & Dragons, at my house. I was drawn to her because her life was worse than mine. She was the daughter of two alcoholics in a broken marriage, with a mother who blamed her children for the breakup. Back when the mother suffered a nervous breakdown, this girl (who was only thirteen at that time) was left to care for her six-year-old sister. After the mother's discharge, more problems followed, such that the girl didn't want to go home. This was why, late one Saturday after a long night of D&D, I found this girl asleep on my mother's couch. Knowing her story and that she had no place else to go, I stayed up all night watching over her so that my mother didn't find her and demand explanations.

As the sun came up, so did her eyelids. She blinked a few times, staring at me. Then her face scrunched up in confusion. She looked at the sunlight creeping in through the windows. "Have you been there all night?" she whispered.

I nodded.

"Don't you have to go to work in a few hours?"

I nodded.

She stared at me for a long time as if my elaborate replies didn't make sense.

"Why?"

"I wanted you to get a good night's sleep."

Again the odd, long stare.

I didn't know it then, but that was the moment Robin Planck fell in love with me.

It was also the instant that the downward spiral of my life stopped and slowly began to go in the other direction. Robin suggested that I go to a community college. I honestly didn't think that was possible. Given that she was the valedictorian of her high school class, I knew she was more intelligent than I, so I took her advice. I didn't get much out of the education, but I was able to land a job as an illustrator for slightly more than minimum wage. Robin spent three years working full-time while simultaneously finishing her engineering degree. We both worked sixteen hours a day, seven days a week, and ate peanut butter and jelly sandwiches for lunch and meatless spaghetti for dinner. Sweaters and wrapping up in blankets were a necessity because we kept our thermostat so low that we blew on our hands when writing. But by doing all that, we managed to afford a house.

Once Robin graduated, we got married, and from that point on, every year has been better than the one before. Most of it wasn't easy. Neither of us benefited from a mentor, a supportive family, a wealthy relative, or a lottery win. No opportunities fell into our laps. Doors were usually closed, several locked, but one way or another we found our way in.

I'm not suggesting we had it harder than anyone else. After all, I am a straight, white, American male, so my basement is a roof for many others. Still, when comparing myself to everyone I knew, I suspected I was the least likely to succeed, especially at something as challenging as becoming a novelist. The idea wasn't realistic enough to even contemplate.

It was a fantasy. And yet here I am.

So for me, the idea of an unlikely character beating the odds and achieving the impossible isn't something that exists only in books. It's the story of my life: the tale of a young boy destined for failure, who, through the heroics of one woman and the generosity of a legion of readers, has achieved dreams heretofore unimagined.

Thank you for proving that critic wrong and supporting me for so many years. You've turned a fantasy into reality, and I hope I can return the favor.

Michael J. Sullivan
January 2023

Esrahaddon

BOOK THREE OF

The Rise and Fall

MICHAEL J. SULLIVAN

Prologue

PERCEPLIQUIS, FOUNDER'S DAY, SPRING, 2120 IR

As he rushed up the Grand Marchway toward the Imperial Palace, Esrahaddon prepared himself to kill. This process took far less time and effort than he was comfortable with. Literally about four seconds, or the amount of time required to take four quick steps. He'd killed before, but so many of those he was about to slaughter were innocent—some would even be children. The others, while not guiltless, had been corrupted by lies. In another place and time, he and they might have been friends. Oddly, what bothered Esrahaddon the most was not what he was about to do, but that he so readily accepted the undertaking.

It's always easier to destroy than to build.

This was about to be the worst day in the lives of so many people, the tragic end of the greatest era of mankind, which made Esrahaddon wonder why it was such a beautiful morning. That it happened to be Founder's Day was more than a little ironic. The holiday fell at the same time each year: mid-spring. People planned weddings or trips during the holiday because it was believed to have the best chance for good weather. Despite this, Esrahaddon had rarely seen a pleasant Founder's Day. Always too cold, too hot, or pouring down rain. But this day, of all days, the holiday weather was flawless. The sky was blue, the air warm, and the blossoming trees were at their peak. This would have been the best Founder's Day in recent memory. Instead, he was about to make it the most infamous in history.

Esrahaddon waded through the rivers of people pouring into Imperial Square. To his right stood the stone rotunda of the Cenzarium, and to his left was the more brutish columned façade of the Teshlor Guildhall. Before him, at the terminus of the boulevard, rose the great, golden-domed palace—the seat of the emperor of the world. Esrahaddon marched past the Ulurium Fountain, across the Memorial Green, to the very steps of the palace. Not a single imperial guard was on duty. No one noticed. Everyone was too busy celebrating.

That was part of the plan.

Entering the elegantly marbled hall, Esrahaddon was engulfed in the scent of incense that made him think of the umbra trees and abbra berries from the land of his birth—the smell singularly out of place here. The palace was a marvel: large, beautiful, and extremely well built. The building had stood for more than a thousand years, and the empire for twice as long.

But all that was about to end.

Two Teshlor Knights faced Esrahaddon as they stood guard before the magnificent golden doors. At his approach, each man reached for his sword. With a word, Esrahaddon commanded the doors to melt. The resulting wave of molten metal engulfed the two guards—their screams lost in the revelry of the city's celebration. An instant later, Esrahaddon walked over the solidified pool of gold where parts of two men protruded.

The reception hall and corridor—normally congested with dignitaries, diplomats, ambassadors, delegates, legates, envoys, emissaries, council ministers, aides, administrators, and servants—lay empty. In that silent vacuum, Esrahaddon's anger grew. The emperor was inside with his family. They would be hiding somewhere—down by the tomb, he imagined.

I'm done playing games.

Esrahaddon flexed his fingers. He was free to act at last, free to take his revenge, free to show everyone what he was truly capable of. All he needed was to find the emperor. Esrahaddon followed the corridor where he once more saw the murals etched into the polished stone like burnished details on glass. The images told a story, and Esrahaddon had seen them before, but this was the first time he recognized the man mysteriously repeated in each coronation picture.

He reached the throne room and found it empty.

Hearing a pounding noise echoing down the hallway, he headed that way.

More knights appeared in the corridor. Above them, a two-ton block of stone fell from the ceiling, killing the lot. With a flick of Esrahaddon's finger, the block blew apart. Stepping around the crushed knights, he reached the stairs and headed down. The pounding grew louder.

Deeper into the palace he went.

At the bottom of the stairs was a hallway that ended in a small, square room. The light of his robe revealed a vaulted ceiling, and at the center was a great statue of Novron. The walls were filled with cubbyholes, which themselves were stuffed with piles of rolled scrolls. On the far side was a stone door, closed tight.

Knights were busy pounding on the door, desperate to get in. At his approach, they turned and attacked. He opened the floor, letting it swallow them in a single bite. This left only the door. Esrahaddon had reached the Vault of Days. Inside, he could hear the emperor, his wife, and his daughter crying.

Esrahaddon placed a hand on the stone portal and shook his head.

How had it come to this? How had it gone so wrong?

Memories flooded him—a voice from the past. *"Killed his own mother . . . So vile, even a lion refused to eat him . . . Only a child but he's as evil as a new moon is dark . . . This is all your fault, boy."* This last one hurt the most, the words chilling.

Esrahaddon felt the cool stone against his palm as he pushed the door open.

"This is all your fault, boy."

PART ONE

Awful Things

YEAR 2100 IR

CHAPTER ONE

Tigerwolves

TWENTY YEARS EARLIER
IMPERIAL PROVINCE OF CALYNIA, SUMMER

"This is all your fault, boy," his father said, glaring down at him. Eleja was a big man by any standard, hard and fierce. His bare arms displayed lean muscle, while cracked hands adorned with callouses held tight to his hunting spear. To a seven-year-old boy, Eleja was a giant—an angry one.

Ezra said nothing.

Outside their little home, people sobbed as the sun set and the last light faded. The men had spent all day making more walls, trying to defend their tiny village. But even as young as Ezra was, he knew the bamboo and jungo leaf panels provided only the illusion of a barrier. Maybe that would be enough. After all, animals weren't smart. Ezra wasn't bright either, but even he could tell the village defenses would be useless.

The tigerwolves, the largest and meanest kind of hyena, began their high-pitched squeals and chuckling laughter as soon as the sun vanished and shadows flooded the valley. There were more of them that night, many more than before, and they were closer. The sounds scared Ezra. Animals shouldn't cackle.

Ezra, his aunt, and her two boys remained inside their mud-grass-and-stick house—ordered there by his father. To Ezra, their home, like the jungo-leaf barriers, provided only the perception of shelter. The door was nothing but a woven mat that rolled up with the pull of a string.

Animals might not be smart, he thought, *but they aren't stupid.*

Maybe some hyena were. They certainly looked dim-witted with their high shoulders and low-slung heads. But the striped ones, the tigerwolves, were cunning and vicious. And like dogs, they could dig. So if the mat door confused them, they could go under it or through the walls.

The home was cramped and smelled of smoke and tulan, which was drying among the rafters. Members of Haddon Village harvested and sold the red leaves in exchange for salt and fish oil at the seaside town of Shahabad. But this year the crop was thin. The wet season had been dry. Rivers became rock gullies and lakes little more than circles of cracked mud. Haddon had seen droughts before, or so Ezra had been told. The last one had been seven years ago—a few months after Ezra's birth. Animals came then, too. That time it had been a pride of lions. Some days nothing happened. As many as three nights would go by, and people talked about the terror being over. Then someone else would disappear. The cats were quiet and quick. Fifteen villagers were killed that year. Ezra's mother had been one of them—the last one.

Ezra had been with her. She was gathering abbra berries and rom nuts along the eaves of the forest. She didn't dare go in; everyone knew the Erbon Forest was a place of unspeakable horrors. Some had names, others did not. Only hunting parties went under the forest canopy, and those who ventured too deep never returned.

A narrow trail through an open field connected the village of Haddon to the port city of Shahabad. This path and the meadow they farmed were considered safe, and people didn't stray from them. Ezra's mother had carried him in a basket and set her new son down in a patch of dry grass. Then the lions attacked, and they tore her apart. Ezra couldn't remember the moment—not really. His recollections came from after-the-fact retellings by village elders who had found Monsara's shredded body. They said his blanket was drenched with her blood. The mystery that remained since that day—the one that had baffled everyone including Ezra—was why the starving lions had ignored a helpless baby. It made no sense for them to attack his mother when he was so easy to snatch. But even more curious was why the pride had left Monsara's body behind and had chosen that moment to leave Haddon Village for good. No one had answers, but many made guesses. Ezra's father was always vocal about his.

"This is all your fault, boy," his father said again, perhaps thinking Ezra hadn't heard him the first time, even though Ezra stood close enough to feel the spray of his spit. There was sweat, too. His father's skin glistened, and drips gathered, rolling over the hills and gullies of Eleja's wrinkled forehead before entering the forest of bushy brows that ran together, joining forces in their reproach of Ezra. "Did you call them?"

"What?" Tadesha asked, confused. Ezra's aunt had her arms around her two little boys, pulling them close as they huddled on the mat beside the pit. The three were rocking and praying to Novron for protection. "Who? The tigerwolves?"

The old man didn't answer. He continued to stare at Ezra, who shook his head. This did nothing to satisfy his father. "You're doing it again. I know you are. You brought lions to kill your mother and called the tigerwolves for the rest of us."

"The drought brought the animals," Tadesha said softly.

"And just like before, *Ezrrra* made the drought," Eleja declared, dragging out his son's name as if it were a lie that needed to be exposed to the light of day.

"No. I didn't," Ezra whispered.

"He's always been trouble," Eleja went on, talking to Tadesha or maybe to himself, possibly to Novron. Everyone else was speaking to the god that night, and his father was as faithful as they came. The family had little, but Eleja always found a coin to put into the wooden box at the church in Shahabad. "Not a bit like Kedea, Nocea, Jaomo, and Ado."

"He's seven."

"All *my* sons are strong, tall, brave, and fit." Eleja waved his left hand out and up in a violent motion. "This one is sickly and weak. He picks at his food, stays in the house, and draws pictures on the walls instead of learning to fight and hunt."

"He's seven," she repeated, but without much conviction.

"That may be, but he *is not* my son. He's . . . he's *something else.*"

This wasn't the first time Ezra had heard this. Eleja often told the other men of the village that his wife had been unfaithful. He proclaimed her death was Novron's punishment for her betrayal. But maybe this was the first time Tadesha had heard it, or perhaps she simply didn't like him speaking ill of her dead sister.

"You're crazy," Tadesha said, her voice rising. "What are you accusing Monsara of? My sister was a good woman! And Ezra isn't *something else*, he's just a boy. What do you think he is?"

"The forest is full of Awful Things. And if the village suffers, it's all *his* fault."

Tadesha straightened herself. She was a bony woman with a skull-like face dominated by sunken eyes and yellow teeth. Everyone said she was so devoted to her deceased husband, Blar, that she refused to take another man after he died. But Ezra thought Tadesha was alone because no other man wanted her. People said that Blar was old and no great prize, but it was also said that Tadesha had been lucky to have him—luckier still that he gave her a pair of sons before passing.

With a final, hateful glare, Ezra's father left the house, dragging the butt of his spear and leaving a line in the dirt beside a set of bare footprints that led away—footprints Ezra knew he could never fill.

When Ezra turned back, Tadesha was hugging his cousins, Jaydan and Nomax, so tightly that they winced. She stared at Ezra with cold eyes. She *had* been supporting her sister's memory, not defending her nephew.

Maybe she agrees with Father. What is she seeing when she looks at me? And who am I if I'm not Eleja's son?

The attack came later that night.

Ezra had managed to fall asleep on his mat beside the big water urn. The woven carpet of grass that had belonged to his mother was thin and frayed. It had an ugly, rusty zigzag pattern that didn't quite line up, a stain that smelled of dung and sweat, and a corner that constantly threatened to unravel. The mat was also his most beloved and cherished possession—the only connection to the one person who had loved him.

His other two treasures were a clay cup and a colorful feather. The misshapen mug had been cast aside because a chip and a crack made it leak. Ezra had found the feather about a year ago near the big rock. Almost a foot long, the plume was bright yellow and blue, and Ezra thought it had to be the most beautiful thing ever. He'd never seen a bird with feathers such as that. Imagining that it must be magnificent, he'd tried drawing the bird on the walls of his house, guessing at its wondrous shape. Ezra hoped someone might see the drawing and say, "Oh, that's a *something-something* bird," giving him the chance to ask questions and learn where he might catch sight of one. That never happened. He considered showing the feather around and inquiring about it, but he was afraid someone would steal it, or—and he felt this to be the worst possibility—that they would know exactly what kind of bird it came from and claim it was nothing special. He feared this because the feather *was* extraordinary. Too beautiful to be of the village, it had to come from someplace else, someplace better: a softer world of brilliant colors, where things with such magnificent plumage could fly. Ezra often imagined that the feather had been left just for him. that the bird had dropped it in his path as a sign, or perhaps a message. What the bird was trying to tell him was a mystery, something for Ezra to figure out. He kept the plume under his inherited mat, taking it out only when he was alone. Looking at it made him grin, and because of that power, he knew it was magic.

That was the other reason he kept the feather hidden. Magic was evil. Ezra's father and Novron, the Son of Maribor, had said so. Any magic—even reading—was forbidden. Once, a Monk of Maribor had come to their village. Everyone was happy to see him until they noticed he carried books. The elders sent him on his way, calling him a sorcerer of Uberlin. A goat was slaughtered that night and every building painted with its blood to purify the village. For weeks afterward, conversations centered on the evils of the outside world and how fortunate they were to live in such a blessed place as Haddon.

If a Monk of Maribor is cast out for having books, what would the elders do to a boy hiding a magic feather? Not to mention a boy who had killed his own mother. Or was it Novron who killed her as punishment? He would never dare ask, but he guessed his father would say both were true. That was the way with Eleja.

Ezra couldn't tell if it was the screams or the growls that woke him. The sounds were similar. The throaty snarl of a striped tigerwolf was much like a man groaning out in anguish. Such a noise was a terrible thing to wake up to, and Ezra's eyes snapped open. Most of the cries came from outside where a big fire had been built, but one scream issued from across the room. This wasn't the growl of a tigerwolf; it came from Aunt Tadesha.

Her prayers to Novron had not worked. Ezra watched as his aunt was jerked by her foot. Using a series of violent tugs, a huge tigerwolf with wild eyes hauled his aunt toward the doorway. She screamed and kicked at the beast with her free foot while she clawed the floor, scratching shallow lines in the packed dirt as out the door she went.

The tigerwolf didn't have the slightest trouble getting past the mat on the string.

Cowering, abandoned by both Novron and their mother, Ezra's cousins cried. Ezra did, too. The night was filled with screaming—screaming, crying, growling . . . and laughing. But only the animals laughed.

Ezra's brothers weren't there. Older and armed with spears, they would be fighting. His sisters weren't around, either. They both had men now, and that night they were with their new families. With Tadesha gone, Ezra was alone with the wailing Jaydan and Nomax.

Shut up! he screamed in his head. *You're just asking for—*

Another tigerwolf entered. It ducked its dog-like head under the door's woven mat, lifting it up to look inside. One of its eyes was blind and milky. Its ears were big, like a bat. And all around its face, its fur was soaked with blood that dripped from long chin hairs that created a deep-red beard.

Is that Aunt Tadesha on its face?

Framed in the firelight, creeping in slowly, the beast kept its head low, shoulders high, tail tucked.

It's not an animal at all. This is one of those Awful Things that Father said the forest was full of.

The blind, milky eye looked at the screaming cousins, and the animal showed its teeth.

"No!" Ezra shouted.

The monster's head turned, and its good eye found him.

Ezra felt under the mat and drew forth the feather. He pointed it at the animal. The plume was long and drooped lazily—quivering. "Stay away!"

With labored wet breaths that smelled of rotting meat, the beast took a step toward Ezra. Then it crouched, growled, and finally cackled.

Terrified and expecting to die, all Ezra wanted was for it to stop laughing—for all of them to stop making that noise.

Another tigerwolf entered the house, then another.

They all laughed.

Ezra continued to point his feather but closed his eyes. "*Stop it!*" he screamed. "*Stop it! Stop it!*"

The laughing ended, and the tearing began.

Ezra woke on his back in the center of the village with the sun on his face. He wasn't alone. A circle of men surrounded him. All the elders were there. So was his father.

"See?" Eleja said, pointing down at him. "What did I tell you?"

The others nodded with serious expressions.

"Not a scratch," Kenja said. He was the Chief Elder, the biggest and oldest, and on his shoulders was the drape of the leopard skin that went by the name of the Great Oska.

The men stood shoulder to shoulder in a ring, and above them was the blue sky and a high sun that told Ezra he had been sleeping a good while.

"What happened?" he asked.

They ignored him.

A fire was burning somewhere—a big one. Ezra could hear snapping and crackling. He heard crying, too, but that was faint and muffled. Inside a house, perhaps. In the gaps between the fence of men's legs, all he was able to see was smoke.

"What do we do?" Ashah, the Second Elder, asked while holding his spear in two hands.

When Kenja hesitated, Ezra's father spoke up. "He must be killed."

Who? Ezra thought. *Me? Why?*

"He's just a boy," Kenja said.

"He is not," Eleja declared. "He's a demon spawn. That's why trouble always comes—he draws it, causes it! He's the reason for the drought that saw fifteen of us die. And now this." His father shook his head in disgust. "So vile, even a lion refused to eat him. Only a child, but he's as evil as a new moon is dark."

Several of the elders nodded at this.

It is *me. I'm the one. My father wants me dead.*

"What happened?" Ezra asked again, more earnestly this time, but once more they acted as if they couldn't hear.

"We cannot kill him," Kenja said. "It is dangerous. We all saw that."

"Should have listened to me. Should have killed him while he slept," Eleja said. His lips were wet, his teeth showing, and he breathed as if he'd been running, but there was no sweat on him.

"Wouldn't have mattered," Kenja proclaimed. "The lions didn't kill him. The hyena couldn't, either. There must be a reason for that. He is protected. Trying to harm him would only bring wrath."

"Novron will protect us."

"If Novron wants this boy dead, then he can do it." Kenja clapped his hands. "We shall banish him. Give him to the forest."

"A child cannot hope to survive in the Erbon—" Ashah said.

"Not a child," Eleja said, "a demon spawn. We need to—"

"Novron will decide," Kenja declared, and he clapped his hands once more in judgment. He faced Ashah. "Or do you suggest that our Lord, the Son of Maribor, cannot protect an innocent child, should he so wish?"

"He's not innocent." Eleja spoke with such frustration he spat with the effort.

"And are *you* saying Novron cannot kill a child—spawn of a demon or not—should it be his will?" Kenja asked.

Eleja panted and sputtered but said nothing more.

"What happened?" Ezra asked a third time, pleading for them to answer.

"How say you?" Kenja asked the elders, and each in turn nodded in agreement.

Ashah pulled Ezra to his feet. "Food and water?" he asked Kenja.

"Novron will provide, should it be his will," Kenja said. Then for the first time, he addressed Ezra. "You will leave Haddon and never come back. If you do, we will try to kill you."

Without another word, the circle of men dispersed, and Ezra could see what was left of the village. Most of the homes were gone, flattened as if by a mighty wind. The feeble walls the men had spent all day building were blown outward. One was high in a tree at the edge of the clearing. The watchtowers were toppled, the stones of the well scattered, baskets and pottery flung in all directions. And everywhere, there were bodies. Some were villagers—Ezra spotted Tadesha, her throat ripped out—but most were the striped carcasses of tigerwolves. There might have been as many as fifty, but it was difficult to say. They appeared to have been torn apart.

The only building unaffected was Ezra's home.

Not a scratch.

"Go," Kenja ordered, and pointed at the forest. "Leave, and never come back."

All the survivors of the village stared at him, Jaydan and Nomax among them. His cousins looked at Ezra in horror.

What did they see? What happened?

Ezra had nothing. His feather and cup were lost, and they were sending him away without even his mother's mat. All he had left was a single drape of plain cloth tied with a string. The garment measured less than his height in length, yet it was long enough to wrap twice around his waist and once between his legs. Seven years and three full moons old, and Ezra would be alone for the first time.

He cried all the way across the field, past the big rock where he had found the feather, and up to the start of the forest where the great umbra trees held hands with stalks of jungo plants. The greenery created an intimidating barrier that separated the world Ezra knew from oblivion.

No one went into the forest except the bravest of men, who hunted in groups of twenty, each armed with spears. Even they ventured there only to slay a single kapa, the long-nosed pig the villagers roasted on each of the four Feast Days. The great Erbon Forest was no friend to the people of Haddon. It was the Other, the place in which all terrible things lived.

Two men, Kenja's sons, had followed him. Tall, lean, and as stern as their father, the pair climbed atop the rock and watched as Ezra reached the eaves of the forest. They stared at him without a line of kindness on their faces.

"Why?" he half-shouted, half-cried, nose running. His hands squeezed into fists. His body shook.

One of Kenja's sons pointed firmly at the trees. The other folded his arms tight across his chest.

Ezra hitched a breath, lips quivering, eyes blurred. Turning, he looked at the shadow-line that divided the sunny brittle grasses and dusty patches of the field that had always been his home from the darkness of the unknown forest canopy. Ezra had never once been inside. Where he stood was as close as he had ever come, and that was with his mother—the day she died. He didn't know the exact spot. Many had told him, but they each mentioned different places. It didn't matter. Everyone agreed she had died at the eaves, and that's where he now stood.

He looked back again, and once more received the adamant point and the folded arms.

Sobbing so hard that the stream of tears ran unchecked down his neck and chest, Ezra bowed his head in resignation and stepped into the forest, into the darkness of shadow, into the Realm of Awful Things.

CHAPTER TWO

The Forest

Ezra pushed past the massive jungo leaves, many of which were just as tall and decidedly broader than himself. He dodged around the kala plants with their poisonous pink flowers. Deeper and deeper he went until Ezra was fully behind the curtain, under the leafy blanket—gone from his world and into the Other.

Up close, the trees were massive. The stately umbras had smooth gray bark and appeared like old women—curvy and decidedly wider at the base than higher up. Some, perhaps the older ones, had bark that peeled back, revealing a pale underside. Other trees had bodies that seemed made up of hundreds of other trunks all woven together. These were the eske trees that looked like stretched dough or torn flesh, and Ezra had always thought of them as gruesome. Nothing here was familiar, nothing safe, nothing pleasant. Looking back, he could no longer see Kenja's sons, or the rock, or the field.

What had happened? The question remained unanswered.

Something bad, he was certain, and something *he* did, or they wouldn't have cast him out. Ezra was guilty of a crime so terrible that even a child could not be forgiven.

But what was it? Perhaps it is so bad they don't want to speak about it.

Ezra couldn't recall anything that happened after the tigerwolves entered the house. He had pointed the feather, closed his eyes, and cried. That was all.

I must have fainted.

Women did that sometimes. Men did, too, if it was hot and they were out too long in the sun. But such a thing was shameful. Men weren't supposed to faint, or cry, or draw pretty birds on the walls. But no one had ever been exiled to the forest for fainting.

"He's seven," Ezra's aunt had said, but age didn't matter to his father. Men were big, brave, strong, and they always knew what to do. Ezra was small, weak, cowardly, and ignorant of everything. *I can't be his son. How could I be?* That was why they sent him to the forest. *I belong here, not in such a wholesome place as Haddon. I'm one of the Awful Things.*

He knew it was true as soon as the thought landed. *I should never have been born. I deserve to die, and now I will.*

He waited.

Tigerwolves would be on him soon. They would drag him away by his feet. Or perhaps the lions that had killed his mother and given him nightmares all his life would leap out of the shadows. *How much would it hurt to be torn apart?* Ezra closed his eyes, held his breath, and cringed in expectation, but all he heard was the rustle of leaves in the wind. He fell to his knees, placed his face in his hands, and sobbed. He cried until his stomach hurt. At any minute, his death would come, so he waited. Then he waited some more, and then some more.

After a good deal of time, Ezra grew bored. He looked up and stared at the underside of the trees. Big and solid as stone, still they swayed. A leaf came free and spiraled down, hitting the forest floor only a foot away. It landed without a sound. But there were plenty of noises. Now that Ezra had stopped crying, he heard them—birds mostly. They tweeted, cawed, and whistled. Insects droned, and frogs peeped. Some creatures made sounds Ezra couldn't identify—chirps and plunks and chuckles. Something tapped repeatedly on wood, making an eerie echo. Then he heard a whooping sound, which he concluded must be a monkey. The forest was surprisingly loud, as if an angry argument were underway and everyone shouted at once. Even the trees creaked.

Out of the din came music—beautiful and serene, as if someone were playing a flute. But it wasn't an instrument, it was a bird. Looking up, he saw it high in the trees, and its long tail feathers were a brilliant yellow and blue. Ezra held his breath as he stared. The bird was perched on a high branch on one of the ladylike umbra trees and caught in a shaft of sunlight. It was beyond anything Ezra could have imagined, as it was unlike any bird he'd ever seen. Not only was it yellow and blue, but also orange, green, and black. It had normal-looking wings, but its tail feathers—each a perfect match to the one he'd treasured for nearly a year—were twice its body length. Still, the bird had yet another set of feathers that draped down from its back to well past its feet, gratuitous plumage that served no obvious purpose other than to look amazing. Ezra thought the bird wore these extra feathers like Kenja wore the Great Oska.

"You're in the forest?" Ezra asked the bird, shocked. "You're in the Realm of Awful Things?" The Erbon was certainly a different world, which agreed with his belief that the bird was not of the village and yet . . . "But you're not an Awful Thing—you can't be. You're beautiful."

The bird flashed out gorgeous wings and flew deeper into the trees.

"Wait!" Ezra shouted, jumped to his feet, and ran after it.

He might have only been seven, but forests seemed made for someone his size. He moved swiftly, leaping logs and ducking under branches as he chased the bird. Stopping to catch his breath, he lost sight of it. Then the melody started again, that music similar to songs played after meals—except that his uncle was an amateur compared to the Magnificent Bird. Ezra crept toward it and was rewarded with another view of those brilliant feathers, now higher in the canopy. The bird took flight once more, and the chase began anew. This went on until finally Ezra collapsed. Panting and looking around, he had lost all trace of the bird. He waited, trying not to breathe so he could hear better. But the song and the bird were gone.

By then, Ezra was deep in the forest. He no longer had any idea which way Haddon lay.

I can't go back now even if they let me. I'm lost.

Ezra once more recalled his fate, the impending doom that the bird had only briefly distracted him from. With it, the sadness, guilt, and fear returned. He thought he might cry again, but just then, he realized he was thirsty. The running had done it. But he had no water, and he would find none. The drought that had driven away the herd animals and caused the tigerwolves to feed on the villagers was still raging. Even the well had been desperately low. Ezra recalled how Aunt Tadesha had complained that the gourds always came up half full.

If the animals can't find water, what chance have I?

A gentle breeze blew through, and one of the plants he sat beside brushed his face. He swept it away.

Perhaps I ought to travel downhill. Water is more likely to be found the lower I go. Isn't it?

Another breeze, and the broad green leaf slapped him again. Ezra pushed back, snapping the plant stem. He hadn't meant to. It was only that Ezra was trying to think, and the leaf—

Out of the broken stem a drop of liquid appeared. Touching it, Ezra brought his finger to his tongue. *Water.* Bending over, he sucked on the snapped stalk. He got a little more, but only a little. Then Ezra stood up and looked around. He was standing in a patch of green plants—lots of them. Jungos, spikers, even some abbra berry bushes. And there were many more he didn't know—forest flowers, shrubs, and ground cover. Ezra had worked long hours in the village gardens, carrying water from the well to give to the stunted vegetables, and they had never looked so lush as this. All the grasses in the field around the village were burnt and yellowed, and many patches had returned to dirt. But here everything was enormous and flourishing.

Here wasn't a big place. The patch of lush plants extended only a few feet around him. *Smaller than my house,* he thought, then reminded himself, *not my house anymore.*

Ezra got up. As young as he was, even he knew plants didn't grow without water, and they sure wouldn't get this big and green without a lot of it. He couldn't remember the last time it had rained. Uncle Hebus—the amateur flutist—was fond of saying, "There's a time for everything." He even had a song about it, though Ezra only remembered one line: *Green grows the abbra berry, early in the year; summer is the time of plenty; winter's nearly here.* The time for rain wasn't late summer. That was the time for broiling heat, dead grass, and fighting to keep the olla pots filled. But those things were true in a normal year, and this wasn't one of those. Even in spring, Ezra couldn't keep the clay pots, which seeped water to the vegetable roots, filled. There had even been talk about what to do if the well went completely dry. But here . . .

Ezra pushed back the plants, sticking his head into the bushes and searching for their secret. He found none, but where his hands touched the dirt, it was cool.

Digging with bare fingers, he found moisture. Puzzled, Ezra frowned at his dirty hands. That's when he heard the drums.

Haddon had one that was hauled out and beaten at each funeral. Ezra guessed he was hearing the start of the ceremony that would bury Aunt Tadesha and whoever else had died the night before. But this sound did not come from Haddon's funeral ceremony. For one thing, he heard more than one. For another, the funeral drum was a tall instrument made of hardwood, like a giant chalice with goatskin stretched over the top. Slapping it made a high, hollow ring unless you hit the center. Then it would make a lower tone, but nothing so deep as what Ezra was hearing as he stood in that little patch of green.

His second guess was thunder, but thunder heralded rain, and rain no longer made visits to Haddon. While Ezra was now in another world, he didn't think it so far, nor he so fortunate, as to be in a place that had rain. Also, the sound didn't come from overhead but off to his left, in the direction the Magnificent Bird had flown. Ezra officially gave it this name, assuming the authority based on his growing belief that he alone had ever seen it, and that they were both of the same universe—both members of the Realm of Awful Things.

If it wasn't the funeral drum of Haddon, Ezra was at a loss as to what it was. His entire understanding of everything ended at the forest eaves. Being in a new world, it might be anything. Still, Ezra was scared. Loud, deep, hollow sounds were frightening. They suggested something big and dangerous that had no fear of being heard.

The forest is full of Awful Things.

Ezra gave up trying to solve the mystery of the green patch and searched for a place to hide. He considered climbing a tree, but the umbras were too smooth to scale, and there were no nearby eskes to scramble up. The other ones, those with branches he could reach, were too small to help.

Boom, boom, boom.

Was it louder? Closer?

Ezra found a large rock that an umbra tree clutched with its roots. Part of the rock was tilted up, as if the tree had been working to lift it. Smaller rocks—or likely broken portions of the big one—lay beneath, creating a tiny gap. Not quite a cave, it was better than the open forest. Being small, Ezra was able to squeeze in, and he found the crevice was deeper than he had first thought. Delighted, he pressed himself down, twisting into what he believed was a cleft. Ezra discovered his mistake when he fell, or maybe not so much fell as slid. While the trip down wasn't far, it was enough to leave him in the dark. He was under the rock, beneath the tree, and for the moment, he was happy. Pleased to be where it was cool, glad to be hidden. *Whatever is making that sound won't find me in here, and even if it does, it can't get me. Nothing making that big of a noise could fit.*

Ezra lay on moist dirt, staring through the opening at the muted forest light—waiting. The drumbeats were muffled, made softer by his refuge. The pounding could be anything. Might not be drums at all.

What if they were footfalls of some monstrous beast, like a giant or a dragon?

Uncle Hebus had all sorts of stories about the forest: songs about spiders, lizards, lights, and talking trees. None ever had happy endings.

Ezra listened to the drums pound, which he no longer thought were coming closer. On the other hand, they weren't getting farther away, either. The pounding beat continued unaltered, and what had been frightening slipped into an almost comforting constant. Ezra was back to waiting for death, and in addition to being thirsty, he realized he was also tired—a strange sort of exhaustion—despite having slept late that morning. Lying on his stomach with his cheek pressed to the cool ground and his mind focusing on the regular, rolling rhythm that played like thunder, he discovered the weariness taking priority. It made no sense, but who knew if sense was allowed in the forest. And in between one beat and the next, Ezra fell asleep.

Plunk, plunk, plink. Ezra could hear the drums, but they sounded strange. Less throaty, higher pitched, the beats came with greater pauses in between. The bird was in the tree, looking back at him over its shoulder as if it was showing off those stunning tail feathers and that extra plumage that draped it like a wonderful robe.

"This way," it told him, and its voice was music. "She's waiting for you."

Ezra opened his eyes, but everything was dark. Lying on moist dirt, he was chilled. Looking up, he could see the exit from the hole. But it was night, so he couldn't see much else. The outside was a shade lighter than in the hole, but that was it. Something tiny crawled over his stomach, and Ezra shivered. Sitting up, he frantically brushed himself off, then pulled his knees tight to his chest, hugging them. Remembering everything, he felt like crying once more but wondered if he had the tears. Back in the village, water had been limited to only a few cups a day, and Ezra hadn't had any since he'd left—except for the little tease he got from the plants.

Maybe if I chewed on them?

The drums had stopped, but there was another regular sound. This one didn't come from outside. This came from deeper in. *Plink, plink, plunk.*

Water? Perhaps I ought to travel downhill. The thought revisited him.

The problem instantly presented itself: darkness. Ezra couldn't see anything except the pale exit framed by the silhouettes of stone and tree roots. *If I go down, I'll lose that. I got lost in the forest. What happens if I get lost down here?* This very sensible argument was countered by the far more obvious, *what is there to lose?* The debate was destroyed by overwhelming thirst and the tantalizing dripping sound coming from somewhere below.

Not too far, he thought. *I'll still be able to get out—I think.*

Down he slid, feeling his way with his toes, guided by his ears that homed in on the regular *plink, plink, plunk.* Soon he lost sight of the exit. A small panic gripped him as he realized he wasn't at all certain how he might find it again. *Maybe in daylight it will be easier? Best to spend the night down here anyway.* Predators roamed in the dark. Tigers would be on the move—jaguars, wolves, and snakes, too. The constrictors were known to eat even the big cats. A hole seemed a good place to be, but if so many Awful Things were outside, who knew what was down there?

Worse things? The thoughts played in Ezra's head unheeded as his feet and ears listened only to his thirst. The route was down. This was all he knew, and the trip was made entirely on his back with legs outstretched, reaching for understanding like the antennae of a bug. The only serious concern that impacted his desire for a drink was the very real possibility of a drop. This worried Ezra; it didn't stop him. He was supposed to die anyway—unless the Lord Novron saw fit to reach out a hand and do something. But if his own father had called for his death, what hope had he of some distant god caring?

Ezra did not fall off a cliff. The descent deeper into the cave was a smooth one, and soon the sound of the dripping water was so close Ezra found his heart racing in anticipation. Didn't matter if it was brackish, muddy, or tasted of metal, Ezra was going to drink until he exploded. That had been his plan. Then he saw the light.

Below, and a little bit beneath a short ledge, Ezra saw a blue-green glow. It provided a welcome visual understanding to everything he had previously known only by way of toe-tips and heels. He saw a stone chamber that looked enough like the mouth of a monster—complete with upper and lower teeth—to worry him. But in the place where the tongue ought to be, a blue pool glowed. The illumination was less than what was produced by half a moon on a cloudy night, but after the absolute darkness, it might as well have been the sun. With its assistance, Ezra made quick work of slithering down the last bit of the descent until he was near the water's edge. The cavern pool was so still that what Ezra had thought to be lower teeth rising from the floor were actually the reflections of the ceiling. *Plinks* and *plunks* came from smaller puddles in the same chamber, each beneath ceiling-teeth that dripped. But their pools didn't glow. The light came only from the large, still pool—from something below the surface.

Lying on his stomach, Ezra put his face to the water and sniffed. It had no odor, nothing bad, at least. Putting his lips to the liquid, he sucked and drank. The water was cold, clean, and wonderful. He swallowed several mouthfuls, more than was ever allowed in Haddon. He felt gluttonous, greedy, and decadent but couldn't care less.

I'm an Awful Thing, after all. It's what we do.

Then Ezra stopped. Something wasn't right. The water was fine, and nothing had changed except that the clear surface of the pool was blurred from the ripples he had created. No, it was something else. Then without knowing how, he realized he wasn't alone.

Ezra pushed up on his arms and peered around the cavern. Spotting three figures, his eyes went wide. The trio sat less than fifty feet away, watching him. They weren't from the village of Haddon, nor could they have come from Shahabad. They did not appear to be human.

All were distinctly different from one another: different colors, sizes, clothes, and expressions. They shared only three common features: long pointed ears, a general lack of hair, and rather startling dark vertical pupils set in yellow eyes that glowed faintly in the dark.

He watched them, and they stared back. No one said a word.

Ezra fixated on the yellow eyes. He'd seen them before. Some lizards had eyes like that—the big ones with long toothy snouts that lurked just below the surface of the lagoon in Shahabad. But mostly they reminded him of cats . . . of *lions.*

Not knowing what else to do, Ezra greeted them with a wave and a hopeful smile. "Hello?" he offered, as friendly as he could.

The three glanced at one another then back at him with what Ezra guessed to be an expression somewhere between confusion and amusement. The smallest was quite obviously blue—not a bright or uniform hue but a dark and uneven color. He had clever eyes, a tiny nose, and tall ears that pointed at the ceiling, and each lobe was decorated with a trio of brass rings. The biggest figure was green and looked downright mottled, with his arms a murky myrtle color, his neck a sea green, and his ears a light lime. He was also the hairiest. No hair grew on the crown of his head, but there was plenty of it on the ends of his ears and quite a lot above his eyes, making the most remarkable brows. The last figure was pale gray with brown blemishes, making him appear three days dead. He had a terrible scar down the side of his face, three deep cuts—one tracking above his eye, two below—that looked to have come from a large claw. His ears flopped down, showing a pink underside.

The three sat in a circle around a cache of assorted bags. Two were made of dark leather, others of canvas, and a few of soft cloth. Some were open, and what looked to be food lay spread on the floor.

The blue one peered hard at him and asked, "Who are you?" His voice was quick, sharp, high, and nasal.

"I'm Ezra."

"Ezra?" The three looked at one another.

He nodded. "Eleja's son, from Haddon Village." He pointed vaguely over his shoulder. Then with a concerned grimace, he asked, "Is this *your* water?"

All three looked at the pool, appearing puzzled. "Whaddya mean?"

"I'm sorry if I was stealing."

"Stealing? It's a pool of wadder," the pale one said. His voice was soft, but he suffered a speech defect because his lower jaw stuck out farther than his upper. "What do we care?"

"In Haddon, you're not allowed to just drink water. You're only allowed a little each day." Ezra held up a hand, his fingers slightly apart, indicating something small. "I get half a cup in the morning, a full one at midday, and another half cup at night, but that's all."

The blue one grunted—Ezra had no idea what that meant—then waved his hand at the pool, and as he did, Ezra noticed he had nails on the ends of his fingers that were surprisingly long. "Drink all you want. We don't care."

Ezra grinned, and bending back down, he sucked up another few mouthfuls, delighting in the cold, clean taste. Coming up for a breath, he said, "Your water is much better than ours."

"It's not *our* water."

"Oh?" Ezra said. "Whose is it?"

"It's just water."

"But you live here."

All three shook their heads, which caused the blue one's earrings to jingle.

"How about you, Ezra of Haddon?" the blue one asked. "You don't live here, either, obviously. So, what's your story? What brings you down into the bowels of Elan?"

"Hiding." Ezra dropped to his stomach again and took a second indulgent drink.

"From what?"

"I don't know." He slurped and swallowed again. "I heard pounding—drums, maybe."

"Oh. That'd be the Krun Ba Ran. You know about them?"

Ezra shook his head, and wiping his chin with his hands, turned over and sat up to face the three. This time he noticed how unusual their clothes were. Like the bags, they came in different materials and colors. The blue one dressed in a lightweight, black cloth shirt and loose leggings as simple as Ezra's own, and had a necklace of large, sharp teeth. The pale one wore heavier cloth, with a leather belt. He was barefoot. The big one wore a thick leather tunic and skirt with black metal studs and buckles. He also had leather boots, and on either side of his broad belt, he wore a pair of long, curved blades.

"The Krun Ba Ran is what your kind call goblins," the blue one said.

"Are they dangerous?"

He nodded, and his earrings jingled again. "Rumor has it they're known to eat young fish like you."

"But I'm not a fish. I'm a boy."

"That's just a figure of speech."

"A what?"

"Never mind."

"Can they get down here?" Ezra glanced back toward the way he'd come in.

The blue one looked at the other two. No one answered.

"You're from da village, den?" the pale one asked. "What you doing out here so far from home and so late at night?"

"They sent me out."

"To do what?"

Ezra thought about this for a long while, then shrugged and said, "To die, I guess."

This caught the attention of the big one, who until that moment had been preoccupied with searching for something in one of the leather bags. Now he looked up. "Why?" His voice was low, deep, and suspicious.

"I dunno," Ezra admitted.

"What happened?"

"I dunno," he repeated. "They just told me to leave, and that if I ever came back, they would kill me."

"Seriously?" the pale one asked.

"That's brutal," the green one said, twitching his bushy, black eyebrows, which fluttered like dragonfly wings.

"Nice home you have," the blue one sneered. "Or had. No clue why they banished you?"

Ezra shrugged again. "I think it had something to do with the tigerwolves. They attacked last night."

"Umm, yes, we heard them." The big one closed the bag he'd been rummaging through. Then he stood up and walked a couple of steps away where Ezra noticed rolled-up blankets. He also observed how the big one hunched over as he shuffled forward, his arms long and his hands . . . his hands were, they were . . . "The striped hyena make a racket, for sure. All their food done run off, so they figured they'd eat you, I suppose." He raised his voice to cover the distance, and it echoed across the cavern.

"Men fought them off?" the blue one asked.

Ezra was still staring at the big one's hands, trying to understand what he was seeing. "A few, I think. The rest . . ." Ezra hesitated. "I don't really know what happened. I was in the house, and three came in. One had a milky eye and looked like he was gonna attack Jaydan and Nomax, so I pointed a feather their way and told them to stop."

"You pointed a feather at a trio of striped hyena and told them to stop?" the blue one asked.

Ezra nodded as he continued studying the big one's hands that didn't look like hands at all.

"Did they?"

Ezra shrugged. "Next thing I knew, I woke up outside, surrounded by the elders, who told me to leave."

This brought a round of furrowed brows, which was a thing to see on the big one's face.

"What happened to da tigerwolves?" the pale one asked.

"Some were killed by the men with spears, I suppose. A couple, at least."

"And the rest?" the big one asked, his hands making a clicking sound.

Ezra remembered the village, the smoke and the blown-down houses. "They . . . they looked . . . they were torn apart, I think. Ripped to pieces so that I couldn't tell how many there were."

Ripped to pieces—yes. Ezra realized what he was seeing at the end of the big one's arms . . . claws—massive, powerful talons that he was clicking together, making a loud sound that echoed in the stony chamber.

"Also," Ezra went on, "the houses in the village and the watchtowers, and walls. They were all blown down—except mine."

All three stared. Then they exchanged nervous glances. They licked lips, rubbed chins, and scratched bald heads. No one spoke for a long time. Eventually, the blue one asked, "Still got that feather, do you?"

CHAPTER THREE

Goblins

The three had offered Ezra some of their food—flatbread with a berry preserve spread on it. They watched him eat. The big one left for a bit. He walked in the direction Ezra had entered, then returned after just a few minutes. He never said anything, but when he came back, he looked at the other two and shook his head.

"Is your faffer named Ezra, too?" the pale one asked.

"Don't be an idiot," the blue one said.

"What? Sometimes day do dat—name offspring after parents."

"He already told us his father's name is Eleja. That's right, isn't it?"

Ezra nodded as he chewed.

"Oh," said the pale one. "Sorry."

"Is there anyone else at your village named Ez-ARE-ah?" He spoke the word with a slow precision. "Someone older?"

Ezra shook his head. "Just me."

The blue one sat back, resting against a bag of canvas held closed with leather straps—two of which looked to be the sort to go over the shoulders. He glared at Ezra with a frustrated frown, like the boy was a jammed door or a knot in a string.

"Who are you?" Ezra asked. "I've never seen—"

"Us? What'd you mean, who are us?" the blue one replied as if the question was ridiculous.

Confused at the rebuff to what Ezra thought to be such a simple, normal question, he shrugged. "What are your names?"

"Oh, ah . . . I'm Niblick. Clawed-face here is Dank," he said, hooking a thumb at the pale one. "And the big guy is Mashie. Probably could have guessed that though, right? How's the bread? Like it?"

Ezra nodded, and not out of politeness. The bread was spongy-soft, with just the right number of brown spots where it had stuck to the inside of the oven wall. And they had given him a whole sheet, and plenty of berry spread.

"Great, that's great. This village of yours probably doesn't feed you either, right?"

Ezra opened his mouth to reply, but Niblick went on talking. "Look, ah . . . maybe this will sound strange, maybe it won't. But were you, ah . . . I don't know, expecting a package?"

"A what? A package?"

"Yeah, you know, a delivery, a gift, or maybe payment for something or other. I'm just asking if you were expecting to receive something—something unusual, something from far away?"

Ezra shook his head.

"No, of course not. That's ridiculous. You're just a kid, aren't you?"

"A kid who blew up a village and ripped apart more than a score of striped hyena," Mashie said, his voice a low growl. Of the three, Mashie was the most disturbing. The claws had a lot to do with that, but his tone—and the way he wore a judgmental frown as if it were his favorite outfit—helped as well.

Ezra stopped chewing. "What do you mean I—"

"You think *that's* strange?" Niblick asked his fellows. "I'm still wrestling with why a clan of tigerwolves would attack a village to begin with. That's not normal, right? There's a drought, sure. Their usual prey migrated, looking for greener grass. Fine, I get that. But why didn't they follow the herds? Why stick around and make a suicide attack on a village of healthy humans? Hyena are scavengers, aren't they?"

Mashie shook his head. "Some are, but the big striped tigerwolves? They kill most of their food."

"Okay, but have you ever heard of them attacking a village?"

"Not so much, no. Tigerwolves are not the bravest hunters," Mashie acknowledged, "but desperation is a strong incentive, and it's not a big village."

Niblick didn't look convinced. "Okay, ah . . . Ezra, the three of us are, ah . . . going over there a little way to talk a bit. You stay here and eat. Have as much as you like. Enjoy yourself. You look like a starved rabbit, so go ahead and feel free to gorge yourself to death. It's fine."

Getting up, he waved for the others to follow, and all three walked across the cavern, away from the pool. The light barely reached them as they stood like ghostly figures facing one another in a little clutch. Ezra took the invitation to grab up another piece of the flatbread and more of the berry preserves.

"What do we do now?" the pale one asked. "We gonna take him back?"

Ezra wasn't looking, but it was impossible to mistake the owner of that muddled voice. Dank's question was faint, but in the profound silence of a cavern that turned droplets striking pools into resounding retorts, he could hear them surprisingly well despite their distance. He wouldn't have guessed it and didn't think they had, either.

"It's not supposed to be a kid," Niblick's fast-talking, nasal voice replied. "It isn't, right? She would have told us if it was. Why didn't she tell us?"

"Maybe she didn't know."

"Probably doesn't know a lot of things. But a kid? A *human* kid? It doesn't make sense. Look at him. He's all soft and . . . I don't know—*new*. It can't be him. Gotta be someone else. Ezra could be a common name around here, for gripe's sake. How do we know?"

Niblick had his arms folded and was tapping his foot, making a dull, slapping sound. Dank appeared like a turtle trying to retreat into its shell, and Mashie stood in his same stooped manner, his arms at his side and those big claws dangling.

"Ever seen hyena attack a village like they did last night? It's strange, is what I'm saying, right?"

"This is Krun," Mashie said. "Lots of strange things here."

"What's in da package?" Dank asked.

"I don't know," Niblick replied. "Why you asking me? How am I supposed to know?"

"You was wiff her from da start. She talks to you."

"Not that much. Not about *it*."

"But you've seen it?"

"Sure, it's small. You know, like this big." Niblick held out his hands, but Ezra couldn't see because Mashie stood in the way. "And light—real light—even though she's got it wrapped in heavy canvas."

"You touched it?" Mashie asked.

"Sure, I picked it up. It was on the ground and in the way, so I grabbed it to, you know, move it aside. She threw a fit. Ripped it out of my hands. Told me never to touch it again. Since then, she's never let the freaking thing out of her sight. Sleeps on it."

"Would you tell us if you knew what it was?" Mashie asked.

"Suppose that depends on what it is, but probably not."

"Why not?"

"Because both of you are idiots."

Ezra finished the bread and sat back, dusting his hands off. His movement caught their attention.

"Dink he can hear us?" Dank asked.

"He's human," Niblick said. "Got human ears. Can't hear his own heart beating. Wouldn't even be able to see us if it weren't for the lichen in the pool. And he's a kid, for gripe's sake. What are we supposed to do with a kid? This is nuts—downright *walnuts*."

"So we're taking him wid us, right?" Dank asked.

"No other choice," Niblick said. "Do you see another choice? I'm looking around, and I'm not seeing other options here. This is riddlebag ridiculous. No, what am I saying? It's beyond that. It's a mingle-mangled mess—a gallimaufry of errors."

"I'll hold him while you two truss him up," Mashie said. "He's little. Shouldn't be a problem."

"Ah . . . big guy, do I need to remind you about the feather?"

Mashie thought for a moment, then cast a look over his shoulder at Ezra. "I don't see no feather. Kid didn't have one when we found him. I don't think he—"

"Mashie, in the name of freaking Uberlin." Niblick shook his head, and even at that distance, Ezra heard the earrings. "When I said you were an idiot, I didn't know you were stupid, too. It's not the feather. Kid just thinks it is. Here, try this. Take a deep breath, hold it, and concentrate real hard. If this is *the* Ezra, he's not gonna be just some normal human kid. There's something scary-special going on here, follow? So grabbing him might not be the wisest course of action, get me?"

"What do you suggest? You got a better idea, smart guy?"

"I don't know, maybe. Granted, I'm just pulling this one off the top of my head, but how 'bout we—I'm thinking—*ask him?* Invite him to come? You know, like normal people."

"We're not normal people."

"Sure, sure, but he don't know that. Look at him. He's sittin' there eating our food, having a grand old time. Anyone else would have screamed and run away the moment they saw my face or heard your claws clack. This kid ain't innocent—he's oblivious. Besides, what else has he got to do? Doesn't sound like he has a full schedule to keep, does it? What exactly are his options? He's exiled. His people kicked him out with a death-on-return guarantee. And he's an infant. If the desperate hyena don't eat him, the lions or jaguars will. Even if they don't, the kid don't know nothing about surviving in the forest—he'll starve, or poison himself, or maybe your relatives will catch wind of his scent and put him in a cage to be the main course at the next Feast of Uberlin."

"Ankors arc not all alike," Mashie said, "and you'd be wise to remember that."

"But you do eat humans, right? Especially the young ones? You like the soft meat."

"You shouldn't judge what you don't know."

"So we're asking him to come back wiff us?" Dank asked.

"Sure, why not?" Niblick said. "We'll bring him back, and maybe she'll let us see what's in the package, or at least learn something about this mingle-mangled mess. How in Phyre did I get involved in this crap? That's what I want to know, that's all."

"Day put a price on your head," Dank said.

"Thanks, Dank. Thanks for that reminder. I knew we had you around for a reason. Just couldn't come up with it."

"Is dat why you're doing dis?" Dank asked. "To find out what da package is? You dink it might be valuable?"

"No, you poor excuse for a Klune moron, I think Rex Nexziria sent Hekkabah across the Green Sea all the way from Arkum to this remote village on the frontier of Krun to deliver a worthless bundle of manure."

"Why would he—"

"Never mind. You're both idiots—did I mention that? I think I did."

The three broke their clutch and returned to Ezra, Niblick in the lead.

"So look, here's the deal, kid," Niblick addressed him. "You come with us, see? And ah . . . we'll . . . we'll watch out for you—you know? Ah . . . take care of you, feed you, keep you from gettin' eaten, that sort of thing. Okay?"

"Okay," Ezra replied. He had already decided to accept the offer before they asked. Niblick was right; what choice did he have? Going with them was better than dying, and now, having heard their discussion, he was curious. *Who is this Hekkabah? What is the package? What does she want with me?* But more than anything, these three had reacted as if they knew what had happened in the village.

"A kid who blew up a village and ripped apart more than a score of striped hyena."

"It's not the feather. Kid just thinks it is."

Maybe if he went with them, he would find out. Besides, so far, these three strange people had treated him better than anyone in his entire life, except for his mother. They had given him good food and let him drink his fill—so much so that he was feeling a little sick.

Ezra also knew that if he said no, they'd take him anyway. And he'd rather not be *trussed up.*

"Where are we going?" he asked.

"Not far," Dank said. "Just a few miles norff down to da beach—well, it's more of a cove, really. Nice place. It's where my family live—and where she is."

"Who?'

"Hekkabah."

"Who's that?"

"You'll find out," Niblick jumped in. "She has a present for you—or so she says. Let's gather up and get going while it's still dark."

"You don't want to wait for morning?" Ezra asked.

They all looked at him as if he were a talking donkey.

Ezra nearly tripped on a sizable branch that the others apparently saw but failed to warn him about as they plunged through the foliage, following no visible path. Mashie was in the lead, nearly invisible, blending in with the greenery. Niblick walked beside Ezra, and Dank was behind them—a following gray ghost.

Ezra was surprised by how much he could see in the forest at night. He had expected to be blind but discovered he could discern the outlines of trees, branches, even the ground—all of it revealed in silvery moonlight that gave a sense but no details, perception without depth. Yet understanding was there. He knew to step around rocks and over branches that he couldn't recall having seen. Maybe he was noticing more than he thought, or just good at guessing. Previously, devastated by confusion and without clues, he had been overwhelmed. Nothing had made sense. And while little of that mystery he called *yesterday* had been solved, he now found a *kind of* footing in a *pseudo-world* with *sort-of* friends. Not being alone changed everything for the better, despite not knowing if his new companions planned to help or ultimately eat him. At least he had a direction that led somewhere other than the grave—or rather, he hoped so.

They're goblins. The idea had fluttered around the edges of Ezra's mind since the moment they met. It kept pushing in; he kept pushing back. Ezra didn't want them to be goblins. He wanted them to be strange-looking folk from another village. Odd fellows perhaps, but that could be expected from distant neighbors. They couldn't be goblins; they spoke the same language he did. *Goblins couldn't do that . . . could they?* The claws made that a hard sell. Mashie's green skin added to the struggle.

Goblins were evil, which made sense, as they were the "spawn of Uberlin"—the *god* of evil. That's what his father called them. Uberlin and the goblins were the ones that had killed Novron the Great, the savior of mankind, his father's personal hero, and the most revered of all things in Haddon. The village had four feast days, all of them revolving around the First Emperor: his birthday, which took place conveniently on the same date the sun was reborn; the spring festival of Founder's Day, the holiday commemorating the establishment of the capital city of Percepliquis; Coronation Day, marking the end of the Great War with the elves and the moment Novron was crowned emperor; and finally, The Day of Sorrow, which was not a holiday at all, but a remembrance of Novron's death. Given that Novron died on Founder's Day, the Day of Sorrow was always observed on the day before as a memorial of fasting before the feast of Founder's Day. Novron was the absolute, the constant, the one true thing that could not be disputed. He was their god, and everyone in Haddon prayed to him.

Even at seven, Ezra had found that curious. Ezra imagined that gods were immortal and couldn't die, but this one had. When Ezra asked, he was told that Novron's dying was exactly what made Novron so special. Ezra didn't feel that explained anything, but he also didn't want a beating. Too much curiosity was considered a hallmark of trouble. Knowledge was a curse.

"Education befuddles the mind and confuses the heart," his father had explained on several occasions. The last time, he had clarified the explanation with a leather strap. Ezra didn't grasp the idea any better, but he had learned to stop asking questions, and maybe that was the true lesson.

Since Novron's death, the imperial legions—the army of the emperor—fought goblins daily. That's what Uncle Hebus had said. He used a flute rather than a belt, which was why Ezra had turned to him for answers. Although his uncle's stories and songs were great fun, they never burdened themselves with anything resembling understandable explanations.

Ezra had never seen a goblin or an imperial soldier, but then he hadn't been anywhere other than the field around the village and the port city of Shahabad, where the big boats bobbed. These were apparently places that neither the army of the emperor nor forces of darkness visited. Still, goblins were supposed to be green, wicked-looking clawed creatures that lived in the forest and ate people. Odds were good these were them, and running off with three goblins seemed foolish, but so did running off without them. Oddly, Ezra realized that he had chosen to join the trio in the same fashion he'd decided to step around and avoid tripping on a branch he never saw. In that instant and for a fleeting moment, he felt he'd touched on something profoundly important. And then it was gone.

A bright light appeared and vanished off in the trees to their left.

"What's that?" Ezra asked.

"Huh? Oh. I dunno," Niblick replied.

"A glow bug," Mashie said. "Haven't you ever seen a glow bug before?"

"I've seen fireflies in our field, but that one was huge and bright blue."

"Yeah, glow bugs are a little bigger, I guess. Don't ever follow them, though. They fly toward muck bogs. Get in there, you never gonna come out. Sucks you right down."

"Nice," Niblick said. "You'll find, ah . . . Mashie is full of uplifting tidbits like that. The guy is a wizard of forest lore—all of it scary as daylight in a snowstorm."

"What's a snowstorm?" Mashie asked.

"White stuff that falls from the sky—frozen rain. Stuff collects on the ground, blankets everything in bright white. Sun hits it, and you're blind as a Guron cave fish."

"What's a Guron cave fish?" Ezra and Mashie both asked.

"It's a fish—doesn't have eyes. You two don't get out much, do you?"

They continued pushing through massive leaves, scrambling up fallen logs the size of roads. Ezra saw another light, this one white, stationary, and solid. Coming closer, he realized it was a flower. Huge and bell-shaped, it bent under its own weight, the long tongue-like petals glowing with a white radiance. Several of the flowers blossomed on a vine that spiraled up the trunk of an umbra tree, as if decorating it for a party.

"Amazing," Ezra said.

Mashie paused and glanced at the blossoms. "Don't touch them. They're poisonous. Got a liquid—a resin on 'em. If you get it on your fingers and touch your eyes, or mouth, or both, within an hour you're blind and choking on your own vomit."

"Uh-huh." Niblick's earrings jingled. "See? What'd I tell ya? Guy's a walking marvel of nightmarish trivia."

"Rather I didn't tell ya?"

"Not saying that, just fascinated by your wonderful home. I love a place where death is everywhere you look, and even some places you don't. I tell ya, I am absolutely terrified every time I need to take a piss. Can't do it. Takes me an hour to conclude business. I'm always sure I'll be eaten by a giant snake or the ground will just freaking swallow me, you know?"

"You're not from here?" Ezra asked.

"Are you kidding? No. I hate this place. All these trees and plants—and have you seen the bugs? I nearly died when I saw my first spider. Thing's the size of a dog, and not a cute little mutt either, but a full-sized hound, you know? They got these webs the size of a ship's sail. Well, I thought to myself, what's a thing like that eat, you know, birds? I figured it had to be birds—crows and vultures and crap like that—but no. They eat bugs. Can you believe it? Got mosquitoes the size of hawks here. And I don't even wanna talk about the caterpillars with a billion legs and pincers the size of one of Mashie's claws, or beetles that can cut the trunks of small trees with their mouths. And noisy! For gripe's sake, all night long there's this racket, this chittering and chattering like everything out there is eating everything else. And in the daytime, same thing, only the birds join in with their whistling and chirping. But you heard that yourself, right? It's all walnuts, I tell ya."

While Niblick was speaking, Ezra had noticed movement in the trees to their right. Large dark figures appeared and disappeared in the shadows that were everywhere in the forest. "There's something out there. Something big. More than one, I think."

"You're just seeing 'em now?" Niblick said and made a hiss. "Humans—how do you survive?"

Mashie led them around a huge eske tree and, without turning, said, "Lions."

"Lions?" Ezra said, startled. He stopped walking and stared out into the darkness that he realized was everywhere.

"What's wrong?" Dank asked, coming up from behind.

"Dunno," Niblick said, staring at him, puzzled. "Kid's got a problem with lions, I guess. What's wrong, kid?"

"Lions killed my mother. I was with her. I was a baby."

"Oh, okay." Niblick nodded, jangling again. "Sure. I can see that. But ah . . . don't worry. They're not gonna bother us. We've got Mashie."

Ezra looked hopeful. "Is he a lion-hunter?"

"Huh? No. He stinks."

"What?"

"Seriously, the animals of the Erbon hate the smell of the Ankor Ba Ran. They ain't gonna come anywhere near us."

"Why are they following, then?"

Niblick glanced off to the side. He pulled down a huge jungo leaf to get a better look, then shrugged. "Why they following, Mashie?"

"They could be really hungry and smell the kid. Starvation makes them take dangerous chances. But most likely, they're looking for an easier meal than us." The big guy slashed a broad-leaf bush with his claws, cutting it in half and granting them access ahead. "Lions are just as happy scavenging our leftovers as hunting their own. They follow the Ran like dogs follow humans, hoping for bones."

"What's a Ran?"

"You never heard of the Ran, kid?" Niblick put his hands on his hips. "They keep you buried in a hole in this village of yours, do they? I'm only asking 'cause from what you told us so far, it sounds like something they'd do."

"What are they?" Ezra asked again.

Mashie was starting to leave them behind. Niblick smiled and swept his hands forward in a grand invitation for Ezra to go ahead. "Probably best to keep up with the smelly one if'n you don't want the lions to eat you."

Armed with understanding, Ezra was able to make out the silhouettes of big cats creeping through the trees alongside. He trotted to catch up to Mashie.

"It's people," Niblick said, when they caught up and slowed down. "That's what the *Ran* is. The three of us are technically all Krun Ba Ran—*Western Sea People,* on account of we all come from the same general branch of our collective family tree that crossed the ocean after everything went to crap and sank under the sea. But that don't mean much, 'cause all the tribes are different. Mashie is from the Ankor Clan of the Gur Em Ba Ran. That's why he's so big and scary."

"What's *Gur Em* mean?"

"This." He pointed up and around. "A godforsaken jungle. That's what his people call home."

"*This* is the Erbon Forest, not the Gur Em," Mashie said. "The Gur Em is farther to the east, where the mountains rise sharp and high in the mists. The Erbon is nothing like the Gur Em."

"Whatever. It's all the same thing to me."

Mashie made a sound that might have been laughter, or a clearing of his throat. "Not if you think the spiders here are scary."

"Moving on . . . Dank is a Klune. His folks live along the coasts and rivers in these cute little cottages they build on stilts right out on the water. They're fishers mostly—and that's also a stink you can't get off. But unlike Mashie's, *that* particular perfume can attract cats and pigs and flies and every other cursed irritant on the face of Elan. Honestly, every nuisance in the world loves the smell of old fish. Why? No idea. Walnuts, that's what I say."

"What about you?"

Niblick grinned. "I'm Urgvarian Ba Ran," he said with pride. "We're the real deal, the true Ba Ran. We got saltwater flowing in our veins. Our ceiling is decorated with stars, and we fly free with the wind and the waves. So you see, different tribes, same people. The word *Ran* in the old language really just means *people.* So technically, you're Ran, too. You're *Human* Ran, I suppose. But for all practical purposes Ran means folks like us."

"You said the Krun Ba Ran were goblins."

"That's what your kind calls our kind. I don't think they mean it charitably. That's sort of a nasty word, so you might want to keep to yourself. Technically, if you want to put a fine point on it, we prefer *Uber* Ran—Great Ones—that's what we used to be called before we broke apart and went our different ways. It's all the old language. The sort Dromeians still remember. That's where your kind gets a lot of the old terms. You probably know them as Dherg, or dwarfs, but over the years they've muddled a lot of it. The Arkum Ba Ran are the only ones who still use it. They never crossed the sea. They're still in the Old Country—or what's left of it—the *pure ones.*"

"Pure ones," Mashie scoffed.

"Being Krun Ba Ran, Mashie is an advocate for the New World Order. Isn't that right, Mashie? He likes his dog-spiders and murderous flowers. He also likes that our rex is on the other side of the Green Sea."

"Rex?" Ezra asked.

"King, monarch, chief, whatever. A long time ago, it's said, my kind ruled the world. We had an empire and a great city. I dunno. It's probably just a load of crap, but that's the story. Then came the war, and now that great city is under the sea. There's this big crater where it used to be. Musta been one heck of a war, I tell you. It wiped out almost everything. A whole section of the world blew apart and sank under the ocean. All that's left now are the tops of the mountains that make up a bunch of scrawny islands. That's where Arkum is—the last city of the Old World."

"Wasn't the war did that," Mashie said. "The rivas destroyed it."

"Careful, my friend. Say that in mixed company, and you'll—"

"They did."

"Everyone knows that, Mashie, but no one *says* it. At least no one who wants to continue to enjoy the luxury of breathing . . . through their noses and mouths, I mean."

"What's a riva?" Ezra asked.

"For gripe's sake, kid, you're nothing but a bottomless pit of questions, aren't you?"

No one spoke for a few minutes as they continued through the dark of half-seen trees, leaves, and following lions.

"What is it?" Ezra asked again. "What's a riva?"

Niblick rubbed his chin and said, "Just about the scariest thing still in the world."

To this, Dank and even Mashie nodded.

"There were, ah . . . five originally, only two left. And yeah, Mashie's right. They say the rivas tried to destroy the world. Some say they failed because not all of them showed up for the fare-thee-well-and-kiss-my-ass-goodbye extravaganza.

Obviously, Elan is still here, but they took out a sizable chunk. They were the ones who blew up the Old World and sent us all swimming into the sunset. Fun group of guys, let me tell you. I'm guessing one of the reasons Mashie prefers this side of the Green Sea is because our ruler—Rex Nexziria, who resides on the other side—is one of the two remaining rivas." Niblick grinned at Ezra, then shook his head, rattling his earrings. "And here I bet you thought the whole world was that little cow manure village of yours—the one that don't feed or water you. If you manage to beat the odds and live . . . boy, are you in for a surprise."

"Are you going to eat me?" Ezra hadn't planned on saying it; the words just came out. Niblick, Mashie, and Dank all paused to look at him. Then for the first time, he saw them laugh together. Not surprisingly, Niblick was the loudest—his was a high-pitched cackle. "Waves rolling, kid, you sure are something."

"You said Mashie's people eat young fish like me."

"Wow"—Niblick's ears rose a bit—"you really listen, don't you? Smarter than you look. Brave, too." He called to the others, "Starting to think we might have got the right one here." Niblick smiled at Ezra, his ears drooping a little. "Naw, kid, we ain't gonna eat you. Not gonna lie, though. There are some Ba Ran that do. Some of them even eat our own kind. Those are real *goblins*. But we're not them. We're civilized. I mean that. Seriously, ours is the oldest civilization there is. We started everything, according to the Arkums. Of course, few believe them. Hard to do that when you're out here in—"

Mashie held up a claw and clicked his talons. Niblick and Dank froze. Ezra took an additional step and looked over in confusion. "What—"

Niblick stopped him with a stern stare and a slashing motion across his neck. Then they all waited. The three Ba Ran watched the trees like they might get up and move, and not in a good way.

Lions! Ezra thought and felt a panic rise. *They're coming!*

Peering out, however, he saw that the lions were gone.

Then without any sound that Ezra heard, faces emerged out of thick brush on either side—Ba Ran faces. Ezra felt he was an expert on the subject, having spent most of the night with three. Now he was surrounded by a dozen or more. All looked like Mashie—big and muscular, with rows of sharp teeth and long arms ending in massive claws that they began clacking loudly. They pressed in on all sides.

"What are you doing, Mashie?" a low voice asked. It belonged to a particularly big Ba Ran who squared off with their guide.

"What's it to you, *mackerel?*"

The Ba Ran facing off with Mashie scowled and pushed out his chest, appearing to grow taller. "I am Klon Vex."

"Klon, eh? Whose Klon are you, Vex?"

"There's a rumor you're escorting an Arkum. Where is she?"

"None of your concern."

"What is she doing here?"

"Also, none of your business."

Klon Vex spotted Ezra. "You have a human child with you."

"What?" Mashie spun. "Well, will ya look at that. Musta snuck up on all of us."

Vex glared at Mashie. "What are you doing with him?"

"What's it to you?"

Once more Vex squared off with Mashie. "This is my territory."

"This is imperial territory," Mashie said, "which makes me wonder just who you're serving, *Klon*. Can't be Ghazel Da Ran Zar Bar; you're too far from Aoz Hilus. So who is your master?"

"Where is this Arkum female?"

"My business. Understand? Ain't got nothing to do with you. So, nice to see ya—have a great day—so long."

Klon Vex looked angry, and this did nothing to improve the Ba Ran's demeanor. He raised a claw.

Mashie clapped it with his own, holding it firm. "I know you want to make a big impression on the members of your new school, but I spent thirty-four years in the combat rings in Gur Em, proper five-on-five combat. I faced eight teams, and I was the only survivor. I also know most of these you got with you, and they know me. You wanna fight, it's just gonna be the two of us. I'm okay with that; the question is, are you?"

He let go of Vex, who bared his own impossible collection of jagged teeth.

Niblick, who had been uncharacteristically quiet until that moment, spoke up. "You can tell the Ghazel Da Ran, or whoever you're reporting to, that Hekkabah Zar, daughter of Geth and Zanna, is a priestess from the Temple of Uberlin in Arkum. She's the real deal, a genuine Rona Zar, and she was sent by Rex Nexziria himself. So if your boss has a problem with her, tell him to take it up with the riva."

Vex's foaming anger vanished. His puffed-up posture deflated, and when he spoke, his voice was smaller, too. "What does she want here?"

"Him." Niblick pointed at Ezra. "Apparently."

"A human child? What does she want with that?"

"Let me tell you, your guess is as good as ours on that one. Our job is just to find and fetch. We don't ask questions—not of a High Priestess of Arkum Temple; that's for sure."

"Who are you?" Vex asked.

"Who, me?" Niblick looked around as if it might be someone else, then shrugged. "I'm nobody. Just one of a million Urgvarian sailors, Your Resplendentness."

"What did you call me?" Vex's shoulders rose again.

"Relax, it's a compliment. Now if you don't mind, the night's not getting any darker, and I'm sure we both got places to be before the sun raises its ugly face."

This appeared to settle the matter, though Mashie and Vex continued to glare at each other for a time before breaking off. Then as silently as they came, Klon Vex's Ba Rans melted away.

"For a minute there, Mashie," Niblick said after they had moved on, "I thought you were gonna start telling them your theories on riva world destruction and other popular heresies."

"Vex is a piranha," Mashie said. "He bets on the rings but wouldn't dare enter one, and he acts all superior. Thinks he's better. And, worst of all, works for the highest bidder. There are rumors he serves humans."

"Yeah, I got that he's not the most watertight ship in the fleet, but he did have a small army with him, and we got the kid to think about. That's all I'm saying."

"Yeah, well, just make sure that's *all* you're saying."

"It is, trust me. I'm not nearly as stupid as the three of you."

"What did I do?" Ezra asked.

"Are you kidding? You're a human infant that ran away from home and took up with a band of bloodthirsty goblins. Are you insane?"

"I didn't run away. I was . . . I was . . . *banished*." Ezra felt tears rising. They came on without warning, without reason. "Sent away to die by . . . by people like Klon Vex."

"Relax, kid, I didn't mean nothing."

"*Bastard* Ran," Ezra said.

"What's that?"

"That's what they are. Human, goblin, doesn't matter. They're all the same tribe—*Bastard Ran.*"

"Hey, what'd I tell you about using foul language. *I* can say *goblin*—not you. But I get your point. It's a universal tribe, isn't it? Only why sugarcoat it? They're not Bastard Ran; they're undoubtedly *Izuto Ran.*"

"What's that mean?"

"Trust me, it's exactly what you want it to mean, but . . ." He looked around. "That's another one of those words you shouldn't say. At least not until you're a little older."

Ezra wiped his face and looked at Niblick. "*Am* I gonna get older?"

"I dunno. Only one way to find out. And honestly, kid, I'm almost as curious as you are."

CHAPTER FOUR

Hekkabah

The sunrise that next morning was the most beautiful thing Ezra had ever seen, and that included the Magnificent Bird. In a way, they were similar—both so colorful, so majestic, so awe-inspiring, and so very different from his drab village.

Ezra and his escorts reached a ridge where the trees stopped in a near-perfect line. The ground fell away sharply, revealing a rocky cliff and a sheer drop that went a long way down. Below and running out as far as Ezra could see was water. The sun was just above the horizon, a brilliant yellow that was impossible to look at squarely. It faded to pink then blue as it dissolved into a sky bigger than anything Ezra had known. Where the sun touched the water, it made a straight golden line that pointed directly at him as if it knew he was there.

"Never seen the ocean before either, eh, kid?" Niblick asked.

"I saw it at Shahabad, only there the water was dark and small, a place where ships bobbed. And it smelled of fish."

"You were looking at a dock or harbor. That out there is the Green Sea." Niblick had a stick in his hand that he'd picked up along the way and had been using to smack the big leaves aside. Now he used it to point at the vibrant horizon. "Off to the left a smidge is a point of land. Can you see it?"

Ezra nodded as he noticed a small bit of solid blue that almost blended away into the sky. Across from it was another. "One to the right, too."

"Exactly. Between them two headlands, that open water you see—that's the big one. Out there is the open ocean, so huge it doesn't even have a name. It's like the sky, right?" He gestured overhead with the stick. "No one divides it up. No one calls one section one thing and another something else. It's all just the sky. Same with the ocean." He looked back out at the sunrise. "You go that way for a couple, maybe three, days with a good wind—and you'll come to a bunch of islands: The Ba Ran Archipelago, otherwise known as what's left of the Old World."

"That's where you come from?"

"That's where *we all* come from, kid." He stared for a minute, then frowned, shook his head, and added, "If you believe in that sort of stuff."

"Where do we go now?" Ezra asked.

"Down."

Niblick found a path Ezra hadn't noticed that cut through the rock along the face of the cliff. At times, they lost sight of the ocean as they turned back in a zigzag pattern where some trees managed to find enough soil to grow. Each time the water reappeared, they were lower, and the ocean closer. Soon Ezra heard booms. They came in a slow rhythm from down below. He looked to the others, but none appeared to care.

"What's that sound?"

"What sound?" Mashie asked, concerned, and looked behind them.

"That booming."

"Booming?"

Niblick rattled his earrings as he shook his head. "He means the waves."

This made Mashie smile, which still looked a bit like his frown, but Ezra was starting to recognize the difference. Mashie had a face like an old shoe, worn and ugly, but dependable.

At the bottom of the cliff, they walked out on bronze sand so soft that Ezra wanted to lie down and roll. Great humps of water churned, rising with white crests before turning murky as they crashed and spread out in a froth of bubbles, which smoothed the sand as if it were an unruly carpet.

Niblick led them to the water's edge, bent down, and washed his hands in the surf. "Waves are nice to fall asleep to, sometimes fun to play in, and a bitch in a storm 'cause they can rear up like a mountain, and when they come down, they can swallow ships whole. This is a beach, by the way. Thing you got to know about them is that they come and go."

"They come and . . . they leave?" Ezra stared at the vast sandy stretch, mystified.

"Twice a day, actually, but they always come back."

Ezra had a hard time believing this. *Where could such a thing go?*

He looked up at the sheer cliff that created the cove and at massive rocks that stood offshore as islands that appeared to once have been part of the cliff. Trees and bushes still grew on top of several, and waves crashed against them, throwing up white plumes. These did not have *beaches*. Their bottoms appeared to have been eaten away as if they were fruit and a giant had devoured each to its core. Now the ocean had changed color from the golds and pinks of the sunrise to a stunning turquoise near the shore that shifted to a dark blue at the horizon.

The four traveled alongside one another down near the water where the wet sand made walking easy. They left clear tracks that the waves took away in their constant effort to keep the place tidy. Often the water washed in and ran over their feet, rising as high as their ankles. It felt wonderfully cool and thrilling, like the tongue of a friendly dog. When it rushed back out, the sand around Ezra's feet was pulled with it. The sensation tickled as the ground was stolen from beneath him.

"There's so much water," Ezra said. "If the elders knew, we'd be able to drink as much as we liked."

"Oh, you don't want to drink this water, kid." Niblick was fussing with one of his ears, digging with his pinky finger in search of something. "It's salty."

"Salty?" Ezra's eyes widened. "That's wonderful. My village paid nearly half a year's crop to buy just a couple sacks."

"Yeah, sure, salt's good, only not in your drinking water. You drink that stuff and a funny thing happens. The more you drink, the thirstier you get."

Ezra narrowed his eyes, certain Niblick couldn't be telling the truth. Beaches that disappeared twice a day, and water that made you thirsty if you drank it? There was no reason to lie about such things, so it had to be a joke, only he couldn't see how it was funny, and no one was laughing.

"It's not nice to make fun of me," he said. "I know I'm not smart, but you don't have to be mean."

"I'm not lying." Niblick took his finger out of his ear. "It's the truth. Why would I be mean to you?"

"Because I'm human."

"Not really, not yet. You're still just a kid. You're like a tiger cub, cute and sort of cuddly, you know? One day you'll grow up, get teeth the size of my hand, and four sets of claws bigger than Mashie's. You'll be able to take my head off then, and that could be a problem. But right now? You're just a cute little cub. So why would I be mean? If you think about it, teasing a tiger cub is a pretty freaking stupid thing to do."

"Everyone in my village is mean. They said I was terrible because I'm small and weak and a coward. They told me I shouldn't draw pictures or daydream about beautiful birds or wonder what's beyond the forest. They hit me and took away my food. My father said I was evil. He asked the elders to kill me."

Niblick sighed. "Waves rolling, kid, you're really not selling me on this village of yours. Sounds like you were born in the armpit of the world, populated by the sort of people you've heard exist but really can't bring yourself to believe they do."

"They told me that Haddon is the most wholesome, wonderful place there is."

"Seriously?" Niblick smirked. "And you think *I'm* lying to you?"

Overhead, a white bird with tapered black wingtips cried. It soared in a circle, its shadow running across the sand. There were more, perhaps a dozen, such birds soaring. None of Ezra's escorts appeared to notice.

"Go ahead," Niblick said. He took a couple of steps out into the surf and pointed down. "Scoop up some water and taste it. See for yourself."

Ezra bent down, cupped a bit in his palm, and lifted it to his lips. The salt was powerful. It exploded on his tongue and coated his throat, making him swallow repeatedly. But still the feeling remained.

"Salty, right?"

Ezra nodded.

"Leaves your mouth feeling kinda dry?"

He nodded again.

"See? I'm not lying to you—not about the water, not about anything. So believe me when I tell you that you're small and weak because you're young—like a tiger cub. You'll grow out of it. You're not a coward. I've known you for less than a day and figured that out. And you're definitely not stupid. I can tell that *because* you daydream about birds and have the curiosity to wonder what's beyond the forest. I'm not lying, kid. Got me?"

Ezra nodded a third time, then wiped tears from his face.

"Aww, for gripe's sake, what now?"

"I . . ." Ezra struggled to hold his lips tight for a moment until they stopped quivering. "Thank you."

Around midday, Ezra saw tracks in the sand that weren't their own. A little later he spotted part of a net half buried in the sand. Farther down he found broken pottery shards. Rounding one of the cliff faces, they entered another deep cove. Here, hidden by the sheer cliffs, a pretty beach surrounded a tranquil lagoon, and in the cliff wall was a cave. Partway between the water and the cliffs, a dozen small houses were built high on stilts. Narrow ladders led up to round wooden homes with peaked grass roofs. Clothes hung drying on the railings, and barrels full of water were at the foot of the steps. Several tiny boats were drawn up on the sand, but a large one with a mast sat in the water tied by a rope to a tree. Its black sail was furled and lashed to the beam the way Ezra had seen them in Shahabad.

"At least that's still here," Niblick said.

Out of the cave crept a handful of pale people who looked like Dank. They called out using words Ezra didn't understand. In return, Dank trotted ahead to greet them, and they gathered in a group, making chittering sounds.

"What are they saying?" Ezra asked.

"Your guess is as good as mine," Niblick replied. "I don't speak Klune. How about you, Mashie?"

"Don't know Klune or Urgvarian, for that matter."

"Such is the state of the Ba Ran Nation." Niblick frowned. "Here we are, three Uber Ran, all speaking the imperial language because we can't understand one another's. No wonder the empire pushed us into the sea. Of course if we did understand one another, there'd probably be a lot more disagreement, followed by a lot more blood."

By the time they caught up to Dank, they were halfway up the beach where dozens of red-and-yellow clay pots with pointed bottoms sat deep in the sand. Many rope nets were hung out on wooden racks where several were being worked on. Small crates lined with fine mesh contained bulbous gourds that were painted with white stripes. Other pale Klunes came out of the cave, all of them appearing thin and desperate as they watched the four approach.

"She still here?" Niblick asked Dank.

"Inside." Dank pointed toward the cavern.

"Okay, c'mon, kid. Let's go see the priestess and see what she says."

"What if she says to eat me?"

"Remember that ocean I showed you? And how big I said it was? It's also dangerous. There are the storms I mentioned, a considerable lack of fresh water, monsters, and you name it. Riding the ocean is like being on the back of a wild boar that don't like you up there and will do anything to knock you off. So most Ba Ran—unless they're Urgvarian like me and my kin—they don't like being out on it. And the Arkum Ba Ran, well, they hate it most of all. Hekkabah is an Arkum, and she crossed that ocean." He paused to let that sink in. "Then she got me, Mashie, and Dank and brought us here so we could find you. We've been looking for about a month. That seems like a lot of trouble for a scrawny little meal, don't you think? Besides, I told you, 'We're civilized.'"

Niblick, Mashie, and Dank escorted him up around the platform houses, where Ezra smelled something wonderful cooking. They climbed the embankment onto the rocks and into the mouth of the cavern. The sun shone across one wall and reflected off a big pool of water just inside, providing plenty of light and revealing a large chamber with openings to tunnels that ran off into darkness. Carpets and pillows covered much of the cave floor. Brass plates and tin pots were set near a huge firepit filled with cold coals. Mats with blankets were spread out, and on them lay people who looked like Dank. Ezra thought this odd but figured that they might sleep during the day. He changed his mind when he realized these Ba Ran looked sick. They had damp towels on their heads. One moaned. Another shivered.

A female was moving between the beds. She was green, with long, red hair done in braids and decorated with strings of wooden beads and metal cuffs. Her ears were just as pointed as the others but were small, and Ezra could barely see them poking out from under her ornamental hair. A silver ring pierced her nose, hanging down and resting in the divot of her upper lip, making Ezra believe this was the common cleft's true purpose. Her eyes were different from those of Niblick, Dank, or Mashie. While exhibiting the same vertical pupils, they were almond-shaped and angled, which, when coupled with her pronounced cheekbones, gave her a wickedly stern expression. She wore a sleeveless black dress with bright yellow swirls that made Ezra think of falling stars. Before she said anything, the grace in her movements, the intensity of her gaze, and the way she stood with her shoulders back and head up convinced him this was not a person to trifle with. She was more than impressive. She was scary.

At their approach, she stopped rinsing a cloth in a halved calabash bowl. "Ezra?" she asked, sounding shocked.

He nodded.

She looked to Niblick, Mashie, and Dank before refocusing on him.

She let go of the wet cloth, leaving it to soak in the bowl. Then using her skirt to wipe the damp off her fingers, she circled him slowly and tilted her head. "You are only a child. I did not know you would be so young."

"See?" Niblick said, and he started to shake his head.

She glared at him, and Niblick froze before his earrings could make a single *clink*.

This, then, was the famous Hekkabah—the source of the mystery, the one who knew his name and professed to have a *gift* for him. Like her ears, hair, eyes, and posture, her speech was different from the others. She seemed less acquainted with the local language and more accustomed to a vocabulary that required the rolling of the tongue and sharp, precise inflections.

"It's all the old language . . . The Arkum Ba Ran are the only ones who still use it. They never crossed the sea. They're still in the Old Country—or what's left of it—the pure *ones."*

She continued to study Ezra, still circling, the way tigerwolves and lions did before attacking.

"Are you going to eat me?" Ezra asked because he hated the waiting more than the pain. The seconds leading up to a beating always proved worse than the punishment. Even when he knew what was coming, when he'd experienced it before, the waiting was still the worst part.

"Eat you?" Hekkabah glared at Niblick. "What have you been telling him?"

"Exactly what we know—nothing. Maybe if you filled us in a little more, we could screw up better."

"And yet it appears you managed to underachieve just fine. How did you encounter him?"

"He found us," Niblick said as the others sat down where they'd been standing. "The drought has this massive clan of striped hyena taking out their frustrations on just about anything that breathes. We holed up in that cute little cavern with the blue pool. We were just settling into breakfast when guess who walks in and says 'Hello'?"

"And you brought him *directly* here?"

"No, we took him on a whirlwind tour of the imperial cities of Urlineus, Rolanina, and Ra Mar, then topped it off with a night of debauchery at a series of bog houses where we introduced the kid to smoking tulan and slamming shots of hohura and Green Gurlin."

"Are you done?" she asked, unamused.

"I don't know. You tell me."

"Why not go and check on your ship? We had a high wind yesterday. Broke some branches."

"Fine," Niblick said and turned to leave. Then he stopped and looked back. "She ain't gonna eat you, kid. I've no idea what she *is* gonna do, but barbecuing is unlikely. As I said, you won't make enough of a meal. C'mon, Mashie, let's go see what they did to the *Great Excuse*."

The pair threaded their way back through the beds, heading for the light of the beach.

"You should check on your family," Hekkabah told Dank.

The pale Ba Ran looked concerned. He nodded, causing his floppy ears to sway. He gave Ezra a smile and a wink. Then he climbed deeper into the cavern, leaving Ezra with the Arkum priestess.

Hekkabah took a moment to pick up the cloth she'd laid down. She rinsed it again, then folded and draped it on the forehead of a shivering Ba Ran. "Give it time. It will work," she whispered.

"Come with me," Hekkabah told Ezra and led him deeper into the dark, up to the mouth of one of the tunnels.

Ezra was relieved she stopped before going inside. He would prefer to be out on the beach with those marvelous waves, or at least in the part of the cavern where the sun was bright. Still, he was happy she didn't take him into the dark. The tunnel frightened him.

Out in front of the tunnel's mouth was a carpet and a sleeping mat not unlike his own. Two small canvas sacks and a pair of clay pots rested alongside a handful of calabash gourds. A black cloak that matched Hekkabah's dress lay on the ground, covering something that Ezra thought might be food or perhaps a wadded blanket.

"It is not much, but I call it home," Hekkabah said. "Sit down. We need to talk much, you and I." She handed him a small bowl filled with cooked whitefish, abbra berries, and nuts. "You must be hungry."

He smelled the food. There was a spice he wasn't used to, but the aroma was wonderful. She was right, the all-night hike had left him famished. Tilting the cup to his lips and using his fingers, he scooped some into his mouth, chewed briefly, then swallowed.

"What are you doing?" she asked.

He looked down at the bowl. "You gave it to me?"

"Do you not know how dangerous it is to eat anything offered to you by a strange female out in the wilds? Have you not heard of the Tetlin Witch? She is known to use food to capture children such as you. What if I am her?"

"You're not."

"How do you know?"

"Because you are Hekkabah Zar, daughter of Geth and Zanna, a priestess from the Arkum Temple of Uberlin, and a genuine Rona Zar."

Hekkabah's eyes widened. "How do you know all of this?"

"Niblick talks a lot."

She smiled. "Yes, yes, he does." She seated herself across from him on her mat and folded her legs. "Do you know what any of that means—those words you just said?"

"It means you're not the Tetlin Witch."

This made her smile broaden, though it was clear she didn't want it to. In that moment, Ezra realized there was a beauty about this strange person. She didn't look like any woman he'd ever seen because she wasn't a woman, and yet he thought she was attractive in the same way the Magnificent Bird was beautiful.

"How do you know my name?" he asked.

"I was told your name when I was sent to find you."

"Who sent you?"

"Someone very important."

"Rex Nexziria?"

Again the surprise. "You know a lot of names."

"Niblick talks—"

"Talks a lot. I know."

Ezra looked back into the bowl. The first mouthful had been excellent, and his stomach rumbled. "Can I have some more?"

"By all means. Now that we have determined I am not the Tetlin Witch but simply a priestess of Uberlin, you should eat up."

Ezra took another handful and chewed.

"That does not bother you, either?"

"What?"

"That I'm a goblin, and I worship Uberlin? Your kind hate Uberlin, and they kill goblins on sight. We have been at war with your empire for hundreds of years. I am the enemy of your people. Does that not interfere with your eating with me?"

"My people sent me into the forest to die. Your people gave me food and water and protection from lions. I like them more than mine. And you shouldn't use the word *goblin*. It's not nice."

Hekkabah let out a surprised laugh and stifled it with a hand over her mouth. "I believe you *are* the Ezra De Haddon I am looking for."

"What are you going to do with me?"

Hekkabah gave a glance to her cloak, lying on the ground. She sighed. "I am not sure now. I was supposed to give you a gift, but this gift is not for a child, which means . . ."

"What?"

"That there is more for me to do."

Ezra wasn't sure he wanted to know what that meant, so he changed the subject. "Is it from Rex Nexziria?"

"In a way." She rocked her head from side to side, suggesting it wasn't.

"What's a riva? Niblick said it was the scariest thing still in the world."

She thought about this, then nodded. "Niblick talks too much, but he is not stupid. Rivas were the commanders of the forces of the god Uberlin when he made the First War against his own family in a time long, long ago."

"Niblick said Rex Nexziria was a riva."

"He is—one of the two that still live."

"And he sent you to find me?"

She thought about this for some time, giving Ezra the chance to eat more while he waited. Finally, she reached a decision. "No," she told him. "To be honest, Nexziria will kill me the moment he discovers where I am."

"Then who sent you?"

"You're such a smart child. Have you not figured that out?" She grinned at him. "I am his priestess, after all."

Ezra finished his meal in silence as Hekkabah watched him. At times, she would stare at the ceiling of the cavern as if she saw something. Ezra would look, but he never noticed anything. When he finished, he set his bowl down and waited, but the priestess continued to sit and stare.

"No one has died," Dank said to Hekkabah as he returned from the shadowy interior of the cavern, wearing a smile.

"It was close with a few," the priestess replied. "Izilu . . ." She shook her head. "I thought I had come too late, but she made it through the night. The fever is gone. She will be good now."

"Dank you." Dank looked around the cavern with tears in his eyes. "When I went in search for help, I didn't dink dar was a chance. We are da *Ghazel*, da Forgotten Ones. What hope did I have? I wanted to find an Urgvarian commander wid a ship, get him to come pick us up, take us away. Sorry to say, I didn't dink much of you when we met, or your offer, but I couldn't find anyone else who would help."

"Most of you would have died on a ship."

Dank nodded. "I want to say I'm sorry, and to dank you—dank you so much for helping my people."

"It is not true," Hekkabah said.

Dank's ears drooped. "No, I'm truly dankful. I—"

"Uberlin has not forgotten us."

This caused Dank to tilt his head.

"Come along, both of you. All of us need to talk."

The priestess led the way out of the cavern and past the stilt-supported homes to the beach, where the waves continued to roll without pause. Strong gusts of wind buffeted Ezra's hair and threatened to knock him over. *What a wonderful place*, he thought, as once more he saw the white birds with black-tipped wings skim over the waves. It was sunny yet cool, and the ground was so soft he could sleep anywhere. The beach lacked tall grass, providing no cover for lions or tigerwolves to creep up. And if there was a storm, he had the cave. Ezra imagined a storm would be nothing in a fortress such as that. This world of the Other, this place of Awful Things, was not living up to its reputation.

"Go," Kenja had ordered, pointing at the forest. *"Go and never come back."*

Why would I ever want to?

Hekkabah took them down to where the big boat rested on the sand. It had one tall pole standing up in the middle and two wrapped in canvas resting on the deck. The whole thing leaned to one side because its bottom wasn't flat. There were other coils of rope—a lot actually—inside and on the sand. Wooden barrels and crates were lashed to the boat, and Ezra could see steps that went under the deck to what had to be a tiny place inside. Lots of palm fronds were scattered all over. Mashie stood to one side, his arms folded, while Niblick circled, pulling the fronds off the boat and pausing to stare as he scratched his chin.

"Well?" Niblick asked as they came up. "I see the kid's still alive. Did we get the right one? Are we done here?"

"You did very well," she replied.

"Great." He picked up another frond. "You were right about that storm. Made a mess of things, but the *Great Excuse* is seaworthy—or as seaworthy as she ever was. Just need supplies and high tide, and we can set sail."

"Did she give you the package?" Mashie asked.

Ezra shook his head.

"The time is not right," Hekkabah declared.

Niblick said, "What's that supposed to mean? What are ya gonna do? Leave it with Dank to give to Ezra later? As much as I love the great white underbite, are you sure you should? I mean, you've been a bit hypersensitive about trusting that thing to anyone. I'd swear it was your child. So how's that gonna work?"

"It will not," she replied, "which is why we are all going to stay."

"Stay?" Niblick said. Still holding the palm frond he'd just picked up, he walked over to face her. "What? Until when? Are you saying you have to wait until the kid grows up? Are you nuts?"

Hekkabah brushed sand off the hem of her skirt. "You have some other pressing engagements?"

"Yeah, I gotta live the rest of my life." Niblick pointed the palm frond at her. "You know, there's a rumor that while we were gone, you took a trip of your own."

"They say you went to the human town," Mashie added.

Dank came closer. He stepped up alongside Hekkabah and looked at the priestess, concerned, which for Dank was a distinct lowering of his ears and a frown.

"I did not have everything I needed for the medicine," she explained.

Dank's ears rose, his mouth opened, and his eyes widened. "You went to Shahabad?"

"I went *near* Shahabad. I traded with people living outside the town. I kept my hood up and painted my hands and face. They likely thought I was one of those wild people, the outcasts that live in the deep forests, the half-breeds."

"Tenkins," Mashie provided.

Niblick dropped the frond and dusted his hands together. "So at best they think you're an outlaw, and at worst they know they have an encampment of goblins living down the coast."

"I do not think they care either way. These were poor people. They needed me as much as I needed them."

"What did you give them?"

"Silver," she said. "I do not think they will seek to kill a person willing to trade riches in return for simple herbs and minerals. This is an opportunity for them."

"Is that how they think back there in Arkum? These are humans you're talking about here. You don't have them where you come from, so allow me to explain exactly what they'll do. Regardless of whether they think you're a goblin, a Tenkin, or a really handsome green-skinned one of their own, they will figure there's more silver to be had. And, yeah, they will definitely see it as an opportunity. They're gonna come down here looking for you, and when they find a pretty village of sickly goblins basking on the beach, they will be overjoyed. You know why? Because it isn't merely okay to kill us, it's their sacred freaking duty. They're gonna slaughter everyone. Then they'll look for the source of the coins and will no doubt be disappointed to find only your purse rather than some massive silver mine complete with a smelting furnace and coin press."

"They do not know where we are."

"They're looking. We brushed up against an Ankor patrol outside of Haddon that knew about you being nearby. How does that happen? You been putting up signs or something?" He looked at Mashie. "Who do you think Vex is working for?"

"No one nearby."

"Why is that?"

"There aren't any Ghazel Da Rans out this far. Aoz Hilus is the closest stronghold."

"But he said this was his territory."

"He was lying."

"What if he wasn't? You said the claw-for-hire worked for humans, right? What if he's working for one now? What if he's employed by the governor of Calynia, or one of the legion officers who thinks he's clever by taking advantage of an idiot who lost his moral compass and replaced it with a bag of coins?"

Mashie thought a moment, then shook his head. "Imperials don't hire Ba Ran."

"That you know of, but it doesn't need to be an imperial, just someone with something to offer the likes of Vex—someone who can grant him a *territory*."

"Just tiny villages like Haddon out this way."

"The people here are very poor," Hekkabah said.

"Shahabad isn't poor," Dank said. "And it isn't imperial. Da port is controlled by a legion deserter named Banka."

"A warlord stole an imperial city?" Niblick asked. "How'd he manage that?"

"Da same way my people live here. Dis is too far off da map for da emperor to notice. Banka rules all da villages and little docks in da area."

"That seals it. Somehow the warlord knows about an Arkum and is hunting her, but either he doesn't know she's a Rona Zar, or he's not telling his underlings because as soon as I mentioned it to Vex, he changed his mind about pressing the issue." Niblick looked at the boat. "We gotta get out of here. Give the kid the thing, and let's go."

"No," she said.

Niblick looked at Ezra and sighed. "Fine, we can take him with us."

"No, we cannot."

"Why not?"

"Where can we go with him?" she asked.

He shrugged. "I dunno. Aoz Hilus, maybe."

"Not there," Mashie said with the same tone as a dropped boulder hitting the ground.

"Ah . . . okay." Niblick glanced over. "I can understand that. Sure, not Aoz Hilus, but somewhere else down that way. There are lots of ports."

"Yes, and in every one you are wanted for treason," Hekkabah said, "and Mashie for murder. There is no place across the straits for you."

"What about Arkum?" Niblick offered. "We could go to your hometown. You could put in a good word for us with your boss, get us jobs in the capital, maybe. That'd be nice, wouldn't it?" He looked at Mashie, who nodded.

Hekkabah shook her head. "Our best chance is to stay hidden in the forest."

"Our best chance of what? We can't go to Arkum? You're like a bigwig there, aren't you? A Rona Zar is a huge deal, I thought."

"We cannot go to Arkum—we cannot go east at all—and absolutely not with him." Hekkabah pointed at Ezra. "How can we take a human boy to the Old World? I was sent to give Ezra De Haddon the gift, not to drag him back to certain death."

Niblick folded up his lips, forcing two lower incisors to peek out as fangs. "But the rex will protect him, right? I mean, Nexziria wants him. Isn't that what this is all about?"

Hekkabah looked at the sea. "Perhaps you are right. Humans may come looking. We will need to leave here and go deeper into the forest. We will find a safe place and build a new home, and there we will raise Ezra to manhood so that I can finally fulfill my task and give him the gift."

"Raise him?" Niblick laughed. "Hold on, the kid's like, what? Five or something? I didn't join up for a life sentence here."

"Foolish is the raindrop that believes it chooses where to land."

"Isn't that a lovely sentiment? Just like a priestess. But you didn't answer my question. What about Rex Nexziria? He's not going to wait years to get word, is he? And I hope you aren't expecting me and Mashie here to babysit while you go back."

"I cannot go back."

"Why not?"

Hekkabah moved past Niblick to the boat. She walked down to the low side. After wiping off the railing, she sat.

Niblick followed her and, putting his fists on his hips, he asked, "Why can't you go back? I thought . . ." He stopped and scratched his chin. "Wait a minute." Niblick's eyes narrowed. "You told us you got the package from Nexziria."

"I did."

"Sure, sure, but did he *give* it to you?"

She didn't answer.

"Hekkabah, tell me he gave it to you. Please, tell me the ruler of all Ba Ran gave you that freaking package and politely asked you to deliver it for him."

Hekkabah developed a sudden obsession with brushing out the wrinkles on her skirt.

"Oh—for the neglect of the Missing God! You stole from Rex Nexziria? You robbed a riva, then decided to involve all of us? This is treason, you understand?"

"You are already wanted for treason. You were on trial when I met you."

"Mutiny is one thing. Stealing from a freaking riva is . . . it's beyond walnuts; it's coconuts is what that is!" Niblick began pacing, kicking up sand when he turned. "This is . . . this is a problem. We got nowhere to go, and a riva is hunting us—a freaking riva! He's out there right now, searching. It's only a matter of time. You can't hide from him. And when he finds us, when he . . ." Niblick looked like he might cry. Then he stared at Ezra and shook his head, jangling his earrings. "Aww, kid, I really wish you still had your lucky feather."

"Lucky feather?" Hekkabah asked, and looked at Ezra.

"Dat's why day kicked him out," Dank said. "When da striped hyena attacked, he killed 'em all."

"With a feather?" She looked at Ezra, drew herself off the boat, and moved closer. "Did you?"

He shrugged. "I don't know. I didn't mean to."

"Were you tired afterward?"

"I fainted. Woke up late, but, yeah, I was tired. Still am, sort of."

Hekkabah turned her head as if she heard something, but all Ezra noticed were the waves and the birds crying overhead. She slowly raised her hand to her mouth, and her eyes widened as if she might be sick. "That is why he sent me," she said, then nodded. As she did, her free hand came up to join the other, covering her lips.

Ezra looked to Dank, whose ears were down. He appeared just as mystified as everyone else. Even Niblick lost his demanding stance to peer at her, puzzled.

Hekkabah knelt in the sand before Ezra and took his hands in hers. She stared at his fingers. "You have power."

"What? Like an oberdaza?" Mashie asked. His tone did not appear pleased.

Ezra had never heard the word before, and he didn't like the sound.

Hekkabah shook her head. "More than that. Much more."

"Aww, for gripe's sake," Niblick exploded. "The kid's an Artist? You gotta be kidding me. He's gonna be a Cenzar when he grows up? I was really sort of kidding about the whole tiger cub thing, you know?" Niblick threw his hands up to the sky. "Waves rolling, Hekkabah, why didn't you just let me die? All they was gonna do was hang me."

"How *many* hyena?" she asked Niblick.

"Huh? I don't know. Who cares?"

"How many were there?" she asked Ezra.

He shrugged because he didn't know.

"I'd guess about fifty," Mashie said. "That's what we saw before the attack. That's what drove us into the cavern. Cute little cats are one thing. Fifty striped hyena—well, you don't mess with that, not when they're hungry enough to attack a village."

"How many animals survived?"

Mashie looked at Niblick and Dank. "Didn't see *any* hyena afterward."

Hekkabah nodded, still holding his hands. Her fingers were warm and soft. "You are powerful," she told him. "How old are you?"

"Seven."

Hekkabah let go of his hands. "Seven?" She said the word like it was bad. She stood up, breathing heavily. She brushed her braids back and held them out of the way as she stared at the sand beneath her feet with a suspicious glare.

"For gripe's sake, what now?" Niblick asked. "Are we all gonna die seven times or something, each time more horrible than the previous? Or is it that the riva will keep us alive seven years as he—"

"I had a son," she said.

"You . . . *had?*" Niblick softened. "What happened to him?"

She didn't answer. Hekkabah continued to stand before Ezra, and he noticed her lips quiver.

"The riva?" Niblick guessed.

She nodded.

"And your son was seven?"

She shook her head. "No, but he would have been seven if he had lived."

"Hekkabah, Ezra's a human boy, not a replacement."

"Yes, he is." This time she touched her throat and the necklace that lay there. "That is what this is all about. I was sent to bring Ezra the gift. I expected no payment in return, but this is my reward, the chance to raise the son that I lost, a child endowed with the power of Elan."

"And now we come to it," Niblick said. "Pray tell, who was it that sent you?"

She straightened up, took a deep breath, and placed her hands on Ezra's shoulders, "The Lord God Uberlin."

"Yeah," Niblick sighed, drawing the word out. "That's what I was afraid of. We've now officially gone beyond the realm of nuts entirely. This is pistachio land. I know you're a priestess and all, but that's a bit hard to believe, given that Uberlin has been missing in action for what, a few hundred thousand years? I don't even know how long. I'm not that good with numbers, and I'd have to be, to work that one out—because he's been gone that freaking long! So you're saying we gotta stay here and raise this kid from a cub to a real tiger, with a riva hunting us and—"

"Hunting me. Rex Nexziria does not care about you, does not know about him—just me and the package."

"Whatever. I'm just saying we're doing all this because you had what? A dream?"

"Was not a dream."

"Oh, so you actually saw him? Spoke to Uberlin, did you?"

"No."

"Of course not. Which makes this one giant riddlebag of gallimaufry. How in the world did I get into this?"

"You made the mistake of saving my life," Mashie said.

"Oh yeah, you're right. I should hate you most of all, my big stowaway. In Aoz Hilus, there must have been what? Twenty-five ships on that dock? But you hid on mine."

"I didn't ask you to stop them."

"Coulda, woulda, shoulda—oh, the regrets we must live with."

"Glad you did."

"That makes one of us, and even you might regret that, big guy, when the riva comes knocking. You know they don't actually kill you, right? I mean, they do, but they keep your soul locked up in their pile. I'm guessing Nexziria's pile is pretty big by now."

"It's not a pile," Hekkabah said. "He turned the bones into bricks and built a fortress the size of a mountain."

"Anyone else just feel a chill?"

"So what are you going to do?" Hekkabah asked. "Stay or go? I have no power to keep you, no authority to command."

Niblick sighed and kicked sand. "How's that even a choice? Of course I'm gonna stay. No one ever said I was smart. I did, sure. I said it hundreds of times, but *no one else* ever said it. So I guess I'm just as much an idiot as the rest of you."

"Or maybe," Hekkabah said, "maybe you are simply a raindrop."

"Yeah, that's it. I'm a freaking Uberlin-forgotten raindrop."

"I would prefer if you stopped using the Lord's name in vain the way you do."

"Seriously?" Niblick shook his head. "Uberlin abandons us—his own people—and you—"

"He did not abandon us. He has a plan."

"Does that plan include allowing the empire to push the Ba Ran into the sea? Leaving us with no home?"

"An invasion is coming," Mashie said. "Everyone is preparing for it."

"They always say that, but even if it's true, the empire with their Cenzars and Teshlors will just obliterate us again."

"Not this time," Hekkabah said.

"Why not?"

She looked at Ezra. "Because Rex Uberlin did not forget his people."

"Whatever." Niblick took a moment to let his fingers run along the side of the boat, a frown on his face. "So where we doing this? Where we gonna live?"

Hekkabah smiled. "Let Ezra decide."

"Really?" Niblick rolled his eyes. "Okay, fine, sure. I mean, who really cares, right? Go ahead, kid, you decide. Just make it close to fresh water. I don't want to be hauling buckets a mile. Anyone know how to build a house?"

"I thought the Ba Ran lived underground in holes," Ezra said.

"Sometimes, but caves are cold and wet. Dank would probably like it. Personally, I would prefer the deck of a ship, fresh air, fresh fish, lots of fish . . . too much fish actually. How about you, Hek? What was your home like?"

"I used to live in a palace."

"Hmm. Okay, you win."

"Where would you like to live, Ezra?" Hekkabah tugged lightly on his hands as she grinned at him. "Where would you like to grow up?"

Another bird flew overhead, but this one wasn't white, and it didn't soar. Ezra caught the sight of flapping wings and bright blue-and-yellow tail feathers. The Magnificent Bird landed briefly in the nearby palm. Then after glancing over its shoulder at him, it flew off again.

"That way," he said.

CHAPTER FIVE

The Nyphron Church

IMPERIAL CAPITAL OF PERCEPLIQUIS, AUTUMN

The moment he entered the city of Percepliquis, Mawyndulë felt the thrill of hope. Two hundred and twenty-some years had passed since he last entered between the lions. The giant stone statues with their paws stretched out before them marked the start of the city and were the first recognizable landmarks declaring he was back. The city had grown far beyond its founder's intent. Lavish villas sprawled across the hillsides, large and small shops displayed garish signs, and apartment buildings rose several stories. Just outside the city proper, shanties cobbled together from scavenged materials formed their own small towns. As if to prove things could always get worse between the lions' paws, a village of impoverished tent dwellers grew up like weeds around a carefully cultivated flower bed. So much had changed. The city had grown, and so had he.

This time will be different, he thought.

"Your Grace," Theopol addressed him, "I see we are coming upon the home of Councilor Lucian Hargrave. Shall I request an invitation for a midday meal? I'm certain he will be eager to have you, and we still have so far to go. The city is always crowded this time of day, and it might be hours before we reach Imperial Square."

Theopol was his general secretary, his senior assistant, the one entrusted with—as the title implied—his master's many *secrets*. Mawyndulë had several secretaries, servants, groomsmen, couriers, and even a tailor. He had no bodyguards, no protectors—he didn't need them.

This time will be very different.

"Shall I order the coach to stop?" Theopol placed a hand on the door.

"I am not hungry. I would like to push on."

Mawyndulë couldn't imagine suffering the revulsion of entering a human's house. They would expect him to eat from their bowls and drink from their cups, even sit in their chairs. The very thought made him feel nauseous.

"At least allow me to procure you a proper litter. These cobbled streets are an agony to suffer riding on a hard axle. And litters can more easily navigate the congestion."

Mawyndulë considered this. Theopol was right on all counts. For a human, he was remarkably intelligent. Litters were far faster and more comfortable and the preferred mode of urban travel for the wealthy and powerful—but therein lay the problem. Mawyndulë wasn't entering Percepliquis as himself but rather as the humble Bishop Venlin, the pious leader of the Nyphron Church. Were he arriving as himself, it would have been wholly appropriate to be carried on the backs of humans. But were that the case, the city would be on fire and most of the humans would be too dead and dismembered to carry anyone. Despite being his secretary, Theopol would not be privy to this one secret.

"I am but the servant of Novron," he explained, as if Theopol had never heard this declaration before. So much of this role was superficial repetition that it bored Mawyndulë. He could only imagine the weariness it must inflict on those constantly around him. They didn't show it, and this caused him to ponder whether they were better actors than he, or if they simply believed so deeply in his illusion as to accept that this was how the truly devoted acted. "I do not require a litter, nor will I burden the backs of my fellow men with my weight."

As Venlin, Mawyndulë often said things like this, knowing that in any sane world laughter would result.

"Of course, Your Grace," Theopol said, without so much as a smile. "My apologies. Please forgive me."

Mawyndulë stared at Theopol, reading the story in his eyes. He was near tears, not because he was embarrassed or upset at the rebuke, but because he was actually moved by the humble sanctity of the man he knew as Venlin. The creature was choking up with emotion because Mawyndulë had turned down a free meal and a more comfortable ride.

How is it they ever beat us in the war?

Mawyndulë knew exactly how. He'd been there in the front row, a witness to the whole thing. The Fhrey had been betrayed by one of their own: Nyphron. The very one Mawyndulë had arranged to be killed a bit over a thousand years earlier, the one he was now teaching the humans to worship as a god. Centuries ago, when Mawyndulë was the prince of Erivan, living in the palace of the world-ruling Fhrey, if anyone had told him how his life would turn out, he would have assumed them insane—insane, but remarkably creative.

Mawyndulë stared out the window of the coach, not much more than a wagon with hard bench seats and a canopy—all the better to appear the modest servant of the Murdered God. The city's buildings were taller than on his last visit. Nearly all were more than five stories, a few as high as ten, if the windows were a true indication. The residences of these towering hives flaunted elaborate balconies with colorful sunshades and gardens complete with topiary trees. Some of the public buildings, such as the imperial library—which he took special notice of as they passed—encompassed a whole city block. Rising like an island on a plateau and marked by a bank of marble steps, the Imperial Repository of Tomes and Knowledge was fenced in by a towering colonnade of marble pillars. The thing looked more like a temple to a god than a storage shed for ink-stained parchment.

As the wagon rolled along, Mawyndulë noted the various colors of marble: pink, green, rose, and white. These were further subdivided: fine grain or coarse, bluish-gray or semi-translucent. Each came from a different part of the empire and were used in architecture to show off. It was well known that the best marble was saved for statues or other monuments, such as the Arch of Novron, which Mawyndulë noted as they passed under it. The crime, as he believed it to be, was the way they painted so much of it. Mawyndulë liked the purity of naked stone, but the city insisted on covering the marble in horrible garish colors of rusty-red and turquoise. They painted the statues, too, which was to be expected. Left white, they looked too much like ghosts. The architects and builders of Percepliquis had a thing for red and blue-green . . . and gold, lots and lots of gold, much of which wasn't paint. Percepliquis was the physical embodiment of bragging.

The coach rolled by theaters, bathhouses, open squares, markets, sporting arenas, vast neighborhoods, and artisan shops. And they passed temples—temples that he noticed were dedicated to Novron.

"How many temples are in the city?" he asked Theopol.

His secretary thought a moment. He did this a lot. Theopol was the sort terrified to make a mistake, so he spent extra time deliberating on everything before saying a word. For a long time, Mawyndulë had thought him mentally slow, but eventually he recognized the familiar hesitancy that used to accompany his father's assistants—servants who could be killed for a misstep. The virtuous Venlin had never threatened anyone, yet his people tripped over themselves to please.

Theopol opened his mouth to speak, then stopped and quickly dug into a satchel by his side. He pulled out a small pamphlet and quickly thumbed through the bound stack of what had to be a hundred pages.

"What is that?"

"A guidebook, Your Grace. I purchased it in Rodencia in anticipation of coming here."

"The city of Percepliquis has a guidebook?"

"Oh yes. And it is very helpful. There's even a street map." He held up a woodcut-printed page that looked to be a confusing series of crosshatched lines. "It lists the best bathhouses, how to avoid being cheated when buying a quatra of wine or oil—"

"And how does it say to do that?"

"There's a standard amphora kept in the Cenzarium that you're supposed to compare it to."

"And where is the Cenzarium?"

"In Imperial Square, across from the Teshlor Guildhall. The Cenzarium was formerly the Aguanon—a temple to Ferrol, but that changed back in 1880, around the same time the imperial library was built. Incidentally, the Teshlor Guildhall was formerly the Imperial Administration Building, and before that it was the original palace where Novron and Persephone first ruled."

"Sounds fascinating," he lied.

"Oh, it is! There are also dates of city festivals—they hold ninety-nine a year, the grandest being in fall, what with the harvest and all. The book lists all the best shows in the city as well. Apparently, no one likes the tragedies, with everyone overwhelmingly preferring comedies and the ones with fighting. In the back, there's a yearly prediction of the best chariot team to bet on—Red Team is favored, but, alas, this book is six years old." He flipped it over and looked at the end sheets. "I suspect they make these but once a decade. Still, I can look for a more current one now that we're here."

"And the question of temples?"

"Oh yes, ahh . . ." He flipped some more, then stopped on a page. "Here it is. There are eighty-two temples in the capital city."

"Eighty-two?" The number surprised him. Mawyndulë knew he wouldn't be establishing the first—but eighty-two! "Oh, wait . . . how many are dedicated to our Lord Novron?"

Theopol looked up and smiled. "All of them."

"All of them? Eighty-two, and all—hold on. Are you saying there are no temples to the Fhrey god, Ferrol, in the city?"

"Not anymore. Most of those have been repurposed, the rest destroyed."

"Where do the Fhrey worship?"

Theopol looked uncomfortable. He was being asked to answer a question he didn't know the answer to, and which wouldn't be found in his trusty guidebook, forcing him to speculate or be guilty of failing his master. "I suspect there are precious few elves still living in the city. Most of them relocated to Merredydd centuries ago."

"What about the *fino*—the Fhrey-in-name-only—the myr, the half-breeds?"

"There are still some, but even they, I believe, have moved to Merredydd. Those with elven features are more accepted there." Theopol frowned. "The church, I regret to report, hasn't had much luck in Merredydd."

The coach was passing through a large intersection, where a tall column caused the traffic to go around a circle.

"Tell Evon to pull over and stop."

The secretary stood up, holding tight to the walls of the wagon, and popped his head out from under the canopy. In a moment, the coach came to a halt, and Mawyndulë climbed out. They were traveling the Grand Marchway, the broad avenue divided by a small garden of fruit trees, and had reached Destone Circle. This was the second landmark Mawyndulë recognized. The column at its center had been erected in memory of Seymour Destone, a monk who had died around the same time as Nyphron. Mawyndulë was still uncertain if Trilos had killed him, or if his mentor had merely taken advantage of a freshly abandoned body. Either way, it was right around here that—

Mawyndulë moved to cross the street and was nearly run down by a cart overloaded with produce.

"Careful, Your Grace!" Theopol shouted. "These people are monsters."

Mawyndulë looked at the cart racing away. Theopol had clearly never known a *real* monster.

Mawyndulë darted across the thoroughfare and down the street whose name he recognized from two centuries earlier—Ebonydale. His eyes searched the north side. *This is where it was,* he was certain. He crossed all the way to the next block, then came back down the south side of the street, where he met Theopol coming toward him with a concerned face.

"What's wrong, Your Grace?"

"Nothing," Mawyndulë replied, still looking around. "I just thought—"

He saw it then. The façade across the street was the same—at least the outline was. Ebonydale had always been a mercantile district. The narrow road crossed the Grand Marchway near the middle of the city and terminated in two different market squares on both ends. Here, just off the Marchway, there had once been a rugmaker's shop called Wegan's Weaving. It hadn't been a fancy place, just a simple family business run by Desmond Wegan, who made quality rugs for common families. The Wegans were some of the first people in Percepliquis to convert to the Church of Nyphron, and for a time Mawyndulë—who back then went by the name of Proust—had lived in their basement. It was really too much to expect that such a place would still exist, but Mawyndulë found it pained him to discover that the little shop was gone. The building was still there. He recognized the outline, but now it was whitewashed and had a tawdry sign painted in violent red shouting NEED MONEY NOW? Several people were lined up at the open door, proving they did.

"What is this place?"

"A payroll lender," Theopol replied without his usual pause. "They loan money to people who can't wait for their normal payday, and in turn, they take a percentage of the person's wages."

"Oh," Mawyndulë said. "A rugmaker used to have a shop here. I don't think he would approve of what's here now."

Theopol looked at him with that expression of awe that always flooded his face whenever Mawyndulë exceeded the bounds of his role of Venlin. He was just being lazy in speaking to Theopol about a memory Venlin couldn't possibly have, but to the general secretary, this was merely one more example of the First Bishop's legendary abilities—his miraculous gift granted to him by a grateful and powerful god.

Mawyndulë continued to stare at the place across the street. "This was where it all started—the church, I mean. Right here is where Mayda and the others began their preaching. They used to live in the basement when it was a rug shop."

"That's incredible." Theopol looked at the line of people coming out the door.

He believes me with no proof. Maybe he'd like to ask how I know but doesn't dare. Such a question would imply a lack of faith.

Mawyndulë remembered Mayda. She had an ugly overbite, and he used to call her Rhapsody.

"I want you to build my church," he remembered telling her before he left. Then he went on to say something like, *"Replace the Aguanon. Throw down their false elven god, shatter their ugly statues, and rededicate that pagan temple to Novron. Make me proud, Mayda."* He never thought she'd actually do it, but two centuries later, with Mayda long dead, the church she built had spread across the world. Every imperial province had one, every village and town—except in Merredydd and Erivania. And now he was coming to assume control of the soon-to-be flagship church being established in Imperial Square.

The little chinless, flat-nosed, short-haired, frowning hunchback managed it after all.

"Let's go see our new church," he told Theopol. "Afterward, perhaps I will look into making this a shrine."

The Church of Nyphron in Imperial Square was a rubbish heap—not literally, but Mawyndulë suspected that if he asked Theopol to look it up in his trusty guidebook he would discover that at one time it had been just that. It wasn't even actually in Imperial Square. His new home, and what he hoped to be the foundation of a new world order, was a full three doors down Ferry Street. The church was at least larger than any of the previous temples he'd spotted on the ride in, all of which were of the tiny shrine variety, just big enough for a statue of Novron and a place to kneel. This was a true building, with windows—although boarded up—and presumably rooms behind them. The place was a generous four stories, judging by the outside, but still tiny compared with the Aguanon across the street. Whether Mayda had had anything to do with it or not, the statues in Ferrol's Temple were destroyed and its purpose rededicated but not to the Church of Nyphron. The grand domed building, so large it formed the east side of Imperial Square, was now home to the Cenzarium, the college of human wizards. Mawyndulë could see some of them standing out on the high steps in their scholarly robes, acting as if they were something special.

"You're displeased," Theopol said, standing in the doorway below the three fake arches that were mere decoration forming the bottom of the balcony above. In front of this clearly repurposed stone building, wooden scaffolding stood covered in wide strips of cloth that protected workers from the late summer sun as they struggled to patch cracks in the plaster façade.

Mawyndulë did not reply.

People struggled to move down the busy street, its surface littered with straw that gathered in the gaps of cobblestone. To the left, a broom merchant had a tent set up, presumably more for the comfort of his patrons than for the array of brooms he had on display. To the right, a cart merchant sold sandals. Between them, on the very porch of the infant church, a man sold grain from open sacks. Mawyndulë climbed up the single step from the street. *One step! The Cenzarium sits atop a mountain of marble. But I have a few inches separating me from the filthy herds of wandering animals.* He looked down. *And it's cracked. The library is a palace, and my church—my grand temple—isn't fit to house pigs.*

The front of the building had three sets of double doors, one under each of the faux arches. He pushed on the center one. It refused to budge.

"Is it locked?" he asked.

Theopol grimaced. "Only the left one works, Your Grace. The other two are broken—sealed on the inside."

Mawyndulë placed his tongue on the underside of his mouth and made a clucking sound that caused Theopol to cringe. Walking around a discarded basket of rags, Mawyndulë moved to the open left door. The interior was a dim and dusty haze illuminated only by angled shafts of sunlight that pierced the broken slats of the poorly blocked windows. As he entered, something flew out of the rafters, its wingbeats echoing.

"This is the best you could manage?"

"Options were few, as you insisted it be on Imperial Square."

"It isn't."

"It is as close as I could get. I knew it would be rough. The place has been abandoned for a year."

"Only a year?" Mawyndulë traced an arc in the dusty floor with the toe of his shoe.

"I have people coming to clean it. In a few days, you won't recognize the place. It will be a palace."

"At this point, I'd be happy with a livable hovel." Mawyndulë shook his head. "Get it fixed. Have at least one room cleaned enough so I can sleep in it. I'll be back in an hour or two." He looked around once more and sighed. *There's humble, and then there's ridiculous.*

Mawyndulë walked back out to his new porch, where the grain seller continued to sit cross-legged behind his open sacks. He offered three different types, but Mawyndulë had no idea what they were. Each appeared to be coarse-grained dirt of varying shades. The entrepreneur's feet were bare and filthy, and he had but one tooth, which he was proud enough of to display with a grin.

"How's business?"

The man looked up and nodded, his shaggy, matted hair bouncing. "Very good."

"How much are you pulling in?"

"Fourteen keng and a handful of pith, on a good day." His voice was full of pride. "I have a small farm a day's walk from here where my wife threshes the grain and looks after my sons and daughters, but no mule. So I must carry what I can on my back. But the crowd here is worth the trip. It keeps my family fed."

"Not bad."

"Is this your building now? I have been selling here for eight months and sleeping inside until I sell out my stock. It is a good place. I understand if you do not want me to sleep in your building, but I hope you will not mind my selling on the stoop."

Mawyndulë smiled. "Not at all. You can sell all you want on my front step. That's perfectly fine."

The grin grew bigger, showing that he did indeed have but the one tooth.

"Yet, as this is to be a church, I must ask that you tithe."

"What does that mean?"

"It means that if you make fourteen keng you will give thirteen to me."

"I will not!"

"Don't you believe in god?"

"Not if he is a thief."

"A thief is someone who takes what isn't theirs. Everything belongs to our Lord Novron, so he cannot be a thief. On the other hand, by taking advantage of his kindness to use his stoop to sell your wares but refusing to share the profits Novron has provided, *you* are the thief. Given this, if I see you here again, I will have your hands cut off because that is how Novron rewards criminals who take advantage of his good and faithful servants."

He smiled at the man, whose grin, along with that awful tooth, vanished.

Leaving the farmer with that happy thought, Mawyndulë crossed the street, threading his way around the flow. A woman brushed by, and he shivered at the contact. *They are all so disgusting.*

Safely reaching the far side of the road, he looked up at the old Temple of Ferrol. The Aguanon, as it had once been known, displayed a simple but perfect design. The triangle pediment supported by eight soaring columns faced the center of Imperial Square and formed the vestibule to that grand rotunda with its wonderful dome. Mawyndulë climbed up the twenty-eight unblemished steps to the plateau that formed its lofty campus. Around the old temple was a new garden with stone pathways, statues, and fountains. Behind everything were other buildings that Mawyndulë had never seen. These weren't as lavish, but far more practical as dormitories and offices. In too many ways, it reminded Mawyndulë of the Airenthenon and the Estramnadon Academy of the Art that he had attended as a youth, before the world ended. The Cenzarium looked out on the Ulurium Fountain that marked the center of Imperial Square.

Just beyond that, on the other side, upon its own hill, stood the Teshlor Guildhall. Having been Nyphron's onetime home, the place was built like a fortress, complete with a wall—a wall that Mawyndulë knew to have dwarven runes chiseled into it. The Cenzarium and the Teshlor Guildhall faced each other like adversaries on either side of an arena. Between the two, on the north end of the plaza, forming the predictable terminus of the Grand Marchway, was the palace itself—an incredible white building with a massive dome of gold that shone brightly in the afternoon sun. This was the center of the city, the heart of the empire, the hub of power and influence. His goal was to harness that power. The days of precision attacks were over. Mawyndulë had a new tactic: overwhelming force through absolute domination. Such a thing took time. He'd already invested more than a century, and by the looks of his church, he had a few decades still to go. But when he was done, the city would be his. After that, the rest ought to be easy.

Mawyndulë studied the three hills and the plaza between them, imagining himself a talented general surveying a battlefield the night before the start of a final showdown. The players were all there: the dominant powers of Teshlors and Cenzars, yoked together and held in servitude to the emperor. For Mawyndulë, it felt like spying a massive boulder on the edge of a cliff with only a pebble holding it in place. He need only apply a series of tiny pushes, pulls, and perhaps a well-timed whack to get the thing rolling. Then he could stand back and watch that massive rock fall and crush the life out of everything. He still needed to be careful, lest he be in the path when the rock started to roll.

His key to victory was taking the high ground, and in this case that meant the three hills of power. He decided to begin with the Cenzars because they were the closest, and the Teshlor Guild still had that irritating rune-marked wall. *I'll need to do something about that. Doubt they check it with the same frequency a shepherd checks his fence. No one is likely to notice if a single symbol is marred. I'll send one of my devotees with a chisel and hammer and the faith to use them.*

Looking up at the Cenzarium, he noted that the self-important-pretenders-to-power who strolled the grounds and gardens in their white and green robes were no match for him, but he couldn't altogether discount their threat. And he wasn't certain what precautions they might have put in place. The good news was that the Cenzars, unlike the Miralyith, were all human. They lived such short lives. Although during his waking hours Mawyndulë maintained a simple glamour that convinced everyone he was human, he had nevertheless waited to return until he could be certain everyone who had been alive during his last visit was dead.

After two thousand years of trying, this time it had to work.

I'll see the city destroyed before I retreat again.

The Cenzarium presented the biggest threat.

Best to get the hard part over with.

Mawyndulë checked his defenses—he didn't want some virtuoso Artist detecting his power and asking questions. With all in order, he put on a fine, I'm-your-new-neighbor smile and walked up the cute marble path through the garden. Either the imperial wizards would see an affable, middle-aged leader of the new church, or a two-thousand-year-old Fhrey outlaw.

Either way, this should be interesting.

Several of the Cenzars looked his way, each wearing robes that sought to imitate the superior Fhrey asica, but they managed only to demonstrate human inferiority. The Cenzar costume looked like a bedsheet wrapped around the wearer once, with an end thrown over a shoulder. This was especially pronounced with the younger devotees, those he assumed were the aspiring wizards who seemed to be limited to plain white vestments. The more accomplished Cenzars displayed longer, finer, green garments. Some of the older ones—teachers, he suspected—wore blue robes that sported distinct velvet or silk panels along the collars, sleeves, and cuffs. These tailored accoutrements likely meant something. He would need to learn all of it: the colors, the terms, the ideals, and even the names of the teachers and students. Mawyndulë planned to borrow techniques he remembered from the old Curator of the Aquila. Imaly had to be long dead, but she was still teaching him. This decade's lesson would be how to manipulate the young and impressionable.

"Masquerading as a human again, Mawyndulë?" a voice asked.

He froze, gripped with panic.

The one who had spoken was an old man with long white hair and a matching beard that grew down to the center of his chest. His robes were gold and blue and of the finest silk. He even wore an embroidered cape held across his shoulders with a gold chain. "I suppose that means you're up to no good again. What's the plan this time?"

Mawyndulë just stared. After a second, bewilderment set in. *It's been over two hundred years. No human can live that long. No one can know who I am. A powerful Artist might see through my illusion, but there is no possibility that anyone could . . .*

Mawyndulë narrowed his eyes as the old man smiled.

"Trilos?"

"Yolric," he corrected.

"Why *Yolric?*"

He shrugged. "I like the way it sounds. Similar, but distinct. It was time for a change. The old name was worn out. Had it for . . ." He struggled, then laughed. "Funny, I don't know. It's impossible for me to determine the number of years I spent in Phyre. And out here the calendar is always changing. We're going by Imperial Reckoning now. Did you know that?"

Trilos had always been chatty, the sort to talk all day and never say anything—nothing useful, at least. Mawyndulë always felt that his mentor concealed vast treasures of knowledge, but he buried it under a trash heap of pointless blather. Like all children who sought the pot of gold at the end of the rainbow, eventually Mawyndulë gave up searching for the fabled riches and went out to make his own.

"What are you doing here?" he asked his old mentor.

Yolric swept a hand out toward the Cenzarium. "Teaching. I've always enjoyed instructing youth in the way of the Art. You remember me doing that off and on back in Estramnadon, don't you? Fenelyus was still my best student. I wonder what became of her."

Mawyndulë stared incredulously. "She became fane, won the war against the dwarfs, gave birth to my father, then died."

Yolric smiled. "I meant after all that."

Mawyndulë never knew what to make of his mentor's "senior moments." *Is he hinting at something profound or just losing his mind—dusty.* The old term was one he had employed frequently as a youth to describe the failings of the elderly mind. He suddenly realized he was not much younger than those he used to mock. Unlike Trilos, Mawyndulë knew his age, and dialing in at two thousand one hundred and thirty years, he was almost as old as Arion and his father when they died.

"You weren't in Estramnadon to teach," Mawyndulë pointed out. Then he paused to look around to see if anyone else was watching this bizarre exchange. Several robed figures surrounded them—walking, sitting, reading, or gathered in small discussion groups—but no one showed any interest in the two of them. He and Trilos were merely Venlin and Yolric, a pair of aging men standing beside a stone bench beneath the changing leaves of a poplar tree, engaging in some pointless small talk. "You were there to see the Door open—hoping to catch your brother in the act and slit his throat. The teaching bit was a guise."

The new Yolric shook his head, causing that silly beard to wag. "Not a guise at all. Unlike you, I don't require a pretense. No one is hunting me. I suspect that you and my brother are the only two on the face of Elan who know I exist."

"Lucky me."

"Indeed. No, I love teaching. I always have, and this place"—once more he waved at the Cenzarium that loomed large and cast a growing shadow that crept their way—"is quite nice. Not as stuffy as the Estramnadon Academy.

Not much hierarchy here. There are elders and students, of course, but after induction, everyone comprises the General Assembly. And it isn't only a school. The elders send representatives to the Grand Imperial Council to advise the emperor, which is nice, but a great many Cenzars also serve as circuit envoys traveling throughout the empire keeping the peace, solving disputes, eliminating threats, and experiencing the world. It gives them an outlet, a way to feel useful. I think that was part of the problem back in Erivan. You had all these young Artists with all this power and no purpose, nothing larger than themselves for which to employ it."

"But why are you *really* here?"

"Same reason you are."

"Oh? You're planning on destroying the empire, too? That could get awkward if we both do it."

"You're part of the convergence," Yolric said. "This is a focal point in the timeline, same as the day you fought Nyphron. Something big is coming. You must feel it, right?"

Mawyndulë only felt concern that he didn't feel anything. "Maybe. Thought it might be indigestion."

"The world is about to wobble again, and this place is the hinge upon which it will swing. Turin will show himself in some form—to thwart you, I suspect. My mentoring you may have been the smartest thing I ever did. It has resulted in so much divergent oscillation—you're like a tornado that comes each spring to stir the pot."

"Care to help?" Mawyndulë asked with a smile that even he felt might look a bit demented.

His new persona, the illusionistic façade that he mentally referred to as *The Mask*, was half drawn from people he'd known. But much of the rest was his true self. An illusion was far easier to manage and maintain if it wasn't trying to do too much. Changing all the leaves in a forest to blue was far easier than making each tree different or eliminating the forest altogether and replacing it with a mountain. Anticipating that he would be maintaining *The Mask* for decades, Mawyndulë had chosen to wear comfortable shoes. The drawback, as he saw it, was that he wasn't particularly attractive anymore. Age had not been as kind to him as it had to Arion.

Over the years, and given his many setbacks, Mawyndulë had suffered long periods of depression. He slept a lot. Whole years and at least one entire decade he remembered as nothing but a haze of self-pity. He'd spent a good deal of his time hiding in the backwater province of Dortha in what used to be the Belgriclungreian Empire, back before Emperor Nyrian annexed the entire dwarven peninsula. Rotting in an impoverished coastal town filled with Dherg hadn't helped his mental state, and he'd grown despondent. There had been days he couldn't find the motivation to eat, much less groom himself. This led to the discovery that he no longer needed to shave his head, as he was going bald. What awful tufts that did remain were a ghastly mottled mix of white and putrid brown. He gave up shaving his face as well but failed to grow the luxuriant, braidable whiskers the dwarfs managed with ease. His was thin and patchy, continuing the piebald tradition started on his head.

As a Fhrey, he believed he was now disagreeable to look at, but after he was forced to use the Art to mask his best racial features, he appeared ghastly. Looking at his reflection brought him to tears. Rather than fight it, he added a darkness around his eyes, allowed his wrinkles to show, caused his scant beard to form into a point, and narrowed his brows into sinister threads of delicate malice. This he felt was his inner self brought to the surface. *If I can't be pretty, I'll be scary.*

Trilos stroked the full, rich, snowy beard of this new body he called Yolric and pursed his lips in thought. "Help you? Perhaps. What's your idea for world domination this time?"

"I'm creating a religion, the Church of Nyphron."

"You are advocating the worship of your vanquished foe?"

Mawyndulë smiled. "It's an unfortunate title especially since I'm recasting Nyphron as Novron the human demigod—something I believe he would have absolutely despised. But *Church of Nyphron* is the name that caught on, so I'm stuck with it. I hope to foster corruption, division, and a general poisoning of the well. I aim to rot the roots, so I can easily topple the tree." He pointed down the hill at the deplorable dump that was now his new home and place of business. "That's my church down there. I'm moving in today."

"How you've grown," Trilos said. "But still so naïve."

"How so?"

"You continue to believe such small things as revenge matter."

"Says the one who has spent millennia fruitlessly hunting his brother for some unexplained slight."

Yolric shrugged. "That's different."

"Oh, I'm certain it is," Mawyndulë said with a patronizing nod.

"I doubt you'll need my help to sow distrust and discord," Yolric went on. "Collapse is the natural proclivity of all that stands. The world expects and, to a great degree, demands it. Should be an easy victory."

Mawyndulë stared, sensing a subtle tit-for-tat in the condescending tone. But as always, his onetime mentor was as clear as morning fog. "So you won't help, but you also won't get in the way?"

Yolric nodded. "Just as before, I'm here as an observer. Waiting for the Invisible Hand." He glanced at the Cenzarium's dome. "But also, as a teacher."

"Then teach them well," Mawyndulë said. "They're going to need it."

PART TWO

New Beginnings

YEAR 2106 IR

CHAPTER SIX

The Longest Day

SIX YEARS LATER . . .
IMPERIAL PROVINCE OF CALYNIA, SUMMERSRULE

The morning sun was starting to filter through the canopy, but Ezra had been up for hours. Working by the light of his grease lamp, he was reaching the end of his essay on the fall of Arencia. Hekkabah had given him five days, but he'd had nothing else to do that night. Sleep certainly wasn't an option. He never slept on the shortest night of the year, the one before Summersrule, the longest day.

"Ezra?"

Looking down, he saw Hekkabah at the base of the barowan tree, using both hands to cup her mouth as she yelled up at him. At her feet was the basket.

Blowing out the lamp and wiping out his ink bowl, Ezra moved to the open deck that surrounded his room. He was the only one to build his place in the branches of the tree. Hekkabah inhabited the big pondok constructed around the base of the massive trunk—the place they had all originally used when first settling the headwaters. Well, all of them except Niblick, who had always slept on the *Great Excuse*, which was still tied up at the riverbank. In truth, Mashie also had little use for the shelter, spending most of his time outside.

"I am going foraging," Hekkabah said when she saw him at the railing. "Come with me."

Ezra had been waiting for something like this, and in his excitement, he nearly burned his hands sliding down the rope. He reached for the basket. She snatched it up, but not before he saw something was in it. "Come along, we have much to do today." Saying nothing else, Hekkabah started off into the trees, following the highland path that went southeast.

Although they had cleared a small patch to grow vegetables, and created a sizable rock pile in the process, the best treats the forest offered were wild. Hekkabah often brought him along when she hunted mushrooms, rom nuts, and abbra berries. He was good at crawling under the bushes and scaling the trees that the elderly priestess found challenging. Most of their foraging trips were in spring and fall. The hot season was less busy, and he had spent most of his previous summers with Niblick repairing the *Great Excuse*, which always needed work despite only being used the one time. That was six years before when the three had offered farewells to Dank and the rest of the Klune and sailed eastward down the coast to the mouth of a small river. At Ezra's urging, Niblick had managed to navigate a short distance up the waterway to where the current became too strong to travel farther. For Ezra, that was far enough. He spotted the Magnificent Bird perched on the high branches of a massive tree the likes of which he'd never seen before. "Here!" Ezra had declared. "This is where we ought to make our home. Right where that tree is."

Niblick had proclaimed it, "as good a place as any." But it was more than that. With fresh water and a nearby hill providing shelter from storms, the little clearing in the forest where the wide, deep river turned into a series of upland cascades was perfect.

Ezra took the bird literally, and suggested they build a tree house on the branch where it had landed. He was quickly coming to believe in the wisdom of the Magnificent Bird, but being seven years old at the time, he also thought a tree house would be great. Hekkabah explained that a tree house fifty feet off the ground was not something she was comfortable living in. Instead, using tools and supplies left in the belly of the *Great Excuse*, they all worked together, and in a few weeks, they'd constructed the pondok, a simple house like those built by the Klune. It took Ezra, with the help of Niblick—who taught him how to make rope, tie knots, and work pulleys—two years to complete his Magnificent Bird's

Nest—*complete* being a relative term. He officially moved in at the two-year mark but continued to work on it, adding levels and decks.

Initially, Niblick justified keeping the *Great Excuse* in good order for fishing the open sea, but the river offered more than they needed, and the forest provided the rest. Ezra agreed with Hekkabah that for Niblick, the *Great Excuse* was just that—his way of dealing with this new life. The boat was a promise to himself that one day the Urgvarian would return home—home being the open sea.

Mashie spent his days hunting in the forest. Ezra recalled how twenty men from Haddon would stalk a single wild kapa. The powerful animal with sharp tusks was dangerous, and men were often severely wounded—some even killed. But Mashie went out alone, dragging back kapas, giant lizards, monkeys, even a small bear. Occasionally he was hurt, but Ezra noted it was on those occasions that the big Ankor Ba Ran smiled more often and sighed rather than complained. Hekkabah treated him with potions and salves, as she did all of them when they were ill. The rest of her time was spent teaching Ezra, and she never lost an opportunity.

"What is Sirdia Ferrillia?" she asked as she swung her legs over a log that Ezra had jumped.

The two were covering familiar territory. After six years, their repeated passage had widened animal runs into comfortable trails that Mashie was kind enough to maintain, using his claws to clip back the underbrush.

"I completed the essay this morning," he replied impatiently, dismissing the topic. He didn't want to discuss history. The here and now was far more exciting.

"That doesn't answer my question."

"Sirdia Ferrillia is the city of Ferrol, the one she established just before the start of the Great War and filled with her kin."

"And where is it?"

He sighed, and to put the subject to rest, he ripped through the information. "Sirdia Ferrillia was built on a rise three leagues northeast of the first city, Erebus, and five leagues east of Dorthineia. Dorthineia was the city of Drome, which, along with the city of Marn, were all conquered by Uberlin, who ruled Erebus. Each of the conquered cities became strongholds for Uberlin's rivas. But as he had five rivas and only three cities to bestow, two were left out. Hitartheon crossed the Eraphus Sea—now called the Green Sea—where she built Borappathin on the coast, and Nexziria quartered the reserve army at Arkum—otherwise known as the City of the Rising Sun."

He grinned.

Hekkabah gave him the look. She was not pleased.

"I'm right, aren't I?"

"It is your tone."

"My tone?"

"You believe all this is unimportant—a waste of time."

"Remembering stuff that happened ten thousand years ago does seem a bit like Niblick keeping the *Great Excuse* seaworthy."

"Thirteen thousand, six hundred and six years ago, and it is important because . . ." She stopped.

Hekkabah did this occasionally, and Ezra determined it was because she caught herself just short of saying something interesting—part of the secret he knew she refused to tell him. The mystery he hoped she'd reveal that morning. He believed this was the day because he had turned thirteen.

Ezra's birthday had never been celebrated. While living in Haddon, he'd only had seven—which his father never acknowledged, at least not that Ezra remembered. The only reason he knew the day was because of Aunt Tadesha. She had been teaching her sons their birthdays, and he had asked after his. She appeared surprised he didn't know, then looked around for his father. Not seeing him, she seemed a bit unsure how to proceed, but eventually relented. "You were born at dawn on Summersrule. If you stand at the well, it is the day the sun lines up with the road to Shahabad. The longest day." After that, Ezra pretended that the celebration held on Summersrule was partially his. In a boy's imagination, the feast, music, and dances were in his honor. The problem with this fantasy was that everyone else received presents on their birthday, but he never did. As the sun rose on his thirteenth Summersrule, Ezra believed this birthday would be different.

He had no real reason to believe this. His new family—Hekkabah, Niblick, and Mashie—never celebrated anyone's birthday. Ezra had no idea if this was a cultural difference between the Ba Ran and humans, or merely specific to these three. They weren't close blood kin, not even from the same clans, so it was possible they didn't even know one another's age, much less their birth dates. But they knew his. Hekkabah had asked him that first year they were together, and Ezra believed he knew why. In Haddon, thirteen was the age when boys became men. They traded in their rakes for spears, joined the hunting parties, and began the long process of proving themselves worthy of a wife.

This must be the year, he thought. *This has to be the day she gives me the gift.*

"So . . . remembering all this ancient history is important because . . . ?" he prodded, hoping she would explain the slip. He did so with an innocent smile as he nonchalantly waved his hand at a cloud of tiny flies that, for reasons known only to the insect world, delighted in swarming his face.

"Because . . ." She hesitated so long he felt certain she might finally say something. "It is important."

"Why?" he pressed.

"Because it is."

Hekkabah took the left route at the fork and moved through the trees, following the narrow path that eventually ran down into the creeks that gave birth to massive jungo and kala plants.

Ezra gave up. If she planned to tell him, she would. If not, all the questions in the world would not hasten the event. "Where are we going?"

"You will see."

"How am I to learn if you don't provide answers to my questions?"

"Because I am not here to teach you answers. I am here to teach you how to learn. And as I have been telling you, I am not the one you should be posing questions to. *My* voice will not be the source of your answers."

Over the years, Hekkabah had told him to be mindful of his feelings—those strange thoughts or sensations of dread or confidence—that arrived unexpectedly. These were the whispers of Elan trying to speak to him, she said.

"You have mastered reading and writing, though your lettering still needs work. You understand the calendar and constellations. You know something of medicine and healing, and it seems you have acquired a fair understanding of history. But your other studies have not progressed at all. I noticed a light in your tree house last night. Did you ask Elan to light it for you?"

"I used embers from the fire."

She shook her head. "And the belt you made for Niblick for Wintertide. Did you weave the braid with your hands, or the Art? Did you etch the image of the ship into the leather with a knife or the power drawn from the world around you?"

"I can't do it."

"Did you at least try?"

"I know you think I can, but I can't."

"It will come."

"It's been six years, and it hasn't. I think you may be mistaken."

She paused, turning to face him. "I will not always be with you, Ezra. And there are certain things you must know, skills you must master and stories you must remember."

"Why? I doubt the monkeys and umbra trees care if I can do magic or know the names of the five rivas."

"Their names are not so important," she said. "What they did is what you need to remember."

"They turned on one another the moment Uberlin disappeared, and their civil wars allowed the Children of Uberlin's enemies to return and defeat them." He gestured at the trees. "See?"

"See what?" she asked.

"No applause."

Hekkabah frowned. "You are very intelligent, but a little too smart."

"I have a good teacher."

This caused Hekkabah's eyes to narrow in that scary way he didn't like.

"It's a compliment."

"It had better be."

Reaching the old dead tree, she turned and headed up the slope. No path went that way, and the old priestess marched through rough ground, pushing aside leafy plants and struggling around thorny bushes. The morning sun was lost here to a denser canopy that left the world around them in a deep shade of twilight.

"You must understand, Ezra, that I am a Rona Zar, a priestess of Uberlin. I am not a daza—not a master of the natural powers. I cannot harness the wind to plow a field or use light to spark a fire. These are gifts that Elan grants to those who are worthy. I cannot instruct you specifically how to develop your power. This is a path you must explore by yourself, a universe you alone can enter and map. That is always the way. So while I can show you the door, you must walk through it to that other world—the place I cannot follow."

"What makes you so certain that I—what makes me *worthy?* I haven't done anything. Well, I made a pretty fine tree house, I'll admit. But—"

"It is not through achievements that Elan grants her gift. The tree that survives the storm while others snap receives more sunlight, more water, and from this grows taller than all the rest. The muscle that is tested becomes more powerful than the idle arm. Pain, suffering, and perseverance against adversity—these are the merits that mark worth. I know daza from the Old World. All suffered as children and youths. Some lost their parents to accidents; others suffered long sicknesses. One was blinded at the age of eight. The more horrible the affliction, the greater the pain, and the earlier in their lives it occurs creates a more powerful daza." She paused to lay a hand on his shoulder. "Ezra, while still an infant you witnessed the violent slaughter of your mother. She was ripped apart before your eyes by lions. Afterward, you lived in a house of hate with a father who wished you dead, in a community that saw you as evil. That is a storm that would have broken many trees. But you . . ." She looked at him with eyes of awe, as if she beheld a thing of beauty. "You are whole. There is not even bitterness, no lingering poison. You still possess the power to laugh."

"You think I can do magic because I can laugh?"

"No," she returned, walking up the hillside, "I *know* you can hear the voice of Elan and that you can wield her power. But because you survived *and* managed to preserve your light, I believe you will be a daza of immense strength."

Hekkabah paused, bent down, picked up something, smelled it, and then dropped it. "You merely need a push." Once more, she turned and pressed into a thicket of brush.

"Where *are* you going?" he asked again.

"This way. Is there a problem?"

"We've never gone up this slope before. Why are we doing it now?"

"Follow me and find out."

Pushing through the thickets and brambles, Hekkabah led Ezra out into open land. They were out of the deep seclusion of the lush coastal forest and up on the highland plateau. Before them, a vast open field of tall, brown grass swayed in a wind they hadn't known existed until then. Ezra had never seen the field before. Mashie had warned everyone to stay away. "Trust me," he had said more than once. "You don't wanna go there. I don't even go there."

Ezra assumed Mashie had gone to the field at least once. He also thought he knew when that was. During their first year, before they learned the lay of the land, Mashie had kept them all fed by hunting the forest. He often came back with cuts and scrapes, but once he almost didn't make it back at all. Niblick said he found Mashie in a hole near the highland ridge. All Ezra remembered was the blood. The Ankor Ba Ran looked like he'd taken a bath in it. Given the number of cuts on his skin, Ezra was certain most of the blood was homegrown. Mashie recovered, but it was a month before he could walk again, and almost a year before he returned to hunting.

This is the field!

"What are we doing here?"

"Tell me about Arencia, Ezra."

He looked left, then right. The field was huge and flat. The grass shoots, nearly as tall as Ezra, were gold on top, running down to a dull green. Already it was late morning, close to midday, the sun brilliant. "There's nothing to be foraged here."

"You say that you finished your essay. So tell me. Tell me about the fall of Arencia."

The two stood at the edge of the forest, the trees at their backs, a golden sea before them that rolled in silent waves. Everything was frighteningly quiet—except Hekkabah.

"Ezra? Please answer me."

He swallowed. "Ah . . . after the fall of Erebus, the children of Ferrol, Drome, and Mari drove the rivas and their armies east to their last stronghold of Arencia in the highlands of Hyphus."

"Except . . ."

"Except Riva Nexziria, who remained with his army in the city of Arkum, worried about an attack on Mynogan, and Riva Hitartheon, who refused to leave Borappathin." He spoke absently, blindly pulling the names and events from the back drawers of his mind while the field held his attention.

"And . . . ?" Hekkabah asked and took a step out into the grass.

Ezra gasped.

"And . . . ?" she repeated.

"And the Uber Ran's enemies surrounded Arencia and besieged it for nearly a year."

She took another step, and he watched her body be swallowed by the grass, only her head visible, bobbing above the fuzzy seed tops.

"And?" she asked, not looking back.

"And then, knowing they couldn't win, the three rivas in Arencia attempted to destroy the world rather than surrender."

"How did they do that?" Hekkabah asked, her voice calm but not casual. Each word was measured. She wasn't oblivious. She knew what she was doing. And as she spoke, she walked on, each step—like her words—deliberate and slow.

Ezra was torn. He didn't want to enter the field but was afraid to lose the priestess to the grass. She hadn't told him to follow, nor had she ordered him to stay. Hekkabah was purposely refusing to discuss anything to do with the situation at hand.

She's doing this on purpose, but why?

He followed her, keeping a pace behind.

"How did they do it, Ezra?"

"They cast a spell, worked together, and tried to cut a deep chord." Irritated with the pointless questions, he rushed the answer, speaking quietly, afraid something might hear.

Doesn't she feel it? All around, Ezra felt . . . *badness.* That was the best description he could settle on. Everything was wrong—worse than wrong—terrible, terrifying. *And she's just—*

"Do you know what that means—*severing a deep chord?*"

"No." This time he whispered and didn't care if she heard.

"Neither do I," she replied, "because I am not a daza."

Ahead of them, Ezra saw a small patch of grass sway *against* the wind. Off to the right he noticed the same irregularity, like a back-pooling eddy fighting the current in the river. While fishing, Niblick had taught him how rings on the surface of water betrayed movement below.

"The whole of Hyphus and most of Mynogan were destroyed," Hekkabah said. "Arkum was the only ancient city to survive, as it was built high on a mountain. Much of the relics of old Erebus were brought there for safety. They were housed in the Temple of Uberlin, where I served as Rona Zar, and where seven years ago I found a stone with writing on it."

"Seven?" Something about the number of years rang in his head, caught his attention when nothing so trivial should.

"Yes, Ezra, seven. Strange how that number keeps coming up, is it not? The number of Rhune clans, the number of Frhey tribes, the number of Dromeian clans, the number of Frhey rulers there have been thus far. Your age when I found you. The age my son would have been if he had lived. The number of stars in the constellation The Great King, which dominates the night sky starting today. The number of jewels in the crown of Uberlin."

Ezra was abundantly aware of everything, of his heartbeats and breathing, Hekkabah's movements, the sunlight and shadows, the singular course of a pair of vultures soaring high above, and the terrible movement of the tassel-topped grass that created still more eddies, more telltale signs of movement below, and the number seven.

"Stranger still is that the stone tablet I found was taken from the ancient palace of Uberlin in Erebus, meaning it was carved about thirteen thousand years ago. Do you know why that is remarkable, Ezra?"

He neither knew nor at that moment cared. What he couldn't understand was why Hekkabah kept walking deeper into danger.

"Trust me. You don't wanna go there."

Ezra trusted Mashie. Why didn't Hekkabah?

Mashie's warning was nothing compared to Ezra's own internal alarms, which exploded in mysterious impressions of dread: screams, snarls, the horror of baked grass, the awful smell of blood, fear so powerful that Ezra struggled to breathe.

"Are you listening, Ezra?"

"Yes."

"The reason the stone tablet with the writing on it was so remarkable is that writing did not exist thirteen thousand years ago. And yet there it was, chiseled in a script I could read—in the language passed down to us from the Gur Em who themselves gained it from your people. And on it was my name." Hekkabah stopped walking and put the basket down.

The basket! Of course! The gift! That's what this is all about!

He'd waited six years, and in that time, Ezra's curiosity had only grown. Having a fine imagination, he had spent numerous nights pondering what it might be. According to Hekkabah, the gift was taken from Rex Nexziria, the riva ruler of the Ba Ran. She also said that Uberlin himself had directed her to give it to him. At one time, he thought it might be a crown, meaning that he would be the next ruler. He figured he was some kind of illegitimate heir to the throne of Uberlin. Being the true son of the god of evil would explain a lot. Like why Eleja hated Ezra and called him the spawn of a demon. But Ezra also wondered if the present was a weapon because Hekkabah had said it wasn't the sort of thing to give a child.

She's going to use it now. She's going to show me what it can do before giving it to me.

"On the stone," Hekkabah said, "I read these words: *'Though it be many centuries after I write this, I know you, Hekkabah Zar, daughter of Geth and Zanna, will be the first and only to understand these chiseled words. Tell no one, and after reading, destroy the tablet. This message is only for you.'*" She looked at him. "You're likely wondering why I am telling you this, are you not, Ezra?"

I'm wondering why we aren't running for our lives!

"It is because your name was also on that tablet. Written in a script that would not exist for another ten thousand years—in words that no one else could read—was a message to me from Rex Uberlin. He ordered me to cross the sea and find a Mari-born male and give him the gift Uberlin left for you. The tablet read: *'You will know him by his given name Ez-Rah and Haddon, the village of his birth. When you find him, you'll know I have not forgotten my children.'*"

She reached out and touched his cheek. "I have found you, Ezra."

Hekkabah smiled sadly, then bent down to the basket. "I have raised you as my own son. But I have not trained you, not in the way Uberlin requires."

She closed her eyes, took a deep breath, and reached into the basket. "Forgive me for this, my son, but you must learn. You must be what our Lord requires." Hekkabah pulled back the cloth that hid the basket's contents.

Ezra expected a great blade of some sort, perhaps a glowing crystal, a whip, or ax. Instead, to his shock he saw the basket was filled with freshly butchered, still bloody meat. Hekkabah drew the dripping flesh out and to his horror began rubbing it on herself, leaving blood smears across her face and arms.

"They can smell it," she told him. "Do something, or just like your real mother, I will die. We both will."

Hekkabah wasn't wrong.

Ezra saw the eddies move in direct lines toward them. This was the pride of lions that had once been so desperate and hungry they had risked an attack on Mashie and paid for it. Now they were desperate once again.

There are seven—four females, two young males, and the pride leader. They are hungry, real hungry, but not weak. The females will lead the attack. The males will wait for the kill before coming in to eat.

He knew this as certainly as his own name, but had no idea how.

Ezra was also aware of a honeybee worker deserting a pretty white flower in favor of settling on a milkweed blossom; that the two vultures had been joined by five, making a total of seven, and were watching with great interest the gathering of the hunting pride; that a gust of wind had snapped the top off one of the tallest stalks of grass; that a pure-white butterfly had also noticed the milkweed and was adjusting its flight to land; and that Hekkabah radiated fear and a rapidly growing belief that she had made a fatal mistake.

The lions came in slowly. At least it seemed that way to Ezra, for whom time had practically stopped. He stared at the basket at Hekkabah's feet, empty now but stained in blood. Seeing it, he smelled the memory of abbra berries and rom nuts that weren't yet in season. He heard his mother's voice. She was singing.

The female huntress—the mother of the other three females—charged Hekkabah from behind. Ezra watched, impressed with their teamwork and timing as her daughters flanked. One even gave a thought to him, but Hekkabah was the primary target. She was the smaller, older, weaker one, and smelled so wonderfully of blood.

Hekkabah turned and flinched as the lioness, still more than a body's length away, flashed claws, dug deep, and sprang.

"No!" Ezra shouted, throwing up his hand.

The bee on the milkweed noticed, as did the butterfly, who promptly reconsidered landing. The vultures beat their wings to fight an unexpected shift in the breeze, and the floundering top of the bent stalk of grass snapped clean as across the field a blast of wind ripped with the power of a giant fist. Hekkabah fell as if brushed aside. The lioness and her three daughters were blown back like a quartet of kittens hurled by an invisible slap. The hunters cleared thirty feet before hitting the ground, rolling, and forming a long swath in the towering grass.

Ezra had no real idea what had happened. His hand had come up unbeckoned, the way his arms would if something were thrown at his head. Only it wasn't merely his hand. He'd brought something else.

The winds that brushed the grass.

While he hadn't planned anything, just as with catching himself in a fall, he wasn't shocked that he had. The flight of lions was his doing. Rather than reacting in disbelief, he accepted the act as being as natural as breathing.

This is what birds feel at the first flap of their wings.

With this truth flooded understanding.

I killed the tigerwolves. My terror tore them apart. That's what Jaydan and Nomax witnessed—that's why the elders drove me out. But I didn't kill the lions that attacked my mother. I don't know why. Maybe I couldn't. Maybe I was too weak.

The idea felt wrong, a dull note, a false answer. All he knew was that these weren't those lions.

The cats shook off the blow, and after a moment came again. Once more the lioness charged.

Ezra held his open palm at her, and in a quiet voice said, "No."

The cat slowed, then stopped. She stared at him. Her daughters waited, confused. The males also waited. The very air waited.

"Leave," he said.

A moment of doubt followed. Ezra felt the anticipation sizzle the air. The cats were hungry and not convinced.

"Be warned," he said and thrust out his arms in a sweeping gesture.

Starting with Ezra at the center, the grass of the entire field lay down. No wind nor gust of air forced this feat. The shoots simply bowed to him. The great sea of gold revealed its secrets: the rocks, ravines, anthills, marmot holes, and the seven exposed and vulnerable lions, whose doubt faded. This was too disturbing to risk, too unexpected to face, and the animals retreated to seek the security of the trees.

When Ezra looked at Hekkabah, she was still covered in blood, but now she was grinning.

CHAPTER SEVEN

Growing the Flock

MEANWHILE . . .
IMPERIAL CAPITAL OF PERCEPLIQUIS, SUMMERSRULE

"His father is the governor of Alburnia," Bishop Venlin explained. "And the boy has dreamed of nothing else other than to become a Teshlor Knight. He is named after the boy's great-great-great-grandfather who met Princess Farilane and witnessed the legendary Battle of Rochelle where Kolby Fiske and Cedric Oslow defeated the Fourth Legion. That's when the family adopted their reverence for the Teshlor Order. The child wishes so deeply to repay the family debt, and it would so please his father if you could see yourself clear to giving him a chance."

Mawyndulë stood before the little desk of the martial master and recruitment officer for the Imperial Academy of Teshlor Knights—a fellow by the name of Morgan Rawlings. He was an old man whose once-black hair had been invaded by white and was losing the battle. A onetime Teshlor Knight of some renown, he had retired to a life of teaching children the sword as headmaster of the famed school of combat.

It takes a certain kind of man to willingly choose that sort of misery.

The Imperial Academy, while not officially part of the Teshlor Guildhall, was physically connected and would have been protected by the Art-blocking Orinfar runes if those dwarven decorations hadn't been *accidentally* marred about five years earlier by some late-night vandal. Still, Mawyndulë always suffered anxiety whenever he stepped through the gate, wondering if some ambitious and clever fellow had noticed the fresh chisel marks around the backside of the guildhall and taken it upon himself to "fix" them.

"I'm not asking that you instate him, only that you provide the boy with the opportunity to prove himself," Mawyndulë-as-Venlin said.

"That's what we just did." Master Rawlings remained disrespectfully seated, his focus on the surface of the desk, where he studied a handful of pages scrawled with poor penmanship. "That's what the entrance exam is for, Bishop."

None of the chambers in the guildhall was luxurious. They were hard, cold, unyielding places—the perfect gardens to grow a crop of invincible men. Still, Venlin found the size of this one surprising. Master Rawlings was the chief trainer of the Teshlors, yet his room was tiny. The office did have its own little fireplace, with a great sword mounted above. The rest of the space was taken up by the simple desk and the bed, mostly hidden behind a drape of red cloth.

"I understand. But surely you can't judge a person's whole character from a single interview," the bishop argued. "Besides, I was of the impression that the academy prides itself on shaping the boys that come here into the men they will be. What point is there in correcting the perfect? All I ask is that you give him—and yourselves—a fair opportunity."

Bishop Venlin gestured to the boy behind him, a well-dressed youth wearing a traveling cloak and a side sword.

"The lad is twelve and a half," Rawlings said. "The training takes a minimum of ten years. Knights graduate at eighteen. You ought to be capable of the math, Bishop. Also, the character of a man is like clay, malleable when young, but once it hardens, one needs to break it to change its shape. If he had come here when he was younger, something might be done. But altering attitudes when the boy is a man, is—"

"Just one more chance, please."

Rawlings stared hard at the bishop. Then something outside the office caught his eye and made the master frown.

"Jerish!" Rawlings barked.

From out in the hallway, a young boy approached. He was holding a broom, which he'd obviously been employing to clean the corridor. Still, he presented himself as straight and tall as he could manage, the broom at his side like a proper pikeman.

"Jerish, this young man is Darius Seret of Alburnia. Darius will be attending here, on a *provisional* basis." He looked hard at the bishop. "Darius has a mark against him. If he gains another, he will be barred from any chance of being a knight. I want you to be his orientation guide."

"Yes, sir," Jerish replied, sharp and clear, but his eyes betrayed his confusion. "Which bed, sir?"

"Yours."

The breath seemed to go out of Jerish, but the boy wavered for only a second before saying, "Yes, sir." Then holding tight to the broom handle, he stepped to face Darius, who stood a head taller and had fuzz on his chin and upper lip that spoke rumors of the man to come. "Follow me, please."

Jerish walked up the corridor toward the dormitory stairs and waited for Darius to follow. As they left, Mawyndulë told Rawlings, "I'm certain that you'll find Darius Seret to be a wonderful asset to your institution. He merely needs some time to get settled and find his feet."

"We teach balance here," Rawlings said. "Finding one's feet is everything. Might I ask why the head of the Church of Nyphron has taken such an interest in this boy?"

"His father asked me to."

Rawlings looked less than convinced. "Does that happen often? People send a bishop of the church on personal errands?"

"His father is a good and faithful member of the church, and while I may be the leader of the church, all that means is that I am the lowest servant to all its members."

"I see."

"Does this bother you, Master Rawlings? You seem dismayed."

"There have been an unprecedented number of recruits as of late with strong ties to your church."

"It is everyone's church, Master Rawlings. We worship the First Emperor, after all. Given that the Teshlor's creed is to serve and protect all the emperors, it seems only sensible that the Church of Nyphron and the Teshlors have close ties.

Who else would you rather adopt into your ranks than those who were born with a reverence for the Imperial Throne?"

"The problem is that we teach loyalty to the *living* emperor, not to a dead one whose edicts are delivered by way of a self-proclaimed bishop."

"I'm not certain I understand you. Are you saying—"

"Don't make me hurt you!" The voice was that of Darius Seret, and it came from down the corridor.

With another frown, which appeared to be his default expression, Master Rawlings got up. "Excuse me, Bishop."

The aging Teshlor strode up the hallway, and Mawyndulë followed.

"This whole place stinks," Darius was saying. "You stink, this hallway stinks, and that fellow—that Master Rawlings—stinks. Him and his test. He told me to kill the kid. Gave me the blade! Explained it as 'kill or be killed.' What did he expect me to do? Let the other brat have a free go at me? Does he think I'm an idiot? But it was all a ruse, a lie, because he stopped me. Did some sort of trick. Caught me off my guard. The bastard."

"Don't speak of Master Rawlings like that," Jerish warned. "It's disrespectful."

"The man is a liar and a cheat." The boys' voices came from just ahead.

"No. Master Rawlings is a great man, but you, sir, are a spoiled, selfish, egotistical coward."

"Take that back."

"Which one?" Jerish asked. "Never mind. They're all true, and I can't take back the truth."

When the pair came into view, they were standing in the empty corridor facing each other. With one hand on his sword, Darius towered over Jerish. The younger boy still held onto the broom. Noticing their approach, Jerish took his eyes off Darius to look their way. The governor's son took that moment to strike him hard across the face.

"Darius, what are you doing?" the bishop asked.

"This disrespectful brat insulted me. Called me a coward. I am putting him in his place, teaching him a lesson. Isn't that right, boy? This is a school after all."

Jerish didn't answer. He wiped his face. His nose was bleeding.

"Now take it back, or I shall strike you again," Darius demanded.

"Stop it, Darius," the bishop demanded. "This doesn't look good. He's nothing but a child."

"If he's old enough to mouth off to the provincial governor's son, he's old enough to learn a hard lesson." Darius looked at the men in the corridor. "Or will Master Rawlings interfere again?"

Rawlings shook his head. "This is between you two. Settle it as you will."

"Hear that?" Darius said. "They're not going to save you. You're all mine. Now withdraw the insult. Apologize this instant for pretending you are equal to me, and I'll let you leave my presence."

Jerish stood straight and in a loud voice said, "For the record and those who came late, Darius Seret has accused Master Rawlings of being a liar and a cheat. He has also maligned the Teshlor Guild and indicated he has no intention of following its rules."

"I have done no such—"

"And he has thrown me to the ground and struck me for denouncing his false accusations." Jerish looked square at Rawlings. "I have done nothing."

"Nothing?" Darius laughed. "You continue to assault me with your words and disrespectful tone. This boy, this common moneylender's son, is so pathetic he can't even cut it in this Academy." Darius looked at the bishop. "He's being expelled, you know. Told me himself."

Darius took a step closer, forcing Jerish to look up at him. He raised a gloved fist. "Take it back."

"No."

Darius struck him again. The blow was harder this time, and landed square, since Jerish made no attempt to move. The weight of the bigger boy drove him back against the wall. More blood sprayed, but he did not fall.

"Darius, please," Venlin begged.

He could tell that Rawlings was already suspicious of the bishop's request. This sort of behavior was only going to inflame that mistrust. The game Mawyndulë was playing was hard enough. He didn't need the pieces on the board taking it upon themselves to be stupid.

"Do it, boy." Darius didn't even give Jerish time to speak before he struck again.

There was a crack as Darius broke the little boy's nose. The blow had jerked the kid's head around. Blood sprayed, leaving a rooster's tail image on the wall.

"I won't ask again." Darius slowly drew the sword from his scabbard.

How stupid can this brat be? Breaking the nose of a younger kid who had told what Mawyndulë knew—and everyone else likely guessed—to be the truth was already putting Darius's admission at risk. The murder of a child in front of the headmaster and a bishop would see the governor's son arrested and very likely executed. Not only would he have made this trip for nothing, but Mawyndulë was also concerned the collateral damage might spill onto him and the church he was building. Mawyndulë couldn't read Rawlings because, like all Teshlors, Rawlings wore the Orinfar, but Mawyndulë didn't need the Art to understand why the old man was letting this happen. His reasoning was clear: *If this is the sort of raw material the church sends us, I don't think the Teshlor Guildhall will be accepting any more applications from child killers, thank you very much.*

In Mawyndulë's youth, even as recently as a few hundred years ago, he would have tried using the Art to interfere. He now saw how that was a mistake. Imaly had managed everything she had done without magic. The Art was for the big stuff; using it for trivial matters not only invited complications, but it was also an admission of defeat. Patience, intellect, and feeding the weaknesses in everyone around him worked better.

But even if Darius killed the boy, Mawyndulë could salvage treasure. "I tried to stop it!" he would say. "I was the only one! The headmaster stood by and watched as a child was murdered right in front of them! Are these the people we want creating the new generation of Teshlors?"

"Darius, this has gone too far!" the bishop shouted, trying his best to sound outraged.

Mawyndulë looked over, hoping for intervention, but Rawlings did nothing.

The shouting brought others. A few boys and another Academy master. Mawyndulë hoped he might have the sense to stop the murder, but this new master also did nothing except show concern as he watched Rawlings.

Darius raised the tip of his blade to Jerish's cheek. "Take it back. Now."

"No." Jerish remained firm, back straight, arms at his sides.

With a slash, Darius cut a red line down Jerish's face, causing him to hiss and retreat until his back was against the wall.

"No wonder you're being expelled," Darius said. "You're a terrible student. Can't seem to learn a thing, can you? Take back the insult, or by the beard of Novron, I will kill you."

Jerish, who had his palm pressed to his cheek trying to slow the spill of his blood, looked up. "What did you say?"

"I said," Darius spoke in exaggerated precision, "take back what you said, or by the beard of Novron, I will kill you." To emphasize this, he raised his blade over his head.

"That's what I thought you said." Jerish looked at Rawlings, frowned, and sighed. "I'm sorry." This made Darius smile, but only briefly. "I cannot allow you to take the Lord's name in vain," Jerish declared with a tone of great regret.

"What? You foolish little mongrel. You deserve this."

"Darius, no!" Venlin shouted as the older boy swung.

This time, Jerish stepped aside, allowing the sword's tip to spark across the wall. He stomped on Darius's foot with the sharp edge of his boot heel, making the older boy cry out. Then he cracked the broom handle across Darius's knuckles. The sword came free and clattered onto the floor. With Darius off balance, shocked, and now unarmed, Jerish took the extra time afforded to him by a bewildered governor's son to wind up before breaking the broom handle across the older boy's face. Darius went down, clapping his head hard against the floor and uttering a grunt that was quickly followed by a cry and a series of moans.

Jerish stared at Darius's bleeding face. He dropped the splintered end of the broom, wiped blood from his eyes, and turned to face Master Rawlings.

Rawlings stared at the boy, stone-faced.

"I need to wash," Jerish said as he moved to the stairs. "I'll clear out my things right afterward. Do I have permission to use the needle and thread?" He put a hand to his cheek, where he had been cut.

"You have nothing to clear out," Rawlings said.

"I have my blanket, sir. I brought it with me. I will take it as I leave."

"You will not," Rawlings said.

"Please, sir. It was given to me by Deacon Kile. It's mine."

"I don't care who gave it to you. It stays here."

Jerish's shoulders dropped, and he struggled to breathe through the blood in his nose and mouth. "Then . . . I'll just go." He bowed his head and walked toward the forward stairs.

"You do not have leave to go," Rawlings said. "You made a mess, and you will clean it. I do not wish to see your blood on this wall."

Other members of the Academy, other boys, had arrived and stood in the rear watching the event, whispering among themselves.

Jerish looked down at his stained tunic. Droplets were still falling from his nose and leaving a tiny trail on his chest and on the floor. He nodded. "Yes, sir," he said. "And . . ." He struggled to get the words out. "And I'm sorry, sir. You were right about me. I'm incapable of restraint."

Rawlings crossed the distance between them.

The speed of the approach made Mawyndulë suspect the master had lost all patience with the boy, and he thought he knew why. Rawlings had wanted Darius to kill the kid. Politically, it would have been a boon, but by some strange fluke the child had laid out Darius and ruined everything. Now out of sheer anger, the master himself would administer the punishment. Mawyndulë fought against a smile. If Rawlings killed the boy, Mawyndulë could petition the emperor for a replacement. A Teshlor more sympathetic to his church.

Rawlings halted in front of Jerish. He took a deep breath and sighed. Jerish looked up, letting the blood drip down his chin.

"Jerish." Rawlings' face retained its indifference. "A Teshlor needs discipline, control, and a firm grip on his temper. I explained that to you." The master stepped around Jerish to inspect Darius who remained on the floor, rocking side to side and moaning through hands that clutched his face.

Rawlings shook his head in disgust. Then he faced Jerish once more. "This institution means everything to you, yet Darius cares nothing for it. You feel unworthy of the Teshlor Guild, while he feels the guild unworthy of him. He is rich and can prosper in any number of endeavors, but when you leave here you would have only an old blanket. You were aware that Darius Seret failed his entrance exam—a test you passed—and yet he was being admitted while you were being expelled to make room for him. Jerish, you were ordered to escort and educate Darius, to help him replace you, to give him everything you had, or ever dreamed of having. None of which he cared about, none of which he wanted or deserved. He insulted you and maligned everything you hold dear. Even after being beat and cut, you still *restrained* yourself."

Jerish glanced at Darius. "Doesn't look like restraint to me, sir."

"A knight does not inflict pain out of revenge, or in response to a slight, but in the service of truth, the protection of the weak, and defense against cruelty. Truth is, Darius was being cruel to one he believed was weak. Discipline is one thing, son"—Rawlings approached Jerish and laid a hand on his shoulder—"but if you had showed any more restraint, you'd be dead. Go get cleaned up. Report for the midday meal, then come back here and scrub this wall and floor. Mind you, I want no stain left reminding *anyone* of this unpleasant affair. But leave your blanket where it lies. Your bed is still yours. You're staying here. It is Darius Seret who will be leaving."

"You can't do that," the bishop declared.

Rawlings faced him. "Oh, I assure you I can. As headmaster and recruitment officer for the Imperial Academy of Teshlor Knights, I have absolute authority over who is admitted and who isn't. Only the emperor himself can overrule me."

Venlin frowned as he produced a scroll from within the folds of his robe. Mawyndulë had hoped he wouldn't have to resort to this. "I didn't want to start things on the wrong foot, you understand. I had hoped Darius would be admitted on his own merit. Even after failing the exam, I still held out hope that he would prove himself worthy." Venlin handed the paper to Rawlings, who noted the imperial seal, cracked it, and read.

Mawyndulë had created the prop as a backup plan, but it came with flaws. If Rawlings challenged it, if he presented it to the emperor—which wasn't entirely impossible—Bishop Venlin would have a great deal of explaining to do. And if it was shown to a Cenzar, they would detect traces of Artistic manipulation, which would really blow the top off everything. The odds of all this happening were so slim, however, he decided it was worth the risk.

The note was short. The less written the better. Rawlings looked up at Venlin and nodded. "Very well. Novice Darius, welcome to the Academy."

Jerish took a breath. "I guess I'll get my blanket after all, sir. But thank you for—for what you said."

"What I said is that as recruitment officer for the Academy, I have absolute authority over who is admitted and who isn't. I also have the same authority over who is expelled. Now, unless the bishop is hiding another note from His Eminence requiring me to banish you . . ."

Venlin shook his head.

"Good, then. Jerish Grelad will remain a member of this school."

"But you only have so many beds," Jerish pointed out. "And you said—"

"Would you prefer to break ice off the crates in the alley as you search the garbage for old bones to gnaw on?"

"No, sir." Jerish wiped his nose, painting his index finger with a bright red line.

You'd think the bleeding would have stopped by now, Mawyndulë thought. He never could stand the sight of blood.

"Do you suspect this guild, which has successfully defended this empire for over a thousand years against a multitude of invaders and ambitious generals, to be incapable of adding an additional bed to the Academy's dormitory?"

"No, sir."

"Then be quiet."

"Yes, sir."

"Now get a rag, put your head up, then go to the infirmary. Make sure your nose is set straight if you still wish to be a Teshlor. Knights don't have crooked noses."

Jerish nodded, and as the others began to help Darius up, Jerish headed back toward the main hall.

"How old is he?" the bishop asked.

"Almost ten," Rawlings replied.

"Are you telling me that boy, who just demolished Darius, is only nine years old?"

"Cadet Grelad?" Bishop Venlin called out as he quick-timed it down the corridor, catching Jerish at the stairs. "Cadet Grelad?"

The boy stopped and turned. "Sorry, Your Grace. I didn't . . . well, no one calls me that."

"No, no, let me apologize. I don't know the protocol here. How do they address you? Trainee? Pupil? Apprentice?"

"Just Jerish, usually."

"Okay," the bishop replied. "Master Rawlings says you're number nine on the leaderboard. That's unusual for a nine-year-old, isn't it?" Venlin tucked his robes tight around his legs as he sat down on the top step.

Jerish nodded. He seated himself respectfully on a lower tier. "They say younger boys don't beat older ones."

Venlin nodded. "Yes, yes. That's what I thought. It seems you are very talented."

"I work hard. Don't really have much else to do. I'm not popular."

"I wasn't either when I was young. I never had a single friend when growing up. Lots of enemies, though." He winked.

"Really?"

The bishop nodded. "Those destined for greatness . . ." He looked into Jerish's eyes. "People can see it, glimpse a hint of the future. It scares them. They know we're different. We don't fit the world they snuggle up in. We live our lives our own way. Often, most of what we suffer is the result of people we try to please or those who just want to hurt us."

Jerish nodded. The boy didn't have the Orinfar tattoos yet and Mawyndulë could read him like a book.

"I'd like to ask you a question, if that's all right?"

Jerish nodded, thought better of it, and said, "Yes, Your Grace."

"Well, it's like this. Rawlings told me you were being expelled for getting into so many fights. Then Darius taunted you mercilessly, and it's clear you were holding back. I suspect you thought that by showing restraint, you would secure your place here, but in the end, you fought Darius. Why?"

Jerish frowned. "He cursed our Lord. It's wrong, isn't it? My mother told me it was."

"Oh yes," the bishop nodded with great sincerity. "Your mother is a very wise woman."

Again Jerish frowned. "Was."

Mawyndulë pretended to look hurt. As the pious bishop, he had decades of practice. Gently, the bishop placed a hand on the boy's shoulder. "I think I understand why you're ranked ninth at the tender age of nine."

"Nine and nine months."

The bishop smiled. He leaned in and whispered, "You are a true warrior of Novron, and our Lord protects you."

"That's what my mother told me!" Jerish exclaimed in shock.

"And she was indeed a wise woman. Jerish, Novron has his eyes on you. Your destiny is in his hands. And I can assure you, it will be like no other. Still, you need to be careful. Your mother was a loyal member of the church, as are you, I assume?"

He nodded. "I believe in Novron."

"Of course, but there is so much more. I fear a war is coming, young Jerish, a terrible war. One that may tear this empire apart. We already see the beginnings with the rising strength and influence of the Cenzarium."

"The Cenzars are our friends."

"They are practitioners of magic, and magic is evil. Novron outlawed it in his lifetime, but over the years, over the centuries, those greedy for power have brought it back. The elves who nearly destroyed us in the Great War were sorcerers, you know. And what do you think they called themselves?"

"Wizards?"

"No—*Artists*, the same as the Cenzars call themselves. The Cenzarium will ruin this empire if they are allowed to. They admire the elves—want to be them. You see how they dress in those fancy robes and sashes. That's how the ancient elven mages dressed. And the Cenzarium—the very building itself—was once the temple to Ferrol." Venlin raised a pointed finger. "They want us to turn our backs on Novron and worship the Fhrey god, but we can't let them. We need to fight, Jerish. We need to defend Novron. I believe I can trust you to do that, can't I, Jerish?"

"Yes, sir. Absolutely, sir."

"You'll need to start attending the church. You must learn the ways of truth and light to be a proper soldier of Novron. Will you do that?"

"Of course."

"Good boy. I'm going to keep my eye on you, Jerish. I suspect you are destined for great things."

PART THREE

Hidden Gifts

YEAR 2112 IR

CHAPTER EIGHT

The First City

SIX YEARS LATER . . .
THE GREEN SEA, SPRING

Ezra marveled at how fast the shore rushed by—far faster than he could possibly run. Niblick had the *Great Excuse* tilted on her beam so that the deck was up at an angle that caused Ezra to hang onto the gunwale. Clouds of spray burst over the bow as they slammed through the waves. Wind was in his hair, sun on his face, and his heart felt buoyant, as his whole family flew aboard the boat that he and Niblick had spent twelve years refinishing. If not for the look of concern on Hekkabah's face, Ezra would have been happier than he'd ever been.

It was clear that she didn't like how fast they were going. Mashie himself gripped the rail with his claws, tight enough to leave marks. But Hekkabah's expression, Ezra knew, grew from more than a fear of speed. What was thrilling to him was something else to her.

The unknown is frightening to everyone, he reminded himself. No real danger existed, but he could never convince her of that.

Only Niblick, who grinned at the wheel, shared Ezra's joy. *This,* they both knew, *is living.*

When they came in sight of the white cliffs, Niblick righted the boat, and Ezra drew down the jib, slowing their pace to a modest coast.

"I still don't like this," Niblick told Hekkabah, as he spun the wheel, swinging the ship around the shoals and revealing the numerous stilt-supported Klune pondoks up from the beach. "It's just stupid exposing ourselves. And what do we get out of it?"

"We do not do it for us," Hekkabah replied, still holding onto the rail. Then she let go long enough to brush the spray from her eyes with one hand.

"That's not an answer."

"The seed of aspiration does not sprout in a garden of selfishness."

"Have you got a proverb for everything? Is that what they teach you in the temple, how to use words to convince people that up is down, based on the rule that if you babble better than the next guy, you must be right?"

"Relax. Nothing looks amiss," she told him. "And the Klune need us. Hergal and Rimzog would have died if we had not come last month. We saved their lives. Is this not reward enough?"

"Nothing's reward enough if the riva or the humans find out where we've been hiding."

"And you so love it there, do you?"

Niblick shrugged. "It's better than dead. Not a lot better, mind you. I'm pretty sure I won't have to listen to Mashie's thunderstorm-snoring in the afterlife, but I admit to a certain irrational fondness for breathing."

The boat bumped against the short dock the Klune had made to spare Hekkabah the trouble and indignity of having to swim through the waves to the beach. Mashie and Niblick tied the vessel to the pier as Hekkabah gathered her things.

Ezra helped her. The priestess had accumulated a fair supply of medicines, cloths, and a number of tools that made Ezra queasy just to look at: the sort with sharp hooks and drills. Among the pile of sacks and bags, he found The Package. Still wrapped in canvas, the bundle looked smaller than the last time—though he couldn't be sure, as he hadn't seen it for twelve years.

Hekkabah caught him staring. She said nothing.

Ezra caught hints of anticipation and worry radiating off her. The impression that presented itself in his mind was that she saw him as a dog off its leash, and a squirrel had just appeared.

Is this a test? Hekkabah had quizzed him before, just as when she had gambled in the big field with the lions. Since then, most inquiries were simple things such as asking him what he wanted to eat, or what to carry on a trip, or which path to take. These all appeared to be harmless, even polite, questions, but Ezra knew better. He knew a lot of things now.

Hekkabah hadn't so much opened a door for him the day she revealed his talent but forced him to see the wide-open threshold that until then he had mostly disregarded. Ezra had a new sense as powerful as sight or hearing, though it reached him on the level more associated with feelings. The world ceased to be a foreign thing, becoming instead an extension of himself. He saw how he and others fit like threads into the tapestry of existence. With practice, he knew he could weave his own patterns and alter those already made, but mostly he was amazed that he could see the design as a design. She'd shown him that the annoying sensations and intuitions he'd been struggling to ignore were valuable messages. The instant he'd stopped the lion attack was the moment he learned a new language, and with it came whispers that allowed him to cheat.

Ezra picked up the other bundles but didn't touch the canvas package. He knew Hekkabah wanted to see if he would—to see if he might demand his gift. He couldn't read her mind, but some things were obvious. What wasn't obvious was that this only became a test the moment he saw The Package. Hekkabah hadn't brought it for that purpose, but for something else. "Why is that here?"

"It goes where I go."

He studied her to no avail. Elan told him nothing. Either she didn't know or refused to say. Frequent and plentiful were the limits of his seemingly limitless power.

"Really?" he said with a side-eye, as he lifted the other bags and placed them on the dock. "Everywhere you go, you take that thing with you? No offense, but that's a little hard to believe as it's not exactly small, you know? Kinda hard to hide a bundle the size of a newborn baby. Where you been keeping it?"

Her brows rose. Then she looked past him at Niblick and pointed a deadly finger at him. *"You!"*

"What'd I do?" Niblick replied, appearing genuinely shocked.

"You have been an awful influence on him." She shook her head. "When he came to us, he was so respectful, so polite. Since then, I've tried to educate him, to raise him to be wise, thoughtful of his words and the power they have, but whenever he opens his mouth, all I hear are *your* words—your disrespect—tumbling out."

Niblick looked at Ezra and grinned with pride.

"Do not encourage it! Ezra will be the Hand of Uberlin. He should not be silly."

"Silly?" Niblick frowned. "I've always seen myself as sardonic, insightful, witty even."

"That makes one of you."

"I didn't mean anything," Ezra apologized.

"Of course you didn't, but now you must explain this to me. Remember that, or one day you will grow up to be *him*."

"There are worse things, you know." Niblick raised his hands to ward off Hekkabah's building retort. "I'm just saying—there are far worse examples in this world than me, and you know it."

This stopped her. Hekkabah sighed. "I suppose so, but that is hardly the bar of excellence I was aiming for." She looked at Mashie, who carried down the rest of the supplies, stacking them on the dock, which vibrated with the arrival of some Klune who ran to meet them. "Are you staying with me or going with them?"

"I'm done with this thing," Mashie replied, slapping the hull of the boat with a claw.

"Hey, watch it," Niblick said. "The kid and I just put a new coat of paint on that this winter."

"How long will you be gone?" Hekkabah asked him.

"I don't know," Niblick said. "Couple days, at least. The kid helped me work on the *Great Excuse* for years. He deserves the chance to see what real sailing is all about."

"And you think a pleasure cruise is less dangerous than spending a week with the Klune? What if you are spotted by a ship?"

"Unlikely. Nobody sails the middle of the Green Sea—there's no point. But if they do, I can handle it. The *Great Excuse* is a fine ship now, and maybe you don't know it, but I'm a pretty talented sailor. Also, I got the kid here—who, by the way—ain't so much a kid no more. He'll be nineteen in a few days, right?"

Hekkabah nodded, and to Ezra it looked forced. She didn't want him to grow up. At least she didn't want to accept it. The priestess who twelve years before had forfeited her privileged life to deliver a package across the sea, had yet to do so. He doubted she'd ever admit it, but Ezra suspected Hekkabah dragged her feet because she had found a new calling, one she was far less willing to cast aside. The aging Arkum Ba Ran had become his mother.

"I was supposed to give you a gift, but this gift is not for a child."

The comment had once led Ezra to believe the gift was a powerful weapon, something dangerous. Over the years, that opinion had changed. What need did he have for a weapon when he could now call lightning? The reason for the delay appeared obvious. The package was some sort of call to action. Hekkabah had more than once referred to him as the Hand of Uberlin. Ezra was destined for something. Presenting the gift to him would leave Hekkabah at the end of her god-given quest but launch his. She would face the end of her purpose with nothing to show for it but a human son who would likely be required to leave her the moment she fulfilled her duty. This concern could only have been stoked by Ezra's increasing desire to see more of the world than their river hideaway.

In recent years, Ezra had taken to exploring deeper into the forest and asking questions about what lay beyond. Niblick, who had explored more of the world than any of them, told tales of wondrous places. Many were the islands, bays, jungles, and ports he'd personally visited. But others were grand adventures told by traders, exiles, and mercenaries—stories of the far west, all of which began and ended with Percepliquis. Hearsay reported that the capital of the Novronian Empire was five miles square and composed of buildings taller than any tree, each with its own private stream of hot and cold water. Millions of people from all over the world lived, worked, and played there. The city had palaces just for books, and arenas like the ones Mashie used to fight in, but big enough to hold full-scale reenactments of famous battles—some complete with ships! Percepliquis was home to not only the emperor but also the Teshlor Guild—headquarters for the greatest warriors in the world—and the famous school for wizards known as the Cenzarium. Niblick referred to the Teshlors and Cenzars with both fear and reverence—not unlike how he spoke of the riva. They traveled in teams, one Cenzar and one Teshlor, and they patrolled the far reaches of the empire on the emperor's behalf, with the power to rattle and awe any high official or military commander into submission. Legend held that two hundred years before, these Teshlors and Cenzars had led imperial legions into battle and driven the Ba Ran off the continent. Ezra longed to visit this place, to see these things for himself, but he knew Hekkabah, Niblick, and Mashie never could. Just as he could not travel back with them to the Old World, they could not go with him to the New, and whenever Ezra had expressed a desire to see Percepliquis, Hekkabah had grown quiet.

"Now, I can't be positive," Niblick said, "but I'm fairly certain there ain't no Ba Ran ships carrying their own personal daza. And I must admit that provides quite an advantage."

"What if an imperial warship spots you?" Hekkabah asked. "They have been known to have Cenzars."

"We're going out to sea. Humans never leave sight of land. We'll be fine. You, on the other hand, should take care. You're only a stone's throw from Shahabad here, and as we know, Warlord Banka isn't our friend."

"Mashie will protect me."

"I'm sure he will, but he's only got two claws. So keep your head down."

"Then I will see you in a few days," Hekkabah said to them as she turned to greet the Klune, who were already in the process of gathering her gear.

Ezra threw his arms around Hekkabah and hugged her.

She hugged him back, but there were questions in her eyes. "Why do you . . . you haven't hugged me like that since you were ten."

Ezra shrugged because he honestly didn't know why. Emotion had overtaken him with no explanation, and he felt a bit foolish.

She smiled. "It is good. I missed the hugs. Thank you."

She and Mashie waved goodbye as Ezra and Niblick cast off. As the dock and the village disappeared, Ezra realized why he had hugged her so tightly. Elan had told him to.

Ezra sensed it long before he saw anything—desolation.

Standing at the rail of the *Great Excuse*, looking east, he waited for the coast to appear. They had been at sea for almost three days, and Niblick had carefully avoided land. According to him, all sailors preferred to stay within shore-sight. Most of those traveling from Krun to the north islands preferred to cross at the Strait of Hyphus, a thirty-mile gap between Calynia and Marn. Niblick referred to it as a "freaking family reunion of Urgvarian ships that were so crowded you could walk the distance using their decks." Instead of going there, they had sailed due north across the open sea for safety's sake. This, Ezra understood to be a dangerous proposition. Humans would never dare such a thing. Even the Ba Ran avoided open water whenever possible. The primary fear was getting lost. East and west were easily determined by the rising and falling sun, and at midday, shadows roughly determined north and south. At night, the stars were a map of sorts, but all of this was precious little to navigate by, and weather interfered. Niblick chose this treacherous route by the simple logic that, as he put it, "No one else would be as stupid." Turned out he was right. They had seen no ships, and no one had seen them.

"Any minute now," Niblick said, coming up alongside him and peering ahead.

Ezra stared at the horizon, straining to see. His feelings picked up impressions, but it was like fumbling in the dark with blind fingers. What he sensed was confusing: ancient sorrow, death, loss. Nothing more specific. Nothing clear or tangible revealed itself, but like licking charcoal, it left an awful aftertaste that was hard to shake.

"There she is," Niblick declared and pointed.

Ezra saw it a moment later, a gray line, which provided even less information than the gossip Elan was whispering.

Niblick moved to the stern and rotated the rudder, turning the ship a few degrees to starboard and aiming them at the appearing line. Once more, the *Great Excuse* plowed the waves, tilting to the side so that anything not tied down would have slid across the rising deck. Water sprayed, and Niblick had that grin on his face that Ezra rarely ever saw on land.

Looking back at the northern horizon, Ezra saw the view had changed dramatically. More land had appeared, two highlands with a gap between them.

"That's the Mouth," Niblick explained. "The entrance."

"There's an entrance? I didn't know there was a *door*."

"Not a door, you buffoon. It's not a house we're going to. You're sure you want to go in?"

"You've been there, right?" Ezra asked.

"Once. It's not the sort of thing you do twice. I'm pretty sure folks stopped having picnics here about a billion years ago. I was just thinking you might be in a hurry to get back, seeing as how she brought the package."

Ezra smirked. "It's not my birthday."

"What's that got to do with it?"

Apparently, Ba Ran didn't give gifts on birthdays.

"I just would have thought . . ." Ezra shrugged. "Back in Haddon, you're considered a man when you turn thirteen, so I figured she'd give it to me then, but no. When I turned sixteen, I was certain I'd get it. Again not so much. Now eighteen has come and gone. I don't know what she's waiting for."

"Me neither. I just hope this gift isn't like fish or something that can go bad. Can you imagine how green and rank a nice tuna steak would be after twelve years in that humid heat?"

"I don't think it's food," Ezra said.

"Any idea what it *is?*"

Ezra shook his head. "Something important."

Niblick frowned. "You've been studying with Hekkabah for twelve years, and that's your most intelligent conclusion? What's she been teaching you?"

"How to talk to Elan, mostly."

"Magic, you mean."

"She doesn't call it that, says it's inaccurate, and . . . I think she's right."

"She also says Uberlin hasn't forgotten us—all evidence to the contrary. How does she teach you magic, anyway? She's not a secret oberdaza, is she?"

"Oberdaza means *crude creator*, right?"

"Something like that, I guess?" Niblick adjusted the ship's wheel a few degrees and checked the sail. "It's originally an Ankor term, and I'm not a linguist. You can ask Mashie when we get back. All I know is that oberdaza dress in feathers, dance poorly, sing terrible songs—and then the world blows up. Exactly the sort of fun times you'd expect from Ankors."

"Hekkabah is not a daza, certainly not an *oberdaza,* but that doesn't so much matter, as I'm not learning magic." He struggled to explain. "It's like when I drew on the walls back in Haddon. I'm learning to use my imagination to create something real, but I'm not doing it alone. I'm joining with the world, and together, Elan and I change things."

"Ah-huh. You know, normally I'd say you were full of crap, but . . ." Niblick pointed up at the black sail that bowed full. "That sail has been full like that for three days. Hardly needed to trim it at all. Never too much or too little wind, and always in the right direction. Now, I've been sailing for decades. I was born on a ship—bet I never told you that. Still, I ain't never experienced such a perfect run of weather as this." He stared. "It's you, isn't it?"

Ezra smiled.

"How?" Niblick asked. "I ain't seen you do nothing. Like I said, oberdaza hop around, sing like dying cats, smoke tulan leaves—even seen some vomit, and others bleed themselves. They howl and shout and scream and wave, but not once did I ever see them do anything as"—he thought a moment—"as *slick* as this."

"Wind is easy. Clouds are . . ." Ezra grinned. "Clouds are fun."

Niblick stared. "You're starting to scare me, kid. How powerful are you?"

Ezra shrugged. He honestly didn't know. Hekkabah hadn't let him find out.

"Too much of anything is bad," Hekkabah had told him more than once, starting the day he commanded lions and persuaded a field of grass to lie down. She had seemed pleased to be right, happy he saved them, but a little frightened, too.

"What about happiness?" he had countered. "Can you have too much?"

"Yes. Happiness is merely a state when everything is as it should be. But if everything is always perfect, there is no challenge, no reason to live, no purpose to exist. Happiness is the reward for struggle, and without struggle there can be no growth. What does not grow, Ezra, is dead—or should be. Still, you must guard against indulgence. Too much will create a thirst. Quenching that thirst makes you drunk. Being drunk invites greater excess. Soon your judgment is lost, and power becomes your only desire. That's when it happens."

"What happens?"

"You change into the worst version of yourself, and eventually lose even that, until all you are is a shadow."

At the time, he hadn't understood, but over the years, he connected the dots and realized she wasn't speculating but speaking from experience. She had witnessed the effects of overindulgence firsthand.

"To answer your question," he replied to Niblick, "yes, I want to go in."

"I doubt you're gonna wanna stay long."

"Why is that?"

"Look for yourself." Niblick pointed out across the water.

They were much closer now, the *Great Excuse* entering between the two headlands that rose on either side. The shore revealed itself. Chalky rock and parched soil formed a shattered landscape where no living thing existed. Here the sky was thick with cold, gray clouds that weren't of Ezra's making, yet they appeared in no way natural. Like bundles of filthy cotton, they were too thick. Rolling and erupting, they were anxious and very angry. Nothing on the land moved except the clouds of ash brought to life by howling winds.

"I suppose you can see now why this is no longer a stop on sightseeing tours," Niblick said. "I'm surprised you wanted to come here at all. I'm even more surprised Hekkabah let you."

Ezra shifted his feet awkwardly.

"She did give her blessing for this little excursion, right?"

Ezra focused on the cliffs rising on either side of the boat.

"Unbelievable." Niblick rang the rings on his ears. "She sure has taught you, hasn't she? Growing up trapped with the three of us over the years has made an impression. I've noticed that you've picked up some of my more colorful expressions and adopted a dash of my wonderfully acerbic wit. You even developed a drop of Mashie's candid, welcome-mister-sunshine attitude. But that old priestess has gotten into your head big-time. You're both as devious as demons."

"I just wanted to see it."

"Well, you're looking at it. Happy?"

"But where's the city?"

"Dead ahead."

Forward of the bow, all Ezra saw was water, not as violent as the Green Sea. The waves were smaller, and in the far distance, he saw hills ringing a massive inland lake.

"I don't understand."

"No one does—but this is it. According to legend, right in front of you was once a massive plateau hundreds of feet high, and on it sat the greatest city of antiquity: Erebus—the First City. Then some ten thousand years ago, give or take a millennium or two, it became this—a crater lake about the size of a small sea."

The wind in the mainsail faltered as the *Great Excuse* drifted into the ring. The lapping waves made a loud sound where they slapped the hull and echoed off the barren hills.

"All around you is the land of Uber, the heart of the Old World. Sort of like Percepliquis is today, I suppose. This is where Rex Uberlin ruled the entire world. Up north was Dorthineia. If you squint, you can barely see the mountains where the city stood."

Ezra could just see jagged tips in the distance, where they blended with the hazy sky.

"Supposedly, that's where the Dromeians used to live. And up that way"—he pointed again, this time to the east—"is Sirdia Ferrillia."

"The City of Ferrol," Ezra confirmed. "And this"—he pointed to the southeast—"is Marn, the land of man. Hekkabah explained it all, but . . ." He took in the devastated landscape. "Words could never describe this. Do you know how it happened? Hekkabah said the city was destroyed by the war. She explained how Uberlin, with his home base in Erebus, nearly won but then he disappeared. Without him, his forces were disorganized, and the children of Drome, Ferrol, and Mari went on the attack. So this place saw a lot of combat, but how could mere fighting do this?"

Shaking his head, Niblick jangled his earrings. "Wanna land?"

"Not really. You?"

"Not especially, no. Always thought it was kinda creepy being here, like something was watching."

Ezra looked around. "You're right. It does feel that way, but . . . whatever is watching isn't looking for us."

"Not yet. So let's not, you know, invite problems. You have a present waiting."

"Not my birthday, remember?"

"Again what's the deal with birthdays?"

"Humans give gifts to people on their birthdays."

"Really? People in Haddon gave you gifts?"

"No. Other people got gifts."

"But you never did."

Ezra shook his head. "I just thought that maybe . . . I don't know. I mean, I never had a mother either, but now I sort of do. So why not a birthday gift?"

"You gotta stop measuring the height of things based on the yardstick that village gave you, kid. It's like a bird taking directions from an ant."

"Yeah, I know, but . . ."

"But what?"

Ezra shrugged. "I can't explain it. Something just tells me it's a birthday gift."

"Sail!" Niblick shouted, pointing off the steering board side of the boat.

Ezra saw it, a dark vertical line on the horizon. "Ba Ran or human?"

"Doesn't matter. If it sees us—"

"It won't," Ezra declared. A moment ago, the sails of the *Great Excuse* had been full of a southeasterly breeze. With a slap of his hands, that died. The Green Sea became as calm as a puddle. Taking a breath, Ezra closed his eyes. He'd never tried this before and didn't know if it would work, but nearly everything he did had a blind first try. Hekkabah told him things she'd seen other daza do—not to mention the riva—but she could provide no details, no insight. Everything from raising the wind to flattening the grass had been built on instinct, coupled with trial and error. Some attempts, like rain, worked the first time; others, like making food, water, or himself fly, continued to fail. Ezra was confident in what he was about to do because weather was always easy and clouds were fun.

The process—an ever-evolving set of ideas, guesses, and discovered methods—centered on getting in sync with Elan and using her power to tweak the world. The more he changed things, the more power he required and the more it exhausted him. He envisioned it as finding a stick, picking it up, and then swinging it to knock fruit from a tree. Picking up and swinging a little stick was easy. Hefting a giant log and hitting a branch had the power to break the entire limb, but doing so was exhausting.

As the *Great Excuse* slowed in the calm sea, Ezra searched for the elements he needed. Only three were required, and he had plenty of each: air, water, and sun. In a way, it felt like cooking with Hekkabah. He had the ingredients, but the amounts and the timing were what made the bread rise. In this case, Ezra began by warming the air with the sunlight, which soaked up moisture from the sea like a sponge. He drew it in, wrapping the boat. Then with a series of finger movements, he lightly pulled up the colder water from deep below. The moment they came together . . .

"It's getting foggy," Niblick said. "I can't see the . . . oh. You're doing that, aren't you? Smart. I was starting to think I was insane. You just don't get fog on the open sea this late in the year. Hope they don't know that, or if they do, realize this is a sign not to mess with us."

When Ezra opened his eyes, the world around him was white. He couldn't see Niblick or the back half of the boat. "Maybe I overdid it."

"No, no, you did good, kid." Niblick's voice came out of the soup. "Course, without wind I got no way to steer, or move, and we're blind as to which way to go . . . but it's good."

"We don't need wind to move or steer," Ezra replied.

"How's that? You're an expert sailor now? Trust me, a ship needs wind, unless you want us to try paddling, which is like wrestling Mashie—neither is particularly fun."

"You didn't need wind to go down the river to the sea. Didn't even put up the sails."

"That's different. We rode the current."

"Exactly." Ezra focused on the water around and below them. In a way, he could almost see the underwater world the way a blind man can "see" a room using his hands and mind to create a working map. Just as he had been aware of the bee, butterfly, and vultures in the field with the lions, he was now cognizant of a school of fish swimming east and the broken remains of a sunken ship that had become the home for countless forms of aquatic life. He also detected different "rivers" that ran below and around them. Some were warm, others cold.

Just a tweak, just enough to bring the warm current up to the boat. Ezra double-checked to be certain he felt land off to his left. *Yes, the warm and sunny shore is right where it ought to be.*

"We're moving," Niblick announced.

"How do you know?"

"Because either we are or the fog is, and I don't see no reason for you to make the fog move."

"A current is pulling us toward the shore."

"It beats paddling, only . . ."

"Only what?"

Niblick came forward. The Urgvarian struggled to peer through the white gloom. "Only I was never able to determine whether that other ship was moving away from us, or at us."

"Away," Ezra said. "Not positive, but I think I'd know if it was coming this way."

Niblick looked at him and smiled. "You know what? I've decided that helping to raise a tiger isn't such a bad thing." He hooked his thumbs in the belt Ezra had made for him out of braided leather. It had an image of the *Great Excuse* etched into it. Ezra had made it by hand back when he was only twelve, before he'd discovered his power. It had taken months. When it was done and Ezra presented it, Niblick had scoffed. He found fault with the tanning, the design, and of course, the image of the ship. Niblick had also worn the belt every day without exception. Now with his thumbs proudly hooked and his chest out, the Urgvarian Ba Ran appeared every bit the master of his realm.

As they drifted, Ezra played with air currents, opening fleeting holes for them to peek through. The first two times they spotted the distant sail. The last four, they saw nothing, and Ezra relaxed his hold on the damp front, allowing it to disperse naturally. He sat down feeling a tad tired, like he'd been holding a rock outstretched in one hand. The wind naturally returned and Niblick went about the process of capturing it in the sails.

Before long, they were gliding once more, and the faint line of land appeared on the horizon.

Smoke.

As the land changed from a vague line to the irregular shapes of hills and trees, Ezra spotted a dirty, black tendril snaking up to the sky. Something on the shore was burning. Given the distance and the amount of smoke, whatever it was had to be big.

"That's not good," Niblick said. He stared at the beach, where several of the Klune pondoks were burning. "That is *so* not good." Then he glanced off to their left. "It was that freaking ship. It's heading back to Shahabad. Blow us in, Ezra. Get us back."

Reaching the docks, they were greeted by the cries of wounded Klune scattered on the beach. Dozens of pale bodies lay in the sand. Ezra spotted two of them face down, floating under the dock. Blood was everywhere.

Niblick paused to tie up the *Great Excuse*, so he was a few paces behind Ezra as he raced up the planks, then hit the beach, where he found more dead and dying Klune.

"Hekkabah!" Ezra shouted over the crash of waves and wails of the wounded.

"Mashie!" Niblick yelled.

Entering the caves, they found a gruesome sight. Fifty or more Klune lay dead, missing arms, legs, and heads. Some were mutilated beyond recognition. Pots, trivets, and tripods were scattered. Hot coals looked to have been used to burn some of the Klune.

"Hekkabah! Mashie!" Their shouts rang out and returned.

"Ezra." The voice was faint, coming from the dark tunnels.

Together Ezra and Niblick crawled into the space at the back of the cavern. They only managed to go in a few feet before they were blocked by something.

With a sound and a flick of his fingers, Ezra summoned a flame that danced on the palm of his hand and revealed that the tunnel was filled with bodies—human bodies. They were stacked one atop another, blocking the corridor.

"Mashie? You in there?" Niblick asked.

"Mostly."

"Mostly? What in the name of Uberlin is that supposed to mean? Hang on, we're coming for you. Did you do all this, big guy? What a mess. There's a lot of dead humans here—a lot."

Pulling the bodies out, Ezra and Niblick cleared a path, allowing light to illuminate the mystery. Hekkabah and Mashie were lying together on the floor of the tiny tunnel. Mashie had an arm around her, holding the priestess to his chest like a baby—both were covered in blood.

"Aww, geez, you two don't look so good," Niblick said.

He was right. Mashie was missing his left claw. A bit of cloth had been twisted tight around his forearm with a stick. Hekkabah was worse. The whole front of her body was soaked slick, her chest rising and falling with great effort.

"Hekkabah?"

Her eyes fluttered, then opened slowly. She saw Niblick first. "Are they gone?"

"Yeah, they were sailing out as we were coming in. But who were they?"

"You were right to be suspicious about Banka," she told him. "He's working for Nexziria. Tortured the Klune until I gave up the package."

"And apparently you were right about Mashie. He protected you."

The Ankor Ba Ran shook his head. "Tried. There were too many."

"But you're alive," Ezra said. "You both are."

Hekkabah shook her head, then coughed.

Mashie answered for her. "Took a sword to the stomach. Just hanging on, I think, waiting for you."

"Ezra," Hekkabah said softly. "The package—Uberlin's Gift—is yours now. It calls for you."

"I don't care about the gift," Ezra replied, surprised to hear his voice crack.

"Just hanging on . . . waiting for you."

Tears were filling his eyes. "I'm going to save you."

He raised his hand.

"No!" she shouted, then coughed again and sputtered. "You cannot." Her head lowered and hung limp for a time.

"I think I can," Ezra said.

Hekkabah's head came up. "You *must* not. I am going to die, Ezra. I am going to die, and you must let me."

"What?" He was baffled. "I don't . . . why?" The flame on his palm grew brilliant, causing the three Ba Ran to squint. "I don't understand. I can save you. I'm positive I can."

"Loss is gain; death is life . . ." Hekkabah looked at Niblick and put on a weak smile. "Up is down."

"What are you talking about? I can—"

"No! Death is not something to be feared, Ezra. It is not some wrong to be fixed. Death is necessary. Death is part of life. Fighting the end is the way of the riva, the way of the raow. This is my last lesson to you. Learn it well."

"Niblick," she addressed him. "Dank is dead, but there are many suffering Klune still alive. You must take them away. The agents of Nexziria will return for me. They will want my head. Take them away. Take them east. Take them back to the Old World. Save them, Niblick."

"The kid can't go to the—"

"Ezra's path is no longer with you. Take him back to the tree house. Leave him there."

"What? That's walnuts. Why?"

"Do it!" she wailed with desperation. "Do it or so help me I will haunt you the rest of your days!" Again she sputtered and gasped, her head going limp.

"Okay, okay. For gripe's sake, fine. But can you at least . . ." He paused. "Hekkabah?"

The old Arkum priestess lay still beside Mashie—too still. She wasn't breathing.

"Hekkabah?" Ezra reached out and placed a hand on hers. "Hekkabah?"

CHAPTER NINE

The Tree House

The familiar bend in the river appeared, and Niblick dropped the jib. Getting up the river had been easy, with Ezra providing unwavering power, and they tied the *Great Excuse* to its usual berth. Niblick and a Klune named Lark, one of the few uninjured refugees who was well on his way to a career as first mate, tied off the vessel.

Ezra stood at the rail, looking at the tree house he had built on the branch where the Magnificent Bird had landed. It all seemed so long ago. The bird had been right. This place, at least, had always been safe.

None of them had a clue why Hekkabah had ordered Ezra to be dropped off at the tree house. General consensus concluded that she had died before she could tell them. This left Ezra to guess. He took what he knew of her last words into consideration. Given that Hekkabah had ordered Niblick to gather the wounded and sail east, knowing the killers would return for her head; that Niblick was to drop Ezra off at home on the way; and that she refused his help, thus ensuring her death, Ezra determined she wanted to be buried at the tree house.

"I used to hate this place," Niblick said, once the boat was properly secured. "Not so sure why now. It was okay here. Boring, but at the moment, I feel that boring is underrated. You know, I don't think I ever noticed, but this place is actually very nice—cozy even."

He was right. The sun was piercing the canopy at points, sending brilliant golden shafts to the floor of the forest, which was blanketed with flowering ground cover. And then there was the tree. Mashie had called it a barowan tree. All Ezra knew was that it was the biggest he'd ever seen—and it was beautiful.

The deck of the *Great Excuse* was carpeted with wounded Klune bundled in blankets. Their heads, arms, and legs were wrapped in makeshift bandages, but they were all stable. Ezra had seen to that, and for the first time, he felt the acute drain of his strength. There were too many to fix them all, even if he knew how. Some were easy. He could see a broken bone or a cut and understand how it ought to be. But others suffered internal wounds. And then there was Mashie.

I have no idea how to reconstruct a hand, much less a claw.

He could look at the one for reference, but that only provided the outside. There were muscles, ligaments, veins, and other things he knew nothing about, and creation was, as far as he could tell, impossible. His exhaustion came as much from stress as exertion. Most things Ezra did were trial and error, and he was uncomfortable performing exploratory attempts on living people. He had healed Mashie's wound, creating a smooth stump, apologizing he couldn't do more.

Together, Niblick, Mashie, Ezra, and Lark took Hekkabah down the gangway. She lay on the charred remnants of a pondok's wall, and they carried her as proper pallbearers should. Niblick offered to help dig the grave, but Ezra shook his head. "I can do it. You have wounded to save."

"Yeah, I do got that."

They stood over Hekkabah as a soft breeze stirred one of her red braids, and Ezra noticed how much less vibrant they were. Gray had slipped in without him noticing.

"What about after? Won't you and Mashie be killed if you go back?"

"Twelve years is a long time. Doubt anyone is still looking for the likes of us, if they ever were. Besides, neither of us have ever been to the Old World. No one knows us there. Should be easy to hide."

"What about the riva?"

Niblick pointed at Hekkabah. "She was the one the rex wanted—her and that package. Now that she's . . . well . . . and he has the package back, I can't imagine Nexziria giving two diseased rat tails about us."

"How about you?" Niblick asked. "What are you going to do—I mean after you bury her?"

"Find the one responsible—and kill him."

Niblick nodded. "Starting to sound like Mashie, but that makes sense. You got her brains and cunning, my colorful wit, so it only seems fair that you got Mashie's vengeful spite."

Niblick glanced over, but Mashie didn't even look up.

"Anyway, good luck with that, kid."

Ezra stared at Hekkabah's face—at her wickedly stern expression aided by pronounced cheekbones. He had thought her scary once. Now all he could remember was how she had taught him to read, pulled splinters from his thumb, wiped his eyes, made him soup when he was sick, hugged him when it stormed, and curled up next to his bed in that tree house she hated when he had nightmares about lions and tigerwolves. "I won't need luck," he replied. "Blowing someone apart is a lot easier than replacing a claw."

"Sure. Yeah, I guess I can see that, but ah . . . do me a favor, won't you?"

Ezra looked over and was shocked to see tears in the Urgvarian's eyes as he stared at Hekkabah. "Take your time; make it hurt. You see, I don't . . ." He wiped his eyes. "I don't like many people, but . . . I liked her. She was aggravating, and could be annoying, but she saved my life. Wouldn't even be standing here if not for Hekkabah. Still can't wrap my head around that. An Arkum Rona Zar saved my life. It's riddlebag ridiculous, really—but she did. No one else would have. So make it hurt, will ya?"

"You'll hear the screams."

"Sadly, by then, I won't be close enough."

Ezra nodded. "Yeah, you will. It will be that loud."

Niblick nodded. "Goodbye, kid—my little tiger." The sailor hugged Ezra, as did Mashie, who nearly crushed him. "I don't think we're gonna see each other again. So I want you to know that I'm proud of you. Don't let the world mess up what we made here, okay? I just wish you could have had your birthday present. Wish I could have seen you open it—seen what it was. But by now, it's probably halfway back to Arkum. Too bad. She risked so much to give it to you."

Ezra dug the grave by hand. Not literally—he employed the same tools that they utilized each year to prep the garden: shovel for the dirt, mattock for the rocks, and an ax for the roots. But he didn't use magic. He could have. He was certain of it. Ezra had a growing sense of what was possible and what wasn't. Gray areas remained, in the same way a person might look at an oyster and ponder whether it was edible or not. Hekkabah had been right about the word *magic*, though; *magic* didn't adequately describe the things he was able to do. By its very nature, that term symbolized the mysterious and inexplicable. What Ezra did was explicable to the point of mundane—as simple as making a sound by clapping his hands.

But isn't everything like that? he thought. *No one looks amazed if someone claps, but does anyone really know why slapping palms together makes a sound?*

On the surface, in the Realm of Commonplace, everything is mundane. But at its core, in the Kingdom of Undiscovered Details, there lies magic, the difference being familiarity. Though Ezra had only formally met this power six years prior, he had lived with it his whole life. Nothing about his talent felt foreign or strange. Forming a cloud in a clear sky was nothing to be marveled at. He was shocked that others lacked the ability. Like walking, speaking, reading, writing, or growing facial hair, these were things he might have assumed came naturally to adults. Still being something of a child, Ezra found it harder to accept that he had mastered an ability valued by those of any age but possessed by few. If anything was magic, it was this idea that a strange, young, exiled pauper, who was raised by goblins in the jungle, possessed a power for which kings would kill.

The effort to dig the grave, lower Hekkabah's body into it, and cover her—first with a shroud taken from her bed and then with all that dirt—took him the entire day. When finished, when at last Hekkabah was laid to rest, he chose to leave her grave unmarked in case Rex Nexziria sent others to search for her. They might find the tree house, but in a frighteningly short time the forest would remove all traces of this scar he made in the dirt. He alone would know the final resting place of the most remarkable person he had ever known, a priestess of Uberlin and the closest Ezra ever had to a mother.

Night had settled in, and Ezra was alone and exhausted, as much from the exertion as from grief. He'd cried through most of the digging but saved just enough tears to break down entirely when the time came to cover her face with the black, moist soil. He sat with his back against the trunk of the barowan tree, listening to the sounds of the night. His knees up, held fast by his arms, Ezra was reminded of his first night in the forest, in the Land of Awful Things.

The sounds no longer frightened him. They were the music of his youth. He knew the source of each: the howler monkey's deep-throated growl, the tree frog's rhythm, and the cricket's trill. He also no longer feared the lions or tigerwolves, nor did he worry about food and water. But one souvenir of that first night remained just as durable as ever: loneliness. In a strange way, he felt as if he had traveled in a circle. Older and educated beyond the comprehension of anyone in his village, he hadn't managed to budge from the darkness where they had cast him.

"You will leave Haddon and never come back. If you come back, we will kill you."

Ezra wondered what they would do if he returned now. Killing him might not be so easy anymore, and he played with the idea. In the morning, he had planned on traveling northwest up the coast toward Shahabad. If he took the road—the easiest route—Haddon would be on the way. *Perhaps I will—*

A light emanating from behind him illuminated the forest with a stark pale brilliance. Ezra sat up, stunned. He turned, but the trunk of the barowan was huge and blocked his view. Scrambling around, the light was gone before he could see the source.

He waited, listening. After several moments, he took a chance. "Who's there?"

No answer.

Ezra sat, closed his eyes, and concentrated on the universe around him, searching. The Erbon Forest was a hive of life, and finding anything specific was challenging, especially when he had no idea what he searched for.

It was like a lightning bug the size of the Great Excuse.

He expected Elan to be shouting, directing him with all haste either toward or away from the source, but he found nothing unusual.

Ezra waited, and waited.

The night was warm. He was tired. Before long, the waiting conspired with his exhaustion, and he fell asleep. Light woke him, but not the light of day. Opening his eyes, he was blinded. So he covered his face, turned away, and crawled to the far side of the tree trunk, then looked once more. The light ceased, but not before he saw that it came from the direction of the garden. Getting up, he cautiously walked the little path to the sad patch of struggling vegetables.

None of his companions had been gardeners. At the age of seven, Ezra had been the expert, and all he knew was to water regularly and pull the weeds. They spent weeks prepping the garden until they had a hill of sticks and a mountain of stones. The sticks they used in fires; the stones remained in a pile, which looked ominous in the dark. Again Ezra found nothing out of the ordinary but the year's crop that would never be harvested—at least not by the planters.

"Who's here?" he called, turning left then right but with little hope of reply.

None came, and he waited, watched, and listened. Eventually, Ezra returned to the barowan tree. He gave a few more glances toward the garden, then at a loss, he decided there was no imminent threat. The forest was full of oddities. This was just another one, and he was too tired to investigate any further that night. Ezra climbed to his bed and went to sleep in his tree house for the last time.

The morning came with its usual slanted, filtered light, but quieter than ever. Niblick and Mashie rarely went to bed before midday, and Hekkabah never seemed to sleep. Ba Ran were by nature more nocturnal than humans, and Ezra usually awoke to the sound of hammering or loud conversations. That morning the silence was both eerie and heartbreaking.

It's all gone. My mother, my family. And without them, even my home is no longer where I left it.

An overwhelming unease washed over him.

I don't belong here anymore.

Everyone who had made the place special was gone. The time of his childhood was over. He had outgrown the tree house, and lingering in that dead memory felt so wrong he shivered, as if realizing he'd slept in a grave.

A grave.

Struggling to keep from a monumental, debilitating breakdown of sobbing, he avoided looking at the freshly turned dirt and focused on packing what little he had into a satchel he had once used to gather nuts. In it, he placed the ink stick and a couple of his most recent quills, along with some reed paper. Ezra had little in the way of clothes. As he had grown taller, Hekkabah traded for cloth and created a tunic for him. But she was no more a tailor than a gardener, and the thing was lopsided, poorly sewn, and stained from years of hard use.

I have little more now than I did leaving Haddon.

He took a few berries and nuts, but food would not be a problem. Water might, so he set out to fill a gourd at the stream. He was just capping the container when he saw blue and yellow fly by. He looked up with a smile when he heard the flute-music, a sound he hadn't heard in years—a sound that lightened the darkness smothering his heart. Not everyone had left.

"Where have you been?" he asked.

Spotting the Magnificent Bird perched on the rock pile near the garden, Ezra looped the string to the bottle gourd over his head and slowly approached.

That's where I saw the light.

Ezra knew the world formed itself in patterns. Veins in his hands, branches of trees, and the lines in leaves all mimicked one another. He couldn't determine if this tendency to find similarities granted him the ability to alter reality, or if altering reality gave him the insight into patterns. He also rarely understood the meaning of the similar designs—only that they appeared the same. In the case of veins, they all suggested a kinship—something living, something growing. Now he sensed another pattern: the bird and the light. This was more complicated and subtle, but he felt it. Elan was suggesting the bird and the light were of the same weave, close relatives in a land of strangers. Realizing this truth, Ezra knew chance had not caused the bird to rest on that stone pile.

"Do you know what the light was?"

Ezra stopped when he was an arm's length away. The bird showed no fear.

"What's going on? What do you want? Why are you back?"

The Magnificent Bird began scratching the stones it perched on.

"You're not serious?"

The bird replied by cocking its head. Then with a squawk, it flew up into the trees.

Ezra stared at the mountain of stones. "You honestly want me to dig in this pile of rock? I have a warlord I need to kill, you know?"

With one more squawk, the bird threw out its wings and flew away.

"That's just rude." Ezra looked down at the pile. It was huge, the accumulated debris of twelve years of agricultural excavation. *This will take hours.*

Ezra began to half-heartedly toss aside the stones. He wasn't committed, not fully. He couldn't accept his own conclusion that the bird who had first led him to Niblick, Mashie, and Dank—and later to the barowan tree—was actually instructing him to dig in a pile of rocks. Ezra no longer embraced the idea that the bird was special. As a child, he'd thought so, but as a child, he'd respected his father. There was no reason to dig in a rock pile that Ezra had helped build, but the top stones were small and light. After removing them, he felt he might as well take off one more layer. By midday, he had refilled the bottle gourd five times and was soaked with sweat, his hands dirty and scraped from the effort of taking down half the pile. He had built a second, nearly identical pile alongside. At that point, committed to digging all the way to the dirt, he found something. He was at the level of stones that marked year three of their gardening adventure. Pushing more rocks aside, he struggled to understand what he was seeing.

This is . . . magic. It must be.

He whirled and looked toward the grave of Hekkabah. Nothing out of place. She was still dead, still buried.

"How is this possible?" he asked as he pulled the canvas-wrapped package from the stone pile.

Finding nothing else, Ezra carried the bundle back to the base of the barowan tree and laid it down, baffled. "You said it was taken," he said to the grave. "How can it be here?"

"Ezra, the package—Uberlin's Gift—is yours now. It calls for you."

He'd waited twelve years for the gift she'd promised. The mystery of what it might be had tortured him. Now holding it alone in the forest, he was terrified to look.

The bird. The light. The package being where it couldn't possibly be. What is this thing?

He could have cut the old twine but took the time to untie the bindings as if this were a sacred ritual. Once the package was free of its bonds, Ezra unfolded the first flap and was rewarded with a treasure: a small bit of reed paper, and on it, writing in Hekkabah's neat hand.

> Ezra, if you are reading this, it means I am dead, and you have opened the other package, finding an old blanket and my silly riddle. You have figured out the meaning—as I knew you would—and dug in the stone pile where I am now secretly burying this. Just as I was told to find you, I was told I would die before the time came to deliver it. I did not understand until I found not a man, but a child. Now it makes sense. As I do not know how I will die or who might die with me, I am burying the gift away from our home in case it is attacked and burned—though I have my doubts fire will harm the gift.
>
> This, then, is the reason I traveled across the world to find you. Here is the Gift of Uberlin, once sealed in a tomb

of enchanted stone that even the rivas could not open. I alone was given the secret. In the attempt to obtain it, to take it from Rex Nexziria, my son, five brave and valiant friends, and my dearest Seleion were killed. The fruit of their sacrifice—the lives of seven good people—lies in your hands. What you hold is one of the greatest relics of all time: the Gry Erlikon, one of Uberlin's five surviving treasures, and a god's gift to man.

Go now, and be the person Uberlin needs you to be.

Ezra pulled away the canvas to reveal a gray robe.

He stared at it, confused.

The robe was odd—nothing like the rag of his youth, nothing like anything he'd ever seen, but also nothing special. It was clean, and instead of sweat and dirt, it smelled like the sweet fragrance of salifan. After so many had died to bring it to him, Ezra felt guilty to be disappointed by the gift, but a robe? He had expected that opening the package would answer a million questions. Instead, it only added one more.

Sitting on the rock, Ezra waited to be noticed. It wouldn't take long.

He was wearing the robe.

Ezra had put the thing on, not because he liked it, nor because of the drama surrounding the gift. Truth was, it didn't suit him. He'd spent his whole life wearing little more than his loose cloth leggings and a tunic, but the shirt was a disaster. It was stained and torn, so he gave up the tunic for the robe, but he did so reluctantly.

Grudgingly, he admitted that the robe might be better than his ratty shirt. It managed to keep him surprisingly warm at night, cool in the day's heat, and dry even when Ezra allowed rain to fall on him. He also imagined he looked impressive in it, mostly because of the length and the hood. The material was also soft and light. But the most remarkable thing was how it instantly changed color the moment he put it on.

Now outside the village of Haddon, Ezra waited on the same rock where the Magnificent Bird had left a feather for a boy to find—the boy who now wore the same stunning colors of blue and yellow. The Awful Thing had returned, but he was now magnificent.

Staring at the cluster of homes, Ezra was surprised to find the village of Haddon tiny. Even the rock was small. The very stone where the sons of Chief Kenja had climbed up and stood that day—one with folded arms and the other with a pointing hand, ordering him to leave and never come back—turned out to be the size of a pig, and a small pig at that. Ezra counted eight pathetic hovels. They weren't much more than mud huts. In comparison, the Klune pondoks were architectural wonders. The well was where it had always been, but it too looked diminished somehow. The sacred source of the village's water and life was but a hole lined with poorly set rocks. This was spring. There was no drought. But the field grew scarce and sickly plants.

Our garden near the barowan tree is better than this.

Men were coming out of the field or fetching spears from the huts. Everyone looked at him—at the Awful Thing that had come out of the forest—the Other.

As they approached, he struggled to identify anyone. *I barely recognized the rock and the well. What are my odds of picking out Ashah, Jaydan, or Nomax?* He was confident he'd know his father, Kenja, and Uncle Hebus, but he didn't see them in the gathering crowd.

"Who are you?" a man asked. He was muscular, sweaty, and trying hard to appear fierce and dangerous as he threatened with his spear. "What do you want here?"

"I am Ezra, son of Eleja and Monsara. I used to live in that hut back there on the left." He pointed, then dropped his arm and shook his head. "Waves rolling, did everything here shrink? There's no way my mother, father, two sisters, and four brothers could all have lived in that clump of dirt. I think we even had a dog for a while." He tried to remember but wasn't sure. "Anyway, I'm just passing through. Thought I'd say hi to my dad, see how the garden is growing—which is clearly not well."

"Ezra?" one of the younger men said.

The eyes gave him away.

"Nomax?"

"This is Ezra," Nomax told the others. "The evil one, child of a demon, who brought death to the village years ago."

"Wow, Nomax," Ezra said. "Congratulations. You're the first thing in this village that hasn't really changed at all. I mean, sure, you're taller, and starting to sport some chest hair, but you're still a little bastard."

"Leave us, evil one!" The big fellow took a step closer, which was still twenty feet away, but jabbed forward with the spear nevertheless.

"Really? I've been away twelve years, and this is how you welcome me? You know, I actually had this crazy idea that I might help you. I could fix that well so it never goes dry. I could teach you how to build real houses, the sort that don't include worms. I could revolutionize your agriculture, show you where and how to get salt without having to sell half a year's crop to buy it."

"We don't need evil here."

"Or intelligence—yeah, I'm getting that. The real question is how, for gripe's sake, did I ever come from this place? It just baffles the mind—mine obviously, not yours. You're likely still surprised every time you let go of something and it falls. Still, it's sad because there are probably hundreds of villages like this growing ample crops of stupid."

"Leave! Leave now!"

"Fine, but can I at least speak to my father? I did come all this way. At least he can't possibly let me down. Eleja was a hateful ass even when I was a boy, and wine gone to vinegar can't get any worse."

The one with the spear jabbed at the air between them again. "Eleja is dead."

"Oh." Ezra hadn't expected that. He searched his feelings and found none. He was neither sad nor pleased. The best he could summon was relief. *At least I don't have to deal with that now. This is a clean break. Whatever the future holds, there's nothing behind to look back at.* "What about Hebus or Kenja? I should at least thank the chieftain for not killing me."

"They are all dead."

"Really?" He looked at Nomax. "Jayden?"

His cousin shook his head.

"Was there a plague or something?"

"I will tell you," the spearman said, "and then you go."

Ezra studied the miserable village again, spotting the cup tethered to the well post where he had once received his two daily cups of water. "It will be hard to say goodbye to this place." He glanced at the guy with the spear, then back at Nomax. "And certainly after such a touching family reunion, but ah . . . sure."

"Lord Banka," the spearman said, "punished them for failing to pay for his protection."

"Banka." Ezra nodded. He looked back at the feeble garden, the gaunt faces of the people. "Looks like I was living here during your heyday. Okay. Not that I should—I mean you haven't been exactly hospitable—but I'm going to do you a favor—mostly because I planned to do it anyway." Ezra stood up and made a show of brushing out the nonexistent wrinkles from his new robe. "I'm off to kill Banka, and that way you'll be able to keep *all* your food, and no one should be *punished* for *lack of protection* anymore."

He waited.

So did they.

Ezra sighed. "That's fine, no thanks are necessary. Sorry about your brother. Have a good life, Nomax. You should try to get out more often. There's a whole ocean just over that way."

Ezra hated that village but couldn't help feeling a sense of loss. His childhood, bad as it was, now felt erased. And somehow that was worse.

Ezra walked north along the path where, if he stood at the well on his birthday, the trail lined up with his shadow.

CHAPTER TEN

Rappaport and Wardley

PORT CITY OF SHAHABAD, SPRING

Rappaport breathed in the steam from her coffee, drinking in the view. She and Wardley sat at an outdoor café with a fantastic panorama of the Shahabad harbor below. Ships and fishing boats, all painted bright colors, bobbed with the rhythm of the sea.

They don't call them cafés here, she reminded herself.

In Calynia, these open-air coffee shops were known as *jaffes*, which was a variation on the word *café*—or vice versa, she supposed, given that coffee was an import. Using the proper term was important, as getting it wrong had been known to cause fights.

Culture, she mused, *is like a drop of ink on a wet page. It splatters and bleeds, but never far. What does spread isn't the original black but rather some form of gray, as the native paper absorbs the ink but never fully surrenders to it. The ink despises the loss of true color, and the paper hates the change forced upon it.*

Rappaport saw something different. She did not focus on the loss but on the gain. The blending of cultures was not less of each but more of something wholly new. The merger was a floodplain inundated by muddy water. The land might loathe the deluge that left it covered in silt, but such fertile banks brought forth blossoms.

"Everyone here wears linen; a sheer muslin seems to be the choice of the more well-to-do," she said. "Not a whole lot you can really do with such flimsy material, but given the weather, I can certainly see the benefits. Does it get cold here?"

"What does that have to do with anything?" Wardley replied.

"I'm interested in clothing. You must know that by now. I designed this dress-coat myself. Usually, I have a vest on beneath it, but the heat and humidity here . . ." She fluttered the lapels of her jacket. "I really am starting to see the benefit of the sheer muslin and light linen. Alas, I must sacrifice for fashion."

Rappaport slouched as she placed her feet up on the neighboring chair, the ceramic cup held on her chest by both hands. Beside her, Wardley sat upright, both feet on the floor, chin up. *Stiff posture aside, at least he looks like he belongs here.* With weathered features, dark beard, and that intense look in his eyes, Wardley might have been a native. His clothes gave him away.

Neither of them was making an attempt to blend. This wasn't that sort of assignment. So while not as distinct a statement as hers, Wardley stood out by wearing his uniform.

"Well?" he asked, cracking another one of those big nuts from the complimentary basket on the table.

"I'm thinking."

"About fashion?" He spat shells onto the floor. The fieldstone patio was strewn with yellowing hulls, the accumulated refuse of a dozen tables.

"I *can* do two things at once. Part of the training, actually." She sipped her coffee that was ridiculously strong—practically soup. "You probably want to kill him, right?"

"Why would you say that?"

"You have three swords. Carrying those around all the time must give you an itch, if only to justify the effort of hauling them."

His brooding expression slipped into a scowl. "I thought you were smarter than that. There's a rumor you were third in your class."

Her time to scowl. "There were only three in my class."

"Oh, right." He smiled. "Now, tell me what we should do—and show your work. Dazzle me, my dear."

She sighed, blowing away the steam, her eyes still on the bobbing boats. "We can't simply kill him because another would take his place and the problem would remain. We could go all ancient-Miralyith and make an ugly example in the hopes that it would scare any would-be copycats. Might even slaughter a couple dozen lackeys, even some innocents, to drive the point home. But such cruelty would sow a festering hatred against the empire, creating greater problems down the road."

"And I couldn't condone such acts," Wardley said, "as I have a code of conduct. A fact that, despite all your education, you seem to have forgotten."

She smiled. "Wasn't meant as a serious option."

"A joke? What passes for humor among young people today is frightening."

"More like me thinking out loud. You wanted me to show my work, remember? Also, we prefer *irreverence* over *humor*," she said as if she'd been appointed spokeswoman for her entire generation.

"I'd prefer you get on with it." He popped another nut into his mouth.

Rappaport looked out over the bluff at the harbor. The water was turquoise, the sky blue, the rest wreathed in green. *Such a lovely place to be pondering such ugly things.* "We could hire him, I suppose. There's a certain poetic justice in corrupting corruption, but rewarding bad behavior would—again—make for a bad example, and provide a road map for others to follow."

She sipped her coffee. Either the cooling made it more palatable, or the powerful bitterness had disabled her ability to taste. "We could also arrest him, and haul his butt back to Percepliquis where he could be tried for atrocities. This would provide a sense of justice rather than brutality, even if the emperor executes him, as the locals here wouldn't actually witness the punishment."

"I'm sensing a *but*."

She nodded. "Removing him is always the problem. Taking him out leaves a power vacuum that, once again, others are waiting in line to fill. Now, we could leave him here, punishing him in some other way. A public whipping, maybe, or perhaps a disfiguring mutilation. The sort that is visible to all, making him a living reminder of the cost of challenging the empire."

Wardley spat shells, then peered at her.

Rappaport thought this was at least a viable possibility, but the expression on her partner's face disagreed, and she knew why. "Granted, a public weakening would invite others to see an opportunity, and they might replace him themselves. And the problem again would remain."

Wardley nodded. "And so?"

Rappaport sighed. "I've only got one more option."

"Which is?"

"We replace him with someone of our choosing and make certain this new agent has the power to control the situation. Be best if this new *imperial employee* was seen as responsible for the elimination of his predecessor."

Wardley smiled. He raised his cup in salute and drank.

"That's not just coffee, is it?" she asked.

"I hate coffee," he replied, "unless you dress it up a bit. I'm one of those people who adds so much extra stuff that it's no longer recognizable as coffee."

"You put liquor in it, didn't you?"

"Hohura, a local favorite. You can only get it down here, as it spoils so quickly. Great stuff if you don't mind going blind before your fortieth birthday."

"You're fifty-six."

"Then I guess I'm safe." He smiled and took another sip. "Old humor."

Rappaport frowned. "Ha. Ha. Ha."

Wardley shrugged. "It's funnier if you're drinking what I am. Care for some *cream* in *your* coffee?"

She genuinely laughed at that. "Oh, you do *not* want to get *me* drunk."

"You get ugly, do you?"

"Dangerous." She set her cup on the little table between them, sat up, and looked around. "So I suppose the next question is, who do we elevate, and how do we decide?" Rappaport felt a sensation brushing past her like a hot wind, except there was no wind. And rather than soothing, the perception raised tiny hairs on the back of her neck.

She turned and spotted a man walking up the street past the *jaffe*. He was tall and slender to the point of lankiness and had a skin color that suggested he was native to the region. He had the patchwork beard of a young man and hair that did not appear to have ever been cut. There was a wild recklessness about him, a savage fury. If she hadn't looked with her eyes, Rappaport might have concluded an angry tiger was running by. The oddity was the outfit. This two-footed feral beast wore the most remarkable clothing she'd ever seen. He was dressed in a perfectly tailored bright blue-and-yellow robe adorned with the most stunning embroidery she'd ever beheld.

"What's up?" Wardley asked.

"Dunno," she said, standing, her focus fixed on the robed man.

"Why do all of you need to be so secretive? If you ask me a question, I'll reply truthfully, but—"

Rappaport abandoned their table. Moving quickly, but not so fast as to draw attention, she pursued the robed tiger. She dodged through the city streets, which were rudimentary compared to Percepliquis, but chaotic and confusing. Chickens wandered free, carts blocked passages, people lay in the road. They weren't dead, not even sleeping, but perhaps trying to. The eastern world was something Rappaport had yet to properly codify. Every second, she experienced a new smell, sight, or sound. This was exciting and normally welcomed, but at that moment she needed to concentrate. Rappaport felt like a fisherman who had casually cast a line and snagged what might be a whale.

Wardley caught up.

"You left me with the bill, you know?"

"I'm not being secretive," she defended herself. "The Art isn't simple or orderly. Truth isn't always built on facts, it's . . . well, it's Art. Everything is communicated in vague sensations that need to be figured out. Everything is a puzzle until it isn't."

"And what vague sensations are you getting?"

"That man up there in the fancy robe. See him? Just going past the pipe stand?"

"Looks like a kid."

"I would estimate he and I are near the same age."

"Like I said, a kid."

She frowned. "Anyway, he's bright."

"You mean—what? He's an Artist?"

"Not just an Artist, he's radiating power like the sun, and he's not even trying to hide it. And that robe he's wearing. I've never seen anything like it. I can't even guess what it's made from. And look at his feet."

"They're dirty."

"They're bare. What sort of person who can afford a robe like that goes barefoot? And I'm getting all kinds of strange signals off him."

"Good or bad?"

"Violent, that's for sure," she said. "Whoever he is, he's wound up, pulsing with power, and intent on something."

"Is he a Cenzar?"

"Don't think so."

"Then we've got a rogue."

"That would be my guess."

"Great. And here I thought this was going to be a quiet, relaxing day."

Ezra marched up the street toward the big house on a hill that numerous residents of the city had declared to be the home of Lord Banka. He didn't have much of a plan and wondered if this was a problem. Since discovering his ability to alter the world to suit his needs, Ezra had lost much of his traditional fear. He could find food and fresh water, persuade animals to leave him be, start fires, and even convince flames not to burn him. These were the practical features of his gift. More amusing tricks included controlling weather. Ezra could make it rain, or not. He could gather clouds in any shape he wished, and he could raise wind and form currents in water, even reverse the flow of rivers, though that made a terrible mess. Each of these things Ezra had done, but he sensed there was more, much more. Even after six years of exploration, he was certain he had tapped but a fraction of his potential. Ezra had gained a glimpse of how powerful he was when alone in the forest, and after finding a dead tree, he tried something new. He focused violence on the trunk in a way he would never do to a living thing.

The tree blew apart.

What bothered Ezra the most was that destroying the tree took less effort than reversing the river or raising a wind. This was the first true lesson he had taught himself: Creation was impossible, alteration challenging, but destruction came naturally to the world.

As he walked the streets in Shahabad toward the home of Lord Banka, he didn't feel the need for a plan. His intentions were simple. Ezra was going to obliterate Banka and everyone and everything around him.

I suppose that is a plan, after all.

This wasn't his first visit to Shahabad. Ezra had been there before as a child, when much of the village of Haddon came to trade. All he remembered was how big and busy it was—so many buildings, so many people. The whole experience had been overwhelming, little more than a blur. All he recalled clearly were the big lizards down by the docks. Some people would feed the beasts meat scraps and be thrilled as they fought over them. The giant reptiles used to terrify Ezra. His brothers noticed and threatened to feed him to the lizards. Jaomo and Ado had picked him up and held him over the railing that separated the walkway from the beach where the lizards sunbathed. *My whole family were Izuto Ran.* The world, Ezra was coming to realize, was filled with them, and as far as he could tell, their local headquarters stood at the top of the hill he now climbed.

Reaching the crest, Ezra beheld the house of Banka. Bigger than other homes, it sat on prime land, overlooking the sea. The foundation and the lower half of the walls were stone, the rest a slipshod post-and-beam construction filled with wattle and daub, none of which was exactly plumb. While it was by far the largest, grandest building Ezra had ever seen, he had expected more. Hekkabah had filled him with stories of grand fortresses built in the age of Uberlin, now occupied by rivas, and in his head Ezra had imagined Banka's abode to be like that. Ezra had fantasized about storming a colossal, black stone battlement. This was just a house.

"You, there!" a man shouted. He had a sun-beaten face, a long, curved sword that hung from a red sash belt, but only a few teeth. Until that moment, he had been leaning against the side of the big house's wall. Now he pushed off and came at Ezra. "Who are you?"

Ezra replied with a question of his own. "Is this Banka's house?" He felt there was little doubt, but given the cataclysm he was about to unleash, he felt it best to be certain.

The man grinned, displaying a lot of dark gums. "This is Lord Banka's *palace*." He lifted a hand and rested it on the hilt of his sword. "Give me that robe."

"Why? Do you do the laundry around here? Doesn't matter; it's not dirty."

The man's upper lip curled back, showing still more of his unpleasant gums. "Smart mouth for a kid. Don't force me to take it. Hand it over. I don't want to dirty my new robe."

Two more similarly thuggish men appeared from around the sides of the house.

"What do we have here?" the one on the right said, and Ezra thought the two could be brothers.

"Back off, both a-ya. I seen him first. He's mine, and so is that fancy robe."

"Bosh! You ain't wearing it yet."

"Excuse me," Ezra interrupted. "Any chance you three might have been part of the group who killed all those Klunes down the coast about three days ago? It was quite the slaughter. Most of the Klune were old, sick, and children, so it wouldn't have taken much. Were the three of you part of that or do you know who was?"

Ezra didn't actually expect them to answer, but to his surprise all three nodded. Like anyone, they were proud of their work.

"That was us." Mister No-Teeth indicated all of them with one thumb. "We work for Banka, which is all the more reason you need to hand over *my* robe." He took a step closer. "Last chance, kid."

"No, I don't think so." Ezra shook his head. "Your last chance expired three days ago when my mother died. I imagine she would have told me not to do this, but you killed her, so, in a way, it's your own fault."

Ezra decided to start slow.

"Sorry for—" The man stopped, his eyes opening wide.

Instead of ripping a hole in the world, Ezra had merely summoned the air from the three men's lungs. This was the first time he'd done anything like it, but the process was stunningly simple, and altogether not much different from summoning a breeze. Having aided Mashie in gutting animals he hunted, and assisting Hekkabah in healing the sick and injured, Ezra had a good sense for what was inside the human body. Two sacks of air that Hekkabah called lungs were inflated and deflated when animals and people breathed. But if the lungs lost *all* air, they collapsed, and people died. All three men exhaled dramatically then dropped to the dirt. They weren't dead, not yet, but would be soon.

There were others on the street that had seen the exchange. Someone even gasped. Ezra ignored them and climbed the steps to the door that had been conveniently left open. It was, after all, a nice warm day.

Rappaport looked at Wardley, who stared back at her. "Did you see that?"

The two remained on the street outside Banka's "palace." The warlord had commandeered the best house in Shahabad, but that wasn't saying much. The backwater port was blessed with a wonderful natural harbor, but being so far out, it served little more than local fishing vessels and a few trade ships supplying the tiny town of Rochelle on the far side of the bay. The best that could be said for Shahabad was that the port was culturally authentic, anachronistically rustic, and drenched in buckets of character. Sophisticated it was not, and Banka's abode reflected this. By Percepliquis standards, the house on the hill might have been used as a poor man's barn.

"Kid's an Artist, all right," Wardley replied. "What's he doing here? You think Banka has an Artist on retainer? If he does, this routine extraction just became a priority."

"No, Banka's men didn't recognize him and certainly didn't know he was talented. Also, did you catch that bit about the slaughter of Klune and the murder of his mother? What's Klune? Do you know? Is it a place, a people, a creed?"

Wardley shook his head. "I don't know. I've only worked down here a few times. Most of my routes were up north."

"Who or whatever Klune is, it seems clear Banka finally picked on the wrong family."

"You said the kid is strong?"

Rappaport nodded. "Normally, you don't feel talent walk by. This guy practically knocked me over. He's not trained, or he would have dimmed himself."

"Does he know about you?"

"Doubt it. Beaming the way he is, it's not likely he can read anything. If you're singing at the top of your lungs, it's hard to hear a whisper."

"What'd he do to Banka's men?"

"Suffocated them. Efficiently, too. Usually, the technique would be to prevent a person from breathing in or out. The average person can remain a threat for a full two minutes, and live for several more. This guy literally sucked all the air from their bodies. Never heard of that. Effective, though. Nasty, even."

They weren't the only ones to witness the instantaneous death of three of Banka's men. Word was spreading, and people began to appear on the street, creeping closer.

"What's your evaluation?"

"I'd say we're dealing with a homegrown manifestation of unusual potency. This guy has suffered a lot, and it's fueled a monster."

"Can you handle him?" The old man looked at her with real concern. He had a habit of pretending to be a rock, but she often caught glimpses of another truth lurking beneath. Wardley reminded Rappaport of her father. Both pretended infinite strength and absolute indifference, but that masquerade slipped when she was in trouble.

"Sure." She smiled at Wardley. "It's sort of like you seeing a seven-foot wall of muscle who you can tell hasn't ever been in a real fight before. So given he's likely to kill Banka—who we need erased anyway—do we wait out here or follow him in? I'm inclined to let him do our work for us, particularly since he seems to have a grievance that I am willing to bet is more than warranted."

"You just don't want to kill Banka and know I would make you do it."

At this, Rappaport grinned.

"Sometimes it's part of the job, Rap. You'll need to face that one day."

"But it's such a *nice* day, Wardley."

He sighed. "Come on, let's keep the rest of these people back, in case the kid gets a little irresponsible with his—"

Too late, Rappaport thought, as she sensed the massive surge.

CHAPTER ELEVEN

The Warlord

PORT CITY OF SHAHABAD, SPRING

Inside, Ezra encountered two more thugs and realized a new truth: They were all the same. This wasn't a revelation whispered by Elan but rather his own conclusion. He felt suitably knowledgeable on the topic, given the sheer number of bullies he'd known over his short life. The entirety of his birth family, the vast majority of his village, Klon Vex, and now these stalwart fellows all drew a consistent picture on the walls of his mind. Each believed steadfastly in the virtue of power because each was stronger than those around them. Size and muscle were all that mattered. This was what his father had meant when he disowned Ezra.

"Not a bit like Kedea, Nocea, Jaomo, and Ado. All my *sons are strong, tall, brave, and fit."*

If his father had made that same statement today, Ezra would have also added: cruel, callous, and conceited. As Ezra was none of these things, he also could not be Eleja's son. There was a convenient homegrown logic there. Ezra realized—now more than then—that when his father had said, *"He is not* my *son,"* what he meant was, "I don't *want* him to be my son."

Strength is the only virtue recognized by the powerful. And to those who use spears and clubs, power is muscle and physical speed. All else is worthless, for in their insular worlds they cannot imagine any other form of strength, mostly because they lack the capacity to imagine. In Banka's men, Ezra saw what he now understood to be all that was wrong with the world. Ignorance born from a blind reliance on brute force dominated in the way large trees denied sunlight and water to the ground, stifling the growth of flowers. For what good are flowers? What virtue is fragile beauty?

Ezra did not face men but the root of evil, both source and symptom. As it turned out, his father was wrong. Ezra *was* tall and strong, brave and fit, but only because he had managed to find a tiny patch of sunlight in which he was free to grow. Now came the time to educate these smothering, canopy-spreading trees—time to teach them the potential of a single seed.

Ezra did not feel the need to chat, and both of these greeters kissed the floor before even seeing him. They dropped not unlike the pair of puppets Hekkabah had made for him one year. The ease with which he killed these previously perceived monsters delighted him in much the same way as crushing wasps. Deep within him, a warning whispered, but Ezra refused to pay attention. For days, he had looked forward to this. He assured himself now that he was fulfilling a promise to himself and Hekkabah in ridding the world of monsters.

Beyond the fallen puppets, Ezra entered a great hall. The high, beam-raftered ceiling looked like the spine and ribcage of a giant beast. From these wooden ribs hung iron wheels decorated with candles. Below, long tables were covered with cups, buckets, pots, and plates. In the center of the room, a kapa pig roasted on a massive spit, filling the room with the savory scent of cooking flesh. Round shields and sets of crossed spears decorated the walls, along with fabric banners depicting one of the reptiles he'd once seen on the beach—the ones that fought over scraps. As many as twenty men sat at each table on long benches. Most were drinking, talking, laughing. A pair in the far corner sang. Women, dressed in pointless sheer cloth, served the men. Cages lining the wall were filled with songbirds, a leopard, and a tigerwolf.

On the far side of the room, in a large alcove on a raised platform, sat a man on a wooden chair. He had a full, dark beard, long hair, and he wore a knee-length tunic, a crude copper crown, and what appeared to be a linen blanket over his shoulders. Sitting with legs swept over an arm of the chair, he struggled to hold a ridiculously large goblet.

Laughter, singing, and conversations trickled off as Ezra entered. Heads turned to watch him descend the three steps into the hall.

The man with the goblet was one of the last to take notice. He pulled his legs off the chair's arm and leaned forward.

"Are you Banka?" Ezra asked.

"I am *Lord* Banka," the fellow said, raising his voice in a threatening manner.

"Nice robe," a man at one of the tables taunted with a hungry tone.

"Very nice robe," another agreed.

What is it about my clothes?

Once more the warning sounded. Elan was waving her hands, trying to catch his attention, but again Ezra ignored the alarm. He was too busy at that moment to listen.

"The ladies and animals ought to leave," Ezra said. "The four-legged ones, I mean."

The room grew quiet. Anyone who had been making jokes, stopped; anyone not paying attention, started.

Banka scrubbed his beard as he produced a manufactured chuckle. "These are not *ladies*. These are my slaves, and the animals my pets. And tell me, infant, why should they leave?"

"Because I don't wish to hurt innocents, but . . ." He looked at the faces of the ladies and found a distinct lack of virtue. "Okay, sure, I can see your point. Who am I to judge? Right?"

"Indeed," a deep raspy voice said from the crowd. "Who *are* you?"

Ezra looked around the hall for the source of that comment. There were more than a score of men, a half dozen women, animals, lots of smoke from the spit, and the whole of the place was dark.

"Whoever he is," Banka said, grinning, "he's here to fight. I sense fire in his belly."

"That might be last night's dinner you're picking up because I'm not expecting this to be much of a fight."

At this, benches scraped the stone floor as the men around the room stood. Nearly all had daggers. Some, slick with grease, glistened in the firelight. Three men moved to where they had left swords. One took a spear off the wall.

"And the women and animals?" Ezra asked. "Last chance to be a decent human being."

Banka laughed. "Oh, child. They are mine, and my property stays with me. To deny them such wonderful entertainment would be cruel. Although, I agree this show will be short and uneventful. No doubt you're here to avenge some small slight I have done to you. I do not find that odd. That threats such as this are rare is the surprise. What I find bewildering is that you invited yourself to a fight but neglected to bring a weapon. I do not think you thought this through. But then, that's the way with the young and vengeful."

The warlord looked to his guests and laughed. The men laughed, too.

"Fine," Ezra said. "Apparently, an ass is just too small to stuff a conscience into."

The men with weapons crept toward him, not out of fear—they were all smiles—but more as a means of getting as close as possible before he bolted. But to their evident surprise and delight, the young man in the nice robe didn't flee. Didn't even try.

With a word he knew everyone present wouldn't understand, Ezra thrust out his hands to either side, and the home of Lord Banka blew apart. The four walls and the thatched roof exploded outward, exposing everyone to brilliant daylight. Tables toppled, cages rolled, and chairs blew out of sight. Everyone except Ezra flew off their feet. Some landed better than others. One's head was crushed when he hit the foundation with his skull. Another was flattened by falling beams. The survivors suffered broken limbs, backs, and necks. The flying tables, benches, rafters, and support pillars were heavy timber and battered the occupants bloody. Wailing voices of shock and anguish quickly faded to a frightening silence. A moment later, thatch began to float down.

Ezra had intentionally spared Banka most of the blast. The warlord lay on the ground beside his toppled throne, looking at the carnage around him in shock.

Ezra stepped forward. "You have intimidated, tormented, and stolen from the surrounding communities for years. You also, more recently, slaughtered a village of innocent Klune. But most importantly, you murdered my mother—Hekkabah."

The warlord's eyes grew large, and his hand came up to block the sunlight so he might see the child's face clearer.

He recognizes the name.

"Killing her was a mortal error, one that you will now pay for." Ezra raised his hands, causing Banka to throw up his arms in defense. *Does he think I plan to throw something at him? Someone's in for a surprise.*

Using his fingers and arms, Ezra began a complicated pattern in the air, muttering as he went. As he did, he embraced the memory of Hekkabah's dying breath, the bloody stump of Mashie's arm, and the cries of a hundred Klune on a blood-covered beach. In a dramatic flourish, he separated his fingers and swept his arms out almost as if he were dancing.

Nothing appeared to happen. Ezra knew differently and was anxious to see how long it would take.

Banka waited. His eyes shifted around the room. He turned and looked behind. Finding nothing amiss, he stood up and smiled with relief. "I thought—"

Then it happened. Banka staggered and clutched the fallen chair for support.

"I have a couple of friends, sort of uncles, really," Ezra began in a friendly, conversational tone as he continued to approach. "I promised you'd scream loud enough for them to hear. As they are very far away by now, you'll need to be loud."

Banka shook his head, blinked, then shook it again. "What—what did you . . ."

"Are you familiar with the siafu ant? The siafu help rid the Klune's homes of rodents and other pests. Each year, right on time, the ants march in the tens of millions like a spring river. They flow through the Erbon, eating anything that moves. No one knows why, but each year they come. The Klune vacate their houses, spending a couple days on the water in their boats, letting the siafu pass through. Interestingly, the ants don't harm furniture, walls, or floors. They don't even touch the Klune's food. They only eat living things: insects, spiders, rats—even dogs and cats if they're forgotten and trapped in the house. You see, they love flesh. At this moment, thirty-three siafu ants are crawling around inside your skull. I'd have invited more, but there's just not enough room in your head—at least not yet."

The warlord's eyes went wide.

"With millions of siafu, it doesn't take long to clean a village, but with only thirty-three it could take a while. Of course, these ants are gonna want to get out before they die, so they have more incentive than most."

Banka cried out and raked at the hair on his head.

"It ought to take some time for them to devour the entire contents of your skull. Without air, I expect they will die long before they finish the job, but I don't think that will matter as—"

"Greglion!" Banka shouted, his terrified eyes searching the ruins. "Greglion!"

"Yes, Banka?" that same deep raspy voice replied.

Standing in the rubble, Ezra saw a Ba Ran. He lacked the hunched back and claws of an Ankor and was neither pale gray or sea blue, which ruled out Urgvarian and Klune. His skin was a dull green like Hekkabah's. And Ezra could see why he was hard to spot in the crowd. He was wrapped in a dark cloak complete with hood. A Ba Ran in the halls of Banka struck Ezra as surprising, as was the fact he appeared calm and unconcerned despite the strange events.

"Help me, Greglion! Help me! Get the ants out of my head!"

"Two problems with that," Greglion replied as he carefully picked his way through the rubble. He moved toward Banka, stepping over the partially roasted pig, which still had the spit rod through it. "I honestly have no idea how he got them in there in the first place. And secondly, even if I did, I have no reason to help you."

Ezra didn't like the Ba Ran's voice. None of the Ba Ran he knew could win a contest for beautiful vocals, but this one was truly disturbing in its back-of-the-throat rasp.

Banka cried out in anguish again and followed this by banging the heel of his hand against his forehead. "You need me! Only I can get the Gry Erlikon. That's what it's called, isn't it? Your master will kill you if you return empty-handed. That's what you said! So you do need me! You *need* me!" He practically screamed this last sentence, even as he collapsed to the floor, raking his head and face with fingernails that left bloody cuts. "Help me!" he pleaded.

"That's just it, Banka," Greglion said. He reached the warlord and stood peering down at him. "I don't need you anymore because I've found it. In ancient Uber, *Gry Erlikon* means *Robe of Light*." The Ba Ran focused on Ezra. "And that is indeed a *very* nice robe."

"Rex Nexziria sent you," Ezra said. "You're responsible for Hekkabah's death. You and your master."

"Smart boy. And might I say, I didn't much care for the old blanket that was brought to me."

Banka screamed in anguish.

Hear that, Niblick? Hear that, Mashie?

Ezra faced Greglion and thought a moment. "I obviously must kill you as well, but before we get to that, I'll need to know how to find Nexziria so I can eliminate him, too."

The Ba Ran's brows rose. "Arrogance should take lessons from you, child." He smiled. "I like that. I also must admit, I adore the ant thing." He looked down at

Banka, who was lying on his back, drooling, jerking, mumbling, and whimpering. "I wasn't kidding. I don't know how you managed it." The Ba Ran leaned against the downed chair. "I see no reason to fight. I was only sent to kill Hekkabah and return the robe. Give it to me, and we're done. Then you can go on to erase this whole disgusting growth they call Shahabad with Rex Nexziria's blessing."

"Sorry, this robe was a birthday present from my mother, and I'll be happy to demonstrate how I did the ant trick—right after you tell me how to find Nexziria."

The Ba Ran shrugged. "Rex Nexziria dwells in the Fortress of the Rising Sun in Arkum—that would be the island just north of Myno and Gan, the mountainous one at the far end of the Ba Ran Archipelago. Really can't miss the riva's home. The fortress is Old-World massive, built using blocks formed of the crushed bones taken from millions of victims over the last ten thousand years."

Ezra smiled. "Wonderful. And for being so cooperative, I'll skip the lesson on ants."

Gathering strength from the warmth of the sun, Ezra released a torrent of blue fire that struck the Ba Ran. After several seconds, Ezra laid off, to find the servant of Nexziria standing unharmed.

He stared dumbfounded.

"Fire?" the Ba Ran said, shaking his head. "So pedestrian. After the ants, I honestly expected something more creative. You truly are just a child, aren't you? Some local village talent. Likely lots of you around here. This place is ripe with misery. All that youthful pain manifests into power that runs unrealized down these primitive drains. You're the exception because Hekkabah took you in for reasons that now no one will ever know. Maybe she had a plan. Perhaps she intended to set up a fiefdom here with you as her muscle. Who knows? Problem is, Hekkabah was no daza. She couldn't teach the craft, which explains the ants. Ignorance coupled with imagination will come up with bizarre *things* and *crazy* solutions. So while you can somehow manage to summon ants and stuff them inside a living head, you likely have no idea how to perform a simple shield, do you?"

Ezra didn't.

For so long he had believed himself at the top of the food chain. Ezra was certain the world no longer held any danger. Now he had second thoughts.

The agent of Nexziria nodded with modest sympathy. "Too bad."

Ezra felt the air around him move. Overhead, the sky darkened as clouds began to swirl.

"Goodbye, brazen child."

A flash of light blinded Ezra. A second later came the boom of thunder.

With her shoulder and hip still throbbing after flying through the air and slamming onto the road, Rappaport managed a decent enough shield to save Mister Fancy Robe from being scorched to a black spot by a lightning bolt. She deflected it into the ground—where it wanted to go anyway.

Wardley was off to her far left, moving slowly. She imagined he'd suffered worse than she had. They'd been outside the building when it blew. Not too close, but not far enough away, either. The gust had tossed Rappaport twenty feet, onto the street's hard stone. She'd come down on her elbow, hip, shoulder, and cheek, none of which was happy, each remaining in close competition for the squeakiest wheel. Getting to her feet took longer than was safe. Somewhere in the backdrop of her mind, she heard a strange conversation about *ant tricks*, someone yelling for help, birthday presents, a *next aria*, and *try air lick con*. These last two she figured were the lingering effects of slamming her head against a slab of rock. She was, however, certain that the local talent they had been following had unexpectedly encountered a trained Artist, and like metal meeting flint, sparks flew. Or in this case, lightning bolts.

Why Rappaport threw the shield was more complicated than the act itself. She didn't know either of the combatants. This was Rappaport's third trip out of Percepliquis and her first one outside Rhenydd. The province of Calynia was as alien to her as life under the ocean. All she knew came from books, teachers, or, more recently, Wardley, who was managing the dual role of partner and tutor. This battle might be the result of some ancient clan feud, and her interference could well result in the province citizens rising en masse to challenge the might of the empire. Odds were against that, but Rappaport tended to always err on the negative side of anything she was involved in. Coming in third in a three-person class did that.

Maybe it was the pain that had flooded off Mister Fancy Robe as he walked past her in the jaffe or the comments about his mother's death and a slaughtered village that put her on his side. It might also have been nothing more than the fact that she found him a dash attractive—certainly more than his opponent.

In the end, she simply didn't want to see him—or anyone—fried, and so she raised the shield.

It saved his life, which she thought was good, but now the goblin was looking her way. At least, she thought he was a goblin. The thing had green skin, fangs, massively pointed ears, a nose like the beak on a hawk and he was completely bald. Despite the unfamiliar features, she recognized the expression.

He didn't like what I just did.

Adding injury to insult, Wardley was taking his time getting up from the pile of stones that had hit him. Her mentor on this job wasn't a young man, and old bones broke easily.

Rappaport was far from helpless. She had practiced in Artistic combat, but only in classroom settings. This would be the real deal, and this guy looked about as scary as . . . well, a goblin. Taking a deep breath, she forced herself to calm down while at the same time siphoning the power needed for battle. With the nearby ocean waves, warm sun, and wind, power would not be a problem for either of them.

"Sometimes it's part of the job, Rap. You'll need to face that one day."

The sky churned with boiling clouds. Wind picked up, blowing Rappaport's hair. Ashes from a fire pit that had been at the center of the building blew across the street.

"I am Cenzar Rappaport," she shouted over the rising wind. "Duly appointed imperial envoy and personal representative of Emperor Nareion Nyphronian. You are both under arrest for murder, destruction of property, high crimes against the empire, and unregistered, unlawful use of the Art. How do you plead?"

A massive tornado formed near the dock.

Mister Fancy Robe wasn't doing anything. This was the green goblin's reply. At first, Rappaport was confused about why he had formed the funnel so far away. After watching it rip apart and suck up the debris from houses, boats, and shops, she understood he was loading his weapon.

Rappaport gritted her teeth. She'd never tried to kill before. Combat had always been carefully monitored. This was the first time she aimed for the center and threw lethal weight into the attack. It was frightening to exercise such power, even against a goblin, but so was that tornado. She generated a blast of incendiary light, something she always felt to be elegant and neatly precise. Igniting in a straight line, the beam flashed between them.

The goblin's shield held, but that wasn't all. The blast was reflected back at her. With no time to build a shield, Rappaport fell to the ground to avoid having a hole burned through her chest.

The goblin chuckled. "Cenzars are supposed to be powerful daza. But you are not. You're just a little girl who should run before my cyclone arrives. No pathetic shield will save you from that."

Cyclone? Rappaport had heard the word before. Cyclones were the near-eastern equivalent to hurricanes, not *twisters*, not in the traditional sense. Tornadoes were tight funnels of swirling air, but they were usually only a few hundred feet wide and lasted only a few minutes. Cyclones were rotating storms hundreds of miles across that lasted for days. Tornadoes, like the one ripping the harbor apart, were side effects of hurricanes. Looking up, she saw an eye forming overhead. The eyes of these storms, she was told, could be big, miles wide. Rappaport had a feeling this one was going to be goblin-sized.

"Give me the Gry Erlikon," the goblin said to Mister Fancy Robe, "and I'll allow you both to walk away. Defy me, and this part of the world will be destroyed, and you along with it."

Dirt, dust, and ash filled the air. Pebbles and thatch pelted Ezra as he stood in the ruins of the old building, facing the Ba Ran who stared at him, awaiting an answer.

Too much had happened too quickly for him to process. Banka was dead. He'd stopped moving some time ago. Most, if not all, of his men had died, too. The women were injured—Ezra couldn't help that—but none of them was dead. They had scattered. Protected by their cages, the animals suffered the least from the blast, something for which he was grateful. Ezra didn't want to consider the fate of the songbirds.

Before him, not much more than fifteen feet away, stood the Arkum Ba Ran emissary of Rex Nexziria. He was a daza of considerable skill and power. Off to the side stood a young woman in strange clothing, bleeding from an abrasion on her cheek. She, too, was a daza—one of the imperial Cenzars Ezra had heard about. He wasn't sure, but Ezra thought she had saved his life. This had made both of them targets, and a violent storm was coming.

"Give me the Gry Erlikon, and I'll allow you both to walk away. Defy me, and this part of the world will be destroyed, and you along with it."

"Destroy me, and you'll destroy the robe," Ezra countered, pretending to be brave as well as smart. In truth, he had no idea what he was talking about, but desperation pushed him to try anything.

The Arkum Ba Ran laughed—it came out as a cackle. Then he shook his head. "I do not possess the power to so much as stain that garment. Now give it to me, or I will pull it off your dead body."

Ezra looked at the woman, who peered up at the rising storm with fear. *Whoever she is, she can't stop it, or she would have done it by now.*

Boats in the harbor began to break against one another. Masts snapped, and sails flew through the sky. The grass roofs of homes added to the debris in the air. Ezra's hair and robe whipped violently. He staggered with the force of gusts that felt like a big man shoving him with both hands.

I can't stop it, either.

This was no ordinary storm he could convince to calm down. This was born of intent. Ezra had no idea how to affect that, how to disarm the rising wind. Elan was frustratingly silent on the matter.

She's mad at me. I didn't listen, so here's my punishment.

"Time is running out, child."

Ezra saw movement behind the Ba Ran. An old man holding a sword in each hand rose from the rubble and charged the emissary from his blind side. The agent of Nexziria sensed him but was too late to do more than defend.

Ezra felt a barrier go up. He couldn't see it, merely felt the same sort of tremor that had saved him from the lightning. Given the context of the situation, it didn't take a genius to deduce that a wall had been raised by the Arkum Ba Ran. The man had no idea what he was about to slam into, and Ezra watched, cringing on the inside, as . . .

To Ezra's surprise, which was nothing compared to the shock of the Arkum Ba Ran, the man passed through the shield as if it wasn't there. One sword slashed the emissary, but an instant later a powerful gust of wind blasted the man through the air, tossing him aside like a clump of thatch. He hit the ground hard, grunting, his swords scattering.

"Wardley!" the woman cried, and dozens of rocks, sticks, beams, shards of glass, and a clay pot shot at the Ba Ran. The potpourri of projectiles shattered off his invisible shield and exploded in bursts like tiny clouds.

With a backhand, a stomp of the Ba Ran's foot, and a word of force, the woman flew backward, slamming into the wall of the building across the street.

"The robe! Now!" the emissary demanded. His face was twisted in pain. Ezra saw blood soaking his shoulder, blood dripping from his hand.

Ezra couldn't understand why he was asking. Even with Elan's continued silence, he believed this daza could kill him. Ezra had power, but he didn't know how to use it. *But why not kill me and take the—the robe!* That had to be it. The Ba Ran's earlier bravado—he *was* afraid of damaging it.

No, that can't be right. He tried to hit me with a bolt of lightning. Then what? Was it just to scare me? Does lightning not affect fabric? Can he not harm me while I wear it? Does he really not want to hurt me?

Truth was, Ezra hadn't a clue. He was still the ignorant little village boy holding out his limp feather at a growling tigerwolf.

Tigerwolf. For a split second, Ezra considered opening the cages to the leopard and hyena and coaxing them to attack. He knew he could. But if Ezra, at the age of seven, before ever knowing anything about magic, managed to kill fifty tigerwolves, he was certain this Arkum daza would have no trouble doing the same.

The cyclone intensified by the second. Many of the buildings near the coast were shorter or missing altogether, granting Ezra a clear view down the hill. The ships were gone. Massive waves had consumed them and erased the docks. Water flooded the city, rising rapidly. Trees were down everywhere. When the storm reached full force, everyone was going to die, including Ezra. Then the Ba Ran could collect his prize and take it back to Arkum, whether he was still wearing it or not.

Ezra pulled off the robe.

"Throw it to me."

In the rising wind, Ezra imagined that tossing the robe into the air would leave it somewhere in the next valley, but what did he care? What did concern him was that he expected the moment he gave up the robe, he'd be killed—along with the other two. He wasn't certain of that, but it seemed likely. It was, however, a sure thing that if he didn't give it up, he would die. By complying, he was betting with very poor odds, something Niblick would have chided him for.

"Stupid, kid—real stupid," he imagined Niblick saying. *"Not that I'm a genius, mind you, but come on!"*

The robe didn't blow away. It fell at the emissary's feet.

Ezra waited for death with only one regret. He would have liked to thank the man and woman, whoever they were, for trying to help him. He wasn't worldly, but Ezra felt certain that someone risking their life for a stranger was an uncommon occurrence. The woman hadn't moved from where she had fallen at the base of the stone wall across the street. She was still alive. Still breathing. The man moved but hadn't gotten up. He merely rocked from side to side.

When Ezra looked back, the Ba Ran was holding the robe up with both hands, admiring it. He appeared so distracted that Ezra thought it might be possible to just walk away. If he was quiet enough, the Ba Ran might not notice. Ezra moved back, stepped on a ceramic cup, and broke it with a loud crack.

He cringed.

The Ba Ran took no notice.

He really doesn't care about me at all. What is it with this robe?

Ezra could admit that the robe was nice, but not *that* nice. Hekkabah lost her son and several friends to obtain the thing. Then she abandoned her world to cross the sea and give it to him. And now this *goblin* was standing in the middle of a rising cyclone with three enemies around him, gawking at a gown. Granted, the *enemies* were pretty much vanquished, and he stood in the eye of the storm. But it still seemed strange. Nearby roofs flew away, the shingle sort this time. The front half of a big boat flew across the street and slammed into a two-story building, cleaving it in half.

"This is walnuts," Ezra muttered, and he took another more careful step back. As he did, the Arkum Ba Ran put one arm into the sleeve of the robe, then the other. He drew the front closed and grinned up at the sky. Ezra had no idea why.

Only then did Ezra realize the robe was no longer blue and yellow. In the gathering darkness of the storm, the robe had turned a deep pulsing red.

Okay, so it changes colors, Ezra thought. *Cute and kind of awesome, but . . .*

The Arkum emissary's face appeared to do a reenactment of Banka's when the warlord felt the ants in his head. His eyes went wide, his teeth gritted, but instead of clawing at his head, the Ba Ran grabbed for the front of the robe, tearing at the cloth to open it. As he did, the red light of the robe grew brighter, shifting from deep ruby to a bright blood color. The Arkum Ba Ran began to scream. He tried to pull it over his head. This was a mistake. The moment the flamingly brilliant red material covered his face, the Ba Ran shrieked a muffled cry and collapsed.

He didn't fall over. This was something Ezra was certain about and later relived in nightmares. The Arkum Ba Ran appeared to melt like a candle until only the robe remained, lying crumpled on the ground.

The clouds overhead immediately broke up. Shafts of sunlight pierced the gloom. The wind died. The storm was over.

CHAPTER TWELVE

Riddle of the Rogue

PORT CITY OF SHAHABAD, SPRING

"I am way too old for this," the man said for the third time. He sat with his eyes closed, legs out straight on the street, his back resting on the upturned bow of a good-sized schooner that had come to rest upside down and halfway through a warehouse wall. According to the inverted letters painted on the stern, the boat went by the remarkable name of *Storm Rider.*

The woman sat cross-legged next to him. She clutched her bowed head; long locks of brown hair dangled all the way to the ground. Both remained, understandably, dazed.

Ezra gave them time. He felt he could be generous in that regard. Having killed Banka and his men, Ezra considered his life's quest complete, presumably leaving him entire decades with nothing to do. Nexziria still lived, but given the trouble Ezra had had with the riva's servant, he didn't think it such a great idea to take on the master—not yet, at least. He was calling his revenge good enough and opting to walk away while he still had feet and legs. That left a huge problem.

What now?

Expecting that the answer might take a while to sort out, he was fine with waiting. He still had a *thank you* to deliver, and it would be better if both recipients were conscious when he bestowed it—no sense repeating himself.

The woman raised her head with a grimace, eyes squinting. The sunlight seemed to hurt. She stared at him for a moment as she struggled to focus, then looked past him at the city below. Slowly, her eyes widened, and though she didn't utter a sound, her mouth opened as if she might.

"I could really go for another coffee, extra strong," the man said.

"Sorry, Wardley," the woman replied. "I don't think there is any more coffee."

"Technically, I'm more interested in the *sweetener*. I feel like I broke every bone in my body."

"Not even close," Ezra said. "You fractured a femur, shattered your ankle, and splintered the big bone between your elbow and shoulder. Oh, and you snapped two ribs and cracked a third."

"Really?" He opened his eyes. "'Cause I don't feel *that* bad. Everything aches but—*whoa.*" The old man's sight settled on the view down the hill, leaving him speechless.

"What happened to the goblin?" the woman asked, finally shifting her gaze away from the devastation to look at him.

Ezra sat topless, wearing only his leggings.

"You gave him your robe, I see. Is that why he let us live?"

"Not exactly."

"Where is he? What happened?"

"Hard to say."

"Look." She closed her eyes again. "I'm not up for guessing games at the moment. It's not easy for me to think right now. My head is throbbing. So could you please just explain what happened, and do it as simply as possible?"

"Sure. The reason your head hurts is because it was busted like a melon when you hit the wall. And yeah, I gave him my robe."

"And?"

"It ate him."

She opened one eye. "That might be a little too simple." Running fingers through her hair, the woman examined her head.

"You're better now. I fixed you." Nodding at her companion, Ezra added, "Him, too. Honestly, the both of you were . . ." He made a grimace. "Enough said."

"Who *are* you?"

"Ezra of Haddon. And you are an Imperial Cenzar. Is that right?"

She started to nod, then stopped, moaned, and whispered, "Yes. My name is Angela Rappaport. That's Reese Wardley. He's a Teshlor Knight. We work for the emperor."

"Nice to meet you."

"Same . . . I guess," she said.

"Yeah, I appreciate the repair work." Wardley stretched his shoulder, wincing a little. He focused once more on the devastation below. "It would appear there was another solution to the Banka problem that we never considered, Rap."

"What's that?" she asked.

"Destroying everything. Can't have a power vacuum without a vacuum."

"What's a vacuum?" Ezra asked.

"He just means there's nothing here to be lord of anymore," Rappaport said.

"Yeah, it's something of a mess." Ezra pointed farther up the hill. "The dockside office is up on that ridge now."

"Anyone alive?" the woman asked, looking down at the harbor.

Ezra shrugged. "No idea."

"You didn't go down and look?"

"No. To be honest, I was only staying here because I wanted to thank the both of you for helping me out. I haven't met too many people who—"

"There could be people dying down there!" she said with a raised voice that caused her to wince.

"Quite a few, I would think." Ezra nodded.

The woman appeared dumbfounded. "Why don't you do something?"

"What do you mean? Why? I don't know any of them."

"What difference does that make? They're people, and they need help. What more do you need?"

"A reason?"

Again she donned that shocked face. "You helped *us* without a reason."

"I was returning a favor. You saved my life by putting up that shield that stopped the lightning. Something I'd love to find out how to do, by the way."

"And do you know why I shielded you?"

"Actually . . ." Ezra thought. "No. I have no idea. Why did you?"

"Because you were a person who needed help. I was there, and I could." She struggled to her feet. "By Novron's beard, were you raised by animals?"

"No, Ba Ran Ghazel."

Despite her throbbing head, Rappaport managed to organize a rescue squad. She and Wardley gathered healthy survivors into teams and began searching for the less fortunate. Into this effort she recruited the former Mister Fancy Robe, who reluctantly helped. Even after an entire day of working with him to find, rescue, and heal dozens of people, the man remained a riddle—perhaps more now than before. His attitude, his lack of empathy for his fellow man, even his speech was strange—unusual even for Shahabad. She almost believed he *was* raised by goblins. That was another thing. His humor was off. She could never tell if he was joking.

"How you doing?" Wardley asked when, at the end of the day, he found her exhausted and sitting on the beach, listening to the waves. The moon was rising, casting its reflection on the ocean like a line of chalk on a rough blackboard.

"Tired."

"How about the kid?"

"Esrahaddon?"

"Is that his name?" Wardley asked.

She nodded. "I think so. That's what he said, at least. Of course his accent is a bit thick."

She looked to where Esrahaddon slept on the sand, still topless, with what appeared to be a bedsheet wrapped around his lower half. The fate of the robe remained a mystery. The man lay on his back, chest to the stars, one arm behind his head. He was thin, but his shoulders were broad and so lean that every muscle lay legible. "He's fine. A little too fine. Look at him, he's just so . . . comfortable. How can anyone be that at ease sleeping practically naked, without a roof?"

"He's exhausted. You should understand that. Consider what you had him do. That can't be easy, can it?"

"No—no, it's not," she conceded. "But that's another thing. He's powerful and has the endurance of an ox, *and he can heal.* Do you know how hard that is?"

"Healing?"

She nodded. "Not all Artists can do it. Imagining a storm or an earthquake is actually easier than the detailed intricacies of muscles, bones, and tendons, much less the other, more complicated stuff. The most I've ever managed is simple bone-mending. The Cenzarium doesn't teach much in the way of healing arts to the General Assembly. That training is considered too difficult and too dangerous. You must practice on real people, and apparently mistakes have been made. Healing can also lead to other, forbidden practices." Rappaport hoped Wardley didn't ask what those were and was pleased when he didn't. Maybe he already knew. The man had spent decades working closely with Cenzars. As her teacher, Wardley often feigned ignorance, pushing her to solve problems, but likely there was nothing he didn't know.

Rappaport slid closer to the Teshlor and spoke in a whisper, just in case the Calynian was only pretending to snore. "But think about that. The man is a healer, but he lacks empathy. How's that work?"

"I carry three swords, but I'm not a murderer." He smiled at her. "Besides, he *has* empathy. He saved our lives."

"But he never even thought to help the people in the city. He's an Artist, a powerful one, and it never crossed his mind he could make a difference down here? If we hadn't pushed him, he'd have walked off to Novron-knows-where." She frowned and followed it with an exhausted sigh.

The Calynian wasn't the only one who had had a big day. She'd been slapped against a wall like a fly, hitting her head—*busted it like a melon*, as Mister Empathy had put it. Then she spent the rest of the day using the Art to find the trapped and the near-dead and did her best to dig through collapsed homes and flattened businesses. With the Art, she pushed aside walls, lifted timbers, shattered rocks, and siphoned water, mostly because she wanted to save the Calynian's strength for healing. By the end of the day, he was doing both and making her look inept with the effortless ease he performed each act as she lay panting on the sand.

"Still . . ." she forced herself to say, "it is hard to be angry with a guy who saved your life."

Wardley grinned at her. "You saved his first. So maybe that means you win."

"This isn't a competition."

"Isn't it?"

Rappaport frowned, then stood up and stretched. Her back still ached, both from injuries and the work. That day they had rescued one hundred and twelve survivors—only a fraction of the city's population, which she estimated to have been over a thousand. They found plenty who were crushed or drowned, but Rappaport guessed most had been swept out to sea. "I'm so tired."

"Go to sleep."

"I can't. How can anyone fall asleep under an open sky? Besides"—she hooked a thumb at the Calynian snoring on the sand—"I've got Mister Gemlock Box here to figure out. Have you encountered a rogue before? Do you know what we should do?"

Wardley frowned. "I'm not supposed to give you answers. My job is to let you act, allow you to get your feet wet, and only haul you out if it looks like you're going to drown."

"Can I have a hint?"

Wardley considered this, scrubbing his beard as he did. "I can tell you a story."

"I love stories. Is it going to put me to sleep? If so, I'll lie down."

He smiled but didn't look happy or even amused. He seemed sad.

"Sorry, I didn't mean to be flippant."

He shook his head. "It's just not a pleasant story."

Rappaport nodded. She sat down and, pulling her knees up to her chest, made a sincere showing of giving him her full attention.

"I was paired with Cenzar Macklin. This was years ago, and Macklin was senior. We were responding to a report about an Artist causing trouble in a village on the far side of the East Bernum River, in Rhulynia. The Artist claimed to rule a forest in the area. So Mac and I went in."

Wardley stared out at the dark ocean. The waves rolled in, crashing once, twice, three times. He just kept staring.

"And?"

He sighed. "And we found her. Mac and I explained that she did not rule the forest; the empire did, and she was required to return with us to Percepliquis to face charges of unlawful use of magic and a handful of other minor crimes. She disagreed. Mac and the rogue went at it. Even with my armor, I couldn't do much. She was smart and knew how to handle Teshlors."

Again Wardley pondered the ocean and the rising moon.

"And?"

"And it really wasn't much of a fight. Mac was . . . *killed*."

The pause before the word *killed* made Rappaport suspect he hadn't merely dropped dead. Wardley was a private man of few words unless he was joking or drunk. At that moment, he was neither, and he was sharing a lot. Something worse had happened that day, but she'd rather stick needles in her eyes than ask.

"She let me go because of Farilane."

"*The* Princess Farilane? The historian who died hundreds of years ago? *That* Farilane?"

He nodded. "The rogue asked me questions about her, then let me go after strongly suggesting I should never come back."

"What happened to her? Were others dispatched?"

"They never told me."

Wardley returned to spying on the ocean, a miserable look on his face, like he had swallowed wrong.

"So you're saying, 'Be careful; rogues are dangerous?'"

"Not exactly. But to be honest, this guy"—he tilted his head toward the Calynian—"is cream and honey compared to Ruby Finn."

"Ruby Finn? I've heard that name before." Rappaport struggled to recall her first year's historical studies. "Ancient history, I think. Ruby Finn would have to be ridiculously old, though."

"She is," Wardley said. "I looked her up. I needed to know why Mac died, and why everyone refused to speak about it. Turns out Farilane met Ruby Finn and wrote about her. Ruby's purist Fhrey grandparents couldn't handle the embarrassment of a mixed child and literally sold her to a workhouse when she was still quite young, then pretended she'd never been born. Turned out Ruby was talented."

Rappaport nodded. "The Art is known to manifest in people who suffer emotional pain early in their lives. Being both rejected and sold to a workhouse as a child would certainly qualify."

The prevailing philosophy taught at the Cenzarium was that talent manifested itself through emotional suffering at a young age. The younger the age and greater the suffering, the deeper the personal well and the more powerful the talent. Rappaport was not a prodigy by any means. She'd shown no signs of talent until puberty. She *had* suffered, but late in her youth, and not as terribly as most of those she met at the Cenzarium, none of whom had been sold into slavery by their family.

"It gets worse," Wardley said. "A friend was being beaten, and Ruby, who was still young and still unaware of her talent, *lashed out*."

"What happened?"

"Ruby destroyed everything and everyone around her . . . including the friend she was trying to help."

Rappaport couldn't recall having ever read that part and now had no words.

"The empire hunted her as a demon—this was before the formation of the Cenzarium. Authorities found her a few times. She defended herself, killing scores of legionnaires and local officials. Finally, Ruby hid away in that same forest where Mac and I found her."

"What did she ask you about Farilane?"

"She asked how she was doing."

"Seriously? What did you say?"

"I said she died around three hundred years ago. Ruby didn't like that, which made me nervous. So I showed her my medallion." Wardley lifted the dragon emblem off his chest and turned it over, revealing the image of a beautiful woman on the back. "I explained that Farilane was revered by the Teshlors, and we worship her memory. That's when Ruby told me to leave. Wasn't anything I could do. Ruby Finn might not have been a demon, but the empire made her into one. Found out later the forest where we stumbled on her—the Mystic Wood—is off-limits to everyone. A kind of miniature Ryin Contita—no-man's-land—right there on the far side of the East Bernum River. Of course we didn't know that because no one talks about it. Ruby Finn and the Mystic Wood are something of an imperial embarrassment."

Once more, Rappaport looked down the beach at the snoring Calynian. "You're thinking if we try to force him to come back with us, he could become another Ruby Finn? Another imperial embarrassment? Another demon that can't be exorcised?"

Wardley didn't answer.

"But if we leave him here, he'll certainly run afoul of imperial law, and the same thing will happen. Won't it?"

She waited, searching his face for an answer. "It's pretty important, Wardley. I think you need to weigh in. I don't want to be responsible for something this big."

"That's part of being an imperial envoy. Out here in the provinces, we are the word of the emperor, and like him, we are investigators, judges, and if necessary . . . executioners."

"Sometimes it's part of the job, Rap. You'll need to face that one day."

He's not saying . . .

"I won't kill him, Wardley."

"Then what will you do?"

"I don't know. I . . . I can't . . ."

He placed a hand on hers. "This decision is yours, Angela. I know you don't like it, but it's part of the training. And so far, it doesn't sound like you're drowning."

Ezra awoke with sand in his mouth.

The sun was surprisingly high. Seagulls called and flew overhead, their shadows making circles on the sand. A few shore birds wandered the wreckage-covered beach, exploring the remains of the disaster while keeping a safe distance from him. He rarely slept late, but he had that morning. Ezra couldn't remember having been so tired.

Sitting up, he noticed the old man was gone. The woman, Rappaport, sat just a short distance down the beach, looking out at the churning waves as they rolled and crashed, the foam nearly reaching her feet. The morning sun was on her cheeks, the wind whipping her hair. He watched her for a moment, wondering if Rappaport was typical of western women. Ezra hadn't seen many women at all. He remembered a few from Haddon, but that was years ago. Since arriving in Shahabad, he had spotted others. The old and young wrapped themselves in layers of light colorful cloth so that only their eyes were visible. But while local ladies shrouded themselves in mystery, by comparison, Rappaport seemed naked. She wore no paint or veil, and her clothes weren't only inappropriate for the climate, they were tight. She dressed in trousers that defined her legs. And that thick, long-sleeved, embroidered jacket, buttoned closed, had to be smothering.

He liked what he saw. She was pretty, but more than that, he perceived a courage of conviction in her attire, a brave self-confidence unafraid of standing out and being different. Three other things he realized he liked about her—three things he'd never before found in another human being: intelligence, kindness, and the ability to craft magic.

Rappaport looked over. For a long moment, they stared at each other. She squinted, causing her forehead to wrinkle. A modest smile graced her lips. *What is she thinking about?* It came as something of a surprise that he cared.

Ezra stood up, shook his hair out, dusted the sand off his body, then walked over. "Morning." He dropped down on the sand beside her.

"Slept well, I assume?" she asked. Her voice was crisp and precise, lacking the melodic undertone he was used to hearing. The western accent, as exotic as it was, had all the music of an ax chopping wood.

"Very. Did you stay up all night?"

"Most of it." She looked at the waves. "I had some things to think about."

"Am I one of those things?"

"Why would you say that?"

"Because yesterday you declared I was under arrest for murder, destruction of property, high crimes against the empire, and—how did you put it?—the unregistered, unlawful use of the Art."

Surprise shone from those clear eyes of hers. "Wow, you recited that word for word."

He nodded. "My Uncle Niblick used to say it was easy for me to remember things because my head was like a bucket that was so empty there was plenty of room to hold stuff."

"Sounds like an insult."

Again he nodded. "You have to know my uncle. Pretty much everything he says *is* an insult. So am I still under arrest?"

Rappaport's lips tightened. "You should be, but you did help us so much. You see, imperial law restricts the use of the Art. Only properly trained and certified Artists are allowed to employ it."

"You've been trained, then?"

"I have."

"And that's why you know how to make a shield that stops lightning?"

She nodded.

"That was *really* impressive. I wish I knew how to do that. It's easy to push water or create heat. Such things are natural and self-evident, but an invisible wall—I don't even know how to approach such a thing."

He felt the surge of emotion radiate off her at the same time he noticed her eyes grow a little wider and the corners of her lips rise. *What is this? Delight? Relief?* Both were certainly present, but the best way Ezra was able to interpret the impression into a word was *glee.*

I've made her happy somehow.

She was grinning. "There's a lot more you could learn: all sorts of techniques, methods, established patterns, and best solutions. All of it is taught at the

Cenzarium in Percepliquis. Not only is it the premier school for Artists, but it's the only one."

"I've heard of it."

"Not surprising. It's where all the Cenzars are educated. Have you had any schooling, Esrahaddon?"

The way she said his name and birthplace together was strange—like one long word. Maybe she had misheard him, or maybe in the west everyone included their hometowns in their names. *Perhaps she, herself, came from "a port."* Either way, he liked it. Esrahaddon sounded far more sophisticated and grown up—more like Rappaport.

Just looking at the way she dressed, hearing how she talked, the words she used, the command with which she spoke, he understood Rappaport was worldly and educated. She was everything he wasn't— but all that he wanted to be. Ignorance, he knew, was what doomed his village to suffering. Hekkabah had shown him the value of learning. She was wise and practical. Niblick was smart. But Rappaport was intelligent . . . educated.

"Does this Cenzarium teach anything else?"

"Of course. They teach everything: history, logic, all the philosophies, and the law. It's really all part of the same thing. The more knowledge you have, the better you can wield the Art."

"And the *Art*. This is what you call magic, yes?"

She nodded, then took a deep breath and looked him in the eyes. "Esrahaddon, it is illegal for you to use the Art unless you've been trained to do so by the Cenzarium. But if you came back with us to Percepliquis, I'm pretty sure I could convince them to admit you as a student. Is that something you would be willing to do?" Her eyes and lips strained with concern.

She's desperate for me to say yes, terrified I'll refuse.

"What if I say no?"

Rappaport looked frightened. She reached out and took his hand, holding it gently with both of hers. "Please don't."

Eager as he was to set her mind at ease, her touch made him hesitate. If he said yes, he was certain she'd take those hands back.

Bowing her head, she looked at the sand between them and swallowed hard. "Look, you seem nice. You're a little strange—a bit feral—but basically a decent person. That's not merely what the Art is telling me; it's what I saw yesterday when you helped heal the villagers and took care of Wardley and me. You're not dangerous—well, no, I mean you are, but you could also be a huge benefit to the empire—to the world. You proved that yesterday. I sense you're at a crossroads. The Art is telling me this moment is wildly significant. You can either go left or right. I want you to choose what is right. The Art is a blessing, a gift, but it can be used to help or hurt. And . . . Esrahaddon." She stared hard at him. "I can't allow you to hurt people."

Ezra was only half hearing her, his focus still on the warmth of that hand on his.

"So will you come home with me?"

Ezra took an instant to consider all the other opportunities and appointments he had lined up. He speculated on how being invited by a beautiful woman to join the world-renowned college for Cenzars in the legendary capital of Percepliquis might interfere with his long-term plans and various life's goals—which is to say, he struggled not to laugh.

Ezra smiled. "I think I would like that *very* much."

Rappaport could tell that the old Teshlor wasn't entirely pleased with her solution to the rogue talent problem. The young man had murdered a host of people, and as Wardley probably saw it, Rappaport was rewarding him. Teshlors, she had learned, were all about right, wrong, fairness, and justice. They followed a rigid code of conduct and expected the rest of the world to do it, too. Cenzars saw things differently. Justice, fairness, right, and wrong were only ideas, and these concepts were only virtues if they made the world a better place for the majority of people. For the most part, they did, and this was why she and Wardley were able to work together. This was also why they often suffered arguments. But while Wardley was disappointed in her decision, he didn't fight it. She wasn't drowning, and he conceded that, if Esrahaddon had not walked into town, Wardley would have insisted she deal with Banka almost exactly as Esrahaddon had.

This still left an unresolved issue. Lord Banka had not only been a criminal who extorted, tortured, and murdered those unfortunates who lived in and around Shahabad, but he had also been the only real leader. With the city in shambles and the docks destroyed, the inhabitants of Shahabad and all the surrounding villages that relied on the port for goods would suffer.

The shock came when Wardley announced he was staying.

"You can get the kid back to Percepliquis on your own just fine," Wardley told Rappaport as the two stood on the headland overlooking the desolation of the port. "You don't need me, but these people do. Without someone acting in authority, chaos will finish the job the goblin Artist started. You'll get a new partner, which is good, because I think I've taught you all that I know—not that it was much, but it was what I had to pass on. And I'm not as young as I used to be. I can't take these circuit trips. Sleeping on the ground is for kids. No, I think I'll stay on here and see what I can do."

"But you'll come back to Percepliquis sometime, right?" Rappaport asked.

"Eventually, I suppose. The empire won't be happy about an old Teshlor taking over and running his own town any more than they would approve of having you as a governor. That sort of thing is a bit too dangerous. We already have enough power. But I imagine it will take the bureaucracy a while to deal with this dot on the map, a couple of years maybe. By then, I'll be ready to retire. I'll get myself a little patch of land to fade away on."

Rappaport stared at him, feeling guilty as if this were all somehow her fault.

"Relax," he said. "Everyone gets old."

"You don't need to pretend. I knew before the fight. Esrahaddon healing you didn't surprise me. I'm a Cenzar, remember? You really can't hide it from us."

Wardley looked surprised. "You didn't say anything. You ought to have reported me to the guild."

Rappaport rocked her head. "I figured you had your reasons for keeping it quiet. Did you remove the tattoos on purpose? Were you wounded? Scarring, maybe?"

He shook his head. "No, nothing as romantic as all that. I just got old. Tattoos, they seem permanent when you get 'em, but everything wears out. Some of the lines faded and blurred. Wrinkles probably didn't help, and I've got a lot of those."

"You could have had them redone."

"Didn't want to. It's hard to explain, but I feel different. Sunsets are more beautiful. Music—" He widened his eyes and smiled. "Music is amazing. Even food tastes better. And I can dream now."

"You didn't dream?"

He shook his head. "I used to, when I was young, but never after the Orinfar was put on me. Funny how I didn't even notice—didn't notice a lot of things until the tattoos wore out and it all came back. It was like regaining sight that I forgot I'd had. I didn't want to give it up again. I found it . . . comforting."

"Dangerous, though."

He nodded. "Yeah. I still have the markings on my armor and sword, and I figured that would be enough, but the armor doesn't go all the way around my body, so . . . it helps, but it's not the same. I know that because I can dream with my armor on. Anyway, it's just one more sign that it's time to hang up the sword."

She hugged Wardley, realizing only after letting go that it was the first time she had. Rappaport struggled not to cry. *He's just so much like my father, and I'm losing him again.*

Rappaport and Wardley's wagon had survived the disaster without a scratch, as had Leap Frog and Cantankerous, the two horses that Rappaport insisted pull the thing. Esrahaddon had never seen a horse before and couldn't understand why these two would want to haul a big heavy cart.

It didn't take long to get the rig loaded and hitched. Rappaport did all the work. She had a routine, and although Esrahaddon tried to help, he only got in her way.

"Take care of yourself," Wardley told Rappaport. Then he peered at Esrahaddon, who had managed to find his seat on the front bench. "And you take good care of her, you hear me? If she doesn't make it back to Percepliquis safe and sound, I'll come after *you*."

"We'll be fine," Rappaport assured Wardley. She hugged him and kissed his cheek.

They both smiled, but Esrahaddon felt an overpowering sadness pouring off the pair.

"Thank you, Wardley. Thank you for everything you taught me."

"You'll make a fine envoy. And I didn't do much. I only sanded down a few rough edges."

"You made me a better person."

Wardley hesitated. He clenched his teeth and swallowed a few times. Then he nodded. "Thank you. Now get out of here. I have work to do, and you're just getting in my way."

Rappaport climbed up, threw off the brake, clapped the reins, then waved as she drove the pair of horses up the road that curved around the downed trees. The devastation was horrific. Palm fronds, thatch, and splintered wood were everywhere.

"Can he do it?" Esrahaddon asked.

"Wardley? Of course. The well is fine, and there's plenty of food—for now. He'll mostly have to just clean up and rebuild, and that will simply take organization. Wardley is good at that."

"But there will be those who won't listen to him despite that uniform. There could be trouble, and he's old, and breaks easily."

"Wardley is a Teshlor Knight. He'll be fine." She said this, but her emotions disagreed.

She looked over, narrowed her eyes, and instantly her emotions disappeared. Then Rappaport stared as if she'd caught him peeking up her dress.

"What?"

She frowned, but said nothing except to the horses, which she encouraged to move a little faster. They quickly cleared the debris field and were up on the open road heading south toward a town Rappaport called Wesbaden, which she had said was much bigger than Shahabad.

"You've never been on a wagon before, have you?" she asked.

"Never saw one until today," Esrahaddon replied.

"What do you think?"

"Jarring. Walking would be more comfortable."

"But this wagon comes with its own bed, roof, floor, pots and pans, food, water, wine, extra clothes—you name it, we've got it. Speaking of clothes, it is still early spring, and as we head northwest, the weather is going to change. It's going to get colder. Do you have anything else to wear?"

"Sort of." He said this so quietly she almost didn't hear.

"What's that mean?"

"I still have the robe."

"The robe? Oh—the *robe!* The one that ate the goblin? Yes, I can see why you might be reluctant to put that on again. So maybe we can get you something when we reach Wesbaden or Rolandue."

"You shouldn't call them that. *Goblin* is an insult. It's offensive. He was an Arkum Ba Ran."

"Really? I've never heard anyone . . ." That's when the realization landed. *He wasn't kidding about being raised by goblins.* "The Klune," she said. "The ones you said were slaughtered—they are gob—ah—Arkum Ba Ran?"

"The Klune are a different tribe of Ba Ran, but yes, they are what you'd call goblins. Only nothing like what you probably think. The Klune are a kind and gentle people."

"What do they wear?"

"I'm sorry, what?"

"What do they wear? What sort of clothes? They do wear clothes, right? I'm . . ." She pulled on the lapel of her jacket. "I made this myself. I didn't use the Art, either. I sewed it by hand. Took forever. Apparel is an interest of mine, a hobby really."

"What's a *hobby?*"

"Something you do just for fun." She thought a moment, then decided to ask, even if it might be taken as an insult. "How is it you know the imperial language so well? Most people around here, they speak it, but the accents are so heavy I can hardly understand them. And to be honest, your accent was more pronounced yesterday than it is today."

He shrugged. "I'm good with languages, I guess. I grew up with a family of four people, each of whom spoke a different native tongue. So maybe that's *my* hobby."

They rolled on into the dense forest, which Rappaport knew would persist very nearly until they reached the city of Wesbaden. Shahabad and the ocean were no longer visible behind them.

"So you grew up near here?" she asked as the two rocked in tandem with the uneven road. The imperial network was terrible this far out. She had been spoiled by the broad, tree-lined avenues that surrounded her home.

He nodded. "A tiny village not too far away." He looked at her and smiled.

"What?"

"They would have no idea what to make of you. Probably think you were a demon."

She stared at him. The man was so very different from anyone she'd ever known. Curiosity overwhelmed her. "Esrahaddon," she said, "one of the things you'll learn at the Cenzarium is that the Art is manifested in a person through pain and suffering—a terrible hardship faced at a young age. With me, it was my father's death. I was twelve. My mother, father, and I lived in a pleasant enough neighborhood in East End—that's a part of Percepliquis. My dad was a dock foreman. My mother sold quilts. Everything was great until my father became sick. Something from the docks, they said, something that came in on a ship from far away. He was bedridden for a year. Never got better. I watched him withering away, suffering, in pain. Without my father working, we didn't have money. We lost our house, but relatives took us in. Still, my mother . . . she couldn't handle it. She just sort of shut down. Stopped talking. Stopped doing anything. I had to force her to eat. So here I was, this twelve-year-old kid taking care of my father and my mother. I wanted to cure my dad, I wanted to fix everything, but all I could do was hold his hand while he died. One night when I was thirteen, I woke up from a nightmare, alone in the dark. So I lit a candle because I was scared. But . . . the candle was on the other side of the room, and *I* never got out of bed. That scared me more than the dream, and I kept it a secret.

"To support my mother, I worked as a pot scrubber, a maid, and a serving girl at a public house, anything to make money because mom still wasn't talking. When I was eighteen, I applied to the Cenzarium. Didn't think they would take me because I couldn't do much more than light candles. But they admitted me. I never had to worry about my mother after that. They took care of her because, from then on, I was a Cenzar. I was somebody because Cenzars are revered, agents to the gods, sacrosanct." She looked over. "Don't answer this if it makes you uncomfortable, but . . . do you know what happened to you? What hardship you might have suffered that manifested the Art? It's fine if you don't know. Many have no memory at all of their youth."

"I know." He nodded. "And it's okay. I don't mind. You see, my mother was torn apart by lions in front of me when I was an infant. My father hated me after that, blaming me for her death, believing I was evil and asking to have me killed. Then my village was attacked by fifty hyena. I watched them drag my aunt, screaming, out of our home by her foot so they could eat her. At the age of seven, I was driven out into the forest. I was told they would kill me if I ever came home. I would have died if not for a small group of Ba Ran Ghazel who took me in and raised me like one of their own. Then three—no, four days ago—Banka and his men slaughtered most of the Klune, maimed one of my adopted uncles, and murdered my adopted mother."

Rappaport continued to stare ahead at the tunnel-like road that wound through the forest and said nothing as the big wagon wheels creaked.

"So, yeah," Esrahaddon said, "pretty much the same as you."

THIRTEEN

The Proposal

IMPERIAL CAPITAL OF PERCEPLIQUIS

Sadarshakar caught up with Hanis in front of the Baths of Barbaree. The junior councilor remained on the street, staring at the bathhouse made to resemble an Old-World temple, complete with double rows of dark marble columns.

"Going in?" Sadarshakar asked.

Hanis didn't answer, didn't take his eyes off the front steps.

"We are seeing the emperor today. Our first private meeting. You do want to look your best, and Barbaree is the finest public bath in the city."

Hanis refused to move or speak. He had his jaw fixed, lips pressed, eyes narrowed as if he were trying to mentally melt the bathhouse with his stare.

Around them, the city flowed by on carts, wagons, and sandaled feet. After more than a decade of traversing those streets, Sadarshakar barely noticed. The shouts, songs, barks, and bells were all white noise. Nothing but another complication that worked against his efforts. The city had a current, but it never coursed his way.

"I should go in," Hanis finally said, his tone bitter.

"Go ahead. I'll wait."

Hanis turned to face him, then with an angry scowl, he huffed, breathing deeply through his nose. Turning back, he glared at the entrance where lesser men trotted up the stone steps and greeted one another.

For a moment, Sadarshakar thought Hanis might do it. For the last eight years, a week hadn't gone by that he didn't threaten to go in, but that morning, with the two of them slated for a private imperial audience, Sadarshakar knew the contrast galled his friend. They could enter the palace and chat with the emperor, but neither of them could take a bath in a public bathhouse.

"There's no law against it," Hanis grumbled. "No legitimate reason whatsoever." He pointed at the Baths of Barbaree as if trying to stab the establishment with his finger. "Every other council member, every municipal administrator, every guild master and corporate captain bathes in there—they conduct business, strike alliances, discuss policy! Yet you and I are barred by the whims of the ignorant."

"Those *whims* busted your lip, blackened your eyes, and dislocated your jaw. The last time you defied the ignorant, they taught you a lesson, and I was forced to speak on your behalf at the council debate, defending an argument I didn't even agree with. Can't even remember what it was now."

"I didn't do anything!" Hanis snapped at him. "I simply wanted to clean myself."

"Yes, but you made the classic blunder of being Frhey."

"It's getting worse, Sadar. You know it is. The church—they sow seeds of hate everywhere."

Hanis wasn't wrong.

When they first came to Percepliquis, Sadarshakar recalled, most of the inhabitants viewed the Church of Nyphron as a joke. Everyone understood that the new religion had found popularity in the distant, more isolated provinces that lacked education, out where people were born, raised, married, and buried in the same village. These were places that still interred loved ones with stones in their hands. The sophisticated population of Percepliquis was certain that an institution that proclaimed such obvious absurdities could never catch on in the imperial capital. That was then, and *then* was only ten years ago. Now the red dragon symbols were everywhere. FREE THE EMPEROR! was painted across the marbled walls of the imperial library. Councilors introduced suggestions that a list be made of all inhabitants with Fhrey blood in the capital and that hearings be held to ascertain the truth to the claims that the emperor was being controlled by elven magic. And on all these subjects, the normally outspoken and opinionated councilors—those usually blessed with reason and intelligence—remained surprisingly quiet.

"Come on. We have a big day today," Sadarshakar told him. "Besides, I need your mouth in full working order."

Hanis hesitated.

"Don't dwell on your failures. Focus on your successes."

"Like what?" Hanis shot back but conceded to leaving the bathhouse and accompanying Sadarshakar down the street.

"Are you serious? You have Vendis Shipping as your patron! You live in that swank townhouse two blocks from Imperial Square. Do you remember the Realm of the Rat King? I honestly thought we'd have to settle for nothing more than that apartment."

"As I recall, you liked it."

"I was willing to make the best of a bad situation."

The two traveled west on Ferry Street. The morning sun behind them shone off the dome of the Cenzarium, which rose above the rooftops of the shops and administrative buildings. While Sadarshakar ignored the city's daily routine, disruptions stood out. "Oh, look, the pottery shop is gone," Sadarshakar said, noticing the missing sign. A squadron of carts full of bolts of cloth was parked in front of the shop. "Looks like a tailor is moving in."

"We've been here twelve years and eight months, Sadar!" Hanis blurted out, not even looking at the old pottery nook. "And we have accomplished nothing! We failed to block the provincial tariff levy and got nowhere with our effort to introduce independent reviews of provincial appointments, which the governor of Merredydd set as our chief priority—you remember that, right?"

"Given that my grandfather is the governor, I'm not allowed to forget. For a year he began every correspondence with 'My Regrettable Grandson.'"

Either Hanis didn't grasp the toxic abuse Sadarshakar was describing or he didn't care. The Fhrey often exhibited more than a fleeting addiction to narcissism.

"Today will be different. We meet the emperor in three hours and finally will have our chance to do what we came here for—to fulfill our dream of becoming emissaries to Erivania."

Hanis paused. He stopped dead in the street. "Do you really think so? Dear Ferrol . . ." He looked around. "If we could get out of here, if we could cross the Nidwalden, meet real Old-World Fhrey, see the ancient city . . . that would be . . ." He bit his lip and Sadarshakar saw his eyes well up with tears.

"You really hate it here, don't you?"

"And you don't?" Hanis wiped his face and resumed walking toward Imperial Square. "We are the grandsons of legendary heroes. We are councilors to the emperor, but no one respects us. We are despised. No, that suggests a level of peer acknowledgment. We are loathed like mold on bread. And it's only getting worse. Once, people such as these worshiped us as gods. Now we can't even bathe in their presence."

Sadarshakar knew that Emperor Nareion Nyphronian, son of Nordyan, grandson of Nyrian, was only two hundred and twelve, but the ruler of the world appeared old. His eyes were bright and alert, and he moved with confidence and grace, but Nareion was already showing gray on his temples and lines on his face. He looked to be a Fhrey starting his third millennium, but of course, he wasn't Fhrey. The emperor was the result of seven generations of mixed breeding with humans. Nowhere was that more obvious than in the shape of his ears, almost entirely without angle or point. He retained a sharpness to his jawline, distinct cheekbones, and his eyes were noticeably narrow, with angled brows, but all else appeared human. Given the rarity with which Nareion made public appearances, Sadarshakar understood the seed the Church of Nyphron used to grow its wild accusations. From a distance, Nareion could easily be mistaken for a man in his late fifties.

That morning, Sadarshakar and Hanis had waited near the end of a long line that stretched outside the door of the Imperial Throne Room and down the Hall of Memory. Both were disappointed at this. Being council members, they had anticipated a private meeting. Sadarshakar imagined sitting down with the emperor in a small office, perhaps sharing a glass of wine as they leisurely discussed the past ten years and their thoughts on the future. In his head, Sadarshakar had run through a variety of conversations where he smoothly shifted the topic to their plan of traveling to Estramnadon. The emperor would be impressed with the idea and the combined genius of their arguments. The meeting would conclude with a second bottle of wine to toast the new adventure. He knew his expectations might have been a bit idealistic, but never had he dreamed the two would wait all morning at the tail end of a queue.

The others in line comprised a wide assortment. Some appeared to be beggars, others wealthy merchants. The woman directly in front of him was impossible to categorize. She was small, dressed in a strange knee-length jacket with wide lapels and several buttons that served no purpose. She also wore the barbarian-styled trousers, which as he understood it, even the barbarian women didn't wear.

Chancellor Evictarus read out her name. "Imperial Envoy Rappaport, come forward into the presence of His Grand Exalted Eminence."

The woman approached the dais, accompanied by an older man with a white beard who was dressed in a fine robe. They both knelt, and when the chancellor bade them rise, the man moved off to the side. Apparently, he was only there for moral support.

Hanis and Sadarshakar were now at the front of the line and stood between the two Teshlor honor guards at the threshold of the five-story gold doors that marked the rotunda known as the Center of the World. Tall narrow windows and statues of every emperor, sculpted from white stone, lined the circular wall. The floor was an inlaid map of the known world that stretched from Desolatia to the Ba Ran Archipelago, almost all of which was highlighted as controlled by the imperium.

Across the vast chamber, the small woman stood before the grand throne, whose back rose to support the dome like some great tree. In addition to the emperor, who sat, and the chancellor, who did not, Empress Amethes stood, her hands clasped before her. Two others stood beside the grand chair. On the left was Gaylord Sire, a Teshlor Knight, his armor buffed to a mirror's luster. On the right stood an elderly man in an elegant robe with bell sleeves and embroidered trim, who Sadarshakar assumed to be the famous Cenzar Offman.

"You have recently returned from Calynia," the chancellor said. He did not speak very loud, but the dome served to carry the conversation across the chamber. "There was some trouble. Please explain to His Eminence what happened."

"Teshlor Knight Reese Wardley and I were on circuit through Wesbaden where we heard of trouble in the north at a small fishing port known as Shahabad." The woman spoke with clarity but not much volume. "A man by the name of Banka had set himself up as warlord of that region and was extorting revenue and loyalty from the surrounding villages. En route, we learned Banka had committed an abundance of atrocities. Wardley and I concluded it would be necessary to remove Banka, but we were still working out how to replace him when we encountered a rogue talent."

Cenzar Offman, who had been looking down, raised his head at the words. Indeed, everyone near the throne, including the emperor himself, appeared to shift from polite listening to attentiveness.

"How did you *encounter* this rogue talent?" Offman asked.

"While we were en route to Banka's stronghold, the talent entered first. Just as we arrived, the building exploded, killing nearly everyone inside."

The vast chamber went silent. Even those behind Sadarshakar and Hanis quieted.

"What happened then?" Emperor Nareion asked.

"That's where it gets a bit strange, Your Eminence. It seems the talent was out for revenge against Banka, which did not surprise us. But there was another person present—a Ba Ran Ghazel, who had power."

"An oberdaza?"

"No, Your Eminence." The woman's associate now stepped forward. "From what Rappaport told us at the Cenzarium, the ghazel she encountered was no mere witch doctor."

"Rappaport is a recent addition to the General Assembly," Offman said. "This was her first mission, correct? How could she be in a position to evaluate—"

"The ghazel conjured a cyclone with enough intensity to devastate the entire region, which did destroy the city," her bearded associate stated.

"Go on," the emperor commanded Rappaport.

"Both Wardley and I fought the ghazel . . ." She hesitated. "We both failed."

"How is it you are here if you failed?" the empress asked with a tone of concern.

"The rogue talent saved us."

"How?" Gaylord Sire asked.

Rappaport shook her head. "We were both unconscious at the time. When we awoke, the talent had already taken it upon himself to heal our wounds, and it seems they were extensive."

"He healed you?" Offman asked, looking shocked.

"Yes, sir. And afterward, he assisted us in saving hundreds of survivors. To be honest, he actually did most of the work because Wardley and I were still suffering from our injuries."

"And what became of this ghazel Artist?" the emperor asked.

"I can't say for certain. It appears he was killed while we were unconscious."

"And the rogue?"

"We didn't feel it prudent to leave him at large, but given the assistance rendered, it was hard to arrest him. Instead, I have returned with him to ask that he be considered for enrollment into the Cenzarium. Furthermore, Reese Wardley volunteered to remain and assist in the recovery efforts at Shahabad until a more suitable replacement arrives."

"And does this talent have a name?" the emperor asked.

"Esrahaddon," she said.

"And does Esrahaddon wish to be admitted to the Cenzarium?"

Rappaport nodded. "Oh yes. He has a lust for learning."

"Very well." The emperor looked at Offman. "Do you see any problem with admitting this Esrahaddon?"

"He'll need to pass the admission requirements."

"Oh, I think he's already crushed the admission requirements, don't you?" Rappaport's associate asked. "The lad blew apart a building, saved the lives of a trained Teshlor and Cenzar, defeated a powerful oberdaza, healed the envoys, and went on to rescue and heal hundreds of innocent bystanders. If we raise the entrance bar that high, Offman wouldn't qualify."

This caused the emperor to chuckle and the empress to cover her mouth.

"Who is that with the woman?" Sadarshakar whispered to Hanis.

"One of the Cenzarium elders. I think his name is Yolric."

"He didn't hear us out," Sadarshakar said. "He didn't even listen. We waited for hours, and he couldn't be bothered to let us speak."

"The man is not fit to wear that crown!" Hanis declared.

Sadarshakar cringed as people looked over. The pair were just outside the palace, walking back through Imperial Plaza, which, like on any other day, was filled with people. He took hold of his friend's arm and led him farther away, toward the fountain, where the spray of water would help mask their indignation and possibly save them from execution. "While I tend to agree, try to keep your voice down. And the emperor isn't a *man*."

"He's more a man than Fhrey, and he proved that with his words, not the mere shape of his ears."

Sadarshakar couldn't disagree. There was a tinge of self-loathing in the emperor's utter refusal to continue their discussion the moment he ascertained the topic of their proposal. "I can't believe he wouldn't even listen. I hadn't gotten to how much increased trade could be acquired, or the limitless possibilities of technological, medical, and magical advancements that might be gained. What good is it to have a province we have no contact with? We don't even know what goes on there. Everyone could be dead on the far side of the Nidwalden, and we'd never know! They might have been invaded by goblins from the outer sea. Giants could have returned and come down out of the north. They could need our help."

Hanis was nodding. "It's not that he fails to protect them—which is the first and foremost duty of any ruler—but what kind of emperor refuses to so much as acknowledge a whole nation of his people? It's as if he's embarrassed they exist. This is a clear declaration that the emperor is biased against Fhrey. He didn't even let us state our case before denying our request."

"Asking to be emissaries to Erivania, we were volunteering for a hazardous trip to improve the empire. And he wouldn't even hear it."

"You didn't see him treat the woman ahead of us that way." Hanis scowled. "He sat and listened on the edge of his seat while she admitted to failing—a defeat that resulted in the destruction of an entire port city! He practically gave her a hug—because she's human, and while Fhrey can do nothing right, humans can do nothing wrong. This whole empire hates our people. It acts as a millstone around our necks. We have nothing in common with them. The Instarya ought to secede."

PART FOUR

Unexpected Challenges

YEAR 2113 IR

CHAPTER FOURTEEN

Eber-On-Aston

TEN MONTHS LATER . . .
IMPERIAL CAPITAL OF PERCEPLIQUIS, WINTER

"How *are* they treating you, Ezra?" Rappaport asked, bounding into the upper deck of the Cenzarium's reading room. Her face was flushed with the cold, giving her cheeks badly needed color. She wore a heavy traveling coat. The woman refused to wear a cloak. Conformist she was not.

"You're back!" Esrahaddon shouted. Jumping to his feet, he nearly knocked over the book-laden table. Then he stood there, stupidly fighting the urge to sprint the length of the room and hug her.

Ezra—or Esrahaddon as he was now known by more people than he previously knew existed—was suffering from a terrible bout of loneliness. The boy from the backwater village had braced for the inevitable mockery, bullying, and prejudicial hatred he expected to accompany being a clear foreigner in a strange land. But nearly a year later, he was still waiting. No one insulted or made fun of him. He heard not a single derogatory comment about his humble origins. Everyone had been perfectly polite, answering his questions, providing all necessary help. But he couldn't say he'd made a friend—no one came close to filling the holes left in his heart by the loss of his tree house family.

And it wasn't like he had a lot of candidates. Intimidated by the complexity of the capital city, which was nothing like the Erbon Forest, he remained mostly in the Cenzarium, where he had no peers. Those he encountered were much older, more advanced and experienced members of the General Assembly. He was the youngest resident of the Cenzarium and its only student.

Unlike the imperial legion and even the more discerning Teshlor Guild, the Cenzarium couldn't recruit pupils. The college of wizards did not create Cenzars from ordinary individuals. Instead, they discovered talent at random. Because of this, decades might go by without a single new inductee. As it happened, Rappaport's three-member class was considered rather large. Since that time, Esrahaddon had been the only new addition. Even Rappaport, it turned out, was a full four years his senior.

The two had grown close over the weeks it took to travel from Calynia to Percepliquis. At first, he was the guide, introducing Rappaport to the language, food, traditions, and local customs that he took for granted. Later, as they moved north, *she* became the teacher. He had no choice but to trust her, and that reliance developed into fondness. She became his only friend on that side of the world, but shortly after arriving in Percepliquis, only a day after enrolling him, Rappaport had been sent away on another mission.

Esrahaddon had fought his homesickness by burying himself in work. The Cenzarium alone was a universe of information, and like a starving mouse dropped into a silo full of grain, he gorged himself. Esrahaddon read everything he could, studied every lecture given, and practiced the Plesieantic Incantation, Crystal Matrix, and Torsonic Chant until he dreamed them at night. He barely ate and rarely slept. Seeing Rappaport again was like spring after a long, dark winter. At least he imagined that's what it would be like. This was his first cold winter.

Seeing Rappaport again, he found it hard to just stand and watch her cross the room. But open expressions of affection were not practiced in Percepliquis as they had been in Calynia. On the riverbank outside his boyhood tree house, he would have embraced and bestowed a dozen kisses, but in the Cenzarium, they didn't even shake hands.

"Indeed. I have returned and just in time," Rappaport said. She cleared a spot on the table and sat on it. "I hear you're going out on a mission. First time, right?"

Esrahaddon nodded. "I'm only an observer, though."

She nodded. "You'll do that a few times. And it's important, too. The real world is *so* different from here." She waved at the vaulted ceiling, lined with paintings of a Fhrey god bestowing gifts on his people. "Witnessing some of the crazy things that happen and how a seasoned team deals with them helps prepare you for anything—well, not *anything* I suppose. But you do learn a great deal. Who are you going with? Do you know?"

"Lysander Lawson, but I don't know who the Teshlor will be. Maybe Wardley. Did he come back with you, too?"

"Wardley is officially retired now."

"Really?"

"Got himself a little vineyard in southern Rhenydd. His family is from there. They all used to work on an estate together. To hear him talk, it was this idyllic life harvesting hay with his father and brothers, barn dances at night, and fishing on holidays. Well, now he owns his own little patch of paradise."

"Good for him."

"Yeah." She nodded, looking at the floor with a dash of sadness on her face.

"Miss him, don't you?"

"Little bit." She looked up. "But I missed you, too!" She smiled, and he knew she was telling the truth.

Even without the Art, he could tell that, and all at once, Esrahaddon found it hard to breathe.

"So tell me what you've learned," she said. "Who do you like and hate?"

"I don't *hate* anyone."

She stared intently. "But you don't *like* anyone, either?"

He shrugged. "That's hard when I don't know anybody. They all keep to themselves. I'm used to a more social existence, but it is better than being beaten, I suppose."

She laughed. "No one *beats* a Cenzar—even a Cenzar novice. That's a recipe for cataclysm, but I suppose I understand. When I was here, there were three of us, and we talked, compared notes, ate together, studied, explored the city as a group. Have you been out?"

He tilted his head side to side. "A little, but the place is a tad overwhelming. There're so many people, and they all speak with different dialects and slang. It's hard to understand. I don't want to accidentally offend anyone. Since I'm also not supposed to use the Art, I'd rather avoid situations where I might have to. Besides, I have a lot of catching up to do." He clapped the stacks of books. "I find it amazing how little I knew—how little the people of my village knew—about the world, its history, and its innovations. Did you know that crushed volcanic ash, combined with lime and water and mixed with rubble, will pour out like mud, but in a short time harden into rock—and it will do so even underwater? They use it to create the footing for piers and bridges."

"I see," Rappaport said, making Esrahaddon wonder *what* she saw.

"So where were you?"

"I had to finish my circuit of Calynia. That's a big province down there. Wardley and I had only just started when we crossed paths with you. I got a new partner, a fella called *Wilbur Jenkins*." She spoke the name with a pronounced sarcasm as if the two words were somehow absurd.

"Oh?"

"Yeah—why?"

"Just the way you said it. Seemed . . . is he nice?"

She hesitated, which surprised him. "He's not like Wardley."

"What's that mean?"

"Wardley is old-fashioned, but open-minded. Jenkins is . . . well, for one thing, he's religious—a member of the Church of Nyphron." She leaned in as if to share a secret despite the chamber being empty. "He didn't care for my clothes."

"Oh, that probably didn't go over well."

She shook her head. "We learned to avoid certain topics." She paused, then added, "We actually didn't talk a lot." She slapped her thigh. "But what about you? Where are you going? Do you know?"

"No place exciting. We're only expected to be gone a week—maybe less. Some little village in Rhulynia had a few kids go missing recently, and they asked for help. Lysander expects we'll find they broke through the ice on some pond and drowned or got lost and died of exposure. Supposedly kids in these parts disappear in winter all the time."

Rappaport nodded. "Not every trip involves a warlord and a cyclone. It should be good, though. Lysander is a *decent* sort."

"That's overwhelming praise. How can anyone live up to that?"

She smirked. "Oh, he's fine, except he tends to be a bit outspoken. Let's just hope the Teshlor assigned to the team isn't like Jenkins, or your trip will be a loud one. You might even make some friends."

"I doubt I'll be making friends anytime soon. Don't think I really need them. After all, I've got you."

Her face showed sadness—pity. "Your problem, Esra, is that you have trust issues. I'm not saying your caution isn't based on some evidence, but the whole world isn't like Haddon or Shahabad. Sometimes, you need to take a chance, risk getting hurt, and believe in someone other than yourself. You trusted me, and that worked out okay, didn't it?"

"So far." He grinned.

"Watch yourself, young man." She hopped off the table. "C'mon, I'll take you out to dinner. You might want to put your heavy wool on, and definitely wear your cloak. It's freezing out. I'll meet you at the front doors." She turned to leave, then stopped. "Whatever happened to that nice robe . . . the one that—you know—ate that fellow?"

"Still got it."

"You haven't put it on again, have you?"

He shook his head.

"That's probably smart. You might want to show that thing to Yolric. You've met him, right?"

Esrahaddon shook his head.

"Oh, really? Probably seen him though: old guy with the long white beard? He's the resident genius—knows everything. Really nice, too. But if there's something I learned when traveling, even as an Artist, warm clothes are very nice in winter. So when you do head out, take everything you can wear. Constantly using the Art to keep yourself warm is a pain."

Esrahaddon returned to his little room with its small bed, study table, bookshelf, cabinet, trunk, and tiny fireplace, which at that moment was filled with cold, white ash. He grabbed his heavy woolen cloak from under the bed, then stopped. Next to the cloak, rolled up and tied in twine, lay the old—now once again, gray—robe. He tentatively touched it as if he were poking a dead body to see if it would move. Nothing happened.

It's like the thing is looking at me.

Esrahaddon hadn't dared to wear it since the previous spring. He was afraid to touch it but was always aware it was there. A moment of melancholy washed over him. The robe was the only tangible thing he had that connected him to his past—to Hekkabah, Niblick, Mashie, Dank, and his old life in the deep forest by the sea.

Hekkabah and so many others I never knew died to bring this to me, and I'm too damn scared to even wear it now.

He recalled how amazingly cool it had kept him on the hot nights, how warm on the chilly mornings, and completely dry even during pouring rain.

Getting back to his feet, he left the robe where he'd found it. That evening he had a wonderful meal with Rappaport, where they talked late into the night about her adventures in Ra Mar and the easternmost imperial fortress of Dur Guron. And on his way back, he realized she was right. His heavy wool was not enough protection against these northern winds. He'd need to think of something.

"You hate dwarfs, too?" Lysander asked Griffith with a disgusted shake of his head as the two rode their horses just ahead of Esrahaddon. Griffith's mount was white, Lysander's black. Their tails swished in opposing rhythms.

"I don't *hate* anyone. There you go, putting words in my mouth. I never said anything like that. All I said was that too much education can be a bad thing." The Teshlor Knight wore the same uniform as Wardley had—that same metal armor that Esrahaddon imagined was a nightmare to live in—but he was a considerably different man. For one thing, he was a great deal younger.

"Too much—or any?" Lysander asked.

"That which is beyond necessary is too much."

"Necessary for what, exactly?"

"To live a normal life."

"And what is *normal?* Who decides what *normal* is?"

The Teshlor sighed with exasperation. "Normal is normal. Everyone knows what it is."

"Really?" Lysander asked, with that condescending tone that Esrahaddon had come to recognize as the dialect of the Cenzarium. Lysander appeared older than Griffith. How much his senior, Esrahaddon had no idea. The beard had a lot to do with it. People in Calynia had them, but no one in Percepliquis did—except Cenzars, which invariably made them look older. "As a member of the General Assembly of the Cenzarium," Lysander went on, "I'm one of the most educated human beings on Elan, and I haven't the slightest clue what *normal* is."

"There you go. Too much education makes you stupid. Was it your intention to prove my point?"

"You're calling me stupid?"

Griffith grinned. "Well, you're the one who doesn't know what *normal* is."

Lysander looked back at Esrahaddon so he could see the Cenzar roll his eyes. "What does all this have to do with dwarfs?"

"I don't know," Griffith said. "You're the one who brought them up. You tell me."

The two had been at it ever since leaving the city. That was nearly three days ago. The arguments appeared to drift from the value of education, which Lysander was for and Griffith against, to religion, which Lysander was against but Griffith was for. A number of other topics exploded in between. The most volatile centered around *elves*, which was odd, since they both seemed to agree that elves were bad, but for different reasons. Esrahaddon found the whole thing bizarre, since the emperor himself—the one they both swore a mortal oath to—was at least partially elvish. As a novice, a student in his second year, Esrahaddon was expected to pay close attention to his mentors, to learn from them, but their arguments were so repetitive and ridiculous, he had stopped listening.

All three traveled on horseback, something Esrahaddon had never done and wasn't particularly pleased with. He understood the sense of a wagon, even the necessity for horses to pull it, but riding on the back of an animal was wrong. The wagon housed food and supplies for everyone, including the horses. Asking them to do their part by hauling provisions didn't seem so awful, but expecting one to carry *his* weight and *his* gear violated Esrahaddon's sense of decency. He might have refused if the Art hadn't allowed insight to his mount's feelings. Her name was Ester, and she was not upset. While not thrilled to carry his weight, Ester accepted it as part of life, which made her no different from any worker—no different from everyone, he supposed. Life, it turned out, was chock-full of undesirable chores, and animals had it no better or worse than people.

Esrahaddon was informed that their destination was due east of Percepliquis, but winter made off-road travel nearly impossible. A lengthy, roundabout route that followed roads and made use of established bridges would be necessary. Their trip began by crossing the Yardley Bridge over the West Bernum River and entering the imperial province of Instarya. Then the three of them followed the road to Merredydd through snow-covered hills decorated with frosted trees. The following day Esrahaddon spotted a beautiful city perched on a high cliff. Instead of entering, however, they avoided it by veering north and circling around it until they rejoined the road on its far side.

"That was Merredydd," Griffith had told him. "The city of *elves.*"

Lysander responded by stating it was the seat of the province of Instarya, which was predominately inhabited by imperial citizens who were descendants of the Fhrey who helped build the empire. This launched a day-long debate that didn't end until they reached the Grandford Bridge. At this point, the trio turned south, crossed the Gula River, and entered Rhulynia. This was a rural, sparsely populated province, and the roads weren't much more navigable than the fields.

Their second camp was in deep snow. Lysander used the Art to clear the ground of snow and moisture and then warmed it before they pitched their shelters. But as the night wore on, the wind pierced the canvas tent. Being banned from using the Art left Esrahaddon suffering chills. Wrapped tight in his blanket, wearing nearly everything he'd brought, Esrahaddon was still cold. But not cold enough to open the little leather satchel, which contained the robe. He'd brought it *just in case*, having no idea what *case* might warrant putting on a potentially man-eating robe.

By morning, the weather was colder, but Lysander had a grand fire going, and everything was fine, except for the continued bickering that ruined the otherwise transcendent peace of a world gowned in unblemished white. Esrahaddon had never seen snow until that first winter in Percepliquis, and he found it astounding and wonderful. The cold he could do without. He wasn't used to it and hadn't felt warm since the trees lost their leaves. That was something no one had told him about, and for weeks, he had been certain some terrible blight plagued the city.

Esrahaddon had expected meals on the road to be simple affairs, but he discovered quite the opposite. Traveling with an imperially anointed Cenzar was nothing short of luxurious. They enjoyed fish, bread, and cheese, along with something called noodles. And there was soup, cider, and eggs. While the food was all real, the preparation owed everything to Lysander's Art. And the man was a great cook. Esrahaddon also felt he was showing off for Griffith.

"Have they replaced him yet?" Lysander asked Griffith as they finished breakfast.

"Replaced the academy master? Of course. We're knights but still soldiers. We live and die for the emperor. We don't wallow in self-pity."

"In the Cenzarium, we call it compassionate grief, or if those words are too big or alien, you could just say—we have *feelings*. But I suppose you must beat that out of your cadets, right? Can't have them thinking or feeling, or they might get it in their head not to obey."

"It's called discipline. You don't give a man the power of life and death over his fellows and say *go have fun,* like you do in your school."

"And yet—no calamities have resulted because we teach facts and reason. Armed with that, anyone can make the right decision."

"Facts and reason but not the truth."

"Oh, let's not get into *truth* again." Lysander shook his head and downed the last swallow of his cider. "I'm tired of beating my head against that wall with you. My only point was . . . I wanted to offer my condolences. I liked Master Rawlings. As far as Teshlors went, he was a good one. It bothers me that the Cenzars seem to mourn him more than his fellow knights. I feel like he deserved better."

"We mourn. We just don't let it get in the way of our duty."

"But the tournament was canceled, right?"

Griffith shook his head. "It was held. News of Rawlings' death didn't arrive until near the end."

"But I heard the final match was called off."

"Oh, you're talking about cadet Jerish Grelad. He forfeited his final match. I have no idea why. Giving up is not something the Teshlor Academy teaches. That whole thing was just strange."

Griffith stared at the last manchet roll. He looked at Esrahaddon. "Yours or mine? You can have it if you want, but I'm going to take it if you don't."

"It is all yours, sir. I'm good."

"Lysander does make a killer manchet." Griffith snatched up the golden-brown roll.

"Mixing butter into the dough is the key," Lysander explained. "But what do you mean by strange?"

"Hmm? Oh, right. Ah, it's just that Jerish was one of the finest students to come out of the academy. He's been at the top of the leaderboard ranking since he was old enough to enter the Summersrule tournaments. The day Rawlings passed, he had petitioned and received permission to enter the live-blade competition."

"Why did he need permission?"

"It's only for the older boys, the seventeen- and eighteen-year-olds, those close to graduation. Jerish is only fifteen. Despite that, he beat his first two opponents handily and was about to fight Darius Seret in the final competition. If he'd won, he'd have become the youngest cadet to ever do so, but then he just quit, which was strange because he was known to be this brutally dedicated competitor. All he ever wanted to do was fight. When the other boys went into the city to enjoy themselves, he stayed and practiced alone—all day, all night, even in the worst weather."

"You keep referring to him in the past tense. Was he expelled, or—he didn't die, did he?"

"Oh no." Griffith chuckled. "At least I don't think so. I don't know what happened to him. I haven't heard a word about the lad since the tournament this last midsummer. He might be gone. A lot of cadets fail in their last year or two."

The more Esrahaddon heard about the Teshlors, the more distasteful he found them. If it hadn't been for Wardley, he would have written them all off as Izuto Ran. This Jerish kid certainly seemed to be—or at least have all the makings of—one.

Cleanup with a practicing Cenzar was also a snap and a clap, and soon they were once more on their way. Their surroundings became more rural until eventually they bordered on wilderness. Finally, as the sun was setting, he spotted smoke rising in the near distance. Hoping they might find better shelter for the night than a wind-whipped sheet of cloth, Esrahaddon was happy. Then Lysander pointed at a village hidden among the trees and said, "That's it. That's Eber-on-Aston."

"Been here before?" Griffith asked.

"Nope," Lysander replied. "You?"

"Don't get up this way at all."

"Smaller than I expected," Lysander said as they approached and could see the whole of the town.

Esrahaddon counted fewer than twenty buildings: crude wood constructions that spewed smoke from stone chimneys. Split-rail fences enclosed a small number of dirty sheep and some thin cows. A river—the Aston, Esrahaddon presumed—ran nearby, much of it locked in ice. And all around were the stumps of recently harvested trees. While the forest and hills were velvet white, between the buildings the ground was trampled and dirty. Villagers bundled in layers of tunics, trousers, chaperons, and boots caught sight of them and began to gather in the clearing between the buildings. Some carried pitchforks, axes, or mattocks, which made Esrahaddon wonder if they had been using them or just picked them up for the greeting. Looking at the group of roughly thirty men and older boys with the women and young children peeking out of thresholds, he recognized all of them. These strangers were no different from the inhabitants of Haddon. This village was but another version of home.

"Who are you?" someone shouted from the presumed safety of the herd.

In reply, Griffith threw back his hood and opened his cloak to show the dragon emblem. At its reveal, the villagers gasped. Lysander did nothing. Esrahaddon followed his lead. The men with farming tools promptly set them aside.

"Agenperals," one said with enough awe to suggest they were gods.

Esrahaddon had never heard the word. "Do they speak a different language?" he inquired.

"It's just what they call us in the provinces," Lysander explained. "A condensed and backward slang for *imperial agents*."

"Up in Warica they call us agempors," Griffith said. "Agents-of-the-emperor. In summer, they can identify us from a distance just from the clothes. Spotting armor and robe riding side by side, they're quick to sweep their town clean of any evidence of crimes."

The crowd parted as they entered the village, each face a mix of terror and fascination.

"I am Griffith Simmons, Second Order Teshlor Knight, agent of His Imperial Eminence Nareion Nyphronian. This is my partner, Cenzar Lysander Lawson. We are here to investigate the recent disappearance of children from this village."

"Assuming this is Eber-on-Aston. Is it?" Lysander asked.

Several nodded.

"Wonderful."

"Is anyone willing to stand forth and speak for this community?" Griffith asked.

One of the taller men, who had dropped his pitchfork at their approach, raised his hand. "I'm Hal Haston, son of Hagis, nephew of Uthor Eber. One of the last Ebers to have lived here."

Like the trees of autumn, Hal's once-dark hair was changing color and falling out. Aside from this, Esrahaddon couldn't tell much, as all else was buried beneath layers of poorly fitted wool. Even the man's hands were hidden in mittens.

"Wonderful," Griffith said. "Is there a warm place where you can explain in detail what happened here? And perhaps a place to properly house our animals?"

Haston led them around the fenced enclosure to a barn built of poorly spaced, warped planks. "We don't have horses here, but maybe this will do?"

"Should I see to the animals?" Esrahaddon asked. Not that he knew much about horses and their needs, but he wished to be of some use.

"No," Lysander told him. "You're not a servant. You're a student. The whole point of you being here is to watch and listen. Can't do that in a barn."

"What about our supplies?"

Griffith chuckled. "The boy thinks the locals are going to rob us, Lawson."

The Cenzar showed an amused smile. "Trust me, Esrahaddon, when I say they will treat that gear like fine crystal. As *agenperals*, our presence can cause provincial governors and legion generals to forget their own names. Keep in mind, out here we carry the power of the emperor. That makes us both judge, and if necessary, executioners of the sentences we dole out. Our job is to enforce imperial law, just as the emperor would, but in less time and with a lot less pageantry. And a Teshlor Knight and a Cenzar are more formidable than a legion."

Esrahaddon remembered the way Wardley and Rappaport had been tossed aside like toys, which did nothing to better his assessment of the imperial army. He gave a glance to Ester as two young men led her away. He wasn't at all concerned that he might lose his things to a thief. Rather, Esrahaddon was terrified some fool might take it upon himself to open his satchel and perhaps seek to air out his robe. He wasn't certain what Lysander and Griffith—the judges and executioners—would do, should a villager be eaten by his clothes.

Hal Haston led them into a humble house, a small cabin with a single room with a loft above. A fire was smoldering, and Hal quickly bolstered it from a messy pile of wood beside the hearth. An unmade mattress was boxed in on one side of the room, and a pair of hardwood chairs stood on the other. Bags, crates, barrels, nets, tools, and lots of firewood were strewn about with little sense of order, and two blankets hung from a line near the fire. These he quickly pulled down and threw without care into the shadows. Then he stood with his back to the fire and offered the chairs to his guests.

He's terrified. Esrahaddon sensed the fear rolling off him. *Surprised, too.*

Griffith sat upright in one chair, and Lysander reclined in the other, extending his feet toward the rekindled flames. Esrahaddon remained standing near the entrance but off to one side to avoid the draft of air that grew colder as the sun set. The cabin had no windows, but the gap at the top and bottom of the door provided visual confirmation to what the Art told him: Night had arrived.

Hal jammed a splinter of wood into the coals, catching a flame, then he cupped it with his hand and moved around the room, igniting three clay oil lamps. "I don't have much to offer you. There's still some cider left. I think it's hardening, but it's still far from vinegar."

"I think we're fine?" Lysander looked at Griffith, who nodded.

"Just need to establish some details," Griffith said. "From your messages, you report that several children have gone missing, and one as recently as this week? If so, we most certainly need to begin a search immediately."

Hal was nodding but biting his lower lip at the same time. "Not exactly children."

"How's that?" Griffith asked.

"They were young, but not children. The youngest was fourteen."

"How many?" Lysander asked. "The report we have says four."

"It *was* four—now it's five. My own teenage daughter disappeared yesterday."

"You have my condolences," Lysander said.

Griffith asked, "Number of boys versus girls?"

Hal pulled off his mittens. "All . . . girls."

"Really? Where were they last seen?"

"Going into the Forbidden Forest."

This admission stalled the questions from both Griffith and Lysander, who looked at each other in silence.

"There's always been tales of an evil witch that lives up in these woods," Hal explained. "Been around since before the Ebers settled here. The girls started daring each other."

"Imperial law restricts anyone from entering the Mystic Wood," Griffith stated, his tone strange.

The man had been confident to the point of arrogance, defiant in the face of Lysander's logic, but now Esrahaddon heard something different, and he struggled to determine what it was. The Art was useless. Teshlors guarded themselves with ancient markings that shielded them from magic. Esrahaddon could only guess from the drop in volume and suddenly somber pitch. *He's concerned, worried . . . afraid?*

"Why only girls?" Lysander asked.

Hal shrugged. "It's a game. Never caught on with the boys, I suppose. Instead, the lads challenge one another to cross the river on the ice floes."

"What's wrong with your kids?" Esrahaddon asked.

Both Griffith and Lysander scowled at him.

"This is Esrahaddon." Lysander introduced him as if apologizing. "He is a student, a Cenzar-in-training, here to *observe only*. You won't hear him speak again."

Esrahaddon frowned. While bad enough to be reprimanded at all, it was worse to be belittled in the presence of one such as Hal Haston, who reminded him so much of the Haddon Village elders. He had his own questions, inquiries that he felt neither Griffith, who hailed from rich Maranonia, nor Lysander, the son of a silversmith, could begin to imagine, since neither had grown up in a small village or had ever been exiled to a forest.

"If they were seen going in," Lysander asked, "why weren't they stopped?"

"Until recently, it was only the other girls who saw. When the first one didn't come back, they were too scared to tell anyone. I suppose they figured they would be blamed. When the others started disappearing, I thought they had woke up something in that forest that came and took them. I guess others did as well 'cuz two families—both with daughters—up and left our village altogether. When Edee disappeared, she was the fourth. I saw her go in and mentioned it to my daughter, and then she—" He lifted his head, his lip trembling. "The witch took them all. Why do we have to live in the shadow of this monster? You're agenperals. You can do anything. Go kill that witch so nobody else dies."

"You'll need to stay here," Lysander told Esrahaddon as the two entered the rickety stable.

It was damp, musty, and smelled of rotting hay and wet animals. A single tallow lantern hung from the center rafter's crossbeam. Lysander lit it with a flick of his finger.

"Stay? I don't understand. Because of what I said?"

Lysander found their horses. All three had been stripped of their tack and looked to have been brushed and blanketed. They noisily ate grain from the angled trough designed for cows, their hot breath steaming.

"Here," Griffith said, entering the stable and holding up something tiny in his hand.

"Whose is it?" Lysander asked, meeting him under the lantern and taking what Esrahaddon finally saw were strands of long hair.

"One of each," Griffith replied. "Took them from their pillows and brushes. Even out here, girls have brushes."

Lysander inspected the hairs in the light of the lantern. "These will do." He got on his knees and with his hands swept away the straw from the dirt floor.

Griffith spotted their gear reverently set on a table and walked toward it. "You know what he's doing?" The Teshlor wasn't asking for himself. He already knew—*would have to, given he fetched the hair.*

"He's going to cast a location weave by burning the strands of hair and studying the smoke that rises from them. Although . . ." Esrahaddon paused, since Lysander had picked up a small hooked tool and begun to draw a circle around himself in the dirt. He followed this by marking symbols inside the circle. "Those are . . ." He looked at Griffith. "Aren't those the same symbols you wear to *block* magic?"

Griffith held out his helm. Apparently, tattoos weren't enough. Inside, Esrahaddon saw the same symbols engraved on the metal. Only . . . Esrahaddon looked back down at the dirt drawing Lysander was making. "They're backward."

"They are," Lysander agreed.

"I don't understand."

"The Orinfar creates a null space, a bubble of sorts that cuts off contact with Elan, and as a result the Art cannot be manifested within nor penetrate the barrier. However, by reversing the symbols, the opposite is enacted. Instead of blocking the power of Elan, the circle invites it, giving the weave a boost."

"Is that necessary?"

"No, but it helps, particularly with location spells. Long-distance weaves are impractical in the same way it is unrealistic for me to shout and expect the girls to hear me. They're simply too far away. The more power I have, the louder my voice and the greater my effective range. This circle will essentially help funnel the active power of the Aston River into my weave, giving me the resources to search a massive area and hopefully locate the direction of each girl."

"But we already knew that," Esrahaddon said. "They went into the forest."

"We are not taking *Hal Haston's* word for that."

Lysander began his weave.

The man was an accomplished Cenzar, and he managed his construct quickly and efficiently. Then he held out a single hair between forefinger and thumb, and just as he had lit the lantern, he burned the strand. Gray smoke peeled off, drifting southwest. He sighed and shared a look with Griffith. Neither appeared happy.

Esrahaddon was about to ask his question again when Lysander performed the weave with a second hair. This time Esrahaddon didn't see any smoke at all.

Lysander did this three more times, still no smoke. Then the Cenzar stood up and carefully placed the remaining strands in a small pouch on his belt. He stared at Griffith.

"So only one is still alive?" the Teshlor asked.

"So it seems. Makes sense. The last one disappeared only yesterday."

With that, they both looked at Esrahaddon and frowned.

"You'll have to stay here," Griffith said.

"So I've heard, but I haven't been told why."

"You don't need to know. You simply must follow orders."

"He's not a Teshlor recruit, Simmons," Lysander said. "We teach our pupils to be curious, question everything, and seek answers."

"Too much education." Griffith shook his head and turned away.

"Esrahaddon," Lysander said as he gathered his things, and the two began prepping their mounts, "you must stay here because we cannot be responsible for you breaking imperial law."

"I still don't understand."

"Entering the Mystic Wood is forbidden—by order of the emperor. Not even Teshlors or Cenzars are allowed to go in. Simmons and I are about to break that law because we are certain an innocent young woman is lost in those woods, but just like her friends, she'll freeze to death if we don't find her soon. While we are knowingly defying the emperor, we cannot allow you to do the same. So you must stay here."

"Why is the forest forbidden? Is there really a witch?"

They looked at each other. "We don't know," Lysander admitted. "Information about the Mystic Wood has been kept secret. Few know why." He looked at Griffith. "Perhaps if the emperor were more like the Cenzarium, we'd be able to make a more informed decision here. As it is, we must enter this problem blind."

The Teshlor Knight made no comment as he cinched the four-horned saddle on his white horse.

"So I just wait here?"

Lysander nodded. "If for some reason neither of us returns by tomorrow night, you should go back to Percepliquis. And if that becomes necessary, I hereby grant you permission to use the Art to aid yourself. Do you understand?"

"Yes."

"Good. With luck, we'll gather up this stray villager and be back by morning."

The Art was telling Esrahaddon something very different as his mentors left the stable. The night was cold, and dark, and he didn't think luck was with *any* of them.

Hal Haston offered to vacate his own home to provide Esrahaddon with a bed. The Cenzar-in-training refused, claiming that if the barn was good enough for his horse, it was fine enough for him. Truth was, Esrahaddon didn't like Hal. He reminded him too much of Kenja. Esrahaddon recalled how Kenja had initially fallen over himself by being gracious to the Monk of Maribor who had visited Haddon. But when he found the monk's book, he was accused of being an evil sorcerer, and he was lucky to escape with his life. Given that Esrahaddon was a literal sorcerer, he felt it best to stay close to his horse.

In the corner of the barn, Esrahaddon created a nest out of the straw to sleep in. As he did, he thought about how similar Eber-on-Aston was to Haddon. Both were tiny, isolated communities on the edge of a terrible forest. Eber-on-Aston had ample water from the river, but it also had snow and killing cold. In appearance, they were different, but in essence, they were the same. *And if the elders of Haddon exiled me to the forest as punishment, isn't it possible Hal Haston sent five girls to the woods as penalty for some offense?*

Esrahaddon didn't think it required genius to guess at the crime.

"The witch took them all. Why do we have to live in the shadow of this monster?"

Esrahaddon had heard something similar before.

"He's a demon spawn. That's why trouble always comes—he draws it, causes it!"

Esrahaddon blew out the lantern and shivered as the night wind blew through the gaps in the walls.

Hal must have believed the girls were witches, so he cast them out. Or perhaps they were offered up as sacrifices to an imagined monster. No limits defined the irrationality of the ignorant.

He'd thought to tell Lysander this before he and Griffith left, but he knew they would never believe him. How could they? The fifth was Hal's own daughter. Neither Griffith Simmons nor Lysander Lawson had likely heard their fathers petitioning for their children's deaths out of fear of the unknown.

Esrahaddon curled up in his nest, closed his eyes, and went to sleep.

CHAPTER FIFTEEN

The Forbidden Forest

IMPERIAL VILLAGE OF EBER-ON-ASTON, WINTER

Esrahaddon awoke to see Hal Haston leading Ester out of the barn. She wore her saddle and bridle, as well as much of Esrahaddon's equipment. Taking these supplies, which weren't actually Esrahaddon's at all but had been provided by the Cenzarium, was Hal's mistake. Esrahaddon spotted his big copper pot on the ground beside the horse. The loop on the pot handle was held by a poorly tied strap secured by a thief who had little experience with knots. The pot clanging on the hard dirt was what had awakened him.

Hal looked back, wide-eyed, then pulled hard on the horse, trying to force her out of the barn. The moment she cleared the door, Hal tried to jump up into the saddle. Esrahaddon, having lived in a forest of unexpected nightly alarms, was quick to his feet and tackled Hal to the snowy ground, where the two slid clear of Ester's hooves as she danced aside.

Hal was shorter, but thick and sturdy, possessing the build of a man who'd lived his life with an ax and plow. Esrahaddon was taller and younger, and while he was forbidden to use the Art, he'd been trained in hand-to-hand combat by an Ankor Ghazel arena fighter. They came up, and Esrahaddon landed the first punch to Hal's face. It was a solid blow, but Hal took it and came back with a swing of his own that Esrahaddon ducked.

"Be mindful of your footing," Mashie had drilled into him. *"Plant your feet. Use your weight. You haven't got claws, so slam those knuckles—and aim for the soft, vulnerable spots."*

Esrahaddon got a solid punch into Hal's stomach, but again the man didn't seem to feel it. Grabbing hold of Esrahaddon, Hal threw him to the snow. Before he could get up, arms grabbed him. Hal was seized as well.

"What are you doing, Hal?" a big, bald man in just his nightshirt and boots shouted as he wrestled Hal into submission. He was aided by eight men, who looked to have come out with little more than their nightclothes on. "Are you insane? You're fighting an agenperal? You'll get us all killed!"

"He's a trainee. A novice."

"So? Why you fighting him?"

"He's trying to steal my horse!" Esrahaddon shouted.

The bald man with the bare legs and boots stood in the muddied snow between two camps of gathered men. One group clustered around Hal, holding onto his arms and legs as the man struggled. Another gang did the same to Esrahaddon, though he stopped struggling, causing most of those holding him to relax their grips.

The bald man looked at Ester, then grabbed Hal by the collar and jerked him roughly as if trying to wake him from a dream. "Tell me you didn't. Tell me you're not that stupid, Hal. Tell me you didn't try to steal an imperial agent's horse."

"He's not a—"

"You think it matters?" the man exploded. "Holy mother of Novron! When them other two come back—"

"They'll kill me!" Hal shouted, spit flying from his mouth. "That's why I wanna be gone. On this horse, I'll be miles away."

"You can't run from magic, you idiot! They'll hunt you down."

"Got to catch me first, and I plan on being real hard to find. No agenperal's gonna waste months or years chasing the likes of me. I'm not worth it."

"I don't understand," said one of the men holding Esrahaddon. "Why are they going to kill Hal?"

"Because he killed those girls," Esrahaddon answered. "Didn't you, Hal?"

Esrahaddon knew the answer. Elan had been pretty up front about this one, but Esrahaddon felt certain that even without the Art, he would have put it together. "They never went into the forest. Did they, Hal?"

"How do you know that?" the bald man asked. He looked shocked, and more than a little worried.

Esrahaddon felt it then. The reek of guilt just oozed from the bald man, and another piece of the puzzle fell into place. "You knew. Everything that he did—you knew about it."

The bald man didn't answer; he didn't need to. The Art told Esrahaddon the rest. "Why didn't you tell anyone? Why didn't you tell Lysander or Griffith?"

"Because Hal's my little brother," the bald man admitted.

"You're . . ." Esrahaddon looked back and forth, only then noticing the resemblance. The lack of hair had thrown him. The older brother showed Hal's future, but for now the hair made them appear different. "Oh, I see. Out here on the edge of the forest, if you're family, murder is okay?"

"I didn't know," the older brother defended himself. "Not at first."

Around them, more people arrived. These had taken the time to dress. Most were women, who approached slowly with blankets around their shoulders. They fanned out to watch, and like a herd of cattle, they huddled in a circle, creating a fog with their combined breath.

"Then little Edee disappeared, and Hal said he saw her go into the forest. We couldn't go look because no one is allowed in. That didn't stop Edee's parents, though. They went in—went in and never came out."

All around the circle, heads nodded.

"The rest of us learned from that lesson, so we built a big bonfire and took turns shouting into the trees, hoping she was just lost and would see the light and hear our voices. When that didn't work, we sent for you folks."

The older brother squared off with the younger.

"Hal didn't like that. He was pretty upset, and that's when I realized he was lying. Still, Hal figured he'd be safe because not even the agenperals are allowed in the forest. Isn't that right, Hal?"

The rest of those in the circle started talking to one another. And more than once, Esrahaddon heard the words, "Hal lied?"

Hal turned his face away. He struggled, but the men held him tight.

"Guess I shoulda known," the brother said, staring at Hal. "He's always had a *thing* for young girls. Ya like to hear them scream, don't you, Hal? When we were young, he pulled their pigtails just to make them squeal. His wife tried to tell me. Tried to convince me, but I didn't believe her—I didn't *want* to believe, not about my little brother. After you were done, you killed them, didn't ya?"

Hal said nothing.

Someone arrived with a torch and held it up to reveal their faces. Hal was scowling, teeth bared. The wind blew snow off a nearby roof. It fell with a *thrump*, and several in the crowd jumped.

"They're not all dead," Esrahaddon declared. "Lysander performed a test. It proved at least one victim is still alive in the forest."

"That's Elinya," the brother said. "Hal's daughter. She was friends with Edee. She believed what Hal had said. But . . . unlike the rest of us, Elinya went in to look for her best friend."

"Look, the agenperals might not come back," Hal appealed to his brother. "That girl's parents never did. And Elinya sure hasn't. There's a reason that wood is forbidden. If the agenperals don't come back, no one is gonna know anything."

"*I* know," Esrahaddon said.

"Yeah." Hal nodded. "This helpless, agent-in-training who punches like a girl. If he went into the river—"

"But you still killed them!" someone shouted.

"I didn't kill anyone. There's no proof I did nothing, just this kid trying to win points with his teachers. Think about it. You all live here. You know me. None of you thought I did nothing until he said so. And them agenperals . . . they don't think I did nothing. It's just this kid here."

"And your brother," Esrahaddon said.

"Oh, he don't know nothing, neither. Do you, Bo?"

"Shut up," his brother said.

Hal raised his voice. "If you think I'm gonna let you pin this on me—forget it. If I go down, I'll take everyone with me. I'll say this whole village knew everything, and my brother helped. Everyone will pay the price for trying to scapegoat me. But if the agenperals never come back . . ."

"If they don't return, this one will run and tell the emperor," Hal's brother said, and he hooked a thumb in Esrahaddon's direction. "He'll send soldiers."

"That's right," Hal said. "And everyone here will hang, and this village will be burned to the ground. Then it won't matter what I say. The emperor will just erase this place as a warning to everyone else. Of course if something happens to this kid, if he disappears, no one ever has to be the wiser, right? We could say he went into the forest after them. They can look—they'll never find him, but that don't mean he didn't go in. And if the agenperals don't come back, if none of them do . . ." He grinned at Esrahaddon. "Well, it will be a long time before more agents are sent, and we can just say, sorry, never saw them, never got here. Don't know nothing."

"You still killed them girls," the brother said. "I know you did. Your own daughter is still out there. It's possible they'll save her."

"Possible, but unlikely. You know as well as I do that there's something awful in these woods. Something old and dangerous. Agenperals are forbidden like everyone else because just like everyone else they're helpless against the witch. So what's everyone gonna do? Fight me and die, or join me and live?"

"What *are* we gonna do, Bo?" one of those holding Esrahaddon asked.

"I don't know," the older brother replied. "But I'm freezing; that's for sure. Can't think when I'm this cold." He looked at Esrahaddon and frowned. "Look, I haven't decided nothing yet. I gotta think on this, but I can't have you starting trouble. Colin, Lenis, put him in the root cellar. Lock him in." He looked at his brother. "I'm not killing no agenperal-in-training if there's a chance the other two are coming back. We should know by sunset tomorrow. I'll decide what to do then."

"You're making a mistake," Esrahaddon said as they pulled him away.

"Maybe," Bo replied. "But I've already made so many, one more can't hurt."

The root cellar was just what Esrahaddon expected—a hole in the ground with a heavy timber door held fast by iron hinges and a sliding bolt. He'd caught a quick glimpse of the interior before they slammed the door. The space was small, with a dirt floor, stacked stone walls, and massive logs overhead. It was half filled with sacks and crates. The lack of windows left him in the dark. He'd hoped for a sliver of light to leak under the door or around the hinges, but the villagers were careful about their food stock. To prevent mice or bugs from getting in, they employed a previously unseen level of craftsmanship, and the seal was tight. In the silent, black world, his two most prominent senses were shut off, leaving the others to do the heavy lifting. He could smell the musty, earthy scent of roots and vegetables, and he could feel the damp cold. At least there was no wind in the cellar. He felt around a bit. Everything felt clammy. After banging his head on a low beam, he found what felt like a wooden crate and sat on it. Then he stared out at the dark.

Esrahaddon wasn't blind, though. Far from it. He still had the Art. While he was forbidden from active use, passive employment was allowed, mostly because it couldn't be blocked. Elan spoke to everyone. The only choice people had in the matter was whether to listen or not. Most didn't. He was learning to, and at that moment, listening was all he could do.

Looking with the Art, for him, was like staring through frosted glass. Nothing was in focus. He could see movement, light, and shadow, but not much else. The sun was up, he knew that. Villagers performed their daily functions as if the world hadn't stopped. Strange how that was always the case. Floods, droughts, wars, storms—they all rolled through. But those who toiled continued their drudgery as if it were a joy they couldn't live without, not even for a day.

That was likely the truth of it, he guessed, minus the joy part.

Ester was still around. He sensed a horse. If there had been more than one, he might not have been able to tell. If Ester was still in the village, so too, he believed, was Hal Haston. They were waiting for sunset, he guessed. If Lysander and Griffith returned before then, Bo would hand over his brother, throw himself on the mercy of the agenperals, and likely hope that not killing Esrahaddon would garner enough goodwill to keep him and the village safe. If they didn't return, it was probable that Bo and Hal would come to the root cellar with an ax, a rope, or maybe just one of the knives they slaughtered lambs with. Esrahaddon figured one of the brothers would hold him down while the other slit his throat. Then they would toss his body into the Aston and let it carry away the evidence. Hal would take his horse and gear and disappear—exiled for his crimes, but also to cover their tracks. If the agenperals returned the next day or the one after that, the village could declare that the Cenzar-in-training took his horse and went home. The fact that he never made it back to Percepliquis wouldn't be their fault.

What neither Hal nor Bo nor anyone else in the village appeared to know was that being a Cenzar-in-training only meant he wasn't *allowed* to use the Art—it didn't mean he *couldn't*. Lacking that information, they also didn't know that Esrahaddon was only forbidden to use the Art until sundown. *"And if that becomes necessary, I hereby grant you permission to use the Art to aid yourself."* What Lysander meant by *"use the Art to aid yourself,"* Esrahaddon felt was broad enough for him to interpret as he wished. The fact was, even if Hal and Bo came for him before nightfall, he had every intention of ignoring Lysander's restriction. He wanted to be a good student but wasn't about to die on the altar of principle. He also wanted a solid excuse for what he imagined was going to be a questionable conclusion to the affair. While officially a member of the Cenzarium, he was still the product of his childhood, and he realized he hated Eber-on-Aston nearly as much as he did Haddon. Just as Hal planned to simply erase all witnesses to his crime, Esrahaddon was thinking along the same lines, except his version of *erase* could be a good deal more comprehensive.

From time to time, Esrahaddon stood up to stretch his legs. The cold damp made him tense up and he didn't want to be stiff when they finally came for him. He also dug through the sacks, following his nose to find carrots, radishes, beets, some apples, and winter squash. He ate a carrot and an apple, and later some of the squash and a beet. Then he had another apple as a means of fighting a growing thirst.

As the day passed, he began to worry, not about his fate but about Lysander and Griffith. He honestly didn't need their help and would enjoy exacting revenge on good old Hal the child-killing monster and even his brother Bo, who preferred to keep his options open. But if the sun set and the Cenzar and Teshlor still weren't back, what did that mean? *"A Teshlor Knight and a Cenzar are more formidable than a legion,"* Lysander had said, and Esrahaddon had a hard time imagining a whole legion marching into the forest and *not* coming out.

"The witch took them all. Why do we have to live in the shadow of this monster?"

Was that just Hal inventing an excuse?

"Entering the Mystic Wood is forbidden—by order of the emperor. Not even Teshlors or Cenzars are allowed to go in."

"Is there really a witch?"

The day passed. Lysander and Griffith did not return.

The last rays of sunlight had faded. Esrahaddon knew this as well as he knew he was thirsty, and in much the same way. He didn't see thirst, didn't hear it. He felt it somewhere inside him, but where exactly he wasn't certain. The same was true about the passing of the day. He also sensed the coming of Hal. Nothing so clear as sound or as accurate as sight had preceded him, but he was coming.

Esrahaddon stood up and positioned himself against the supplies, facing the door.

A dozen possibilities ran through his head. Even after hours spent contemplating what he'd do, Esrahaddon remained undecided. He considered escaping, hiding and watching them enter the root cellar, then locking them in by changing the door into a solid wall of stone. He could also cave the place in, burying both. Esrahaddon liked that idea, as it was so tidy. But while these appealed, in an elegant, minimalist aesthetic, they denied him the satisfaction of revenge. These two were owed punishment, not for what they'd done to him, but on behalf of the four young women Hal had murdered. Esrahaddon was certain Hal Haston hadn't mercifully bludgeoned them from behind and dropped them into the river.

"Ya like to hear them scream, don't you, Hal?"

The man had tortured the girls in some manner. It felt only proper that Esrahaddon should balance those scales. A quick and tidy death was the proper reward for having lived a good and decent life. Hal deserved something messy. This forced Esrahaddon to rule out making the man explode, like he had done to that tree in Calynia, and unfortunately there were no siafu ants to put inside his head. He was still pondering the right demise when the door opened and Hal entered, holding a torch in one hand and a small scythe in the other.

"Time's up, little apprentice. Your masters aren't coming back, and I must leave. Before I do, Bo says I gotta toss you in the river. You'll like it. There are four pretty girls who'll keep you company."

Hal was grinning. He had a hungry, deranged look in his eyes. His lips were wet as he kept licking them, his breathing heavy. Despite this, Esrahaddon saw a line of drool running down his chin.

He's so eager, so excited. It's as if I am one of the girls, and he plans to . . .

Hal closed the door behind him. Then he planted the torch in the iron sconce beside it. "Take off them clothes."

"So you really did kill those girls?"

"Of course I did."

"But you did more than just kill them, right? What did you do?"

"Whatever I wanted. Just like I'm gonna do now."

Esrahaddon bit his lip. "You're making this so hard. You're like a mosquito bite. I mean, you itch something awful, making me want to scratch hard, but I know I'll pay for it later."

"Not later, boy. Right now." He raised the scythe. "You're all alone, just like the others. Your masters ain't coming back."

"If only I could be certain of—" Esrahaddon stopped, then smiled as the idea hit him. "Excellent idea, Hal. We can go find them together."

"You ain't getting out of here, boy. Not alive, at least."

"Oh, Hal," Esrahaddon said with false sympathy and a comical frown. "You're a bit confused. You have me mixed up with the others you've killed. I'm not a fourteen-year-old girl."

Hal reached down and began to unbuckle his belt. "I'm not that picky."

"You're not understanding me. I'm not a young helpless boy, either. I'm a member of the Cenzarium. And this really isn't your day."

"Oh, I think—"

The torch went out.

The scythe rang when it hit the dirt.

Then the root cellar exploded.

Esrahaddon didn't need to cause that much devastation. He could have simply opened the door and walked out, but after being cooped up and made to wait, feeling that itch build up for so long, he had to scratch at least a little. It felt good to let go. Destruction was always so easy—and he had to admit it was more than a little fun. In his mind's eye, Esrahaddon saw it like he was plucking a chord, a massive string like the sort found on a lyre. The resulting vibration, the tone, had the ability to rip apart the world. He'd picked it lightly when he burst the tree, plucked it harder when he destroyed Banka's palace, and now he gave the chord a good solid flick. The result ripped the ground apart. Soil, rocks, and vegetables blew into the air. Massive timbers flew like bits of straw. It rained dirt and pebbles from a cloud of snow, and when the dust cleared, all that was left were two people standing in a massive crater.

There had been a hay barn nearby, but it was no longer there. A wagon was also missing, but no one was dead, no homes damaged, no one hurt—though food might be scarcer that winter.

Hal was on his knees, screaming.

Moonlight revealed him staring in horror at his hands, or more accurately, where his hands used to be. Now his arms ended at the wrists. They hadn't been cut off; no blood was visible, and nothing was on the ground except the scythe. It was as if he'd never had hands at all.

Not surprisingly, the whole village turned out.

In order to help them see, Esrahaddon set Hal's house on fire. Witnessing the home burst into a blazing torch caused everyone to stop moving as if they were terrified to activate some further calamity.

"Bo?" Esrahaddon said, standing inside the blown-out crater on a patch of untouched ground. The flickering firelight illuminated his dark face. "Send someone to fetch my horse. Make sure she's properly saddled, and that all my gear is on her."

"You did this?" Bo asked, coming slowly out of the shadows.

"Oh yeah. Like it?" Esrahaddon grinned. "Kinda felt the place needed a little sprucing up, you know? I can do more if you like." He glanced up beyond the shacks at the rising forested hills. "Actually, I was thinking it would be fun if I animated the trees. You know, give them the power to move and such, and let them have their revenge. I think they'd like that given how they've had to stand there year after year and watch all of you murder, butcher, and burn their friends and family. I mean, really, what kind of messed-up world is that for them to be trapped in? Can't help but feel sorry for the poor bastards. Just imagine being forced to stand there as your family is literally sawed and axed right in front of you. I imagine they might very much enjoy expressing their displeasure."

They all took a moment then to look at the trees, and he could see it in their eyes. Like the people of Haddon, the inhabitants of Eber-on-Aston were terrified of the forest, but the fear came from the Awful Things it hid inside. They had never seen the forest itself as a threat—until now.

"Chad, Newly," Bo called, "get the man's horse saddled."

Esrahaddon walked to the well. The bucket was full of ice. "You see, I'm a novice—but not because I can't do magic." He thawed the ice with a slight flourish of one hand so he could dip the communal cup in and take a drink. "I just need supervision because I'm not trained to understand what I *shouldn't* do. Left to myself, I'm a bit like a baby giant—I just don't know enough not to crush the little people." Esrahaddon lifted the water cup toward Hal's brother as if offering a toast. "Feeling little, Bo? Your brother does. Old Hal, he's starting to understand what a mouse feels, trapped between the paws of a bored cat. I'll be taking him with me into the forest to look for my teachers. There's something poetic in that, don't you think? Hal being forced to go where he said everyone went. That's really what tipped it for me. I like poetry."

Esrahaddon finished his drink, then walked over to stand before Bo, who stared at him, horrified.

"The rest of you will stay here. No one is to leave. Everyone is guilty, to some degree, of failing to assist imperial agents with an investigation and putting said agents in peril. I actually don't know all the laws yet. That's second- or third-year stuff, but I'm guessing that cooperating in a conspiracy to murder the direct representative of the emperor—even if it is only to murder a Cenzar-in-training—is pretty close to insurrection. I'm guessing the punishment is death, but like I said, I don't actually know the laws yet. As a result, we'll need to wait either for my teachers to return, or for new agents to visit. But either way, *everyone* stays here." Esrahaddon walked up close to Bo. "You'll likely run." He looked up at his bare head. "Sadly, you have no hair. And I am going to need something I can burn to locate you in case you flee. I think a finger or two will be fine."

After a good long drink at the village well, Esrahaddon rode Ester southwest into the forest. The moon was bright and reflected off the snow, providing ample light to see by. Hal followed on foot, tethered by a rope to the rear horn of the saddle. Because the man had no hands, Esrahaddon had tied the rope around his neck, which was easy, convenient, and added a necessary incentive for Hal to keep up.

Esrahaddon had no clear idea where to go. He'd seen the direction Lysander and Griffith had gone in, but he hadn't been so careful as to pinpoint the exact spot. Didn't seem important at the time. The snow around the village was trampled flat, leaving no tracks. This area extended quite deep into the trees. Some places were icy, others trodden enough to show dirt or grass, mostly around fresh-cut stumps where there were also chips of bright blond wood.

So they're able to enter a little bit, even cut some trees. Whatever is in here doesn't seem too partial to the forest itself. That rules out tree spirits or a forest god or anything primordial like that.

Esrahaddon was fairly certain none of those things existed beyond the fear-filled minds of the ignorant, but freeing himself of ingrained childhood lessons was nearly as hard as casting aside his belief in the need to eat and drink. He could reason all he wanted that breathing was silly, and yet some things couldn't be erased with mere education. Knowing and believing weren't always allies, and sometimes there was good reason for that. He had, after all, seen a robe eat a person.

This trafficked region of the wood extended far enough into the trees that Esrahaddon was unsure where the official Forbidden Forest began. He saw no sense in asking Hal or anyone else. At this point, they would only lie or refuse to answer. He wished he'd taken a few strands of Lysander's hair. He knew the location weave. They had taught him the simple exercise his first week in the Cenzarium. Esrahaddon had been tasked with finding a white mouse that'd been hidden behind a concealed door on the upper story. They provided him ten small pale hairs. He found the mouse using only three. This was a record of some kind and impressed his instructors. Everything he did appeared to impress, but also . . . *frighten* them. They didn't show it, but the Art revealed their trepidation. Hekkabah had warned him against arrogance, but conceit was hard to fight when he regularly filled experienced experts with hidden awe.

But I'm not an idiot, he reassured himself. The encouragement was needed because he suspected he might be letting arrogance get him into trouble. *I know this is dangerous. Just because I can find a hidden mouse like nobody's business doesn't mean I'm a god.* Part of him insisted he was doing it to save the lives of his friends. Only they weren't his friends. He'd just met them both and honestly didn't care much for either. Lysander was sensible but zealous in his push to force his beliefs on everyone. Griffith was quiet but appeared to be the typical thug who believed actions were better than words and deeds more profound than ideas.

So why am I doing this? I have orders to return to Percepliquis. Rappaport is waiting. I could be having another lovely meal with her. All I need do is turn Ester around and gallop home. If I did, and I didn't bother to untie the rope, the "Hal problem" would take care of itself.

He ventured deeper into the forest. The trodden snow gave way to pristine fluff, and he faced a truth. *I'm better than they are, and I want to prove it. I will return to Percepliquis with my grateful instructors and have them explain how the novice saved their lives.*

Even in his own head, the words sounded a tad unrealistic: the fantasy of youth—the product of pride. *But what is arrogance but the unrealized, unproved capabilities of a person? Once tested, once confirmed, arrogance transforms into courage and confidence. Novron never doubted himself, and as a result changed the world. Life is a series of wagers, and the greatest gambles are best made while young, when there is less to be lost and more to be gained.*

Esrahaddon concluded he was simply playing the odds.

At last, he and his prisoner came to the end of the village's influence. Progress slowed as Ester and Hal both struggled with the increased depth. Overall, the snow was less than a foot deep, but it drifted in places such that if he pushed Ester, she might stumble, and Hal most certainly would be jerked to death. Esrahaddon didn't want that. Not yet.

Just as Esrahaddon had found with the Erbon, this equally maligned forest appeared to be falsely accused of malevolence. The evergreens were beautiful, attired in their white gowns of glistening snow. Even the naked trees were bedecked with an attractive icing that gleamed in the moonlight. Everything sparkled in a most festive and enchanting manner. This pristine blanket of white also told wonderful stories that the foot-packed snow kept to itself. One of those secrets Esrahaddon spotted just a few feet off to his right: the tracks of two horses that had ridden side by side. He veered over and followed their path.

Looks like I don't need a hair after all. Finding Lysander and Griffith would be far easier than he'd imagined. Finding them, however, might not be the hard part.

"What do you know about this wood?" Esrahaddon asked Hal. "About this witch you spoke of?"

"Give me back my hands, and I'll tell you."

"Sorry, can't do that."

"You could if you wanted."

"If you had cut *my* hands off—with an ax, let's say—could you put them back on? Of course not. Same here. So stop being foolish and tell me what I need to know."

Hal didn't answer.

"I only ask because if this witch does exist, and if she managed to defeat my teachers, there is a good chance we will encounter her. If you aid me, there's a possibility that we might also save your daughter." He looked back and saw no interest, no value in that direction. "And," he added, "Lysander and Griffith will most certainly take that into consideration when they sentence you, which could be the difference between imprisonment and execution. Remain silent, and it's possible we'll both die." He watched Hal trudging behind, trying to keep to the easier tracks the horse opened up. "You might suspect that is the smarter option, but I'm thinking death by a noose is preferable to death by a witch. I'm no expert, but I suspect witches are similar to you in that they like to terrorize their victims. Living out here, deep in these woods where no one is allowed, she has the luxury of time and the curse of loneliness and boredom. Might keep you alive, torturing you for years."

Hal still said nothing.

Esrahaddon considered forcing him to talk but doubted it was worth the effort. Hal didn't seem like the educated type. All he might reveal would be foolish, useless hearsay. That's all the inhabitants of these villages ever knew: superstitions and made-up stories — the Uncle Hebus tall tales that tried to explain the unknown through a filter of fear. Villagers who actually ventured out, who learned the truth and brought it back, were ignored, belittled, insulted, and, if they persisted, beaten. Lifetimes lived in fear of what turned out to be nothing was too humiliating a fate to face. Men found it easier to *be* wrong than to *admit* it.

As the forest grew denser, Esrahaddon noticed that among the tracks left by the pair of horses was a single line of footprints. These were older, less defined, mostly filled in, and they often disappeared altogether. They were the footprints of a young woman.

"The stories are old," Hal said.

Esrahaddon didn't turn, but he did slow Ester a bit.

"Some say they go back thousands of years, before the Great War, and there was an ancient evil here even then — a witch. But most of the stories only go back about two hundred years. They say the witch killed a princess and the emperor couldn't do nothing. The witch is too powerful. So he made the forest forbidden to all. They say she's an ancient evil, something immortal from before the birth of the gods."

"There was something before the birth of the gods?" The question was rhetorical, but Hal, being the genius he was, didn't catch that.

"There was Chaos."

"Which is another way of saying there was nothing."

"Chaos ain't nothing. Can't be if from it came all things."

Esrahaddon opened his mouth to cast a sarcastic rebuke—his Gift of Niblick—then he thought about it and realized Hal had a point. Everything did have to come from somewhere, except how could everything come from anywhere? If it did, where would that come from? The answer . . . Chaos. Chaos was chaos. It had no rules, made no sense. Chaos didn't need to come from anywhere because *coming from* was logical, a common sense that didn't exist in chaos. Logic, reasoning, judgment, argument, facts—all of this came *out* of chaos, and only with them did a path begin. Esrahaddon saw it all clearly, aided by the analogy that he was following tracks in the snow. Everything that made sense left a trail that could be followed back to its origin, but at some point, that trail ended at a cliff beyond which was nothing at all—chaos. None of this was helpful in their present situation, and yet, Esrahaddon felt that Handless Hal might have stumbled on a fundamental truth that wiser men had missed. Chaos was indeed something. It was, in fact, the source of everything.

The night grew darker. Moonlight faded. Either clouds were rolling in, or the evergreens were growing dense enough to block it. Esrahaddon had a sense that it was a bit of both. The night was also growing colder. This wasn't strange. Even in the Erbon Forest, the nights were always coldest just before the dawn.

So why do I think it strange?

"Your, ah . . ." Hal said. "Your pack. It's glowing."

Esrahaddon turned around to see the satchel hanging from the rear horn of his saddle looking like it housed a lit lantern, except the light was milk-white.

"Is it supposed to do that?" Hal asked.

Esrahaddon ignored him but stopped Ester.

Been almost a year. Why now?

Esrahaddon climbed down and stared at the pouch, unsure what to do. He'd been terrified of the thing ever since it consumed the Arkum emissary. Clothes weren't supposed to eat people. Where he'd gotten the courage to pick it up and stuff it into the satchel, he couldn't recall. All he knew was that there was nothing but a greasy stain on the ground where the emissary had been. The stain was what stayed with him as he exiled the robe to the back of the wagon and later under the bed in his Cenzarium cubicle.

"What is that?" Hal asked, awe and fear raising the pitch of his voice.

Esrahaddon thought that was a very good question.

"I was supposed to give you a gift, but this gift is not for a child."

"Are you listening, Ezra?"

"It is because your name was also on that tablet. Written in a script that would not exist for another ten thousand years—in words that no one else could read—was a message to me from Rex Uberlin. He ordered me to cross the sea and find a Mari-born male and give him the gift Uberlin left for you. The tablet read: 'You will know him by his given name, Ez-Rah, and Haddon, the village of his birth. When you find him, you'll know I have not forgotten my children.'"

Esrahaddon had never known his real mother, but he believed she had loved him. He always felt that she hadn't simply been killed by the lions, but that she had fought to protect her son. Maybe that was true. But what he did know—knew for a fact—was that *Hekkabah* had loved him. She had given up her own life to raise an orphan boy of another race. He remembered how she'd hugged him when he cried; healed him when he broke his leg; taught him everything she knew, and protected him for over a decade. Who he was had more to do with her than anyone. And Hekkabah had sacrificed her life and the lives of family and friends to give him that robe. And while he hadn't received it on the longest day of the year when the sun lined up with the road to Shahabad, the day the robe came to him had, in many ways, been the start of a new life.

"What is that?" Hal asked again.

Esrahaddon unbuckled the strap and flung the flap free. Only a portion of the robe was visible, but it was enough to illuminate the forest, making the world sparkle.

"A birthday present from my mother."

With a deep breath and clenched teeth, Esrahaddon removed the robe from the pouch and pulled his arms through the sleeves. Most robes that closed in the front were held fast by a sash or belt, but this required neither. The two sides came together and secured themselves such that the robe almost seemed a single piece. The sleeves and hem were the perfect length. From his first wearing, he recalled how the hood acted as a high collar until he pulled it up.

The white light had vanished the moment he touched the robe, and once he put it on, the color shifted from gray to blue-green. Expecting the worst, Esrahaddon stood beside Ester, waiting. If the robe consumed him, what would happen to Hal? Without hands, he would be hard pressed to untie the knot around his neck. He'd also find it challenging to climb on Ester's back, and if he failed, if he fell and spooked the horse, the rope would snap his neck.

"What?" Hal asked, uncomfortable with Esrahaddon staring at him.

Esrahaddon looked down at himself, at the Robe of Light, what the emissary had referred to as the Gry Erlikon. He brushed his palm across it. "Nothing. Looks like we're okay."

Climbing back into the saddle, he urged Ester onward through the snow.

CHAPTER SIXTEEN

The Witch

MYSTIC WOOD, WINTER

For the last mile, the forest had seemed to grow thick and dense, leaving only a single navigable path. This route resembled a tunnel around which all the trees' branches curled like taloned claws. In the unrelieved darkness, Esrahaddon had a mind to try out the light-weave that Asure, a fifth-year Cenzar, had shown him. Yet before he uttered "Venderia," the prompt for the weave, before he even opened his mouth, the robe eliminated the need by brightening. A soft, white light shone from it and illuminated the world around them. Esrahaddon froze for a moment, unsure what that meant. He waited, and when nothing more occurred, he concluded that . . . *apparently it means, "You wanted light; here you go."*

"Robe of Light," Esrahaddon muttered as if that explained the situation, which it did just about as well as the phrase *act of God*—which was to say, not at all.

He was feeling better about his new attire. In retrospect, he should have realized that it wouldn't make sense for Hekkabah to give him the robe if wearing it was dangerous. The moment he slipped it on, he felt warm. If not for his wind-kissed face and hands—and all the snow around—Esrahaddon might have assumed he'd entered a lovely summer's night. Still, he was accustomed to the idea of clothes being tools—an item he used for a purpose. The emphasis being squarely on *he used.* Esrahaddon hadn't done anything to make the robe glow. The thing had brightened on its own.

How did it know? That one thought was disturbing. Clothes can't *know* anything. Cloth isn't capable of contemplation. Yet even if it were, how could it be aware of what Esrahaddon was thinking? *Maybe it wasn't. Might have been a coincidence.* This thought did little to help, as that conclusion merely suggested that the robe itself desired more light.

Esrahaddon shoved the *how and why* onto his Consider Later pile, since the *here and now* was far more pressing. The robe's radiance revealed the rise of a hazy mist obscuring everything more than twenty feet away. Esrahaddon didn't need Elan to tell him he was close, but that didn't stop the old lady from talking. Esrahaddon felt that familiar alert rush through him. Something big was about to happen. In only another few steps, he saw it. Just ahead, the trail ended at an iced-over black pool. On the far side was a steep cliff, and in its face was a half-moon wooden door. Stained, scratched, and weathered, it looked as old as time itself. All around the pool and jutting up out of it were bones and body parts. To one side and tethered to the sickly trees stood two horses—one black and the other white—saddles still on. Footprints, those of the young woman and the fresher, deeper marks left by Lysander and Griffith, all led to the ice-covered pool.

Esrahaddon dismounted and stood peering through the mist at the door. The hill appeared sheared away, as if the result of some violent blow, and the door was covered in dripping layers of frozen ice like melted wax.

This is where nightmares come for ideas.

"That's her house," Hal said. "Gotta be." He had his arms around himself as he stood shivering in the snow. "You see the foot?"

It was impossible not to. Jutting up out of the frozen pool, the single five-toed appendage protruded as far as the ankle. The skin was pale and nearly as white as the snow that dusted it.

"Doesn't that bother you?" Hal asked.

"If it wiggled, it would."

They both looked, waited. It didn't move.

Esrahaddon untied Hal. "Go knock."

"What?"

"Knock on the door. Ask to see the lady of the house and see if she'll come out to talk."

"Are you insane?"

"Obviously not," Esrahaddon smiled. "If I were crazy, I would go knock."

Hal held up his two stumps. "Can't knock. Ain't got no hands."

"But you have an elbow. Try that. If that doesn't work, use your head. Literally."

Hal didn't move.

"Okay, let me make this easier. Either you can walk over there and rap politely on that creepy door, or I can announce myself to the mistress of this place by throwing your body across the pool and bouncing it off the door. And I will continue to do that until someone comes out, or your bones become so pulverized that you no longer make enough noise."

As if to emphasize this, the robe brightened a little. Hal noticed, and the point was driven home, mostly because he assumed Esrahaddon was controlling the light. Once more, Esrahaddon wasn't certain whether he was pleased or frightened. If nothing else, the robe appeared to be on his side and acted like a wildly luminescent guard dog growling at Hal through the beauty of aggressive white light.

Hal grimaced, then with some difficulty swallowed, and slowly began to walk out across the pond.

"Take courage, Hal. Remember, your loving daughter is probably on the other side of that door."

"I don't give a snake's ass about her!" the man shouted back, his voice harsh and quavering. "She's the idiot that came out here. That's probably her lousy foot!"

Esrahaddon heard the ice moan and pop with Hal's weight. The moment he reached the center, a crack appeared. It zigzagged from one end to the other.

Hal stopped, afraid to move. "Oh, by the white of Novron's beard!"

"Actually," Esrahaddon said, "Novron was clean-shaven. And if he did have a beard, it wouldn't have been white—more of a golden blond."

"Shut up!" Hal shouted. He had his arms out now as if he were walking a tightrope.

"Keep going."

Hal moved slowly, but he advanced, sliding his feet rather than lifting them. "There's something under the ice. Something moving. I can see it. Oh geez, it's an eye! An eye! And it's looking up at me!"

"Keep moving."

Another pop, then another crack fissured across the surface of the pool. This one intersected with the other, making an X right at Hal's feet. "You're almost there."

Hal knew it and pushed his luck with the last few steps. He reached out and tried to knock with a hand, which he didn't have. His stump made a dull, fleshy *thump*.

"Elbow, Hal. Use your—"

The ice beneath Hal shattered, and down he went, faster than Esrahaddon could have imagined. Black water splashed the door and dripped down, freezing into tears as it went. The hole Hal fell into vanished as the water refroze in seconds. Esrahaddon saw movement underneath. Peering through the ice, he saw Hal was still alive. He beat on the ice with his stumps. Then his terror-filled face pressed against the underside like it was a glass window. He shouted and a series of bubbles exploded from his mouth. Then something else moved. A huge dark mouth with rows of pointed teeth rose and snatched Hal away, leaving only the dark pool and the black ice that covered it.

"Bye, Hal," Esrahaddon said.

Just me and Ester now.

He straightened himself and looked out across the ice at the door.

It wasn't really there. It was, but it wasn't. Looking through the frosted glass of the Art, he saw all of it flickering, a telltale feature of things manifested with the Art—the essence of the Art itself, which those who understood it could detect as a distinct form of illumination. What he was looking at was something made to appear like something else: *an illusion*. Esrahaddon knew this.

But what had killed Hal wasn't fake.

Someone with a great imagination had gone through a good deal of trouble, and he hated wrecking it, in the same way he hated destroying a beautiful spiderweb built across a walking path. But he disliked getting smacked in the face with a web even more. He appreciated the time and the work, but he also had no choice.

There wasn't much power in the area. The trees were dormant—in fact, pretty much everything was asleep. The wind was the best generator. While not blowing much, it was enough. Destruction never required a lot. He brought the wind in, funneled it, and cast out with devastating force. Nothing appeared to happen. The door, the pond, the trees were all still there. The snow hadn't so much as drifted.

"That wasn't very nice," a voice said from behind him.

Spinning, Esrahaddon saw a woman step out of the mist to stand in the center of the tree-tunneled path. She was dressed in a green gown that draped and wrapped, but it had no buttons, ties, or belt. Despite the weather, she wore no shoes. She had rusty-red hair long enough to reach her hips and skin so pale that the foot in the pond could have belonged to her. She wasn't old, not the hag he had expected. In truth, she was beautiful. *But* . . . he cautioned himself . . . *this is a place of illusions.*

"So many visitors today," she said.

Whoever she was, she had power. Esrahaddon could feel it flowing off her like heat from a bonfire. Despite this, Elan wasn't ringing the alarm bells. Still, he sensed a whisper of caution. This was no lion he could convince to walk away, no warlord he could infest with ants.

"Where are the owners of these horses?" Esrahaddon asked.

Her eyes tracked to the animals. "The Teshlor and the Cenzar? They're dead."

Esrahaddon was surprised at the bluntness, stunned at the news, shocked that it affected him as much as it did. "You *killed* them?"

"Just like your friend."

"He wasn't my friend."

The woman shrugged. "This is my realm. They trespassed. My laws are very strict."

"I'm fairly certain this land—this place—belongs to Emperor Nareion."

"Nareion?" She said the word as if needing to hear how it sounded a second time. "Have they crowned a new one?"

Esrahaddon didn't reply. It didn't sound like a question.

"They think I'm insane," she said. "Maybe you do, too. Do you?"

"I have no idea. I don't know anything about you."

"That's fair." She nodded. "I'm not. Insane, that is. The problem is simply that I can't stay focused on any one thing. One idea always leads to another." She pointed at the horses. "Perfect example right there. The world isn't black and white. By looking at those horses, or speaking to their riders, you might think so, but nothing is so simple as that. If you paused to consider how many shades and hues of black and white there are, you would realize that the idea of *one or the other* is just lazy. And it isn't shades of gray, either. That, too, is an inaccurate shortcut. Reality is an infinite number of colors. Most don't see that. Maybe only I do. Does that make me crazy?"

She looked up, took a deep breath, and turned slowly around in a full circle, making her gown flare. "The deep chords are why you're here. You want to strum them, hit them hard, listen to the tone, to the music they impart. In that way, we're a lot alike—us and the old rivas. Only they didn't just play them, did they? They cut one—tried to sever it. Can you imagine snipping one of the pillars of the universe—one of reality's supports? They wanted to destroy the world." She twirled, arms out, palms turned up. "Didn't work . . . *obviously*. Everything is still here." She stopped and sighed. "But they rent a whole continent in the attempt. Can you imagine the devastation? Killed everyone involved instantly. Probably died believing they succeeded. Still, how amazing was that? What must it have been like to break a chord?"

"How do you know about the rivas?" Esrahaddon asked. He knew of them through Hekkabah and Niblick, but they had given him the impression that humans had long forgotten the Old World and its ways. Nothing in his time at the Cenzarium had made him suspect anything different. There were no books on the subject, not even in the legends section. Everything appeared to start with some vague myth about an exodus from the east, brought about by flooding, but with no mention of the cause.

"Oh, it's all there, isn't it? Nothing is ever lost," she said. "Elan keeps a close record. You just have to ask the right question and listen for the answer. But you need a good ear. Takes time to learn how to listen. To understand the nuances of the language. Humans don't have that much time." She took a step toward him. "For example, I know that you're here to kill me, although I suspect that you don't know that yourself yet. You will. The real problem is that before you even know you ought to kill me, you're already wondering if you can."

She moved to the horses and lightly clapped the rump of Lysander's mount. "You want to, don't you?"

At that point, he didn't know what he wanted. Lysander and Griffith were dead. He knew this not merely because she said so, but because Elan confirmed her statement. The woman's words *felt* true down to his bones and beyond. She had killed them, and he felt a loss, but not one so great as needing revenge. Even if he did, he wouldn't admit it to her.

Esrahaddon shook his head.

She laughed. "I don't mean kill me. I mean play the deep chords. I can feel it in you. You'd love to strum the big ones that you know are there. Imagine the rush of power! How wonderful to hear that sound, the music that they make. Even a single note would be transcendent because it was one of the notes played by the symphony that created everything. For perhaps only a moment, you would be one with all—with life, death, time—everything that is, was, and will be. You have the hunger just as I do." She flashed him a wicked grin, spun, and walked two steps away, then stopped. As she did, her gown slapped the backs of her calves.

Big, lazy flakes of snow began to fall, illuminated by the robe and turning the tunnel into a world unto itself, a sort of fairyland. Esrahaddon felt as if he were in the deep end of some terrible lake and not at all confident in his ability to swim.

"The truth is . . ." she said, still facing away, snow catching on her hair, "you really aren't here to kill me. That's the irony. I'm supposed to kill you."

She turned slowly. Arms at her sides, she presented no threat. Went to an effort to show it. Then she tilted her head slightly down so that she looked up at him. That's when he noticed her eyes were green. "The sad part is that you don't have a clue why, and that isn't because of something you've done but something you will do."

Maybe she is *insane.*

Esrahaddon hadn't spoken to many deranged people before, so it was hard to gauge. Sane or mad, the situation was bad. Either he faced a lunatic who might do anything, or a perfectly rational lady intent on murdering him. That hearth-like radiation of power he felt flowing off her—far greater than even what he'd sensed in the presence of the ghazel emissary—suggested that despite his new ability to throw up a shield, she was more than capable of destroying him. She clearly had had no trouble with the combined might and experience of Lysander and Griffith. What chance did a Cenzar novice have?

"Has he visited you?" she asked.

"Who?"

"I can see both of them, you know. Two brilliant points of light shining out in the cosmos like pieces on a game board. They are blind to each other, but I can see them—the last gods to walk this world. There is another, but she's quiet—for now."

The green-gowned enigma stared at him for a moment, then licked her lips. "You *haven't* seen him—the older one, I mean. Maybe you won't, but he has his eye on you. I've seen him. He came here—said this place was special. Told me centuries ago he raised one of his daughters in this forest—the younger one, the one he named after himself. He does that—name things after himself. Thousands of years later, they still call this place the Mystic Wood, after her."

She looked up and caught a snowflake on her tongue. "The snow is real," she explained, her voice becoming girlish, reveling in a silly delight.

Esrahaddon really didn't care. He felt like a knife was pressed to his throat.

"He—the older brother," she went on, the taste of the snowflake apparently forgotten, "told me you'd come. Told me I'd be able to recognize you by that."

She pointed at his chest.

The robe?

"Said it was once his and that he gave it to you."

"You're saying you talked to *Uberlin?*"

She nodded. "That's one of his names. He has a whole bunch."

"And he told you I would come here?"

"He can see the future as well as we see the past."

"Oh. So, ah, he's the one who . . ." Esrahaddon swallowed. He hadn't liked how this conversation was going and liked it even less now. According to Hekkabah, Uberlin—the first king of the world and the present god of the Ba Ran—had singled him out for some great work. This was the one bit of knowledge he had never fully accepted. Hekkabah was a priestess of Uberlin, and this, he felt, had always made her judgment suspect. Now he had to deal with this second opinion that appeared to verify the first, except that according to this new report, Uberlin wanted him dead. "What is this crime I'm expected to commit? The one you must kill me to prevent. Maybe I can just promise not to. What is it I'm supposedly going to do?"

"Destroy the world."

Esrahaddon just stared for a second. "Didn't expect that."

"No one ever does." She brushed the flakes out of her hair. "I didn't expect the crime I'm destined to commit, either."

"Which is?"

"Live forever." She sighed, then smiled. "Would you care for some tea?"

"That depends. Is it going to be poisoned? Is this pre-execution tea?"

She laughed so casually, so carelessly, that for a moment Esrahaddon lost track that she was the likely instrument of his impending death. Instead, what stood before him was a beautiful woman wearing a stunning gown, in an enchanting snowfall illuminated by his own robe, and laughing warmly, genuinely amused with him in such a manner that he felt his spirit lighten. Shockingly, he found himself able to set aside the fact that she had killed two men—technically, three—that he'd recently known.

"I'm not going to kill you, Esrahaddon. I like you too much."

"But a god who knows the future foretold you would, right? Kill me, I mean?"

She rocked her head side to side. "I was given a choice." She smiled at him. "I'm just now making my decision."

"In that case, sure, tea sounds great," he said and perhaps never meant anything so vehemently in his life. He felt as if he were wandering in some nether universe where all normal rules failed. Tea was normal, and at that moment more than any previous, Esrahaddon was thirsty for normal.

She cast a hand out, and the forest changed from winter to spring. A lovely, flower-outlined path led to an oasis where a cascading waterfall plunged into a sparkling moonlit pool.

"Come with me. Let me show you my home." She led him up the path. "By the way, my name is Ruby Finn."

A young woman waited beside the pool. Small, with a round face and large eyes. From her clothes, which were of the same cut, color, and fabric as the poor farmers of Eber-on-Aston, he guessed her to be Elinya, Hal's daughter. The only oddity in her attire was the tiny silver pendant with a blue gemstone that she wore around her neck. A strange luxury for someone so poor. He hadn't expected to see her—not alive—and now he felt a pinprick of regret at Hal's death. But only a slight jab, given that Hal's last words—or very nearly so—were, *"I don't give a snake's ass about her!"*

"This is the vale," Ruby said as they walked toward the pool. "The sacred heart of the forest. Can you feel it?"

Esrahaddon thought she was speaking metaphorically, but he did sense something. Ruby was right. Understanding the language of Elan took study and practice. Not only did one need to be a good listener, one also needed to be gifted at interpreting symbols, sensations, motion, and sounds—even smells, as it turned out. Past positives needed to be categorized and remembered, and the subtle differences understood. Time and immersion were the best teachers of any language, and while he hadn't the years behind him, he did have a talent for languages. What he perceived was like a lingering scent, faint but distinct, and it smelled of laughter and the howl of a wolf.

"We are not the first of our kind to tread this ground. I am convinced that this was also the home of Suri." Ruby said the name like everyone ought to know it.

"Who?" he asked.

She looked at him as if he'd spat on her.

Then she caught herself. As understanding filled her face, it was quickly followed by a disappointed frown. She stopped walking as if all the ambition had drained from her, and not just for the tea.

"You're too young." She stood staring at him, devastated as if his youth were a curse. "We can't go yet. I should have noticed." She continued to peer at him, studying every line and curve. "You're a bright yellow fire. There's no orange, no red, and utterly no chance of blue. I just thought you would come on the day, but I guess not. We'll need to wait."

The young woman near the pool, who had been sitting among the flowers at the edge of the water, stood up. She'd been watching them but hadn't moved or made a sound.

"Wait for what?" he asked.

"I was given a choice. It wasn't easy—still isn't. Your being here makes it better. You seem nice. You're like Farilane, in a way. You're not myr, but I can sense the pain in you, the scars. I guess that's why I failed to notice your age. You *seem* older. Suffering does that . . . *if* it doesn't break you. Breaks a lot of people, though. Already, you drink from a deeper well than those others, the ones on the black and white horses. While older, they lived in a world infinitely smaller than the one you breathe in. They lacked a whole dimension and so couldn't begin to comprehend what's happening. They didn't see the shades of gray, much less the colors. But that doesn't change the fact that your furnace has only kindling. You need logs; you need hot coals if either of us is to survive the mission."

"We're going on a mission?"

"I have no choice about killing, merely whom I kill. And if it's not you, it's the other one. And that's not going to be easy, which is why you must come."

Esrahaddon liked the idea of murdering a mystery person only marginally better than he liked the idea of being murdered. "Who must we kill?"

She looked up as if he pulled her from a thought. "Hmm? Oh, Mileva Hitartheon."

Esrahaddon had not expected to recognize the name. He had lived in isolation in the jungle along a narrow strip of beach. On a world scale, he knew almost no one. He didn't know Mileva Hitartheon, either, but he knew the name. "Mileva Hitartheon . . . the riva?"

"Yes," Ruby said. "One of the two remaining generals of Uberlin's army. She lives not too far from here—although I don't suppose you can call it living, exactly. But then that's the whole point, isn't it?" She toggled a finger between them. "Just as Mileva and Suri did, we also face the ancient problem."

"We do? What problem?"

"You feel my power, don't you?"

He nodded.

"And I can feel yours. We're both like . . ." She looked around, searching. "I don't know, like . . ." She knelt down and picked up a pebble. Then she hefted the hem of her gown and put the pebble on it in the same way Esrahaddon remembered girls doing in Haddon when they collected nuts but didn't have a basket. Ruby then stretched out the material until it was taut. "See how the pebble sits there?"

Esrahaddon nodded.

"Now put a bigger one next to it," Ruby instructed as she continued to hold her skirt stretched out.

Bewildered, Esrahaddon did as told, picking up a fist-sized stone and placing it on the spread material. The weight pulled down on the fabric. As it did, the little pebble rolled into the depression created by the stone.

"See?" Ruby said, grinning.

"See what?"

"The pebble is everyone else. You and I are the stones. Suri, whom you inexplicably have never heard of, was also a stone—a *big* one. So is Mileva."

"I still don't—"

"The fabric is reality."

Esrahaddon stared at the hem of her dress that still contained the rocks, and while he didn't think he understood, he did realize there was something to understand, something profound.

"The size of the stone reflects the level of power?" he asked.

"The capacity for it, yes," she said. "People like us, we bend the very fabric of reality merely by existing. And because we stretch things out, we leave permanent marks after we're gone. This place was home to Suri more than two thousand years ago, but you can still feel her echo, still make out the little dip where she stretched the fabric. Being able to alter reality to such a degree is . . . addictive. Power is a thirst that can never be quenched. The more you drink, the more you want. We all face it—even the pebbles, to some degree. With us, however, it is a true problem because we have the ability to alter the cloth, to purposely warp reality to suit us."

"What are you saying?"

"You and I are the seeds that rivas grow from because we have the power to change the rules, to warp the weave, to become immortal."

"So did this Suri person become a riva?"

"No," Ruby said, "she was able to resist the craving. Easier for her, I think. She was human, lived less than a century, and was raised by Tura—the Mystic the forest is named after. It's harder for me because I had no one and have lived longer. That's why I got the visit."

"Uberlin?"

She nodded. "Left alone, it was a sure thing. I'd already started thinking in those directions. He explained the nature of the path I'd be taking. Was a sobering conversation, I might add. I actually got sick just listening. Emptied the contents of my stomach just over there." She pointed toward the trees.

"How do you know he wasn't lying?"

She looked at him with a sympathetic smile. "One doesn't get physically ill from a rumor. It was the truth—*my* truth. But I have a choice. He let me know that."

"To kill Mileva Hitartheon or kill me? I don't understand. How does either alter your situation?"

She let go of her skirt, and the stones rolled away. "I honestly don't have a clue. He wasn't lying, but he also wasn't telling the whole story. All I know is, I like you, but I suspect I won't like Mileva Hitartheon."

"If Uberlin can tell the future, wouldn't he have known which choice you'd make? And if so, was it ever really a choice?"

She nodded. "For him, no, but for me . . . yes because I didn't know what I would do until now. If he hadn't told me about you, about a young man in a robe of light, this night would have transpired differently."

"And you're okay with me destroying the world?"

She smiled. "I exaggerated. He didn't actually say that."

"What *did* he say?"

"He said you would destroy the empire."

They never did have tea.

She left him alone for some time, and when she returned, it was clear that once she concluded they weren't about to embark on a life-altering mission, she was eager to be rid of him. When he realized she was granting him liberty to go, he was equally eager to be on his way. Being with Ruby Finn in her realm of eternal spring was the stuff of make-believe—a land of fairy tales and glowing toadstools. He felt a bit like the time Niblick and Mashie had gotten him drunk on what Mashie called *home-brew bog*. The experience was interesting in its novelty, but it soon wore off and left him wishing for a means to wake up from the effects. That same attitude rushed him now, made more dire by the challenges he knew awaited him back in the *normal* realm. Back there it was still winter, and he was alone in a forest, in a land he didn't know, days from Percepliquis. His teachers and guides were dead, and he wasn't entirely certain he knew the way back. If he managed to return to the city, he'd face the unpleasant task of explaining what had happened. His hope of returning as the hero was replaced with the fatalism of being the lone survivor. How that would turn out, he couldn't foresee, but he knew that procrastinating would not improve his situation.

"Before you go," Ruby said as if they had just concluded a long farewell discussion, "there are three things I must ask of you."

Esrahaddon was both concerned and pleased—concerned because who could guess what such a person might ask, and pleased because Ruby was *asking*, not *demanding*. This indicated he had the option to decline, but like so much associated with Ruby Finn, he guessed this, too, might be an illusion.

"First, I would ask that you take the horses. They don't belong here and don't deserve to be left freezing in the forest."

Esrahaddon had every intention of taking Lysander's and Griffith's mounts back with him and was happy to nod his agreement, feeling he'd gotten off easy with the first request.

"Second"—Ruby gestured at the young woman who dutifully waited—"this is Elinya. She is an innocent who also does not belong here. Now that you have two extra horses, I ask that you take her away with you as well."

Again Esrahaddon felt he was getting out cheap with this second wish. He would be retracing his steps past the village and could drop her off on the way.

"And finally, I ask that you return here in . . ." She thought a moment while staring at him. "Seven years—that should do—but no, not in winter. Come back in spring. Yes, come back seven years from now—be here on the first day of spring. Then you will come with me to Borappathin to destroy Riva Mileva Hitartheon."

Here was the hook—the catch that he dreaded.

Can I say no?

He figured she was giving him his own Choice of Destiny. He could refuse, but if he did, she would be forced to kill him, something he felt she could manage in her sleep.

Seven years—interesting that she chose that number—it's a long time. Either one of us might be dead by then. The decision to accept was an easy thing but one that would haunt him for years to come.

Esrahaddon rode Griffith's white stallion, Grygor, named after a mythical giant. He would have preferred to be back on Ester, as he had grown fond of her, but the horses were particular about the order in which they walked. As Esrahaddon needed to lead the line of three, he was forced to ride Grygor because that horse refused to follow anyone—least of all Ester. All the Artistic persuasion in the world wasn't going to change that. Lysander's black mare came next in the line of ponied animals, with Ester happily bringing up the rear.

Elinya rode on Ester.

Esrahaddon had suggested his old mount because Ester was the smallest, oldest, and most agreeable of the animals. Lysander's horse—whose name he couldn't remember—was willful and skittish. Grygor was stubborn, independent, and huge, making him uncomfortable and a bit scary to ride. As a result, the young woman traveled well behind him as they walked in single file back through the snowy forest.

Elinya didn't say much, which Esrahaddon appreciated.

Ruby never said why she hadn't killed Elinya, but he assumed that, like the horses, the young woman was deemed innocent of trespassing—a crime within the realm of the Mystic Wood that was consistently punished by death.

Their silent journey through the moonlit corridor of snow-bedecked forest was magical, in the traditional sense of the word. Mystically sheltered in the Robe of Light that still illuminated the path with a soft glow, Esrahaddon felt like some ghostly spirit or noble member of the mythical fairy race known as crimbals. Here he was, riding a powerful charger and leading a train of splendid animals with a Lady Fair in tow. Elinya could also be mistaken for a fairy herself, as her radiant youth mimicked the forever-spring of woodland immortals. The primary source of this fairy-tale fantasy rested in the quiet of their passage. Every forest Esrahaddon had ever been in was a chaos of noise—especially at night. Here he couldn't even detect their own passage unless Grygor stumbled.

After a time, the utter lack of sound became disconcerting. Riding alone, it might have been creepy, but with the young woman, it felt rude. As of yet, he hadn't spoken a word to her. *What might she be thinking? All manner of awful things, I suspect.* Being at the back of the line made conversations awkward, but he had to say something. He turned as best he could, putting one hand on Grygor's rump. "I'll drop you off in your village. We aren't far. Should be there before morning."

"I do not wish to go back to Eber-on-Aston," she replied.

This surprised him. "But it's your home."

"It *was* my home. Now it's just a place, and an unpleasant one." Her voice was impressive. Not powerful like an orator, but clear and strong in a manner that Esrahaddon would not have expected from someone who had respectfully waited by a pond like a willing prisoner. There was a polite willfulness in her tone, a well-mannered defiance that left no room for argument or offense. "All my friends are dead. They were killed by my father."

"How did you find out? Did Ruby tell you?"

"Yes—but I didn't believe her. I knew my father as a kind, decent man who loved me and wouldn't hurt anyone."

"What changed your mind?"

She lifted her head to look directly into Esrahaddon's eyes. "When I discovered he didn't care a snake's ass for me."

Esrahaddon cringed on the late Hal's behalf as if he himself had been party to the crime. "You heard that?"

She nodded. "So, no, I don't want to go back to Eber-on-Aston. I hate that place."

Esrahaddon found it impossible not to sympathize. The world had turned around, and now he played the role of Niblick, Mashie, and Dank, having found a wayward orphan from an ignorant community alone in a dangerous forest.

"I can't leave you out here," he said.

"I won't go back," she declared with that impressive quiet determination.

Esrahaddon was at a loss. With three horses and plenty of supplies, he could easily take her back to Percepliquis. But what then? How could she survive in a city, with no relatives, friends, skills, money, or valuables? She'd have no roof over her head nor means of obtaining food. He knew from experience how disorienting it was to come from a rural province to the bewildering mayhem that was the capital city. She wouldn't have the first clue how to take care of herself. He might as well toss her into a pit of starved lions, and yet . . .

"So look, here's the deal, kid. You come with us, see? And ah . . . we'll . . . we'll watch out for you—you know? Ah . . . take care of you, feed you, keep you from gettin' eaten, that sort of thing, okay?"

Esrahaddon sighed. Elan was at it again, and this time he wasn't the one she was focused on. The world had given him a great gift in his time of need. What a thankless child he would be, not to do the same for another.

"Okay," he said, "I'll take you back to Percepliquis with me, but I'm only a student there. I don't have a house or anything of my own. I have no idea how I'm going to manage it, but I'll try to take care of you. Maybe I can ask the Cenzarium to help. They supported Rappaport's mother. Maybe if I ask nicely, they'll take care of you, too. I'll see if there's some way to spread the word around that you're under my—under the *Cenzarium's*—protection. That ought to keep the street snakes away."

"There are snakes in the streets?"

"Bad people," he clarified. "There are a lot of them, the sort that would want to hurt you, but Cenzars are . . ."

"Scarier than snakes?" she offered.

"I was going to say *respected*, but yeah, they're what you said, too. But you're going to need to do as I say. When we get back, I'm probably not going to bother reporting *everything*. I'll explain about your father and how Ruby killed Lysander and Griffith, of course, but I don't see any reason to get into her wanting me to help kill a riva. And I don't want you to say anything, either. Okay?"

"I'll do anything you ask." The defiant tone was strikingly absent in that statement.

What does that mean? A simple 'Sure' would have sufficed. Is that some kind of misplaced hero worship because I saved her life?

For a fleeting moment, Esrahaddon savored the flattery, something that he'd never known before. The idea that anyone could be showing an interest in him was shocking, and she was pretty, in that down-home, backwater sort of way. But Esrahaddon didn't want to become entangled with an ignorant young woman from a backward provincial village. He wanted to leave that part of himself imprisoned in the past. He hoped one day to win the affections of an educated, urban, sophisticated sort—the sort to challenge and push him to be more than he ever imagined possible.

He didn't want someone dressed in the same cut, color, and fabric as the poor farmers of Eber-on-Aston. He wanted someone who made her own clothes.

Upon returning, Esrahaddon was forced to tell his tale several times before the leaders of the Cenzarium. He expected the council would be monitoring him for falsehoods, so his plan was simple: don't lie. That was his genius. He simply ended his report where he found Elinya and where Ruby had let him leave in exchange for taking her and the horses with him. He also skipped over anything to do with the riva, the robe, and the prophecy that Esrahaddon would one day destroy the empire. He honestly didn't think that little bit of fortune-telling would help his standing in his new home. Besides, he determined omissions weren't lies. Luckily, no one asked why Ruby let him leave when she had killed Griffith and Lysander for the same offense. Perhaps they assumed he had no idea. After all, Esrahaddon was a mere novice, a student. How could he know the mind of such a person as Ruby Finn?

The two elder Cenzars who interviewed him accepted his report and offered regrets for Esrahaddon's misfortune.

"I can't believe Lysander would be so foolish as to enter that forest." Isilpor-Sond cursed under her breath.

Small, old, and brown, she reminded Esrahaddon of a rom nut. Having only been at the school for less than a year, he didn't know many people, and certainly not the elders. Seeing her, hearing the Cenzar speak, Esrahaddon suspected Isilpor-Sond was from Calynia, which gave him hope on a number of levels.

"The man knew the law," she went on. "I just don't understand what he was thinking."

Esrahaddon stood under the great dome before the old rom nut and Cenzar Offman. The two couldn't be more different. Offman, with his white beard and matching robe, was as pale as a dead fish and the very embodiment of the dignified old wise man. He stood oddly straight as if proud of being tall.

"Will the emperor take action, do you think?" Isilpor-Sond asked Offman.

"No," the old man replied. "What can he do? This whole incident will be quietly buried." Offman glared hard at Esrahaddon. "You will speak to no one about this, do you understand?"

Esrahaddon nodded most sincerely. He wanted nothing more than to forget the whole affair, except . . . "What about Elinya?"

"Who?" Offman asked.

Isilpor-Sond replied, "The young woman he brought out of the forest."

Offman made a sour face. "What about her?"

"She needs help," Esrahaddon explained. "She has no place to live, no money, no friends or relatives."

"You should have taken her home."

"She didn't want to go."

"That doesn't matter." Offman scowled. "This is the Cenzarium, not a charity. You saved her life. That's enough."

Esrahaddon took an unconscious step forward. "Not if she dies of starvation and exposure. Being sheltered here in this palace of yours, you might have failed to realize—it's winter. And in winter, it gets cold outside."

Offman's scowl was wiped from his face; anger filled the vacancy. "Watch your tone, boy. You're a first-year student here. I presume you'd like to stick around for a second. Now, unless you'd care to join this village peasant on the street, I—"

"Oh please, Offman," Isilpor-Sond said, waving her hand as if pushing away the very thought. "Don't make idle threats. He's a student, certainly, but he's still an Artist, and we don't abandon power to the streets. If we did, we might not have any streets." She smiled at her colleague, who frowned in return. "On the other hand . . ." Isilpor-Sond fixed Esrahaddon with a vicious gaze. "Offman is an elder of this community. He is on the Imperial Council, our representative and advisor to the emperor. And even if you don't feel that this demands respect, just remember that everyone deserves to be treated with understanding and compassion."

Esrahaddon immediately replied, "Including Elinya?"

"How dare you!" Offman exploded so loudly that Esrahaddon watched his fingers for movement.

"Oh, it's fine, Offman." Isilpor-Sond held up a diminutive hand. "If you were as effective with your arguments before the emperor, we'd have half the problems we do now." She peered down at Esrahaddon and grinned at him. "That was a very clever response."

"I mean no disrespect," Esrahaddon assured her. "I honestly don't know either of you well enough for that."

Isilpor-Sond began to chuckle.

"I just know that—look, you took care of Rappaport's mother when she was here. Why can't you do the same for Elinya?"

"What is she to you? Do you like her?"

Esrahaddon didn't care for the question. It was personal, and he didn't have an answer. The ride back from the Forbidden Forest had been nothing like the trip he and Rappaport enjoyed when he first came to Percepliquis. They had talked for hours each night getting to know each other. The journey with Elinya had been so very different. For one thing, they almost never spoke. She'd said little, but then, little needed to be said. Her story, he knew, was not that different from his own. He could see it in Elinya's eyes and the way they looked right back at him; the manner in which she walked with determination through the snow and returned with far more wood in her arms than was necessary for a fire. And then there was the way she smiled when she tasted the food, or grinned when they came out of the forest and saw the city for the first time. Esrahaddon didn't see a village peasant. When he looked at her, he saw himself—but only the best parts.

Upon reflection, their ride back had been oddly quiet, but also surprisingly comfortable as if they were best friends who'd only just met. The experience turned out to be a little too comfortable for him. Elinya was a pair of old shoes that fit the contours of his feet exactly. What an easy downhill stroll it would be to make friends with her—to share hardships and victories—only to realize too late that he was in love.

He couldn't do that to Rappaport. She'd been so good to him. How awful would that be? And why would he? Rappaport was incredible, unique. *The woman made her own clothes, for gripe's sake!*

"As you said," Esrahaddon replied to Isilpor-Sond. "Everyone deserves to be treated with understanding and compassion, but I brought her here and feel obligated to see she's taken care of."

"I see," the elder Cenzar said. "Well then, I suggest you do just that. You handled Eber-On-Aston, Ruby Finn, and even found the courage to lash out at Cenzar Offman. You are well on your way to being a Cenzar, Esrahaddon. I presume that finding employment and lodging for a young woman will not be a task beyond your talents. Good luck to the both of you."

PART FIVE

Tutors

YEAR 2116 IR

CHAPTER SEVENTEEN

Lost and Found

THREE YEARS LATER . . .
IMPERIAL CAPITAL OF PERCEPLIQUIS, SUMMERSRULE

Esrahaddon looked up moments before Rappaport knocked. The door was partially open, but that wasn't how he knew it was her. Over the years, he'd discovered she had a distinctive *signature*. She masked the aura of her talent well, but knowing what to look for, he found it like hearing a familiar voice whispering as she approached.

Without waiting for permission, she pushed the door wide and stared at him in surprise. "What are you doing here?"

Esrahaddon, who had been lying on his bed reading, put a finger on his place and sat up. He made an act of looking around. "This *is* still my room, isn't it?"

Rappaport folded her arms, tilted her head slightly, and smirked. "It's your birthday, idiot. And it's Summersrule. Why are you still in here?"

He shrugged, which was preferable to admitting he had nothing better to do. "Just catching up on some light reading."

She entered the little cubicle he'd called home for the last four years to see what he was reading. This allowed him a better look at what she was wearing. Rappaport had on her traditional Summersrule outfit: a high-collared, brilliant-yellow coat over an extravagant white blouse, matching breeches, and knee-high tan riding boots—all adorned with brass buttons. If anything, her flamboyance had grown since they first met. Most people wore bright colors on Summersrule, but Rappaport competed to outshine the sun.

"*The Lost Princess?*" she queried, reading the title upside down.

"Biography of Princess Farilane," he replied.

"I guessed that much. A bit ironic, don't you think?"

"How so?"

"The princess was famous for her near nonstop adventuring, but here you sit in this dank little hole reading about the life of another."

Esrahaddon looked around again. "You think it's dank?"

She sighed and sat beside him on the mattress, which hissed under her weight. She put her hands between her knees, and without looking at him, she said, "It's been three years, Esra."

He nodded. Rappaport was the only one in whom he had confided the full story of his trip into the Forbidden Forest.

"She's probably forgotten all about you by now. And even if she hasn't, what is she going to do, come knocking like I just did? This is the Cenzarium. While she might be the queen of her forest, Ruby Finn isn't going to be sauntering in, demanding we hand you over."

Esrahaddon pointed at the book on his lap. "According to this, she gleefully played with two First Order Knights, Imperial Prince Nordyan, and what was then the whole of what would become the Cenzarium, including Martasen Dray. She didn't even kill them, hardly hurt anyone. This account says she embarrassed everyone until they gave up or she grew bored. The author wasn't certain. I'm thinking Ruby could walk in here if she wanted to." He closed the book and set it aside. "I was blindsided the first time. Don't want it to happen again."

Rappaport hefted the book, weighing it in her hands. "Got this from the Cenzarium library?"

He nodded.

"You know there's a bigger library in the city, right?"

Esrahaddon shook his head.

Rappaport rolled her eyes. "Amazing. Four years, and no one . . . well, I suppose they all just figured you knew. Who thinks to mention there's a sky outside?" She paused, staring at him. "You do know about the sky, right?"

He frowned, and she laughed.

"It's just so stunning that you don't know, given that it's literally the size of an entire city block and was founded by Farilane herself. A lot of the books—the heart of the collection—were hers. Those are the books she saved, the ones she discovered and brought back from the farthest reaches of the known world." She smiled. "Stuff she did when *out* and not cooped up in her bedroom."

"Must have been an amazing woman."

Rappaport's brows rose. "Oh, from what I've read, she would not like you saying that."

"That she was amazing?"

"That she was a *woman*. She was daughter to the emperor, so she was part Fhrey. Proud of it, I heard. You have at least read *her* book, yes? *The Migration of Peoples?*"

He shook his head. "I didn't see it."

Esrahaddon had spent the last four years devouring nearly everything in the Cenzarium's library, studying old lectures, and paying close attention to talks and demonstrations. He thought he was educated. In comparison to the brash boy from Calynia who had swaggered into that very room four years prior, he was. But compared to Rappaport, he still felt like the ignorant provincial, the backward boy from the superstitious village.

Maybe she sensed it with the Art, or just saw it on his face, but at that moment Rappaport took his hand and looked him in the eyes.

The sun has serious competition this year, he thought.

"You never stop learning," she told him gently. "And you know things I don't. You speak, what? Eight languages?"

"Five, but also four dialects."

"See? I know one and a half, and zero dialects."

"So you've read this *The Migration of Peoples?*" he asked while still holding her hand and not caring much about books at all.

"Actually, no." She took her hand away to open and flip absently through the book. "It was written over two hundred years ago, so the prose is stiff and formal, and it's about ancient history. I actually don't know too many people who have read it. Everyone says they want to, wish they had, or think they should, but, well, the thing is really long, mostly about dwarfs and elves, and isn't a page-turner."

She closed the book and dumped it onto the mattress beside her. "I really don't think you need to worry about Ruby Finn. To my knowledge, she's never left that forest of hers. So as long as you don't go there, you'll be fine."

She stood up and took a step toward the door.

Esrahaddon hadn't seen Rappaport in months. She was constantly out on circuits, as was the norm for newly minted Cenzars. She popped in to see him whenever she returned. They had a few meals together and got caught up with the news of each other's lives. Hers was filled with wild adventures to distant places, in the company of often-infuriating Teshlor Knights. His were tedious accounts of Life Under the Dome. Her visits were the highlights of his life and always too brief. He hated it when she left.

"Where you going?" he asked. "You just got back from Farington, right? We need to catch up. You need to tell me all about the frozen north."

She looked at him, bewildered. "First, Farington isn't in the frozen north. You're thinking of Landeria, in Hinterlandia. And second, there isn't time for that."

"No? Then why did you come by?" he asked.

"To wish you a happy birthday and remind you not to be late. Normally, things here are relaxed, but for this, they really like punctuality, and I know how heedless of schedules you can be."

"What are you talking about?"

Rappaport's eyes widened. She put her hands on her hips and glared. "You're being inducted into the General Assembly in twenty minutes."

"Oh, right," he said.

"Oh, right, indeed. You forgot, didn't you?"

"Kinda." He looked for his shoes. "Is it really that important? It's just a ceremony, right? They pour oil on my head, sing a song, dance around, stuff like that. And then nothing really changes."

"No one is going to sing or dance. And yes, life is going to change. You'll be a full Cenzar."

Esrahaddon found one shoe but hadn't a clue where the other had run off to—*of course, one shoe can't run, can it? Must have "hopped" off.* "Yeah, but how does that differ from what I am now?"

"You'll legally be able to utilize the Art outside these walls, for one."

"Don't usually go out."

"Which is the second thing that will change. You'll get your first assignment. Your first real job."

Esrahaddon found the shoe's mate hiding beneath the bed. *Shoes are always so predictable, which is why they're always so easily caught.*

"Is there anything you're hoping for?"

Esrahaddon sat back on the bed to pull his shoes on. "I'd love the Calynia Circuit, the one you were doing when we met. One day I was even thinking I could be governor of Calynia. Then I could make some badly needed changes in that province. Educate the people so they don't starve or die of thirst out of ignorance, and warlords wouldn't be able to prey on the poor."

"Big dreams," Rappaport said. "And most likely unattainable. They don't generally send people to places they know. Too much chance of corruption. Anyway, you'd best get ready."

"Got my shoes on."

She laughed. "You'll need to change your clothes."

Esrahaddon stood before the Cenzarium Council of Elders in the rotunda beneath the dome—the underside of which was painted to resemble a blue sky. He stood on the gray marble circle that marked the exact center of the room. It being midday on Summersrule, a column of sunlight shone down through the oculus, striking the spot with a diameter equal to the opening in the ceiling. While Cenzars were notorious for their abhorrence of rules and traditions, Esrahaddon had submitted to wearing the classic pure-white asica of a novice practitioner of the Art, mostly because Rappaport told him to. The combination of white robe and midsummer sun pouring down on him in an otherwise dim chamber had to be stunning. This was obviously the point and the reason that Rappaport, ever the fashion maven, had insisted.

Esrahaddon stood, hands clasped, head bowed, and smiled as a thought crossed his mind. *If only Niblick could see me now.*

"The kid's a Cenzar? You gotta be kidding me."

The chamber resounded with a massive clap like thunder. The tolling rang, echoing for a minute, then Cenzar Offman stood and spoke. "With education comes understanding. With understanding, wisdom. With wisdom comes control. With control, peace."

The tolling rang again. There was no bell, no gong. The sound was made with the Art.

Cenzar Isilpor-Sond stood next and addressed the chamber. "Today we recognize Cenzarium Novice Esrahaddon, come before us this Summersrule 2116 of Imperial Reckoning. In the four years he has been with us, Esrahaddon has met or exceeded expectations in accordance with the Suriah, Dibben, and Dray codes. I now call on anyone present to speak if they dispute this or wish to offer reasons Esrahaddon should not be admitted to the Cenzarium General Assembly." She paused, waiting. All was silence. "Very well. Cenzar Yolric."

Yolric stood. "Esrahaddon, do you now swear before this assembly and all you hold dear that you will protect the peace so dearly won, work to improve the world in accordance with the will of Elan, and serve, to the best of your ability, the empire and its interests?"

It was the order of the oath that Esrahaddon fixated on, and how only the last portion was set apart by the qualifier, *to the best of your ability*. Peace came first, then improving the world as per Elan's will, and then, if possible, do try to serve the empire, won't you? Not a mention of obedience to the emperor. Not until that moment did Esrahaddon realize how protective of their independence Cenzars were. The oath made clear that the Cenzarium was not in thrall to the emperor—merely allies, and in many ways custodians and watchmen.

Given the terms of the oath, he didn't hesitate. "I do," Esrahaddon replied.

After the ceremony concluded, Esrahaddon changed out of the official all-white novice uniform and back into the Robe of Light, which he had continued to wear after his return from Eber-on-Aston. Then Esrahaddon and Rappaport spent the holiday celebrating. They had a meal at the Mighty Quail, which strangely did not offer poultry of any kind. Instead, the pair tried the fried spider, which neither of them liked. But they did enjoy the miniature pork chops. Afterward, Rappaport took him on a tour of the city, pointing out both where she grew up in East End and the Farilane Memorial Library.

"The other day we experienced a thunderstorm in the Cenzarium's Sun Room—literally inside the room, you understand," Esrahaddon told her as they sat on the marble steps in front of the library.

Rappaport laughed. "Typical. Do you know there's a crypt underneath? The Cenzarium used to be a temple to the god Ferrol, and they buried high priests down there."

"I didn't know that," Esrahaddon replied. Then he took the last bite of a caramel candy they had bought at a confectioner's shop. He took care not to get any of it on his robe. Not that it mattered. The thing never got dirty.

"No one else did either, until two long-dead corpses got up and began wandering the cellar—presumably looking for a bottle or two of wine. Weaves were always unraveling, especially in the novice wing. If the general population of this city had any idea what really went on, we'd be banished."

Rappaport looked up at the fading light and sighed. "Well, now you know where the library is, so my job is done, and it's getting late. You're seeing the emperor early tomorrow, right?"

"That's what Offman told me."

"Sounds ominous. And you definitely don't want to be late for him."

The day had gone so well that Esrahaddon was feeling brave. He also knew that the emperor would give him an assignment, and he would likely be required to leave soon after. This felt like a now-or-never moment. "You're right," he said, then added, "Perhaps you could spend the night with me so as to ensure I get up on time."

Rappaport stared. She bit her lip and looked down at her hands. As she did, a sadness stole over her face. "I think not."

"Why? I'm a full Cenzar now—no longer an innocent student."

"For one thing, you're leaving tomorrow. The emperor will give you a circuit, and you'll be gone likely for a year or more."

"All the more reason," he argued. "Besides, you'll be here when I return, and we can—"

"That's the second thing." She was shaking her head. "I won't be. I'm going up north."

"They're sending you back? For how long?"

Rappaport took a deep breath and straightened her back. "I won't be coming back."

"What do you mean you won't be—

"I'm getting married, Esra."

He stared at her. "You're . . . what?"

"I was hoping you'd come to the wedding, but it looks like you'll be on assignment."

He didn't hear her. In his head, Esrahaddon was still repeating the sentence with the word *married* in it, trying to work it out as if it were a particularly perplexing puzzle. *Married? Rappaport?* "I don't understand."

"Tomorrow morning. You're seeing the emperor, and he'll—"

"I mean, I don't understand about this wedding. You never mentioned anything."

"I haven't seen you, remember? I've been on circuit up north for the last year and three months."

"That's where you met this person?"

"His name is Adham."

"Is he a Teshlor?"

"Absolutely not." She looked disgusted.

"Is he a—an Artist?"

Rappaport shook her head, then laughed a little. "He's a tailor. A good one. Has his own shop in Farington."

"Are you going to stop, you know, serving as a Cenzar?"

She frowned and gave him one of her appalled looks. "Of course not. I just won't be taking circuits. I'll hold a permanent position in Melenina. After my last trip, I qualified for a post assignment. I'll be serving as advisor to the provincial governor."

"Oh," Esrahaddon said. He didn't know what else to say. He was starting to feel a little sick and regretted that last candy. "So this is, what? You're saying goodbye?"

Rappaport bit her lip. "I didn't want to ruin . . . I didn't want to say anything until now, this being both your birth and induction day, but I don't want to just disappear, either. You're a Cenzar now. You'll be fine."

Esra was oddly both hot and cold. He was starting to sweat yet felt chilled at the same time. He couldn't keep looking at her, so he shifted his focus to the five tiers of marble steps below them and the faceless shadows of people and wagons that flowed obliviously past. So many witnesses.

"I'm sorry, Esra," Rappaport said, her voice so soft it bordered on a whisper. "I really am."

"For what?" he said, then struggled to swallow, surprised by how hard it was. He glanced up and saw her face. It looked pained.

"Esra, you've never been very good at concealment."

He nodded. "Ah . . . betrayed by Elan herself."

"You'll be fine. You're still young. You'll find someone. What about that young woman you brought back from Eber-on-Aston? I heard you found her a room on Carvo Street and a job in the Garment District. I heard she's pretty."

Esrahaddon didn't want to talk about Elinya. He realized he didn't want to talk at all.

"Thank you for telling me," he said, forcing the words out. "And I hope you'll be happy."

"Oh, Esra, don't be that way, please. I care about you, I do. It's just . . . I'm in love with someone else. I didn't plan it. Just happened."

"Like magic."

"Yeah . . . like magic."

The sun set, its light quickly fading as they sat on the marble steps, and as its last rays died, Esra knew he'd never visit that library again.

Esrahaddon paused when he reached Carvo Street.

He'd been walking aimlessly ever since Rappaport left him on the steps of the library. Hours must have passed. The throngs of revelers that had flowed through the streets had dried to a trickle. The post lamps were out, the barkers and vendors silent. Esrahaddon had no more sense of time than he had recollection of where he'd been, what paths he'd taken to arrive where he stood.

He had wandered through more of the city that night than in the four years he'd lived in Percepliquis, but he'd seen none of it. The buildings and people were invisible to him, the sounds but a distant drone, like rain on another's roof. None of this was surprising, given that his mind was elsewhere. In his head, Esrahaddon walked through memories as he cried on and off within the privacy of his hood. The bouts came in waves. His mind tortured him with the special moments—those that had been and the many that would never be. His favorites were the early ones, the long days and hot nights spent under the southern stars when it was just the two of them traveling to Percepliquis. Rappaport seemed different then. His knowledge of Calynia, of the local language, culture, foods, and wildlife had impressed her. She was also awed by the sheer power of his talent. No one had ever looked at him the way she had: as if he were important—certainly no one as worldly and intelligent as Rappaport. To him, she was nothing short of amazing. And in his reflections, every one of those days was sunny, warm, and wonderful. Now they appeared as a distant candle whose singular flame had been snuffed out with a delicate hand. All that remained was a rising whiff of damaged smoke, the only evidence of the happiest time of his life—a moment when everything had been possible. Now nothing was.

Exiting the marketplace of Ebonydale Square—where wine jugs, party hats, and little flags, the fleeting remnants of a short-lived happiness, had abruptly and unceremoniously been transformed into discarded trash—Esrahaddon entered Carvo Street. The narrow lane ran straight, trapped between a continuous series of five-story stone buildings, like a river wedged at the foot of a deep canyon. Windows, square and simple, were plentiful—not one was graced with glass. Since the night was warm, many shutters were open. The few windows still showing burning lamps cast haphazard rectangles of light across the little lane and up their neighbors' walls. Carvo Street lacked the cultivated trees and gardens, the small shops, statues, and fountains of the wealthier neighborhoods. This block remained a dense hive for worker bees. At one end, they bought food at the market; at the other stood the massive warehouses and mills where they labored. Whole lives exhausted themselves along that constricted roadway.

Before he knew it, Esrahaddon had walked half the street's length. In addition to the lamplight, conversations spilled out the windows. "I'm just asking you not to leave it on the floor," a weary woman pleaded.

"Are you going back tomorrow?" another person said from a different window.

"What choice do I have?" a hopeless man replied from the same room.

"Come to bed, I'll warm you up," a new, younger voice said from farther up.

"It's the middle of summer. It's hot," the lover answered.

Then with the sound of a creaking bed, came, "So . . . I'll give you chills."

Nearing the end of the street, Esrahaddon stopped and looked up at the last of the dingy brown stone buildings. This one, mostly dark, was the apartment building where he'd gotten Elinya a room. Esrahaddon had stood where he was now on several occasions. *Might even be the exact spot. Probably a depression in the stone by now.*

He'd come to see her, to make certain she was happy and taken care of, but had never climbed the stairs, never knocked on her door. He didn't want to intrude—didn't want to make her feel that she owed him anything. He did see her on occasion out on the street or at the local market, which he had no real reason to visit. Elinya was always polite, and her gratitude was too easy to confuse with affection. She never ceased expressing her gratitude for her new life despite his assertion about having no part in it. He had told her that the Cenzarium handled it all. This always made him feel awkward. He didn't want to lie, but he also didn't want her to feel obligated to him, mostly because he liked her. He couldn't help it. They had so much in common that they could share a million words with a single look. Where Rappaport had been exciting, Elinya was comfortable, and Esrahaddon knew that spending too much time with her would be like curling up in a soft, warm place—eventually he would fall asleep. She might make him happy, but that wasn't what he wanted.

I don't want someone who's like me. I want someone who is different, someone who can help me *be different. I want Rappaport.*

He admired Rappaport, obsessed over her. To him, she was a whole new world wrapped up in a yellow coat, strange and thrilling. Still, no matter what he did, no matter how hard he tried, he couldn't stop walking down that street. Esrahaddon couldn't prevent himself from standing in that spot, staring up at Elinya's building.

She's probably sleeping, like any sane person. He took the effort to count the rows, and finding the third floor, he spotted a light in one of the windows. He wasn't certain which was hers.

It isn't prudent to call on her now, he thought. *I want to but only because I'm miserable and lonely. It's not fair to her. She'd be very polite, fall over herself to be inviting, swear she hadn't fallen asleep with the lamp burning, but wonder what in Elan I was doing here. Probably suspect I was drunk. And what would the neighbors think? I'd be giving her a terrible reputation—a man showing up in the middle of the night in a dark cloak and hood. Besides, Elinya most likely has a boyfriend, or maybe she, too, is married. No. I would know if she was. But she has likely met someone by now, probably some guy at the fabric mill—a tailor.*

I guess I should go home. The thought was perfectly sensible, and inevitable, but Esrahaddon couldn't bear the idea of crawling back into his little room again. A place that had once been a paradise of hope would now feel like a prison. *I'll spend the rest of my life just wandering the halls of the Cenzarium and probably die alone in that cell.*

He walked on, continuing northwest and entering the business end of the Garment District. Here the buildings were tighter, taller, and darker, as windows were few. Every street seemed an alley, every building a dark fortress. On one wall was the red dragon symbol and the demand FREE THE EMPEROR! *What an ugly place,* he thought, and as he was finding fault, mostly because his emotional free will was transitioning from sadness toward anger, he spotted movement. Out of a second-story window, a young boy made a daring leap to a drainpipe, then slid to the street. The moment he touched down, the kid bolted away. Shouts exploded in his wake. An ugly face peered out the same window as men in workers' clothes burst out of doors, running in pursuit.

"Watchmen! Sentinels!" the boy cried as he ran.

They all rounded an alley, and though he could still hear them, they disappeared from sight.

Mildly curious, and looking for any reason to avoid turning around, Esrahaddon followed, nearly stepping into another mound of manure in the process. The city's side roads, he had discovered, were practically carpeted with the stuff. Streets were cleaned nightly, but the main avenues took precedence, while these lesser streets were often skipped, and he guessed the holiday interfered with the routine. Rounding the corner, Esrahaddon was rewarded with a clear view of six men. At least half held torches, and two held the kid. These weren't small individuals, and Esrahaddon was surprised it required two in order to restrain what appeared to be a ten-year-old.

Luck was with the kid. As two members of the City Watch trotted up in their black-and-red tunics, one asked, "What's going on?"

"Nuthin'," declared one of the brutes holding the boy, with all the eloquence of a bullfrog suffering a busted lip.

"These men are criminals," the boy shouted. "They are kidnapping young women and selling them into slavery!"

This was met with a moment of murderous silence as the men stared at the sentinels and the City Watch glared at the men. Then one of the sentinels said, "That's an awfully serious charge, boy. Where's your evidence?"

"Right around the corner." The boy pointed farther up the street. "They have a wagon loaded, ready to go. They're taking them to Landeria."

"Are they now?"

"Boy seems convinced," the sentinel told the men holding him. "Gonna have to investigate."

"You ain't got ta investigate nuthin'," the tallest of the brutes said with a confidence that suggested violence as collateral.

The sentinel put a hand on the grip of his sword. "Shut your mouth while you still have one. And take your hands off the boy." Both watchmen had blades, the workmen only fists.

The thugs scowled in silent response but released the kid.

"Okay, boy, take us to this wagon full of slaves. And the rest of you lads, you come, too. Don't go running off. I know most of your names and where you live."

Making no effort to hide himself, but keeping a fair distance, Esrahaddon followed as the group moved farther up the narrow street past a series of huge barn doors.

"This must be the wagon here," one of the thugs said and laughed as he pointed at a cart left in the alley, loaded with open rain barrels.

"It's in here," the kid said, indicating the last set of barn doors. Bright lights burned inside, and some rays leaked out through a narrow gap. Painted on the stone above the doors, twelve-inch-tall letters read EVARBURTON & SONS. A sentinel stepped forward and slid back the double-tracked doors. Light flooded the street, clearly revealing the shadowy actors in this late-night play. The watchmen were a pair of toughs distinguishable from the brutes they questioned only by their uniforms, neither of which appeared in the best condition. The workers looked exactly as Esrahaddon had expected, fitting a standard of loutish, vulgar ignorance that men proudly flocked to as if it held worth. The boy, however, was odd. Thin, small, and lithe, he lacked the anticipated feral qualities of a street creature, the most obvious being that his face was clean and his clothes fit.

The exposed interior revealed a stocked warehouse within which was a parked freight wagon in the process of being hitched to a pair of horses.

"Does look like a wagon," the watchman agreed. He moved to the rear door and found it locked with a chain. "Why don't you open that for me?" he asked one of the men holding a torch.

"Cain't do that."

"Why not?" the sentinel asked, his voice gaining a sudden sharpness.

"Because he doesn't have the key," a big man explained in a loud voice as he appeared from inside the warehouse and moved slowly toward them.

This fellow was perhaps the fattest person Esrahaddon had ever seen. He waddled rather than walked across the floor, dressed in an expensive blue silk wrap. Esrahaddon estimated that the cost of the fabric alone must have amounted to a fortune because of the additional yardage necessary. The man had three chins, and his jowls were less cheeks than sacks. His hands appeared inflated, his fingers only stubby nibs protruding from fleshy globs. Esrahaddon could only assume they were fingers, based on how each bore precious-metal rings. "Hello, officers," the man greeted them. "How is your holiday evening going?"

"Just fine, Mister Curtalus. How are you?"

The massive individual grinned and clapped his belly. "Wonderful—at least, I was until all of this racket broke out. What appears to be the problem?"

"Boy here says these men have kidnapped some women and have them locked up in this wagon."

"That's absurd. This wagon belongs to me, and these men are in my employment."

"Yes!" the boy shouted. "And Randolf Curtalus runs the slavery ring! He's the chief accountant for all the businesses involved! You need to arrest him!"

The big man laughed, making his face and tiers of chins jiggle. "What an imagination, and what a sorry state of affairs. Allow me to explain that this boy was hired to work at Evarburton because he begged for a chance—and I expect he was starving. I gave him an opportunity to better himself, but today we caught him stealing. He slipped out a window just a few moments ago. Now out of desperation he is bothering you good men of the watch."

"I understand," one of the sentinels said. "These homeless street thieves are a menace in the city. And I can certainly understand what a terrible and ungrateful thing it is for him to repay your kindness that way, but . . . I'd still like to see what's inside the wagon."

Mister Curtalus frowned. He clapped his belly again, taking several loud sniffs through a nose that didn't look up to the demands of that body. "Oh, very well." Curtalus produced a purse from a belt previously hidden by folds not merely of silk. From it he took four yellow coins. Reaching out, he dropped two in the palms of each watchman. "There now, as we can all see, there's nothing untoward in the wagon. Be off with you."

The sentinels nodded. "Appreciate the cooperation, sir. And good night to the rest of you fine men."

"What? Wait!" the boy shouted as the pair in black-and-red uniforms walked away.

They came right past Esrahaddon but walked on without noticing. Only then did he realize that the robe so blended with the night that he had a hard time seeing his own arm.

"As for you"—Curtalus focused on the boy, who started to bolt but was grabbed and held once more—"I don't know who you are, but I don't want to see you again. Lassiter, take him to the river and see that I don't."

"Brig, get some rope off the back wall," Lassiter ordered. "Miles, fetch a sack and fill it with those extra bricks the mason left next to the hearth."

"How many?"

"I don't know. He doesn't look that heavy. Ten, maybe?"

After the sentinels rounded the corner, Esrahaddon stepped forward, entering the patch of light pouring out of the warehouse. "So . . . what? You just gonna drop the kid in the West Bernum River?"

Everyone spun to look at him.

"It's not a bad idea, I guess," he went on, heedless of their surprise, "but the rope will eventually rot, won't it? And then the body is gonna float up. Maybe by then it won't matter. What's one more dead kid in the river, right? Fish might even nibble enough to make any chance of identification impossible."

This made the boy grimace.

"Who in Novron's name are you?" Lassiter asked.

"Novron's name? You're speaking for a god now, Lassiter. Good for you. I like to see people try to better themselves, 'cause you know this henchman business isn't gonna get you anywhere. But mouthpiece of a god—that does sound impressive on any resume."

Randolf Curtalus, who hadn't managed to get too far, returned by way of his previously established process of waddling. "Now, what have we here?"

"A crime, apparently," Esrahaddon replied. "I do believe I saw you paying off two of the City Watch to ignore your activities here. That seems more than a little shady, don't you think?"

"These men are slavers!" the kid shouted.

"Yeah, kid," Esrahaddon replied, "save your energy. I heard the whole thing. The wagon is full of women bound for the illegal slave trade up north in Landeria."

The men began to slowly pick up wooden dowels that looked to be parts to a loom, or maybe unfinished table legs. They also might just be cheap clubs.

"I think we're gonna need another bag and more bricks," Lassiter said.

"I wouldn't do that." Esrahaddon shook his head as the workers began to clap the clubs against open palms in the bizarre but consistent ritual of intimidation he'd seen so often in his youth. "I'm not looking for trouble."

"Oh, I see," Curtalus said. "You're looking for a handout like the one I gave the City Watch. I'm afraid that's not going to happen in your case."

"Of course it's not. And if you let me finish, I can tell you why." The men, now suitably armed, spread out into a circle. "As I was saying, I wasn't looking for trouble. Truth is, this is my birthday—my birthday, can you believe it? And the love of my life just informed me she's marrying some other guy. So as you might expect, I'm in a pretty lousy mood, and while I *was* in no way looking for trouble, turns out I sure would *love* some."

This made all of them hesitate. Even Curtalus looked confused.

Esrahaddon held up his index finger. "Funny story. Not only is it my birthday, but I also was just inducted into the Cenzarium's General Assembly. And look at the present the love of my life gives me for such an auspicious occasion. A tailor, for gripe's sake! She's marrying a freaking tailor."

"You're no . . . Cenzar," Lassiter said.

"Officially anointed just a few hours ago. Which means I can now legally do this." He snapped his fingers and the cart loaded with rain barrels exploded so violently, the metal hoops ricocheted off the building's walls. A shattered board pierced the left barn door, and one of the cart's wheels whizzed past all of them as it entered the warehouse, shattering a wooden crate in the back. Afterward, and for what seemed to be a full minute, they all listened to the rain of splintered wood.

"I love doing that," Esrahaddon said. "It's just so satisfying, you know?"

"I caught my wife in bed with my brother a few years back," one of the men said with a dull look on his face, his eyes still staring at the broken wagon wheel in the back of the warehouse. "I kinda wanted to kill someone."

Esrahaddon clapped his hands and pointed at the guy. "Exactly!"

Everyone, especially the man he'd pointed at, flinched.

"You fellas seem a tad nervous," Esrahaddon said. He focused on the man with the cheating wife. "So what did you do?"

"Honestly?" The dullard shrugged. "I can't say I'm proud of it, but I took it out on our cow. Beat her pretty bad."

"Yeah, that's precisely how I feel now." Esrahaddon looked over at a wide-eyed Randolf Curtalus and smiled.

"Why you looking at me like that? Don't be looking at me. I haven't done anything wrong. This kid, this kid here, he doesn't know what he's talking about."

"Are there women in the back of this wagon?" Esrahaddon rubbed his palms together and the chain that locked the wagon door melted like wax, the molten links dripped onto the floor where the metal hissed.

"Well, ah, okay, sure, there are a few, but they're workers, not slaves. We have another mill up north. They're just transferring to a better job."

"And you always lock traveling workers into wagons, do you?"

"Look, they want to go. You ask them."

"I will." Esrahaddon took a step forward, then paused to look at the circle of men. "You still holding those clubs?"

They each let go, creating a hollow clatter. Even Lassiter, who had been holding the boy, let go of his charge. The kid shuffled away, rubbing his wrist, but he lingered to watch.

Esrahaddon opened the rear door of the wagon and found it filled with eight women, four on each side, seated on benches facing each other. They stared out with terrified eyes.

"See!" Curtalus said. "They aren't tied up or gagged or any such thing. These women want to go, don't you? I don't have no place for them here. Can't pay them anymore. They want to go where there's work, don't you?"

All the women looked too frightened to breathe, much less speak.

"I don't." The voice came from the dim interior in the back of the wagon.

An instant later, everyone gasped, and several of the men retreated as Esrahaddon's robe brightened. The light filled the area, illuminating the wagon's interior. One familiar head was tilted forward, looking around the others, a silver blue gemstone pendant dangling from her neck.

"Scarier than snakes?" Elinya asked with a hopeful expression.

Esrahaddon smiled. "Oh, you better believe it." He turned to Curtalus. "This is not your lucky day."

The color of the robe began a frightening shift from white to red.

"Wait!" the boy shouted, throwing his hands up. "Don't kill him."

"Excuse me?" Esrahaddon said.

"He's not the only one involved. There were abductions in Vernes, Neith, Rionillion, and Rodencia. The slavers have an extensive network, but he knows the names, the safe houses, the contacts."

Esrahaddon stared at the boy. "Who are you?"

"Me? I'm nobody," the kid replied.

Esrahaddon narrowed his eyes at the child and raised one eyebrow. "Perhaps—perhaps not."

CHAPTER EIGHTEEN

Meet the Tutors

DAY AFTER SUMMERSRULE . . .
IMPERIAL CAPITAL OF PERCEPLIQUIS

Jerish Grelad had only just entered the palace when he was forced to accept that he was hopelessly lost. All those years of reclusive training returned to curse him. He'd rarely gone out into the city, barely left the academy wing of the guildhall, never explored as the other boys had. If the palace hadn't been in the same square as the guildhall, if it hadn't been huge, brilliant white, and capped by a shimmering gold dome, and if the Teshlors—including those in training—didn't march past it each year as part of the Founder's Day Parade, he'd have never found it. Once inside, his luck ran out.

For some reason he couldn't now recall, he had thought he merely needed to enter the palace and everything else would present itself as obvious. As it turned out, just getting inside had been a trial. The big front doors were closed to visitors, for whatever reason he still hadn't learned. Instead, guests were forced into a massive courtyard, where a crowd of dignitaries congregated. Jerish had assumed they were all waiting to go in. Turned out they weren't. The well-dressed merchants in their tall hats, military officers in polished metal, and orators in white robes all gathered to accost those with real business in the palace, who were funneled inside through a small side door defended by palace guards. Although he had set out early, Jerish found himself running late by the time he figured out the proper way to gain entry.

Faced with the massive labyrinth of hallways, doors, and stairs, Jerish had wandered, searching for clues. He had found none, and when he reached a four-way intersection, he felt a sense of overwhelming frustration. Just then, he spotted a brown-haired boy in a simple tunic running barefoot through the corridor.

"You there! Hey, kid! Hold up!"

The boy stopped. "*Me,* sir?" The kid pointed at himself.

"Yes, you. Look, I'm late for a meeting with the emperor. Can you show me, or tell me, the way to the—well . . ." He gestured at the four corridors. "Can you point out which hallway leads to wherever the emperor receives guests?"

"Who are you?" the boy asked.

"I'm Jerish Grelad."

The boy folded his arms over his chest and frowned. "And who is *Jerish Grelad?*"

"Oh." Jerish paused for a moment. No one had ever asked him that before, and he didn't quite know how to answer. His first thought was to offer his father's name and place of birth but didn't see how that would explain anything to this kid. Caught unprepared, and unable to clarify something as simple as who he was, he felt ridiculous.

The boy waited, but his deepening frown and rising brows revealed a growing dismay and a dash of amusement, which was somehow worse.

"Look, I've just graduated from the Teshlor Academy, and I was—"

"Oh, so you're a Teshlor Knight, then?"

"Ah . . . no. I'm just a graduate of the academy. I won't be a knight unless the emperor bestows that honor on me, and he won't if I don't report on time to wherever he is. You see, I'm supposed to—"

"You don't look like a Teshlor. Where's your armor?"

"Haven't gotten it yet. And I won't if I don't manage to see the emperor."

"I don't know," the kid said slowly as he leaned back against the corridor's wall, studying Jerish. "Who's to say you're not a spy? You could be a vicious assassin hired by the Brundenlins, chosen for your skill at portraying a bumbling dim-witted idiot, just to get close enough to the emperor, then *wham!* You plunge a dagger into his throat, slicing through his carotid artery, spewing blood everywhere, shouting '*Death to tyrants and tall folk!*' "

"Look, kid, I'm not an assassin. I don't have a dagger, and I don't even know what a Brundenlin is."

"What about swords?"

Jerish smirked and held up his arms. "Do you see any?"

"That's my point. Teshlor Knights are supposed to have swords—three, in fact—and don't tell me you expect the emperor to provide you with *those*, too. I mean, do you think the emperor is some sort of charity box? That he gives gifts to all who take the time to visit him?"

"No, but because I've not yet sworn allegiance, I'm also not allowed to carry weapons into the palace. Look, kid, I just need to know where the emperor is."

"To kill him?"

"No!"

"Do you at least have a badge or something to prove any of what you say is true?"

"I'm not a knight yet, so no."

The boy frowned and tightened the fold of his arms. "Then I believe we are at an impasse because I don't know who you are, and I'm not a traitor."

"Fine, can you at least direct me to someone in authority? A chancellor or someone?"

"Is that who you're here to kill? The chancellor?"

Jerish rolled his eyes. "No, I'm here . . ." He sighed and shook his head in resignation. "Never mind. I'll just keep looking, I guess." Jerish picked the middle corridor and set off down it.

"Not that way," the boy said. "That way leads to the kitchens, and I don't think the emperor is brushing up on his culinary skills this morning, do you?"

"Okay." Jerish returned to the intersection and took the left corridor.

"Nope."

Jerish stopped, then sighed and turned around. "So it's this way," he concluded, choosing the last option and passing the kid. "Could have just said that."

"You could still be an assassin," the kid called after him. "So when you get caught, don't mention me, okay? As far as you're concerned, we never met. Got it?"

"Agreed. Who are you?"

"Me? I'm nobody."

Esrahaddon entered the Imperial Throne Room of Emperor Nareion. He hoped this time to witness something more impressive than a roasting pig, a score of drunks, a few whores, and a couple of caged animals. He was *not* disappointed.

The double golden doors to the throne room—or the Center of the World as it was also known—were five stories high. Beyond them, the massive rotunda was illuminated by tall, narrow windows interspersed with white marble statues of the previous seven emperors. The floor beneath the dome was polished stone and had an inlaid map of the known world. Three men on the far side of the chamber watched him enter. Two stood. One sat. The seated fellow was a middle-aged man. He had a dash of gray at his temples and confident but intelligent eyes—the sort that focused with intent. For a *myr*, Nareion appeared surprisingly human. And that extended to his clothes. Rather than a godlike gown of glistening gold, he wore a loose linen tunic and workman's trousers. If it weren't for the imperial throne he sat on, which rose and spread out into the underside of the dome like the branches of a great tree, Esrahaddon might have guessed he had the wrong room.

To the left of the emperor and dressed in mirror-like metal, Teshlor Knight Gaylord Sire, imperial advisor and bodyguard to the emperor, stood in the same manner as a suit of armor on a display rack. To the right waited the far less rigid and far older venerable Cenzar Offman, who had recited the Cenzarium maxim at Esrahaddon's induction ceremony the day before. He wore the same ceremonial robes of black brocade decorated with shimmering gold-and-silver thread, as if he only had the one outfit.

"Your Imperial Eminence," Esrahaddon said and knelt, "I am Cenzar Esrahaddon here at your request."

"Your *request?*" Gaylord Sire remarked with abundant disdain. His expression was displeased, his eyes doing that blind stare of the dim-witted, the hallmark of those who bash things for a living.

"Did I get the date wrong?" Esrahaddon asked.

This made the emperor smile. "No, you did not. And yes, I requested your presence. You may stand."

As he got back to his feet, the big doors banged open and into the room ran a child. He bolted across the marble map of the world, running on bare feet and skidding to a stop at the dais. His chest heaved, and a guilty grin spread across his lips as he stared at the emperor.

Nareion frowned. "Not even a bow?"

"Sorry," the boy said and knelt briefly, still grinning as he looked over at Esrahaddon. "Hi."

Seeing the kid's full face, Esrahaddon recognized him as the well-dressed street scamp from the night before, the kid who had narrowly avoided death by brick-bag.

"You know my son?" the emperor asked.

Esrahaddon blinked. "I can't say we've ever been introduced."

"Then allow me—this is Nevrik. Believe it or not, this wild animal before you is the crown prince of the empire and the future ruler of the world." Nareion stared at his son, his sight descending to the boy's dirty bare feet. "Scary, isn't it?"

No one dared answer.

"May I?" Nevrik asked, gesturing at the steps before the throne.

Nareion rolled his eyes. "By all means, please do continue to diminish the regal majesty of the Imperial Throne Room. But do so quietly."

The boy smiled and sat down on the cascade of steps, crossing his legs. This brought him eye level with Esrahaddon, who stood at the bottom.

"Esrahaddon, Offman here informs me you were officially inducted to the General Assembly of the Cenzarium yesterday. Is that true?"

"It is."

"And of course, you know it is customary for the new Cenzars to swear allegiance to this throne, and this empire, and obtain their first assignments?"

"I do."

"You do, *Your Imperial Eminence*," Gaylord Sire insisted, frustration and anger bubbling up in his tone.

"I do, Your Imperial Eminence," Esrahaddon rephrased, realizing he was starting to dislike Gaylord, and how not surprising that was.

"Most Teshlor Academy graduates spend the night before this meeting in quiet contemplation," Nareion continued. "Cenzars spend the evening meditating, reflecting, that sort of thing. At least this is what I'm told, but I suspect both Teshlors and Cenzars act like a groom taking advantage of their last night of freedom by getting hopelessly drunk and rampaging throughout the city. You wouldn't be the first Cenzar who needed to apologize for some minor catastrophe, but then again, that's not how you spent your night, is it?"

"No," Esrahaddon replied, then looked over at Gaylord. "Am I expected to say the whole Imperial Eminence thing every time I speak, or are we good with that now?"

This drew suppressed smiles from Offman, the emperor, and the prince. Gaylord sneered. He took a step forward, but Nareion stopped him by the raising of a single finger. "I think we can dispense with some of the formality for now. Mostly because last night our newly minted Cenzar managed to cripple, if not destroy, a terrible curse that has plagued this empire for years."

"Mister Curtalus talked?"

Nareion narrowed his eyes at Esrahaddon. "I said we would relax the formalities. Don't presume that means we're best friends. You speak when I indicate you should do so. The Cenzarium requires its members to be creative, and I recognize the need for, and grant the privilege of, this freedom, but never forget this throne rules all, and I demand absolute obedience and respect. Is that understood?"

"Yes, Your Imperial Eminence."

Nareion frowned. "I can see why he picked you."

Esrahaddon didn't like the sound of this and desperately wanted to ask, "Who picked me and for what?" But he didn't dare push his luck. Offman's strained face suggested that silence was indeed the wiser course of action. As a result, Esrahaddon remained rigid, waiting.

"Back to what I was saying. You took it upon yourself to investigate the northern slavery cabal that has managed to elude every team I have sent to investigate. You found the heart of that hive right here in Percepliquis and single-handedly captured what we now believe is the hive's queen. Yes, Mister Curtalus *was* most cooperative, and now that the head has been removed, I've dispatched a special envoy team to Landeria to deal with the appendages."

Esrahaddon wondered if this last remark was metaphorical or literal. In all his studies, Esrahaddon hadn't focused much on emperors. Common sense suggested they couldn't maintain such a massive realm and shy away from violence. Nor would he begrudge Nareion a swift execution of Mister Curtalus. Esrahaddon would have killed the man himself if the boy—the prince, as it now turned out—hadn't suggested otherwise and provided an irresistible argument to boot. After what the glutton had sought to inflict on Elinya, Esrahaddon preferred to hope the surface of Elan was no longer burdened with Curtalus's weight. Still, this revealed that the emperor was no kindly father figure, and Nareion would just as easily order Esrahaddon's execution if it pleased him. Perhaps this was what Offman was communicating with his concerned face and lack of words.

The emperor sat up, even leaned forward a bit. "This action, combined with your deeds both in Shahabad and Eber-on-Aston, are to be rewarded. Furthermore, Cenzar Offman reports that your prowess with the Art is considerable, and I have even heard words of praise about you from Bishop Venlin. All of this—"

A massive *boom!* exploded behind Esrahaddon.

Jerish tried his best to quietly close the insanely tall doors behind him. Given their size and assumed weight, he shouldn't have been able to so much as budge them. Much to his chagrin, he found they swung with the ease of a toy top. Together the pair of golden giants slammed. The resounding *boom* was deafening.

Everyone in the room glared, including the man on the big chair. Mortified at announcing his late arrival with such undignified, disquieting fanfare, Jerish froze.

"Your Imperial Eminence," Gaylord Sire spoke as if it pained him. "This is Jerish Grelad."

"Come forward, Jerish," Nareion ordered.

Jerish strode toward the dais, taking some solace in the fact that only five people were present to witness his debacle. Even so, one was the emperor of the world, which didn't bode well for his future, and the other was the legendary Gaylord Sire, renowned as the greatest living warrior and Jerish's personal hero. The presence of these two individuals did help make up for the lack of a larger crowd. Also before him were two men in affluent Cenzar robes, and seated on the steps before the throne was a small—

It's the kid from the hallway! The one who lied.

Turned out the direction Jerish had guessed at the four-way was the right one. The kid knew it and purposely sent him running down the wrong corridor—the one that actually did lead to the palace kitchens. If not for a kindly cook, Jerish might not have arrived at all.

Jerish approached until he stood beside the young Cenzar, then knelt.

"You're late," the emperor said. "Why?"

Jerish looked at the boy, who stared back at him.

"I—I have no excuse, Your Imperial Eminence. My only consolation is that not having been ordained into your service, I am incapable of disgracing the title of Teshlor Knight. With your permission, I will withdraw and—"

"You have no such permission," the emperor snapped. "Stand up."

Jerish got to his feet. He didn't dare look at the emperor. Instead, he stared at the boy, who eyed him curiously.

The emperor looked at Gaylord. "He's here for a knighting, correct?"

"Yes, Your Imperial Eminence. Jerish Grelad is one of our more accomplished graduates. Our only one this year."

"Right, and such things don't take long, but your tardiness has caused a disruption in my schedule. So now you'll need to wait outside until—"

"Him," the boy suddenly said.

"What's that?" The emperor looked down.

"I want him as well."

"Are you serious? Why? Because he was late?"

The boy shook his head. "No. He wasn't late. He was on time. A bit early, in fact. I made him late." The boy smiled. "I accused him of being an assassin and sent him to the kitchens."

"You did what?" The emperor dropped his head into his hands, then shook the whole lot. "That explains why your mother keeps apologizing for you. I assumed it was for something specific, but now I see she merely feels bad for birthing you."

"Mother apologizes for having me?"

The emperor smirked. "Who's being gullible, now?"

The boy frowned.

"Not so nice, is it?"

"My point is that I told him if he got into trouble, he shouldn't mention me. Well, he kept his word." The boy stood up. He descended two steps until he was eye to eye with Jerish. "And you still have no idea who I am, do you?"

"No," Jerish replied.

The boy looked at the emperor. "That's why."

The emperor nodded, then turned to Gaylord. "And you say he is an accomplished graduate?"

"He has excelled since coming to the guild."

"Top of the leaderboard?"

"Actually, Your Imperial Eminence, he has refrained from entering the competition for the last four years, but prior to that he maintained the highest position possible for his rank, constantly beating boys several years older."

"Why have you refrained from the competition?" the emperor asked.

Jerish remembered the empty bench where Master Rawlings used to sit. "I had already beaten them all, Your Imperial Eminence. I saw no reason beyond humiliation to continue to do so."

"Are you the one who refused to fight Derek Seret's boy a few years back? What was his name?" The emperor snapped his fingers several times while looking back at Gaylord.

"Darius, Your Imperial Eminence," Jerish supplied. "And yes, that was my last competition."

The emperor looked again at Gaylord. "Darius never graduated, did he?"

"No, Your Imperial Eminence. Darius was found guilty of actions unbecoming a Teshlor. As he had only completed five years of training, he was expelled."

"Strange that he was ever admitted in the first place," the emperor said.

"Yes, Your Imperial Eminence. Master Rawlings made one of his very few mistakes with Darius."

The emperor looked at the boy. "Very well. As you wish."

The boy smiled.

"Call for the clerk," the emperor told him, and the boy rushed off.

The emperor stood and stepped back to speak to Gaylord a moment. Then he addressed a woman and a man who had returned with the boy. They called Offman over, and the five spoke softly.

"You *really* don't know who the kid is?" the guy in the fancy robe standing beside Jerish asked. "That whole thing about the kid's mother apologizing wasn't a big enough hint?"

"I have no idea who the child's mother is, so no."

The robed man acted like he tasted something sour. "That's . . . that's amazing, but I guess you get hit on the head a lot, huh?"

The emperor and his advisors returned, but this time he remained standing.

"Both of you kneel," he ordered. "Esrahaddon of Calynia and Jerish Grelad of Warica, do you solemnly swear to protect and defend the empire, its laws, its people, and to serve and defend the imperial family to the best of your ability until death renders its final judgment?"

"I do," Jerish said, and after a few seconds, so did Esrahaddon.

"Then rise, Teshlor Knight Jerish and Cenzar Esrahaddon," the emperor said, "for you are both hereby designated as duly appointed officers of the empire and granted all the powers and responsibilities associated with that charge. And in light of your already exemplary achievements, you are both rewarded with the honor of receiving as your first task the prestigious position of official tutors to Prince Nevrik. You will educate him in the ways of letters and the blade, as is appropriate for a future emperor. Nevrik has run wild for too long. Be firm with him, and wary. He's shrewder than his age would lead you to believe—but not so smart as he thinks. I'm entrusting the two of you quite literally with the future of the empire. Make him a better ruler than all that have come before, and I'll consider your charge fulfilled."

CHAPTER NINETEEN

Teaching the Prince

IMPERIAL CAPITAL OF PERCEPLIQUIS

"Tutor?" Esrahaddon asked Offman the moment he walked out of the throne room. The newest Cenzar had lain in wait in the corridor outside for the elder man to exit. Offman was the quintessential Cenzar, with his lavish robes, wrinkles, and knowing demeanor. Not as eccentric as Yolric—who was known for his sage white beard—Offman sported a more stately, trimmed version that gave him a wise, but smarmy, appearance. "I'm to be a nursemaid to a child?"

"It is an honor," Offman replied with his signature stiff and stuffy manner that worked so well for staged formal occasions but made the man look like an idiot in real ones. "You should be grateful. You could be trapped in the frozen north or sent to the wilds of—"

"Calynia?" Esrahaddon suggested. "Because we both know that's what I was aiming for." Prior to full membership in the General Assembly of Cenzars, Esrahaddon had discussed his desire to work his circuit years in that province. At the time, Offman indicated such a thing was possible, which left Esrahaddon hopeful—until five minutes ago. "I know that place. I know the people. I understand the problems they suffer. I could do some real good, I could make a difference. And there's an opening. Rappaport is off that route.

She's up in Melenina now. You need another Cenzar in the south, and I'm perfect for the job. I speak the language, know the customs, understand where the problems are."

Offman opened his mouth, but Esrahaddon had anticipated his response and didn't feel the need to wait for it. "I know the policy against envoys having ties to the routes they patrol, but I've got no family down there. One cousin, I guess, but he hates me, and I have a similar fondness for him. For once, you could have someone who doesn't spend all their time struggling to understand the province. You could appoint a Cenzar who can walk in with ideas ready to go. Besides, I'm not a scholar or instructor. I haven't the first clue how to educate a child. Having me teach this kid is just—"

"Prince Nevrik is *not a kid!*" Offman raised his voice, which surprised Esrahaddon, as he didn't think Offman had more than one volume. "He is the son of the emperor."

With a frown, Offman glanced back up the corridor at the two Teshlor guards that stood watch outside of the throne room door. He gave an irritated shake of his head and began walking.

"What am I supposed to do?" Esrahaddon demanded as he turned to follow. "Teach him how to use a knife and fork? How to chew with his mouth closed?"

"You must teach him to be a good ruler." Offman's voice was back under control as the two moved swiftly through the Hall of Memory, decorated with its relief images of imperial history.

"Something I have no experience with and will never live to see, by the way. He'll not take the throne for a thousand years after I'm buried. So whatever I do manage to cram into that privileged little skull of his will have been forgotten centuries before it matters."

"It is a privileged position that will allow you to remain in the city and work in the palace, where you will have the opportunity to meet and speak with provincial governors, military generals, merchant lords, artists, philosophers, and engineers, not to mention the imperial family themselves. You will have more influence and be more respected and sought out than any provincial envoy or governor. It is honestly the very best you, or any Cenzar, could hope for."

Esrahaddon certainly understood that this was the position *Offman* saw as ideal. The man was jealous, and Esrahaddon's absolute disregard of Offman's dream was what likely caused the loss of control. But Esrahaddon and Offman were barely the same species.

"I'm going to be a babysitter."

Offman made an audible *humph.* "The prince chose you. That right there should indicate the child's desperate need of education. It's done. Deal with it."

"I don't even know how. What do I do? Is he supposed to come to my room in the Cenzarium or something?"

Offman stopped in front of the depiction of the Battle of Big Meadows and faced Esrahaddon. "He is the prince. He doesn't leave the palace. You go to him. Beyond that? It's up to you how you go about teaching the boy. His education begins tomorrow. One word of caution: Failure is not permissible."

Esrahaddon frowned. "That's four words."

The Imperial Garden was a glass-domed courtyard, lush with flora transplanted from all over the empire, though as Esrahaddon recognized, most were from Calynia. Massive blooms of scarlet hibiscus and various orchids climbed up broad-leafed jungo plants. He plucked an abbra berry from a plant near an artificial pool fed by a waterfall and tasted it. The fruit was sour.

Four iron seats had been placed along the gravel walkway, perhaps more as decoration than for use, as they weren't comfortable in the slightest. Nevrik arrived—running as usual. *Does this kid have a slow speed? Can he understand what walking is, or must I teach him that, too?*

He looked nothing like the street waif Esrahaddon had first met, nor did he resemble the kid who had flopped onto the dais steps. The prince was dressed in a crimson three-quarter-length silk coat embroidered with black thread. A short standing collar left a gap at the center of his neck. Beneath the coat, he wore loose white trousers, and as always, his feet remained bare. He stopped running as he approached the iron seats and assumed a statelier stride, his back straight, chin up—the proper gait for a prince. The kid's hair was brushed and drawn back to reveal slightly elongated ears that Esrahaddon chided himself for not noticing before. The narrow eyebrows tilted up, the sharp cheeks, and pretty—near-feminine—features screamed Fhrey blood, but Esrahaddon hadn't detected any of it when Lassiter had him by the throat. *Why would I? He was just a scrawny street kid in trouble.*

"Good morning, dear teacher," Nevrik said with a bright smile as he padded up the walk, tossing something small between his hands as he played catch with himself.

"Don't smile at me, you little monster," Esrahaddon growled. "I should have let them throw you in the river."

Those sliver-like brows tilted up. "But then you wouldn't have found Elinya, and by now she'd be the toy of some fur-covered, drooling brute, her neck chained to a block of ice as she skinned seals on the porch of her master's snow hut, making a bassinet for her new barbarian pup."

"How old *are* you?" Esrahaddon shook his head in disbelief. "If I judged by both your appearance and your mouth, I'd be forced to guess infant-brat going on cynical old coot."

"Really? Truth be told, I'm actually an adorable nine-year-old prince going on all-powerful emperor with a long memory." He flopped more than sat beside Esrahaddon and kicked his long legs out, still playing with what looked like a polished stone. "How's she doing, anyway?"

"Who?"

"Elinya."

"None of your business." Esrahaddon paused. "Wait, how do you know about her? How do you know her name?"

"You two seemed to know each other," the prince said. "I was curious about the Cenzar who saved my life, so I poked around. Turns out you brought her back with you from your first assignment. A messy thing at a tiny village. You saved her life, or something, then asked that she be made a ward of the city." The prince sat up. "You *have* seen her since last night, right? Since saving her from the wagon?"

"I'm supposed to be teaching you all the things a proper young boy needs to know to assume control of the entire world. So tell me, can you so much as read?"

Nevrik frowned. "Of course I can *read*. Good at arithmetic, too. That's how I figured out that Curtalus was smuggling slaves from the businesses he oversaw. Circuit envoys kept reporting to my father that they couldn't find the source of the imports. They listed the names of all the businesses involved and each had two common features—an accountant named Curtalus and slaves that were always sent on Summersrule. Because no slaves had yet been sent from Evarburton, a business Curtalus practically ran, I applied for a job."

"Risky. Why not just tell your father and let him investigate?"

"I'm not merely an adorable nine-year-old; I'm also a bored one. Do you know how dull it is being prince? If they could store me in a bundle of cotton on a high shelf until Daddy died, they would." He tossed up the stone and caught it. "So, *have* you? Visited her, I mean? You haven't. I can tell."

"I'll need to get you books. Do you know much about history? Future rulers ought to understand history."

Nevrik looked dour. "What's past is past, isn't it? I prefer the future. It's considerably more alive, for one. Tastes better, too. Speaking of which, what do you say we go out and grab a bite? Don't worry. I'll tell them who I am, and they won't dare charge."

Esrahaddon ignored the boy. "I'll need to bring all the history books I can find. What about philosophy? Literature? Music?"

"She seemed nice," Nevrik said, and standing up, he began to wander the curving garden path, studying the plants.

"Who?"

"Elinya,"—he paused before a large orange hibiscus bloom—"you should visit her. Bring her flowers or something. Apologize for taking so long. You could use me as an excuse. Say you've been appointed to teach the prince and have been very busy as a result. That'll impress her."

"Not if she's ever met you." Esrahaddon paused to wonder how extensive the prince's investigation had gone. "Has she?"

"No. I've never met anyone—not as Prince Nevrik. I'm not allowed to . . ." The prince's words ran out as he stroked the hibiscus bloom like it was a pet.

"To what?" Esrahaddon asked.

"Never mind." He shook his head, which still hung with miserable portent. "But you should see her." Nevrik plucked the bloom and whirled around. "Give her this. Tell her it's an imperial flower from the palace garden. One of a kind. That will impress her, too."

The prince turned back to face the plants. A hand went to his face, rubbing his eyes and cheeks.

"What's wrong?"

"I, ah—I shouldn't have plucked the flower. Now it's going to die." He turned and looked up and down the path. "Where is Jerish? He's supposed to be here, too."

"I don't know."

"Some educator you are. Here." Nevrik handed him the little stone he'd been playing with. Looking closer, Esrahaddon realized it was a tiny onyx figurine of a cat.

"What's this?"

"A present."

"Where'd you get it?"

"I made it. I carve stuff." He flopped back onto the bench, and his head did that weighted dip again. "I have a lot of time." The boy looked at Esrahaddon and smiled, then his eyes narrowed. "Your robe. It's a darker blue now than it was a moment ago."

"Yeah, it changes color."

The prince's eyes widened. "Really? Where'd you get it?"

"The god Uberlin."

Nevrik grinned. "Sweet."

It was not without some personal frustration that Esrahaddon found himself once more on Carvo Street, staring up at the third-floor windows of the last building.

At least it's daylight this time. I don't appear quite so sinister a figure.

This was true, yet there were far more people to witness his loitering. Unlike his previous visit, this time the street was alive with residents, most dressed in cheap belted tunics. With the weather being so warm, some men folded down their tops and wore only their skirts as they carried water, hauled stone, and drew carts. Women hung out clothes to dry on drooping lines. Carts with colorful canopies had been rolled in and offered bushels of fruits, nuts, and vegetables. A group of strong-backs worked fixing a hole in the street, and one older man sat on a chair with a sheet over him as a younger man with an apron gave him a shave. Baskets with coins were lowered by rope from the upper floors. Bakers, making their rounds, picked up the coins and placed loaves inside the baskets, which were then hauled back up. This system worked for several other commodities as well, including milk and wine.

The most popular spot by far was the rectangular cement pool where a spigot made to look like a lion's mouth eternally spat out fresh water. There, a crowd gathered to fill amphoras and buckets. These public fountains were everywhere in the city, fed by multiple aqueducts. The overflow followed a trench into a gutter that ran to the sewers, flushing away all waste.

Esrahaddon watched this hive of continual activity with genuine interest. This was a world removed from the ones he had experienced. Here was a thriving community of equals. No violence, no obvious poverty. Most appeared happy and purposeful. He pondered the nature of human communities, how some were cruel and violent, glued together by fear; how others were open and free, with no structure at all. Each had its virtues and drawbacks. But this place that lay somewhere in the cosmic middle impressed Esrahaddon as a home he might have chosen for himself.

He also realized he was intentionally wasting time. Not only had he picked up the bad habit of lying to himself, but he'd also adopted the urban vice of procrastination. In a place where survival didn't require constant effort, *dilly-dallying*—as they referred to it—was all the rage.

Nevrik is right, he silently admitted, and mentally sighed.

That the spoiled imperial child he had been forced to educate should be the one to offer him sage advice about his own life felt vaguely insulting and only served to make the act that much harder. The realization that his real father would counsel against him seeing Elinya again, but that his adopted ghazel mother would very likely praise the act as compassionate, ultimately drove Esrahaddon to cross the street.

Esrahaddon entered under the archway to the open-air steps and received a few curious glances and several suspicious stares as he climbed into the apartment complex. At the second-floor landing, he found two young children playing with what he hoped was a small cat. On the third floor he discovered the thick savory aroma of cooking food. What it was, he had no idea, but all at once he realized he was hungry.

Esrahaddon had never actually seen where Elinya lived. He knew the building. He'd walked by it on a few occasions but never climbed the steps, never knocked on the door. He wasn't even sure which door to beat on. This turned out to be less a problem, since all the doors on the third floor were open. Children ran along the balcony, going from one home to another. Old men stood along the railing, looking down, talking.

"Can't keep going like this. Why'd we even fight that war?"

"They need to be sent back home to Erivania. That's what I think."

"Honestly, what we really need is another war. That's the problem. This empire was founded on conquest. Take that away and what have we got: a bunch of lazy louts getting drunk in the streets. And we are the ones to pay for it!"

"If we had a real emperor, instead of—"

Heads turned toward Esrahaddon, and the men glared. They looked him up and down, and expressions hopped from irritation to concern. The Art revealed fear rising near the level of flight.

They're not fools. They know a Cenzar when they see one.

Concerned that one or all might resort to jumping over the rail to escape, a potentially life-threatening act, he offered a friendly smile. "Pardon me. I'm looking for Elinya, formerly of Eber-on-Aston. Any clue where I might find her?"

Still stiff, still wary, the men acted as if Esrahaddon were a lion asking directions from a set of cooked steaks. They slowly nodded. No one found the courage to speak, but two pointed to the right.

"Thank you." Esrahaddon tossed them a kindly wave and walked down the balcony, as half-naked children continued to dodge by, oblivious to the wandering man-eater.

Seeing the number of apartment doors, Esrahaddon regretted coming and had begun reconsidering just how virtuous this visit was when he saw her. Elinya came out of an open door, carrying a carpet and a curved hoop. She threw the rug three-quarters over the rail then proceeded to beat the dirt out of it. She'd struck the thing five times before realizing she was being watched. Looking up, she gasped. In shock, she let go of the hoop and the carpet as both her hands came to her face. The hoop fell at her feet, but the carpet went over the edge to the street below.

"Oh no!" she cried, looking over the rail.

Esrahaddon looked, too, and saw that the rug had toppled a basket containing two jugs of wine. The amphoras hit the street and shattered in a burst of red that stained the stones and the carpet. The woman pulling up the rope scowled. "Elinya! You stupid little fool. Look what you did!"

"I'm sorry!" she cried.

"Sorry? Sorry doesn't do anything! My money is gone. Do you have coin to pay for this? You don't, do you? You don't have a job anymore."

Elinya covered her face with her hand as she began to cry.

"It's not her fault," Esrahaddon declared. "It's mine."

The distraught woman below threw her hands up to the sky. "Well, that fixes everything, doesn't it? I sure hope you're a wealthy merchant willing to pay for what you've done."

"Nope, not a merchant. Haven't got a coin to my name."

"Well, that's just wonderful, isn't it? That's just . . . that's just . . ." The woman began to cry, too. "My husband will beat me when he gets home. He'll say it's my fault." Three children rushed up to hug her legs.

Behind him, Esrahaddon sensed the men watching. Their fear was shifting to anger. Elinya began to shake with her tears.

I'm just a ray of sunshine in this place, aren't I?

He raised his hands and hummed.

This simple act halted Elinya's tears as she watched him.

She doesn't know what's coming, only that something is.

The anger behind him, the fear, the sadness, were boiling reservoirs of potential power, making the act as easy as lifting a feather. Tapping it, rather than the sun or water pouring from the spout, held the added benefit of sapping the growth of collective rage. It calmed everyone—or at least sapped enough strength to kill thoughts of violence.

First, the many bits and pieces of shattered clay reformed into amphoras. Then the wine leaped up off the cobblestone and climbed out of the rug's fibers, traveling through the air as a pink cloud to reinsert itself into the narrow mouths of the pots. Corks snuggled back into the amphoras' throats. Then the carpet stretched out flat. The wine jugs rolled onto it, and the carpet flew up, carrying the restored, refilled amphoras to the woman just below.

The carpet hovered before her. The woman didn't move. She stared at the sight, frozen.

"Take your wine," Esrahaddon told her. "It's just a carpet. It won't hurt you. No teeth, just cute tassels."

This drew a nervous laugh from Elinya, who was now leaning over the rail, watching.

Pretty much everyone on that side of the building viewed the spectacle with open mouths.

"Take it, Leah," someone shouted at her.

The woman reached out with trembling hands and snatched the pots off the rug to the sound of applause. Then she and the children drew away from the balcony. Free of its passengers, the carpet flew up to the third floor and presented itself to Elinya, who grabbed it. A moment later, she dropped the rug, stepped over it, threw out her arms, and embraced Esrahaddon, squeezing him tighter than he would have believed her capable of.

"Thank you so much."

"Was the least I could do, having startled you like that."

Elinya shook her head. "Not for the rug—well, for that, too—but mostly for finally climbing the stairs. I've seen you outside before, and I've watched you walk away. I always hoped you would come up. I prayed you would. I missed you so."

CHAPTER TWENTY

Finding Space

IMPERIAL CAPITAL OF PERCEPLIQUIS

"How did it go?" Nevrik asked Esrahaddon on the following day when they once more met on the same awful wrought-iron garden bench.

We've got to find a better place to do this.

Not only was the bench a physical pain, with its unyieldingly upright metal, but the rain drumming on the garden's glass dome turned out to be irritatingly loud. They could have held their instruction in a bawdy dancehall and had more peace.

"Did you see her?" Nevrik pressed.

Esrahaddon stared at the prince.

"Elinya, I mean?"

"I know what you meant, but we're here today to discuss the books I gave you yesterday." Esrahaddon had lent out five leather-bound tomes from the Cenzarium's private collection to the prince. He had no idea if such a thing was allowed, as he hadn't bothered to ask. If a full-fledged member of the General Assembly couldn't lend books to the emperor's son, something was terribly wrong in the Land of Novron.

Esrahaddon hadn't expected the kid to read all the books in one night. Some were pretty thick. But he hoped Nevrik would have consumed some of the text so as to spur a discussion that might give the prince an interest in learning more. The books he gave Nevrik were ones Esrahaddon had read himself, but then he'd be hard pressed to find books in that collection that he hadn't. These five were on ancient history—mostly concerning the founding of the empire—all written in the last century. Esrahaddon had once thought this odd until—ironically—he *read* that writing had been outlawed for the empire's first eight hundred and fifty years. There had been a reprieve under Emperor Nolyn and his son—a span of nearly seven hundred years—but surprisingly, few bothered learning to read, and even fewer wrote. When Emperor Nurgya was killed, the orthodoxy cracked down. The Estermons reinstated the old rules, and for three hundred and forty-six years, authors were criminals and books were destroyed. Few written documents survived the purge except those protected in secret monasteries until Princess Farilane made literature legal again.

"Did you read the books?"

The prince put up an obstinate face. "I asked first."

Esrahaddon frowned and folded his arms.

"C'mon." Nevrik sat up with the nervous energy of every boy, future ruler of the world or not. "Education doesn't need to be a grind. I'll learn more if I enjoy it and I'm not forced."

Esrahaddon smiled. "In the dwarven language, *grinder* literally means teacher."

"Why does that not surprise me? Look, tell me and I promise I will discuss whatever you want."

"Fine." Esrahaddon folded his hands on his lap. "Yes, I saw her."

"And?"

It pained Esrahaddon to admit, but he saw no reason to lie. "She was in trouble and was happy to see me."

Esrahaddon expected the kid to gloat, to hit him with "I told you so," or "See, I was right," but the boy continued to surprise him.

"What kind of trouble?" Nevrik asked, leaning forward with a concern that seemed convincingly genuine.

"She was let go from Evarburton after the incident with Curtalus. She has no income, no way to pay her rent. They're going to evict her in three days. Do you know what *evict* means?"

The prince frowned. "I'm nine, not a moron. So what did you do about it?"

"What do you mean?"

"How did you fix it?"

"I didn't."

Nevrik looked dumbfounded. "Don't you like her?"

Esrahaddon smirked at the boy. "You might be shocked to discover that while I'm an all-powerful Cenzar, I have no money. The Cenzarium provides me a modest room and food, but that's it. If I were a circuit envoy, I'd have a stipend. But I'm not. Instead of being useful to the world, I'm trapped here with you."

"And if you weren't," Nevrik told him, "Elinya would be chewing on her seal blubber stew right now wondering if she'll lose all her fingers to frostbite, or just the three."

"Where do you get this stuff?"

"When you spend the majority of your time alone, you develop an imagination or go mad. Although I'm not sure that's an either-or thing. I've gone through eight imaginary friends. All died horrible deaths. That says something, don't you think?"

"You're a really odd kid, you know that?"

Nevrik shook his head. "How would I? I don't know any other kids. Aside from my parents and little sister, you're the only person in years I've had a real conversation with—one that has included more than three words—two always being *Your Highness*."

"You said more than that to Curtalus."

Nevrik nodded, "Okay, sure. But that adventure was unique and unsanctioned, a momentary flash in my otherwise gray existence."

Esrahaddon leaned back as far as the unyielding chair allowed and studied the boy. "That *was* the only time you've ever been outside the palace, wasn't it?"

Nevrik rocked his head side to side. "Well, yes, but—I mean—it wasn't just that one night. I watched the place for almost a week. Got terribly lost the first time." Nevrik smiled. "Thought I'd never make it back. Can you imagine? Emperor's son dies of starvation lost in the streets of his own capital city. How embarrassing would that have been?"

"So you've never had a friend—aside from the invented ones you brutally murdered?"

"I didn't murder them. They died of their own stupidity. Besides, you're my friend now—you and Jerish, who is tardy once more. Oh yes! I had a conversation with Jerish that lasted more than five words." The kid grinned. "Sent him in the wrong direction so he'd be late for the audience with my father. That was fun."

Esrahaddon nodded. "I'm starting to see why the imaginary friends killed themselves. I think maybe I'd prefer to keep our relationship professional."

Nevrik, who couldn't hold still any longer, stood up and began once more to wander the garden path. "What are you going to do about Elinya?"

Esrahaddon rolled his eyes. "Back to that, are we? I got the landlord to let her stay another three days. I'll see if I can help her find another job, but I know very little about this city. I have no connections, no influence."

Nevrik spun. "You're a Cenzar!"

"Yes, and I've considered turning her landlord into a frog, but I don't see how that would help. Do you?"

The boy frowned. "It's not right. Elinya did nothing wrong. She shouldn't be punished for Curtalus's crimes. She's the victim, not the criminal."

"Congratulations to both of us. I've managed to teach you something, and you've successfully learned your first civics lesson: *Life's not fair*. Shall we move on to what you read last—"

"Don't you care about what happens to her?" The boy was outraged, planting fists on nonexistent hips.

Esrahaddon did care. Truth was, he hadn't been kidding about the frog thing. He'd considered it far more seriously than he should have. No one liked the threat of living their days out as a toad. But the landlord had his own troubles, his own bills. So in three days, if nothing presented itself, Esrahaddon would invite Elinya to live with him in his tiny cell in the Cenzarium. This might cause some issues, but he would face those as they arose. Then a thought flickered into his head. He was tutor to the prince, and the emperor's son seemed keen on helping Elinya. "You could ask your father to step in."

Nevrik, who was looking at the flowers, let out a sad laugh. "Doesn't work that way around here. I've been asking for a pony since I was seven." He gestured around. "Do you *see* a pony?"

Jerish Grelad entered the garden, appearing exhausted. He was wearing armor: a long formal coat, made from leaves of gold-colored metal, and a plumed helm like the head of an eagle resting on top. These were the new duds, the official uniform of a Teshlor: not as polished as Gaylord Sire's but shinier than what Esrahaddon remembered Wardley or Griffith wearing.

"There you are," Jerish said, looking relieved as he marched up the garden's meandering path.

"How nice of you to actually show up," Esrahaddon said. "What a wonderful first lesson to teach."

Jerish acted as if Esrahaddon didn't exist, and he knelt before Nevrik. "My apologies, my prince. I was required at the guildhall yesterday. It won't happen again."

Esrahaddon sensed a dead space where once the Art had revealed a young man. "He got his tattoos. Bet he's still sore."

Jerish looked up. "Actually, I am. It's not a pleasant process."

"And you got your armor and swords, too, I see," the prince remarked, delighted, the way young boys often are with shiny or sharp things.

"I have, Your Highness."

"Can I hold one? I've never touched a real sword."

"You will soon enough. May I rise, Your Highness?" Jerish asked.

"Oh yeah, sure. Sorry."

Jerish stood and looked around the garden. "This won't do. We'll need a much bigger space. An open field. I suppose we can go to the training grounds at the Teshlor Guild."

"I'm not allowed to leave the palace," Nevrik said.

"You aren't?"

"Hasn't got any friends, either," Esrahaddon said. "Except imaginary ones, who apparently committed suicide to escape his company."

Nevrik stuck out his tongue.

"Why aren't you allowed to leave?" Jerish asked.

Nevrik shrugged, pretending ignorance, but the Art was singing a different song, which caused Esrahaddon to notice the pattern. He assumed the kid was acting out, trying to gain sympathy. After all, what could an imperial prince really have to complain about? But now he was lying about it, hiding something.

"There must be some place in this palace where we can practice," Jerish said. "Some place big, sheltered, and, most of all, vacant."

"Does it have to be outside?" Nevrik asked.

Jerish thought a moment. "Well, no, I suppose not, but I can't imagine an indoor space large enough. We're going to be swinging sticks and eventually live blades. There needs to be room to move freely, and I'm afraid if there's any furniture, we'll destroy it."

"That won't be a problem," the kid said. "There's really only one issue."

"What's that?" Jerish asked.

"Do you have a problem with dead people?"

Jerish followed the prince through several corridors and down three staircases. At the bottom of each set of steps, the corridors were noticeably narrower, the ceilings lower. Jerish had the sensation of delving into a deep cave that closed in on all sides. This was not what he was looking for. He needed a wide-open area where he could demonstrate and drill the prince the way Jerish had learned in the Teshlor Academy's courtyard. They came to a three-way intersection, where three statues of long-bearded men holding shields stood, and here they turned right. Then they came to a T-intersection where a stone door stood beside a marble table. Words in a language Jerish couldn't read were chiseled into the arch above the entrance. Even if he could have read them, he wouldn't have had time because Nevrik asked for help opening the heavy door. Only then did Jerish notice that the Cenzar was still with them.

Jerish didn't like him and realized that the stories the experienced circuit knights had told of the Cenzar's arrogance appeared warranted. This *Esrahaddon* fellow seemed quite full of himself. The sheer cavalier attitude and relaxed demeanor before the imperial prince was appalling. He displayed a total lack of respect. Jerish only hoped the Cenzar didn't plan on making a habit of joining them every day. Didn't see why he would. For that matter, Jerish couldn't grasp why there was a Cenzar tutor at all. A Teshlor Knight could train the emperor's son to defend himself, or fight if he needed to lead a battle one day, but what could a Cenzar teach him? And Esrahaddon would only be a hindrance to the prince's combat education.

Beyond the stone door was yet another staircase going down. Here, there were no wall lamps, and the steps descended into darkness.

"My prince, this doesn't seem a likely place to practice martial arts. And as we lack a torch—"

"Hey, Grinder?" the prince called to Esrahaddon, and cast a smile over his shoulder. "Can you do anything to illuminate our way? There are lamps down here, but they don't usually light them."

"Why did you call him—"

An unnatural white light appeared behind them. Jerish turned to see that the Cenzar's robe was glowing.

"Or sure, that works, too," Nevrik said, and without further comment, he walked on.

Jerish stared at the glowing robe, stunned.

"You're losing your student," Esrahaddon told him. "Probably be bad if on your first day he was eaten by a troll or something."

Jerish turned back, found the prince far ahead, and ran to catch up.

As Esrahaddon walked at the tail end of their tiny procession, the robe's light cast their shadows forward. Disturbingly stretched figures of darkness danced with lanky limbs ahead of them, creating a fiendish shadow-play on the stone walls where ghostly images had been etched. Depictions of forests and fighting men were chiseled into a series of panels that likely told a story, but most of it was hard to see, and Jerish was in no mood for studying. This place was disquieting and growing more so with each step. The glowing robe didn't help.

"How is it your robe creates light?" Jerish asked. "Is it some spell? I didn't hear you say anything."

"He got it from the evil goblin god," the prince explained. "No telling what it can do, but it also changes colors with Esrahaddon's mood, or perhaps it's the *robe's* disposition. Which is it?"

"No idea," the Cenzar replied, "but don't call them *goblins*. That's offensive. The proper term is *Ba Ran*."

"Offensive to whom?" the prince asked.

"The Ba Ran, of course."

The corridor ended at another stone door. Nevrik was capable of pushing this one open by himself, and once more the Cenzar's light revealed what darkness hid: a small square room with a vaulted ceiling. In the center was a statue of Novron. The walls were lined with cubbyholes filled with scrolls.

"What is this place?" the Cenzar asked as he poked around, looking at the scrolls.

"The family crypt's record room," Nevrik explained. "The scrolls list all family members interred within, histories, other stuff, I guess."

"Other stuff, *you guess?*"

The prince scowled at the Cenzar. "It's not like I read them. I'm not *that* bored."

"I'm sorry, my prince, but this isn't going to do," Jerish said. "We need someplace open. Someplace bigger. A courtyard, a playing field, or something like that."

"I know," he replied and cast open a door on the far side of the room. The prince disappeared into darkness. "Esrahaddon, there are candles in sconces on the walls inside. Can you light them?"

"What? Am I also your personal lamplighter now?"

Jerish followed Nevrik into the blackness. Even with the glow of the Cenzar's robe, he could see little but the floor, yet the sound of their footsteps echoed in what had to be a vast chamber.

"Venderia," the Cenzar said, and light filled the hall as more than a hundred wall lamps burst into flame.

They stood in what appeared to be a great ballroom, the walls decorated with gold and polished silver. The lamplight bounced off the many reflective surfaces, making the hall as bright as Imperial Square at midday. Looking at it, Jerish thought it might be nearly as large. Statues of white marble—mostly of women in long gowns or robes—stood in niches, and beside them were small doors that appeared to be made of glass.

"This is the Vault of Days," the prince said, his voice echoing.

"What's it for?" the Cenzar asked.

The prince pointed across the room at another door. "Over there are the emperors' tombs. That's where all the rulers are, lying on shelves in fancy stone boxes. There are twelve boxes, but only six have occupants. Not sure if the tomb's designers were being conservative or optimistic. But out here is where everyone else of note has been stashed: the wives, daughters, beloved servants, family cat, that sort of thing. That's who these statues depict. Behind the mirrored doors are their coffins—not that I've actually peeked. I'm not that curious, and to be honest, not that brave." The prince stepped out toward the middle of the chamber, extended his arms, and rotated in a circle. "As you can see, there's plenty of room, no furniture, and no one *ever* comes here."

Jerish walked around, looking up at the startlingly high ceiling, and the beautiful marble tiled floor. "It's perfect. Won't even need to worry about the weather. Of course I'll need to get some equipment. Some posts, a walking beam, bats. I'm certain I can borrow some from the guildhall."

The prince smiled.

"Why can't you go out, Nevrik?" the Cenzar asked, folding his arms and glaring at the emperor's son.

Instantly, the prince's smile vanished. "What do you mean?"

"You know what I mean. Why aren't you allowed out? Did you do something? Are you being punished?"

The Cenzar's tone was harsh, even cruel, and Jerish didn't care for it. This was the prince, after all, and this Esrahaddon fellow was treating him like a street orphan.

Nevrik shook his head.

"Then what is it?"

"He doesn't have to tell us," Jerish said.

"I think he does." Esrahaddon continued to stare at the prince.

"Nevrik is the emperor's son."

"Figured that out all by yourself, did you?" the Cenzar asked. "Congratulations. You must have been the genius of your class." The Cenzar advanced on the boy, his robe changing from yellow to orange as if he were a bonfire. "Answer me."

Jerish stepped forward and grabbed Esrahaddon's arm, pulling him back. "Leave him alone."

"Be careful what you grab onto," the Cenzar told him. "This robe ate the last guy to mess with it. And that silver tea set and those scribbles you're wearing won't protect you."

"You think that glowing robe will protect *you* from sharp steel?"

The Cenzar looked down at himself. "I honestly don't know, but we both ought to be too terrified to find out."

"Stop it!" Nevrik shouted, his voice magnified by the hollow chamber. The prince began meandering about, shoulders up, head down, elbows held tight as if bracing against a storm.

Esrahaddon watched him. *Turns out he's still just a nine-year-old after all.*

Nevrik slowed to a stop, then turned to face them but didn't meet their eyes. "Look, it's not just me. None of us go out anymore."

"Who *exactly* are you talking about?" Esrahaddon asked.

"My family. We never leave the palace."

"It's true, then?" Jerish asked, recalling the many times he'd heard the stories and seen the slogan painted on walls. "The imperial family is being held prisoner?"

Nevrik started to laugh, then stopped himself. He thought a moment, then nodded. "In a way, I suppose."

"Why can't you go out?" Esrahaddon asked.

"It's too dangerous," the prince said. "According to Father, there are people—*lots* of *powerful* people—who would like nothing more than to kill us."

"The emperor of the world can't safely walk the streets of his own capital city?" Esrahaddon asked.

The prince nodded. "Nine years old—never been drunk, kissed a girl, or been in a fight, but I have a host of enemies who want me dead. Ain't being me grand?"

CHAPTER TWENTY-ONE

Conspiracy

IMPERIAL CAPITAL OF PERCEPLIQUIS

Everything about Isilpor-Sond was captivating. She was small enough to be a dwarf, old enough to be a Fhrey, and dark enough to be an eastern Calynian. Her hair was white, her eyes gray, and it was said she rose before dawn every morning and walked the ten-mile circuit around the entire city on bare feet, stopping to chat with shepherds and farmers. Rumor also held that she enjoyed drinking Gurlin Bog, chewed grenesta leaves, and spat the juice out through the gap between her front teeth. Isilpor-Sond was also the *unofficial* head of the Cenzarium because the Cenzars couldn't have a *real* leader. The very concept of hierarchy remained antithetical to the organization's creed: Knowledge, Creativity, Equality, Cooperation. More than that was the sheer improbability of attempting to dominate people with the innate power to reorganize reality. If controlling inherently independent artists was like herding cats, managing magic-wielding Artists would be tantamount to putting a bit into a tiger's mouth in the hope of going for a ride. Therefore, Esrahaddon considered her to be less the *head* and more the *heart* of the Cenzarium.

That evening, Esrahaddon had his choice of speaking to any of the three local Cenzar elders. As advisor to the emperor, Offman was the official liaison to the palace; Yolric, whom Esrahaddon had only seen the one time at his initiation to the General Assembly, was known to be the eccentric Lore Master; and, of course, Isilpor-Sond. Esrahaddon chose Isilpor-Sond because a dark, diminutive, bog-drinking, grenesta-juice-spitting old lady seemed like his sort of people.

He found her with feet up, asleep in the gallery overlooking the Cenzarium campus garden. "Excuse me?" he said.

With eyes still closed, she replied, "Why? Did you farrow?"

"I'm sorry, did I what?"

One eye opened. "Farrow, break wind, expel an unpleasant odor from one or more bodily orifice?"

"Ah . . . no. I meant for interrupting your nap."

"Wasn't napping. Was resting me eyes." She pulled her feet off the opposing wicker chair. Each foot hit the floor with a heavy slap. "Sit down, Ezra of Haddon, and tell me what's got you buzzin'. Nice robe, by the way. Get that in the city?" Both her eyes opened, and she stared at him with a quizzical look on her face, which now that he had the opportunity to really see it, was as wrinkled as a walnut shell. "No, of course not. What am I thinking? I'm not, that's the problem. Where *did* you get that thing?"

"Present from my mother."

This made Isilpor-Sond laugh, for what reason Esrahaddon had no idea, but it seemed a good joke, since she went on for nearly a minute. When at last she recovered, she wiped her eyes and brushed away a wayward strand of that shockingly milk-white hair. "That's good. Okay, we can speak on that matter later. Tell me, what's the problem?"

"I've been robbed. Everything in my room is gone."

She didn't so much laugh this time as outright guffaw while pounding her fist on the arm of the chair. Then she held up the other hand, warding him off as if terrified of more comedic assaults. "You're hilarious! I hadn't heard that about you."

Esrahaddon blinked, confused, wondering if she was hearing the same words he was speaking. "I'm not joking. I went to my room just now and found it—"

"Your things were moved, dear boy." Again she wiped tears from her eyes.

"To where?"

She took a moment to breathe, then replied, "Your permanent residence."

"My what?"

Using her elbows on the arms of the chair and gritting her teeth while expelling a grunt, Isilpor-Sond hauled her thin frame to a full upright position. "You're in the General Assembly now, a full Cenzar with all the perks that come with that. Did you think we were going to keep you in that little cell for the rest of your life?"

That was exactly what Esrahaddon had thought. He hadn't even questioned it. Having lived in a dirt-floored hut and then a tree house he'd built as a child, the cell had been the finest accommodations he'd known.

"You're upstairs in the posh wing." She winked. "Being tutor to the prince grants certain benefits."

"I thought we were all equals."

"We are, and don't get your hopes up. It's merely a fact of reality that in a square building, at least four people get corners, and those corners have windows on two walls. And because you will be here full time, unlike many of our colleagues who travel frequently, it was agreed that you ought to have a corner." She wiped her mouth with the back of her hand. "You weren't here for that meeting. You've been gone a lot. Busy with the new project, no doubt, so we helped you out by throwing your crap in the new place. Hope nothing was broken. Pasiturn was in a hurry, had a thing to get to. Most of us used our hands; he used the Art. Telekinetic transfer was never Pasiturn's talent."

Esrahaddon just stared.

She grinned. "I'm funny, too, right?"

"Are all Cenzars a little crazy?" he asked quite sincerely.

Isilpor-Sond nodded. "Oh, absolutely. And personally, I believe that's another fringe benefit of being us. People sort of expect it, don't they? At least they don't seem surprised. Now tell me, how is it going with the imperial imp?"

"Fine, I suppose."

"Except?" She stared a moment, then shrugged. "Sorry, but you're radiating a cloud of confusion big enough to forecast rain. I'd love to drill down on the topic of this robe you're wearing—which on a normal level is nice, but when seen through the Art, *it's amazing*. Makes you look like a god. But that's not why you're here. And the robbery isn't, either. You knew, or guessed, that your things weren't stolen."

"True, but only because I have nothing of value to steal. Not really."

"And so, what is the real purpose of this visit?"

"Oh, well, it's something the prince said that I found . . . puzzling."

"Which was?"

"He said no one in the imperial family leaves the palace, for fear of their lives because there are several people in the city who want to kill them—*powerful people*. And I just couldn't understand how that is possible. With the combined might of the Teshlor Guild and the Cenzarium, the palace and city guard—not to mention the legions—the members of the imperial family must be the safest living creatures on Elan." He shook his head. "I suppose it was just a child's imagination. But Nevrik . . . I don't know, he doesn't seem . . . I mean, he's smart. Pretty mature, too, and he appeared genuinely upset."

Isilpor-Sond watched him thoughtfully for a long moment, then nodded. "There is a meeting of the Cenzars tonight. You need to be there."

Esrahaddon wondered if the old woman was, herself, confused. "The next General Assembly meeting isn't for three weeks."

"I didn't say anything about General Assembly, did I?"

"I don't understand."

"I know. That's why you need to come."

"This is mine?" Jerish asked as he stared at the room. Four complete walls, a door, a chest of drawers, a trunk, and a bed with a headboard, fine blankets, and a pillow. Jerish looked around—only one bed. "This room is *all* mine?"

Asurkan nodded. "You're a big deal now, my friend—a full Third Order Knight and tutor to the prince." Asurkan was dressed in his casual tunic and soft shoes. He still had biscuit crumbs from dinner caught in his new beard, which had yet to fill in.

Asurkan, along with Vicks and Spencer, had been the trio considered most likely to make knight when Jerish was in the academy. Jerish and Spencer were the only ones who actually did. Most, like Logan and Sigur, just disappeared, it seemed. Jerish had never known what happened to them. Hanson, they said, got a position with the palace guard. So did Vicks. Gareth became an officer in the legion. Easton joined the city sentinels, where he would likely make captain by the time he was twenty. And of course, the disgraced Darius Seret went back home to Alburnia, where no one knew about his failures. Asurkan was the only one who stayed on at the guild, where there was plenty of work to be done. He didn't wear the emblem, but to those who knew him, that didn't matter. Still, it likely mattered to Asurkan. The failed knight tried to mask his discomfort with casual bravado by leaning on the door frame, thumbs in his belt, yet Jerish noticed a tone of deference in the man's voice.

Jerish had never learned why Asurkan failed to make knight. He was a good fighter, respectful, and decent. Maybe Asurkan didn't know either, and he stayed in the hope that a mistake had been made, and it would be discovered.

"Where does that door go?" Jerish pointed.

"Open it and find out."

Jerish did, and his mouth dropped.

Years ago, when he first arrived at the Teshlor Academy, a boy named Logan had helped him find—what he learned was called—the *lavatory*. Jerish recalled Logan saying, *"Rumor has it that knights have private ones that adjoin their rooms."* That was the Logan from that first day, the Logan he thought of as a friend. Then Logan betrayed him and joined up with Darius Seret. Jerish preferred to remember the *other* Logan.

"There's a stand for your armor over here," Asurkan explained, gesturing at a wooden rack in the corner. "No window, though. Thirds don't get windows."

Jerish nodded as if he understood. He got the part about the window, but it was the *Thirds* he didn't, and sighed. *Barely a knight and already ignoring the Code.*

The Knightly Virtues, of which there were eight, made up the Teshlor Code handed down by Jerel DeMardefeld. One was honesty. *To possess honor, a man must first strive to be honest to men, to women, to children, to great and to small, to the good and to the villainous, but mostly to himself. A knight does not make excuses.* Jerish wasn't certain, but acting like he knew something he didn't was also likely to violate the codes of courage, integrity, and sincerity. Regardless, it was wrong.

"Actually, Asur, I'm a bit embarrassed to admit that I don't know the difference between First, Second, and Third Order Knights, but I suspect I should. Can you tell me?"

Asurkan smiled and nodded. "They explained it all to Spencer before he left on his first circuit. Maybe being a tutor, you didn't get the usual orientation? Anyway, it has to do with the cache of trust you've built up with the emperor and how much imperial power you're allowed to wield. Thirds don't have much. For example, you aren't allowed to kill anyone."

"What if someone tries to kill me?"

Asurkan shook his head. "Not even then. You're a Teshlor. You shouldn't need to kill to defeat. You're also not likely to be put in a position where that would even come up. Thirds are like interns. Circuit Knight Thirds always go out with an experienced Cenzar to cover for them. If you're working in the palace, there isn't much chance of a problem. Now Seconds *can* kill in defense of themselves or others. They also have some judicial powers and can rule on, and dish out, punishment for lesser crimes. But your First Orders, well, they're like the emperor himself. They can do as they see fit. Execute for high crimes, remove governors from office, establish new towns or provinces—you name it. They also tend to be ridiculously good fighters. Gaylord Sire is First Order. You can tell by the emblem. Thirds have bronze, Seconds silver; Firsts get gold."

"Gotcha, thanks." Jerish resumed looking at his new room. "There's a shield here." Jerish pointed at the heater shield on the wall. On it was an emblem of twisted and knotted vines surrounding a star supported by a crescent moon.

Asurkan nodded. "Master Lynch sent that over as a gift. Says it matches your sword. I hung it for you."

"My . . ." Jerish pulled the spadone from the simple leather loop on his back. On the center of the pommel was a small engraving that matched the one on the shield.

"Also, Master Ipstich had this made for you." Asurkan opened the wardrobe and pulled out a scabbard of gold and silver. "Said a sword like that deserved a fine home."

Jerish let the great blade slide in, where it settled with a clank.

"Are you going to the meeting tonight?" Asurkan asked.

"There's a meeting?"

"Yeah." He chuckled. "Has been one every new moon."

Jerish stared.

Asurkan rolled his eyes. "You're going to have to connect with others more, Jer. The real world isn't like the academy. You don't get points for single-minded isolation. You need to get out, meet people, make friends."

"I don't do *friends* very well," Jerish said.

"Then I'll be your friend until you find a better one."

"Thanks." Jerish appreciated the offer but knew friendships didn't work that way. They required two people making the effort, and Jerish didn't know how. But while he had the chance, and seeing as how Asur appeared to know everything, he asked, "Say, Asur, do you know anything about people threatening the imperial family?"

Asurkan looked shocked and shook his head. "Should I?"

Jerish shrugged. "It was just something the prince said. He mentioned that the emperor thinks powerful people in the city are bent on killing them. It's why they rarely ever go out, why no one ever sees them."

"If that's true, all the emperor has to do is tell us, and this whole guild would turn out to hunt them down. Someone would be in a world of hurt."

"Yeah, that's what I was thinking. It's just so odd."

"Meeting is at sunset. You can tell me what was discussed tomorrow."

"You're not coming?"

Asurkan clapped his chest. "No emblem. Meeting is for knights only."

Esrahaddon and Isilpor-Sond didn't need to go far, since the meeting was held in the Cenzarium rotunda. As far as he could tell, all but one of the Cenzars in the city were there.

Looking out over the many seated beneath the dome, each wrapped in their version of the obligatory Artist's robe, he counted twelve whose faces he could connect names to, among them Isilpor-Sond, Offman, Sebastian, Asura, and Pasiturn. Rappaport and Yolric were the only two he knew who were not there. Rappaport was up north, likely in Farington. She'd left five days ago, the morning after Summersrule, to marry her tailor. Maybe they had rushed things, and she was already married. Five days. Depending on what level of depression he was in, it felt like five years or five minutes. Esrahaddon tried as best he could not to think about it. He worked at walling off that part of his life, sealing away rooms that had once been filled with warmth and laughter but now collected dust. The Cenzarium taught concentration and techniques to isolate the mind, to make it a fortress against distraction. He never thought he'd have need of such things just to fall asleep.

Esrahaddon sat beside Isilpor-Sond on the cushioned but less-than-comfortable benches that lined the round hall. "What's this all about?"

"Patience," she told him. "Just listen."

Before long, Offman strode to the center, to the very spot where Esrahaddon had stood for his initiation. He looked around for a moment, then formed a closing weave, and the doors all slammed. He followed this with a seal, and Esrahaddon knew the rotunda was locked tighter than any fortress.

"Cenzars," he began in a voice that carried easily in the room. "We meet once again to discuss the state of the imperium and the strength of the peace, and alas, the news has not improved. It has, in fact, worsened. The emperor is now contemplating the appointment of an Imperial Council oversight committee to monitor and regulate the Cenzarium."

This brought everyone's attention, with a few muttering the rhetorical, "What?"

"The Teshlors are poisoning the emperor's opinion of us. Every day, Gaylord Sire continues to fill Nareion with absurd lies about how we are the greatest threat to the empire. He insists that Novron outlawed magic for a reason."

"What reason?" Pasiturn asked.

Offman shook his head, wagging his beard. "That's just the problem. He never says. If he did, I could argue. I could prove him wrong. But by keeping the topic in a cloud, the poison seeps in, and no antidote can be administered. This is their technique, you see. They put forth that Fhrey and dwarfs are evil; that they should be purged from the empire but never say why or provide reasons. They complain about the financials, insisting that we need to return to an economy of conquest, but fail to explain what is wrong with the present state of peace or who we ought to attack and why. They utterly reject education, declaring it a bridge to corruption—and by corruption they mean, of course, magic. To them, knowledge drives men to believe themselves to be gods, and this very concept they deem as *evil.* They want so badly to return to the Days of Yore—by which they mean the era before the establishment of the Cenzarium—the days when magic, reading, and writing were outlawed. And with each passing day, I see the inroads they make into the mind of the emperor. It is like the wearing away of a coastline by the slow but ever-constant lick of corrosive waves."

"What about the wall?" asked one of the faces Esrahaddon didn't have a name for.

"They still push for it, but the emperor hasn't yet consented."

"What wall?" Esrahaddon asked Isilpor-Sond.

"The Teshlor Guild has been fighting for the emperor to build a wall around Percepliquis for years. They say they want it to protect us from the goblins, but everyone knows it's really to prevent the Merredydd Fhrey from being able to enter unnoticed."

"Why is that a problem? They're imperial citizens, right?"

Isilpor-Sond rolled her eyes. "We're talking about Teshlors here. They hate all Fhrey. They also want a wall built around Calynia."

"The whole province? It's huge."

She held up her hands, nodding. "Teshlors equal crazy."

Offman went on. "It is becoming more and more apparent now that the Teshlor Guild's goal is to eliminate the Cenzarium and take direct control of the empire. This oversight committee is the first step." Offman paused and his face darkened. "This is something we cannot allow. Should they succeed in gaining the emperor's confidence, if they turn him against us, we must act. We do not serve the emperor, but rather the empire and the peace. If necessary, we may need to cut off the blossom to allow the plant to survive."

"It's us," Esrahaddon whispered. "The Teshlors are making the emperor believe that we are out to destroy him. The Cenzarium are the *powerful people* he fears."

Isilpor-Sond smiled. "It's been a long time coming, but the guild and the Cenzarium are destined for a showdown. Imperial Square isn't big enough for the two of us. We can't allow them to endanger the peace. Unfortunately, the emperor is caught in the middle."

Jerish entered the Great Room in the east wing of the Teshlor Guildhall. Over a thousand years ago, it had been the throne room of Novron. Now the massive rectangular chamber with its antiquated braziers, mammoth dwarf-hewn stones, and narrow windows was the Teshlor Guild's assembly hall. The old throne was still on the dais, with two other chairs on either side. On the ground floor were rows of benches where a score of knights sat.

Jerish looked for a familiar face and spotted only Kendel, who had graduated from the academy when Jerish was in his first year. He still remembered Kendel's amazing battle with the great Osfelt, which had ended in a draw. Assuming Kendel wouldn't remember him, Jerish took a seat at the end of a row near the back.

Up on the dais in the center chair was a white-haired knight with a close-trimmed beard, whom Jerish guessed to be Andreas Ranier, the Guild Lord. To his right was Gaylord Sire, shining bright in his golden armor. *Did he put it on for the meeting, or does he wear that stuff all the time?*

Jerish was new to wearing armor. All assembled, the metal outfit appeared to be one piece, looking like a long formal coat made from the layering of gold-colored sheets. The suit also appeared to be comfortable. It wasn't. While great in a fight, where the leaves of metal granted wonderful freedom of movement, it wasn't the attire one lounged in—or wore to a meeting in the safety of the Teshlor Guildhall.

On the left chair sat Bishop Venlin.

Jerish hadn't spoken to the bishop since he was ten. He had no interest in meeting him now, having failed utterly to keep his promise of attending the church. The demands of the academy had been intense and left little extra time. He'd also forgotten. None of these was a valid excuse. The Code didn't allow for them. Best that he found time in the future, showed himself to be trying, then apologize. Jerish trusted his back-row invisibility to get him through the night, and uncharacteristically slumped down on the bench.

The white-haired knight stood up, and the casual conversations stopped.

"Honorable Knights of the Order of Teshlor!" he shouted. "Keepers of the truth, of the Code, of the Promise, of the legacy of Griffin the Great, hero of the Battle of Grandford. Hear me now. I stand before you with terrible tidings. Speak, Gaylord. Tell them what you told me."

Andreas sat and Gaylord Sire stood up and stared about the hall. He appeared to be searching every pair of eyes, his face grim and serious. "My brothers," he began, "the time we have long feared is upon us. Today Cenzar Offman proposed"—he paused as if unable to go on—"limiting the powers of the Imperial Throne."

This sent a hum through the benches that Gaylord and Andreas quieted with a show of their palms.

"Pretending to act in the *best interests* of the imperium, the Cenzars are suggesting that we establish a *written* set of laws that all citizens of the empire must obey—including the emperor!"

"But the emperor's *will* is the *law*," one of the knights in the front row said. "How can he be subject to any law?"

"If that were possible, the Cenzarium would try to control the gods," Venlin said.

"Knowing them, they think it is!" Gaylord said.

"It's all lies," Andreas declared in a booming voice. "They seek to take control of the empire. The emperor stands in their way, and so they must destroy him. By inventing rules that the emperor must obey, they will be able to find him guilty of some breach. And using that as an excuse, they will kill him and the imperial family."

"It will never happen," another from the front row said. "The emperor won't do it."

"He will," Gaylord said. "What you don't understand is how the Cenzars bewitch him. The imperial family does not wear the Orinfar, and the magic is powerful and silent. It works like a poison. Nareion is falling more under their thrall every day. I see it when Offman speaks to him: the way the emperor nods; the way he agrees with everything the old sorcerer says. The emperor is rapidly becoming our enemy. Soon the Cenzarium will be ruling, and they will order our slaughter."

"They might find that harder than they think," another said. Jerish didn't know who. Everyone on the benches with him could have been the same person, as all he saw were the backs of their heads.

"And you may be underestimating their magic. If we let them strike first, we will lose."

"This seems a huge jump, from a request for written laws to civil war," Kendel put forth.

"You're young, Kendel," Andreas said. "You haven't witnessed what we have. The Cenzarium has long sought to take control. They don't accept any kind of authority, except their own. They refuse to take a proper oath to the emperor—only to the *empire*. They don't believe in the gods, not even in Novron. They want to abolish not only the Teshlor Guild, but the legions, leaving the empire helpless."

"How can order be maintained without soldiers?"

"Oh! They say the solution to that is to *educate* everyone. They profess that only the unlearned commit crimes—out of ignorance—and that educated men will always do what is right. All we need to do is teach the people right from wrong, and crime will disappear!" Andreas rolled his eyes.

"The truth is," he resumed, "that they want to teach us all to read so they can use words to control everyone. Then they will invite the Fhrey back to be our overlords."

Bishop Venlin nodded. "Oh yes, this is the truth of it. The Cenzars love the Fhrey. They love their magic and will stop at nothing to return to the time when mankind was a slave to the elf."

"Why would they do that?" Kendel asked.

"Many people suspect that some, perhaps all, of the Cenzars *are* elves and use magic to hide their true nature. It is said that humans—real humans—don't possess the power of magic. Only elves do, which explains why none of us can cast spells."

This brought a silence to the hall. Even Andreas stared at the bishop. "That would truly be a nightmare come true."

"What proof do you have that the Cenzars are elves in disguise?" Kendel again.

"You've seen it yourselves. But you've been lulled into ignoring the true nature of the Cenzars, just like a frog slowly warmed in a pot of water doesn't realize it's boiling before it's cooked. Haven't you noticed the way they wear the elven asicas, the fact they reside in the ancient Aguanon—the ancient Temple of Ferrol? They openly fight for Fhrey rights, don't they? Always insisting the myr are equal citizens? And all of you have heard how they insist the emperor is an elf, even though anyone who's seen him can tell he is human. Don't believe your eyes, they say, believe us instead! All of it is lies. Falsehoods told to return rebellious humans to the yoke of the elf, to win the war they once lost."

This again left the hall in silence.

Finally, Andreas stood once more. "No matter how unpleasant it would seem, we must begin to prepare for the inevitable."

Heads nodded.

"You must also resolve that the emperor himself," Venlin added, "manipulated by magic, will likely be turned against us. And if no other means can be found to save him, as an act of *mercy* and for the greater good of the empire and all mankind, Nareion may need to be sacrificed."

Until that moment, Jerish didn't know that silence could grow quieter. It was as if the very wind outside had stopped.

It's them, Jerish realized. *The powerful people threatening the imperial family are the Cenzars.*

Esrahaddon was coming out of the meeting, and with a lot to think about, he took his time walking through Imperial Square. At that late hour, few people were in the plaza. The evening was warm, and the sound of the fountain loud. Nearing the middle of the square, he slowed to look across at the Teshlor Guildhall. What he saw was the pinnacle achievement of the brute. This fortress of stone formed the epicenter to the same sort of people that had exiled a seven-year-old to a dangerous forest because the child was different: the sort of purveyors of ignorant violence who had slaughtered the Klune and killed Hekkabah and maimed Mashie. What they didn't understand, they destroyed.

"Cenzar Esrahaddon?" A man approached from the dark.

"Yes?"

"Good evening to you, sir. I am Bishop Venlin of the Church of Nyphron." The man wore a great smile and pointed at the church on the south end of the plaza. "I have long hoped to meet you."

The bishop was a feeble-looking gent with a broad forehead and sunken eyes. Like some reanimated corpse, he personified exactly the sort of figure no one hoped to witness coming at them out of the dark. The smile was disarming, at least, his words respectful, his tone friendly.

"Why is that?" Esrahaddon asked.

"I've heard so many wonderful things. You're a bit of a celebrity, don't you know?"

"No, I don't," Esrahaddon replied in a flat tone intended to warn off the bishop. He was in no mood to chat, so he walked on by. Then he recalled something, stopped, and turned to face the happy zombie. "Did you speak to the emperor about me? He said you spoke on my behalf—that you *praised* me."

"Oh, indeed I did."

"Why? This is the first time we've ever met. You know nothing about me."

The undead cleric's grin broadened—not at all a good or wholesome look. If Esrahaddon hadn't possessed the power to obliterate the entire square, he most certainly would have been nervous. This was the face of a hungry monster from a children's fairy tale. No, not a face—a mask. Were this a horror story told around a campfire to impressionable youngsters, Esrahaddon would expect the bishop to rip off that smiling visage to reveal the fanged truth beneath. But by then, of course, it would be too late.

"I know that your significant talents are wasted as a nursemaid to a child," the bishop said in a sympathetic voice. "If it were up to me, you'd be appointed governor of Calynia and given a free hand to reform that barbarity of a province."

Esrahaddon peered at him, surprised. He hadn't told that particular objective to many people, yet it was far too specific to be coincidence. "Who have you been speaking to?"

As innocent as fresh water, the bishop rolled his shoulders. "I speak to everyone."

"That must take a ridiculous amount of time."

"Which is why it has taken this long to get to you. My apologies." He offered an odd little pout, as if he were a five-year-old pretending regret for spilling milk.

"And why is that? Is this why you wanted to meet me? To sympathize with my lack of appointment?"

The pouting zombie shook his head. "No. I have a proposal to suggest, but . . ." The bishop looked around the dark plaza. "I was hoping you would be kind enough as to humor an old man and hear me out. My church is just there." He pointed at the gaudy Temple of Novron, whose clean-cut stone declared it as the most recent addition to the square. Marble steps led to columns that held up an entablature topped with a pediment, all of it no more than an elaborate façade hiding the truth that the heart of the church was a hodgepodge of onetime shops and warehouses that had been cobbled together. "Please, allow me to play the host and provide us with a more comfortable . . . and secluded place to talk."

Esrahaddon found himself more intrigued by the bishop's desire to speak privately than anything else. *Why would the head of the Church of Nyphron want to speak to me at all?*

Without waiting for a reply, the bishop set off at a quick pace, waving for him to follow.

"It's not the palace, but we did what we could with what we had," Venlin said as they passed through the façade into the darkened interior. A small, plaster-walled room lit by a single wall sconce oil lamp formed an antechamber at the far end of which were tall double doors. "Real estate is hard to appropriate on the square. It took nearly two decades. This portion used to be a sandal merchant's shop—or was it the broom maker's store . . . I forget now." He moved to the double doors. "This next portion I ordered built myself. My general secretary calls it the *nave*—something to do with ships. Theopol once served on a boat of some sort, I suppose."

Venlin pushed the doors in to reveal a long, empty room with a tiled floor lined with pillars. Constructed from large blocks of heavy stone, the walls were thick, the ceilings low, and there were no windows at all. The place felt less a house of worship and more a fortified burrow. Esrahaddon wondered whether the church was short on funds, as few oil lamps burned, leaving the interior a dark and foreboding place. At the far end was a raised dais where an altar—consisting of a wooden cabinet, three broad doors, and a marble top—supported two candles. Beyond it were two alabaster statues. One depicted a strong, handsome man in the prime of his youth, kneeling, sword in hand. Looming over him was a powerful, larger-than-life figure with a long beard and flowing robes, who was in the act of placing a crown upon the younger man's head.

"Like it?" Venlin asked.

Esrahaddon walked up the nave to get a better look at the statues. "Who are they supposed to be?"

"Our Lord Novron and his father, the god Maribor."

"I've seen sculptures of Emperor Novron—they're all over the city. None look like this."

"I know. Incredible, isn't it? This work of art was created by a talented young man from Alburnia named Burke Thatcher. What you're seeing here is the only accurate depiction. The others are propaganda, pushing the notion that Novron was an elf. You've met the emperor. Does he look remotely like the city statues of Novron? Or does he look more like this?" The bishop sighed as if this was a battle he had fought all too often. "Esrahaddon, you're an educated man. Do you honestly believe that mankind fought a desperate war for years, losing thousands of lives in the hope of throwing off the yoke of elven oppression, only to bow to an elven emperor? Novron is our savior. He showed us their weaknesses, taught mankind how to fight, how to defend, and he taught us the Art of magic that you study today. In fact, he stole it from the elves. Without the Art—as I suspect you've already been informed—mankind would be powerless against another conflict with Erivan."

"Don't you mean *Erivania?*"

"Not if there is another conflict." The bishop continued walking toward a smaller room off to the side. "This is the very threat that caused me to suggest that the Cenzarium seek to establish an Imperial Code of Laws."

"We already have that." Esrahaddon left the white statues and followed the cleric.

"No, we have a set of rules that can be set aside whenever the emperor feels like it. A law is a law by virtue of its supremacy. No one, not even the emperor, can be above it." He led Esrahaddon into what appeared to be a cloakroom, where the bishop set about the task of lighting a candle.

"Venderia," Esrahaddon said, and the candle gained a flame.

Bishop Venlin jerked back, obviously shocked, then caught himself. "Thank you. That must come in very handy. There are two more over there."

Esrahaddon illuminated the little space, revealing a narrow bed and a small table with a single bare wooden chair.

"Already I see the emperor being swayed by the Teshlor Guild against the Cenzars," Venlin went on, taking a seat on the bed as he offered the chair to Esrahaddon.

This isn't his room . . . is it?

"As the head of the church, I usually try to avoid politics, but I see a dangerous threat looming. Did you know that no human army had ever won a battle against the elves before the arrival of Novron? Once, we even thought they were gods. Their life span is so long that no one noticed them aging. Their death rites are so secret, no human had ever seen an elven corpse. They were the firstborn, the Children of Ferrol. In combat, they were feared above all things. There is an old poem that goes:

'They came with hardly a warning,
thousands both beautiful and terrible.
They came on brilliant white horses,
wearing shining gold and shimmering blue.
They came with dragons and whirlwinds,
and giants made of stone and earth;
They came and nothing could stop them.
They are coming still.' "

"Nothing could stand before the elves and their magic. Even without the Art, their speed, eyesight, hearing, balance, and ancient skills are beyond the abilities of man. Only by virtue of overwhelming numbers, Novron's keen leadership, and most of all, the Art, did we prevail." The bishop crossed his legs, intertwined his fingers around his knees, and leaned back. "For a long time, I—like many—believed in a balance of power: Teshlors on one plate, the Cenzarium on the other, and the emperor acting as the fulcrum. But now, the fulcrum is tilting. At this point, I'm positive that if the Teshlors get their way, they will—out of ignorance—strip mankind of its most important defense: magic."

"I wasn't aware the Church of Nyphron condoned the Art," Esrahaddon said.

"Everything not kept in check is bad." Venlin held up a hand as he spoke as if this were part of a sermon, a universal wisdom. "The Art has a terrible addiction to it, a temptation to always try more, to reach further, to explore the outer reaches. This is dangerous, and what our Lord Novron warned against. But honestly, I'd rather chance it than the alternative. I fear another war with the elves is brewing, one we might not win. But the empire will stand a far better chance with magic than without. That's why the Code of Laws is so important. It will help support the fulcrum and keep it from tipping too far."

"And if the emperor refuses?"

"As I've already pointed out, you're an educated man. You must see the benefits that would result from sweeping away the old, now pointless, holdover traditions and replacing them with an empire run by the most educated and gifted leaders that our society can produce."

"Are you suggesting that the Cenzarium lead a revolution against the emperor?"

"I'm saying peace is better than war with the elves. Maintaining that peace is paramount and transcends any one institution. But I am only a cleric of a church. My opinion matters little."

"And you think I can make this happen? Is that why you wanted to talk to me?"

The bishop shook his head. "Of course not. To be truthful, I'm not even certain how we got on this subject."

"Then why did you invite me here?"

"Oh yes! Almost forgot. I wanted to let you know I've lined up a job for Elinya."

This blindsided Esrahaddon like a silent bull. "You did what?"

"It's nothing much, but I spoke to Ingram Evarburton. He's been looking for a suitable home manager. The man owns half of West End and simply doesn't have time to deal with household trifles like managing a staff of cooks and maids. I suggested Elinya. Said it was the least he could do, given that it was his fault she was homeless and destitute."

"I don't think Elinya knows anything about running a—did you say Evarburton, as in Evarburton Textiles? Doesn't he own the Green Chariot Team?"

Venlin nodded. "And three-quarters of the Garment District. He was embarrassed to discover that his business was being used as a front for that awful slavery operation. Once he discovered how kicking the poor woman to the streets had angered the Cenzar who exposed the slavery operation—the same one who is now tutor to the prince—Ingram begged to make things right. I suspect Elinya will have no problems in this new position of hers, no matter how little experience she has."

Esrahaddon realized somewhere along the way that he'd left his mouth hanging open as he merely stared dumbfounded at Bishop Venlin.

PART SIX

A House Divided

YEAR 2120 IR

CHAPTER TWENTY-TWO

Granting Wishes

NEARLY FOUR YEARS LATER . . .
IMPERIAL CAPITAL OF PERCEPLIQUIS, SPRING

"Did you see that?" Hanis Orphe asked.

"Just keep walking," Sadarshakar replied as he noticed his friend slowing.

"He threw a rock at us." Hanis slowed down further.

"Luckily, he has terrible aim. Keep walking."

They were once more traversing the ever-hostile battleground of Imperial Plaza. What Sadarshakar had once viewed as a unique and exciting opportunity to wade through the amazing Crossroads of the World, he now saw as a daily ordeal. Sadarshakar had taken to wearing a cloak with the hood up, but Hanis refused to conceal his heritage.

Hanis stopped.

Pride will kill us yet.

"Let it go, Hanis," Sadarshakar said. "Do you want another beating?"

A man in a white wrap approached. Sadarshakar hoped he might only appear to be coming at them, yet as the distance diminished, so did his optimism.

Hanis's hand went to the dagger that he had gone to the trouble of concealing.

"If you stab them, they'll kill us."

"Maybe that's best." The fatalism in his tone declared a foregone conclusion. Hanis had reached his limit.

Maybe that's what happened to Ronelle and Pryne. Sadarshakar had always had his doubts that the two previous Merredydd councilors had died in a coach accident. *Like Hanis, they probably became fed up, refused to suffer the insults, stood up for themselves against the mob, and were left to bleed out in a sewer somewhere.*

Sadarshakar watched the man approach. *No doubt about it, he's coming straight for us.* Hanis would get them both killed that very afternoon. *Whatever happened to all my dreams? All my plans?*

"Pardon me, councilors," the man in white said to them. "You're the Fhrey representatives to the palace, correct?"

Hanis whirled, chin up, teeth showing. "So what?"

"I've heard the two of you talking on more than one occasion, complaining about the emperor and humans."

How wonderful! A witness. Sadarshakar felt his heart drop into his stomach. Next would come the accusation of sedition, followed by a crowd, and then palace guards. Or perhaps a Teshlor or two would show up. He and Hanis were, after all, practically standing on their porch.

What geniuses we are to talk so openly outside the palace.

Hanis was not deterred. "I stand by what I said! I'm not afraid."

The man came up short, appearing puzzled. Then he smiled and raised his hands as if taming a wild animal. "You misunderstand. I'm on your side. I fully agree with everything I've heard you say."

Surprised and suspicious, Sadarshakar studied this would-be agitator-ally who at first glance did not invite trust. Of medium height and a bit thin, he appeared frail. His hairline had retreated for higher ground, but a single lock, brushed into place, had been ordered to guard the gate. The man's eyes exhibited a sunken darkness as if he were sick with plague or perhaps wearing some morbid makeup: the sort used by actors portraying the risen dead. His jawline and chin were home to a thin growth that Sadarshakar imagined might be a beard.

"Who are you?" Sadarshakar asked.

"I'm Bishop Venlin of the Church of Nyphron." He pointed across the plaza to the four-story tabernacle.

Sadarshakar could still remember when it was a shoddy storefront wedged in between the doors to a broom merchant and a sandal maker. There had been a feeble sign out front with a hand-drawn symbol of a dragon—not the Imperial Dragon's head on a gold shield that adorned the flags and Teshlor emblems—but a crude creature caught in flight. Since then, the church had expanded, swallowing the whole block, and the dragon symbol was etched in marble above the grand doors.

"And you say you're on *our* side?" Sadarshakar asked skeptically. "We are Sadarshakar Sikaria and Hanis Orphe, the Imperial Council delegates from Merredydd."

The man continued to smile and nod.

Believing this wasn't clear enough, Sadarshakar added, "We're Frhey."

"I know."

Sadarshakar looked at Hanis, puzzled.

"Your . . . *church*," Hanis began with contempt, "teaches that we are vile creatures who are imprisoning the emperor against his will and are the source of all that is wrong in the world."

"True, but I'm also the man who convinced Vendis Shipping to sponsor the both of you and provided your house—the one on Estuary. Picked it out myself. Loved the fresco of the swan. And while you might not know it, the thugs who treated you so poorly at the Baths of Barbaree some years back no longer frequent that establishment. I'm not saying it's safe for you to wash there, but I can guarantee those particular individuals will never interrupt anyone's bath again."

The two councilors exchanged dumbfounded expressions.

Sadarshakar felt as if he'd been hit with a bucket of cold riddles. He had no idea if any of that was true, although he and Hanis had found it strange when Vendis Shipping made the offer after everyone else had refused. The townhouse was perfect, and there was indeed a painting of a swan in the dining hall. Sadarshakar recalled snippets of conversations suggesting the previous owners had left unexpectedly—some said unwillingly.

The white-robed enigma before them inspired a myriad of questions. Whether he was telling the truth was but the first layer of these, and beneath the possible lies were more concerning conundrums. To begin with, how did he know Vendis had sponsored them? Such things were not public. *And how is it that Venlin knows about the incident at the baths that took place thirteen years ago, which neither I nor*

Hanis have spoken about to anyone? The foundational level of this mystery mansion remained: Why was the leader of the Church of Nyphron speaking to them at all, if not to harm them in some way?

Sadarshakar folded his arms. "I think I can safely speak for both of us when I say, 'We're confused.'"

"If I were you, I certainly would be. But let us not chat here like old wives gathering our daily allotment of gossip. How about we have a meal at the Pig and Plum, or if you'd rather, we could walk down to the wharf and see what's fresh." He looked around at the sky as if it spoke to him. "Yes, I think the wharf will be better. Come along. My treat."

Sadarshakar shook his head at Hanis, who hesitated only a moment before following the bishop down Ferry Street.

"This isn't a good idea," Sadarshakar whispered as the two followed a little distance behind the cleric. "Might be exactly how Ronelle and Pryne met their end."

"I don't care. I'm done being afraid."

Sadarshakar spotted at least two others following at a distance. Small, unarmed, and dressed in formal wraps, neither appeared threatening. They also made no effort to hide. One noticed Sadarshakar looking at him, smiled, and waved. *They're a happy sort, at least.* "Look, you want to commit suicide, fine. But I'm not so eager to visit Phyre. I still have a few thousand years ahead of me."

"No one is forcing you."

"You are," Sadarshakar said. "I can't abandon my co-consul."

Hanis appeared surprised by this. He thought a moment, then nodded. "It is a bit like being invited into a spider's web, isn't it?"

"And I feel very much the fly."

"Okay," Hanis suggested, "we won't go anywhere that isn't public. No alleys or closed buildings."

"And neither of us will eat or drink anything offered—unless he eats and drinks first."

Hanis nodded. "Agreed."

Venlin led them to Harbor House, an eatery on the docks where the daily menu hung from the porch by their gills.

"Nothing to look at," Venlin apologized, dipping his head under a massive tripletail the size of a small pig, which hung by a hook. "But the food is excellent.

They serve a good lionfish here, but I'd stay away from the urchin." He put a hand to his stomach and made a face.

The bishop found them bench seats at the secluded rear of the elaborate, wind-weathered shack that extended onto the wharf. The smell of fish and the lap of water dominated the atmosphere as a jug of wine was delivered while they were still in the process of sitting down. Venlin poured everyone a cup, and without waiting, he drank from his.

"I realize you have questions, but allow me to cut through the bulk of your concerns by saying I have watched your careers with interest since you first arrived in this city." Holding his cup of wine in both hands, he reclined against the railing beyond which was the green blue of the West Bernum River. "At this moment, you likely presume nefarious intent, but rest assured, this is not the case, quite the opposite. I hope to help."

"Why?" Hanis asked. "Why offer aid when you preach hatred against us?"

"Because we share a common goal. It is no secret that the Church of Nyphron advocates a separation between the races. Humans fought and won a costly war to be free of Fhrey influence, and yet here we are. And I've heard you say you feel Instarya would be better off as an independent realm. It is self-evident that humans and Fhrey would both be happier and healthier without having to accommodate each other. Truth is, humans and Fhrey have nothing in common. The tragedy is that all this could have been avoided if there had been a clean break between us at the end of the Great War. But that was then. No sense wishing for what never happened. The future is our focus."

Sadarshakar was checking the whereabouts of the happy pair of followers, spotting them still out on the street, when a large plate of oysters, mussels, and shrimp arrived. Sadarshakar and Hanis waited, allowing Venlin to take the first bites.

Venlin continued, speaking in between mouthfuls. "Hostilities are rising. The people are growing dissatisfied with this pluralistic society that struggles with its own identity and which set of values it wishes to prioritize. Even the best intentions will fail in an environment that seeks to please all in an empire of such a dichotomy of interests. The truth is that it doesn't need to be this way. We all suffer out of adherence to false traditions. The idea that '*we shouldn't because we haven't*' is absurd. I speak of course of your marvelous plan to establish open communications with Erivania."

Wiping his mouth, Sadarshakar said, "I have the suspicion all of this isn't the result of overhearing a few conversations in the plaza."

"Of course not." Venlin waved a glistening finger at them and was about to say more when the main course arrived. A pair of spiky, tiger-striped fish were set on the table between them. "Oh, you must try this. Lionfish is one of my favorites. Expensive, but excellent."

He took a swallow of wine, then went on. "The Church of Nyphron is everywhere now. In all the provinces, cities, and towns. All the guilds, corporations, professional associations, trade unions, cartels, and secret societies have devoted members on their rolls. Many, such as the Vendis Shipping Corporation, are literally presided over by my followers. Those that resist find themselves the subject of boycotts, or vandalism, and in some rare cases, violence—or at least the threat of it. None of this is my doing, you understand. But my followers are quite enthusiastic and committed to the cause. So you see, I have eyes and ears all over the known world. Little escapes my attention."

"You have spies in the palace?" Hanis asked.

"Absolutely." Venlin tore the head off one of the fish and dug in with his teeth. "Allow me to begin by saying I adore your idea of contacting Erivania, and I believe the two of you are ideal for the task. A pair of pure-blooded Fhrey of esteemed families will have the very best chance of being received warmly. Your youth and passion are infectious and can't help but generate a positive first impression. Once you open the doors, our two societies will finally have a choice. Those Fhrey who would rather not be subjugated by human prejudice and hatred will no longer need to. Fhrey like yourselves will be free to return home to Erivania."

"Home for most of us is Merredydd," Sadarshakar said.

Venlin nodded. "Which, after establishing alliances and trade with Erivania, will enjoy the greater freedom and increased power that comes from not being the only pro-Fhrey vote in the imperial council. The first step toward that goal is to send representatives to the Old World and say hello."

"Except that the emperor doesn't agree." Sadarshakar tasted the fish and was impressed. The dish appeared to be no more than a fancily dressed white fish, but the flavor was rich, spicy—even a bit hot. He'd never even heard of lionfish, but this was indeed a treat. If nothing else, they were getting a fine meal out of the meeting. After the awful start to the day, and as the wine began to kick in, Sadarshakar was in a much better mood, and he could see Hanis felt similarly. The marvel was that the two owed this recompense to, of all people, the leader of the hated Nyphron Church!

"Eight years ago, we proposed the idea and he forbade us to go," Hanis muttered with a mouth full of fish, tearing pan bread with greasy fingers. As he did, a servant appeared, holding a bowl of warm water, his arms draped with towels.

Venlin smiled and nodded. "A rather high-ranking officer in the navy once suggested that when stupidity gets in the way of doing what is right and good that it is better to ask for forgiveness after ultimately succeeding than it is to behave like everyone else and do nothing. I didn't invite you to this meal merely to eat. This is a demonstration of intent and resources. Just as I had this costly meal prepared in advance on the mere assumption you would join me, and just as I arranged for two—shall we say—less-than-popular Fhrey to be treated like princes by one of the most conservative trade corporations in the empire, I will also pledge to fully fund your expedition to Erivania. Take whatever you deem necessary: wagons, chariots, oxen, tents, servants. I don't care. No merchant in this city will charge you. All will know you go with my blessing. Just don't tell the emperor anything until you return with the wonderful news that Erivania sends their regards, hopefully along with tribute."

CHAPTER TWENTY-THREE

Seven's Shadow

IMPERIAL CAPITAL OF PERCEPLIQUIS, SPRING

Cenzar Esrahaddon sat on the plush, cushioned chair in the main room of the Imperial Repository of Tomes and Knowledge, otherwise known as The Farilane Memorial Library, or just The Library, as there was only one in the world. There was also only one high-backed, winged chair in the building. Stationed before the grand hearth, away from the main doors, with a sturdy, private table alongside, the chair was the most coveted seat in the library. The chair's wings were designed—the creator said—to catch and trap the heat of the fireplace. Given that the wingback had been first introduced in the dead of winter, it became an instant hit. The seat was so beloved that it had its own name. Legend held that long ago there had been two such chairs and that collectively they were known as the Owl's Roost because not only did they have "wings," but their popularity kept them occupied all night. When one of the chairs was lost, however—no one was able to tell Esrahaddon how—the widowed chair was apparently too singular for such a grand title and the phrase eroded and condensed over time to the less majestic and more individually appropriate Oswald.

Esrahaddon regularly visited the library but rarely got to sit in Oswald. The chair was always in use, and he was forced to make do with one of the less comfortable couches or the hard seats at the main table. In the winter months, those were the worst because they were in direct line with the front doors. Now with the arrival of spring, Oswald was in less demand. Being nearly midnight, the library—as far as Esrahaddon could tell—was empty.

The night remained warm, leaving the fireplace dark and dormant. Silver candelabras, not up to the task of illuminating the vast building, provided islands of light amid an ocean of darkness. Esrahaddon had been there for hours—time he divided into a pair of epochs that he designated *Before* and *After* to mark his conquest of Oswald. In the Before time, the library had been filled with people. Most were dressed in the colorful but cheap garb of merchant clerks, who kept to the east wing where the records were kept. The rest were richly attired palace officials, who went west into the sections on culture, economics, and history. In the After time—the Oswald Era—the place remained a dark and silent tomb—better for reading, but a bit *too* quiet.

On Esrahaddon's lap lay a big book: *The Migration of Peoples* by Princess Farilane. He'd read it twice already. This time he studied the words as if he faced a test. He didn't. The days of tests were over. It had been a long time since Esrahaddon had graduated to the General Assembly and begun his new career as tutor to Prince Nevrik. Four years had passed since he'd last seen Rappaport and vowed never to set foot in the library. That pledge had persisted only a few months, since his duty to educate the prince had forced his hand. In retrospect, he was embarrassed by his childishness, happy only that it hadn't lasted longer.

His eyes were hurting again.

Esrahaddon gave them a break, switching his focus to the chamber around him. He did this often, and each time he was amazed by what he saw. The walls rose four stories, marvelously crafted into tiers of marble arcades. Towering pillars ringed the coffered dome and supported the great arches joining the arcades to each other. Around the rim, a colonnade of white marble was interspersed with what—from ground level—appeared to be life-sized bronze statues of twelve men, but they were actually twenty feet tall.

A far cry from the dirt-floored hovel where I was once beaten for drawing pictures of birds on a wall.

Great chandeliers of gold hung around the perimeter of the room, but in the After hours, they had been extinguished to save on tallow. Still, the candles in the silver candelabras provided enough illumination for Esrahaddon to make out the words chiseled into the feature wall that greeted all who entered:

I ALSO WANT TO TAKE THIS MOMENT TO EXPLAIN THAT FROM THIS DAY FORTH, READING AND WRITING WILL BE LEGAL IN THE EMPIRE. BOOKS AND SCROLLS WILL BE TREATED WITH CARE AS THE TREASURES THEY ARE. EVERY MEMBER OF THE EMPIRE SHOULD BE ENCOURAGED TO LEARN THIS MIRACULOUS SKILL AND THOSE WHO EXCEL AT IT SHOULD BE HELD IN HIGH REGARD. A GRAND BUILDING — A REPOSITORY, A PROTECTORATE, AND A RESOURCE FOR THE PUBLIC USE OF BOOKS — HENCEFORTH KNOWN AS A LIBRARY — WILL BE CONSTRUCTED IN THE CENTER OF THIS CITY. ANYONE WHO WISHES MAY GO THERE AND READ ANYTHING THEY LIKE. MY PERSONAL COLLECTION WILL FORM THE SEEDS OF THIS BOOK GARDEN THAT WILL, I HOPE, FLOURISH AND GROW.

— PRINCESS FARILANE, FAREWELL ADDRESS, 1880.

The other reason Esrahaddon nested in Oswald was the chair's location, which was at the library's center, in the heart of The Princess Farilane Collection. He was finding her more fascinating with each day.

How late is it? He rubbed his eyes. *I'm falling asleep here.*

He was loath to give up Oswald. *It will likely rain tomorrow. The late crowd will be bigger. No way I'll get him again. But sadly—*

The fireplace ignited.

A powerful blaze fueled only by a month's ash illuminated the whole of the room.

Startled, Esrahaddon peered around one of Oswald's wings. He hoped to see Pasiturn, maybe Offman, or perhaps even Rappaport grinning at him, as it would be the sort of joke she might play. Instead, he was disturbed to find himself alone.

Standing up, Esrahaddon set aside the ancient tome and studied the room. Nothing moved. The place was silent except for the fire that crackled. Then as suddenly as it had started, the fire went out. Likewise, all the candles in the library died, leaving him in total darkness.

It lasted but a second.

The robe came to his aid, filling the space with light: not the warm glow of flickering flame, but the stark white luminance that drained all of color. In that moment, he realized he wasn't alone, or at least he wasn't anymore.

Esrahaddon staggered backward, bumping against Oswald as the light revealed a person standing only a few feet before him. "Elinya?"

The woman stood in a simple white gown, the whole of her appearing ghostly in the robe's eerily pale light. Breaking the pallor was a strange red glow emanating from her necklace pendant.

"Why are you still here?" she asked, her tone urgent, nearing the level of panic.

Esrahaddon couldn't tell if she was frightened or angry, but she was clearly upset. Her eyes were wide, her body held stiff.

"I was just reading."

"Reading?" She glared at him, dumbfounded. "The seven years are over!" She shouted this at him and touched the pendant.

"Elinya, calm down!"

"Today was the first day of spring. You were supposed to go back to Ruby Finn." She began to cry.

"Yes, I know, but why are you so upset?"

Elinya wiped her tears and stared at him with glassy eyes. "Haven't you ever wondered why she didn't kill me?"

"Because you weren't a threat. You were innocent. You—"

"No! I trespassed. That's a crime to her—a crime punishable by death! But she didn't kill me. Do you want to know why? Look!" Elinya pointed at the pendant.

"I see that. It's glowing. Why?"

"Midnight has passed. The last day is over and—"

From somewhere deep in the shadows of the library Esrahaddon heard what he could only define as a growl but not the sort made by any natural animal: too deep, too loud, too malevolent to be of Elan. The sound did more than resonate in his ears. He felt it both physically and—more disturbingly—through the Art. The whole of the marble building resonated with that malicious rumble.

Elinya's expression was no longer a mystery. She was terrified.

Esrahaddon peered into the shadows but saw nothing. "What's going on, Elinya?"

"I can't do it," Elinya apologized, as new tears spilled. She backed away, and as she did, he noticed she held something in her other hand, something she kept hidden behind her. "I'm sorry—I just can't."

The Art was useless for clues. The woman was a blinding light of fear. He could detect nothing else.

A crash startled both of them as in the shadows a freestanding bookshelf toppled. Esrahaddon spotted movement. Something large approached out of the darkness. A vague, shadowy form that appeared loose and fluid whipped between the stacks. Esrahaddon once more heard the growl, then a hiss as a set of three glowing red eyes appeared. They gleamed so brilliantly that they acted like hooded lanterns, revealing the two humans in their stare. One side of Elinya was bathed in the robe's white light, the other cast in red by the thing's gaze.

"Get behind me!" Esrahaddon shouted as the shadow beast let out a triumphant cry.

Elinya ran to his protection as Esrahaddon raised a defensive shield.

The beast slammed against it. The impact shook the library and drove Esrahaddon backward far enough to collide with Elinya. "Sorry," he said. "This thing's powerful."

Esrahaddon sought strength but found little in the cold marble of the library. He groped blindly outside, finding morsels of vitality in the life-energy of passing late-night pedestrians, a spring breeze, and those few street braziers still burning. A lack of options concerned him. Despite being in a city as massive as Percepliquis, on that paved block in the middle of the night, there simply wasn't a lot of power to tap. The problem instantly lost priority when the beast took a massive bite out of the shield.

The creature was an ethereal shadow with little more substance than thick smoke. Out of that dark haze, a head with catlike ears, a short snout, and massive teeth took momentary shape. The mouth opened, bit, and tore away a section of Esrahaddon's defense.

"That's not good," he said to himself, but behind him he heard Elinya whimper.

The creature paused to chew and swallow. Then to Esrahaddon's amazement, the shadow beast grew larger and appeared to gain more substance. This was no illusion. The Art confirmed the thing's increased power.

"That's *definitely* not good."

The creature lunged forward, hitting what was left of the shield. The defense held, but this time Esrahaddon was driven to the floor. Behind him, Elinya screamed.

"Get out of here!" he ordered as he struggled to rebuild his shield.

He had no idea what he was fighting, or how to go about it, and he was quickly realizing the creature was going to win. The best he could do was give Elinya time to escape.

The beast sank fore and rear claws into the magic wall and once more took a bite.

Esrahaddon cursed as again the monster grew bigger and stronger. "I'm feeding the stupid thing."

With all four claws, the beast tore apart the remaining defense.

"Run!" Esrahaddon shouted, and summoning what reserves he had left, he blasted the shadow creature with what he guessed was enough raw power to obliterate half a mountain.

Instead of killing the thing, the monster inflated, growing so large it filled the chamber. Its head reached near the top of the dome. The creature lost its smoke quality, becoming solid—a giant hairy beast with three blazing eyes, clawed paws, and saber fangs.

"Ah, for the neglect of the Missing God!" Esrahaddon swore as one massive claw crushed Oswald into splinters. The three eyes shone their blood-red light on him.

Needing no more encouragement, Esrahaddon bolted for the exit. Elinya hadn't run, but she did so now and in the wrong direction. The insane woman charged *at* the beast.

"Elinya!"

He finally saw what was in her hand—a dagger.

No! Elinya—no! Esrahaddon had no idea what the monster was, but he had just hit it with everything he had and only made the thing happier. A dagger—a tiny blade in the hand of a slight woman—didn't stand a chance.

Before he could summon resources, before he managed any protection at all, the now-furry giant lunged at Elinya. Still charging, she held the dagger before her with both hands.

At the collision, Elinya went sprawling across the floor. Driven from her grip, the dagger flew, ringing as it hit the floor. Both slid, spiraling across the polished tiles.

The monster howled in rage. Lifting a paw, it looked at it, then howled again. A moment later, the creature staggered.

"Elinya? Are you all right?"

Still on her back, she raised her head and nodded.

The monster wavered, stumbled. Then the towering furry brute collapsed. The whole of it dispersed like dust when it hit the ground, creating a gust of wind that blew back Esrahaddon's hair.

Reclaiming power from that expulsion, Esrahaddon refilled his Artistic coffers. "Venderia!" he shouted, and every candle in the library caught fire, revealing the entirety of the chamber. But all that could be seen was a fallen stack of books, a shattered chair, Elinya getting to her feet, and the dagger that lay twenty feet away, still spinning.

Esrahaddon moved to pick it up.

"Don't!" Elinya said. "There might still be poison on it."

"Poison?" He watched her rush over, clutching a cloth in her hand.

"It can't be seen, so I can't even tell if it's just on the blade or also on the handle. I don't want to take a chance. It's pretty deadly." She wrapped up the weapon.

Esrahaddon stood befuddled. He looked at Elinya, at the dagger as she carefully picked it up with the cloth, and then at the place where the giant shadow beast had exploded into nothingness. He ran a hand through his hair and shook his head. "Okay, I got nothing. What happened?"

She shrugged.

"What do you mean?" He shrugged back. "What was that thing? Why were you here? Why do you have a poisoned dagger? How did a dagger—poisoned or not—kill *that* thing?"

"It's special poison. Magic can't stop it."

"Special poison? Where did—what are you, a secret assassin or something?"

"No! Ah, I mean, well, I guess—I don't know. You see—"

The glow of the pendant faded, and she looked down.

"What's that mean?"

"I don't know. It turned red at midnight, then glowed when I got near here. That's how I found you. But I don't know—"

The pendant flared as the necklace tightened, the silver chain shrinking around her throat like a noose. She dropped the dagger, and her hands came up, clawing desperately at the jewelry.

Esrahaddon reacted more on instinct than plan. With a snap of his fingers, the chain broke and fell to the ground. The glow of the gemstone faded to blue, but around Elinya's neck was a thin red line where the chain had started to cut into her skin.

Another few seconds and it would have severed her head from her neck.

Elinya stood wide-eyed, repeatedly swallowing as she rubbed her throat. Staring at the chain, she began to shake, then with a cry, she kicked the pendant away like a dead mouse.

When she burst into sobs, Esrahaddon gathered her up in his arms. "It's okay. It's over." He looked around at the room, searching for evidence this was true, but felt his heart sink when he heard footsteps. *What now?*

The night librarian trotted in but stopped when he saw Oswald's corpse, the fallen shelving, and scattered books. He spotted them. "What are you doing?"

"Honestly? I have no idea. As far as I'm concerned, this is one big riddlebag of gallimaufry."

Esrahaddon was exhausted by the time he and Elinya reached the Cenzarium. It was only a bit more than five city blocks away, but it felt like the other side of the world. The battle with the shadow monster had weakened him. He felt tired and a bit groggy. Esrahaddon had never used that much power before—and it had been all him, no help from his surroundings. Having no idea what was going on, and unsure whether it was over, he sought the best sanctuary he could find, bringing Elinya along. No way was he going to let her out of his sight, not now.

Once they were safely through the big doors and inside the rotunda, he said, "Tell me what you know." He held one of her hands, while in her other she still clutched the poisoned blade—carefully wrapped. "Where did you get the dagger?"

"Ruby Finn."

He'd already guessed, so no surprise there. "She gave you the pendant, too?"

Elinya nodded, her eyes red from crying. She looked as exhausted as he felt.

Finally safe, Esrahaddon was able to think about more than mere survival. His mind reran events and landed on two standouts: *"Haven't you ever wondered why she didn't kill me?"* he remembered Elinya saying. And also, *"I can't do it."* When she said those words, he'd barely registered them because at the time they didn't make sense. Now he thought he understood.

"I have no choice about killing, merely whom I kill," Ruby had said. *"And if it's not you, it's the other one."*

But if it's not the other one, it's me.

"You were supposed to use that dagger to kill me, weren't you? That's why it's covered in a *special*, magic-resistant poison: the sort I can't save myself from. If I didn't return to Ruby Finn by midnight tonight, the first day of spring, you were supposed to do the deed. Am I right? That's why she let you live—because you promised to be her assassin."

Elinya's lower lip trembled, her eyes taut. "But only if you failed to fulfill your vow," she countered. "I thought you would. Any good man would keep their word. But you—you're beyond good. You came from nowhere and saved me from the forest. You took me away from that horrible village. You found me a new home, a job. Then when I was locked in that wagon, you saved me again, me and all those others bound for slavery. And when I lost my job, when I was about to lose my home—again you appeared at the last minute. But that time you didn't merely save me, you gifted me a whole new life as mistress of a wealthy estate! Esrahaddon . . . you're—you're my hero, my savior, my magical guardian. I actually pray to you at night and believe you can hear me. So when the pendant turned red, when I was supposed to . . ." She hesitated, then swallowed the words that should have come next. "I took the dagger, I tracked you down, but . . . I couldn't do it. I'd rather kill myself." She bit her lip, then looked into his eyes. "But why? Why didn't you fulfill your vow to Ruby Finn?"

Esrahaddon took a breath through his nose and straightened his shoulders. "I was, ah . . . I was busy."

"Busy?" She stared at him incredulously.

"Um, I was nervous. It's ah . . . it's . . ." He looked at his feet. "Okay, sure, I admit it. I was scared. Happy? There you have it. Your *wondrous hero* is a coward." He took a breath and faced her again. "I fought just the servant of a riva once, and it wasn't pretty. I should have died twice over. Still not sure why I'm alive. Rivas are just about the scariest thing still in the world. Even Ruby Finn, who is wildly more powerful than I am, needs help. *My* help. That doesn't make me feel confident. Not even a little bit. So yeah, I was hoping she'd forget or not be able to get to me here, or maybe Mileva Hitartheon might even just drop dead. You never know. Stranger things have happened. I mean, a giant shadow monster just attacked us in the imperial library. Nobody expected that. I sure didn't." He was talking fast—talking too much because he was tense: another inherited trait from Niblick, which just got him remembering.

"Rivas tried to destroy the world. Obviously, Elan is still here, but they took out a sizable chunk. Fun group of guys, let me tell you. And here I bet you thought the whole world was that little cow manure village of yours. But if you manage to beat the odds and live, boy, are you in for a surprise. You know they don't actually kill you, right? I mean, they do, but they keep your soul locked up in their pile."

Elinya didn't say anything. She only nodded.

The silence hurt.

For years, Esrahaddon had seen her as an ordinary villager like the ones he remembered from Haddon. She was a symbol of an unpleasant, embarrassing past that he wanted to bury and forget. He had never once considered how she might see him. *She prayed to me?* That both disturbed and made him feel horrible. Not only had she thought *way* too highly of him, Esrahaddon had also managed to destroy that beautiful, fragile fantasy before he ever knew it existed.

"I'm sorry," he offered.

She shook her head. "I didn't keep my word, either."

"Thanks for that, but where I was a coward, you were brave, and now we're both in trouble."

Elinya looked around the darkened chamber. They stood below the dome's oculus, in the very spot where Esrahaddon had stood when anointed with the title of *Cenzar*. "Are we safe here?"

"This place does have enchantments protecting it, but I honestly don't know if it can stop Ruby. She might be outside right now conjuring who knows what. We need to talk to someone."

"Who?"

"Maybe everyone. And until I have a plan, I don't want you out of my sight. We both have targets on our backs, and a very serious hunter on our trail."

CHAPTER TWENTY-FOUR

The Story Retold

"Where is this pendant now?" Isilpor-Sond asked. Like everyone assembled, she looked groggy after having been roused from sleep.

Esrahaddon had started with her; stopping him part way, Isilpor-Sond had called the rest. She hadn't sounded a full alert, merely woke the Council of Elders, or at least the ones who were in residence. Each province had an appointed elder, all of whom made the pilgrimage to Percepliquis once a year for Full Assemblies. But at that moment there were only the three: Isilpor-Sond, Offman, and Yolric. All of them had been sound asleep. Now they gathered under the dome, seated on a circle of mismatched chairs dragged from nearby rooms.

"The pendant is at the library," Esrahaddon said. "I assume."

"You assume?"

"We were in a bit of a hurry. I wasn't dotting every *i* on our way out. Did I mention the twenty-foot fanged shadow beast that ripped apart my shield and guzzled enough raw power to have destroyed the entire city?"

"Let's not exaggerate," Offman said. The old man, always so poised, looked rattled to have been shaken out of bed.

"I'm not."

"You already said how tapped out you were. No resources available, remember?"

"I pulled from myself," Esrahaddon explained.

Offman made a dismissive sputtering. "No one has that kind of power, and it only hurts your story to claim you do."

My story? He thinks I'm lying?

"This isn't a pissing contest, boys." Isilpor-Sond pushed her way back into the discussion. She focused on Elinya, who shrank away into her chair, difficult to do given that she'd chosen the most uncomfortable seat—a hard wooden thing. She looked scared. Being grilled in the middle of the night by senior members of the Cenzarium, most of whom treated her like a suspect in a murder trial, didn't encourage verbosity.

"What made you think the poison would work on this beast?" Isilpor-Sond asked.

"Nothing." Her voice was that of a bashful insect.

"Then how did you know it would work?"

"I didn't."

Offman stood up and violently swept an arm, making his long sleeves flutter. "Then why did you attack it?" His tone was biting—an accusation illustrated by sarcasm.

He doesn't believe either of us.

"Offman, please," Isilpor-Sond was stern. "I know you like your sleep, but this could be important."

Could be? Even she isn't convinced. I wonder how all of them will feel when a giant shadow beast cracks the dome like an egg.

"I'm merely pointing out a lie when I hear it. If this woman didn't think the poison would work—as she says—she'd be knowingly committing suicide by charging the monster."

"Yes," Elinya said.

"Yes, what?" Isilpor-Sond asked.

"Yes, I expected to die." She refused to look at any of them, staring at her hands folded in her lap. "Ruby said she would kill me if I didn't do what she asked. I didn't, so I thought the beast was there for me. If I died, I thought Esrahaddon would be safe."

"You tried to sacrifice yourself for Cenzar Esrahaddon?" Isilpor-Sond asked.

Elinya nodded.

"Why?" Offman asked, that bass-note of skepticism still playing in his voice.

This time Elinya remained silent, eyes down, mouth not merely shut, but sealed.

"It doesn't matter," Isilpor-Sond said. "If this is true, then Ruby Finn has become active."

"It means nothing of the sort," Offman declared. "Honestly, Sond, I'm stunned that you are giving any credence to this. Even if something did happen at the library, why pin it on Ruby Finn?"

Isilpor-Sond looked at Esrahaddon. "Tell them what you just told me, the rest of the story—the part you left out seven years ago."

Esrahaddon recapped his adventures with Lysander and Griffith, which was interrupted thrice by an impatient Offman, who, like the rest, had heard most of the tale before. Each time, Isilpor-Sond frowned and motioned for him to calm down and listen.

"Then she asked me to take the horses and Elinya. In seven years' time, I was to go with Ruby to Borappathin and destroy Riva Mileva Hitartheon." Esrahaddon sat back and waited.

Isilpor-Sond waited, too. She was watching their reactions.

Yolric had none. He continued to stare at Esrahaddon much the way he had since the meeting began. While Esrahaddon found a familiar strangeness in Isilpor-Sond, and a strange familiarity in Offman, Cenzar Master Yolric was a different thing altogether. With his stately mane of white, he had the appearance of an elderly lion in repose, but fierce eyes hinted at something more. Studying him was quite the same as peering into a night sky and trying to conceive the whole of it; at first glance, contrast was all that stood out, pinpricks of light set against darkness, but closer scrutiny revealed an infinite depth that Esrahaddon was certain few ever noticed.

That night, beneath the grand dome of the Cenzarium, Esrahaddon took special note of Yolric because Cenzar Yolric took special notice of him.

Unlike Offman, who spent most of his time at the palace, or Isilpor-Sond, who wandered the city and farms, Yolric was never anywhere, and Esrahaddon had little interaction with him. The Cenzar master was spoken of highly and often by the other members as being *the* master of lore and was considered by many to be the most powerful Cenzar alive—perhaps the greatest who'd ever lived. In the eight years Esrahaddon had been at the Cenzarium, he'd only ever seen Yolric at his graduation. Back then, the legendary master had looked through Esrahaddon as if he hadn't existed. Now standing under the dome with Offman and Isilpor-Sond, Yolric appeared spellbound by him as if the master of lore had never seen anything so strange.

Offman, however, silently exploded. His eyes went wide, and his mouth dropped open in shock. Esrahaddon had seen a growing anxiety as he spoke, but it was the name Mileva Hitartheon that overflowed the Cenzar master's cup.

"You can't be serious!" Offman declared as if willing it to be so.

"The seven years have passed," Isilpor-Sond said. "And now Ruby is sending Esrahaddon a not-so-subtle reminder of his pledge."

"You call *that* a *reminder?*" Esrahaddon asked.

Offman was shaking his head, but Esrahaddon didn't know why. His mouth remained open, but no more words came out. His gaze began roving about the room like a dog off a leash. Soon his feet followed suit as he started to wander across the marbled floor.

At least the old man seems to have lost his doubt.

Isilpor-Sond focused on Yolric. "What are *your* thoughts?"

The master of lore, who hadn't once ceased to stare at Esrahaddon, replied, "Where did you get that robe?"

"Delightful, isn't it?" Isilpor-Sond said. "I've been curious about it myself, but—"

"Where did you get it?" Yolric's tone stiffened to the point of incrimination, as the old lion's hair seemed to rise.

"It was a gift."

"From whom?"

"My mother . . . mostly. A birthday gift of sorts."

Yolric began to shake his head. "You're telling me the edges. Fill in the gaps."

The ancient master of lore, previously so patient and described by so many as affable and easy-going, glared at Esrahaddon with such cold intensity that he nearly raised a shield.

"The one who raised me, Hekkabah, was a priestess of Uberlin. She was told to give me this robe. She took it from Rex Nexziria, then crossed the sea to Calynia, found me in the jungles, and bequeathed it the day she died."

"Who told her to give it to you?"

Esrahaddon hesitated. He felt the story was already pushing the boundaries of credibility. Answering that question would shatter what little remained. Offman would certainly declare him insane, and he might take Isilpor-Sond with him. Still, under the demanding gaze of the old master, Esrahaddon saw little choice. "Uberlin."

"Uberlin?" Offman spouted, following his eruption with a nervous laugh. "The Lord of Darkness? God of Evil?"

Esrahaddon nodded. "That's what she said."

"And you believed her?"

"Yes. She was my mother."

Isilpor-Sond circled Esrahaddon, studying the robe. "It is a remarkable thing. There's power in it."

Esrahaddon shrugged. "It lights up. Changes colors, too. I don't know how, but when I can't see, the robe glows. I think the different hues mean something, but I'm not sure."

Isilpor-Sond laughed. "Esra," she said, "I can't say the true nature of this garment, but I can tell you it's more than a colorful lantern."

Yolric came to his feet. "He wears the Gry Erlikon—Robe of Light." Yolric said these words in a deadly serious tone. "Regalia of state, imperial habit of Rex Uberlin. Once feared as the uniform of the greatest tyrant the world has ever known, I don't believe this has been seen beneath the sun since the Aesirian Age."

Isilpor-Sond backed up a step to reassess, while Offman appeared more perplexed than ever.

Esrahaddon looked down at himself, placing a hand on his chest. "It's just a robe."

"That's just a robe like Ruby Finn is *just* an Artist, or you're just a boy from a backwater village." Yolric shook his head. "I didn't even notice you. Wouldn't have, except for the robe." He shook his head, those eyes of his sweeping the room, cutting through it. "This can't be a mistake. He couldn't have announced you with any more fanfare than if he had lined up the stars to spell out your name."

"Who?"

Yolric looked at him with obvious exasperation. "Uberlin, of course."

All three stared at the Lore Master.

"We need to speak to the emperor," Yolric said. He glared at Offman. "Immediately."

Immediately turned out to be five and a half hours later, since Offman was unable to arrange an audience before the sun had risen and the emperor of the world had eaten breakfast.

They weren't alone.

Esrahaddon had assumed that a private consultation with the emperor was as possible as Offman impressing him with competence. Neither happened, which did not surprise him, but Offman displayed irritation when, in addition to the normal guards, he saw Gaylord Sire standing alongside the throne.

The emperor hadn't changed much from the last time they'd met, nearly four years before, though he did exhibit that dull, stiff expression seen in those for whom rising early was uncommon. He yawned a good deal and rubbed his face as if trying by force to wake himself up. The rest of them likely presented a far less alert countenance. None had slept.

Emperor Nareion surveyed the room with a perplexed look. "Master Isilpor-Sond, Cenzar Master Yolric, Advisor Offman, my son's tutor Cenzar Esrahaddon, and . . ." He peered past all of them. "And who's that?"

"Elinya, Your Imperial Eminence," Offman answered for all. "She's unimportant."

Esrahaddon was never able to clearly assign a label as to why he hadn't warmed to Offman, but comments such as that played a big role.

"Then why is she here?"

"Because she can't be left alone," Esrahaddon spoke up, once more drawing a nasty look from Gaylord. Nothing, it seems, had changed between them. Esrahaddon gestured at the emperor, saying, *he asked.*

"I assume we will learn more about that soon. But this is a strange group," Nareion said. "And an odd hour. I'm guessing this is important, and by *important,* I mean *unpleasant.*"

"Ruby Finn is active," Isilpor-Sond announced. "And she's taken an interest in Cenzar Esrahaddon."

"An *interest?* Does this have something to do with his visit to the Forbidden Forest?"

She nodded and asked Esrahaddon to explain his lapse in reporting for the third time. Having had practice, he'd pruned the tale down to a concise presentation that, while it never made him look good, no longer gave the appearance he was a total bumbling idiot.

"Why didn't you tell us this years ago?" Gaylord barked.

"I was sort of hoping to forget the whole thing. I had no intentions of going back to that forest. Couldn't, as imperial law forbids it."

Gaylord wasn't satisfied and was about to say more when the emperor spoke first. "What's a *riva*, exactly?"

Esrahaddon nearly repeated his Niblick quote but bit his tongue and waited for one of the others to explain. All of them looked at Yolric.

"They were the generals of Uberlin's army," the Lore Master replied.

This was the first time Esrahaddon had witnessed Yolric in the emperor's presence, and he noted that the Lore Master's tone lacked the formal deference of the others but failed to draw the same ire from Gaylord.

"Uberlin?" Nareion asked. "Isn't that supposed to be the mythical god of evil or something?"

"He's not a myth. Eons ago, the people of the world lived perhaps not so much in harmony but in peace. Then Uberlin set himself up above everyone else—demanded that all others kneel before him. Those who refused were tortured and killed. When some fought back, Uberlin invented war, and all at once, evil was let loose on the face of Elan. That conflict destroyed the Old World and drove those who survived west." With a wave of his hands, Yolric indicated the throne room as evidence.

"But these rivas, these generals of Uberlin, they would be long dead. So who—"

"No, they are not," Yolric interrupted. This was too much, and Gaylord's eyes flared, but still the knight held his tongue. "The rivas remain—two, at least."

The emperor appeared not to notice the disrespect, asking, "How is that possible?"

"Uberlin chose his military leaders from the greatest sorcerers of that age. Trained by Uberlin himself, they were frighteningly powerful, so much so that they ultimately found the means to defeat death. This comes at a terrible cost. Their bodies are still of Elan and cannot avoid inevitable decay. To fight this decline and maintain a vessel suitable to contain their spirit, they must consume others of their kind."

"Other rivas?"

"Other *people*. By consuming their flesh and imprisoning their bones, the rivas deny these victims entrance to Phyre, and in turn, they control these spirits, which they harness as slaves to protect and revitalize themselves. But decay is an ongoing march, and always more victims are required."

"I recall this creature," Nareion said. "A legend, a wives' tale, something I heard as a child, only it wasn't called a riva, but something else."

"A *raow*," Yolric supplied.

The emperor snapped his fingers. "Yes, that's it."

"They are very similar, except the difference between a raow and a riva is not unlike the difference between an eight-pound house cat and a six-hundred-pound tiger. And keep in mind—a single raow was known to wipe out whole villages and turn cities into empty towns."

Nareion chuckled. "You make it sound as if it would take an army to defeat one."

"No, not at all," Yolric replied. "An army would undoubtedly lose such a contest."

"I don't believe a word of it, Your Imperial Eminence," Gaylord declared. "This is all a bunch of Cenzarium rubbish. They seek to frighten you with fairy tales. This *Borappathin* that the Cenzars speak of is none other than Castell Blythium, a legion outpost. The empire has held that fortification for over a thousand years—and we've never had a problem with it."

"Princess Farilane did," Esrahaddon said. "According to her writings, she discovered corruption at Blythium on an unprecedented scale."

"Corruption in the legion is as common as a mosquito in a swamp." Gaylord belittled the idea just as much with his manner as his argument, shaking his head and grimacing. "What she didn't find was an all-powerful demon-thing."

"But the mere presence of such a creature—something as evil and powerful as Yolric describes—could substantially poison men's minds," Isilpor-Sond said, "warp their values and influence decisions. And to Esrahaddon's point, Castell Blythium has always been . . . *strange*."

"Perhaps that would make some sense if such a thing as a riva were there—if, in fact, such a thing exists at all." Gaylord dismissed the diminutive woman with a smirk. "But if it did, how do you account for such a thing going unnoticed for *thousands* of years?"

Esrahaddon watched, amazed at Isilpor-Sond's self-control as she responded pleasantly as if Gaylord had just flattered her. "I think it's obvious the riva somehow hides itself."

"Why? Why would it do that? If it is so powerful, why would it even have a care?"

Isilpor-Sond thought a moment. "I don't know."

"It hardly appears to matter," the emperor said, then shifted in his seat and leaned forward. "Tell me, Cenzar Esrahaddon, what is your plan? What do you intend to do with this riva?"

Reading the emperor was difficult. Esrahaddon's first impression suggested a simplistic, mostly human man with all the typical foibles associated with a person in such a powerful position: arrogance, pride, ignorance, callous indifference. But the Art and his own reasoning suggested otherwise—so had his time with Nevrik. The prince was no ordinary child but rather a deep well of unplumbed complexities. Even after four years, Nevrik continued to surprise Esrahaddon. A son such as that was unlikely to rise from a classic, stock ruler of a father. Just as Nevrik wrapped himself in layers of lesser truths, Esrahaddon suspected that Nareion also presented a false front. Flattery would likely fail. And while disrespect wasn't tolerated, the emperor disapproved of submissiveness.

In the face of uncertainty, the truth, blunt and unvarnished, always seemed the best bet. "Ruby Finn wants my help in killing this riva." Even as he said it, he second-guessed his choice. In this case, the truth sounded ridiculous. "And," he looked at Elinya, "I gave my word."

"I see." Nareion frowned. Still watching Esrahaddon closely, he asked, "And Cenzar Master Yolric, how formidable would you say this creature is?"

"Rivas are beings of the ancient world. In their day, the likes of Mileva Hitartheon commanded armies far greater than the imperial legions, ruled cities that would put Percepliquis to shame, and wielded power unimaginable."

The emperor pursed his lips and nodded. "Did you hear that? Given what Cenzar Master Yolric just said, dear tutor-of-my-son and four-year-experienced Cenzar, how is it you expect to . . . *kill* this thing?"

Esrahaddon sighed. "I have no idea. I simply don't have a choice. As far as I see it, I either go and die or stay and die. The only difference is that at least if I go, Elinya should be safe."

"If only it were that easy." The emperor shook his head. "But I have an empire to protect. If I allow you to go and attack this creature, that would most certainly invite retaliation. If this thing is as powerful as Master Yolric says, not only is it a foregone conclusion that you and Finn will fail, but your actions will also expose this empire to a serious threat. At present, this *unimaginable power*—if it exists—has been content to sleep inactive in a distant outpost. So either it isn't there—as Gaylord suggests, which means nothing need be done—or it is, and it would be foolish to poke it."

"If I don't go, Your Imperial Eminence," Esrahaddon said. "Elinya and I will die. Keeping me here is a death sentence for both of us."

"The Cenzarium can't protect their own against a single renegade?" Gaylord asked with unabashed contempt.

Hearing it, Esrahaddon noticed how similar Gaylord Sire was to Offman. Like a reflection in a mirror, the two were exact opposites, flipped versions of the other yet still the same.

"Ruby Finn is a remarkably powerful rogue," Isilpor-Sond explained. "The effort to remove her as a threat has always been deemed a cure worse than the disease. Left to herself—just as with this Mileva Hitartheon—she hasn't been a threat."

"Until now," the knight jabbed.

Isilpor-Sond looked at the warrior, puzzled. "Are you agreeing or disagreeing with me, now? I can't tell."

"Emperor Nareion," Yolric said, "both Ruby Finn and Mileva Hitartheon pose a serious threat to this empire. While you can forbid Esrahaddon from challenging this riva, you have no authority over Ruby Finn, as she has never granted you any. This isn't a choice between gambling and letting sleeping dogs lie. The decision before you is merely which adversary to fight. You can allow Esrahaddon to go with Ruby Finn and risk the *possibility* of starting a dangerous war with a powerful enemy, or accept the *certainty* of open warfare with Ruby Finn. In some respects, it's less a choice of who to fight and more of where you want the battlefield to be. Mileva is on the distant frontier, but Ruby is on your doorstep. Chances of winning a conflict with Ruby Finn are better than going to war with a riva, but both will be hazardous."

Emperor Nareion got to his feet, and descending the steps, faced Yolric. "Your counsel has always been remarkable. Having you refuse to be my full-time advisor is irksome, but having you here has always been invaluable. So, Master Yolric, advise me now. What path do you believe the wisest?"

"It is better to have a rogue Artist on your doorstep than a riva on the horizon. Let Ruby Finn and Esrahaddon eliminate that threat for you."

"But by your own admission, they have no chance."

Yolric nodded. "This is true. Alone, Mileva Hitartheon will destroy them and add their bones to her pile, but they won't be going alone."

"Are you suggesting I send a legion?"

"No. As I said, an army won't defeat her. They would only get in the way."

"Then what?"

"I will go with them."

The emperor tilted his head in surprise. "Master Yolric"—the emperor smiled—"no offense, but you're not a young man. I would go so far as to suggest that for a human, you're close to ancient."

"Yes . . . yes, I am. And so is Mileva Hitartheon."

Before any more was said, it was clear from the look on Emperor Nareion's face that his mind was set. Esrahaddon felt no relief. Instead, he knew his first foot had slipped into the grave. Having Master Yolric along was little comfort, as Esrahaddon wondered if he'd survive the trip, much less be an asset in a confrontation with one of five beings that had nearly destroyed the world. He felt confident that the old master's reputation was largely honorary. Esrahaddon had stood beside the blazing sun of Ruby Finn's power; by contrast, Yolric was a weak candle.

Everyone waited for Nareion to announce his decision to approve the mission. Once he did, Gaylord Sire exploded.

"Your Imperial Eminence! You can't accept this blatant manipulation."

"What are you talking about?" Nareion asked.

"Four sorcerers burst into your throne room unannounced, and you grant them whatever they want? You're playing into their hands, giving them the freedom to rendezvous with a notorious and powerful criminal!"

"What are you suggesting, Gaylord?"

"I'm saying there is a reason we always pair a Cenzar with a Teshlor on provincial circuits. Checks and balances, Your Imperial Eminence. This so-called mission staffed by such a partisan party reeks of subversion."

"So you are advocating that I also include a Teshlor in their number?"

By the look on Gaylord's face, this was not at all what he was saying. Esrahaddon didn't need the Art to know the knight believed he'd just witnessed an insurrection. Gaylord was likely under the impression that the Cenzarium had, before his very eyes, bewitched the emperor into agreeing to the first step toward the total overthrow of the empire. He couldn't just stand there silently watching. But he also couldn't accuse the emperor of being an idiot.

Gaylord hesitated for so long that Esrahaddon thought the knight's mind might have locked up for good, but then he took a breath and said, "Yes, Your Imperial Eminence. I believe it would be prudent to have at least one Teshlor accompany them."

For the first time, Esrahaddon was a bit impressed with Gaylord. This was the best the Knight Advisor could hope for. He saw it and had the intelligence to restrain himself.

"Do you have a suitable candidate?" the emperor asked.

"I, ah . . ."

He clearly did not. The premier Teshlor Knight and representative of the entire guild was winging this.

In a burst of inspiration, Esrahaddon spoke up. "What about Jerish?"

"Jerish Grelad?" Nareion asked.

"Yes, Your Imperial Eminence. I've been working with him these last four years. We already have a rapport, and he's available."

"He's not. He's my son's tutor."

"Just as I am. I don't suspect we'll be gone that long. Nevrik will manage. Probably appreciate the break."

"And if you die?"

"Then *two* new tutors can be appointed. Checks and balances, Your Imperial Eminence. We wouldn't want your son's education being too one-sided."

The emperor looked at Gaylord. "Jerish is young and untested in the field."

"We are the same in this respect," Esrahaddon said. "Graduated on the same day. Assigned our first tasks at the exact same moment. You remember, don't you, Gaylord? You were there."

Esrahaddon guessed it wasn't proper to address an imperial advisor by his first name, but his inner Niblick was clawing to get out. He was rewarded by the sight of the emperor fighting down a smile.

The knight wasn't pleased, but it was more a general concern than a specific one. He'd lost the battle and knew it. Sighing, he nodded. "Jerish is a fine example of a knight, an upstanding representative of the guild."

"That concludes it, then," the emperor said. "Esrahaddon, Jerish, and Master Yolric will travel to the Forbidden Forest and make contact with Ruby Finn."

"Elinya will be coming as well," Esrahaddon said.

The emperor instantly lost whatever goodwill Esrahaddon had built with him. Nareion folded his arms and glared. "Are you assuming rule of this empire? Is what Gaylord Sire suggests true?"

Esrahaddon shook his head. "I honestly have no idea what the Knight Advisor is suggesting, and I am not usurping your authority—merely stating a fact. Ruby Finn is intent on killing Elinya because I failed to return on time. The imperial library was nearly destroyed as a result. I cannot abandon her until I settle matters with Ruby."

"You cannot or will not?"

"Feel free to choose whichever you prefer, Your Imperial Eminence, but this is not negotiable."

"Negotiable?" Nareion's eyes widened.

"Please, Your Imperial Eminence." Isilpor-Sond stepped in. "Cenzar Esrahaddon is exhausted. None of us have slept in quite some time. He also barely survived an assassination attempt only a few hours ago. This woman, Elinya, saved his life while risking her own. It is understandable, is it not, that he feels an overwhelming debt to her? I suspect even the Knight Advisor can understand such an obligation. Honor demands it, does it not?"

Gaylord refused to agree, but he also passed up the opportunity presented to him.

"Please, Your Imperial Eminence," Isilpor-Sond went on, "forgive a young man his passion to do what is right."

Emperor Nareion stared hard at Esrahaddon. He shifted his glance briefly to Isilpor-Sond, then back. "Be careful, Esrahaddon. I sense a willfulness in you, one that is certain to result in trouble."

Esrahaddon didn't say it, but he came so very close. He clenched his teeth to trap his inner Niblick: *Oh, I think that ship left the dock decades ago.*

CHAPTER TWENTY-FIVE

Training Lessons

Elinya continued to follow directly behind Esrahaddon. No amount of coaxing would persuade her to walk alongside him. She followed as if they were back on horses in the Forbidden Forest, likely feeling that way as he led her through the palace corridors. What had become a mundane workplace for Esrahaddon would be just as shocking as a magical spring within a winter wood to Elinya—just as frightening, too. All of it had to be.

They were alone.

Offman had stayed in the throne room, attending to the day's other imperial business. Isilpor-Sond and Yolric had begun a conversation in earnest as they left the throne room together. No one had said anything about departure time, but as this was *his* endeavor, Esrahaddon guessed that would be *his* decision. And given that Ruby might send another *reminder* at any moment, he had decided to leave as soon as possible. Yolric was likely gathering his things. Elinya probably didn't have any—nothing suitable for a cross-country trip, at least. And Isilpor-Sond—if she were smart—was already assembling the necessary horses and gear they would need. And Isilpor-Sond was very smart.

Only one thing remained.

"What are you doing here?" Jerish asked, pointing a wooden sword at Esrahaddon. The Teshlor stood over the fallen figure of Nevrik like a would-be, but weapon-poor, assassin.

"Am I early?" Esrahaddon feigned ignorance as he studied the new obstacle course the knight had set up, consisting of posts and dangling stuffed sacks. While they shared the Vault of Days as a location to teach Nevrik, they were rarely in the room together. Jerish had mornings and Esrahaddon afternoons. Most of the barbarian toys were put away in a corner by the time he arrived.

The Knight Tutor, dressed casually in a cloth tunic, frowned as he lowered the point of his false blade to his side and extended a hand to help the prince up.

"Given that I haven't slept"—Esrahaddon stretched—"it's a little hard to tell."

"Perhaps you ought to introduce us to your . . . *guest with a dagger?*" Jerish asked, looking beyond him at Elinya, who remained near the entrance, holding the knife and the cloth with both hands.

"Do you *still* have that thing?" Esrahaddon asked. "How did you take it into the throne room?"

"I had it wrapped," she said, shrouding it once again.

"Elinya!" Nevrik exploded with glee.

The woman jumped and took a step back, her face filling with fear as the prince started toward her.

Jerish grabbed the boy and held him back, which wasn't as easy as it used to be. The prince, now twelve years old going on thirteen, had grown ridiculously in the last few years, and was nearly as tall as Esrahaddon.

"That's Elinya," Nevrik told Jerish. "That's Esrahaddon's girlfriend. The one he's—"

"I think that's more than enough introduction," Esrahaddon said.

"What's with the dagger?" Jerish asked again, still anchoring the prince in place.

"Don't worry," Esrahaddon said. "She's supposed to kill *me* with it, not Nevrik."

Jerish nodded. "I can understand that. But if that's the case, why hasn't she?"

"Your concern is touching." Esrahaddon shot Jerish an exasperated look. "I'm guessing *empathy* isn't in your butchering curriculum this decade."

The prince freed himself from Jerish's grip.

"But now that you mention it . . ." Esrahaddon turned back to Jerish. "We"—he toggled a finger between Elinya and himself—"were both attacked only a few hours ago by a giant shadow beast that not only obliterated Oswald and nearly took down the imperial library, but it also came exceptionally close to killing us."

"Did a dead-raising spell go awry?" the knight accused, without a hint of humor or surprise.

"Who's Oswald?" Nevrik asked.

Esrahaddon stepped forward to face off with Jerish. "You know, if I heard you'd just fought off a giant shadow beast, I would at the very least ask what happened to it. Even if you don't care about my welfare; that could be important information, don't you think? Oh, wait." Esrahaddon slapped himself on the forehead. "Of course you don't. That's the whole problem."

"You're disrupting my lesson," Jerish said firmly, but not so much as to sound angry. Jerish never appeared angry, just excessively serious. The Teshlor had a thing about showing anger, and happiness, and fear, and . . . pretty much all emotions were shunned, except irritation, which he was in the process of displaying in abundance.

Esrahaddon knew why, and it had little to do with his disrupting the session. Jerish was peeved because he'd brought Elinya into the Vault. The rule had never been agreed upon, not even discussed, but neither he, Jerish, nor the prince had ever revealed using the Vault of Days as the prince's classroom. There had been no visitors, no guests, no spectators, which allowed them precious solitude and the undivided attention of the prince. And while this may have been the original reason for the discretion, after four years the secret had become an unspoken tradition. And Jerish was all about tradition.

"Looks like the session was going well, too." Esrahaddon grinned to ensure that Jerish understood the sarcasm. "Do you beat the boy when I'm not here? Tell him it's part of the training and always make certain the marks are in places his clothes will conceal?"

"Absolutely not!" Jerish proclaimed, scrubbing his reputation like a spot of insinuated rust on his armor.

Esrahaddon smirked. "Well, of course *you're* not going to admit it. You're not *that* stupid." Esrahaddon paused, then cocked an eye at him. "Are you?"

"He doesn't beat me." Nevrik dusted himself off. "And you know it."

"Of course I do," Esrahaddon said. "Because I'm the smart one. Mister Whack-you-with-a-stick can't even accurately identify sarcasm."

Jerish started to speak, then stopped and thought better of it.

Esrahaddon had seen this many times, wondering just how much it took to elicit an honest response from the man. "So, what's with all this?" Esrahaddon gestured at the stuffed canvas sacks hanging from posts in a circle around a balance beam raised a foot from the ground. "Thinking of taking up carpentry, Jerish? Building a practice gallows?"

"I am teaching Nevrik the basics of the Sebeka discipline—or was until you interrupted."

Spotting black cloth around the prince's neck, Esrahaddon asked, "Blindfolded?"

Nevrik nodded.

"He wants you to walk this beam, and hit the bags with that stick, blindfolded?"

"And he moves them each time—after my eyes are covered."

"Sadistic."

"Kinda." The prince nodded with a frown.

Jerish looked at both of them, puzzled, and Esrahaddon guessed he didn't understand the word, which opened the door to a dozen potential insults, most filled with more words Jerish likely wouldn't know.

"I think that's quite enough," the knight said. He looked at Elinya. "My apologies, madam, but I can't allow my session with the prince to be interfered with."

"We aren't interfering," Esrahaddon said. "Your session is over."

"We've barely begun!"

"And I know how disappointing that must be, given that you stayed up all night constructing this inhumane playground, but . . ." He looked at Nevrik, who was pulling the blindfold over his head. "Well, I suppose *you* aren't disappointed."

"What are you talking about?" the knight demanded.

Finally, they had come down to it, and Esrahaddon forced away a smile.

After it had been decided that Jerish would go with him on the adventure, the Knight Tutor needed to be told. A guild errand boy or Gaylord himself would eventually have informed him, but not until Jerish resurfaced around midday. Esrahaddon could have told them where to find the Knight Tutor, and might have, regardless of "the tradition," but it wasn't merely keeping the classroom secret that caused Esrahaddon to hold his tongue. He relished the idea of personally bringing the bad tidings to his adversary. There was a certain satisfaction in: "If I must go down, you're going with me."

Over the past four years, Esrahaddon had attended the unofficial but regular Cenzarium meetings that reported on the constant efforts by the Teshlor Guild to poison the emperor's opinion of Artists. And each time he met Jerish, the knight added evidence to every argument—expressing disdain for reading or even thinking. With time, Esrahaddon came to realize just how crucial his post as tutor had been. His task was to fight the false narrative of the Teshlor Guild so that when Nevrik became emperor, he would be a good ruler. The ultimate mountaintop would be convincing Nevrik to abolish the toxic Teshlor Guild altogether, if at all possible. Better yet for Nevrik to convince his father to do away with such childish things as toy soldiers and knights in armor. Sooner rather than later.

This was an ongoing battle. Esrahaddon saw the effects of a morning spent with Jerish in the way Nevrik would compliment the knight and recount the excitement of performing some foolish stunt. These were sparks Esrahaddon needed to stamp out before wildfires bloomed. The idea of being away, of leaving the prince entirely to Jerish, was unacceptable, even dangerous.

Jerish took a step forward until the two were a hand's width away. "Why is His Highness's training being interrupted?" His tone was more aggressive than before: louder and lower in pitch.

Esrahaddon did not move except to lean in. "By order of the emperor, you and I are going on assignment." He looked at Nevrik. "We'll be gone—I don't know—a couple weeks? I honestly can't say."

"What?" Jerish was flummoxed.

Esrahaddon could no longer help himself, and he grinned as he moved away, feeling he had won the conflict—but then he knew he would before he entered.

"Where are we going?"

"Castell Blythium." Seeing the not-unexpectedly dull eyes looking back at him, Esrahaddon added, "An imperial fortress on the eastern sea about four days travel on horseback, presently the headquarters of the Fourth Legion."

"Why are we going there?"

"It's . . . complicated. But we are leaving right away, so you'll want to get whatever gear you need together. We'll be meeting outside in Imperial Square in another couple hours, I expect."

No more questions, no arguments, no protests or demands for verification were offered. Jerish merely nodded, looking even more serious than ever.

Incredible. And this man has been appointed an equal educator to the next emperor of the world.

Esrahaddon touched one of the bags, giving it a slight push and letting it swing. He looked at the Teshlor. "Can *you* do it?"

For once, Esrahaddon didn't have to paint him a picture. "Yes," Jerish replied.

"Show me."

"Doesn't seem we have the time."

"Does it take that long? Or are you lying about your prowess?"

The accusation of deceit was Esrahaddon taking advantage of the obvious weakness in the knight's character. The Teshlors were all the same, creatures of trained habits. Forcibly instilled with beliefs intended for control, they provided marionette strings for literally anyone looking to manipulate them. By virtue of his conditioning, Jerish was helpless to disobey.

He took the blindfold and wrapped his eyes. "Move the bags."

Nevrik did the honors, shifting the posts' positions. "All set."

Jerish then felt out with his foot for the balance beam. The moment his toe tapped it, he was off. With blinding speed, he mounted the joist, and seeming to dance along its length, he struck each bag so quickly, the only proof of his success was the swinging of the subsequent sacks.

He dismounted and removed the blindfold, a self-satisfied grin on his face.

"Impressive," Esrahaddon said, nodding.

Then turning around and walking toward Elinya and the exit, he snapped his fingers and every swinging bag exploded in unison, spewing the straw stuffing into the air.

"Bastard," Jerish muttered.

CHAPTER TWENTY-SIX

Departure

Arriving in Imperial Square, Jerish was stunned to find such a distinguished gathering near the Ulurium Fountain. Imperial Square was always full of people with business at the palace, the Teshlor Guild, or the Cenzarium. Some were sightseers, visitors to the city taking in landmarks. Others were on their way elsewhere, just passing through the central intersection. Usually, Jerish spotted some church people. They were easily identified by the red flying-dragon symbol stitched on poor clothing. But that morning, a small crowd of well-attired people encircled two wagons, which were being loaded and hooked to their respective team of horses. What made this group stand out the most were the twelve imperial soldiers that stood guard in a rough perimeter, watching the plaza's population for any sign of a threat.

Jerish spotted four Cenzars wearing—not the basic robes of the rank and file but—the fancy gowns with velvet stripes on the sleeves and bright colored stoles. Two wore floppy tam caps. Aside from Esrahaddon, the only other Cenzar Jerish recognized was Offman, who—along with a short lady Cenzar—stood in a tight cluster nearest the wagons.

Elinya, whom Nevrik had identified as Esrahaddon's lady, stood off to one side, not far from the Cenzarium group but not close to anyone. She appeared uncomfortable, out of place, but still held the cloth-wrapped bundle that he knew held a dagger. Small, quiet, and timid as a mouse in a field of short grass, she was cute. Not at all the sort of woman Jerish expected Esrahaddon would be interested in. Long-legged ladies with painted eyes were what Jerish would have imagined. Elinya wasn't that.

There were also church dignitaries, including Bishop Venlin, who spoke to several people as he moved about the gathering like a bee in a rose bush. The greatest surprise, however, was the presence of both Gaylord Sire and Andreas Ranier, who moved to intercept Jerish at first sight.

"Have everything you need, Jerish?" Andreas asked. The aging warrior kept his white hair and beard closely trimmed, giving the man an elegant yet rugged appearance that Jerish admired. Andreas was a legend in the guild, known for his blunt words and honesty. He was the sort everyone aspired to imitate.

"Yes, sir!" he replied, stunned that the Guild Lord knew his name.

Gaylord looked him over. "You have oil and a good rag for that spadone, Jerish?"

"Oh, ah, yes, sir." He pulled the rag from the wrist of his gauntlet. "Keep it right here."

"Good. Thing's an antique, but a treasure." He looked at Andreas, "That's Jerel DeMardefeld's blade."

Andreas looked surprised.

"Rawlings left it to him."

Andreas nodded. "Did you know he was the Chosen of God? Jerel, not Rawlings, of course. He was known to have spoken to our Lord Novron. Jerel was very religious and dedicated his entire life to Novron's service. He called him *The One*. That's where Jerel got the sword, you know, a reward for his steadfast loyalty."

Jerish stuffed the rag back into his glove. "I do take good care of it."

"Excellent."

"Ah, sir, might I ask what this is all about? Esrahaddon said the emperor ordered me to go on a mission, but I have no idea what it is or what's expected."

"Yes, yes." Andreas nodded and drew him off to the side—directly away from the Cenzars. "That's actually what we wanted to speak to you about, son. You see, we don't know, not for certain."

"There are rumors, of course," Gaylord said, his voice low. "They are off to meet with a sorceress called Ruby Finn. Some say she is a demon, an emissary of Uberlin."

"That's gossip," Andreas chided. "She *is*, however, *an elf*—an elf who lives only a day's travel from here but *well* outside imperial jurisdiction."

"How is that possible?" Jerish asked.

"No one knows. It's all very hush-hush—some secret of the Cenzars. She squats in the Forbidden Forest where no one—not even the emperor himself—is allowed to go, for reasons no one is willing to talk about. She's been there for centuries. Now all of a sudden, the Cenzars have been ordered on this *mission*—not by the emperor, you understand, but by Ruby Finn!"

Jerish was puzzled but thought little of it. He wasn't a worldly person and didn't—nor would he expect to—understand the complex workings of the political machine that comprised the imperial government. He had no aspirations in that direction. Jerish did not want to be a First Order Knight like Gaylord Sire nor Guild Lord like Andreas Ranier. For him, paradise would be to faithfully serve the emperor with his sword, his courage, and his faith until he was too old to effectively do so. Then he hoped to retire to a small bit of land where, having recently discovered he liked goat cheese, Jerish thought he might raise a few of the animals.

"Originally, only Esrahaddon was supposed to go," Gaylord explained. "He's the one she ordered to report to her. Yolric volunteered to accompany him, and the Ancient One never goes anywhere. The only reason you're on this mission is because I insisted. You see, they didn't want any non-Cenzars to go but couldn't push too hard or they would need to answer difficult questions—questions that their tall tale about ghosts and monsters would fail to answer."

"We suspect that the Cenzars are planning something," Andreas said. "Something big. This Ruby Finn has been acting as an interchange, a message broker between the ancient Erivan Empire and their seditionist henchmen: the Cenzars. The elves are preparing their assault and want to coordinate with their inside spies. They plan to launch a three-prong assault on the Imperial Throne—a surprise attack launched out of Merredydd directly on this city, a massive invasion over the Nidwalden, and at the same time an internal strike on the palace and the guild by the Cenzarium."

Jerish stared, stunned, and nearly dropped his travel sack. "I didn't know—no one has . . . When is this supposed to happen?"

"We believe it will be soon. We don't know exactly, but this mission suggests an immediate threat. It's the only thing it can be," Gaylord said. "Yolric is the one who controls the emperor. I've seen it many times. When he speaks, Nareion's resolve crumbles, and he agrees to whatever the old enchanter wants. The fact that Yolric is going on *this mission* is proof that final preparations are being made."

"What do you want me to do?"

"We need you to be our eyes and ears. Don't let them shut you out. We must know what they are up to. Find evidence of their treason that we can present to the guild."

"The guild? Why not the emperor?"

"The emperor . . ." Andreas frowned and sighed. "Nareion, we fear, has been compromised. He may be irreparably under their influence. It is even possible he will order the legions to join the Erivan army and welcome the Merredydd elves into the palace. He's no longer himself, you understand. They have befuddled his mind. Emperor Nareion will likely be the one to present his crown to the elven ruler and smile while doing it."

"But if we can find proof of their treason," Gaylord said, "we will order a preemptive strike on the Cenzarium, take direct control of the legions, and Andreas here will become acting emperor until Nevrik is old enough to take control. The boy is doing well?"

"He's still learning the basics. He's good at balance, but his arms need work. He's a bit scrawny."

"I meant his mind. Does he show signs of being bewitched? Can you tell if Esrahaddon is enchanting him?"

Jerish thought a moment. The prince did seem strangely fond of the Cenzar. During practices he frequently complimented Esrahaddon and cited some bit of pointlessly arcane knowledge. "I'm not sure how I would know if he were."

"That's always the problem. They're so crafty," Gaylord said. "Be careful, Jerish. You're outnumbered by an enemy who will stop at nothing to get what they want."

"Find us a reason, Jerish," Andreas said. "Open the gates for us, so we can rid the world of Cenzars, and this plague of magic, forever."

"I wonder what they are telling him," Isilpor-Sond said as she looked across the plaza at Andreas and Gaylord chatting in earnest with Jerish. "If not for their tattooed runes, I'd listen in."

"I never learned that weave," Esrahaddon said, tying up the mouth of his little travel bag. "Would be handy to know."

"It is, which is why we don't teach it." She smiled, then nodded toward the knights. "Of course, they aren't a complicated lot. The topic of that conversation is easy to guess. They're telling Jerish to keep an eye out for anything they can use to embarrass us in front of the emperor." She pointed a firm finger at him. "Don't give them anything." She sighed. "Although it won't matter. Even if you don't, they'll lie and say you did."

"Lie?" Esrahaddon said. "I don't think Jerish knows what *lying* is. The man is an idiot, and a brute, but he takes this honor thing of theirs seriously."

She chuckled. "I keep forgetting how young you are. What are you, twenty-five?"

"I'll be twenty-seven in a couple months."

She nodded. "Lying is like colors. They come in all different hues and shades. It's quite easy for an honorable man to tell an untruth, so long as he believes it. If I tell you a sea serpent is in a pond and send you to look, and if you go there and see the surface being oddly disturbed by something below, you will believe that you saw the beast. So when you later tell others of the monster in the pond, you aren't lying. You're telling *your* truth. The problem begins with going to the pond with expectations rather than an open mind. Granted, that's a hard nut for anyone to crack."

"Harder for those with minds shut so tight they smother for lack of fresh air."

"Don't be so arrogant," she said, but without the bite of a true rebuke. "Everyone, and I mean *everyone*, suffers this malady. No one treads the surface of Elan who doesn't believe with all their heart and mind in one thing or another that is wholly untrue. Merely suspecting you believe an untruth is devastating. Accepting the real truth and giving up the lie is worse than beating any addiction. I should know." She spat grenesta juice through the gap between her front teeth.

Offman, who had been checking on the horse teams, returned. His eyes watched the Teshlors as he meandered through the line of men carrying crates and barrels. "They're evil, you know."

"Evil?" Esrahaddon said, surprised. "That's an odd term for a Cenzar to use. I didn't know we believed in *evil*. I thought we understood that people acted badly merely as a result of not knowing better."

"True," he said. "Problem is, everyone *knows better* than everyone else." Offman frowned. "Wish I knew that listening weave."

"Wouldn't help," Esrahaddon said. "All three of them are runed."

"Oh, right." He scowled. "Good point."

Isilpor-Sond gave Esrahaddon a wink.

"Still, if there is true evil in the world, we're looking at it," Offman declared. "Ignorance, hate, paranoia, and the absolute conviction that it is good and right to force others to accept their values."

"According to her"—Esrahaddon pointed at Isilpor-Sond—"that's a universal pastime."

Offman pursed his lips and squinted his eyes. "Perhaps, but they excel at it."

Esrahaddon glanced at Jerish, who was standing straight and holding on to a stuffed sack, which looked remarkably like the ones Esrahaddon had exploded only hours before. "I doubt he'll be a problem."

"He's a Teshlor," Offman stated. "They're always a problem."

"Let me rephrase. I doubt he'll be *the* problem. Both of you do realize I'm hunting a riva? The odds of any of us ever returning are . . . not so good."

Isilpor-Sond waved a dismissive hand. "Not to worry, Esra. Yolric will take care of you."

Esrahaddon spotted Yolric on the far side of the wagons, speaking to Bishop Venlin. "Yolric is . . . an old man."

"He's a lot more than you think he is," she assured him. "He is, in fact, the greatest of us. Rely on his guidance. He'll see you through this."

"I hope so," Esrahaddon said as he looked back at Elinya and tried his best to offer her a hopeful smile.

Mawyndulë, in the guise of Bishop Venlin, approached Trilos, presently in the form of Cenzar Master Yolric. "Going on a trip?"

"What? Think me too old, do you?"

"You're too old to still be breathing," Mawyndulë replied. "I thought you wanted to be on hand for the big show. It's almost curtain time, you know? I sent a pair of young fools to Erivan to poke the beehive, and it won't be long before your wobble is teetering again."

Yolric was fiddling with his beard—doing what, exactly, Mawyndulë had no idea. The thing was ridiculously long and thick.

Might be picking out lice. Do dead bodies have them? Maybe he has maggots.

"It would appear the Invisible Hand is waving for me to follow it east."

"Why don't you just say Turin? You're talking about your brother, right?"

He began stroking the beard, as if it were a pet. "He's certainly involved, and he does most of the grunt work in the corrections, but there's always been a problem with the theory that the Invisible Hand *is* Turin."

"Which is?"

"The *Why*." Yolric licked his lips, or at least those of the corpse. "No other living thing has ever been more responsible for disrupting the intended course of the world than my elder brother. So why has he been working to counter our petty interferences? I used to think he was irritated with us for upsetting his master plan for total domination, but now . . . well, it's almost as if . . ."

Mawyndulë stared at him and waited. "Oh well," he said at length. "I thought you might actually say something worth hearing. No such luck, I guess."

Yolric shrugged. "All I know is he's up to something that is big and important, and I want to be there. You see, when we were young boys, even then he had the power of foresight. Not like now, but enough. He would drop a stone on a hillside and challenge me to guess where it would finally come to rest. Even as a child, he was an arrogant bastard and relished lording his ability over me. The last time he tried it, when he dropped the stone, I kicked the rock into the wheat field before it hit the turf. 'Didn't see that, did you?' I asked him. He was angry, so very angry at being humiliated—at being wrong."

"So you're going to go off and kick his rock?"

"Exactly. Whatever he has planned for Esrahaddon and Ruby Finn, I'm going to ruin it."

Mawyndulë looked at the young Cenzar and sighed.

"What's wrong?"

"I was planning on using him. Esrahaddon is powerful, and like all of them, so easily manipulated. In another month, with just a dash more *guidance* he'd have led my war to destroy the empire. But now you're going to kill him."

Yolric looked surprised. "I'm not my brother. I'm not the evil one. I don't kill people."

Mawyndulë pointed a finger and made a sweeping circle indicating the whole of the bearded Yolric corpse. "Folks just vacate the premises to accommodate you taking over their bodies, do they?"

"They don't leave on my account. Many have been so *unaccommodating* that I was forced to *rent* the occasional raccoon. Meager living space, but the opposable thumb is worth it."

"So you're not going to kill him?"

"Won't need to. Mileva will eat all of them."

Mawyndulë shivered, recalling the years he had spent in Borappathin before it became Castell Blythium. Those were the dark days directly following his defeat at the hands of Nyphron. How many years he'd spent there, he honestly couldn't say. What he remembered was that staying in that place was like living in a haunted house where there were far worse things than ghosts.

"How is it . . . why didn't she bother us?"

"I told her not to."

"Old friends?"

"Old enemies."

"But you won't interfere this time?"

"Oh, I'll interfere. That's why I'm going. I plan to kick that stone deep into the wheat field."

When it came time to leave, Esrahaddon took Elinya's hand and helped her climb onto the wagon. She was no longer dressed in the thin white shift, which Esrahaddon, in his inexperience, had failed to realize was an undergarment. Elinya had apparently rushed out that night without bothering to dress. As he hadn't let her out of his sight for much longer than a few minutes at a time, he was curious.

"Nice outfit. Where'd you get the clothes? Isilpor-Sond?"

"Sort of." Elinya offered him a rare smile. "She sent someone to fetch them from Evarburton's estate. These are mine—what I wear when I'm working."

"Really?" The little fabric-belted ocher dress that looped over one shoulder was simple but stunning.

She nodded. "I know. It's very nice, isn't it? But then Evarburton owns most of the Garment District, and they needed me to appear respectable in my new position." She touched the wide torque necklace. "I have this, too. Looks gold, but I think it's only brass. Oh, and this . . ." She slipped on a beautiful red cloak with black lining that appeared to be reversible. The quality was impressive. "I usually change after work, terrified I'll damage something, but whoever fetched the clothes didn't know that, I guess." She took a moment to draw up the hood—to hide.

As she did, Elinya set the wrapped dagger on her lap.

Esrahaddon smiled and shook his head. "I keep thinking of you as this poor, defenseless villager, but you aren't—not anymore. You've become quite the woman, Elinya. And I guess I should have said this earlier—thank you for saving my life."

She shrugged. "You saved mine first."

"My sincere apologies, Jerish," the ancient-looking Cenzar said as he struggled to climb aboard the front bench of the wagon.

"For what, sir?"

"I imagine you were hoping to travel alongside that pretty woman. I know I was." He cast a longing look at the other wagon, where Esrahaddon was taking his seat next to Elinya. "Now instead, you get the feeble old man. Life starts out bad. You come screaming and crying into this world, and it goes downhill from there. Trust me, I've been around a long time, and I've seen some things. Life isn't worth the effort."

"If you say so, sir." Jerish waited until the old Cenzar was situated, then took up the reins and climbed up himself. The bench was set on a curved bit of thin metal, so it bounced with his weight.

"And don't call me *sir*. My name is Yolric, and I don't respond to much else. There's even a good chance I won't respond to that." He winked.

"Yes, sir."

The old Cenzar raised a pure-white eyebrow. "We'll work on it."

Jerish wasn't certain if he was expected to drive or not. He looked awkwardly at the Cenzar, then glanced at the reins.

"Don't look at me. I'm far too old to wrangle a team of horses."

"I don't know—that is—I've never driven a wagon. I've ridden a horse. Part of the training: spears, javelins, ule-da-vars, bows, running, swimming, horseback riding, even falconry. But I guess no one felt that driving a team was something a Teshlor would be expected to do."

"I believe that lever to your left is a brake. You just push it out and pull back. Beyond that I suspect we'll just follow Esrahaddon, or rather the horses will follow the other horses. They usually do."

Jerish nodded, suspecting the old man was right, and a bit surprised at how . . . *normal* he seemed. The Cenzar master didn't insult or demean, or use ridiculously large words, or act superior. He spoke clearly and to the point, and while educating Jerish, he managed somehow to sound humble.

Ever since learning of this trip, Jerish had dreaded the long hours alone with a pair of Cenzars. He expected to be the butt of jokes and the target of insults. He could never win a verbal battle and resigned himself to keeping quiet and letting them have their fun. He would watch, listen, and remember. But now, they hadn't left the plaza yet, and already he had doubts.

"That's always the problem. They're so crafty. Be careful, Jerish. You're outnumbered by an enemy who will stop at nothing to get what they want."

Jerish disengaged the brake as Esrahaddon led his and Elinya's wagon out of the plaza down Ferry Street. Sure enough, his horses gave a tentative step forward, and when he took no action to prevent it, they followed.

"See? You've got this, son," Yolric assured him with a warm, friendly tone, and clapped him lightly on the arm. "You're going to do wonderfully. I would ask a favor, though . . . if, while resting my eyes, I happen to fall off, do be so kind as to stop and gather me up." He smiled and laughed.

Jerish smiled back, confused. *Things were so much easier when all I had to do was fight and be openly hated by those I bested.*

The two wagons rolled one after the other down to the West Bernum River and across the Yardley Bridge.

CHAPTER TWENTY-SEVEN

Merredydd

MEANWHILE . . .
THE ROAD TO MERREDYDD, INSTARYA PROVINCE

Marley Gris was the worst sort of man, but there was nothing Sadarshakar or Hanis could do about that now. They were committed to the venture. There would be no turning back, and in many ways, that helped. Second thoughts were shackled by keys now tossed into a lake. As the first night of their journey came on, the poisonous doubts it inflicted were no longer things to wrestle but merely endure. And yet, Sadarshakar couldn't help being terrified.

"What have we done?" he asked Hanis, who rode alongside.

"Nothing . . . yet," Hanis replied. "What's your problem?"

Sadarshakar looked back over the rump of his horse at the company of men, wagons, and pack animals as they all traveled up the road toward Merredydd. "They all hate us, you know? There's not one of them who's above slitting our throats as we sleep."

Hanis pushed up straight on his horse, a pure-white stallion named Blizzard that Sadarshakar felt his fellow councilor was a little too pleased with. "Not that I will disagree, but you were always the one quick to point out how humans are people, too."

"Yes, but that was before I knew many. I've learned that not all humans are worthy of such a lofty title." Sadarshakar faced forward to once again stare at the back of Marley Gris. "Our guide being a prime example."

The ex-legionnaire, ex-gambler, ex-scout, ex-trapper, and perhaps even ex-human being rode at the head of their party—their hired pilot on this perilous adventure. The man was entirely dressed in crude deerskins sewn together with no more skill than the accidental tangling of string. Even his head was covered with a leather cap.

Hanis nodded. "It's as if he crawled inside the carcass of a moose, and when he was unable to find his way out, he continued to wear it. That can't be comfortable. The sweat stains bear witness to its lack of breathability."

"He was highly recommended," Sadarshakar said remorsefully, more to himself than Hanis, "but no doubt by the most knowledgeable of scoundrels."

"He knows the forests," Hanis said, "how to live off the land, and the ways of the Ba Ran Ghazel. And he's the only one willing to accept the job. Didn't even take an extra breath before agreeing."

"My question is, why?"

"Money," Hanis said.

"We offered the others the same."

"He needs it more. He's an ex-gambler. How does one become an *ex*-gambler except through excessive losses?"

"Or maybe his true plan is to take us out into the wilderness, steal all the supplies the good bishop provided, and leave us as carrion for vultures. Everyone here—all of them—were handpicked by good old Marley Gris. That was a mistake on our part. We should have selected our own handlers, cooks, and huntsmen."

"Of course, because *we know* the right people to choose."

Sadarshakar glared at his partner in crime. "Since when are you so trusting, optimistic, and forgiving of humans?"

"I'm not. I agree with everything you've said."

"Then why the chipper tone?"

Hanis grinned. "Two reasons. First, we are out of that Ferrol-cursed city and on our way to fame and glory as we finally take our first steps on the road to our lifelong dream. That right there ought to put a smile on your face."

Sadarshakar couldn't argue. Despite his earlier misgivings and initial doubts about disobeying the emperor, now that they were on their way, he couldn't help feeling a tad exhilarated. *But at what cost? Jumping off a cliff would be thrilling, too—for a little while.* "And second?"

Hanis grinned. "Being the lifelong pessimist that I am, I recognized the menace of an all-human entourage. While I'm certain I could protect myself from any mischief, I have sincere doubts about you. So I took steps."

"Thank you for thinking about me . . . I think. But what sort of steps did you take?"

"I sent word to Merredydd." Hanis pointed up the road. "I have a reliable friend—Vigish myr Anyval—who knows a member of the Order of the Fauyld and arranged to hire him to act as bodyguard."

Sadarshakar was both stunned and overjoyed at the news. "Truly?"

Hanis nodded with an overflowing abundance of nonchalant self-satisfaction.

Sadarshakar couldn't begrudge his companion's smugness; he felt like kissing the arrogant bastard. "Wait. We can't go into the city, not with this parade of humans."

Hanis held up a hand. "Already solved. We are meeting our new escort at the Lendonlyn Roadhouse." He glanced up at the clear sky and the sun that was resting on the western hills. "Waiting for us now, I suspect. I also requested rooms for the two of us. No sense sleeping in the dirt until we must."

"Outstanding!"

"I thought so."

"What's his name, this sword master?"

"Ulin."

"What sort of name is Ulin?"

"A good Instarya name, I'd imagine."

"And how will we know this Ulin?"

"The Frhey is a Fauyld. I expect he'll find us."

"Are you certain you don't want me to come along?" Marley asked as the wagon train prepared to set up camp on the bank of the West Bernum River. He had his thumbs hooked in his wide belt, which, like all else, was made of some animal hide. Sadarshakar, noticing the man's skin was coarse and darkly weathered, considered the possibility that it might also be made of leather.

"I believe it would be more sensible for you to stay here and keep good order," Sadarshakar said. "Master Orphe and I will spend the night elsewhere and return to you in the early morning. Please have things ready to move out by the time we get back."

"O' course, sir." Marley always said the right things, but his tone never matched the words. Or perhaps it was the hint of a smile or the squint of his eyes that suggested the thinly masked hate. Sadarshakar recognized the signs that he had encountered that first day in Percepliquis when they tried to rent a litter to carry them to the palace. *"Look, you little pixie, none of us are gonna carry your elven ass anywhere. Got it?"* Sadarshakar hadn't *got it*, not then, but after more than a decade of living in Percepliquis, the message finally arrived. Humans disliked Frhey. This was a fact of life, he concluded, one he was able to live with. But in the last two years, he'd come to notice that the dislike had grown to hate, and he'd begun to fear for his safety. Now he saw it everywhere, even in the faces of those like Lucian Hargrave. The imperial councilor had never said a negative word in their presence, but Sadarshakar and Hanis never heard what was said in rooms where they weren't.

"Good evening to you, then," Marley said, touching the rim of his cap. "See you in the morning."

Sadarshakar walked away from the infant encampment to where Hanis waited with their horses. He was brushing Blizzard with the round curry comb—one of five tools the groom had provided. "You should leave that to the groom. You're likely doing it wrong. For example, I think it is proper to take the saddle off first."

"I want to foster a better relationship with Old Snowstorm."

"His name is Blizzard, and I don't think he's very old."

"It's a nickname."

"You gave the animal a nickname? One that means the same as his actual name? That's confusing even for me. Have you considered how bewildering it is for the animal? Isn't it hard enough for them to grasp the concept of one name at all, much less two?"

Hanis scowled. "I'm just sprucing him up a bit. Don't want this Fauyld to think we're slobs." He looked up. "Did you tell Marley we're leaving?"

"Yes."

"Did he seem disappointed he wouldn't get the opportunity to murder us tonight?"

"Didn't mention it to me, but we aren't that close."

Hanis put the brush into the side bag and hoisted himself up on Blizzard's back. "Let's go meet a legend."

Together they traveled down the spur that led off the main imperial route toward the roadhouse. The Lendonlyn was known to them. Neither had frequented the establishment, but they had been there more than once, usually on their way back from an overnight excursion to the Majestics or the ruins of Alon Rhist. Sadarshakar recalled the Lendonlyn's wonderful breads filled with berries or nuts.

The Lendonlyn was a three-story building: first floor stone, second floor timber, and the top a steeply pitched roof of clay tiles punctuated by dormers with tiny windows appearing like the bulging eyes of a frog. An adjoining open-air stable provided accommodations for up to eight animals. That evening, only four of the stalls were occupied—one by a black-and-white cow. With no sign of two-legged life, Sadarshakar and Hanis tied up their own mounts, giving them access to the water trough, then circled around to the front. Glass-enclosed lamps burned on either side of the wooden door, which was held in place by massive, black iron hinges. Overhead, a signboard depicted two frothy mugs clinking in good cheer.

They entered to find a quiet but well-lit common room. Sadarshakar didn't remember much about the outside, but he fondly recalled the elbow-shaped bar, the large open hearth, and the puzzle-piece stone floor. There were always more stools than chairs, and on previous nights when he had visited, the room had always been bustling, resulting in heated competition for the privilege to sit with a backrest. That night, as he and Hanis entered, the place was nearly empty and felt a bit more like the imperial library than the boisterous roadhouse of so many hazy memories.

A slender Fhrey wearing a white apron with damp handprints took note of their arrival and looked across the room at what might be his daughter. She nodded and scurried over.

"Welcome to the Lendonlyn, good sirs." She presented a big smile and extended her arms as if she might hug them both together. "What can we offer you?"

"I'm Hanis Orphe, and this is my associate, Sadarshakar. We have rooms arranged but also are expecting to meet someone this evening."

"You're looking for Ulin?"

Hanis nodded happily. "Yes. Yes, we are."

"She's at the table near the hearth. I'll check on the readiness of your rooms, but is there something I can get you now? Will you be wanting a meal? A drink?"

The delight in Hanis's eyes had gone out, and he stared at the girl with a dumbstruck expression.

"Meals would be wonderful," Sadarshakar answered for them. "And yes, I believe this place sells a nice mead. Two, I think." He looked at Hanis, who continued to appear frozen.

"Right away, sir." With a wink and a grin, the server stole away.

"She?" Hanis said. They both looked across at the fire, where a figure sat on a bench before a big, otherwise empty table. A soft, misshapen hat rested alongside a bowl and a ceramic tankard. Not much else could be determined, as the person faced away and wore a nondescript cloak that draped from shoulder to floor. "There must be some mistake."

"Shall we ask?" Sadarshakar suggested.

The two crept up, drawing no reaction from the seated figure, who seemed lost in the act of eating.

"Good evening to you," Sadarshakar said as he moved around to the fire's side to get a view of the diner's face. Short-cropped hair revealed sharp ears and eyes. She was indeed both female and Fhrey, or a *gyn* in the old language—something Hanis and Sadarshakar had started brushing up on in anticipation of contact with the Old World. "Are you Ulin, perchance?"

The gyn nodded, waited to swallow, then said, "And you must be either Sikaria or Orphe?"

"Sadarshakar Sikaria, and behind you is Hanis Orphe."

Again she nodded, her mouth full. Then turning, she waved at Hanis, who responded with a look of shock. "Have a seat."

Sadarshakar pulled out the bench on the far side and carefully stepped over, but Hanis remained rooted in disbelief. "We were expecting to meet a member of the Order of the Fauyld."

Caught chewing again, she nodded. Then setting down her spoon, she loosened the broach on her cloak and drew it away, revealing the embroidered crest of a blue-and-gold quartered shield divided by a dragon's tooth.

Hanis shuffled around to see what Sadarshakar was looking at. Viewing the crest only appeared to add more confusion to his face. "I don't understand. I assumed the Fauyld was a male-only order."

"Why would you do that?" she asked.

"I just . . ." Hanis peered at her. "I never heard of a female Fauyld."

She shrugged. "Granted, we're a rare breed."

Hanis leaned over the table, looking down at her lap. "Where's your sword?"

She cocked her head. "Over there. Hanging on the wall."

They both spotted a long slender rapier dangling by a belt from a peg.

"I'm here because I was informed that Imperial Councilors Sikaria and Orphe desired to hire a Fauyld bodyguard for a trip east. Is there a problem?"

"Yes," Hanis replied.

"Because I'm female?"

Hanis hesitated. "Because you show poor judgment."

Ulin straightened up at this and wiped her mouth. "How so?"

"You sit with your back to the door, wear your cloak but not your weapon, and . . . and speak with your mouth full."

"I see," she said. "That does sound awful, except that sitting on that side of the table is too hot, but on this side, believe it or not, my back is cold, so I keep the cloak on. I'm not on duty, nor have I any enemies, and given that wearing the sword is awkward while one sits at a bench, I hung it up. And I'm speaking with my mouth full because I'm hungry, I prefer to eat my food hot, and my meal has been interrupted by you two."

Hanis continued to stare.

She looked at Sadarshakar. "And do you share his concerns?"

"Actually, I didn't even think about those things. It's more the fact you're female, and we feel your ability to do the job is suspect on the grounds that males are better at combat, being it's a physical competition."

"So it's proof you want?" She said this more to Hanis and followed the comment with a sigh that told Sadarshakar she'd done this before. Skidding the bench back, she wearily stood, then stepped out into the open space between the tables and tossed aside her cloak.

Ulin was not particularly small—just a tad shorter than Hanis—but she was slender and a bit delicate in appearance, something emphasized by her tightly tailored tunic and snug pants.

Hanis looked at her, then at Sadarshakar.

"I believe she expects *you* to test her," Sadarshakar said.

"How?"

"One would presume with your oft-boasted, finely tuned Instarya combat skills."

"She wants me to—" Hanis stopped and faced Ulin. "You want me to hit you?"

She shrugged. "I want you to do whatever you need to do to convince yourself I can handle the job."

Hanis once more appeared stymied. "I—I can't hit a gyn."

"Haven't even tried," she said. "With all due respect, the Tek'chin is a martial discipline based on finesse, balance, speed, and dare I say, delicacy—not brute force. Furthermore, the blade used is a light, razor-sharp needle of a thing—a *dragon's tooth*, if you will. Our technique isn't to bludgeon. It is an elegant dance—just the sort of thing ladies are often accused of being excellent at. So, come now. Dance with me?"

Hanis drew back his shoulders and squared his jaw in defiance. "I will do no such thing. Come, Sadar, this was a terrible waste of time."

"It will be if we don't at least have supper," Sadarshakar replied. "And I would prefer that bed you promised."

Hanis shook his head and pulled in his lower lip in a violent pout as if he might explode.

Sadarshakar sympathized. He had hoped to return to that troop of humanity with a skilled ally they could trust.

"Honored Councilors, please," Ulin said. "You must believe me when I tell you I am quite capable of protecting you. No one is awarded this crest without completing the training, and no one completes the training without being a master of the sword. And also . . . I could really use this job."

Neither spoke.

"Look," she said. "You don't need to pay me if you are unhappy with my performance."

"That's hardly the point!" Hanis erupted. "If we are unhappy with your performance, it will be because we are dead."

"Okay." Ulin nodded. "But let me ask you this: What are your alternatives? I can tell you now—no one else will take this assignment."

"Why do you say that?" Sadarshakar asked.

"You're going to Erivania and doing so against the emperor's wishes."

Hanis and Sadarshakar looked at each other, stunned.

"We've said nothing of the sort," Hanis practically swore as if he were being arrested.

Ulin noticed the waitress coming with a pair of mugs and swept her cloak off the floor. "Didn't need to," she spoke in a quiet tone. "People aren't so stupid, and your entourage isn't so tight-lipped. I'm not certain that the emperor knows just yet, but he will in a day or two. Fact is, no one else is willing to defy Nareion, nor risk their lives crossing the Nidwalden."

"We aren't asking anyone to *cross* the river," Sadarshakar said. "Only to escort us to it. Hanis and I alone will break the law."

Hanis scowled his displeasure as the presumed innkeeper's daughter arrived with the drinks. "Food will be out soon," she said brightly. "And your beds are being turned down and fires lit for a warm night's sleep."

"Thank you," Hanis managed, speaking as if his lips and jaw were suffering some stiffening malady.

They waited until the drinks were down and the server walked away.

Then Ulin led off. "I'm all you have."

"You can't come," Hanis declared.

"Why not?" she asked.

The junior councilor threw his hands up. "Our whole company is made up entirely of men—*men!* Our guide is a scoundrel of the worst sort. Doesn't it frighten you—this idea of traveling into the wilderness in the company of rough thugs? You could be hurt . . . or worse."

"If such a thing concerned me, I would not be worth hiring, would I?"

"Exactly!"

"But I'm not concerned and, therefore, *am* worthy of the job."

"Why is it you're willing to take the assignment?" Sadarshakar asked.

Ulin hesitated, appearing uncomfortable. "It's personal, has no bearing on the mission, and I'd rather keep that to myself, thank you."

Sadarshakar nodded. "I respect that, but given that we are trusting you with our lives, we won't hire you unless we know."

Ulin straightened herself as she squared off with him from the far side of the table. "What you need to know is that my father was a Fauyld, and his father wasn't merely a Fauyld, he actually learned the Tek'chin from Tekchin."

"Oh, so you're a legacy or something," Hanis said. "The order was somehow obligated to take you, even though you're a gyn, is that it?"

"No." Ulin glared at Hanis as if he'd exposed himself, and perhaps, in a way, he had. "The Order of the Fauyld has never had a restriction on gender. You've been living with humans too long."

Hanis's eyes went as wide as if she'd slapped him.

"The point is, I was raised with a sword in my hand. My entire family has the Tek'chin in our blood. I'm as good with a blade as anyone you'll ever meet."

"What about a Teshlor?" Sadarshakar asked. The comment wasn't serious. He'd thrown it out merely to trip her up, to pop her self-assured bubble. But he watched as she considered the idea.

"Honestly," she began with deadly seriousness, "I'd *love* the chance to test myself against one. I truly would."

Sadarshakar grinned. "Hear that, Hanis? She'll fight a Teshlor."

"Who is your father?" Hanis asked, folding his arms as if building a fortress.

"He was a well-respected Fhrey."

"Was?"

"He's dead."

Sadarshakar and Hanis exchanged looks that agreed they had found the bedrock of the mystery.

"What was his name?" Hanis pressed.

Once more Ulin resisted answering. Slowly, her head lowered until she looked at the table. "Halcyon myr Milyon."

Hanis nodded, but Sadarshakar didn't know the name. "What?"

"Indeed, Halcyon *was* a well-respected Fauyld," Hanis explained. "So much so he was assigned by the Order to protect Empress Sephryn in her later years when she lived in Merredydd. He failed, and the empress was killed."

"My father died defending Sephryn," Ulin said. "He was killed by a Miralyith."

"That failure has been a black mark against the Order ever since," Hanis stated with no hint of sympathy.

Sadarshakar sensed something didn't quite fit. "Sephryn was murdered over two hundred years ago. You don't look much older than Hanis. Why would the Order be compelled to accept the daughter *or son* of a disgraced member?" He focused on Ulin's uniform. The crest wasn't exactly centered, and the cut of the tunic was odd as if it had been tailored secondhand. "That's not *your* uniform, is it?"

Ulin said nothing.

"That's your father's emblem. You had his clothes taken in to fit."

She touched the brilliant white threading of the dragon tooth reverently. "It's why I need this job. I must prove . . ." She looked at Hanis. "I need to erase that *black mark*."

"So you *aren't* a Fauyld," Hanis said, that abrasive, self-satisfied tone rolling back in.

"I'm more a Fauyld than anyone ever has been."

"But the Order apparently doesn't think so."

That did it. Sadarshakar saw the fire ignite in her eyes, and in that moment, he was pleased that her sword was hanging out of reach on a peg.

Ulin kicked the bench away and glared at them. "It's not because of my father, or because I am a gyn that I have been barred from the Order!"

"Why then?" Sadarshakar asked in as gentle a voice as he could manage.

"If I say . . ." She frowned and took a deep breath. "You'll never hire me."

"Oh, I'm quite certain there is no chance of you being employed by us now," Hanis declared. "Am I right?" he asked.

Sadarshakar kept his eyes on Ulin. "Why?"

She swallowed, took a breath, then swallowed again. "Because while my father was Halcyon myr Milyon, my mother was—Amanda Miller." She took another deep breath as if she needed a rest after saying that name. "The empress—the daughter of Tekchin himself—whose death smeared my father with shame was half human, but the Order of the Fauyld doesn't accept myr." She held them both with an expression of contempt. "You . . . you have no idea what it's like living in a city where you're treated as *less than*, where you are deprived entrance through doors everyone else can enter, for no other reason than because you look different, or because you exist not through some arranged marriage but because your parents actually loved each other."

She threw her cloak over one arm, crossed to where her sword hung, and snatched it up. Then with a violent whirl and an angry, quick step, Ulin, daughter of Halcyon, started for the door.

She made it but halfway across the room when Hanis said, "You're hired."

When they returned to the camp the next morning, no one appeared to know quite what to make of Ulin, least of all Marley Gris, who just stared when they explained she was joining the expedition.

"You're bringing a lady Frhey on a trip into the bush? And one that dresses . . . like that?"

"Are you saying you have a problem with me or the way I dress?" Ulin asked, looking down on the man from her saddle.

The guide squinted up at her, focused on the sword lying against her thigh, then pursed his lips as if smelling a trap.

He shook his head. "As long as my pay remains unchanged, I don't care who the good masters here invite to keep them warm at night."

"That's not why they hired me," she said. "So that job is still open if you're looking to augment *your* salary."

Marley's face tightened, but once again he stared at the blade. "I think I'm fine."

"Then I'd say we both are."

The train of heavily laden pack animals, wagons, grooms, blacksmiths, huntsmen, cooks, and general laborers who had been hired to make the trip across the empire both possible and comfortable readied themselves in the crisp morning air. They lined up beside the smoldering coals and faint smoky wisps of their campfires.

"How long does it take to get to the Nidwalden?" Sadarshakar asked Marley.

"How would I know? There's not a man alive—Frey either, I suspect—who's ever been there."

"Well," Sadarshakar said, "I suppose we had best be off then." He looked over at Hanis with a smile. "History awaits."

CHAPTER TWENTY-EIGHT

The Hawthorn Glen

IMPERIAL CAPITAL OF PERCEPLIQUIS

The Yardley Bridge, spanning the West Bernum River, was a massive twelve-arch stone bridge, long considered one of the great wonders of the world. Esrahaddon had, as many still did, assumed it was built in the days of Novron, since everything grand or miraculous was always attributed to that era known as the Age of Myth and Legend. Now he understood this was merely one of the deeply planted seeds of his twisted childhood rearing its ugly head, his father's ignorant ideas embedded intractably into the very foundation of Esrahaddon's worldview. The truth, he later learned, was that the Yardley Bridge had been built by Emperor Nordyan less than two hundred years before. As best as Esrahaddon was able to work out, for about two hundred years after the founding of Merredydd, all traffic heading to the city went by the Havilyn ferryboat. Then Novron built a bridge at the request of the newly established Instarya Province. This had not been a wonder-of-the-world-worthy construction, as it had been constantly in a state of disrepair and remained so for centuries. Then in the late 1800s—when once more the bridge was in desperate need of repair—it was finally torn down to prepare for a new, far more ambitious causeway. At that time, the ferryboat system had been reinstated. Everyone expected it would only be in service for a few years, but it lasted for more than eighty—as was confirmed by Farilane's short essay of her last adventure, *The Search for Truth*. Decades of debate and arguments over the design, not to mention political disagreement with the waning power of the Instarya elves, delayed the project. After the bridge was finally started, construction still took over thirty-six years. That the Yardley Bridge was built by hand, rather than the imperium allowing Artists to complete the project in a couple of days, was cited in Cenzarium lectures as an indication of how the imperium had never fully accepted their alliance. Thinking about it, Esrahaddon concluded that the bridge was indeed a wonder of the world, if it was still possible to wonder at the level of man's stupidity.

Traffic was light on the bridge, and few took any note of the two carts rolling in single file over the great river. This was Esrahaddon and Elinya's second crossing, but they still gawked at the view and the miracle of traveling so high above the water. Below, the river was calm and acted as a mirror reflecting the green trees and gray rocks of the banks and the blue of the overhead sky.

The moment they reached the far side and arrived in the province of Instarya, Esrahaddon veered off the main road, choosing to follow a simple two-track trail that ran due east. No one questioned the route, which surprised him. Perhaps Elinya hadn't paid attention on their last trip. More likely, she didn't care. She was only along for the ride. Jerish, Esrahaddon quickly determined, was of a similar mind. The Teshlor lacked the normal years of circuit training, and his geography was likely limited. Yolric was the odd one. Esrahaddon believed the old Cenzar was well aware they had just turned off the main road and were heading into wilderness. Still, he said nothing.

Elinya continued to sit, bouncing along beside him, exhibiting perfect posture, her hands clasped in her lap over the cloth-wrapped dagger.

"You treat the weapon like a baby," he said. "Are you going to carry it all the way to the castell?"

She looked down at her lap and nodded. "You and Master Yolric have your magic, Jerish his three swords. This is all I have to fight with."

"You're expecting to fight?"

"Isn't that what we are doing?" She looked back at the others traveling close behind. "Are we not champions of the emperor, sent to slay a beast?"

"I'm honestly not certain what we are, but I like your idea. Sounds so much better than . . ." He stopped short of saying a *bunch of cattle heading to the slaughterhouse*. "Look, Elinya, I'm sorry for getting you into this."

She turned her head, pulling aside the hood to see him better. "This isn't your fault."

"I failed to keep my vow."

"So did I."

Esrahaddon chuckled. "So you're saying we are *both* irresponsible failures."

"I don't think I'm a failure."

Esrahaddon realized it *was* still possible to wonder at the stupidity of at least *one* man. "I'm sorry, I didn't mean—I was making a joke, which was not only not funny but also rude. Forgive me." He looked at Elinya—really studied her—noticing her straight back and square shoulders, the firm line of her jaw, and the brightness of her eyes. "To be honest, you're very brave."

"Why? Because I stabbed a shadow? That wasn't bravery, just desperation."

"Which is often the mother of bravery. You also went into the Forbidden Forest and faced a monster to save your friend. No one else did that."

"No one else had a monster for a father."

Esrahaddon looked past the twitching ears of the horses. "I did."

He felt her stare.

"My father wanted to kill me because he thought I was a demon. I was seven years old. At his insistence—and after failing to persuade the village elders to take my life—I was driven into the forest."

She placed her hand on his. "I thought such things only happened to lowly peasant girls."

"You're not a peasant, Elinya," he said, more sternly than he meant to. "And you're no longer a girl." He rolled his hand over, taking hers in his, feeling the warmth of her palm.

"I don't care where we end up." She gave a little squeeze. "And there is no place in the world I would rather be right now. I've served in a wealthy villa, worn expensive clothes, eaten lavish meals, and wanted for nothing, except . . ."

"Except what?"

"I don't know, but no matter how this turns out, I feel more alive right now when sitting beside you than I have in the last seven years."

They traveled until the sun disappeared behind the trees, then set up camp in rapidly failing light. Jerish didn't know why they had pushed so hard. They took only a brief break at a small stream to let the horses drink and catch their breath. This was no way to treat horses, or old men. Yolric displayed no sign of exhaustion and never once complained, but Jerish assumed he was being brave. For a man of his advanced age, bouncing over rough ground for hours had to be a hardship.

"Here, let me help you down." Jerish offered his arms.

"You are most considerate, dear boy. So many in the Cenzarium could learn basic decency from you." The old man touched down on the grass, then immediately went to the horses and stroked their backs. "Poor things. A shame we treat them so. Come, help me free them of this contraption. They did all the work. They should be the first to rest."

Once the harnesses were off, Yolric took a blanket and began rubbing the animals down, telling Jerish to unload the wagon since they would sleep in it. "Better than the damp, rocky ground," he explained.

When Jerish looked over, he noticed Esrahaddon was standing off on a bluff facing east. He was staring down at the long slope that led to a sizable river, the view of which was fading with the light. A breeze blew back his robe. *Just like a Cenzar to leave the work to a woman.* Jerish looked for her, thinking to offer assistance and was surprised to see Elinya already busy building a bed out of blankets in the empty wagon. Their horses were already stripped of tack, groomed, and were eating from food bags.

She caught him looking. "Do you need any help?" she asked.

"Ah—no, I'm fine." He felt a bit embarrassed. "How did you unpack so quickly?"

Elinya pointed at Esrahaddon, then gave Jerish a scary face and wiggled her fingers.

"Magic," he said.

Elinya nodded. "Scarier than snakes."

And just as slippery, he thought.

The fire was made in the same fashion. As soon as Esrahaddon was done with his river-staring, he clapped his hands, and they had an ideal campfire. Jerish frowned at the act and considered making his own, but as it was nearly dark by then, he grudgingly consented to sit by its warmth.

Esrahaddon also played chef. This was good, since Jerish had no talent for food. Luckily, the Cenzar didn't use magic to make the meal because Jerish *would* have refused to eat anything he conjured. *Might as well just slit my own throat rather than consume an enchanted pie of* his *making.* But there was no pie. Instead, Esrahaddon whipped up a strange vegetable dish he called a *malapor.* There wasn't a shred of meat in it. Still, it was filling, hot, and astoundingly flavorful—just no flavors Jerish had ever tasted.

"Where did you get the spices?" Yolric asked.

"Rappaport brought them back with her the last time she was on circuit down in Calynia. They were . . ." He hesitated. "They were my birthday gift."

"Rappaport . . ." Yolric said absently. "She's the one who went up north, isn't she? Married a tailor. Has two kids now. Boy and a girl. I forget their names."

"I hadn't heard that." Esrahaddon put his bowl of malapor down and reached for the wineskin.

"So what's your plan?" Yolric asked.

"Plan?" Esrahaddon looked nervous, even a bit pained.

"About the river," the Cenzar master added. "There's a reason no one directly crosses the Instarya peninsula. Well, there are actually several, but the big one is the river and the lack of means across."

"Oh." Esrahaddon relaxed and took a long pull from the skin. "First, there are many ways across." He wiped his mouth. "For one, Princess Farilane, whose route I am following, swam it." He smiled. "Granted, I don't expect a man of your age to fight across a fast-flowing river, nor"—he gestured at Jerish—"would I expect an armored knight to swim. So I'll make a bridge."

Elinya appeared impressed, and Yolric nodded as if this was a perfectly sensible answer.

Jerish was the sole holdout. "You're going to do what?"

"Make a bridge. Looks to be plenty of stone down there, and with the power of the river, it shouldn't be hard. The real trick will be finding a suitable location. A tall, sharp cliff would be ideal. I'd have plenty of stone to stretch. And then there's the problem of foliage on both sides. I don't like hurting trees, but we'll need enough space to roll these wagons through. So I'd like to find a spot where there is a clearing or maybe a deer trail—something like that."

"Did you say you don't like *hurting trees?"* Jerish asked.

He nodded. "I used to live in one."

Jerish wasn't certain if Esrahaddon was making fun of him or not. Neither Yolric nor Elinya appeared the least bit surprised.

"Should we expect to stay a second night on this side?" Yolric asked. "Building a structure of that size will be taxing."

Esrahaddon shook his head. "Shouldn't be. I'll do it in the morning. Elinya and I will go down to the bank before dawn, so we'll still be able to have a full day of travel."

Yolric raised his snowy brows.

This bravado on Esrahaddon's part—Jerish was shocked to discover—was the thing that surprised the old man. Not that Esrahaddon was going *to make a bridge,* which would no doubt be like the Grand Imperial Yardley Bridge, or that he planned on doing it *in the morning*, or that he didn't like *hurting trees*, or that he claimed to have *lived in one*. The only point of debate seemed to be how tuckered Esrahaddon would be after doing the impossible.

"Well, as long as I can sleep in, I'm happy," Yolric said and reached for more malapor.

"This is really good," Elinya said.

Jerish thought them all quite insane.

Esrahaddon stood on a green hillside. A joyous breeze played with the grass, making it laugh. Overhead, a magnificent yellow sun shone down from a ridiculously blue sky. The air . . . it smelled sweet, somehow fresher, like the scent of a newborn. The field where he stood was vast. Miles of unblemished rolling green. No flies, no mosquitoes, not even bees, but he did see a butterfly. And in this miraculous meadow stood a single tree the size of a mountain. He was under its canopy, between two roots that elegantly clutched the soil, around which flowers of every color grew, yet the tree's trunk was too far away to hit with a thrown stone.

"Go ahead," the boy said. "Drop it."

Esrahaddon looked at the child sitting on one of the roots. Dark hair, dark eyes. He was waiting.

Just then, Esrahaddon realized he was holding a stone in his hand.

"You say it will roll to the stick." The kid pointed down the hillside at a broken twig jammed into the turf. "I say you're wrong."

Esrahaddon looked at his hand as he raised it up, then let go, letting the stone fall.

Before it hit the grass, the dark-haired boy rose and kicked the stone nowhere near the stick.

"Didn't see that, did you?" the boy said with a smug look.

The sky darkened.

A terrible noise shook the world.

Esrahaddon ran to the tree and tightly hugged the trunk.

"Don't worry, it can't get in," the tree told him. "Eton won't let it."

"It's stronger than Eton," Esrahaddon replied. "That's why the sky darkens. It's stronger than Elan; that is why the world shakes. And it is *getting in. Slowly, bit by bit, because they can't stop it. No one can."*

Then as proof, Esrahaddon saw a fly land on the tree's trunk. Soon he saw two, then five. More were coming. "It's getting in."

Esrahaddon awoke just before dawn, swinging at flies that weren't there.

"Are you all right?" Elinya asked.

She was lying beside him in the wagon. The two shared a blanket. Overhead, the stars were just beginning to fade.

"I, ah . . . just a bad dream."

"Oh," she said. "Want to tell me about it?"

"It's nonsensical. Something about a boy kicking a rock, a giant tree, and flies—lots of flies."

Elinya rolled over to face him. "I want to trade my nightmares for yours."

"I don't know. It was worse than it sounds."

"Flies? Really? Even I can kill a fly."

"There was something else, too, something . . . I don't know. Something bad."

"Still rather have your nightmares."

"Why, what happens in yours?"

"I'm under the ice in front of Ruby's door, trapped with my father, and the thing down there with us keeps saying how pretty and *tasty* my face looks."

"No," Esrahaddon said. "No trades. I'm keeping my flies and giant trees, thank you very much."

Elinya sat up, looking around at the faint gray of a lightening sky. "We getting up? Don't you have a bridge to build?"

"You sound excited."

She shrugged. "I've never seen anyone make a bridge, much less make one with magic."

"Well, in that case, by all means, let's not keep my audience waiting."

Esrahaddon stood on the boulder, smiling as Elinya applauded from her perch on the bluff where she sat, legs tucked up like a child watching a puppet show. While the robe refused to get wet, the same could not be said for his shoes, which were soaked through from exploring the riverbank in the dim predawn hours. He wasn't done, but the bulk of the heavy lifting was complete, along with most of the drama. He'd raised a single arch of solid stone from the bedrock below the water. The process was like watching a sea serpent rise up and stretch out across the river, where it turned solid. The bow of the arc was pronounced enough that its reflection on the surface of the water appeared to form a complete circle. After that, Esrahaddon entertained himself by adding a bit more stone on the ends to level the walkway. This made the span less a hump and more an elegant curve. When he was done, the bridge's symmetry was graceful and delicate in its slender profile. Just for fun, he added embellishments: a small knee-high wall on either side for safety, some gutters to take away rainwater, and drain holes to flush it into the river—something he had noticed on the Yardley Bridge. Then just because Elinya was watching and he could hear her gasping and cheering, he traced elegant flower and leaf-shaped designs into the stone. For a moment, he was a child painting on the wall again, only this time someone appreciated what he wrought.

"It's beautiful!" Elinya shouted, in the loudest voice he'd ever heard her use.

Esrahaddon climbed down from his boulder podium, wiping sweat off his brow, then noticed more clapping.

"That's amazing," Jerish said, standing up on the driver's bench of their wagon to gain a better view. "And you made that—just now—you—that's incredible."

Knowing how springy the driver seats were, and after seeing the team of horses shift and cause the wagon to jerk forward, Esrahaddon was equally amazed at Jerish's ability to stand so confidently and successfully.

"The design is odd," Yolric said. "Given the river's width, I would think three arches would work better, allowing for a straight road instead of this humpback climb. In winter, with ice, this will be treacherous."

Esrahaddon made a show of looking around at the flowering trees. "Luckily for us, it's spring. Besides, this is more beautiful for its simplicity, and boats—even those with sails—can pass beneath."

The rumble of hooves and cart approached as Elinya, who had run off, reappeared with their wagon. The day before, she had offered to help drive, having had experience with log-dragging oxen from Eber-on-Aston. The woman was quickly losing her shyness, and she had a great grin as she coaxed the horses down the slope toward the bridge entrance.

"May I?" she asked, exuberant. "I want to be the first."

"Certainly," he said, hopping up beside her.

Elinya licked her lips, her eyes wide and brilliant as she clucked her tongue and jostled the reins to urge the team forward. The *thump, thump, thump* of hooves abruptly changed to *clap, clop, clip* as they trod upon the stone.

Esrahaddon had only guessed at the width. Now that the wagon was on the span, he realized it was a tad snug. "Probably should have made it wider."

"It's fine," Elinya said. "You're nit-picking."

"I am?"

"Yes, you're quibbling over unnecessary details."

"Unnecessary details? Where I come from, nit-picking means to remove the eggs of lice from someone's hair."

"That's right."

He stared at Elinya for a long moment, then shifted away from her on the bench seat.

"Oh, stop it."

The wagon rolled up the incline, and Elinya drew the animals to a halt at the apex so she could take a moment to look around. They were up high, not quite above the trees, but close. To the left and right, the river flowed like a glass snake. This was the East Bernum, which was narrower but faster than the West Bernum, and according to Farilane, it flowed from snow melt out of Mount Mador. Behind them, the low-lying meadowlands lay. Ahead, the steep embankments of the Forbidden Forest rose, marked by soaring pines.

Elinya presented him with a bursting, giddy grin. He wondered if she'd forgotten they were likely traveling to their deaths, either in the forest dead ahead or somewhere farther east. *Dead ahead*, he mused, and sighed.

"Not to worry, Esra. Yolric will take care of you."

Esrahaddon glanced back at Yolric and Jerish, who were also taking in the unique view. *Let's hope you're right, Sond.*

Farilane's essay had described the climb up the embankment on the east side of the river as *harrowing*—this coming from a woman who'd purposely sailed a ten-foot sloop into a storm that had sunk a fleet, jumped off a cliff into a pool of water she *suspected* of being deep enough, and challenged a dwarven lord and his kingdom to a fight she'd won by bluffing. Esrahaddon didn't want to reenact the princess's hardship, so he cleared a pleasant path ahead. He snaked the road around trees as best he could, but had no qualms about rocks, ferns, and what Farilane had called "cat's claw thorn bushes." So they found themselves deep in the Forbidden Forest in just a few hours.

Esrahaddon had prepared himself this time. He knew not to trust his eyes and ears. Ruby was a fan of illusions, and he wondered if the trees—so massive, so tall—were real or just imagination. He took a moment to check, to sense if he was witnessing Art or reality, and was surprised to find no evidence of manipulation. Unless Ruby was more powerful than he'd realized, this temple of wood was real.

Elinya struggled to find a clear route, but as Esrahaddon had expected, a road revealed itself. This was the infamous Greenway that Farilane had encountered. Unlike her, Esrahaddon watched for the enchantment and spotted the deception. This was where the road looped back on itself while the true path lay hidden.

"Through there." He pointed at a tightly packed wall of trees.

Elinya replied with a puzzled face.

"The trees aren't really there."

She looked again. "Even if I believe you, the horses won't."

He nodded, and taking blankets from the back, wrapped them over the horses' eyes.

"What's going on?" Jerish called forward.

"Just wrap your team's eyes. Then follow us."

With that, he nodded at Elinya, who took a deep breath and veered the horses into the trees. A moment later, they entered a new world as if passing through a portal.

This must be an illusion, Esrahaddon thought as he stared at the glen, but he knew it wasn't.

Ancient trees of various species gave the impression of a tunnel formed by gently cupped hands. A stunning canopy of green was pierced charmingly here and there by shafts of sunlight. The tree trunks displayed immense character in their old, wrinkled bark that was wreathed in decorations of white-flowered garlands. These blossom-bedecked ivy festoons drew honeybees and countless butterflies of various colors. Verdant ferns and wide leafy plants decorated a carpet of vibrant moss. Through the middle of it all ran a trail that several creeks and brooks crossed as they spilled down stones, adding a murmur of welcome to a paradise no imagination could have conjured. This place was marvelously enchanting, but it wasn't magical. Still, as he stared, Esrahaddon heard once more the laughter of a girl and the howl of a wolf.

"From here, we walk," Esrahaddon said, seeing no way for a wagon to traverse the narrow path.

"What about the horses?" Jerish asked.

"I don't suspect we'll be going far."

Jerish took a moment to strap on his three swords. Why, Esrahaddon couldn't fathom, except that he was unfamiliar with the world in general and Ruby Finn in particular. Esrahaddon felt a novel bit of sympathy for him. Only a few years out of his teens, and if Ruby Finn didn't kill him, Mileva certainly would.

"What an amazing place," Yolric muttered as they walked in single file down the path. "There's magic here—old magic."

Esrahaddon led the way. He didn't want to, didn't care to be there at all. But he knew he needed to be the first person Ruby Finn saw, or he might be the last one standing. "Ruby told me someone named Suri—an Artist of some renown—used to call this her home."

"Yes, she did, but the magic here is older than her by far. This place was intentionally sheltered. Everything here is akin to a child's nursery."

They crossed over playful brooks, stepping on flat, perfectly placed stones. Brushed through broad patches of daffodils and circled a picturesque pond where two white swans drifted ghostly on the surface within the last residue of a morning mist. Then down a slight slope, they all spotted the cottage. Each one of them made some sort of surprised sound.

Jerish gasped.

Elinya giggled.

Yolric produced a dignified "Hmm."

And Esrahaddon said, "And here I was proud of *my* tree house."

A great hawthorn, bigger and likely older than any other Esrahaddon had ever seen, dominated an open sunny glade. In the center of the trunk was a beautiful half-moon door with a set of steps leading to it. Above and part way up the tree was a round window, complete with a peaked awning and crosshair muntins. As the hawthorn was simply not large enough for a full-sized house, other, larger architectural extensions had slightly more conventional roofs and walls. Up on one side, shaped roughly like a giant beehive, was an attached turret with a conical roof covered in moss. It, too, had a window with crossed sashes.

Outside, a barrel was tucked into the cleft of two roots. And a great flat stone, like a massive table, lay in front. On the sunny side of the tree was a garden. A small pond formed the center and gave birth to three tiny ditches that trickled and laughed and watered the vegetable beds. There were several perfect sitting stones to rest on, and a moss-enriched walkway of flat stones. A waist-high wall draped in ivy formed a half circle that appeared to be the place for putting the unwanted rocks.

I guess everyone does that.

As they gawked, the door in the tree opened and, ducking low, Ruby Finn stepped out. She was dressed just as before in the same green gown and still lacking any shoes. She came down the steps, a frown growing on her face.

Reaching the bottom, she folded her arms and glared at Esrahaddon. "Who *are* these people?"

"Good morning, Ruby," Esrahaddon said in case the others hadn't figured out who the angry redhead was.

"I don't care about the morning," she snarled. "I invited you. No one else. You know what I do to trespassers."

Esrahaddon almost raised his hands as a gesture for her to relax, but being Artists, that might be seen as a threat. Instead, he forced himself to speak awkwardly with his arms down stiff at his sides. "You invited me. I invited them as my guests."

"You had no right."

Esrahaddon rolled his eyes. "You sent a giant shadow beast to kill me and Elinya!"

"You broke your promise."

"A promise made under duress."

"Under what?" She looked confused. "We were in the forest. We weren't under anything. This is my home. My realm and any who—"

"This isn't your home," Yolric said. "You only wish it were. Your home was in Merredydd, but you don't remember that little house at the end of the brick road because you were only a small child when your grandparents sold you to that workhouse in Greenwich. *That's* your real home—the one you grew up in. It doesn't exist anymore, of course, because you destroyed it, along with sixty-three people, forty-two of whom were orphaned children. All that's left of that home is a crater the size of a dried-up lake. You were what? Twelve? Thirteen?"

Ruby didn't answer, but her eyes bore down and her lips pulled back to show teeth.

"You ran and were hunted for years until you found this place. You felt the residue of Suri, and it was like finding a warm blanket and soft mattress." He looked around at the glen. "So much of her still lingers like perfume in the air. You wanted this to be your home because you longed to have what she had. You want to *be* her."

"She understands my pain. I can feel it."

Yolric shook his head, wagging his beard. "Suri died two thousand years ago. All you feel is her echo. All you are is her shadow."

Ruby's hands came up. So did Esrahaddon's, and Jerish reached for his two side swords.

"Don't," Yolric said without moving. His tone was not angry, or frightened, or even particularly urgent. If anything, the Cenzar master sounded bored.

Ruby hesitated. She cocked her head, eyeing him with a sidelong stare as if trying to understand a puzzle by looking at it a bit differently. Then her eyes widened.

"You!" She took a step back and glanced accusingly at Esrahaddon as if he'd betrayed her. "You brought *him* here? You wear Uberlin's cloak, and you brought *him* with you?"

Now even Yolric appeared surprised, and with good reason.

Esrahaddon had been afraid of this. At their last meeting, Ruby showed signs of being less than sane. She didn't tap her foot to a different drumbeat; she heard music where there wasn't any. He even suspected it possible that her intention to hunt a riva was a delusion—he was actually hoping that was the case. In his best scenario, he called her bluff and she forgot why he was there and sent him home. This, however, was the worst possibility. Her delusions got the better of Ruby and she attacked all of them, thinking they were a threat.

"Ruby, calm down," Esrahaddon said. "I'm here as promised. I'm going to help you destroy Mileva, as you insisted. But she's a riva, and they don't die easily. I mean, literally, that's what a riva is—someone who refuses to die—a grotesquely powerful, infinitely ancient raow. These others are here to help. Well, these two are. Elinya is along because I couldn't let her out of my sight until I was convinced you weren't going to hunt her anymore."

He took a breath, trying to sense Ruby's mood. Nothing suggested it had changed, except that she was still listening and not raining fire. "This is Yolric, a Cenzar master, who I am told can aid us. And that's Jerish, a Teshlor, who, to be honest, probably can't."

To his credit, Jerish appeared to take no offense at this. His attention remained on Ruby, his hands on his swords, but he hadn't pulled them.

Ruby focused on Yolric and took a slow step forward. "Why?"

"I'm curious to see what goes on here," the old man replied neutrally, with a nonchalant air.

Esrahaddon hadn't thought much of Yolric when they first set out, but the way he faced her down was impressive.

"You *know* what goes on here. You just heard him!" Ruby pointed at Esrahaddon, who forced himself not to flinch. "We're going to kill Mileva Hitartheon."

"Are you?" Yolric maintained his breezy demeanor. "Are you going to *destroy* a riva or *make* one? Possibly two? That's part of what I'd like to know. And then there's the robe." Yolric glanced at Esrahaddon. "The lad is wearing the Gry Erlikon."

"And you want it?" Ruby accused with an understanding nod as if now it all made perfect sense.

Yolric raised his brows, then knitted them as he considered this. "Interesting idea. Hadn't thought of that—until now." He turned and faced Esrahaddon. "You never wanted to come here. You have no interest in killing this riva. Ruby Finn threatened you and Elinya—that's why you're here. I'll tell you what. You give me that robe, and you, Jerish, and Elinya can go back to Percepliquis free of your Ruby Finn curse. How does that sound?"

"I must kill one," Ruby explained. "Him or Mileva. That's what Uberlin said."

"Did he now?" Yolric mused a moment. "All right. Give me the robe, Esrahaddon, and I will go with Ruby and destroy the riva in your stead. That works too, doesn't it?" he asked.

Ruby considered this.

"Why not just kill Ruby?" Elinya asked. Everyone stared at her, making the woman retreat a step. "Sorry, just seems logical. That's all."

"Because," Yolric said, "I'm not a murderer."

"But you're willing to kill Mileva?" Jerish asked.

"Mileva is already dead," Yolric explained. "Her time was up millennia ago. Eliminating her would only be resetting the natural order." He focused once more on Esrahaddon. "You don't want to mess with Mileva. Trust me, you and Ruby together are still no match for her. And if you know what a riva is, you know they don't just kill you. They eat you, face-first, while you're still alive, and then add your bones to their pile and your soul to their prison for eternity."

"Why aren't *you* afraid of her?" Esrahaddon asked.

"Oh, I'm too old. I don't fear anything anymore."

"Even having your immortal soul locked up for all of eternity?"

Yolric laughed, but it wasn't a wholesome or happy sound. Hearing it, Esrahaddon felt concern, a tiny warning. For the first time, he wondered whether Isilpor-Sond was right, and a truly awful past must have been required to make Yolric the greatest of Cenzars. What kind of incidents could have granted him the courage or apathy to laugh at such a fate?

"Then why don't you just kill Esrahaddon and take the robe?" Ruby asked. She shot a hot look at Elinya and added, "Just seems logical. That's all. That way you get the robe, and no one has to bother with Mileva."

"I just said I'm not a murderer," Yolric replied, raising his voice so everyone could clearly hear him. "Besides, I don't want to do what Uberlin wants. However, at this moment I can't tell what that is. All of this is so odd. He's asked you to eliminate one of his most powerful servants—a task you're not capable of achieving. And out of the mists of time, he sends me the Gry Erlikon delivered on the back of a boy." Yolric shook his head. "No, he wouldn't give it to me that easily. Isn't that right, Esrahaddon? You're not going to give it up, even to save your immortal soul from Mileva."

Esrahaddon shrugged. He had no idea what this was all about, what Yolric was getting at, or what he was trying to accomplish. But Yolric was quite right. "It was a birthday present from my mother."

"Really?" Jerish asked, astonished.

Yolric laughed. "You'd give up your immortal soul over a sentimental attachment? I thought you more intelligent."

"Strange," Jerish said. "I thought him less honorable."

"Hekkabah," Esrahaddon began, "my adoptive mother, who saved my life when I was abandoned to the forest, was a High Priestess of Uberlin. She sacrificed everything she had, her home, her station, her friends and family, even her young son, just so I could have this robe. I still don't know why. But no, I'm not giving it to anyone. Ever. I'll die with this on. Besides . . ." Esrahaddon offered a wry smile. "Maybe you don't want it as much as you think. The robe ate the last fellow I gave it to."

"See?" Yolric said to Ruby. "So now I must decide what Uberlin really wants. Problem is, whatever I decide, I'll be wrong. You have no idea how frustrating that is. I didn't think he could see me—and maybe he can't, but maybe I caught him off guard last time. Now he's taking steps, making better guesses based on ripple effects. There's no way he places that robe within my reach without a good reason. There's something else going on. Something huge because Uberlin is betting the house."

Is Yolric fighting crazy with crazy, trying to confuse her? He was certainly confusing Esrahaddon.

"What are you talking about?" he asked. "Why does everyone want this robe? Sure, it's nice and all, but I've gotten the impression there's more to it. Adding to the mystery is the fact that there are no mentions of a Gry Erlikon anywhere in the Cenzarium or imperial library."

"Wouldn't be," Yolric said. "Documents in the library only date back a few hundred years. The oldest would be the *Book of Brin*, and that only goes back a couple thousand. The robe you wear is over thirteen thousand years old and hasn't been seen in well over twelve, I would say. Most suspected it was lost, destroyed perhaps when they tried to rend the world. That made the most sense."

"But what is it?"

"I believe I already mentioned that it is the Robe of State made and worn by Rex Uberlin when he assumed the throne as ruler of the world."

"So it's just a symbol, then?"

"Oh no," Yolric replied, "this robe is one of Uberlin's five most treasured possessions. The others being his mantle, the Key of Eton, his spear Narsirabad, and, of course, his crown. That robe was famous in its day. Like the mantle, it was created for convenience. You've noticed how it lights up when you need it to, yes? Also, it keeps you warm or cool and protects you from rain. It'll even change size if you gain weight. And it never wears out or gets dirty. All of these things were the robe's primary function while Uberlin reigned—he hated changing his clothes. But rumor holds that when Uberlin disappeared, when he supposedly had a change of heart, he gave up his powers to walk the world like a mortal man. How he managed that, no one alive, and I suspect even few of the dead, could say. But it is suspected that he divided his immense Aesirian heritage and—because he trusted no one—he stored all that power in his beloved possessions. Then he hid them, locked each one up, presumably so that one day, should he have another change of heart, he could regain his birthright and happily return to his earlier hobby of destroying the world." Yolric studied the gown that was, at that moment, giving off a very mild blue-green glow. "To be honest, I didn't believe the rumors. It's hard for me to accept that Uberlin could bring himself to give up power, but the Gry Erlikon, the robe I knew, couldn't consume a person—but Uberlin could."

"So then, you're saying that if Esrahaddon gave you this robe," Ruby Finn thought out loud, "and it didn't eat you, you would have the power of the evil god?"

"Doubt it," Yolric replied. "Uberlin retains his talent of foresight, so he could have seen this moment and may have taken precautions."

"Meaning it would eat you," Elinya said.

"Something like that, yes."

Ruby Finn bit her lip, then said, "But it is just as likely that Uberlin saw that you wouldn't take it, and as a result didn't bother to set any traps at all."

Yolric raised a significant finger. "And that is the crux of my dilemma—always has been."

"But wait," Jerish spoke up. "Does that mean *Esrahaddon* can use these god-powers?"

Yolric looked at Esrahaddon. "I don't know. Can you?"

Esrahaddon shrugged. "Until now, I had no idea they existed. But . . . no. I mean"—he shrugged a second time—"it's just a robe."

"One that eats people," Jerish pointed out.

"I didn't say it was typical."

"Be way too expensive if it was," Elinya said, and once more she drew everyone's stare. "What?" she said. "I spent years working in the Garment Industry. I'm just saying no one could afford that."

"So where does this leave us?" Esrahaddon asked, looking back and forth between Ruby and Yolric.

"Looks like we're going to kill a riva," Ruby replied.

Yolric nodded.

"We aren't all going," Esrahaddon said. "There's no reason to endanger Elinya any further, is there?"

Ruby shook her head. "No, she's free."

"And Jerish can escort her back to Percepliquis—take one of the wagons. We'll take the other."

Jerish shook his head. "I'm supposed to go with you. Emperor's orders, remember?"

Esrahaddon sighed. "Jerish, look, I realize I've been less than kind to you. To be quite honest, one might even say I've been a bit of a bastard—but I'm not now. This isn't that. I made the mistake of involving you in this and—"

"*You* did?"

"Yes, I was the one who suggested you to the emperor."

"I thought Gaylord Sire did that."

"He insisted there be a Teshlor. I picked you."

"Why?"

"So you wouldn't be filling Nevrik's head with dangerous ideas while I was away and unable to counter them."

"And now?"

Esrahaddon attempted to rub the strain from between his eyes. "You heard what Yolric said about Mileva. I know that might sound like a fairy tale to you, but I grew up with people who knew better. The truth is, I don't want you to die—or worse. And I don't want Elinya to be left alone. So I'm asking you, as an honorable knight, to please return her safely to Percepliquis."

Jerish didn't answer. His eyes tensed, his teeth clenched, and he sighed several times.

"He can't," Elinya said.

"Why not?" Jerish and Esrahaddon asked together.

"Because I'm not going back."

"Elinya," Esrahaddon said. "This isn't a game."

"Neither was walking into the Forbidden Forest. In fact, I would say the situation is identical."

"But there's no reason for you to come."

"Yes, there is. Same reason I had for walking into the Forbidden Forest."

Esrahaddon shook his head, showing he didn't understand. "You went into the forest to help your . . . friends." As he spoke, he realized he'd answered his own question. "But, Elinya, you won't be able to. Even Jerish will be of no use. I question if I can be, and just this morning you saw me make a bridge out of nothing. If what Yolric says is true, this is a suicide pact we're making."

"You once told me that desperation can be the mother of bravery," Elinya said.

"I left out that ignorance is the father."

"I lost everyone I cared about when I was fifteen. I spent seven years living in the greatest city in the world, and I felt nothing but alone—except when you visited." She gritted her teeth. "Where you go, I go. And Novron help the Teshlor Knight or Imperial Cenzar who tries to stop me."

Jerish raised his hands. "I'm on your side, dear lady."

Esrahaddon sighed and tugged on the front of the robe. "I wish I did control Uberlin's power."

"What would you do?" Ruby asked.

"I don't know. At this point I'd probably just summon a frothy mug of Green Gurlin and a shot of hohura. I mean, this is . . . this is just riddlebag ridiculous. No"—he shook his head—"as my Uncle Niblick would say: 'It's beyond that, it's a mingle-mangled mess—a gallimaufry of errors.'"

"Your uncle sounds very . . . *interesting*," Elinya said.

"My uncle is a blue-skinned, seafaring, Urgvarian Ba Ran with a real anti-authoritarian attitude and a colorful gift for strange words."

"Must run in the family then," Jerish said.

Esrahaddon looked at the Teshlor and caught a smile. *Did Jerish Grelad just make a joke?*

CHAPTER TWENTY-NINE

Ryin Contita

NORTHERN ALBURNIA

Two days after Ulin joined them, Sadarshakar Sikaria and Hanis Orphe were still following Marley Gris when they spotted the indisputable outline of Mount Mador. The strangely conical shape, a little too perfect to be natural, stood out dramatically on the flat plain. The top was snow-covered and glistening in the setting sun. The sight was everything legend promised. Folklore told of a great Fhrey ruler—a powerful Cenzar—who had created the mountain. No one knew why. Such stories never came with any sensible explanation. They were invented to explain things that had no explanation. Crows were black because they were made last, and Elan had run out of colors; trees used to walk but were rooted into place because one had accidentally stepped on the toe of a god. Silly as they were, the tales persisted, handed down from one generation to the next. Seeing Mount Mador with his own eyes, however, Sadarshakar could see how the story came into being. The mountain did look disturbingly artificial and out of place.

"Do you think he ever bathes?" Hanis asked.

"Marley?"

Hanis nodded.

"I'm almost certain he does," Sadarshakar said. "When it rains."

Hanis smiled, then glanced behind them, as he often did. Sadarshakar didn't need to turn to know what he looked at. Ulin rode behind them.

"It's hard to tell she's a myr." Hañis chose to whisper this. He apparently had no qualms about discussing Marley Gris's poor grooming habits or questionable wardrobe decisions in his typical *outside* voice, but this he whispered. Maybe because humans were known to have terrible hearing, or perhaps because Ulin wore a sword. "She passes really well. I mean, I had no idea, did you?"

"No, can't say I did."

"Do you find her attractive?" Hanis asked, his voice so faint now, Sadarshakar barely heard.

"Yes."

"Really?" He turned and looked again, then frowned. "I don't know. I mean, sure she's got all her parts in the right places, but she's still a myr."

"Got all her parts in the right places? Are you serious? Sounds as if you're sizing up a used wagon. And so what if she's a myr? You just got done saying you couldn't tell the difference. Doesn't that mean there isn't one?"

Hanis scowled. "I've never been able to tell the difference between an edible and a poisonous mushroom, but there's definitely a difference."

"Ulin is no more a mushroom than she is a wagon. She's a person . . . a very attractive female person."

"You like humans, too, don't you?" Hanis shook his head. "I've seen the way you look at a few of the women in Percepliquis."

"Oh, I've done more than look, my friend."

Hanis shivered.

"Wait, hold on now. We've been in Percepliquis for more than a decade. There are very few Fhrey in the city and absolutely no gyns—no female Fhrey at all. Are you telling me you've been celibate all this time?"

"I wouldn't say that." Hanis straightened up in his saddle, lifting his chin a smidge. "And there have been a few visiting gyn."

Sadarshakar started to protest, then he stopped, and his eyes widened. "Not Yimar?"

Hanis didn't reply. He refused to even look over.

"Hanis, she's married to your uncle!"

"At least she's Frhey."

"And family, and . . . by Ferrol, she must be what? Well into her second millennium? It's more like you're robbing a crypt, my friend."

Hanis looked over with a wicked grin and said, "And it's a very *rich* crypt—a very well-off, well-built mausoleum, indeed."

The sun was low when they reached the river. On the far side lay the start of a towering forest the like of which Sadarshakar had never seen. Most of the trees around Merredydd and Percepliquis had long been logged, regrown, and logged again. These massive old-growth trees supported a high canopy that cast everything below in darkness.

"That'll be the Harwood," Marley Gris announced, pulling his mount to a halt. "The start of No Man's Land."

"Ryin Contita, you mean?" Sadarshakar said.

"However you wanna say it don't change a thing, but over that river is the start of the real wilderness. No one's allowed in there."

"But you're all going, right?" Sadarshakar asked. "You were contracted to escort us to the banks of the river Nidwalden, and this isn't that."

"I know. You're right, and we will. You see, the Harwood is forbidden to everyone, and because of that, there's no one to stop us. Anyone we see inside is just as guilty as ourselves, so not much chance of finger-pointing."

"How long do you think it will take to reach the Nidwalden?" Hanis asked as they all dismounted.

"Impossible to say. I've never been."

"Then how will you guide us?"

"I have an old map." He clapped his chest. "And there's supposed to be an ancient road."

"According to this map of yours, how far do you estimate?" Sadarshakar asked.

Marley swished his lips to and fro for a few seconds. "Depends on the condition of this mythical road. My guess is, after two thousand years it isn't much of a highway, which means we'll need to cut a new one. So there'll be a few days spent just scouting the *best route*, then days if not weeks of cutting trees to clear a path large enough for the wagons. And those are some big-looking trees."

"Can't we just leave the wagons and put the gear on the horses?"

"Maybe, but again it depends on the forest. Some are too dense for horses, and a forest that hasn't seen humans or elves in thousands of years is likely to be a problem. I'll know more tomorrow. We'll set up a nice base camp here, and in the morning you and yours can take the day off and lounge away doing what you like. I'll cross this here river down at that shallow bend and spend the day poking around the old Harwood—see if'n I can find this road or not. I'll be able to tell you lads more then. Okay?"

Without much else they could say, Sadarshakar took their personal packs and handed the animals off to the groom, who led them away to the river to drink.

"I hope you weren't planning on being anywhere anytime soon, Ulin," Hanis told her as she, too, handed her animal off. "Looks like this two-week trip might take a year."

"My schedule's clear," she replied and moved off to a nearby tree to make use of its shade.

"Sadar!" Hanis shouted.

Still night, everything was dark as their tent collapsed onto them. The heavy canvas hesitated only slightly, puffing out from air trapped within.

"What's going on?" Sadarshakar asked as the canvas settled over his face.

"I don't know!" Hanis shouted, pushing up on his side of the tent and causing Sadarshakar's portion to come down.

Then a weight landed on Sadarshakar. Something straddled him, a weight pressing on his stomach.

"Here's one!" a voice above him said.

"I got the other!"

"How about the elf bitch?" Marley Gris's harsh voice was unmistakable.

What's going on? Sadarshakar struggled to make sense of the world. He couldn't see, couldn't move much at all. The canvas, and now a man, pinned him down. He felt hands searching him through the canvas.

"Lyle killed her. He and Bo. She was sound asleep."

They killed Ulin! Sadarshakar managed to put it all together. Shaking off sleep had muddled his mind, but it wasn't a hard puzzle. They had hired Ulin to defend against this very possibility.

"Which one have you got, Deek?" Marley asked.

"I dunno," said the man atop Sadarshakar.

"Doesn't matter I guess," Marley mused. "I'd-a liked to have watched them blubber a bit. Them two was all so full of themselves. But I don't care that much. Here, bring me that knife you used to cut the guylines."

Sadarshakar struggled to shove the man off, but the canvas held him like a fly in a web. Breathing was becoming an issue.

"Okay," Marley said a short distance away. "Let's see. We'll start with this one."

"Get off me, you filthy animal!"

"Ah-ha! So you'd be Hanis. Good, I wanted to begin with you. So you don't like the way I look or the clothes I wear, eh? Maybe I'll wear your clothes instead. What do you think of that?"

"Careful how you cut him, Marley," one of the others warned. "There's a slope here. Cut him downhill so his blood don't stain the fabric."

"Bah!" Marley laughed. "Like I'd wear pixie robes!"

"You'd look good in 'em, boss."

"You can't do this!" Hanis screamed. "Let me go! I'm an imperial councilor!"

"Where's the little bugger's neck?"

"I got his ankle, so it must be the other end."

Sadarshakar heard scuffling.

"What's that?" Marley asked.

"I dunno . . . wait, I—"

There was a cry, the canvas pulled sharply, then another scream.

What's going on? Sadarshakar tried again to shove off Deek and had better luck, managing to at least move the man and free an arm, but to no avail. All he could do was slide it under the tent fabric. *Maybe it's Hanis! He has his dagger! He's fighting them.*

Sadarshakar had a mental image of Hanis stabbing upward through the canvas, killing Marley, then slicing away the cloth, leaping out, and proving his Instarya ancestry.

Above Sadarshakar and somewhere on the other side of the smothering canvas, Deek made a muffled *woof!* Then he fell over, off to one side.

Things grew quiet then.

"Hanis? Hanis?" Sadarshakar called.

"I'm here."

There was a sawing sound, then a rip. The canvas came apart, and Sadarshakar saw Hanis crouched over him, dagger in hand. A quick look revealed five dead men on top of the collapsed tent, Marley Gris among their number.

"I take back everything I ever said about your martial skills, Hanis. You saved our lives!"

Hanis shook his head. "Wasn't me."

"But you have your dagger." Sadarshakar didn't understand.

Hanis shook his head. "I was held down. Just now got it. All I did was cut us out."

"So who killed them?"

They both looked around at the darkened slope that led down to the stream running silver with starlight. The moonless night and the nearby trees made it hard to see, or at least it felt that way. With a mysterious killer on the prowl, nothing short of full daylight would have sufficed.

"Do you think the killer—the one who got them," Sadarshakar whispered. "Do you think it didn't see us because of the tent?"

"It?" Hanis was still on his knees. The dagger was shaking in his hand. "What do you think? It must be a monster, right?"

"I don't know."

"It killed eight men in seconds." Hanis gestured wildly with the dagger at the corpses near and far. "They didn't even cry out."

"I heard a couple screams." Sadarshakar fought to breathe. He was panting for air like he'd been running.

"Short-lived ones."

Sadarshakar scanned the landscape and found it so very alien. He'd never been this far out on the frontier before. Who knew what might be lurking so close to the eaves of the Harwood? It was foolish to think they would only be in danger *inside* the wood. Of course it was also foolish to trust Marley Gris and his band of human cutthroats. *Who am I kidding? Hanis and I are a pair of imbeciles.* "This isn't good, Hanis. This is very not good."

"Oh, really? Thanks for that bulletin because I almost thought I was having the time of my life."

"Are you two all right?"

Hanis let out a squeak of fear as both of them jumped.

"Ulin?" Sadarshakar said, seeing the gyn moving toward them, sword drawn.

She chuckled. "You sound disappointed. Would you have preferred a forest monster? Something big and hairy?"

"No! But . . . what happened? They said you were dead."

Ulin cleaned her blade with the tent canvas. The entire length was coated in a dark liquid that in the starlight appeared black, but in daylight, Sadarshakar guessed it would have been red. "They killed the *other* me." She deftly returned the sword to her scabbard, where it slid home without a sound.

"What?" Hanis asked, his voice nervous.

"After dark, I made a mound out of branches and grass. Wrapped it in blankets and my cloak. Put the hood up." She pulled the cloak around and put fingers through two separate holes in the cloth, wiggling them. "Not very honorable, these men of yours."

"You . . . you killed them all?"

"You can count the bodies if you like, just to be sure, but I'm pretty good with numbers, and I ran my blade through eight hearts and four throats. Because I previously counted twelve, I think we can surmise that, yes, I killed them all. Forgive me. But having been stabbed while I slept, I felt no compunction to offer quarter."

"I won't forgive you for anything!" Hanis said. "That was brilliant! Thank you!"

"So does this mean you'll pay me?"

The morning brought flies that swarmed and lighted on the bodies. Sadarshakar couldn't summon even a hint of sympathy for the troop of humans who had tried to kill them, but the flies were disgusting. Of all things, including vultures and rats, he felt flies were the most appalling. Rats and vultures kept their distance, but flies thought nothing of buzzing around his head and landing on his face—even going into his mouth. *Where do they come from? What purpose do they serve? Why are there so many different kinds, and why are they everywhere?* Flies, he felt, were proof of evil in the world. Mindless, pointless, chaotic evil that served no purpose greater than spreading misery.

Sadarshakar and Hanis left the dead where they lay and consolidated the wagons' gear, having decided to push on with their quest. They had discussed this at length during the remainder of the night since neither had slept. Both speculated about whether they ever would again. Ulin had no such trouble. She curled up in a wagon, and at one point they heard her snoring.

"You don't need to come," Sadarshakar told Ulin. "You've earned your pay. We'll give it to you now if you wish, and you can return to Merredydd."

"But you two are going on?"

"Yes," Hanis said.

"You could still use a sword. No telling what's in those trees."

"The Harwood is the start of the Ryin Contita. That whole region is off-limits. After you saved our lives, we feel it is . . . *rude* to ask you to break the law."

"Besides," Hanis said, "I primarily hired you to protect us from . . ." He swept a hand at the bodies.

"I see," she said. "But that leaves me in a bind."

"How so?"

"I took this job not so much for the money as for the other thing."

"To prove yourself worthy," Sadarshakar filled in.

"Yes. But if my two clients—revered imperial councilors beyond reproach—walk into that forest and never come out to tell the tale of how Ulin Myr Halcyon defended them against twelve traitorous human cutthroats, I'll be less than half-paid." She looked down at the pommel of her sword, a beautiful thing with an elaborate hilt and handle. "No one would accept any story I told. So you see, I have a vested interest in ensuring your safe passage both there and back."

"You understand, if we are successful," Sadarshakar told her, "Hanis and I intend to go directly to the emperor and explain what we've done, meaning we all have just as much chance of being executed as rewarded."

She touched the crest on her uniform. "The Order of the Fauyld is not a bashful fellowship. We were founded by Tekchin, a notorious braggart, gambler, thrill-seeker, and nonconformist rebel. Given that I took this job to prove myself worthy of this crest, I need only ask myself what Tekchin would do."

"And the answer?"

"I'm taking the big black stallion Gris was riding. My old nag is worthless but all I could afford. I suspect if we let the rest go, they can find their way back."

"Just going to leave the wagons?" Hanis asked.

"Don't think anyone else will be up this way. Squirrels and chipmunks might get at some of it, maybe even a bear, but we might get lucky. Most will probably be here when we return. Good to have supplies waiting."

"Marley seemed to think horses wouldn't manage the forest," Sadarshakar said.

"That Marley?" She pointed at his dead body. "Still trust him, do you?"

"That reminds me . . ." Sadarshakar opened the front of Marley's buckskin and discovered that in at least one respect, the vile creature was telling the truth. There was a map. A sheet of parchment possessed a hand-drawn illustration of hills, valleys, and rivers. Percepliquis was clearly marked, as was Avempartha, with the most detailed portion centering on the Harwood and its many trails. This was good news in more than merely providing a chart for their course. It also suggested Marley was genuinely planning to take them to the river as agreed. His decision to murder Hanis and himself was just that, *Marley's decision*. Bishop Venlin likely knew nothing about it because Venlin was no doubt the map's cartographer.

CHAPTER THIRTY

In the Shadow

NORTHERN RHULYNIA

"How is it you can leave your tree?" Esrahaddon asked Alurya as she walked with him through the snow-covered forest.

"Same as you," she replied.

"I don't have a tree."

"You have a body—same thing."

"But I can't leave my body."

"You will. Just like me, you have a form born of Elan and a spirit born of Eton. They can separate. The time will come when you die and go to Phyre. In my case, it happens every year."

"You go to Phyre?"

"No," she laughed, and it was the sound of forgotten spring. "I stay here. Phyre is where the Typhons are, and where you will go."

"Why?"

"Because Eton insists on time alone with Elan. He's actually very jealous."

"What happens to me in Phyre?"

"You just wait there a while. Then you come back, just the same as I must return to my tree form in spring. The duration might be different for you—no one really knows, as

no Aesirian has yet died. My guess is that you will get a different body when you return, like the annuals do."

"The Typhons don't come back."

"No," her voice lowered to the sound of a lonely wind. "Nor will they ever."

"Why?"

She shook her head. "The tale of the Typhons is not for one so young as you. Maybe when you're older."

"Are you a . . ." Esrahaddon reached out and touched her. Then he smiled with relief.

"Yes, Turin, I have a real body—but it's only temporary. I can take many forms. I'm this way now for you."

"Why not stay this way?"

"I can't do my job this way. Like this, I'm disconnected from Elan. Not completely, more like you are. You feel her, and she's aware of you, but it's not the same as when I'm rooted. Then . . . well, then we are almost one, which is why Eton doesn't like it."

"What's your job?"

She whirled around, lifting her arms towards the leafless trees. "Remember how this was in spring and summer? That's my job. I am the source of all that's green. I am the blossom on every flower, the heartbeat of every animal, and that includes you."

"You made me?"

She smiled. "I am life, vast and varied. I draw my power from my mother, Elan, and grow in a multitude of forms. You are the first of my greatest achievement—the Aesira. And I love you dearly."

Esrahaddon reached out and hugged her then. "I love you, Alurya! I don't want to go to Phyre. I never want to leave you."

"I love you, too. And we will never be apart for long. Don't worry. As I said, death is only temporary. Eton and Elan have promised me. Phyre will just be a place to rest for a bit, like winter before a new spring begins. You'll see. Trust me."

He pouted.

"All right. Here." Alurya held out a golden fruit. "Take this, but don't eat it yet. This is special."

"In what way?" He studied it, noting how it glowed from within.

"If you eat this, you shall become immortal, and you will never be able to enter Phyre."

"Why don't I eat it, then?"

"Because you might want to go to Phyre. One day, Phyre might be a wonderful place where everyone visits as a respite from this world. A refuge to take a breather in between adventures, sort of how winter is for me. A time for reflection and relaxation. But . . . if it isn't, if Eton goes back on his word and attempts to lock you up as he did the Typhons, then eat it and he will not be able to send you there."

Esrahaddon nodded, clutching the fruit as if it were a magic treasure.

A fly buzzed by. It circled, darted, and landed on a snowy mound.

They both watched it. Easy to do, the way the insect stood out so dramatically against the snow. The pest was only there a moment, then it flew away.

"Did you make flies, too?"

Alurya didn't answer. She looked frightened, which was an answer in itself.

The next morning, Elinya chose to ride with Jerish in his wagon, since the one she'd shared with Esrahaddon didn't really exist anymore. Rather than play the proper host, Ruby Finn had ignored everyone and spent the night *working* on the wagon. By morning, the simple four-wheeled flatbed and bench had transformed into a lavish white coach with gold filigree, four walls, a roof, and two doors—complete with glass windows. Inextinguishable lanterns were mounted fore and aft, and a banded spring system treated the entire riding compartment in the same fashion as the front bench.

"Have you seen the inside?" Esrahaddon asked all of them as they prepared to roll out. "She's got a fireplace in there."

"Do you mind?" Elinya asked him. "It's just that she makes me uncomfortable."

Esrahaddon smiled. "I'll miss your company, but I understand. Ruby makes everyone uncomfortable. Just tell Mister Teshlor to keep his hands on the reins and his eyes on the road."

"I heard that," Jerish said as he checked the straps on his team's harness.

"I know," Esrahaddon replied.

"My lady," Jerish extended a hand to assist Elinya up onto the driver's bench.

She settled in, wrapping the blanket Jerish had provided around her legs.

"Stop being so charming, will ya?" Esrahaddon told Jerish. Then he returned to the luxury coach and stopped short of climbing aboard. The horses were no longer horses. The motley pair were now near-identical white, with lion-like tails, cloven feet like deer, and a single horn protruding from the center of their heads.

"Seriously, Ruby?" he muttered as he climbed up on the bench, which was now adorned with a luxurious cushion and back rest, which he took far less offense to than hitching unicorns to a wagon. "They aren't really unicorns, are they?"

Yolric, who sat beside him, shook his head. "Just an illusion."

"Good." Esrahaddon took up the reins but did nothing. He looked around at the trees for a moment. "Don't actually know the way." Esrahaddon admitted. "It's east of here, but—"

"I know how to get there," the old master said. "Turn around and go back to that road we turned off of, then take a left. Before long, you'll find a north–south trail. We'll need to follow that up to Grandford to cross the Bern, then we'll catch the Imperial Highway down through Cryllion—really shouldn't linger there, not with her—then we'll enter into Alburnia, and reach the provincial gubernatorial seat in Rochelle. Castell Blythium is up on a cliff near there. The Fourth Legion uses the old fortress as its headquarters."

"Oh . . . good." Esrahaddon forced a smile as he released the brake and began the process of turning the coach around. Jerish mimicked him, and Esrahaddon felt disturbed by the way the *unicorns* managed the feat far more deftly than the horses, making him wonder if Yolric was right about *an illusion*. "Never a favorable start to a suicidal mission when you don't even know the way to your own death."

Yolric stroked his beard. "You're optimistic this morning."

"Sorry. I haven't been sleeping well. Been suffering nightmares."

"Given our course and aim, I'm not surprised."

"You'd think that, but they don't include a riva, and nothing bad actually happens, but I feel terrified when I wake up."

"Might be something you ate. Indigestion can do that sort of thing."

"I suppose. It's just that the sensation lingers. Now I'm living in deathly fear of flies, and I have no idea why."

Yolric chuckled. "Count yourself lucky if these are your nightmares. They may change after you meet Mileva."

"Why don't you get along with Esrahaddon?" Elinya asked Jerish after they were out of the glen and rolling steadily down the broad road.

He looked over at her, surprised. This was their first one-on-one interaction, and her opening move was a frontal assault. Jerish had thought he liked Elinya—but this blunt, fair, and honest question removed all doubt. She was nothing like the

Cenzar: no big words, no subtle, underhanded, or sarcastic comments, just a how-you-doing-and-dish-me-out-a-big-heaping-plate-of truth-and-hold-the-sugar-and-the-crap inquiry. He wanted to reply in kind, but it wasn't that sort of an answer despite being that sort of a question.

"That's a taller order than you might suspect, and the answer might not be to your liking."

"I'm a big girl, and we've got a long day ahead."

Jerish smiled. He definitely liked Elinya. "All right. A large part stems from how the Cenzarium is trying to destroy the empire by eroding its ethical foundations. We knights are taught—as all good and right-thinking people are—that courage, honesty, integrity, faith, generosity, respect, and sincerity are gracious and worthy traits. We believe in standing up for those beliefs and for those who are too weak to do so for themselves. By contrast, members of the Cenzarium are our opposites in every way."

Most of what he said Jerish had borrowed from the meetings he'd attended each week. Having heard the same quotes several times, much of it was word for word. This was good, he felt, as it made him sound intelligent and the ideas credible. Left to his own devices, Jerish was certain he would make an explanation of day and night sound like a fever dream.

"They don't believe in Novron," he continued, mimicking his guild orators, "because they see themselves as gods. So they place their faith in knowledge that teaches them to lie and to be cruel and cowardly. They rely on the evil power of magic, which corrupts their hearts as all power does, but magic excels in this regard by its easy solutions and irresistible forces. Cenzars give their true allegiance not to their fellow humans, but to our historic archenemies, the elves. They would rather side with those who millions fought and died to free us from—adopt their ways and their religion—than stay loyal to their own race. Moreover, and most recently, it is believed they are attempting to bewitch the emperor, invite an elven invasion, hand over the empire to their elven masters, and destroy the Teshlor Guild."

He paused and studied her. Esrahaddon would have interrupted him a dozen times already. She hadn't said a thing, hadn't even shown an indication of wanting to.

"On a personal note . . ." Jerish went off script. "Esrahaddon is arrogant, insulting, cruel and thinks he's better than everyone else. He lives for himself and doesn't understand sacrifice."

At this, Elinya's brows furrowed. "You're wrong. I'm not a very smart person, Jerish, so I don't know about all that political stuff, but one of the things I admire most about Esrahaddon is how kind, decent, and understanding of others he is—especially those the rest of the world sees as unimportant or worthless. He doesn't judge."

"That hasn't been *my* experience."

"So what *has* been your experience?"

"That he, like all Cenzars, never had to struggle, never had to suffer. They were born with power and handed positions of authority as a result. They have it *so* easy, they can't understand what it's like to be poor, unwanted, disliked, and discarded. The lack of hardship and struggle makes all of them think they are better, but it's pain and fighting that builds character and makes you a better person. That's what they don't see. I think that's the heart of the matter. I wasn't born to elegant robes. My mother died when I was young, and my father gave me away to the church. I have no money, no title, no prestige except for this uniform and what I made of myself through years of sacrifice and hard work. And because of this, Esrahaddon treats me as worthless."

"I see." She nodded. "I guess he never told you."

"Told me what?"

"About himself." She smiled. "You never told him either, did you? About your past? By the sound of things, you've never had a real conversation with him. What do you two do? Just scream at each other every day? Accuse each other of high crimes against mankind and the empire?"

Jerish smiled back. He nodded. "Sort of, I guess."

Their wagon rolled over a rock, and the bench bounced such that Elinya grabbed the seat to keep from flying off. They were still in the forest, but the trees were smaller, and there were more gaps between them—more light filtering in.

"Esrahaddon is from a tiny village in Calynia," she told him. "He was born in a hovel with dirt floors and drew water from a dying well. His mother was killed less than a year after he was born. She was torn apart by lions while he watched from a basket. At the age of seven, his father asked for him to be killed, believing he was a demon because he drew pictures of birds. Instead, the entire village agreed that Esrahaddon—being different—should be driven alone into the jungles that grown men were afraid to enter. He was found by goblins, who raised him."

She paused and looked over, but Jerish didn't reply. What could he say?

"I only just learned all this myself on yesterday's ride," she went on. "But I now think this last part has a lot to do with why he's so understanding—why he was so kind to me. He learned firsthand how those individuals who everyone taught him to hate were better than his own family. I suspect that's a lesson few learn." Elinya adjusted the blanket across her lap, shifting the dagger that she still carried, still wrapped. "And I think you might also be wrong about the privileged, easy lives of Cenzars. According to Esrahaddon and Ruby, the Art comes to those whose lives were *not* easy. Artists are privileged because they survive hardships that would ruin others. Course, I don't know everything. I'm just a woman from a backward village, except I do know that when I had no one else, *he* saved me. Didn't have to. Nothing would have stopped him from dropping me back in that awful village, or just leaving me where we met. But he took me to Percepliquis, found me a job and a place to live, watched over me. And while I would have done anything he asked—still would—he has utterly refused all but a thank you and is uncomfortable with even that. And yesterday I saw him try to save you."

"Save me? From what?"

"You didn't notice?" She smiled again.

Jerish realized she did that a lot. He couldn't tell if she smirked at knowing more than he did or was perhaps embarrassed at being made to admit such. All he knew for certain was that he liked when she did. Few people he knew smiled—fewer still ever did so around him.

"I can't say I know Esrahaddon very well," Elinya said. "We don't move in the same universe. Compared to Esrahaddon, I'm a bug. Not that he feels that way, but I know it to be true. Still, I can tell when he's sincere. He makes jokes as a way of dealing with things that upset him, but there are moments when, if you pay attention, you can see the truth inside." She looked Jerish dead in the eyes. "He really does believe we will all die. That's why he asked you to take me home. He was giving you an honorable way out. He was trying to save your life as well as mine."

Jerish thought a moment. This all sounded well and good, too good.

"That's always the problem. They're so crafty."

"How do I know he didn't put you up to this? Ask you to tell me this story to gain sympathy, make me more easily manipulated?"

She scowled. "Funny, I never got the feeling you were one of those doom watchers, the sort that could look at *good* and call it *bad* just because your life wasn't perfect." She sighed and stared off at the trees. The morning was showing every sign of becoming a beautiful spring day. "I grew up with a lot of them. Days were always too hot, or too cold, too long or short. Everyone else had it easier, and they always saw the worst in people, even before they met them. And if anyone did something nice, particularly if they were praised for it, they always insisted there was a selfish reason. As I said, I'm not smart, but those values you listed earlier that knights believe in—I mean, to me, doom watching seems sort of the opposite of those. But I suppose if you're always looking for people to make mistakes, you're never going to be disappointed, are you?" She shook her head. "I just don't think I'd want to live that way."

Jerish remained silent. He focused on the road, despite not needing to. Their horses followed the white carriage like it was made of sugar.

What she said about him wasn't entirely wrong. What worried him was that it might not be wrong at all. Somehow that would be worse, though he couldn't, at that moment, see how. She was confusing him. Pretty women did that. While it's easy to find the threat in a charging bear, no one suspects a turtle dove of clawing your throat open.

"Maybe you just need time to get to know each other more," she suggested. "Perhaps the two of you could become friends."

Jerish laughed at this. "You're wrong there."

Elinya started to protest, but he stopped her. "It has nothing to do with Esrahaddon, except that he would be the most unlikely of all candidates; it's just a fact. I don't make friends. Never have."

"You've never had a friend?"

"No. Enemies I'm excellent at, but I have no talent at making friends."

"Why not?"

He shrugged. "I don't know. I guess I'm too strange, too extreme for most people. I take my obligations very seriously. I don't drink or dance, lie or make jokes. In short, I'm as fun to be around as a manure pile on a hot and humid day."

"No women then, I suppose?"

He shook his head, then toggled a finger between them. "This is the longest conversation I've had with a woman in my entire life, and that includes my mother."

"I can't tell if this is just more doom watching on your part, or if you're just being humble, but I like you, Jerish. And I'll be your friend, so there."

He laughed. "You're an excellent fencer, my lady. I do believe I have been disarmed."

"How do you know what it looked like?" Esrahaddon asked.

"What's that?" Yolric replied.

"My robe. You say it's the Gry Erlikon, a thing not seen in twelve thousand years, and you also say the oldest thing in the imperial library is only a couple thousand years old, so no drawings nor paintings of the Gry Erlikon exist. How do you know what it looks like?"

"I'm older than I look."

"You *look* ancient."

He smiled. "I'm older than ancient."

"Are you trying to tell me that you personally saw this robe before—that you're twelve thousand years old?"

"Not trying to tell you anything, just answering your question. But while we're on the subject, are you telling me you weren't expressly instructed to show me this robe on the day you did?"

"By whom?"

"Turin, or I suppose you'd call him Uberlin."

Esrahaddon knew Yolric was what many would call eccentric, but this pushed the boundaries of casual abnormality. "I told you my mother gave this to me. Actually, she left it for me. She was dead. There was a note saying it was for me."

"And there was no instruction to find me?"

Again Esrahaddon wondered if Yolric was a bit too far beyond simply odd. "None at all. I highly doubt my mother knew you existed."

This seemed to irritate the old man.

"Is that a problem?"

"Yes." He sighed, dropped back against the seat rest, and folded his arms roughly over his beard. "It muddies the waters considerably. I can't know if he *wanted* me to see the robe and come along, or if—it can't possibly be a coincidence." He shook his head. "No, the odds are beyond calculating. He must have seen something and guessed. But why?"

"What *are* you talking about?" Esrahaddon was used to instructors at the Cenzarium talking over his head about things beyond his level. Yolric was known far and wide for his arcane knowledge and command of history. Esrahaddon could expect a degree of humbling ignorance when he sat beside him, but this sounded like the ravings of a lunatic.

"My brother," Yolric said. "He and I are at odds. I'm sort of hunting him, and he'd rather not be found. This robe is just the sort of thing he might send my way as a message. But I can't guess why."

"Well, unless your brother is Uberlin, he had nothing to do with it."

He's hunting his brother? As far as Esrahaddon knew, Cenzar Master Yolric had never left Percepliquis. *How does one hunt anything without the searching part? And is it possible for him to have a brother? No one ever mentioned the master having a brother. And what are the odds of two human beings living this long? Is this a joke? It must be a joke.*

"Seriously," Esrahaddon said, "how did you know this robe was the Gry Erlikon? The servant of Riva Rex Nexziria also recognized it. So how is this done? Is it the Art?"

"I don't know what to tell you, Esra. If you saw someone wearing a hat your mother wore every day for years, you'd recognize it, wouldn't you?"

Esrahaddon grinned. *Back to jokes, are we? Or is this a test?* "You can't be twelve thousand years old. Even elves don't live that long, nor do trees. The only thing I know that lives . . ." He smirked. "You're not a riva—are you?"

"No." He chuckled. "Your mistake is assuming I'm alive."

Esrahaddon laughed. *He is messing with me.*

Yolric tilted his head side to side while scrunching his face up, making the hairs on his mustache jut out. "It's really a pointless distinction. Does it matter if you build the house you live in, or move in after the last owner died? The house is yours and you're still a community member, aren't you? No one points and says, 'But you didn't build that house. You simply moved in! So you're not really a land owner!' Right?"

Once more, Esrahaddon had no idea what he was talking about.

"That's what I did."

"Okay," Esrahaddon said merely to acknowledge he was still listening.

"This isn't my first body." Yolric stroked at his whiskers. "It's nice, though. I do love the beard. Never had one like this. Fun to play with. You see, my first body died just about twelve thousand years ago. Like clothes that wear out, I pick up a new one when the current one gets too many holes and tears that I can't mend it properly."

Esrahaddon stared dumbfounded. *What if he's not trying to be funny? What if he really is senile?*

"Which is entirely different from someone like Mileva," the master went on. "Rivas are too stubborn. They refuse to leave their bodies behind, so they go to horrible lengths to keep them patched up. You might imagine how unpleasant it would be if you wore the same clothes for several thousand years. Even if you sewed up the rips, the garment would fade, thin, and wear away until it was as sheer as gossamer. The stink alone would be hideous. I have no idea how she manages."

"Okay. If you don't want to tell me," Esrahaddon said, "just say that. I don't need two Ruby Finns on this trip."

They made good time, reaching the old north–south road that was only a subtle furrow in a vast meadow. Before nightfall, the white coach drawn by a pair of unicorns and the creaking buckboard following it were within sight of the Seven Bridges of Grandford.

"Why seven bridges?" Esrahaddon asked.

"You've never read the epic poem, 'The Battle of Grandford'?" Yolric asked, surprised.

"Sort of." He sighed. "It's hard to get through. I've heard there are modern translations where the text is updated, but the copy in the Cenzarium is . . . I suppose the best way to put it is: *authentic*. The language is a nightmare to penetrate. Had a hard time understanding half the words, like breckon mor, leigh mor, and Dureya. And then there's the whole Great Vowel Shift, where the long vowels move by one place. I used to have to simply run through all the vowels first, just to understand where they fall. And then there are all sorts of references to things that no longer exist, and the slang is utterly unintelligible. Truth is, we have more words now than existed then. What writers today can say in a single word, ancient authors relied on gymnastics and a fortress of word combinations and relationships to achieve. I'm certain it was wonderful in its day, but for a modern reader the text is opaque."

"You're making it sound much harder than it is," Yolric said. "Try reading it aloud sometime. It's beautiful. A true work of art. And you would also know why there are seven bridges."

"You're not going to tell me, are you?"

"I will not encourage ignorance by rewarding laziness with knowledge."

"Fine. I'm exhausted anyway. Let's set up camp. I need to sleep."

The sky was a ceiling of black clouds stabbed by blinding flashes of white lightning. Thunder crashed and rolled like a giant monster trudging closer or beating on a gate. Esrahaddon had never seen the sky so ominous, so violent, so angry—as if a battle raged overhead.

"Turin! Turin, my love!" Alurya called to him.

She was outside her tree, a strange occurrence in summer, but this was a strange day. Wind lashed her hair like it whipped the branches. The storm revealed the undersides of leaves, and gusts showed another side of Alurya.

She rushed forward and embraced him. "Oh, my love, you're safe!"

"Why wouldn't I be? What's going on?"

"Eton has lost his mind. He's betrayed us, and Elan can't stop him."

Esrahaddon looked up at the boiling clouds. "What's he done?"

"It's what he's going to do," she told him, her voice frightened. "He's betraying us. He intends to kill all the Aesira, send everyone to Phyre, and lock them up forever just as he did with the Typhons! He's going to begin with you."

"Why?"

"Because he's mad with jealousy. He knows we've had a child, and he sees you as his rival. He's afraid of you. That's why he locked up the Typhons. And he'll kill you and lock your spirit in the underworld forever. Unless we act quickly."

Esrahaddon nodded. "I still have the fruit you gave me. It's back in the city, I'll—" He started to pull away, but she held on.

"No! There's no time. Here." She held out another fruit, this one more reddish, not so golden. He took it. While smaller, it felt heavier.

"Eat it," she told him. "It's better than the other one. More powerful."

He lifted the fruit to his mouth.

"Only one bite!" she warned.

"Why?"

"One bite of my fruit will make you immortal—two will kill you. And not merely your body, but all of you. Two bites and you will be entirely unmade."

Esrahaddon looked at the fruit, concerned. She had that sort of power?

"Hurry, my love. Time is running out."

Esrahaddon bit into the fruit, chewed, and swallowed. The taste was bitter, and it had a rotten scent. The single mouthful burned on the way down.

"Good. Good," Alurya praised him, taking the remainder of the fruit away. "Now—now you are safe. Now you are immortal."

"I don't feel any different."

"You will. You'll see. Everything is going to be better now."

"I thought it was good before. Alurya, you seem different."

"Everything is going to be different, my love, better than ever. You and I, we can fight them."

"Who?"

"All who oppose us. You'll see. We'll make them pay. Together we'll rule."

"Rule? Alurya, I don't understand. Why are you so—"

"It's just because I'm so happy—happy and relieved you're finally safe and that we will be together forever . . . and no one will ever be able to stop us."

CHAPTER THIRTY-ONE

Rochelle

For Esrahaddon, the next few days passed in the manner of all long journeys. Tedium gave birth to boredom, which led to daydreaming—only it was hard to imagine a future beyond *The Mileva Affair*. Instead, Esrahaddon consoled himself with what might have been. But that, too, had its problems.

He tried to picture his life if he'd never gone into the Forbidden Forest—if he had just ridden back to Percepliquis as he was supposed to do, as the law required. He realized—oddly for the first time—that he had broken imperial law by going after Lysander and Griffith. He had known that his actions were dangerous, arrogant, even stupid, but *unlawful* had never crossed his mind. Likewise, he hadn't wondered about the lack of punishment.

Why was that? Not even a full Cenzar, I ignored the emperor's edict and instead was thanked for my bravery. As a Cenzar-in-training, maybe I was seen as an adolescent and not responsible for my actions?

The point was, if he hadn't gone in at all, no one would have criticized or disapproved. That would have been the right and proper choice—the sort someone like Jerish Grelad would have made. He never would have met Ruby Finn, never been forced to go on a quest to kill a riva, and lacking that heroic feather in his cap, possibly not been appointed tutor.

At this very moment, I could be back in Shahabad reviewing Wardley's work as the Cenzar half of the new envoy team to Calynia.

He imagined introducing his counterpart to the virtues of the virtueless bog houses and suggesting they swing by this little village called Haddon. The conditions there would appall the knight, and together they would make a plan to rebuild the place, make it livable, make it civilized. And he imagined finding a child who drew pictures and kept a feather: a boy or girl who dreamed of a better place. Esrahaddon wouldn't need to take them away to grant their wish. He would make Haddon that better place. Doing so, he felt, would have made his life worth something. He would have done a lasting good. That life would have made sense.

Of course there was one problem with that happy little daydream: Elinya.

If I'd never gone into the Forbidden Forest, we never would have met. Ruby Finn would have killed her.

He looked back at Elinya and Jerish riding elbow to elbow and felt a stab of jealousy. The knight was just her age. He was tall, muscular, rugged, and dressed in all that shiny armor. Not merely handsome, but dashing. Jerish the knight was the sort of man that women daydreamed of. No one fantasized about thin and flimsy Calynians who wore weird robes. Jerish didn't need to do anything but be himself. Esrahaddon was certain he was back there treating Elinya with a level of respect she'd never known. The daughter of Hal Haston was probably suffering a nosebleed from the height of the pedestal he was putting her on.

And she deserves every inch. I just didn't see it.

He did now, but now was far too late. Now they would all die, so where was the point in saying anything? Where was the virtue of admitting feelings that had no future? And what could he say? *I've known you for seven years, during which we rarely spoke, but now that we're about to die, let me confess there's a good chance I'm in love with you?*

The best he could hope for was a slap in the face.

I could try telling her the truth. I could explain that I was young and stupid and thought I wanted something else, something shiny and new. That I confused infatuation with something deeper, mostly because I'd never experienced anything deeper. That sometimes a man needs to be knocked on his ass by a gigantic magical beast to see the value of what has been in front of him all along.

She'd likely spit in his face for that, or at least she should.

I wouldn't blame her.

Esrahaddon couldn't help feeling responsible. The actual reasoning—the cause and effect—behind the guilt was murky and hard to connect with any real logic, but that didn't matter.

I'm no longer in that forest, but I'm still an Awful Thing.

Each of Esrahaddon's well-intentioned daydreams turned to daymares, but still time marched on. The wagons continued to roll, and before long, they were out of the rugged, snowy mountains and traveling down into the coastal lowlands of Alburnia. Following a well-maintained imperial road, they made good time. Below, they could see the hills and valleys that sloped toward the sea, and far to the northeast, Esrahaddon spotted the unmistakable cone-shaped peak of Mount Mador, crowned in white.

Nightly camps were dull, quiet undertakings. Riding a wagon all day was shockingly exhausting, and no one had energy for much conversation. He also guessed that everyone was lost in their own deep thoughts of mortality as time ticked away the days left to them. They ate and went to sleep soon after with only the most obligatory of discourse.

One night, while they were still at a high elevation and in sight of snow, an ugly freezing rain started, threatening to cover everything with a nasty layer of ice. Esrahaddon put a stop to it with a word and a wave. Elinya and Jerish gaped, while Yolric appeared unfazed. Ruby wasn't there. Most of the time she refused to come out of her carriage sanctuary, no doubt cozy and warm. Each night, deprived of the second wagon, Esrahaddon adopted the habit of creating a place for Elinya to sleep. He took great care in fashioning small nests by persuading grass and nearby thickets to arch up and interlock. The results were cozy domed baskets the size of small tents. Most lacked material for more than a single person, which was fine. Jerish and Yolric slept in the wagon; Ruby had the carriage and Esrahaddon his robe.

Before long, they were down in the open valleys again, in a world of river gorges and ocean cliffs, lonely bluffs where wind-lashed junipers stunted by endless whippings populating a sparse landscape surrounded by snowy peaks. Dense fog wreathed tiny seaside fishing villages that most often consisted of no more than a couple of weathered shacks and a rocky dock.

Then by evening on the seventh day, the unicorn-powered white coach with burning lamps rolled into Rochelle, the provincial capital of Alburnia.

Jerish thought the stone house with the thatched roof, standing on the edge of the seaside cliff, might have been abandoned. It had that desolate, forsaken demeanor usually reserved for ancient ruins on windblown heights. Then he saw the barn, the rickety outhouse, and several low stone walls dividing a sheep pasture from crops. He knew it was a sheep pasture because he saw three sheep. And he knew it was a crop field because of the little green shoots growing in perfect rows. Jerish had no idea what was growing. Yet, even with his limited agricultural experience, the knight was confident that the true strength of this farmer was the harvesting of rocks and stones. Despite the sheep and the baby vegetables, the real sign that the house wasn't some deserted farmstead revealed itself as they came fully over the rise.

Competing with the cries of gulls, about a dozen men shouted threats as two of them struggled to load a sheep into a wagon where another animal had already been consigned. The target of their verbal assault appeared to be a small family huddled just outside the front door of the house. Three boys and their father and mother all suffered the heartless wind while begging the men to stop.

The men, Jerish realized, all wore imperial legion uniforms.

"Pa?" The oldest of the boys spotted them rolling up the road and tried to get the attention of his father, but the farmer was red-faced angry and couldn't be deterred.

"You can't take them! You've already taken eight. We need them for wool!"

"Pa!"

"Without wool to sell, we won't have money to pay the tax!"

"Would you rather we take your wife?" One of the legionnaires grinned as he admired the way the wind pressed the woman's gown against her body, both fabric and hair whipping behind her. "She'd probably like to see her daughter again. Wouldn't you, dear?"

The father stepped in the way, blocking her from the legionnaire's sight.

"Pa! Look!" the boy insisted, and finally the farmer turned. They all did, and the shouting match stopped.

"What beneath the moon and sun is that?" The same man who'd threatened the farmer's wife spoke as they rolled up.

"Are those unicorns, Pa?"

"I—I dunno."

"Good day, gentlemen," Esrahaddon called cheerfully, pulling the carriage to a stop before the stone farmhouse. "We're strangers to these parts, and I was wondering if you'd be kind enough to tell me how I might get to the Governor's Palace, or Estate, or House—whatever it's called."

"Who are you?" the soldier asked, and Jerish didn't like the way he said it. *Arrogant* wasn't the word. This was something more. He spoke as if this were *his* land, *his* house, and they were trespassing. Jerish didn't like that at all.

"Name's Esrahaddon," the Cenzar said, pleasant as could be. "And you'd be?"

"Where'd you get this carriage?" The soldier, who hadn't appeared to notice Jerish's wagon for the sight of the filigree-adorned snowball with gold wheels, stared longingly. If the carriage had been a woman, Jerish would have feared for her virtue.

Esrahaddon opened his mouth to answer, then stopped, shook his head, and concluded with, "Way too long of a story. If you could just—"

"I think I'd like me a fine ride like that," said the soldier who appeared to be in command even though he had no mark of rank on his uniform—no insignia at all beyond the Fourth's Rhistian Boar.

Esrahaddon laughed. "Oh no—no, you would not. Trust me."

"What's pulling it?" one of the other men asked, inspecting the onetime horses. He was fascinated by the horns and appeared to debate the merits of touching one.

"Please, gentlemen," Esrahaddon spoke up, "if you could just direct me—"

Five riders came racing up the road, catching everyone's attention.

With an angry growl, the unmarked leader of the legion troop climbed up on the wagon beside the loaded sheep to gain a better look. "Aww, for gripe's sake. Here comes trouble. Fan out, boys!"

"It's Darius!" the farmer's son declared with joy, clutching at his father's arm and yanking hard as if it were a bell rope used to ring in a celebration.

The legionnaires let go of the second sheep, drew swords, and followed the order to spread out. The horsemen slowed as they approached. At the head of the little band was none other than Darius Seret. Gone was his cadet clothing. In its place he wore a new uniform, which matched those with him—black with red trim and a scarlet flying-dragon crest.

"You got no business here, boy," the legion commander declared from his wagon rampart. "Go back home to your daddy before you get hurt."

"The *governor* has empowered me, as High Sheriff, to protect the people of his province," Darius declared. "It is you, Bracket, who has no business here. These are not your livestock. Leave these people alone and return to the outpost at once!"

"Or what, my little child? Are you and your pals going to teach us a lesson? Got a couple more this time, I see. Freddy the Sty, and Mort the Barrel—you're really attracting the best and brightest, Darius. Still not enough. You'd like everyone to think different, but we all know you washed out. You weren't good enough. You're no Teshlor."

"I am." Jerish threw the brake on the wagon, handed the reins to Elinya, and hopped down.

Everyone turned. The legion leader put a hand on the wagon's side and leaned over so as to see around the unicorns and coach.

"Jerish!" Darius shouted, smiling.

"Darius." Jerish nodded back, walking forward to confront the soldiers and coming to a stop before the wagon where the unloaded sheep bent its head and began eating the crushed grass.

Esrahaddon sighed and shook his head. "Jerish, we—"

"I got this."

"We don't need to *get this*, Jerish. We're not here to—"

"I said I got this. Just relax."

"But, Jerish—"

"I'm still a Teshlor," he said, hoping this would be enough. It obviously wasn't, as in reply Esrahaddon gave him a perplexed look, raising both hands as if to ask what that had to do with the rising price of sea bass in Vernes.

Surprisingly, Darius Seret came to his aid. "Teshlor Knight Jerish Grelad, meet Assistant Third Spear Silvas Bracket of His Eminence's Fourth Imperial Legion. He and his expeditionary force are here to pillage the village for their own personal gain. Today it seems they are in want of mutton, or perhaps an alternative for female companionship. It's even possible he's after both."

"Is this true?" Jerish asked.

"Naw, we got plenty of women up at the fort," Bracket replied. "This sod's daughter is one of 'em." He pointed at the farmer. "We collected her, what?" he appeared to ask the farmer. "A year ago, was it? She's coming along fine. Learning the skills needed to please a cohort."

Jerish rolled his eyes. The man wasn't making this any easier on either of them. "By your answer, I must assume the rest of Sheriff Seret's statement of allegation is true?"

"So what?" Bracket asked. "What business is it of yours?"

Darius said, "Knights are obligated to defend the weak from monsters like you. It's not only a requirement of their oath, but a matter of honor. And Jerish Grelad is as *Teshlor* as they get."

"I don't care if he's the emperor himself. This here is our province. We own it and everything in it. And that includes the lot of you if I want. Understand? Besides, I can read a uniform as well as the next fella, and I can see the Teshlor here is a *Third* Rank." Bracket took a step toward Jerish. "You can't kill nobody, not even to save yourself or someone else. Ain't that right?"

"That's correct," Jerish acknowledged.

"That's what got him kicked, I hear." Bracket hooked a thumb at Darius. "Expelled from the Knights' Guild for killing a total stranger—for the fun of it. Only avoided the gallows because he's a governor's son. You don't look like no governor's son to me, Jerish Grelad."

"No, I am not."

"Then I don't expect you'll be killing anyone."

"That's not my intent, no."

"So what is your *intent*, boy?"

"Boy?" Esrahaddon muttered. He stroked a hand down the length of his face, his lips clenching together as if trying very hard to avoid speaking. He glanced at Yolric with a look of expectation, but the old master continued to watch the encounter as if he were in the front row of a theater.

"If it is your intent to ruffle Jerish's feathers, it won't work," Darius said as he got down off his horse. "I nearly killed him once, and he didn't flutter an eyelid. But unlike him, as you said, I'm not a Teshlor of any rank, and my father *is* the governor of this province, so I can kill you."

Darius drew his blade.

"So it's a fight, is it?" Bracket said, drawing his own sword. The legion leader did not appear concerned. "Hear that, boys? We're gonna kill ourselves a Third Class Teshlor who can't kill us, and maybe this time we'll finally send Darius and *his knights* to their grave as well."

"A fight is not necessary," Jerish explained.

"Maybe not," Bracket said, "but it's been a slow day, and I—"

There came a sound like twelve separate ripe melons being ripped open. Before his eyes, Jerish witnessed all twelve legion soldiers explode.

Everyone staggered back. The sheep not yet in the wagon darted off across the field. The one in the cart slammed itself into the railing, trying to follow. The farmer's wife and children all screamed. The farmer himself gasped. The horses Darius and his men arrived on reared and threatened to bolt as their stunned owners fought to keep them still. Jerish himself took a step back, and feeling warm wetness on his face, wiped away the spray of blood that splattered everything in the vicinity. And in the midst of that din rang the sword Bracket had been holding as it hit the ground.

Jerish, like everyone, gaped wide-eyed. Then he whirled and glared at Esrahaddon. "I said I—" He stopped as he spotted Ruby Finn standing outside the carriage, beside the open door.

"Can we go now?" she asked.

"Ruby . . ." Esrahaddon dropped his head into his hands. Then feeling the blood on his face, he grimaced. Jerish found it odd that in that moment of confusion and disaster, he noticed that while the unicorns, the carriage, Yolric, and Esrahaddon were all splattered, there was no blood on Esrahaddon's robe.

"We're almost there now, right?" Ruby asked. "Let's get this over with. There's only so much knitting I can do before I go crazy."

"Before you go crazy?" Esrahaddon asked of no one in particular.

"Who is that?" Darius whispered, standing rigid as a salute as he watched the lady re-enter the coach.

Jerish sighed. "Ruby Finn."

"I told him he didn't want any part of this carriage," Esrahaddon said to the wet spot where Silvas Bracket had stood, where now there was only a pair of empty sandals.

Esrahaddon stared at the governor of Alburnia, lost in one of those rare moments when reality upends expectations. He had begun to formulate an opinion that men in positions of wealth and power would all be like Randolf Curtalus: the embodiment of gluttony and privilege. However, Governor Seret was a dark-haired man of rugged good looks. Furthermore, while Derek Seret was head of state, and chief imperial officer in the province, he stood when they entered and greeted Esrahaddon and Jerish with a bow.

"Greetings, gentlemen, and welcome to Rochelle," he said respectfully. "I only wish conditions were better so I could receive you with more gracious accommodations."

"We don't require anything," Jerish replied.

"That's good because I have nothing to give. Our fields are barren, our stores nearly empty. I don't wish to sound ungrateful, but it has certainly taken you a long time to come. How many men have you brought? Have you found adequate space to bivouac them? That is the one thing we do have—plenty of fallow fields."

Jerish looked at Esrahaddon, who returned the same expression of confusion. "There's only five of us."

"Five?" the governor said in obvious shock "Young man, while the Fourth Imperial Legion is arguably the smallest in the empire, it's still composed of some two thousand soldiers."

Jerish nodded. "I understand that, sir."

The governor looked questioningly at his son.

"They arrived in two small wagons," Darius explained. "And yes, I think there are only five."

"Five?"

Esrahaddon and Jerish both nodded.

Having left Elinya in charge of the horses and unicorns and Yolric in charge of Ruby, the two had followed Darius Seret to the gubernatorial estate, which was on a small island in the center of the Roche River, which divided the little port city. The property reminded Esrahaddon of the many nice villas found in the hills around Percepliquis. The house was three stories and had gables, a centered portico, and stone pillars. Five chimneys marked the roof, and twenty-nine glass windows faced front; one of them was round and set at the portico's peak. Unlike the Imperial Palace, the governor's villa was merely an overly nice home. Darius led them in, and the governor received all three in a room that might have doubled as a fine dining hall. Whatever had been on the imperial governor's schedule that day had been cleared for their arrival.

"Five." The governor repeated as if trying to make sense of the word. "I am aware of the reputation of imperial agents, but does the emperor truly think that four envoys and . . . who is the fifth?"

"Governor," Esrahaddon said, "I sense we are not working from the same source material." He meant this literally. The governor was shifting wildly from relief at their arrival to panic at their lack of numbers, when he should be mildly curious why they were there at all. "You act as if you expected us."

"Of course I did. I just expected you years ago. We have two thousand corrupt legion soldiers tearing this province apart, treating it like their personal playground and private storehouse. As a result, the province itself is facing a debt crisis because I cannot manage trade and taxation while the legion wreaks havoc upon my citizenry. I've been petitioning the emperor for help for years. Isn't that why you're here?"

"I don't think the emperor is aware of your problems," Jerish said. "Who are your normal circuit agents?"

"Normal agents? We have not been visited by any representative of the empire since I've been governor."

Jerish looked at Esrahaddon. "Strange."

Esrahaddon nodded.

"At least you're here now," the governor said.

"Except we are not here to assist you," Jerish said, and Esrahaddon marveled at his utter lack of remorse. "We are here to eliminate Mileva Hitartheon."

The governor looked once more to his son.

Darius stood alongside them, facing his father as if he, too, were part of their notorious gang, and all were facing judgment. They weren't. Esrahaddon knew this but felt guilty just the same. Twelve men—a dozen soldiers in the service of the emperor—had just been snuffed out. Neither Darius nor Esrahaddon was directly responsible, and even if they had been, a provincial governor hadn't the authority to take action. Teshlors and Cenzars were sacrosanct, subject only to the emperor. While Esrahaddon was well aware of all this, he still felt blameworthy.

The governor waited, but when Darius said nothing, he asked, "Do you know who that is?"

Darius shook his head. "Never heard of him before."

"It's actually a her," Esrahaddon corrected.

"Never heard of *her* before, either."

"We believe she is inside the castell," Jerish pushed on with that blunt confidence that Esrahaddon would normally hate, but he knew that in this instance it was necessary.

"Allow me to understand you clearly," the governor said. "My province is dying, but the emperor sent you here to kill a woman hiding in the castell?"

"I believe when our business is complete," Esrahaddon said, "if we're successful, many of your problems may no longer exist. But at the very least, we will report your plight to the emperor."

"I would appreciate that. Thank you." The governor said this with a roll of his eyes and a shake of his head.

"Father," Darius said, "I would like to volunteer to assist them. And I believe my knights will follow me."

"Knights?" Jerish asked.

"Yes," Darius replied, "after I was expelled from the guild, I came home to find things worse than ever, so I began training my own order of knights with the intent of providing my father with a means of enforcing his, and the emperor's, edicts."

Jerish paused to look him over. The man was dressed in worn armor but a new tabard. "You bear the symbol of the Nyphron Church."

Darius nodded. "Bishop Venlin has always been a friend. He supported my bid to be a Teshlor, but when that failed, he provided funds and resources to aid me and my father. In return, we're going to build him a cathedral, a proper home for a bishop in the hope he will spend the hot summer months with us."

"We're trying," the governor said. "But the legion has crippled our ability to do much of anything. Darius has been invaluable to me. His dismissal from the Teshlors was a blessing in disguise. I learned only after he joined that Teshlors are barred from serving in their home province." The governor placed a hand on his son's shoulder. "If that man hadn't attacked your sister, I'd be alone in this fight . . . and likely dead."

"The man you killed," Jerish said, "the one you were expelled for—he attacked your sister?"

Darius bowed his head, but nodded.

"My son heard the screams," the governor explained, "but arrived too late. First Spear Gladius Burke of the Rhistian legion killed my daughter in this very room. He was trying to get to me, and she got in his way."

"And you were let go for this?" Jerish asked.

"It wasn't necessary for me to kill him, Jerish. It was just the two of us, and a First Spear in a frontier legion post is no match for even a fifth-year Teshlor Cadet. But my sister . . ." Darius paused, coughed, and swallowed. "She was dead on the floor between us. Her blood on his sword. I didn't even think. Wouldn't have mattered if I had. Right now, if I could do it all again, the only change I'd make would be to take my time and make it last longer." He wiped at his eyes. "That's why they dismissed me. I never had your restraint, and they knew it."

"Darius," his father said, and he waited for his son to look up at him, "your bravery has never been in doubt, but you and your knights, and a handful of Teshlors and Cenzars, are simply no match for an entire legion. You are truthfully facing an army."

Esrahaddon was struck by a memory. "One of my first field instructors in the Cenzarium once told me a Teshlor Knight and a Cenzar are more formidable than a legion. At the time, I didn't believe him. Looks like we're about to find out because while there are five in our party, tomorrow I think it's just going to be Jerish and me knocking on the castell's gate."

"Jerish, may I go with you?" Darius asked. "My men aren't Teshlors, but I've worked hard with them, teaching all I know. They're good and dedicated. And my father is right. Two thousand is a lot to fight, and I would love to see the inside of that castell."

Jerish thought a moment, then shook his head. "Since a few more swords won't help, and you're not runed, taking you with us would be irresponsible. And regardless of whether we are victorious or not, you and your knights will be sorely needed to serve your father in the aftermath."

Darius gritted his teeth. Whether he was holding back words or actions, Esrahaddon didn't know, but there was anger behind those eyes.

Jerish was still thinking about Darius as he and Esrahaddon left the governor's estate and walked down the gravel path leading back to the bridge and the farm. At the academy, Darius had been one of his many enemies. The senior cadet had even challenged him to a duel—a fight with live swords that was known to end in death or dismemberment on occasion. Jerish had defeated Darius without injury and obtained an apology. After that, the two avoided each other. Then one day, Darius was gone. He was expelled. No reason given. Rumors were many. The most popular was that he had gone crazy and killed one or more people. Some said he was drunk and murdered a bartender. Another alleged that he attacked a woman for rejecting him. That was the sort of reputation Cadet Seret had established at the academy, the kind that allowed people to believe such things. No one would ever have accepted the honorable story of his sister's death. Even Jerish might have held his doubts if not for coming to Rochelle—if he hadn't seen this place with his own eyes. The way Darius had explained his expulsion without excuse, accepting responsibility for his mistake, showed a maturity and honesty not previously seen. But that last look he delivered told a different story.

"Was he lying?" Jerish asked Esrahaddon.

"Who?"

"Darius. I've heard Cenzars can sometimes tell such things. That story about his sister's death. Was he telling the truth?"

"I don't know. It doesn't work like that. I can't read minds. I just get impressions, usually from strong emotion. He was upset when you turned his offer down. That's about all I can tell you."

Jerish nodded. "And that bit about a Teshlor and Cenzar being as powerful as a legion? What do you really think?"

"I think two thousand soldiers is a lot," he replied. "And you can't kill?"

Jerish shook his head. "I haven't earned that much trust with the emperor."

"He trusts you to teach his son but not to protect him. And they train you to fight, then send you out with arms tied behind your back. Yeah, that makes all sorts of sense."

"You don't have restrictions?"

Esrahaddon made a sound close to a laugh. "Ever try to train a cat? The power Cenzars have isn't bestowed by the empire. It comes to us naturally, so there's no sense of obligation, no required loyalty."

"So I've heard."

Esrahaddon eyed him for a moment. "Cenzars don't do what they are told because someone who claims authority dictates it. We act according to what we know is right."

"So do Teshlors, but we are careful to put only good people in authority, so it isn't necessary to discuss and explain every action. This allows us to function quickly and decisively to make certain everyone is, in fact, doing what is fitting instead of what they might think is right."

"Good in theory, until the man in charge decides what is right is what is right for himself rather than the greater good. Then you have a cascading failure of epic proportion. The guild is like a herd of anything. Wherever the leader goes, the rest follow. Very convenient, very easy to conduct, but if the leader goes off a cliff, the rest will, too. You can't herd cats. They act independently of each other. I'll grant you that is often a pain that seems worse than the benefit, but in a storm, fewer trees fall because each is separately rooted."

"So you can kill?" Jerish asked.

"I can, and I have, but I don't like it."

"Who did you kill?"

"Men who slaughtered my family and friends, and who thought it might be fun to do the same to me."

Jerish nodded then looked east. A massive construction project was underway on the far bank of the river. The new church, he guessed. Beyond it, up high on a distant cliff overlooking the sea, was the jagged outline of a fortress.

"I've never killed anyone," Jerish said.

"No? Somehow, I thought that would be a requirement of graduation. The cadet school would visit the local prison and chop off condemned inmates' heads to get a feel for the real thing."

Jerish frowned. This was the very attitude he had tried telling Elinya about. "I *thought* about killing *you* quite a few times. Does that count?"

"That's the second joke I've heard you make. Do you have a fever or something?"

"What makes you think it's a joke?"

The two reached the bridge and crossed to the west bank, working their way back to the coach and wagon—hoping they were still in front of the farmhouse.

"So, what are you thinking?" Jerish asked. "I can *hurt* quite a few, but we'll still be overwhelmed. Can you put them all to sleep, or something fancy like that?"

"Destruction is easier than *something fancy*, and two thousand is a lot of people. I'm not as powerful as Ruby, and I don't want her anywhere near that legion."

"You think she'll kill them?"

"As I said, destruction is easy. She's not about to expend her energy just prior to fighting a riva by trying to merely render an army helpless."

"What about Yolric?"

Esrahaddon didn't answer for a while as they left the gravel and returned to the dirt two-track. The farm was up ahead. It and both the coach and wagon were there and still intact.

"I don't know," Esrahaddon said. "I'm told he's this powerful Cenzar, but I've never seen him do anything. He seems knowledgeable, but since he's a master, I wouldn't expect anything less. Right now, I'm just hoping he can keep control of Ruby. They seem to have a relationship, which I don't understand. Honestly, I think we're going to be on our own for this." He looked up and smiled. "Good news is, the legion should be the easy part."

Elinya sat on the stone stoop of the farmhouse. Yolric had gone inside. She could hear the conversation through the door. The Cenzar master did not shout, but his voice was the loudest, and the family rarely spoke, giving the impression Yolric was having a conversation all to himself. Their sheep had been saved, but the family was terrified. Seeing a dozen men explode did that. Elinya was a bit nervous herself, and she'd recently fought a giant shadow monster with nothing but a poisoned dagger. She still didn't know where she'd gotten the courage to attack it. Madness, she supposed.

The sun was down, and the last bit of day's light was fading when at last she saw Esrahaddon and Jerish coming up the road. They looked tired.

"You're all right!" She rushed out to greet them. Forgetting herself, she hugged them both, Esrahaddon first and the longest and then Jerish.

"And so are you," Esrahaddon told her. How he knew she needed to hear that was one of the many mysteries of the man. "Is everything okay here?" He glanced at the carriage parked off to the side, the unicorns left to graze in the pasture with the sheep.

"Me and Oscar—that's the eldest boy's name—we took care of the animals."

"What about the other two?"

"The wagon horses are also in the pasture. You just can't see them because the house is blocking the view."

Esrahaddon smiled. "That's not what I meant."

"Oh," Elinya said. "The Cenzar master is inside with the family."

"And Ruby?"

Elinya tilted her head at the carriage. "She went back into her cave-with-wheels. Been there ever since you left. I have no idea what she does inside."

Esrahaddon nodded. "I suppose we ought to be happy for small favors." He looked at her, concerned. "Have you been out here all this time? It's getting cold."

She didn't answer.

He frowned, and she loved him for it.

"Let's go inside. By the sound of things, we'll all need a good night's sleep."

"So we're going to the fortress tomorrow? Going to face Mileva?"

Esrahaddon glanced at Jerish, who remained stone-faced. "Yes—yes we are."

This wasn't good news. Elinya was terrified. She could see the fortress up on the hill and had been looking at it for some time. It was wreathed in mist that was already bathed in the eerie light of a rising moon. She saw no details, merely an ugly outline. To her, Castell Blythium looked like a living thing, a monster perched on a precipice on the edge of the sea, and she felt it was watching them—watching her.

They entered the farmhouse. The home was a very simple affair, as the houses of the poor and hopeless usually were. Elinya knew something about that and so in a way it felt familiar, but not in a good way. It was just the one room with a loft for the kids to sleep in. Yolric sat on a wooden bench at a simple table before the hearth, where a new fire had been started. By the look of its slow growth, she guessed they had lit it by conventional means. The whole of the family huddled on the far side of the room, the children clutched by their parents on the bed as if a bear had snuck in and pulled up a seat.

The family all started at their entrance.

"Relax," Esrahaddon said in a cheery tone. "It's just us."

Elinya imagined this gave them no solace. Esrahaddon, for all his wisdom, sorely underestimated his own intimidating presence. Even without a spectacularly bloody demonstration of brutal carnage, a swarthy Calynian in an elegant robe would be as calming an influence to a simple provincial family as a tornado in the bedroom. Not that Esrahaddon had himself done anything, but she knew the family painted them all with the same brush. Oscar had even addressed Elinya thrice as *Your Ladyship*, and once as *Your Highness.*

It's the clothes or maybe the way I quickly and nonchalantly walked around the blood puddles to unharness the unicorns that—

The more she thought about it, the less confusion Elinya had about the titles.

"We'll be leaving in the morning," Jerish assured the family in that formal diction of his that made him sound so commanding. "And no more harm will come to this house or those who dwell in it."

"Thank you," the farmer said in a mouse's voice. His name, she'd learned, was Aldrich Ferguson. They were all Fergusons except for Oscar. He was a Hawkins. Oscar was with the Fergusons because there weren't any more Hawkinses. His eldest brother was the last to go—taken by the legion less than a year before.

"All went well with the governor?" Yolric asked. He said this without interest, more as a polite and expected comment.

"Seems the emperor has been ignoring Alburnia," Esrahaddon said, and sitting on the floor before the slow-growing, smoky fire, he pulled one of his boots off. "There have been no visits to this province from any agents in close to twenty years."

"Why do you think that is?" Jerish asked.

"Mileva," Yolric replied with confidence. "Her influence is powerful. I wouldn't be surprised if she had agents of her own in the palace whose job is to prevent anyone from bothering her."

Esrahaddon turned his boot upside down and shook it. Nothing came out. He wore purple socks, which Elinya found amazing. Real purple anything was expensive. She guessed he made them that color with magic, but the fact he also hid them in his boots was both odd and endearing, and so illustrative of the man. *He's powerful enough to have anything but refuses to show off.*

"Do you think she knows we're coming?" Jerish asked.

Yolric thought a moment. "Possibly not. Even I didn't see this. You need to remember she's dwelt on that promontory for thousands of years, and I don't think she's ever had an unwelcome visitor—nearly no visitors at all. There's been the occasional shipwreck, of course. Bran and Falkirk stumbled in, and the legion came knocking. Twice, I think. But I don't believe anyone other than myself has intentionally sought out Mileva Hitartheon. Most have no idea she's even there."

"Why did you go?" Esrahaddon asked, finger-searching the inside of his boot.

"She helped me out with a problem I was having."

Esrahaddon stopped his footwear exploration. "Are the two of you friends?"

Yolric shook his head. "Old enemies. She helped me once without me asking, so I went to ask why."

Esrahaddon shook out his boot once more. "And?"

Yolric shrugged. "And she was hoping I'd repay the favor with a favor. She wanted me to help find a person of interest to her, but I had no idea who she was talking about. At least I didn't at the time. I've since read up on the subject and have a better understanding of why she thought I could assist her, but I still couldn't."

"Anyone we know?" Jerish asked.

"I highly doubt it. Her name is Muriel. She's an immortal older even than Mileva."

"An *immortal?*" Jerish repeated the word as he continued to stand by the door.

Elinya didn't understand why, then caught him looking at her and realized he was still standing because she was still standing.

She took a seat on the bench beside Yolric.

"It means she can't die," Yolric explained.

Jerish frowned. "I am aware of the word's meaning. I just thought, from the way you said it, *immortal* might be—I don't know—a kind of thing, a creature, or being."

"She's the First Daughter of the Aesira, if that means anything to you."

Jerish shook his head and sat down on the opposing bench.

"Didn't think so."

"Any idea why Mileva wants to find this person?" Esrahaddon asked, pulling his boot on once more.

Yolric leaned forward, placing his elbows on the table. "Revenge. When you're talking about a riva, *revenge* is almost always the reason. Mileva, I think, was . . . I don't know if you can say *in love* with Turin, but infatuated, certainly. Which made her jealous of Alurya because—"

"They were lovers," Esrahaddon said.

Yolric sat up. "How do you know that?"

"I don't know. It's weird, but those dreams I've been having, the ones I told you about?"

"The ones with the flies?"

"Yep. In them I'm someone else, someone named Turin, and I'm talking to someone named Alurya, and it sure seems like they're lovers."

Yolric stared at him, then he looked at the robe, then back at Esrahaddon. "What happened in these *dreams?*"

Esrahaddon chuckled. "They're silly."

"Tell me anyway."

Esrahaddon looked at the rest of them. Elinya sat leaning forward with anticipation. Jerish showed no interest, but perfect posture. Their host family continued to cower on the bed in one hugging mass as the darkness invading the little home was pushed back only by the weak firelight.

"Well," Esrahaddon said, "lots of stuff happened, but I can't recall everything. You know how dreams are, and most make no sense, but let's see . . . Alurya gave Turin a fruit, a strange fruit that made Turin immortal. She did it to save him from Eton, who was angry at both of them for having a child."

"Eton was angry *because they had a child?*"

"That's what Alurya told him. But there was something else." Esrahaddon thought a moment, putting his back to the stone of the hearth. "Something about flies, and the fruit—the second fruit was different. The first she gave him was golden. That's the one he saved and later gave to his daughter . . . his daughter . . . *Muriel!*" Esrahaddon's eyes widened. "That's right, I just had that dream last night. I'd forgotten the whole thing until just now. Turin found Muriel outside the city—don't ask me what city. I don't know. She was asleep under Merriweather—that's what she called the tree. Apparently, she named all the trees. Merriweather was her favorite. Turin woke her up. There was some trouble in the city, but she didn't know about it. She asked after someone named Tribal, Trivost, Tri . . ."

"Trilos?" Yolric asked.

Esrahaddon's eyes flashed. "Yes! That's right—Trilos. This touched off an argument. Something about him being her uncle and Turin having slept with his own mother. Which is bizarre dream logic because I think Alurya is a tree? Maybe she was a tree or became one—who knows. Anyway, it went on for a bit. I don't remember most of the squabble, but then Turin apologized and offered Muriel a gift . . . the golden fruit. That's when she noticed Turin had stains on his hands, but it was too late because she'd already taken a bite.

"Her reaction to the fruit was different from when Turin ate the other fruit. Muriel thought it was wonderful, but like I said, the fruit wasn't the same as the one Alurya gave Turin—the reddish one."

"How did Turin get stains on his hands?" Yolric asked.

"Yeah, that." Esrahaddon grimaced. "Like I said, when I have these dreams, I'm not me—it's like I'm Turin, so it was more than a little unpleasant that—well . . . apparently Turin had just killed Trilos. He'd murdered his own brother—his daughter's lover—because Muriel liked him better than her own father. The whole thing was pretty sick and twisted because the fruit he'd given Muriel made her immortal. But it wasn't to protect her, or even to ensure they would always be together. He did it as punishment. By killing Trilos, he ensured that Trilos's eternal spirit would go to Phyre forever, but Muriel could never enter Phyre because she could never die." Esrahaddon paused, his face tight as if seeing something terrible. "I can still hear her screaming. I never had such vivid dreams before."

"It's the robe," Yolric said. "You sleep with it on, don't you?"

Esrahaddon nodded and looked down with surprise.

"These are not dreams. You're seeing a memory," the Cenzar master said. "Turin's memory. That's why he gave you the robe."

Yolric went to the door and peered out, and by the angle of his gaze, Elinya knew what he was thinking because she was thinking it, too. "Tomorrow we go to Borappathin. This is it, the last night." Yolric whirled on the clustered family, making them flinch. "Tonight, you will provide Cenzar Esrahaddon your bed to sleep on. Make it up as best you can. The rest of you will spend the night in the loft. I will remain here at this table. No one in this house is to make a sound. It is important that Esrahaddon gets the most comfortable night's sleep he's ever had." Facing Esrahaddon once more, he said, "I think you'll dream again tonight. And the moment you awake, I want to hear every detail."

CHAPTER THIRTY-TWO

Before the Gates

The day was cold and gray. No hint of sun shone through the blanket of clouds, the world cast in a dull pallor: a dark, colorless gloom. Esrahaddon paused to look behind at the path he'd made. Many of the holes and drag marks he'd created in the new snow were already gone, erased by the endless silent storm and mean, icy flakes that fell with the patter of rain.

He was alone in that barren wilderness that reeked of death but smelled like ice. Esrahaddon had walked away mid-battle. Blood was still on his face, on his hands, under his fingernails. He could see the dark stains where he gripped his spear, using it now as a walking stick to aid his efforts to plow through the ever-deepening snow. He had left the battlefield the moment it happened. Felt it hit him like a thunderbolt. Something fundamental had broken, something primordial had snapped. The jarring impact was obvious everywhere as if whatever creature held the world in its hands had, through inattention or simple clumsiness, dropped everything. When Esrahaddon saw green leaves begin to fall, he knew. He didn't believe, but he knew.

The snow intensified as the temperature dropped. He heard people calling for him, his army searching for their ruler. He ignored the shouts. He needed to find Alurya. Esrahaddon needed to ask why the trees had lost their leaves and why it was snowing in the middle of summer.

"That's all," Esrahaddon told Yolric. "That's all I remember. Sorry."

Yolric stood at the bedside, hands clasped before him, head bowed like some pious priest of Novron.

Lacking a headboard, Esrahaddon had pushed himself up against the stone wall behind the bed. It felt more dignified and less disorienting. "I know you were hoping for more."

Yolric didn't reply. Instead, he turned away and crossed the floor to the little glassless bedroom window. The rocky sill was splattered white with bird droppings. The Cenzar master looked out at the springtime green, and the brilliant rising sun illuminated his face and beard, making him appear golden. "She was dead," Yolric explained. "When Turin reached her, he found Alurya's tree had withered. I wasn't there, obviously, so I never knew what happened—what it was like. If I had been, I, too, would have gone to Alurya. We all would have. She was our mother. She was everyone's mother. She was life itself." Yolric leaned out the window, where birdsong added melody to the insect percussion of the morning's music, and he took a deep breath. "Which raises a very obvious question."

"Which is?"

"As a teacher, Esrahaddon, it is not the answers we give our students that help them learn but rather the questions we pose."

"Seriously? That's your answer? You basically said, 'I could explain everything, but I feel like being an asshole today.' And just as a point of fact, I'm not asking for the answer. We haven't gotten that far. I'm asking for this question you so arrogantly proclaim was obvious. This was *my* dream, remember?"

"All the more reason for you to figure it out. Come along now. I need to visit an old acquaintance and ask a most disturbing question about the Invisible Hand."

Despite having been born fluent in the language of Elan, as all living things are, it had taken years for Esrahaddon to learn it. Like most men, he had quickly managed to shut out the whispering wind and subtle touches that sought to guide him. Esrahaddon had spent years relearning what once had been second nature. He had no doubt that Ruby Finn was far more adept at hearing and understanding

Elan. *She's had far more time to remember.* Still, Esrahaddon now considered himself above average. He could read the clues, decipher the code, perceive the secrets hidden behind the mundane. Yet it was unnecessary to have the slightest skill to sense what loomed ahead.

Everyone feels it, he thought. *Sometimes the voice of Elan is like that: loud and powerful like the coming of a thunderstorm or the changing of seasons or, it would seem, facing a riva in her fortress.*

As he drove the coach up the narrow seaside road, no one spoke. The only sound came from the cries of gulls and a wild wind let loose in a dismal landscape devoid of trees. Though they had set out on a fine spring morning, dark clouds rolled in as they followed the remainder of the last road east, the one that climbed ever steeper toward an inevitable drop. Light dimmed, and the temperature fell to a humid chill. Rare cliffside plant life in the form of misshapen thorn bushes and prickly weeds grew in the jagged cracks of lichen-covered rock. The road itself hugged the edge of the cliff as if all those who had trodden that path had felt the need to stay clear of the interior, the previous visitors finding comfort at the brink near the sea even though the path meandered alongside a deadly drop. Death, they seemed to have collectively concluded, would be better.

Coming over a rise and around a bend, Esrahaddon beheld it—Castell Blythium—blanketed in a dense fog. This building was not of imperial construction. It held none of the delicate stylings of modernity. Each giant slab whispered of such antiquity as to make Percepliquis faint. The ancient stone of greenish-black, unlike anything he'd previously seen, formed the base and much of the walls. They appeared burned, marred, and singed by fire from so long ago that its soot became a permanent part of the rock. Over this loathsome laminate, a blackish ooze grew. It might have been tar, but Elan suggested it was more akin to blood. *You can't get blood from a stone,* the saying went. Apparently, a riva could.

This is a loathsome place, Esrahaddon thought, and realized he'd been here before. Not this geographic spot, of course, but this scene—at least when viewed through the eyes of Elan. He'd been nearly nineteen when he stood beside Niblick on the rolling deck of the *Great Excuse* and stared into the eternity of what had once been the First City. This remote promontory reflected the same warped desolation, a silence so empty, you just knew it had followed a fatal scream. Back then, it had been the strange void of water that felt so unnerving. Here, Esrahaddon sensed an unwholesomeness about the proportions and dimensions, about the angles and slopes. The fortress's spires were hexagonal, with tops like the points of spears. The most dominant feature was the gate—several stories high, surrounded by walls constructed of stone slabs too massive to have been built by humans, dwarfs, or elves. The double doors were formed of a black metal. Mounted on huge hinges, the pair delivered a powerful, but ambiguous message: *Stay out!* Or perhaps just as likely, *Don't let it out!*

Down below where cliff met sea in what appeared to be a natural harbor, Esrahaddon spotted an eastern-style ship complete with the traditional Urgvarian black sails. *Are there Ba Ran here?* he wondered. Esrahaddon hoped not. While the presence of Ba Ran made sense, since rivas were leaders of the Uber Ran, he did not relish the idea of killing any. Imperial soldiers were bad enough, but Ba Ran were family.

"I want Ruby to stay here," Esrahaddon declared the moment they reached the great gate and he had thrown the brake on the carriage. There were no guards on duty outside: no gate watchers or patrols. The eerie mist that enveloped the fortress created a magical stillness that dampened sound while heightening dread.

The little compartment door to the coach popped open, and Ruby burst out. "I came here to kill the riva!"

"Yes, and by all means, please do." Esrahaddon climbed down using the front spoked wheel, then dropped onto the moist ledge rock. "But not the legion. They aren't part of this."

"If they get in my way, they will be." Ruby craned her neck, looking straight up at the full height of the doors. She was still dressed in the same clothes she always wore, and she was chewing something.

"This is why I don't want you to come in—not yet, at least."

Jerish trotted up, three swords clapping against his armor. "Can we kill Mileva without her?"

Both he and Esrahaddon looked at Yolric.

"Of course not." The Cenzar master, suffering his old age, took time gingerly descending from the heights of the carriage bench. "To be honest, you can't do that even *with* her. You need to understand who Mileva is. She isn't Aesirian, but Mileva walked under the new sun that was more white than yellow, took shade under the first tree, gave many of the plants and animals their names. She's one of The Five, the riva: the generals of Uberlin's ancient army—the world's first and greatest. Under his guidance, and even after Uberlin was gone, they nearly conquered the world. They destroyed Ferrol, Atella, Drome, Havar, and Mari. Then when their enemies retreated and went into hiding, they fought one another. With the rivas divided, their enemies saw their chance and attacked. Even then, even when they were being defeated, they tried to take everyone else with them by destroying the world. Granted, she's alone and much older now, and even rivas wear out. Nothing of Elan is meant to be continuously used. Still, you two are less than children in comparison."

Esrahaddon raised his brows and clapped his sides. "Then why are we even here?"

"That's easy: You're here so Ruby doesn't kill you. Jerish is here because he was ordered by the emperor. Elinya's here because she's in love with you. Ruby is here because she is afraid of death and arrogant enough to believe she can replace Mileva as the new riva of Borappathin, but to do that she needs to prove her worth to Uberlin by removing the old mistress of the house. Why Uberlin wants to *retire* Mileva, his longtime servant, I have no idea. And I'm here . . ." Yolric visored his eyes as he, too, stared up at the entrance. "Well, I'm still trying to work that out, still struggling to see what's really going on, but things just keep getting opaquer."

"But Ruby *is* very powerful," Esrahaddon said. "You can tell that, right? You can feel her—she's a freaking bonfire."

Yolric nodded and looked at Ruby, who stood defiantly straight with both fists mounted on her hips. "But she's not a riva. She has no pile."

"What's the pile have to do with it?"

"It gives them strength," Elinya said softly. "Each set of bones represents a spirit denied freedom. They can't enter Phyre because they can't leave the pile. Instead, they are slaves forced to lend their strength to the riva. Eating their bodies keeps the riva alive, but keeping their bones unburied gives them power."

Esrahaddon realized his mouth was open and closed it. "Elinya? Have you been holding out on me? When did you obtain your advanced education in obscure monster trivia?"

She displayed that now-familiar, ridiculously appealing, insecure smile of hers. "Ruby told me. When I was . . . her *guest* seven years ago."

They all looked at Ruby, who put on a stiff face and folded her arms.

"There was a tree in the glen," Elinya explained. "Ruby warned me not to go near it—an ancient oak. She said a raow was imprisoned in it, and a raow, I guess, is like a riva. She said someone named Tura defeated the raow by first burying the bones that made up the raow's pile. Then she sealed the thing in the heartwood of the tree."

Again they all looked at Ruby.

"What?" she asked defiantly.

"Didn't you think that maybe this was important information you might want to have shared with the rest of us?" Esrahaddon asked, encompassing both Ruby and Yolric in his glare.

"Thought you knew," Ruby said. "You seemed highly knowledgeable about rivas. Never asked any questions, did you?"

"Exactly," Yolric agreed.

"What about me?" Jerish asked. "No one here can claim they thought I was an expert in demons."

Ruby laughed at him. "Oh, you poor boy. Haven't you figured it out? You're our sacrificial lamb in all this. You serve no real purpose. You're only an extra target. And . . ." She looked behind her. "I suppose you did a fine job driving the wagon, didn't you?"

"Wow," Esrahaddon said. "You really would make a fine riva."

"Riva or Phyre?" Ruby pretended to weigh each in opposite hands. "You might call this venture window shopping. It's a big purchase, and I want to be sure the new lifestyle fits before I commit."

"Fine," Esrahaddon said. "It's creepy, and more than a little duplicitous, but why on the face of Elan am I here? Why force me to join you on your twisted shopping spree?"

Ruby shrugged. "Uberlin said I would need you to defeat Mileva. Maybe that robe will do something."

"This robe keeps me warm, saves me money in lantern oil, and gives me nightmares. I don't think it will destroy a riva."

"But we know how," Elinya said. "We have to bury the bones that are in Mileva's pile, just like Tura did. She'll be weak after that, and you'll be able to defeat her."

Esrahaddon and Jerish both nodded thoughtfully.

"There's a problem with that." Ruby addressed Elinya in a smooth, purring tone. She moved toward the woman, and seeing her approach, Esrahaddon felt like a parent watching a tiger slink up to his toddler. "If you remember from that story I told you, the raow hid her pile where it had been safe for decades, maybe even centuries. A riva would need to do a much better job of concealing and protecting her bed of bones."

"But it would be bigger," Esrahaddon said. "Much bigger, right? I was told Rex Nexziria made his pile into a massive fortress. Something that size isn't easy to hide."

"Or destroy," Ruby said. "And I suspect she'd know the minute you removed a single bone."

"It could be anywhere, though, right?" Jerish asked. "It could be miles away."

"No," Elinya replied. "It would need to be close and easy to get to."

"Why?"

"Because she must constantly add to it. Once a month a raow, or riva, needs to eat, needs to consume the body of a living person, starting with the face."

Jerish grimaced. "Why their face?"

Elinya shrugged. She looked at Ruby, then they all did.

Ruby frowned. "Because it's out of the mouth that the spirit tries to escape. You need to be able to catch it, stop the soul from slipping away into the safety of Phyre. Then the spirit must be locked up in the pile, tethered to its bones for all eternity."

"Once upon a time, I sort of liked you," Esrahaddon said. "But you're really losing points here."

"One doesn't achieve immortality without some sacrifices."

"Usually in a comment of that nature, both *immortality* and *sacrifices* are meant metaphorically, but I'm guessing you don't see the problem with that."

"I bet it's inside." Jerish stared at the fortress. "Maybe within the walls themselves. They could be filled with bones. Long ago, some old-fashioned fortifications would build two stockade-style walls—an outer and inner ring—then fill the center with dirt to make them really strong. Maybe these walls are filled with bones."

Esrahaddon nodded. "I agree that the pile is most likely inside and that destroying it is our best course of action. Perhaps Ruby and Yolric can distract Mileva while Jerish and I search. If we find the pile, we'll destroy it, and the two of you can hopefully keep her away from us while we do that." He looked at Elinya. "You stay here with the animals."

"I'm going with you."

"Someone needs to tend to the unicorns."

"They can take care of themselves." Elinya put her knuckles on her hips. "They're unicorns, after all—they have horns."

"Going inside is dangerous, and . . ." Esrahaddon forced himself to say it. "You won't be any use to us. You will, in fact, be a liability. I would need to watch out for you instead of focusing on the fight."

Elinya pointed at Jerish. "You're letting the sacrificial lamb go with you. Besides, I've got this." She raised the dagger. "And it's still poisoned."

"What's on that thing, anyway?" Esrahaddon asked Ruby.

"Vendon pox," she replied as if everyone with even half a brain should know what that meant. "The only known substance naturally immune to the Art."

"Did you make it?"

Ruby looked amazed at his ignorance. "Vendon pox is the venom of a pox worm, or death worm, depending on where you are and who you're talking to. Tricky to get since touching a pox worm causes instant death, and the Art has no effect on it."

"So how did you get it?"

"Turns out someone who dies from touching a pox worm develops pustules on their corpse. These little pimples are filled with leftover poison."

"So you coerced someone into touching a worm for you?"

She smiled.

Esrahaddon ran an exasperated hand down his face.

"That is what you get from rogue Artists left to fend for themselves," Yolric said. "With no guidance, they turn feral."

"*Feral* is another word for *free*," Ruby declared.

Esrahaddon faced Elinya. "It's that important to you?"

Elinya nodded. "I'd rather die than not help."

He stared at her, feeling sick. He wanted to save her, to keep her safe, but at what cost? And what right did he have? How was this different from using his power on a helpless young woman in a forest?

Because that would have been selfish. This is for her own good.

Nice try, he thought. *But it's still what I want, which makes it just as selfish. She's a grown woman, and she knows the risks, just as I do. Everyone who goes in will die—but I'm still going, and if Yolric is right—and I think he is—I will be no more help than Elinya. She tried to sacrifice her life for me. Am I really going to tell her 'No'?*

"All right then," he said, "But Ruby stays here for now. Yolric, if you would be so kind as to keep her company, I would appreciate it. Jerish, Elinya, and I will go in to talk to the legion commander. Ask him to evacuate the fortress. Technically, he's required by imperial law to obey us, but I doubt it will be that easy. Still, we need to at least try. Elinya, you hang back, understand? No heroics."

She nodded.

Turning back to Yolric and Ruby, he finished with, "I don't want another bloodbath like yesterday, so we're going to take this slow. Most of these soldiers are innocent men simply following orders. But once the legion leaves, you two can come in and begin searching for the riva while the rest of us look for this pile."

"And exactly why should I follow this plan?" Ruby asked. "Why should I obey any of your orders? This is my quest. You're here at my command, remember? You do as I say."

"No, you're going to follow my *suggestions*, and you'll do it for two reasons. First, Uberlin said you need me to defeat Mileva. I'm not nearly as powerful as you, so it isn't because of that. I'm guessing your plan is to burst in there and kill everyone, then launch a frontal assault on the riva in her own fortress. A fortress that was designed to withstand an attack by an Old-World army of millions. Some—I must assume—would have been powerful Artists. Such an approach is doomed to fail, so I'm guessing I'm here to provide tactical planning.

"Second, you're about to face an opponent stronger, older, and more accomplished than yourself. Do you want to face her after expending the energy required to kill two thousand legionnaires? Or would you rather allow Jerish and me to mop up the arena first so you can face her fresh?"

Ruby glared at him. Her fur was up, but that was all. She might be insane, but she wasn't stupid.

Esrahaddon and Jerish walked side by side up to the gargantuan doors with Elinya following behind. Up close, the gates were even more impressive and ominous. The heads of the bolts that held the hinges in place were wider than the breadth of Esrahaddon's hands, and the metal face of the gate was scored and dented.

"Do we knock?" Jerish asked.

"Don't think anyone would hear it if we did."

Jerish reached out and pressed his palm against the metal. "Do you think they open in or out?"

"Judging from the hinges, I suspect it doesn't matter."

"It's warm," Jerish reported, then looked up. "Not much sun, but enough for black metal, I guess—I hope."

Esrahaddon didn't know why Jerish *hoped* it was the sun's warmth, but he could make a few guesses. None of them knew what was inside. Darius, the governor's son, had no idea, which likely meant his father didn't either. And if the province hadn't seen imperial agents—if no agenperals had visited in twenty years . . .

No, Esrahaddon thought, *not twenty years.*

Agents had merely failed to inspect the province in all the time Derek Seret had been governor. That didn't mean a thing. There was no reason to believe agents stopped visiting because Derek took office. More likely, imperial agents had *never* visited Alburnia at all.

No, that's not right. In her book, Princess Farilane visited Rochelle, and she had two Teshlors with her. She didn't go into the castell, but she sent one of the Teshlors.

According to her own writing, Farilane reported that the province was rampant with corruption and debauchery. The Fourth Legion was disbanded, then reassembled with all new men and officers before being returned to the post, but it wasn't long before allegations of corruption resurfaced. All legions suffered some disobedience, corner-cutting, and rule slacking, but the Fourth was famous for it.

But why? And why was nothing ever done?

Esrahaddon had thought the neglect was because of Rochelle being so far out on the fringe of the empire, a poor backward borderland. He now suspected Alburnia had been *intentionally* kept isolated, and that since Farilane's time, no one who didn't call it home had ever set foot inside Castell Blythium.

Yes, Esrahaddon thought, *let's hope it's the sun that warms the metal.*

He reached up and let his fingers trace an inch-deep scar that ran on a sweeping angle for several feet, wondering what power could have caused such a gash. "Clearly, we aren't the first for whom knocking wasn't an option."

"Any ideas?"

Esrahaddon nodded. The doors weren't magical, but they were crazy-thick and heavy. Upon touching the metal, the Art hinted at a mechanism on the inside. A big wheel that, when turned, either inserted or withdrew a phalanx of iron bars through the center of the doors. Quite formidable to anyone unable to reach the windlass. Cranking the device, he guessed, would require three men. With the Art, he spun it blindly with two fingers.

A scraping sound followed. Then a clank rang out as both doors came free. One swung a few inches inward. Jerish added to the motion by pushing, but the door barely budged an inch and a half more. He put his back into the effort, Esrahaddon lent his weight, and even Elinya ran up to help. The massive plate of metal shifted inward a few more inches—not much, but enough for each of them to slip inside if they turned sideways.

The door's thickness was revealed to all of them. About two feet.

Jerish looked at the width, then straight up at the height. "How big is a riva? Are they normal size or giants?"

Neither Esrahaddon nor Elinya had an answer. Riva specifics had never entered into Hekkabah's curriculum. As a boy, Esrahaddon knew them as the things of nightmares. He never expected to see one, never suspected a need to know more.

Beyond the great gate was a small corridor open to the sky. Tall stone walls wedged them in.

"An excellent killing box," Jerish observed. He pointed at the ramparts above. "A lot could rain down from up there."

Esrahaddon nodded. "Arrows, oil, rocks. I imagine the weather here is awful during the invasion season."

Jerish smiled as he shook his head.

Esrahaddon had no idea what that meant. While he had a decent command of the Language of Elan, he did not speak Jerish gestures. Perhaps the knight was amused, but more likely he was somehow appalled.

At the far end was a portcullis, but it was cranked high by another windlassed chain and left open. Given the Fourth's reputation, Esrahaddon guessed laziness. They stepped under as if passing beneath a set of front teeth into a monster's mouth. Beyond that was a heavy oak wall and a smaller set of doors within—smaller, but still large enough to drive a herd of cattle through. Esrahaddon thought of cows because the floor was littered in manure. The place was unkempt, neglected, and so far, empty. That luck wasn't going to hold, as already they heard noises from the far side of the wooden wall.

"Young man, while the Fourth Imperial Legion is arguably the smallest in the empire, it's still composed of some two thousand soldiers."

Shouts and some screams came from farther inside. Throwing back the oak doors, they saw why. The courtyard of Castell Blythium was alight with fire. Initially, Esrahaddon thought the place was burning, but quickly realized what he was seeing were several massive bonfires. As odd as this was, these blazing infernos fed by piles of logs were the most normal things to be seen.

Roughly two hundred topless men, glistening with sweat and filth, labored at huge butchering tables as others cranked massive spits over the bonfires. The smell of smoke and cooking meat was powerful, as was the stench of urine. These were the legionnaires. Esrahaddon made the identification only by virtue of their imperial-issued sandals. Most bore tattoos. Several were entirely covered in them. The tattoos weren't Orinfar. He didn't need to see the symbols. These soldiers weren't blocked from the Art like Jerish. Esrahaddon felt the violence radiating from the men in the courtyard as much as he felt the heat from the fires.

"Are those . . ." Jerish began, then paused, overwhelmed by his own disbelief. "Are they cooking . . ."

Esrahaddon nodded. "They're butchering and roasting people."

Esrahaddon pointed to a large banquet table where another thirty-odd men sat drinking what he guessed was blood from several large tankards and eating a shared human carcass. One tore meat off an arm like it was a turkey leg.

"Stay here," Esrahaddon told Elinya.

She offered no protest, her eyes—the whole of her face—wide with horror.

She's probably rethinking her decision . . . I know I am.

With a deep breath, which Esrahaddon regretted as the air was anything but fresh, he passed through the wooden gate and into the courtyard. Jerish caught up and flanked him—hands on the pommels of his side swords.

It took a remarkably long time for anyone to notice their presence, and they might not have if the Gry Erlikon hadn't begun to glow. The robe lit up with a silvery light, a hue Esrahaddon hadn't seen before, but which stood out in sharp contrast with the reddish-orange flickering of the bonfires.

Heads turned, shoulders were tapped, men rose, and a crowd formed.

"Which one of us should do the talking?" Jerish asked.

"You speak *military* better than I. You can relate to your brothers in arms."

"But you have the impressive glowing clothes. And besides, these aren't military men—not anymore, and I don't speak . . . whatever *this* is."

"Depravity, perversion, immorality?"

"I was actually thinking more like *cannibal.*"

One of the bigger men approached. Like the rest, he was stripped to the waist, his tunic folded down into a skirt held up by a wide leather belt that also supported his short sword. Oddly, he continued to wear the red Rhistian legion scarf around his neck. Not all of them did, and Esrahaddon wondered if this meant he was special.

The man stood before them, appearing mildly confused as if he had just awakened to find a staring raccoon in his bed.

Jerish stepped forward. "It's a rough guess, mind you, but I think we're looking at about fifty-eight violations of the Imperial Code. I am Teshlor Knight Jerish Grelad. This is Cenzar Esrahaddon. And you are?"

"I am the hunter's moon, the flame in the fire, the dragon's tooth." The fellow followed this with an overly manic laugh that had Esrahaddon genuinely concerned he might swallow his own tongue. Several others followed his lead, all laughing in a pack until they drooled.

"By order of Emperor Nareion," Jerish began, raising his voice to be heard over the lingering cackles, "on whose behalf we are empowered to speak, you are hereby ordered to leave this fortification immediately—and by *you*, I mean the entire Fourth Imperial Legion. You have one hour to evacuate, so please spread the word to the rest."

Hunter's Moon chuckled. Apparently, he thought everything was funny. "Oh, no need to spread words around. This is us, and by *us*, I mean the entire Fourth Imperial Legion." He laughed again.

"There are two thousand members in the Fourth," Jerish corrected. "I see fewer than three hundred here. Are the rest in the citadel?"

"Oh no. We don't go in. It's dark . . . in there. We's all here. Some of 'em eaten, some of 'em bein' eaten."

"Are you saying . . ." Jerish looked to the fires. "Are you saying you eat your own men?"

"We had some disciplinary problems—some culinary ones, too!" Once more Hunter's Moon began to laugh.

"Look, we really aren't here to share recipes," Esrahaddon said. "We came to see Mileva Hitartheon."

"Never heard of her," Hunter said, sounding abruptly cognizant.

"Really? Then how did you know Mileva is female?"

"It's a feminine name, isn't it?" The man glared at him. "You're the smart one, aren't yah? The big scary Cenzar?" Again he laughed, this time hooking a thumb in his belt. Maybe he was trying to offer a threat by drawing attention to his sword, but what Esrahaddon noticed was the belt itself. A wide braided band with a sailing ship etched into the leather.

"Where did you get that belt?"

"This?" He looked down, surprised. "Had this for years. Took it off a goblin we got locked up."

"Is he still alive?"

"No idea if *it* is—how do *you* know *it's* a *male?*"

"Because I'm pretty sure his name is Niblick. He's my uncle. I made that belt for him when I was thirteen. Where is he?"

"She keeps them . . ." He grinned and pointed at the citadel.

"Are we talking about Mileva now? The one you know nothing of?"

"I like that robe." Hunter drooled and stared, unblinking, at the garment. In that look, Esrahaddon saw no sign of humanity, only the reflection of the silvery light that illuminated the soldier's eyes with a bright, diabolical glow. "It's pretty. Why don't you hand it over before you get blood on it?"

"Where exactly does she keep them?" Esrahaddon demanded. His voice was higher and louder than he'd planned. The thought of Niblick—the person who taught him to tie knots, to sail, to swim, to swallow hohura in one go, and who provided him with the best and most useful parts of his vocabulary—the idea that he was being tortured in some filth-filled pit set a fire blazing.

Hunter just laughed as he drew his sword, pulling it free of the scabbard slowly, making the blade hiss against the metal rim. Several others did likewise as the crowd got up, closed in, and enveloped them. Then Hunter stopped, and his eyes shifted and focused beyond Esrahaddon.

Thinking Mileva might have taken the opportunity to creep up behind, Esrahaddon spun, only to see Elinya just outside the gate, right where he left her. She stood, all alone, in that blood-splattered waking nightmare, clutching herself and looking so out of place in those nice urban-styled clothes.

"I see you brought me a pretty present." In a shout, Hunter commanded all in earshot, "She's mine!"

No one in the courtyard listened. Like drought victims presented with a cool, clean pond, those closest to Elinya charged. She stood frozen in place.

The big oak gates slammed shut, separating Elinya from the pack. The legionnaires threw themselves at the door, clawing at the latch and edges. One went so far as to bite the wood.

"You should be talking me down right now," Esrahaddon told Jerish through clenched teeth, as the Gry Erlikon shifted from silver to red. "Do you remember the bags of straw in the Vault of Days? Remind me that these are innocent soldiers."

"No." Jerish shook his head. "I'm not doing that."

"Go up the ramparts!" Hunter shouted. "Drop the ropes. You can get her that way!"

Without warning, Hunter swung hard at Esrahaddon. The blade came nowhere near him. Jerish swatted the sword-stroke down and nearly drove the weapon from the soldier's grip as the blade's tip jammed into the dirt.

Hunter either failed to see reality or could no longer recognize it. His eyes had gone red, glowing with the robe's new hue. It was easy to imagine him as evil, simple not to feel anything at his erasure. The man was like a wasp or a biting fly: a pest without value but one that could still harm and cause pain.

No, he thought, *I'd have way more regret at killing a wasp.*

It's always so much easier to destroy than build.

The thought crossed his mind, just as it had all those years ago in the Erbon when he first blew apart a dead tree. Now, however, the idea was muffled and fleeting.

Power was everywhere in that courtyard. The place was a veritable cauldron of energy, brewing hate, violence, fear . . . and something else. Underneath everything, he sensed a darkness encouraging it all. A force blew on the hot coals, enticing conflict, begging for destruction. And even as Esrahaddon swept a hand in the air to scoop up the needed strength, he understood that the act pleased this hidden shadow because Esrahaddon had succumbed to the itch of anger and the pleasurable release of violence.

The fires went out. The robe flared. Shouts, cries, and screams were cut off, and silence filled the yard.

CHAPTER THIRTY-THREE

The Legion and the Leash

"What incredible restraint you demonstrated," Ruby said, viewing the courtyard where roughly three hundred men had died. She kicked aside a sword that had managed to impale itself point-first into the dirt, where it stood up like a metal tombstone.

"Shut up." Esrahaddon pulled the soaked belt off what was left of Hunter. Blood was everywhere. Execution by stabbing, bludgeoning—even cleaving off an appendage—produced only so much. Death halted the pump. But when a living body exploded, it was like dropping a bladder of wine from an upper-story window onto hard pavement. The liquid contents went everywhere. Most sprayed across the ground, where the soil was starting to soak it up, creating a gruesome sludge.

"You really showed me, didn't you? Quite the role model, I must say."

Esrahaddon tried to use his sleeve to wipe the blood off the belt before handing it to Elinya, but the robe flatly refused. The blood merely smeared around on the leather. "Hang on to this for me."

Without hesitation, Elinya took the braided band and looped it over one shoulder like a baldric. "How did your uncle get here?"

"I don't know. Niblick and Mashie were going to the Old World across the sea. There's a ship anchored off the point. It's not his boat, though. So maybe Mileva has been trading with the Old World, or just keeping in contact with Rex Nexziria or something, and maybe he . . . I just don't know."

"Any sign of Mileva?" Ruby asked, walking unconcerned through the muck and inspecting barrels and tables as if she'd arrived late for a summer picnic.

"Not yet, which is good. We still have to find the pile. And now, amazingly, I also need to find my uncle, who it seems is imprisoned somewhere." Esrahaddon looked up at the citadel, a brooding body of stacked slabs in the general shape of a building.

"We don't go in. It's . . . dark in there."

"She's inside," Esrahaddon said, feeling the power like a dull hum. The impression he received was that of a loud noise muffled behind a closed door. Unlike Ruby—and Esrahaddon in his youth—Mileva knew how to mask her signature, but no amount of dampening could conceal that amount of power. The vibration made him tingle.

"Still want me to wait outside?" Ruby asked with a dash of venom.

"No," Esrahaddon said. He walked to where Yolric was taking his time strolling into the courtyard. Like Ruby, the old master showed a bewildering lack of revulsion at the carnage. Unlike her, however, he apparently gave it no thought at all as if blind to the bloodshed. "You were inside this place before, right?"

Yolric nodded. "Quite a few years ago, but yes."

"Did you see a pile? Do you know of a place one might be kept?"

Yolric stopped walking to think as if the two could not be done at the same time.

Until that moment, Esrahaddon had been in no great hurry. But now that they were inside the walls, now that he'd announced himself with a massacre surpassing that of Ruby Finn, he felt an urgency.

If she didn't know we were here before, she surely does now.

Yolric appeared doubtful. "I resided here for quite some time, but no, I never saw a pile of bones. Of course I wasn't looking for one, either."

"Do you have any thoughts on where a massive pile *might* be? How it could be disguised?"

He shook his head. "The interior is . . . well, Mileva has many talents, but architecture isn't one. The place is a haphazard maze. There are corridors and stairways that go nowhere at all, and windows that look into furnished rooms with no known entrance. I am above average at navigation, and I swear I got lost nearly every day just trying to find my room. Several nights I settled for sleeping on a couch in a common space for that very reason."

Esrahaddon wasn't certain if Yolric was being serious or not. Either way, his answer was no.

"What about illusions?" Esrahaddon looked at Ruby, as she seemed fond of them.

The red-headed myr was studying a severed hand, holding it up to the light by its forefinger as blood dripped, leaving a trail of damp dots on the dirt. "You know as well as I do," she said, "that the Art glows bright to another Artist. Illusions are like beacons to us, and she's hardly afraid of mundanes. Only Artists can threaten, so unless she's an idiot, she wouldn't use any. Or do you think she's stupid?"

Esrahaddon looked at the citadel again, felt the hum, and shook his head.

"Got a lot of rooms, I imagine," Elinya said. "Wouldn't the most sensible thing be to stuff all of them full of bones, then lock the doors?"

"Maybe." Esrahaddon adjusted his robe, which was back to its normal, non-luminescent, noncommittal gray. "That's actually a pretty good idea."

He faced her and placed his hands on her shoulders. "Still won't wait outside?"

She shook her head.

He sighed. "Okay, let's go in."

Esrahaddon led the way up the stone steps, wondering why he had been elected leader only to conclude he hadn't. This was of his own making. He didn't trust Ruby, whose task this was, and he knew Jerish and Elinya weren't capable. Yolric would have been the obvious choice, but the old man emitted a strong indifference to the whole undertaking. He really did act as if he were a spectator watching the whole thing from behind some magic mirror, immune to the potential repercussions. *I'm up front because I must be, at least so far as I see it.*

On either side of the doors, Esrahaddon noticed numerous windows: tall, narrow things peaked at the top and nearly opaque with dirt but unbroken. The entrance was only slightly larger than might be normal for a palace or an ogre's cave. The doors themselves were made of common wood, reinforced with black iron.

"Should we knock?" he asked Yolric.

He shook his head. "She knows we're here, and she won't answer the door anyway."

Esrahaddon tried the latch. A simple lift allowed them entry. Stepping inside, Esrahaddon was greeted by the overwhelming and repellent odor of mildew, rust, and rot. Elinya was the last one in. She didn't touch the door, but it closed behind her.

Perhaps it's the weight of the door and the tilt of the frame, but maybe it's something else.

The interior was dark. Little sun penetrated the grime-covered windows, but enough came through to reveal a surprisingly conventional, albeit decaying, vestibule. Crumbling plaster walls covered with faded murals or worm-eaten paneling offered rumors of past beauty lost to the brutality of time. The entrance was not large, but it offered two hallways and four staircases—each going in different directions: three up, one down. Also, there were one-and-a-half doors. The half-door was literally half a door, and not the bottom half, either—*that* might have made sense. Instead, it was the *upper* half, set in a wall with no visible means to reach it.

Esrahaddon stared at the plethora of directions, overwhelmed by options. He turned to glare at Yolric. The old man squinted and pursed his lips, then stroked his beard once, twice, thrice. He smiled and raised a finger. "The lady of the house is up those stairs near the fireplace. It's a little bewildering, as I think there's something like forty-seven fireplaces in here. If I remember correctly, though she sleeps in a different room every night, she usually spends most of her time on the second floor."

"She gets lost, too, does she?" Ruby asked.

Yolric shook his head. "Always said it's to confuse the spirits, not all of whom are happy and content to eternally serve her. I imagine those with loved ones waiting for them in Phyre are especially upset. That might also account for the chaotic floor plan, but personally . . ." He lowered his voice. "I still think Mileva hasn't a drop of talent for design, and she's not on especially good terms with logic." Yolric tilted his head up as if looking through the ceiling. "Right now, knowing she has guests, she'll be in the parlor. That's up a flight, first double doors on the right after the statue of the naked woman." Yolric grinned. "It's actually a depiction of Mileva in her youth. While I can't vouch for its accuracy, its artistry is fantastic."

"What about a dungeon?" Esrahaddon asked.

Yolric turned slowly, took a step, and nodded to himself. "Down that way, I think." He pointed at the only descending staircase. "You'll find holding cells. I remember that's where she kept the three men."

"Kept whom?"

"Bran, Falkirk, and . . ." he snapped his fingers several times. "Oh yes, Dibben."

Esrahaddon couldn't care less. "Okay, so, I suggest we head down first."

"I'm not exploring the old lady's cellar," Ruby declared, and she started toward the stairs near the fireplace.

"Hold on! You can't—" Esrahaddon stopped himself, concerned that at this point Mileva might very well be listening. Taking a second to pick his words carefully, he said, "It would be best if you waited until we settled a few matters first."

"You can do that," Ruby replied. "I'm merely going to introduce myself and have a friendly chat. I've been waiting forever and have lots of questions."

"Actually, I feel much the same," Yolric said. "You go on, Esrahaddon, and have a look around. Ruby and I will pay our proper respects to our hostess. To do otherwise would be seen as . . . rude."

"Umm . . . okay," he said because there wasn't much else he could say. Clearly, they had entirely different assessments of the situation. Esrahaddon perceived them as creeping into a highly dangerous monster's lair, intent on sneaking up and killing the thing. Ruby and Yolric acted as if they were visiting a disagreeable great-aunt. How such a disparity existed, he had no idea.

Ruby is the one dead set on killing Mileva—but then she also considered killing me, and we had a pleasant chat while she decided. The whole thing is as bewildering as this house: an ancient stronghold on the outside but with a creepy haunted-mansion interior.

"You two"—he pointed at Jerish and Elinya—"are with me." Both nodded without a hint of debate.

Esrahaddon watched Yolric and Ruby cross the room. As they did, the fireplace came to life. No logs sat in the andiron, but a fire now burned. Several candles lit themselves as well. Both Jerish and Elinya jumped, and even Esrahaddon caught his breath. But neither Yolric nor Ruby appeared disquieted, and on up they went, their footfalls muffled on the threadbare carpet runner.

Without a word, Esrahaddon waved for the others to follow and started down.

These steps were not carpeted. They were stone, well-worn, the edges rounded, the tops cupped—slightly sunken and polished from eons of foot traffic. The steps descended in a wide spiral, the walls made of the same greenish-black stone that, up close, appeared wet. Esrahaddon had no interest in finding out for certain.

They went down much farther than a single story, possibly more than four. At the bottom, they entered a low-ceilinged corridor. Without even the meager sunlight from the first floor, everything was illuminated by just Esrahaddon's robe, which now cast its normal white light. The radiance, however, was limited by the close walls. Jerish pointed out a series of wrought-iron sconces complete with torches.

Esrahaddon nodded and ignited the first one. An instant later, the next in line caught fire. In a long series of bursts coming one after another, the passage was illuminated. The popping sounds continued far longer than Esrahaddon had expected. In the end, an impossibly long corridor with an abundance of little doors on either side revealed itself. With the place adequately illuminated, his robe faded to its usual glow.

"That's a lot of doors," Jerish said softly.

Esrahaddon moved forward and discovered that several were open, and for a brief moment, he was encouraged. If all the unused cells had open doors, finding Niblick ought to be as easy as running down the length of the corridor. Then he approached the first open door and looked inside. The glow of his robe revealed not a detention cell but another corridor. It, too, was lined with doors and appeared to run to a four-way intersection. In at least one direction, he spotted stairs. Hope faded as he realized he was looking for a yellow flower in a field of dandelions.

"It's a maze—a labyrinth. Who knows how big?"

"What do we do?" Jerish asked.

Esrahaddon fully expected Jerish to rebel, to insist they give up. The Teshlor would spew some lengthy and ridiculous legality, some code of law or ethic that detailed, in specifics too arcane for an Artist to fathom, how they could not abandon their imperial mission to rescue a *goblin*. There would also be the argument about how Esrahaddon, being human, couldn't have a Ba Ran for an uncle. And this whole debate would spiral out of control until Esrahaddon was forced to declare he would save Niblick with or without anyone's help. Then Jerish would state flatly that if he saw any goblins—*any goblins at all!*—he would be duty bound to kill the filthy rodents. In that instant, Esrahaddon saw the end. Perhaps it was the riva's influence or the evil that saturated the walls or just the natural hostility between Cenzar and Teshlor brought to a boil by the stress, but they would fight, and in that conflict, everything would fail.

"Look, I don't care what you do, but I'm going to find Niblick. He found me when I was a child—saved my life—and while I call him my uncle, he's more like my father. He raised me. So you can leave if you want, but I'm doing this."

"I was just wondering if there was a spell or something you can use to find him."

Esrahaddon stared at the Teshlor, the torchlight's glow dancing off all that armor. "Oh. Ah . . . yes." He struggled to re-route his thoughts. "There is a spell for locating someone, but I would need one of his hairs or a fingernail or something to burn, which I don't carry around."

"As a rule, I think that's a good thing," Jerish said, looking at the seemingly endless rows of doors as if he hadn't heard, or cared about, what Esrahaddon had just said. "So there's no way aside from peeking in every door to find this Niblick fellow? Esra, there are a lot of doors. Kinda makes you wonder why she has so many."

"There is one thing we can try," Esrahaddon said. "It's risky and unreliable, but it might work."

"Does it require sacrificing Elinya or myself?"

"No."

"Then I'm good with it."

Elinya smiled at this. So did Esrahaddon.

"Okay. Stand back." Esrahaddon put a hand on either side of his mouth. "NIBLICK!" he shouted, making both Jerish and Elinya jump. "NIBLICK, IT'S EZRA! WHERE ARE YOU?"

His voice echoed down the hard corridors, coming back to them more than once.

No answer.

"I could have done that," Jerish said, dismayed. "I figured with all your—"

"That you, kid?" Esrahaddon heard a familiar voice. Weak, faint, and distant, it bounced and echoed its way to them. Without an additional word, they moved as one: quickly at first and then slower as they became unsure.

"Niblick?" Esrahaddon called again. "Where are you?"

"Locked in a cell." His voice was hoarse, and he followed this with a dry cough.

Esrahaddon turned right and trotted down past a line of four doors and came to an intersection. "There are a lot of them. Can you describe it?"

"It's got four walls and a door, but I doubt that helps."

Esrahaddon turned left. "It doesn't, but your talking does."

"Yeah, well . . ." He coughed again. "That ain't as easy as it sounds, kid. I've been in here . . ." He paused. "Ah . . . to be honest, I have no idea how long. It's not like I have a sundial of my very own, you know. In fact, I don't even have a sun. Are there still such things as days and nights, or has that little routine been forgotten? Never used to be a fan of the Big Yellow Eye, but after being locked in a box, you get to missing a whole lot of things you never thought you would. How long do you think, Mashie?"

"Mashie is here, too?" Esrahaddon asked.

"Yeah, somewhere. He's probably asleep. I hope he's asleep. She might have come for him while I was—"

"I'm still here," Mashie's deep voice growled through the corridors.

"Why didn't you answer? It's Ezra. He's here."

"You think so?" Mashie said.

"What, you don't?"

The voices came from the same general direction, and Esrahaddon struggled to move toward them. More than once he came to a dead end and needed to backtrack, passing Jerish and Elinya, who both offered looks of encouragement.

"Given where we are?"

"Good point. Hey, kid, what did you point at the tigerwolves when they attacked your village?"

"My magic feather."

"Was it a lion or a tiger that bit off Mashie's right hand?"

"He lost most of his *left* claw to one of Banka's men. I took off the rest when I tended the wound and apologized for not being able to fix it. Now if you don't mind, I have one for the two of you. What was the primary crop we harvested in our little garden at the tree house?"

They both replied together, "Rocks."

"I'm satisfied. What about you, Mashie?"

"That's the kid."

Esrahaddon hit another dead end and cursed. "This place is a nightmare!"

"Tell us about it. So, Mashie, I was asking how long you think we been here. I wanna say just shy of forever. What do you think?"

"I dunno. Seems *way* longer than that."

"I wish I could give you directions, kid. But it's not like I can precisely recall the exact level, ward, block, or doors we were rather unceremoniously tossed behind."

Esrahaddon made another turn. He was getting close. "Just keep talking."

"For the neglect of the Missing God, kid, what are you even doing here? I mean, of all the nutty places for you to show up, you came here? You realize this is the home of a riva, right? How did you know we were here? Did the old bitch use us to lure you? Is that it?"

"Something moved in here," Elinya said and pointed to a door they passed.

Esrahaddon went back and opened the little slide-aside peek-a-boo window. There was a person inside. A Ba Ran, but he was green-skinned.

"Who are you?" Esrahaddon asked.

The Ba Ran looked up but didn't answer.

"I'm sorry I got you into this, kid," Niblick went on.

Esrahaddon used the Art to mark the door with a white stripe. "Tell me if you notice any more," he said to Elinya. "I can't imagine anyone deserves to be in here. But I want to find Niblick and Mashie first."

"I took the Klune to Myno—no way I was going to Arkum. We did fine for about a year or so, then someone recognized the *Great Excuse* as the ship Hekkabah left Aoz Hilus on. What are the odds? For normal people—astronomical. For me? A sure thing. Next day, Mashie and I were hauled before—guess who? Don't bother. It was Rex Nexziria. Never met him before, and I wish I could still say that. Everything we told you about him being a living nightmare—let me just clarify that was an insult to nightmares. And while I'd like to sit here in this lousy cell and tell you how we bravely kept our mouths shut, I'm sorry to admit we told him everything. By the end—and by *the end* I mean like an hour—I was confessing to crimes I never committed, making things up, hoping he'd just kill me."

"Why didn't he?" Esrahaddon asked.

"He had other plans for me and the Great Right-Hander, as we are the only two in the world who know what you look like. Now, I told him—and I was very clear on this point, at least as clear as a guy can be with a molten metal bar jabbed inside of him—that you never got the present. I guess he figured Hekkabah slipped it to you when we weren't looking or something. So he sent us back to find you. Being Rex Nexziria and not an utter moron, he sent a daza and a loyal crew to ensure we did our best and didn't just disappear."

Esrahaddon led the others to the last door on a long row and knocked. "Niblick?"

"If you're an illusion, I'll kill myself."

Esrahaddon threw the bolt and pulled the door open to see the old Urgvarian sailor. Niblick sat on the floor, his back against the wall of the tiny stone room. He wasn't alone. Another ghazel, one Esrahaddon didn't recognize, sat across from Niblick. Dressed in cheap, ill-fitting tunics, both looked weak and dirty.

When Esrahaddon stepped inside, he felt a strange numbness, a sense of drowning. When climbing a hill, he sometimes experienced a similar sensation of pressure in his head until his ears popped. But rather than merely affecting his head, this smothering enveloped his whole being.

"Don't let that door close!" he ordered Jerish. "Elinya, stay outside."

Esrahaddon took a breath. He was fine, except . . . it felt like part of him was missing—the Artist part. He moved in deeper, approaching his old friend. "You've looked better."

Niblick shrugged. "It's the diet I'm on. Haven't had a lot to drink, either. Come to think of it, being here is sorta like you in Haddon. And I'm not as young as I once was."

That wasn't all. Niblick's face and head were blemished with scarring. He was also missing teeth, and part of his cheek looked to have been removed with something that also nearly took his eye.

"Did she do this, or the rex?" Esrahaddon asked.

"Aside from locking us in here and throwing away the key, the lady of the house has been a peach—to us, at least. The rest of the ship's crew was forced to feed her."

"Feed her?"

"Once a month."

"You mean she eats them."

"Face first, I'm guessing."

"Who's your friend?" Esrahaddon asked, seeing the other Ba Ran getting to his feet.

"Not my friend. That's the Leash, if you get my meaning. He's the daza Rex Nexziria sent with me."

Clearly an Arkum Ba Ran, the Leash looked a lot like Greglion after a long night of drinking at a bog house. Having suffered in the cell along with the rest, that was understandable.

Esrahaddon helped Niblick to his feet. Doing so, he noticed markings around the tops of the wall where, in a nicer room, crown molding might have been. "Orinfar. So that's what's going on." He knew about the markings. He'd been trained to draw them forward and backward for various weaves, like the location spell, and Jerish had them tattooed on his chest, but Esrahaddon had never stood within their stifling effect.

"*Orin*-what?" Niblick asked as they walked to the door.

"Nothing. It's just that this cell is runed."

"You talking about those markings near the ceiling?"

"Yeah. They're Orinfar. They block the Art—prevent magic."

"They do?" Niblick's eyes went wide.

As the two exited the room, Esrahaddon felt the world rush back, and the sensation was like breaking the surface of a deep pool. Niblick turned around, grabbed the door, and tried as best he could to slam it closed. He was a moment too late.

The Leash had followed them out.

Still reeling from the rush, Esrahaddon noticed a plume of power appear then disappear as Niblick's cellmate regained, then immediately muted, his signature.

"Watch out, I told you he's a daza!" Niblick shouted. Just then Esrahaddon's robe began to glow. Seeing it, Niblick rolled his eyes. "Ah, for gripe's sake. That's it, isn't it? You're wearing the gift."

The Leash saw it, too, and his face lit up with more than the robe's glow. "The Gry Erlikon!"

Niblick launched himself at the Leash, knocking him back against the wall before the daza caught himself and with a gesture blew Niblick down the corridor, where the Urgvarian Ba Ran slammed hard into the wall.

A heartbeat later, the Leash attacked with a burst of fire hot enough to melt iron, but thanks to Niblick, Esrahaddon had his shield up, so the fire burned away, leaving only a terrible stench where it had singed the walls. If it had been another legionnaire, Esrahaddon wouldn't have thought twice, but this was a Ba Ran. They were supposed to be civilized.

"Hold on!" he shouted. "What are you doing? I just freed you!"

"You killed my brother!"

"What are you talking about? I don't even know—" Esrahaddon stopped as he realized the Leash really did look like Greglion. He might have guessed, except for the grungy tunic, the fortress diet, and the fact Esrahaddon was obviously terrible at spotting siblings. "Greglion? Your brother was Greglion?"

Perhaps speaking the name confirmed what had only been a suspicion, or maybe it clawed open a painful wound. Either way, the brother's eyes flared, and he thrust his arms forward, palms out. The Leash intended to use overwhelming power to burn through the shield. Esrahaddon altered his defense just slightly, tilting the plane of the shield on an angle. When the blast came, the white-hot arc of pure power was neatly deflected into the now-empty cell, where the beam vanished the instant it crossed the threshold, doing no damage at all.

"Hold on, I didn't kill your brother. He—well—he sort of killed himself. He wanted this robe. I gave it to him. He put it on and . . ."

For a surprisingly long moment nothing happened.

The Leash just stood there, along with everyone else in the corridor.

"And what?" the brother finally asked.

"It ate him."

Another long moment lingered.

"Waves rolling, kid," Niblick's anguished voice came from down the hall. "Don't talk to the bastard. He's a zealot and has orders from the rex to find the robe, then murder the both of us. If you can, kill the son of a bitch!"

Before Esrahaddon could act, the Leash clapped his hands and the opposing stone blocks on either side of the corridor slammed together. Everyone in the corridor—except for the Leash, who had left himself a gap—would have died if not for Esrahaddon's shield still being up. Half as wide as the corridor, it acted as a wedge, catching the stones and preventing them from coming together. Those not in exact line with the shield were struck on one side and bounced off the other. Elinya fell to the floor. The dagger she always held so gingerly spun away. Niblick grunted somewhere behind him. Jerish took the unexpected clap well and remained on his feet.

The Leash redoubled his efforts. Esrahaddon worked to expand his shield. Who would win the battle was not clear, and Esrahaddon was not satisfied with such even odds.

"A little help, Jerish?" he asked.

The knight, who previously seemed content to merely watch, drew his swords.

The Leash reacted quickly with a less forceful but deadly arc of pure power that struck Jerish in the chest. The expenditure of energy gave Esrahaddon the upper hand, allowing him to widen the corridor.

The beam of light did nothing to Jerish, who promptly sliced off the Leash's right hand. The surprise on the ghazel's face was spectacular.

Resistance ended.

Esrahaddon threw the walls back. Then with a blast of his own, he burned a hole the size of a small pumpkin through the ghazel's chest. He collapsed like a soaked sack.

"Thanks," Esrahaddon told Jerish. "But what took you so long?"

"Can't kill, remember? Even cutting his hand off—he probably would have bled to death. I'm not sure about causing death indirectly. No one really explained the rules. And well . . . punching him seemed stupid."

"He was a Ba Ran," Esrahaddon said, surprised.

"Still a life, right?"

Esrahaddon nodded. "Yeah."

Niblick limped up the corridor, breathing hard. He had a cut on his forehead to add to his growing gallery of artwork but appeared otherwise undamaged. He clapped Esrahaddon on the back. "You're a Cenzar now, aren't you? And that's your Teshlor, right? And he knows not to kill me?"

Esrahaddon nodded. He, too, was a bit winded, so he bent down, grabbing his knees to make breathing easier. "Elinya, Jerish, meet my Uncle Niblick—the other one who raised me."

"So that story," Jerish said, "you really were raised by gob—"

"Watch it," Esrahaddon stopped him. "They're called *Uber Ran*. That other word is an insult."

"Oh—ah, sorry," Jerish said as he cleaned his blade and returned it to its scabbard.

"Listen, after what you just did? You can call me whatever you like." Niblick put his arms around Esrahaddon and hugged him. "Good to see you again, kid. And it looks like I was right."

“How so?” Esrahaddon asked.

“It’s not such a bad thing having helped raise a tiger.”

While Esrahaddon took a few minutes to regain his strength, Niblick, Elinya, and Jerish located Mashie and let him out. Mashie looked terrible, which is to say he hadn’t changed much, but he captivated Elinya’s and Jerish’s attention like a rabid dog everyone said was tame. The three sat in the corridor together, while Jerish and Elinya provided a bare bones explanation of what brought them to Castell Blythium, which Niblick called Borappathin. Watching the exchange was fascinating. Elinya and Jerish had never seen a Ba Ran before, likely not even a drawing. They had heard of them. Everyone had heard of goblins. They were *unintelligent, inhuman monsters*, suggesting that only non-humans could be unintelligent and monsters. While Mashie looked every bit the monster, and Niblick had also never been a virtuous beauty—with the last decade doing him no favors—neither could be labeled fiends. And as for intellect . . .

“Okay, okay, so let me get this straight.” Niblick threw his hands up to halt their combined efforts to condense the last few days into a dam release of less-than-organized facts and supposition, which they unwittingly made all the more incomprehensible by talking over one another.

Niblick took a deep breath. “So you’re saying that Uberlin—that no-good, absentee god of me and mine—arranged for the kid here, along with a mentally off-balanced but super powerful daza with delusions of becoming a riva, to come to Mileva’s fortress of death, darkness, and debauchery to kill an old hag that should have dropped dead about twelve thousand years ago? And that the two of you, along with some antiquated Cenzar master, decided to hop on this joyride to nightmarish suffering for . . . what? Kicks and giggles?”

Jerish and Elinya looked at each other for a moment, then nodded.

“Yeah, okay, that makes about as much sense as everything else has lately,” Niblick muttered.

Esrahaddon sat slumped against the cool stone wall in the corridor, the body of the Leash, with the melon-sized hole through him, still in easy view just down the passage. He was feeling a little better, but not great. Killing three hundred men and then the wrestling match with Greglion’s brother had left him a tad tuckered, about the same as if he'd just run a mile. He was sweating, and his limbs felt a bit weak. Nothing strange. It had been a while since he'd done any Artistic heavy lifting, and he was merely feeling out of shape.

"Are you all right?" Elinya asked, moving to his side with a look of concern.

"Just a little exhausted. Believe it or not, what I just did was harder than it looked."

"You held back two entire stone walls from crushing us while I lay on my face," Elinya said. "You deserve a breather."

"Maybe, but I don't know if we have time." He looked up. "We have no idea what's going on up there. Yolric and Ruby could be dead already."

"So, what's the plan here?" Niblick asked. "You're not still intending to go ahead with this walnut idea of trying to kill a riva, are you?"

Esrahaddon got to his feet. "Actually, I am."

"I thought I raised you smarter than this. Humans have made you stupid, haven't they?"

He shrugged.

"We need to find Mileva's pile of bones," Jerish said. "You wouldn't know where that is, would you?"

"Sure, it nearly sank the *Relentless*."

Jerish, Elinya, and Esrahaddon stared at him.

"Nearly sank what?" Esrahaddon asked.

"Our ship—the *Relentless Riva*. The boat Nexziria sent us back west in. She's a beauty of a vessel, real top of the line. Might even be Nexziria's personal warship. Who knows? That's her captain you put a hole through. Which is a joke because he didn't know the first thing about sailing. I had to tell him what to do. And I already mentioned how the crew has been keeping our hostess fed."

"Okay, sure, but what did you mean about—how did a pile of bones nearly sink a ship?"

"Oh, Mileva's pile is stacked under the ocean—thing's like a freaking barrier reef."

"It's in the ocean?" Jerish asked, stunned.

"It's underwater?" Elinya added, sounding defeated.

Esrahaddon thought for a moment. "Niblick, can you take us to it?"

"What, you wanna get up on my shoulders like when you were a kid and have me carry you? It's out in the ocean, kid. I'd need a boat."

"It's still there. Your ship—well, *a* ship, anyway—is anchored in the bay. I saw it as we arrived."

"Really?"

"Yeah," Esrahaddon looked at the Ba Ran. "Niblick, how long have you been locked up?"

"Seriously, I have no idea, but we had a crew of eighty-three when we arrived. If Hitartheon has been eating one per month, which I think is the going rate for immortality, when we let them all out, we should have a pretty good idea. Of course, they're all loyal to Nexziria."

"A promise to get them out of here might change that," Esrahaddon said.

A smile grew on Niblick's face. "Thanks for saving me, kid."

"I'd do anything for you."

The words took the Ba Ran off guard, and the smile rippled like an ocean wave as Niblick swallowed several times, his little eyes growing glassy. "I, ah . . ." His voice cracked. "I really did think I was gonna die, you know? Ever since I went up in front of the rex . . . hope was just a thing I used to have, you know? I'm a ghazel. One of the many forgotten by our own freaking god. It was just a matter of time and a question of exactly how awful it would be. But now . . . now I don't know anymore. Maybe there is a chance." Tears slipped down his face, and he reached out and hugged Esrahaddon. "I'm so proud of you, kid. Hekkabah would be, too."

"I think she's proud of both of us." Esrahaddon hugged him back.

He let go, and moving to face Elinya, he took her hands in his. "I need you to do something for me—for everyone."

"Name it."

"I need you to go back up. Find Yolric and Ruby and tell them we found the pile and we're going to destroy it. Obviously, if *she's* there, don't let her know. Tell them to keep her busy. Can you do that?"

Elinya looked terrified at the prospect of wandering the citadel alone seeking the riva's parlor, but she nodded.

"How are we going to destroy a submerged pile of ancient bones the size of a reef?" Jerish asked.

Niblick grinned. "The kid here inherited my talent when it comes to the ocean."

CHAPTER THIRTY-FOUR

Mileva

Elinya had never liked houses, big or small. It had been with great courage and a whole lot more desperation that she insisted on Esrahaddon taking her to Percepliquis: land of the big houses. She had no idea why buildings made her uncomfortable, why any enclosed space felt smothering. They just did. Even the little shack she was born in—*especially* the dump she was born in—made her sweat. The air seemed thinner, the sounds louder. And under it all, a growing sense that danger was creeping up—danger that would *get her* if she couldn't escape the prison of those walls.

When Elinya had insisted on remaining outside the little tree house in the tranquility of the Hawthorn Glen, Ruby told her that the legendary Suri had suffered a similar affliction. How Ruby knew so much about a person she'd never met and who had died thousands of years before, Elinya had no idea. But given that Ruby made it spring in the middle of winter, she didn't need to explain. Some things were taken on faith.

Ruby explained that Suri suffered from fear of small places because she'd been trapped in a cave-in at a young age. Elinya had never suffered such a thing, but as she crept through Mileva Hitartheon's mansion, she felt the same flavor of fear that she had under her father's roof. This made her wonder if she had experienced a less obvious, more subtle, but just as harrowing entrapment. She hadn't gone into the Forbidden Forest merely to save her friends but to escape an ever-present torment that had no name or face. The similarities of her past to her present were distressing.

Elinya had never learned to swim, despite having grown up on the banks of a river, and at that moment, she felt as though she waded through chin-deep water. She hoped it didn't get any deeper but knew it would. The one consolation—she wouldn't call it a comfort—was that now, the fear had a name and would have a face as soon as she saw her: Mileva Hitartheon.

Having climbed the corkscrew stairwell back to the surface, she felt a smidgeon better. Sunlight, despite being tainted by the filthy windows, was a hint of wholesomeness that held her hand as she continued the journey. Her task was a simple one, her trek short. She only needed to climb a few sets of stairs and deliver a short message, but she knew this was *it*. In everyone's life there was that singular moment that formed the high mark of a person's existence. For most, it could only be seen from behind, by looking back, but she understood that going forward was the act for which she had been born. Elinya also knew it might very well be the act in which she died.

The fireplace and candles were still burning in the vestibule as she followed in the footsteps of Ruby and Yolric. Coming to the threadbare stairs, she climbed once more.

Having the gift—or curse, she wasn't able to decide—of knowing she was reaching the end of her life, Elinya reflected on her regrets. Far from a morbid product of facing mortality, the cold self-evaluation was the best means she had to combat the panic that gripped her, whispering that the air was running out and that she should, too.

Elinya lamented that she had never learned to read. She had visited the imperial library once a week on her day off for years. She had bathed herself raw, put her best clothes on, and put her hair up, then she climbed the grand stone steps and passed through those wonderful doors. Inside, she walked aimlessly, looking at all the book spines as they stood side by side in long rows, like tiny works of art. She dared to touch them, letting her fingertips run over the raised ribs and foil lettering. She would pick the prettiest and, clutching it to her chest like a stranger's newborn, carry the tome to one of the many tables. Elinya would sit alongside all those scholars—all those learned people—and pretend to read, pacing her turn-of-page to match those nearby. She'd hoped that one day she would ask

Esrahaddon, and he might be kind enough to teach her what all the markings meant. She knew he would—he was beyond generous. But now she realized that instruction would remain an unfulfilled dream. That she had touched a book at all, turned its pages, been allowed to enter such a magnificent place as the imperial library was a miracle. And it would have to be enough.

At the top of the stairs, she entered a hallway. A carpet runner continued down its length. The left side was a series of five stained-glass windows that depicted four men and a woman standing on blocks of text that remained a heartbreaking mystery to her. Behind the image of the woman was a familiar fortress on a seaside cliff, leading her to believe that the woman might be Mileva. Since there were five individuals in total, Elinya guessed these could be depictions of the five riva.

If only I could read, I would know.

Down the length of the corridor were periodic half-moon tables set against the walls. One held a blue-and-white porcelain vase of long-dead flowers. About midway was a full-sized stone statue of a naked woman. She posed with her back arched, chin high, hands in fists, eyes focused on some elevated point. Proud, defiant, strong—she was stunning. *Beautiful* didn't come close.

Elinya faced the statue. They were nearly the same height—might have been without the little pedestal. *But we don't look to even be the same species.*

Passing the statue, Elinya watched for the double doors and found them just ahead, both wide open. From the room beyond came voices.

"Is it wine or blood?" Ruby asked in a shockingly casual tone for such a question.

"Does it matter?" replied an unknown feminine voice. "You're looking into the lifestyle, aren't you? Might as well try out a few things. That's why you're here, isn't it?"

Elinya poked her head into the parlor.

By the name Yolric had given the room, Elinya expected an intimate space, but Castell Blythium's parlor was monumental compared to the vision in her head. The room was large, and where it wasn't wood, it was red. Parquet floors were adorned with red-patterned rugs. The lower half of the walls displayed waist-high wood shelving topped with sculpted busts and miniature statues, while the upper portions were covered in ornate, red-on-red floral damask fabric. The ceiling was high and left plenty of room for large paintings and tapestries. The far wall was dominated by a soot-blackened stone hearth that vaguely resembled an animal's mouth—what animal, Elinya couldn't guess. Great brass-urn braziers hung from the ceiling, each secured by a trio of chains. Near the entrance doors was a large table covered in a red cloth and bedecked with a pair of gaudy gold candelabras and a banquet fit for an emperor. Bowls and plates were heaped with all manner of fish and fowl, decanters and bottles filled with wine and spirits. Near the burning hearth was an intimate cluster of chairs and sofas, each upholstered in red velvet.

Ruby stood before the banquet table, small plate in hand, carefully picking delicacies to place upon it. Yolric sat comfortably slouched on one of the sofas. A woman stood before the hearth, as if warming her backside. Dressed all in black, her shoulders bare, her body and head draped in a sheer material that could best be described as a death shroud, she was the very inspiration for the statue in the hallway. She looked to be a youthful teenager: pale skin, dark eyes, and supple lips a hue somewhere between red and purple. The statue, as impressive as it was, remained but a grotesque reflection of the vision before her.

"Who is this now?" Mileva asked, peering at Elinya with prehistoric eyes set in a child's face.

Yolric stood up and walked the length of the room to her. "This is the lovely Elinya. My traveling companion."

"*Your* traveling companion, Trilos?" Mileva asked, apparently surprised.

"She's pretty, isn't she?" He reached out and took Elinya by the hand, then led her into the room, as if they were about to dance. The old man gestured at the table. "Have something to eat, my dear. Mileva was kind enough to prepare a feast. Since we're on the ocean, I would suggest the fish."

"Is it . . . ?" Elinya began, then hesitated, glancing at the lady in black. Like cobwebs, the delicacy of her gown fluttered from the fire's heat.

"It's fine," Yolric said. "Mileva may be a riva, but she's a consummate hostess."

"Oh, but watch out," Ruby added. "I think the wine is blood." She stared at one of the dark bottles with the tall necks and licked her lips. "Does make you wonder what it tastes like, though." She turned to Mileva. "Is it all coppery, like when you bite your own lip?"

"Master Yolric"—Elinya held her nerve by focusing only on the old man—"Esrahaddon asked me to tell you that he found . . ."

"He found what, dear?" Mileva asked, her voice smooth and aloof like a talking cat. Feeling much like a mouse, this helped Elinya not at all.

"He found . . . *his uncle*."

"Uncle?" Mileva asked.

"The other two that came with us," Yolric explained. "I'm sure you're aware they are touring your home as we speak. I told them you're not a gifted architect or interior designer, but they seem fascinated. I didn't think you'd mind. You've never been the gregarious type, and I figured Ruby and I were more than you wanted, anyway. The talented one of the two recently learned from your doormen that an uncle of his is a guest here."

Mileva's forehead pinched in confusion. "Esrahaddon is a ghazel? At present, all my guests are Ba Ran of some ilk."

"No, but from what I understand, he was adopted by them as a child."

"I see." Mileva nodded and smiled. "And you say he found him."

"Is that a problem?" Yolric asked.

Mileva shook her head. "No. One less won't matter. I have a full pantry."

"You have a storehouse of ghazel? How'd that happen?"

"They came by ship. Wanted help. Said that Nexziria sent them and that they had reason to believe the Gry Erlikon was somewhere in Percepliquis. They wanted me to use my influence to find out."

"You didn't help them?"

"They were under the false impression that I served Nexziria. If the robe is in Percepliquis, the last person I want to have it is him."

Elinya continued to look only at Yolric. "I was told to deliver the message that *everything is exactly as Esrahaddon had hoped,* and *that we ought to enjoy our visit as long as we are welcomed to do so.*" She emphasized the comments, trusting that Ruby and the old man would understand she was saying more than the words coming out of her mouth.

"Wonderful." Yolric grinned and picked up a drumstick from some sort of roasted bird before returning to his sofa, making himself comfortable once more.

"This is interesting." Ruby stood before one of the many paintings on the wall. She held a glass of scarlet liquid that she swirled. The painting was the largest in the room: a portrait of a man that had been repeatedly slashed, as if by a dagger. "Did you and Uberlin have a falling out?"

Mileva tilted her head, causing the fragile hood to flutter oddly. The riva's eyes narrowed as tension filled the room. "You know what he looks like? You've seen him?"

"He paid me a visit several years ago," Ruby mentioned.

"Interesting, isn't it, Mileva?" Yolric said. "My brother visits everyone but us."

Mileva remained focused on Ruby. "What did he want?"

"He asked me to kill you."

"And here you are—applying for my job, I assume?"

Ruby shrugged. "Thinking about it." Ruby squared off with the riva. Neither looked as if they were about to fight, but Elinya didn't know how such beings fought. Mileva stood with her tiny hands clasped near her neck in a most proper and posed manner, yet beneath that quivering hood ancient eyes smoldered.

"A bit awkward, isn't it?" Ruby peered at her over the rim of her glass of swirling blood-wine. Then her attention shifted to another painting. Easily six feet in height, the artwork was of a different woman, and as improbable as it seemed, she outshone Mileva. This woman wasn't merely beautiful. This lady was something beyond what words could capture. The closest Elinya could come was *magnificent.*

"Who is this?" Ruby asked.

"Ferrol," Mileva supplied with a crisp, tart tone.

"That's my sister." Yolric pointed at the painting with his drumstick.

"She's stunning."

"She's dead," Mileva said.

Ruby turned back to study Mileva. "You don't look old."

"Should I?"

Ruby gestured with the glass, making a circle that encompassed the whole of Mileva. "This isn't an illusion. This is really you."

"Yes."

Ruby smiled. "I like that." She took a sip, swished for a moment, then swallowed. She stared at her drink and tapped the glass. "I like *this*, too."

"You don't have to kill me to be a riva," Mileva said.

Ruby continued to tap the glass, but now with a more contemplative rhythm. "Correct me if I'm wrong, but *riva* isn't a state of being but a position, a title, one bestowed upon an individual seen worthy by Uberlin. Without *his* approval, you're just another raow."

"Rex Uberlin hasn't been seen or heard from in twelve thousand years."

"Until now."

"So you say. It doesn't change the fact that without him we rivas still abide. Once, we were Uberlin's servants, but that time is long past. And I'd like to point out that it isn't easy being a riva. We all suffered the agony of trial-by-error experimentation. *Raow* is only the first step. We five blazed the trail into immortality, but those secrets are ours. I possess knowledge gathered over twelve millennia. I *could* teach you—help you through the hard parts, show you how to build your own stronghold. *How to eat.*" She tilted her head the other way, as if this granted her the ability to see the world from a new vantage point. "That said, there are three open positions available. Only two of us now, and our alliance is weak, as evidenced by the stores in my pantry." She turned to Yolric. "So strange that they would come asking about the robe. No one has seen it, the mantle, or the crown since Uberlin abandoned his war and his warriors." She took a moment to look at each of them. "Or am I mistaken?"

"I've seen it." Yolric finished his drumstick and tossed the bone into the fireplace. "Turin won't visit, but he sends me his old clothes."

Mileva stared at him so intently, Elinya was certain that if it were her, she might have died. "You have the Gry Erlikon?"

"I don't *have* it; I've *seen* it, and not in passing or by accident."

"So that's why you're here?"

Yolric wiped his greasy hands on the couch. "The only reason for my brother to parade his robe in front of me is to draw me here—to you. Tell me, Mileva, why would Turin want me to come back?"

"Why ask me? You well know I famously have not seen him." She motioned at the shredded painting.

"All right then, let's try something you do know. Why did you help me get out of Phyre, Mileva?"

"I told you—revenge."

"And revenge is always the answer with you and yours. But my question is: Against whom? You said it was Turin."

"Yes! The master betrayed us, abandoned us, left us to die."

"And you told me you wanted my help destroying him." He looked at the tattered painting. "I believe you were telling the truth, but now I think there's more to that truth—isn't there, Mileva?"

She said nothing as she stood alone before the fire.

"I don't think I ever thanked you for getting me out, but the whole affair was so strange. After all, you and I have never been friends, and once Turin became Uberlin, we were enemies. But I must admit, it took a special kind of genius to send messages to the Typhons by way of your murder victims. I'm assuming you threatened to consume their loved ones, sealing their souls forever in your pile if they didn't comply. Brilliant really—sick and twisted—but brilliant. I suppose that's why Turin picked you as a riva. And it clearly worked. Not sure what you offered the Typhons, though, what sort of deal the four of you struck, but they must have agreed, since they did your bidding. Not too many times that's ever happened. But I was there. I saw them cut that tunnel right to the edge of the membrane between the worlds, but even they couldn't pierce the plane. I only recently came to realize you hadn't figured on that. You were certain the Typhons were strong enough to punch a hole for me to escape through. But they couldn't. I had to do that myself." Yolric leaned forward, putting his elbows on his knees. "Don't you find it strange how I chose to do that?"

Except for the flicker of the gossamer shroud, Mileva was every inch the statue.

"I was forced to sacrifice the thing most dear to me to summon the power to make that pinprick I slipped out through, but—isn't it amazing that I chose to give up the one thing you wanted? Your entire reason for rescuing me wasn't to unleash me against my brother at all, was it? No . . . it was to find Muriel. You were positive I would know where to look. Certain I could draw her out."

"By finding her, we would find him," Mileva stated her defense.

"Only I couldn't help you, could I? You didn't foresee that. How could you? You're not an Aesira and have no talent in foresight, but I am, and maybe I did." He clapped his thighs and leaned back. "Sadly, as we both know, I can't remember. I only know what you've told me, and what I later read in that book I brought here, the one that poor girl died for. I still remember the look on her face as she fell. Made me sick. I never meant to hurt her. Just tried to scare the lass. Only afterward did I realize that wasn't possible. Even as she fell, there wasn't a hint of fear."

He sighed. "Couldn't destroy it after that, but I also couldn't read it. I was scared to. Frightened of what I might learn, too cowardly to face what it was that I had lost. But after visiting here and talking to you—and later Bran—I finally did." He bit his lip. "It made me even angrier at Turin. He did everything to keep me from the love of my life: murdered me and sent my spirit to Phyre for eternity, but that wasn't enough. He had to make her immortal, ensuring we could never be together. Turin and I, we had our fights as all brothers do, but I still can't believe he could be *that* sick and twisted. And now this odd development has me wondering *why* about so many things that, until now, I always felt so certain of. It's easy to believe my brother is a selfish, egotistical, jealous, lying bastard. He murdered me, after all. Easy to accept that you want revenge for a ruler who abandoned you and yours to ultimate disaster. But it's the *easy* part that bothers me. Destruction is always *easy. Creation* is hard." He leaned forward once more, his beard touching the floor. "Mileva, why is it spring?"

"I can answer that one," Ruby said cheerfully. "It's a season—happens every year around this time."

Yolric and the riva remained locked, staring hard at each other.

"Why isn't it winter, Mileva?" he asked. "For that matter, why isn't everything dead? Each year, whenever Alurya left her tree, everything shut down. Animals went to sleep, trees lost their leaves, days shortened, and the world grew cold as death. Alurya was life. Without her, Elan is a barren mother, a dead rock. Alurya has been dead for nearly as long as you've been alive, Mileva. I saw her corpse withered and bare. Life itself ended those many eons ago, yet as Ruby says, spring and summer continue to come every year around this time. How is that?"

"I don't know."

"I think you do. I think that's why Turin sent me to see you. I can't begin to fathom why I never realized it before. I should have, but it simply isn't in our nature to notice a *lack* of change. Seasons have always come and gone. The sun also rises each morning. Only if these things stopped would anyone sit up and ask why. I never did, but I should have. We all take so much for granted, but nothing is guaranteed: not the air we breathe, not the sun in the sky, nor the coming of spring. These things have not always been, which means they might not always be. That's what Turin wanted me to see."

Yolric shifted in his seat, casting out his beard like a lady does her gown. "So tell me, Mileva, why has the Gry Erlikon resurfaced? Why did Turin feel the need to send me here, and why do you have a shroud made of flies?"

If he hadn't pointed it out, Elinya never would have noticed. The moment he did, it was obvious. The riva's hood and entire cloak rippled but not from heat waves. It wasn't clothing at all.

Mileva's eyes hardened, and her demure pout bent into an ugly frown. "I was here all the time waiting for him. Serving him. Doing anything and everything he ever asked of me. I killed millions in his name, and I would have died for Uberlin. But he didn't care. Yet the moment *she* died, the instant he learned of Alurya's death, he abandoned everything—including me." She began breathing hard, her arms folded tight across her chest. "He could have come to me. I would have taken him in, cared for him, consoled him, but he didn't want me. He never wanted me. He was always in love with *her*."

"You read the book, didn't you?" Yolric asked. "While I was here, you read the *Book of Brin*."

"Muriel is *his* daughter," Mileva growled. "His and *hers*. Muriel is the seed of Alurya."

"The seed of Alurya," Yolric nodded. "She's what keeps everything alive, isn't she?" Spotting a fly on the arm of the sofa, he said, "But that doesn't explain everything. What are you up to, Mileva?"

She went mute and, except for the shroud of flies, she became as still as the statue in the hall. Now that Elinya saw them, she couldn't see anything else. The mass of insects was hideous and beyond distressing. *How can she stand having them on her—having them all over her?*

"You want to kill Muriel, don't you, Mileva? She's just as much your rival for Turin's affections as Alurya was. In many ways, they are one and the same. Muriel has somehow absorbed her mother's spirit, assumed her role as both nature's mother and the focus of Turin's love. And yet it makes no sense. If Muriel is the seed, and if she is indeed the invisible power behind all life, and if you manage to kill her—if that's even possible—you will end everything. All life on Elan will wither. And with no more meals available, you, too, will pass away. You will win nothing."

"Not nothing," Ruby said. "The other three riva did the same thing for the same reason. They tried to destroy the world, too. Didn't they? Apparently, that's a riva thing."

"Is *that* what you're doing, Mileva?" Yolric appeared puzzled. "Destroying the world out of spite? Reducing everything to . . ." He paused, shaking his head again as if trying to rid himself of the thought. "What deal did you make with the Typhons?"

Mileva threw out her arms and her shroud exploded into a host of flies that buzzed away in a cloud only to return as her cloak. "I'm sick of living like this, and I won't be a prisoner in Eton's dungeon. I'll see the world burn first!"

Ruby stared, dumbstruck, at the riva. Then she blinked and nodded. "I've decided I don't want to be a riva after all. It's not just the flies; it's the drama." She looked once more at Mileva. "No . . . it's the flies."

CHAPTER THIRTY-FIVE

The Pile

Jerish followed in third place as Niblick led the way down the stone steps carved from the face of the cliff on the backside of the stronghold. The staircase went right down to the small harbor where the *Relentless Riva* rocked uneasily at the dock. Jerish had seen ships before. As a child in Rionillion, he had witnessed many big vessels, but nothing like this. The ship was huge, with four great masts of ashen timber and reefed black sails. The leering figurehead carved on the prow was of a monstrous sea serpent with a raging mouth. This was no wholesome vessel, no ship of man; this was a construction of claws—a goblin boat.

Is this it? Is this the secret I came to discover? Is the Cenzarium making an alliance with the goblins?

If Andreas Ranier or Gaylord Sire were there, Jerish felt certain they would tell him so. Everyone knew goblins had invaded the empire and murdered Novron, and that they wanted to murder each and every human and tear down everything mankind had built because they despised all that was good. Jerish knew this to be true, just as he knew Novron was god, Bishop Venlin was his prophet, and the sky was blue. Except . . .

Jerish was suffering a crisis of definition.

Goblin was supposed to mean a gibberish-spewing monster that cooked and ate humans, but Jerish had already met *those goblins*, and they were men: the blood-soaked legionnaires who killed, cooked, and ate their fellow soldiers, and who fell over themselves to do who knows what to Elinya. But while Esrahaddon's uncles certainly *looked* like goblins, Jerish found he liked Niblick and Mashie more than most people. They were friendly but not annoying, and surprisingly welcoming. Furthermore, seeing the displays of fondness and pride exchanged between Esrahaddon and Niblick, Jerish found himself envying such a father figure.

And why are the goblins helping us defeat the riva? If the riva is evil, and the goblins are evil, shouldn't they be on the same side?

They had rescued thirty-two goblin sailors from the cells, and from that Niblick calculated that, if Mileva hadn't ever gone back for seconds, they had all been imprisoned a little over four years. That was another thing. While none of the goblin crew spoke Imperial, Jerish didn't need a translator to understand when the sailors learned the fate of fifty-one of their fellows. Several fell to their knees and openly cried. One poor guy went prone and beat the stone floor with his fists as he sobbed.

Can evil cry?

In all the stories Jerish had been told since childhood, not once did a goblin weep over the loss of a friend.

They all filed up the bouncy gangway and boarded the vacant ship. A great deal of discussion followed. Jerish couldn't understand a word. Esrahaddon joined in speaking what Jerish guessed to be three different languages, as he often appeared to translate for Niblick or Mashie. One of the goblins confronted Niblick. He said a good deal in an angry tone and pointed at Jerish a few times. Niblick replied in a similarly heated fashion, talking even faster than before.

"What's going on?" Jerish whispered to Esrahaddon.

"Niblick is explaining that he is assuming command of the ship. The crew isn't entirely thrilled."

"Is there going to be a fight?"

"No, they don't have a choice, and they know it."

"Because of you?"

"No. Because Niblick is the only real sailor here. The rest of this crew is Arkum Ba Ran."

"What does that mean?"

"Well, imagine you're in a war and you're trapped behind enemy lines. All these green-skinned Ba Ran are your typical tradesmen who just recently picked up their first sword and have practiced with it for a few weeks. They're scared, terrified really. And then there's you telling them that if they ever want to see home again, they need to do exactly what you say. Problem is, you're a stranger, and they're not sure if they can trust you. Thing is, they also know you're a Teshlor. That's what Niblick is, he's sort of a Teshlor of the Sea. They need him, but as with anyone, there's knowing and then there's accepting."

"We don't have a lot of time."

"Niblick will make it quick."

Some more shouting followed. Fewer words of protest were offered. The crew grumbled, but then they went to work pulling in the gangplank and untying the ropes.

"That went better than expected," Niblick said, joining them. "To be honest, I'm a little disappointed. I was hoping we'd have to maroon a few here in Rivaland."

"How far is it to this pile?" Esrahaddon asked.

"It's just around the breakwater—in fact, it *is* the breakwater. You can see it there where the water turns white." He gestured at a spot no more than five hundred feet away at a point where waves crashed.

"Can't we just walk out on that headland?" Jerish asked.

"Sure, but it would take longer and be far more dangerous. That's how *she* gets to the pile, how *she* adds to it. So that's how *she* imagines anyone else would."

"Traps?" Esrahaddon asked.

Niblick shrugged. "I'm only guessing, but I would furthermore presume that the reef likely has no defense at all from the sea."

"Why is that?"

"Because we came crazy close to ramming the thing and nothing happened." Niblick saw that the lines to the dock had been cast off. "Got to go to work. You can help with the wind, right, kid?"

"My pleasure. But can you sail this monster with only thirty-two hands?"

Niblick grinned. "I could sail her with twenty, even less with your help. Waves rolling, kid, it's good to have my little tiger back." He winked, then returned to shouting at the crew. Goblins raised the great black sails and tied off ropes. The moment they did, the massive ship pulled away from the pier and headed out to sea.

The motion increased the pitch of the deck, and both Jerish and Mashie grabbed the rail.

"I hate boats," Mashie grumbled. "And now I got only one lousy mitt to hang on with. You don't seem too happy, either."

"I prefer land," Jerish replied.

Mashie nodded. "Makes sense. You're a fighter. A good one. I can tell by the way you move."

Jerish was surprised by the comment—that a goblin would be so observant. Making it worse was that Jerish hadn't been. So overwhelmed was he by the goblins' strangeness, he hadn't looked at them the way he would men. A quick assessment revealed clarity: Mashie was also a trained combatant, and by the way he held his frame, how he flexed against the rocking deck, Jerish guessed he, too, was a *good one*.

"What happened to your . . . *mitt*," Jerish asked.

The goblin lifted his stub. "Lost it in a battle."

"Sorry to hear that."

Mashie stared at his mutilated arm and shook his head. "Don't care about losing it. I'd have given up both if I could have won that fight, but there were too many."

"You were forced to retreat?"

"No, they gave up and left."

"How is that a loss?"

"Because the one I was protecting died. She was . . ." He struggled. "She was the best of us, and I failed her." He pointed with his stub at Esrahaddon, who by then was with Niblick on a raised portion of the rear deck. "The kid patched me up, saved my life. Kinda wished he hadn't."

Jerish nodded.

In the Teshlor Guild, they were instructed never to lose—never to even entertain that possibility. It was considered a weakness. If you can imagine yourself losing, you likely will. But knights *did* lose. Most died when they lost, but some didn't. They went on breathing but were never the same. Teshlors had a tendency to *disappear*, and although most of their fellow knights wanted to think they lived out their elder years in contented simplicity, raising a family in a quiet village somewhere, everyone knew the truth. Most retired Teshlors eventually took their own lives. And those who failed in battle didn't wait until retirement. For all the education the guild supplied, it neglected to teach what to do after the sword went on the wall, or how to accept defeat.

Jerish had learned all this since leaving the academy, and he'd spent the last few years wondering if Master Rawlings had died of sickness, or by his own hand. Master Lynch had never said, nor ever would he.

"I understand," Jerish said, and he meant it. He also found it beyond bizarre that he was connecting with a goblin on a deeper level than he had with most humans.

Mashie studied him for a long moment as they hung together from the rail, steadying themselves against the rise and fall of waves. In those alien eyes, Jerish was disturbed to see a reflection of himself.

"You don't act like a human," Mashie said.

"I don't?"

"Naw, any other human would have tried to kill me by now. Maybe you're afraid of being outnumbered or trapped on a ship, but that don't explain you talking to me like this."

"Like what?"

"Like a person. The kid's the only human I've ever known to do that. What's your name?"

"Jerish."

Mashie nodded. "You're okay, Jerish, but then the kid always had good luck and good taste in friends."

Jerish was about to explain that he and Esrahaddon were not friends when shouts and pointed arms revealed they were approaching the pile.

Esrahaddon sensed it long before they drew near. The thing radiated power like a massive thunderstorm. But it wasn't thunder that announced the pile's presence, but rather the wails of tormented souls. At least that's how the Art interpreted the pile. With his eyes and ears, Esrahaddon witnessed massive waves crashing relentlessly against bleached bones that barely breached the surface. Less a pile and more a long line that paralleled the coast, the bones formed a macabre reef. Unlike those Esrahaddon had known as a boy in Calynia, no seagrasses or mangroves grew here, and he guessed no clams, crabs, or even fish came anywhere near it. Even the coastline was barren. No trees or grass grew. There was only a bit of lichen on the rocks.

Lichen can live anywhere, I guess.

"I don't want to get too close, kid," Niblick told him. "These surges and a well-timed gust and we'll be wrecked on that thing—not an appetizing vision. I can lower you in a boat if you need it."

Esrahaddon nodded.

"Okay, want me to pilot it?"

"No. You stay here. I know how to handle a skiff. My uncle was a sailor. He taught me well."

Niblick smirked. "Okay, sure, but ah . . ." He rubbed his chin. "Can you explain something to me? Why we doing this? I mean, we got this ship, we got each other, and we got an open ocean just begging to be explored. With this top-of-the-line vessel, my sailing skills, and your magic, we can do whatever we want. We could spend the rest of our lives exploring the world. Maybe there's a place somewhere on the face of Elan that wouldn't scream if either one of us walked in, someplace we could, I don't know, build another tree house."

"You hated that tree house. What happened?"

Niblick shrugged. "I got old."

"I must admit, I'm tempted."

"But?"

"But this is what Hekkabah wanted me to do."

"She did?" Niblick squinted his little eyes.

Esrahaddon nodded. "Yeah. Remember how she used to say that Uberlin hasn't forgotten you? I think this is that. She brought me his robe. Forced me to learn everything she knew about his generals, the riva. Taught me to use the Art. Whether she knew it or not, it was so I could be here at this moment, maybe so you could, too. And . . ."

"And?"

"And I met someone."

"Oh yeah? Back in Percepliquis?"

"No, in a village not much different from Haddon." He pointed back at the fortress. "You've met her. Her name is Elinya."

"She's . . . ?" Niblick turned to look at the fortress. "Wait—what? Do you hate this woman?"

"I think I might be in love with her."

Niblick's eyes went wide. "Are you kidding me? You left someone you care about with Mileva Hitartheon? You know she eats people, right? That's total walnuts. Clearly, I raised an idiot."

"I didn't leave her alone. There are two other powerful Artists with her who are planning to kill the riva."

"Two Artists fighting a riva? That's like two abbra berries fighting my mouth."

"That's why I must destroy that pile. If I do, it will be like knocking out your teeth—the abbra berries will have a fair chance of choking you."

"Well then, why are we standing here yakking, for gripe's sake! Get in the boat!"

Esrahaddon rushed off.

"But be careful out there, will ya? The water around here ain't normal."

"Nothing here is normal."

Jerish saw Esrahaddon climbing into a boat that was being swung off the side of the *Relentless*. "What are you doing?"

"Got to get closer," the Cenzar said.

"Okay." Jerish climbed in.

"What are *you* doing?"

"Going with you."

"Why?"

The goblins began lowering the skiff. The block and tackle squeaked as the ropes were let out, dropping them a bit. There was a jerk, a pause, and another drop.

"Cenzar, Teshlor. We're a team, remember?"

"We aren't battling an army here, Jerish, not even a sea serpent, which I might add, you wouldn't be any more help with."

"You needed me when you fought the Leash, remember?"

"Yeah, okay, sure, but this is a massive pile of bones. What are you going to do, yell at it?"

"At the very least, I can steady the boat."

"Jerish, this is dangerous. It would be best if you didn't come."

"Why?" Jerish wondered if this was the heart of the secret he was sent to uncover. The source of the Cenzar's powers, or perhaps this was where Esrahaddon would make contact with the elven ruler.

"Because . . ." Esrahaddon sighed. "I'm not really sure what I'm doing. I'm making this up as I go. I honestly don't know what's going to happen when I step on that pile, and I don't know what I can do to destroy it. I sorta thought I could use waves, but they've been beating on this thing for eons to no effect. So I don't know. What I do know is that Mileva will protect this with everything she's got and . . . there's no need for both of us to die."

He sounded so sincere, Jerish almost believed him. *Doesn't matter. If he's lying, I need to go to find out why, and if he's not, there's no way I can abandon him.*

"I'm coming."

The boat clapped the water, and the goblins unhooked the lines.

Esrahaddon didn't bother with the oars or the little sail. Using the abundant wind and powerful currents, he persuaded the boat to slowly approach the bone beach. Over and over, water flooded then receded from the top of the pile. The bones must go all the way to the bottom of the bay because they disappeared into the darkness of the churning water.

Destroying it should be easy, he thought. *A lot of things "should be" but aren't. I should be at the Imperial Palace teaching Nevrik or taking Elinya out to a chariot race or a play. I should even be struggling with the idea of asking her to marry me. What I shouldn't be doing is climbing onto a pile of cursed bones in the ocean at the edge of the known world and wondering if I can obliterate it.*

Destruction was always easy. He knew that but sensed he was missing something. *It just doesn't seem sensible for Mileva to leave the pile out here where anyone could blast it into splinters.* Something was going on, or the waves would have ripped it apart years ago.

The boat came up, and on a swell, it skidded over the top, coming to an uneven rest.

"Get ready," Esrahaddon warned.

"For what?" Jerish asked.

"I have no idea."

"I'll get right on that, then."

Esrahaddon stood up in the boat and spread his arms. Power was everywhere: wind, waves, currents, and the sun. The ocean was always a good place to use the Art. Tapping it all, Esrahaddon attempted to affect the pile as he had the dead trees in the forest of Calynia and, more recently, the legionnaires in the courtyard.

Nothing happened.

I knew it.

Reaching out, searching with the Art, he found that the source of that thunderstorm of power wasn't the bones themselves but a shield. Mileva protected her pile with the same basic defense that Greglion had used against him in Shahabad, and that Esrahaddon himself had used against Greglion's brother a little more than an hour ago. The only difference was that where Greglion's shield was the equivalent of an inch-thick wooden fence, this was a four-foot-thick stone wall.

There was nothing he could do.

Jerish watched as Esrahaddon made faces at the pile, but nothing happened. He swept his arms and still nothing changed. Stepping out of the boat, Esrahaddon kicked at the bones and yelped when the leg bone, which appeared to lie lightly on the surface, reacted like an outcropping of granite.

Esrahaddon looked at Jerish, aghast. "It's not gonna work. We can't hurt this thing. I doubt Mileva even knows we're here."

Overhead, the sky grew darker. Around them, waves roiled black, frothing with an ugly foam, as if the pile were a heap of tea leaves that stained the ocean. The pile was indeed made entirely of bones. Jerish spotted ribcages, the broad flat paddles of pelvises, forearms, some with hand bones attached or at least nearby. There were big and small femurs and skulls . . . lots of skulls.

Jerish climbed out of the boat, which rocked with his movement. With a grimace, he stepped onto the pile. The moment his foot touched down, they both heard it.

A bone snapped.

CHAPTER THIRTY-SIX

The Riva

Having delivered her message, Elinya hoped to escape the parlor and return to Esrahaddon. Several times her eyes tracked to the hall, but she was scared to move. She had no magical powers, no special senses, but it took only eyes and ears to register the rising tension in that room. She felt like a bug on the floor in a dancehall for giants. Terrified of being stepped on, she was equally frightened of drawing attention to herself by moving. Bugs that flew got swatted.

Unless they are part of a riva's attire. And who knows what's going on with that.

So much time had already passed that she feared Esrahaddon and Jerish were long gone. But maybe they weren't. She might still catch up. But with each passing moment, that hope diminished. *It's now or never.* In one great burst of courage and determination, Elinya turned and took a step toward the doorway.

"NO!" Mileva shouted—practically screamed.

Elinya jumped and every muscle in her body locked as she froze—except for her neck which, despite all instructions not to, turned to see the awful fate that awaited the bug who had dared to attract the attention of a giant.

To Elinya's surprise, Mileva wasn't looking at her. She wasn't even facing her direction. The riva had turned around and was staring into the flaming mouth of the hearth, and when she looked back at them, her expression had changed. The beautiful youth with the old eyes had left. In her place was the riva. Physically, she looked the same, but the stoic expression and placid gaze had transformed into seething anger.

"No!" she shouted once more, as she cast her glare across all of them. "How dare you!"

Ruby looked to Yolric with a wide-eyed perplexity and raised shoulders, too confused to complete a shrug. "What's she talking about?"

"Esrahaddon has done something to the pile," the old man explained with his usual indifference, as if explaining that there would be a slight delay in that evening's dinner.

His comment pulled Mileva's attention. "You—of all people! How could you?"

Yolric shook his head. "How could I what? Just to be clear, I haven't *done* anything."

"You're with *them!*"

"I accompanied them, yes. I came because this whole affair was manifested by my brother. And since Turin and I are engaged in an epic war of sorts, truth be told, I came with every intention of sabotaging whatever scheme he hoped to execute. Only a funny thing happened on the way: I noticed the leaves on the trees."

"I saved you! I pulled you out of Phyre!"

"Oh, please, Mileva, the two of us have been enemies since that idea was invented. You joined Turin when he put the crown on. You swore allegiance to an evil dictator with aspirations of godhood. I always thought it was because you loved him, and maybe it started that way long ago, but now it's about power. You didn't *save* me, Mileva. You dug up what you believed would be a useful tool. You were wrong. Instead, you unleashed an old enemy. This still leaves me with a huge problem. Is it possible that Turin the Liar is telling the truth? Could he be aiding Muriel? Is she the real Invisible Hand I've been searching for? Either way, I owe you nothing."

Mileva's hateful glare shifted to a sinister delight as she displayed a toothy grin. "I'll add you all to my pi—"

Ruby shot the banquet table at her. The massive counter rammed Mileva hard, driving her into the flaming mouth of the fireplace. An instant later, everything else in the room that wasn't alive or bolted down followed suit, slamming into the opening, barricading the mouth. Then the modest fire that had been smoldering burst forth—with passion, light, and most of all, heat—as flames licked out around the assorted obstructions. A heartbeat after that, Elinya noticed a massive block of stone shake free of the wall, and it, too, rammed into the mouth of the fireplace, punching in like a cork in a bottle, or perhaps, more accurately, like a pestle into a brimming, flaming mortar.

In the silence that followed, Ruby stared at the stone that plugged the hole in the wall. She offered a shrug. "I kind of expected more."

"You shall not be disappointed," Yolric said. "A shield would be good right about now."

Ruby's brow furrowed, but nevertheless she made sweeping motions in the air. She was still in the process when the fireplace spat the stone back out. Blasting across the parlor, the huge hunk of ex-wall hit Ruby dead-on and drove her out the door and into the hallway.

This dashed Elinya's hope of escape. Instead, she slipped deeper into the parlor, made roomier by the furniture-clearing attack by Ruby. Perhaps she could hide behind that pretty tapestry that depicted a bird's-eye view of Rochelle. But there was no room, and she settled for standing still beside it as Mileva emerged from the fireplace with only her pride injured.

The giant block of stone cracked and burst into pebbles. Through the resulting dust, Elinya could see Ruby standing unharmed in the hallway. She brushed herself off, and with jaw set, she marched back in.

"Yes, yes, my dear," Mileva beckoned. "Please do come into my parlor."

~

"You broke a bone!" Esrahaddon shouted at him.

Jerish looked at his feet, obviously concerned. "Is that bad?"

"No! It's fantastic, but how'd you—" The Cenzar slapped his own face. "The Orinfar, you're covered in it. Just like Wardley did with Greglion, you can get through the shield!"

"So, what am I supposed to do?"

"We need to bury the bones."

"What? All of them?" He looked up the length of the reef that appeared to extend for miles. "We don't even have a shovel."

Esrahaddon thought a moment, then snapped his fingers. "Burial at sea. It's a thing, I think. All we have to do is break the bones out of the pile and toss them in the deep water."

"You're sure of that?"

"Not at all, but as you pointed out, we don't have a shovel, and even if we did, it wouldn't be big enough."

"Can't you . . ." He wiggled his fingers in the air.

"Sure, but I can't do anything with this pile. I can't even move a single femur with my hands. Only you can."

"Right." Jerish began kicking and stomping. Bones snapped and slid, but try as he might to help, Esrahaddon could do nothing. "Here," Jerish pulled his short sword and handed it to the Cenzar, who looked bewildered. "There are runes on it. On the blade."

"Oh."

Esrahaddon jabbed it down, and the bones moved as if they were set loosely on top of one another. Seeing this, he began using the sword blade like a rake, dragging bones into the water on the sea's side, where they tumbled into the black water and sank. Jerish drew his hand-and-a-half sword and did likewise. Together they cast scores of stripped corpses into the black water, where they hissed as the water swallowed them.

Then Esrahaddon wiped his brow. With a desperate look at the mild dent they had put into the reef, he said, "If we had an army, this would still take years, and what happens when we dig down below the waterline?"

They heard shouting, and both of them looked back at the ship. Niblick was on the prow, waving his arms. Whatever he was saying, they couldn't hear it over the roaring of waves, but he was vehemently pointing to the east.

"Uh-oh," Esrahaddon said.

"Uh-oh, what?" Jerish followed his line of sight out to sea, where a massive storm gathered strength in the open ocean. Above, black clouds swirled. Beneath, the ocean surface began to spin into a massive vortex. All of it rushed at them with apocalyptic intent.

"We don't have years."

Ruby blasted a stream of fire from her open palms at Mileva. The fire burst against an invisible shield that sent the waves of flame up to the ceiling and down to the floor, scorching both and leaving wide black marks.

Mileva struck back with a beam of white light so bright that Elinya had to close her eyes. When the light faded, Elinya opened them again, and she saw Ruby sitting on the floor, looking dazed.

"That, my dear child, is but a taste of real power," Mileva said.

Ruby rolled to her knees, dodging sideways just in time to evade a second blast of light that cut a crevasse into the floor. Ruby frantically gestured, making strange motions with her fingers, and seemed to sing a song with no words. She'd just finished when she was forced to dodge another blast that left a round hole in the stone wall. The opening made a window to the corridor through which Elinya could once more see the pretty porcupine vase and the dead flowers. As Elinya stared through that gaping, glowing hole, she saw a figure pass by, moving from left to right. Something was moving down the corridor. The suspense was short-lived, as into the room ran the naked stone statue of Mileva. It sprinted past Ruby and charged the riva.

Mileva deftly conjured a glowing blue blade that appeared to grow out of her hand. As she did, the statue gripped her by the throat with one stony fist. Lifting the riva off the ground, it squeezed. Face contorting with pain, Mileva brought the blade up, slicing through the limb at the elbow. The arm broke apart, fell, and shattered on the floor between them.

Showing no sign of pain or remorse, the statue promptly swung at her with its remaining arm. Mileva was ready and severed the other offending appendage. Finally, with both of her hands gripping the sword and tucked to the hilt, the riva cut straight across, dividing the sculpture in half at the waist. It crumbled and collapsed.

Ruby was back on her feet. Her hair clung to sweat that slicked her forehead. With a finger, she summoned the little half-moon tables from the corridor—destroying the vase in the process—and threw them at Mileva. The riva obliterated each with the sword. As she did, Mileva advanced.

Ruby tried to cast a new attack, but nothing happened.

"Not in my house, dear." Mileva laughed at her. "You're fighting a riva now, and all the shadows here are mine." She bared her teeth with hate. "And I really liked that sculpture, you bitch!" The flies that had formed Mileva's shroud left her and, racing in an unnaturally straight line, attacked Ruby, swarming her face. "How do you like the flies now?"

With her cloak of pests gone, Mileva stood exposed in a suit of golden armor. Except for the few visible seams, it could have been her skin. Mileva charged forward, and the blade caught fire, blue flames licking along its edges. In that moment, Elinya didn't see a woman or a monster but a goddess of old. Before her, a vision only myths could capture leaped into battle as only they had the limitless space to house such things.

We came to kill this? Did anyone know? Did Esrahaddon understand? I didn't. How could anyone imagine this?

Mileva struck at Ruby with the sword. The glowing blade hit her shield. The moment the two collided, everything flashed, and the outline of the defensive wall was displayed by the sword. Then as Elinya watched, the blue blade sliced off the top quarter of Ruby's shield.

Through the cloud of flies that persisted around Ruby's face, Elinya saw fear as once more Mileva struck, and again part of Ruby's barricade was sliced away.

Ruby ignored the flies and threw both palms forward. Whatever she was trying to do did not appear to occur. Mileva laughed once more, and this time with a back stroke she divided the remaining—now buckler-sized—shield in half. With a burst of light, the entire thing vanished. Falling onto her back, Ruby screamed, then began slapping her own face as the flies clustered on her eyes and filled her gaping mouth.

Mileva gestured at the ceiling, and a massive stone fell. The multi-ton block missed killing Ruby, but it did manage to crush one leg and the foot of the other. Ruby screamed, but the sound was muffled as her whole face—her entire head—was, by then, a solid mask of buzzing black insects.

"That's better," Mileva said, "isn't it, my darling? No more of this silliness. Now we can begin the process."

The flaming sword vanished, and Mileva moved toward Ruby. She had only managed one step when she was thrown across the room. The riva flew through the air and slammed hard into the wall near where the banquet table had been. She bounced off and fell to the ground.

Stunned, Elinya studied Ruby, but the Artist—suffering from a crippling blow and a mask of flies—couldn't have done anything. Elinya then turned to Yolric, but the old man continued to sit, legs stretched out, hands folded behind his head. Elinya was ashamed of her own spectatorship, but the Cenzar master appeared as comfortable as if he were watching a performance. Still, there was no other answer. "Did you . . ."

He shook his head, wagging his beard. "Not me," he whispered. "But I suspect Mileva's past is returning to haunt her."

Esrahaddon felt a searing pain on his finger as a crab attacked. With a word, he blew it apart, but three more were on him, pincers going for flesh.

"Crabs!" Esrahaddon shouted at Jerish.

"Hail!" Jerish shouted back as the first bands of the growing storm reached them, and with it came a downpour of marble-sized ice that made the sea around them boil.

All of this was accompanied by a growing wind that was already fierce enough to knock them off their feet if they weren't careful, and on an uneven pile of bones, it was difficult to be heedful.

"Wave!" Jerish shouted over the blowing howl.

A second later, a burst of water bashed the bones and exploded in a drenching spray. Despite all of this, the two continued to work hard at dislodging bones. Despite their labor, however, they had hardly scraped the surface of their monumental task.

"This is hopeless," Esrahaddon said as another crab clamped down on the webbing between his thumb and forefinger, making him cry out.

"Nothing is hopeless," Jerish shouted back over the roar of the furious sea. "And we've got help now."

"Help? What help?" Esrahaddon looked up at his partner in bone excavation, thinking the Teshlor had lost his mind—not that such a thing wouldn't have been unwarranted, given their situation. "What are you talking about?"

"Him." Jerish moved out of the way and pointed to his far side where a man was bent over and scooping up bones with his bare hands then throwing them into the water.

"Who is that?"

The hail upgraded from marbles to fist size, forcing Esrahaddon to cast a shield over both of them, creating thunder where ice met Art. Adequately sheltered from the hail, if not from the hordes of man-eating crabs, Esrahaddon took another look and saw it wasn't just one person aiding them. More than a dozen people were on the pile, tearing it apart. Through the veil of falling ice, he spotted men, women, and children of all sorts, sizes, and shades. And beside them were ghazel, dwarfs, and even some elves. Their clothes were odd. More than merely dated, they appeared ancient. One man wore nothing but furs, another only crudely stitched deer skin. Three were legionnaires from the Rhistian Boars.

"Where did they come from?"

Jerish shook his head as he gave up using his sword and began imitating the others by scooping up as much as he could in his arms and heaving them into the waves. He dumped a load, took a breath, then replied, "From the ship maybe?"

"I don't think they're from the ship, Jerish."

"There are more." The knight pointed behind Esrahaddon down the reef.

All along the length of the pile, he saw movement as figures excavated the long line of bones, which, as he studied it, wasn't a line at all but a huge circle.

"They didn't come from the ship," Esrahaddon said. He pointed at the bones beneath his feet. "It's them."

Jerish stopped his labor to look at him. "You mean—are you saying they're ghosts?"

"Sort of." He offered an awkward smile. "I think they're released spirits. The freed ones are helping to break the others out."

They both stopped working and watched as more and more people climbed up out of the water, found a place along the bone pile, and began to clear it. The more spirits working on the pile, the more spirits appeared. Tens became hundreds that became thousands.

Mileva staggered back to her feet and pushed herself up by using the wall for support. In the process, she tilted an oil painting of a great city on a hill illuminated by a shaft of sunlight. The picture's frame looked thick enough to break a foot if it fell in the right spot. No sooner was Mileva standing than she was slammed against the wall again, then a third time. That did it. The painting came loose and crashed with a loud *crack*, but it missed the riva's feet.

"Stop!" she cried and cast out a palm.

Elinya knew she did something, something magical, but had no clue what. Nothing happened visually, but she heard a wail of pain, as if a dozen voices cried out together.

Breathing hard and leaning with her back against the wall, Mileva glared at Yolric. Then she screamed, "They're tearing my bed apart! And my former servants are coming after me!" That youthful face was not so round or childlike anymore. Her features had lengthened, her cheeks not so high. This was the profile of early middle age, the residue born of struggle, stress, doubt, and pain.

"I would expect so," the old man replied. He seemed to be fiddling with his beard, cleaning it of crumbs, or maybe braiding strands.

"My bed, my whole bed! I can't fend all of them off at once!"

"Oh please, don't involve me in your petty problems."

"Petty!"

"You'll find somewhere else to sleep, won't you?"

"You don't understand! It's not just my bed."

"I know it's the source of most of your strength, your—"

"It's more than that." Tears filled Mileva's eyes. "So much more. You don't understand."

Pinned by the block of stone, Ruby lay on the floor, howling in pain and choking on flies. As soon as she spat some out, more insects flew in. And though the Artist battered her own face raw, killing hundreds that created a dark pile scattered around her, still they swarmed. Several worked their way into her eyes, creeping under the lids. More slipped through her closed lips, and a parade crawled in the open gateway of her nostrils. Elinya watched in horror as Ruby's cheeks puffed out from their growing contents.

Don't swallow! Elinya thought. The idea did not come from disgust, but something more primal.

Elinya was not a Cenzar, or Artist of any kind, but she knew the flies were more than insects. They were evil—some kind of ancient corruption that was not of Elan or Eton—and they weren't merely distracting Ruby, they were trying to infest her.

"Why don't you help Ruby?" Elinya shouted at the Cenzar master. "Why don't you do something?"

"Yes, Trilos, why don't you do *something?*" Mileva asked.

"Why?" The old man continued to play with his beard, reclining on the sofa with that insufferable carriage of indifference. "It's strange. I came here to do just that—*something*. I planned to kick the stone before it hit the ground. Didn't much matter to me where the stone went, just so long as it didn't land where Turin wanted. Only now—now I think it ought to land exactly where he aimed it. And because my brother can't see me, can't anticipate my actions, *any* move I make could jeopardize his intentions. So no, I think it best this time that I only watch."

"But he *can* see you!" Mileva shouted. Then she flashed out another palm, generating more disembodied wails.

"No, he can't. I've tested it—proven the theory true. I believe it's linked to his inability to see into the afterlife. Since I've already died, he can't see me. The actions of this body terminated when it originally died. To him, I am but a ghost, a poltergeist invisibly knocking things over and slamming doors."

"Yes, normally, you are a ghost to him, but he can see you now because you're *here!* He noticed when you first passed through Borappathin, just after you escaped Neith when you were heading up to Estramnadon. Only back then he couldn't see much because I had only just started working on things. His vision would have been hazy at best. That he noticed anything at all is astounding."

"You have no way of knowing any of this."

"Yes, I do," Mileva growled in frustration.

"No, you don't. You couldn't. No one could," Yolric said, and it must have been his condescending tone, that infuriating assumption of facts, which sent her over the edge.

"Yes, I do! Because that's why he came here!"

"You said you hadn't seen him."

"I lied. And do you know why? Not to hide the fact. Not to keep you in the dark. No. I lied out of embarrassment. Can you believe that? I am humiliated to tell you that after so many eons, after countless generations of silence, Rex Uberlin—my mentor, my king, my god, my *love*—finally condescended to visit. But he didn't come to see me—didn't care anything about *me*. He only wanted to know about *you*. And why do you think he did that?"

"I don't believe I can trust anything you say at this point, Mileva."

"Don't *believe*, Trilos, just *think*. Turin lured you here to this place so he could see you clearly. Why do that? Why tease you with the robe? It's obvious, you fool. He used it as bait—bait for a trap. He pulled you here to destroy you."

"Destroy me? How?"

"We are talking about Rex Uberlin! No one can know all his powers! Just be certain that whatever he has planned, the ultimate intent is to erase you. You're his great enemy, the only one hunting him, his only threat. You are all that stands between him and total victory. And if you don't help me now, he will obliterate us both."

Yolric paused to think. As he did, Ruby continued to struggle, and Mileva grew older. Wrinkles now lined her face, bags formed below her eyes, sagging skin drooped on either side of her mouth, and her neck hung with loose skin.

"Help Ruby!" Elinya shouted at Yolric.

The old man looked up at her with a slight smile: the same impish expression that had made him so endearing, so approachable, before. It had said: *I know I look scary, and you see me as some great luminary, but I'm really just a kindly old fellow.* Now, however, that same face, that identical smirk, just made him appear insane.

"Help *me!*" Mileva pleaded.

The expression vanished, and Yolric faced the riva. "*How* can he see me, Mileva? What is it about Borappathin that makes this possible?"

"I don't know. He just can!"

"You're lying to me again. That's quite rude. I've never done anything to you. I wasn't even in the war. Turin killed me before it started. So you do know, and I want you to tell—"

Once more distracted by the conversation, Mileva wasn't watching, and again the riva hit the wall. She cried out in pain as her unprotected head clapped the stone.

"That looked painful," Yolric said, then his eyes widened. "Mileva? How are the spirits hitting you? If I weren't in this body, I couldn't touch anything in this world—not easily, at least. That which is of Eton cannot interact with that which is of Elan. So how . . ." He thought a moment then nodded. "It's not *just* your bed, not just a pile for a raow. You've been building something else, haven't you? Building it for centuries. You would have started it even before I returned to Elan. That's what you just said. You're building something—something huge." Yolric stood up. "What deal did you make with the Typhons? In return for their assistance in getting me out, what did you agree to do *for them?* The Agave is closed, the mountain collapsed. And even if it weren't, that place is too small. But if you managed to explain exactly where to dig, certainly by now they could have cleared a tunnel up from the Abyss beneath Borappathin. And if at the same time you dug down, maybe with a *legion* of disposable workers? Then the wall dividing Elan from Phyre would be thin—thin enough that spirits would have sufficient corporeal substance that if they joined forces, they could bash your skull against that wall. Such a thing would also provide adequate means for Turin to see a ghost wrapped in a dead man's body."

"Yes! Yes!" the riva cried at him, her hands clutching her battered head. Her words had lost their music, turning to a sharp rasp as her voice issued from an old throat. "It has taken forever, but I'm nearly finished."

Yolric shook his head. "It won't work, Mileva. The Typhons will hit the barrier like they did before. They lack the power to breach the membrane between the worlds. I was forced to destroy part of my eternal spirit to make the tiniest of pinpricks. As a single Aesira, I was able to squeeze through, but they are far too big."

"This time we have help." As she said this, a fly came out of her mouth and crawled up the side of her face. "There is a greater power than Eton and Elan, Trilos."

Yolric stared at her for a moment, then slowly began to shake his head. "Mileva, no."

"Those two didn't come out of nothing. This world and the universe are not eternal—they were born."

"No, Mileva. There was nothing before them. Eton and Elan came out of chaos."

"Yes, and Chaos wants them back." The ugly frown became an uglier grin. "I have been promised more than you can imagine—more than miserly old Eton and his tight-fisted wife will ever agree to."

Elinya stared at the fly on the riva's face. It crawled to her eye, and Mileva didn't seem to so much as notice.

"Eton can't stop Chaos. As hard as he has tried, he never could. Entropy always leaks in. It has been seeping through his Great Barrier since those two created time. They're nothing but a pair of fugitives on the run. Chaos would have reclaimed them already except for Alurya. Life alone has saved them—ever replicating, ever changing and adapting. Death is only the start of a new cycle, and with each rotation, life becomes stronger and more plentiful. Entropy couldn't get a grip."

"So that's what happened." Yolric nodded as if all this made sense to him. "The robe let me see it firsthand. Chaos infected the source, poisoned the well, and it was from Alurya herself that the disease of destruction spread. Turin didn't invent evil. He was evil's first victim. Alurya wasn't executed, she was quarantined."

"But Eton and Elan were too late," Mileva said. "Entropy's influence escaped. Turin spread it far and wide. It's everywhere now, and there is no cure."

"And the Typhons?"

"Like me, they serve Chaos because Chaos is all there really is."

"The Typhons are traitors to their parents."

"Powered by Chaos, the Typhons will rise up out of the ancient sea and rend this world! They will accelerate the effects of Entropy and erase all life, and with it, the last defense, the only hope Eton has left of keeping Chaos out. Then Eton and Elan will be consumed back into the timeless disorder. You can join us, Trilos. Help me open a doorway. Help me free the imprisoned from Phyre, from Eton's laws, from pain, fear, regret, and want—from rules and punishments of any kind. Help me set reality free."

Yolric appeared stunned. He sat—nearly falling down.

A fly landed on his cheek. He didn't seem to notice.

"You can't be serious. That's—no. Even you wouldn't—couldn't . . ."

The old man's indifference was gone, but Elinya wished it back, for in its place was horror. Seeing such terror in the eyes of Master Yolric was like witnessing a parent cry. Something terrible, something beyond her comprehension was happening, and hopelessness flooded in.

"You think on that, dear Trilos. You'll see we're right. Their marriage, their house, their reality is crumbling—collapsing—because it was never meant to be. Creation is unnatural, which is why it's so difficult and why destruction is always easier. Disorder is the genuine state. It is reality's truth—everything else is a lie."

Mileva then shouted words Elinya didn't understand and didn't like. The whole of the fortress shook. "Don't take too long making up your mind, Trilos. Chaos doesn't understand time, but mine is short." Taking several long deep breaths, the riva smiled at the Cenzar master, then walked back to Ruby.

At her approach, the flies that had covered Ruby left to resume their role as Mileva's smoky shroud. "Goodbye, child," Mileva told her in a strangely sad tone. "I'm sorry. I really would have made you my lieutenant, but now I need something else from you. Something far more important."

Ruby was still coughing out flies as Mileva wove a knot with her hands.

"No!" Ruby cried as she struggled, wiggling as if bound by the wrists.

Mileva continued to toil like a spider working in silk. "Such a pretty face you have."

Bit by bit, Ruby stopped wriggling until she lay flat on her back, entirely still except for her eyes, which darted wildly.

"Open wide," Mileva instructed. Ruby's mouth opened as wide as it could go. As it did, another fly buzzed out and rejoined the shroud. "There now; that's good. That's very good." The riva no longer looked anything like the statue had. She'd deteriorated well into old age, with skin like wrinkled, well-worn leather covered in dark blotches. Hands—thin and bony—worked magic over Ruby Finn's helpless body as the Artist continued to moan.

Elinya looked at Yolric, but the old man continued to sit, muttering to himself—that fly still on his cheek. He appeared just as ensnared by the riva's magic as Ruby.

Mileva crept up closer to her victim. Kneeling down, she took Ruby's head in her hands. Cradling it, she stroked the woman's red hair and caressed her cheek. "They may destroy *that* pile, but I will begin a new one with you."

Elinya stepped forward then, and her first thought was to wonder if Esrahaddon would miss her.

Will he hate himself for letting me come? Will he cry? No. Most likely he won't care. Might not even notice. "Where is that silly, stupid woman?" he might think, then brush it off. The idea that he could love me was just a fantasy—a dream that lives only in my head. It's best this way. I won't be a burden to him anymore.

Just as when she had walked into the forest, just as when she had walked to the imperial library on that first day of spring, Elinya crossed the room. The trip was short. Only a few feet separated her from where Mileva knelt. The riva's back was to her, and she was bent over, lowering her mouth to Ruby's as if to kiss her.

With every step, Elinya was certain Mileva would spin around and out would come that blue sword, or perhaps a torrent of flame, and she would be incinerated. Elinya let fall the cloth from the dagger that had been her ever-present companion for over a week. No longer afraid, she held the weapon with her naked hands. The poison was only supposed to be on the blade, but even if it wasn't, such things no longer mattered.

Might even be for the best. Mileva might eat me otherwise. But no one eats poisoned food. At least I didn't live and die in that awful village on the Aston. I escaped only for a few years, but in that time, I saw the imperial capital. I met the prince. I fell in love with a Cenzar, defeated a shadow demon, and died fighting a riva! How many—even of those who have lived centuries—can claim all that?

Elinya raised the dagger with both hands.

Any moment now Mileva will turn.

She took the final step.

Now she'll kill me.

Elinya struck down.

I don't understand, she thought as she stabbed the riva between the shoulders.

Mileva shrieked. She stood up so quickly that Elinya was knocked to the ground. Out of reflex more than any conscious thought, Elinya crawled away.

The riva tried to reach around and dislodge the dagger but couldn't touch it. She continued to shriek. Spinning, she saw Elinya. For a moment, bewilderment crossed that now corpse-like face. Mileva had slipped from old to unnaturally ancient.

Okay, so this is where I die, Elinya realized.

"It's poisoned with vendon pox," Yolric said. At long last, the old man had left the couch. He stood just behind Elinya. "There's nothing you can do. No magic can affect it. The poison is slow, but that body you've inhabited for so very long will at last die."

"No! No!" Mileva screamed, and as she did, blood spat out of her mouth. "I can't die! I can't go to Phyre! The Typhons!"

Yolric slapped his cheek. The fly fell dead. "Yes, they will be very happy to welcome you to the Abyss. I'm certain they won't be the least bit upset that you failed them. That trio is very forgiving. Aren't they?"

"This doesn't change anything!"

"I think it does," Yolric said. "I think it changes a great deal. I really was here merely to watch. Assuming this isn't one more lie, I just witnessed Turin sacrifice one of his own to stop the end of the world by an enemy I didn't know existed." He looked at Elinya and once more smiled. "He picks the most extraordinary people."

"Wait—no, I don't have to die," Mileva said. "I can just—I can do what *you* did."

"Go to Phyre, fall into the Abyss, sacrifice part of your soul to escape, then wander the face of Elan looking for the recent—and not too damaged—dead to inhabit? Granted, I make it look easy, but it isn't as glamorous as it might appear."

"No, I'll just stay. I won't go to Phyre."

Yolric shook his head. "Dying is like sinking in a ship. Even if you jump out and try to swim, the vortex will suck you down anyway. Without a body to cling to, without that anchor to this world, the current will swallow you down the drain.

You won't have to go through Phyre's gate, but you'll go there. That river has a nasty current."

"A body—yes! I just need to . . ." She looked at Ruby.

"Won't work. She's too damaged. You'll never be able to fix her. Right foot's crushed to dust, and her left leg has been severed, opening her femoral artery. You can't see it under all this stone, but she's lost too much blood. She'll be dead in a minute or two. Which means even if you had such talent, you don't have the time for the repair work."

Mileva turned to stare at Elinya. "You! I'll take *your* body, you evil little backstabber!" Without another word, the riva used her bony fingers to weave a spell.

Elinya cringed.

Nothing happened.

"Trilos, no!" the riva shouted up at him. "Let me have her!"

"Sorry, but that's not going to happen. Elinya did her part. Took great courage, too. I won't let her be punished for being the one person here who did the right thing."

Mileva glared at him.

"And don't look at *me*. I'm not interested in a roommate, and you're not strong enough to evict this tenant."

"I won't go to Phyre! Please . . . please, Trilos. Help me. I know we weren't friends, but you were always the kind one. Please."

The old man frowned. "There is another way. Another *body* you could inhabit."

"Where?"

"Here. All around you." He waved his hand at the ceiling and walls. "This place. This creation of yours. You made Borappathin, raised it, formed it from your own will. It is a *container* of sorts. You will have no hands to weave, no voice to speak, but it will keep you out of Phyre."

Mileva fell to her side. "I feel it." She rolled to her back. "The pox."

"Your time is up. Make a decision. Your ship is going down."

The storm disappeared from the sky. The ocean waters calmed. And like sugar in water, the bone reef began to crumble.

Jerish had no idea if the ghosts were attacking from below the waterline, if that had caused it or something else had happened, but the entirety of the reef lost its integrity and all at once collapsed.

He did as well.

Caught far from the boat when the bones fell away, he plunged into the water.

"Jerish!" he heard Esrahaddon cry, just before his head went below the surface.

Touching nothing, Jerish stroked with his arms and kicked with his feet. All he needed to do was swim the few yards to the boat, only . . .

The armor! The thought hit him hard. *Don't panic!*

He'd been trained to keep his head, to never give up, but this wasn't an enemy he fought. This was *the ocean*. The weight of all that metal pulled him down, and he dropped fast.

Without a thought, he threw off his swords, letting them go, offering them to the sea god in exchange for his life. But it wasn't enough. He threw away his helmet, then reached for the buckles on the breastplate, struggling to free it. He pulled, then pulled again. It popped loose, but there were three more, and that was just on the chest piece.

Even if I get all of it off so that I can swim, I'll be down too far. I don't have enough air! I'm going to die.

"If you can imagine yourself losing, you likely will."

Knights did lose.

Jerish refused to give up, and he pulled at the remaining buckles. His lungs burned. He needed to breathe, knew he eventually would try even if he didn't want to. That would be the end.

Pressure built as he continued to fall. His ears popped. Then the growing compression began to fade.

Still working on his third buckle, he touched down.

I've landed on the bottom of the sea.

He had only seconds. He felt the need to inhale overwhelming him. Death would follow soon after. In those elongated moments before his death, he thought of his mother. How he would see her, how he would be able to tell her he kept his promise. He hoped to see Master Rawlings so that he could apologize for losing Jerel's sword to the ocean. He hoped to also one day see Deacon Kile, and thank him for the kindness that had changed his life. He regretted leaving Nevrik. He felt there was so much more he could have taught him. And lastly, he thought of Esrahaddon, who at that moment was in the skiff paddling back to the *Relentless Riva*. Part of Jerish still wanted to hate him. *Why didn't he help? Why didn't he dive in and try to pull me out? We're supposed to be a team, but Cenzars don't understand teamwork. They are selfish, hateful, arrogant . . .*

No, they aren't.

At least, he's not. He tried to save me—twice. I just didn't believe it. And if this is some elaborate plot to overthrow the empire, it's too complicated for me to see.

Jerish couldn't help himself. His mouth opened, and he inhaled. Expecting lungs full of water, anticipating horrible pain and anguish, Jerish was shocked when he swallowed only a tiny bit of water.

The rest was air.

Falling to his hands and knees, he doubled over, coughing and spitting out saltwater. Jerish was on bones, not sand or seaweed. He hadn't gone to the bottom, only to the pile's debris field. To his bewilderment, Jerish crouched in the center of a circle of nearly dry bones surrounded by a wall of water. Looking up, he saw sky. Then right in front of him, a fish swam by.

This is the most amazing thing I've ever seen.

"Can you please get into the boat?" Esrahaddon said.

Startled, Jerish turned and saw the column of air he stood within also encompassed the skiff, which now teetered a bit on the bones beside him.

The Cenzar had his arms outstretched, fingers wide, palms flat. Facing the wall of water, his face was a bit red and showed strain. "It's kinda hard to hold this much water back."

"Waves rolling!" Jerish exclaimed and clamored into the boat.

"Get your swords and helmet," Esrahaddon told him, grunting with the effort.

Jerish saw his blades lying on the bones. He jumped out, grabbed them, then dove back in.

The moment his body hit the bottom of the boat, water rushed back, flooding up from underneath. He imagined Esrahaddon was controlling how the water returned, as it didn't just fall on them, but it must have been like putting down a heavy object when a person doesn't want to damage it. While the process started slowly, it picked up speed as they began to rise. The motion increased so much that Jerish felt pressed to the bottom. Then as the water walls vanished and the sunlight shone on them once more, Jerish became weightless. He flew into the air, then slammed back down into the boat as both clapped the surface of the sea with an explosion of white spray.

Overhead, the sun was brilliant. Seagulls called to one another, and Jerish lay hugging his swords and laughing wildly for no reason whatsoever.

"Did you say *waves rolling*, back there?" Esrahaddon asked. The Cenzar was beside him, breathing as if he'd run a mile.

"I think so," Jerish managed to get out.

This caused them both to suffer a fit of laughter that made little sense, but that didn't matter when a blue sky was overhead.

"Hey! You two hyena!" Niblick shouted from the deck of the *Relentless* as it inched closer. "You're crazy. You know that right? The both of you are a pair of walnuts."

"No, we're not!" Esrahaddon shouted back. "We're *way* beyond walnuts now, Niblick. I think we just defeated a riva. We're freaking *pistachios!*"

CHAPTER THIRTY-SEVEN

Sailing Home

When the *Relentless Riva* returned to the inlet, Esrahaddon spotted Master Yolric and Elinya standing on the glistening stone pier at the base of Castell Blythium. The wind off the sea blew back Elinya's hair and gown, granting her a valiant, indomitable quality. He'd always thought her pretty but never beautiful or majestic, until now.

"Where is Ruby Finn, do you think?" Jerish asked as the two stood at the rail.

"Honestly," Esrahaddon replied, "I can't say I care all that much." He pointed at Elinya. "That's who I came back for."

Jerish nodded. "You're a lucky man."

Esrahaddon was caught off guard, not so much by the words as by the naked sincerity. In the past, Jerish had always been guarded, never offering opinions, never willingly granting a glimpse behind the veil of his nature.

Maybe he's just tired.

Looking over, he saw that Jerish had the sun shining on him and . . . "You have something on your face."

"Really?" The knight wiped a hand over his mouth. "Is it gone?"

Esrahaddon shook his head. "Nope."

"What is it?"

"I think it's a smile."

Jerish frowned.

"Ah, there it goes. You got it that time."

They both faced the shore as the ship glided up to the moorings. Esrahaddon listened to the creaks of the wooden vessel, the flutter of the sails as they came down, and the soft clapping of waves against the hull. After the storm, the stress, and the panic, this slow drift on tranquil rolling water beneath a warm, bright sun was both surreal and wonderful.

"Thank you," Jerish said while still looking out across the water.

As the ship brushed the fixed fenders on the quay walls, three Ba Ran ran by, preparing to make the leap to shore to secure the dock lines. Piloted by Niblick, the *Relentless* pulled up as deftly as a whale raised by a school of sailfish, and over the side went the ghazel, hauling their ropes.

"For saving my life back there," the knight added.

Esrahaddon nodded. "Yeah, I know what you meant."

"Oh. Well, you didn't say anything, so I didn't know if you understood. You could at least have acknowledged the fact."

"I was being respectful. I assume it's uncomfortable for you, so I didn't want to make a big deal out of it."

"I see. That's, ah . . . that was nice of you."

"But now we're making a big deal out of it."

"Sorry."

Esrahaddon sighed.

The moment the gangway was lowered, Esrahaddon ran down and embraced Elinya who, to his delight, hugged him back. "How did you know to meet us here?"

"You said you were going on a ship," Elinya replied. "Master Yolric knew the way to the dock."

"Where's Ruby?" Jerish asked.

Elinya didn't answer.

"She didn't survive the battle with Mileva," Yolric explained.

"The riva was destroyed?" Esrahaddon asked.

"More or less."

"What does that mean?" Jerish asked.

"Mileva and Ruby were fighting . . ." The Cenzar master nodded his head at Elinya. "Then she stabbed the riva with that little dagger she's been carrying everywhere."

Esrahaddon only then noticed the weapon's absence. After so long, it was strange to see her hands empty.

"I knew that's why she had it," Yolric said, a little proud of himself. "I mean, it was obvious, wasn't it?"

Elinya looked at Esrahaddon, concerned. "I didn't bring it to stab her with. It just—I had it because it was all I had. I never planned anything. You must believe me."

"I do believe you," Esrahaddon told her.

Yolric chuckled. "Oh yes, I didn't mean to insinuate anything nefarious. Few things are serendipitous. The strange or unusual are rarely accidental. Most often, you can spot key elements to the unfolding drama. The hard part is determining exactly how they will be implemented and to what effect. The amount of work that goes into this is stunning. I don't know how Turin manages. He has so many pots on the fire, and each needs to boil at just the right moment. He had to develop that whole spectacle in Eber-on-Aston, setting Ruby up as the block, then involving the two of you and supplying the dagger and the poison, most likely. Any piece missing and the whole architecture falls apart. I'm in awe sometimes, though I suppose it only looks amazing because we don't see the mistakes, the blunders, and missed opportunities. But it's still impressive. Of course I now have reason to suspect he's not working alone—that, in fact, he might not be the Invisible Hand at all."

"What do you mean, more or less?" Esrahaddon asked.

Yolric looked confused.

"What did you mean, the riva was destroyed *more or less?*"

"When Elinya poisoned her, Mileva's body was doomed. Nothing she could do to save it. Vendon pox really is awful stuff."

"She was going to take over my body." Elinya placed a palm to her breast, a grimace squeezing her face. "But Master Yolric protected me."

"He did?" This surprised Esrahaddon. The old man had done nothing all trip, but Esrahaddon couldn't find a reason to complain. The old Cenzar was never a part of this. He was the only true volunteer, and if his one contribution was saving Elinya, then, as far as Esrahaddon was concerned, Yolric did more than his part. "So the riva died?"

"Not exactly. She . . . well, she took a new body." The Cenzar master used both hands to indicate the brooding and antiquated edifice that loomed above them. "That's her up there. She possessed Borappathin."

"What does that mean?" Jerish asked.

"Her spirit inhabits the rooms and corridors. Those windows are now her eyes, the chimneys her nostrils, the door her mouth, the foundation her heart."

"You mean, she's a ghost, and she haunts the building?"

Yolric nodded. "That's a fine way to put it."

"But can she . . ." Esrahaddon thought a moment, trying to calculate the possibilities. This whole idea of a spirit being a thing that took up residence in a body or a house wasn't covered in his Cenzarium education. Hekkabah had touched on it some when speaking of the rivas and how they clung to life at the cost of all else.

In that moment, standing on that sea-sprayed rock, he recalled the old priestess's words:

"Happiness is merely a state when everything is as it should be. But if everything is always perfect, there is no challenge, no reason to live, no purpose to exist. Happiness is the reward for struggle, and without struggle there can be no growth."

He looked up at the towers of the castell. *"What does not grow, Ezra, is dead—or should be. Still, you must guard against indulgence. Too much will create a thirst. Quenching that thirst makes you drunk. Being drunk invites greater excess. Soon your judgment is lost, and power becomes your only desire."*

Was that what happened to Ruby?

"You change into the worst version of yourself, and eventually lose even that, until all you are is a shadow."

"You said Mileva was going to *take* Elinya's body. Can she still do that?" Esrahaddon asked. "If someone unwittingly wanders in through her doors, can she invade them and be free?"

The old Cenzar smiled, making his beard bristle. "I'm quite certain that was her plan, but no. I fixed it so she can't. I locked the door."

"But people will still get in," Jerish protested. "There are windows, and a door can be broken down, and—"

"He wasn't referring to physically locking the building," Esrahaddon said. "Were you?"

Yolric shook his head. "I wove a containment seal, placing it on the building. Even if someone opens the doors to Castell Blythium, it won't matter—Mileva, her spirit—will not be able to escape."

"How does that work?" Esrahaddon asked. "She's not corporeal anymore. How do you bind a spirit?"

"You don't. The enchantment is placed on the structure, not the prisoner." Yolric looked at the others. "I'll explain it on the ride home."

"Do we have to go back through the fortress?" Elinya asked.

They all looked up. No one liked that idea.

"You know, I can take you all the way to Cryllion," Niblick called down. With the ship secured, he left the pilot deck and stood midship beside Mashie, where both leaned over, elbows on the rail. "A lot more comfortable and faster than riding on these roads you got here. And all you got to do is step on board."

"They're my uncles, Niblick and Mashie," Esrahaddon explained.

"We could take a river barge from Cryllion to Merredydd," Yolric suggested.

"If we do that, can we avoid going back up these stairs?" Elinya asked.

"I must admit," Jerish said, "I wouldn't mind skipping the tour of the haunted mansion."

"Might be best." Yolric nodded. "I'm positive I've worn out my welcome here."

"What about the wagons and horses?" Elinya asked.

"I'm sure Darius could use them."

Esrahaddon nodded. "We can stop at Rochelle and let him know."

"And the unicorns?"

"They were never really unicorns," Yolric said. "By now, they'll appear as horses again. Nothing tethers us here."

"Great. I'll have Lark clean out the staterooms," Niblick said. "Smells like they burned a dead cat in there."

"Lark?" Esrahaddon asked.

"Yeah." Niblick smiled. "Wanted to stay on. Go figure. Still my first mate. He's practically an Urgvarian now. I've also got a few bottles of bog somewheres if the lady riva didn't swipe it. We need to celebrate. Right, Mashie? It's not every day I get out of prison, take full possession of a floating dream, kill a riva—making the New World safe for man and ghazel alike—and we see how our little cub has grown. *I just hope I don't get so drunk that I give the old heave-ho to every crew member who gave me the stink-eye.*" He said this louder than the rest then grinned. "A shame most of the Arkums don't understand Marn."

"Marn?" Jerish asked.

"That's the language we're speaking," Esrahaddon said.

"I thought it was *imperial*."

"Of course you did." He saw the now-familiar set jaw of irritated defiance form on the knight's face. "Look, sorry, I didn't mean to insult you. Fact is, everyone thinks that. It's an easy mistake to make. There isn't a human or elf still alive that remembers the origins of our language. I only know because I was raised by the likes of these two and a very learned priestess who spent her life studying such ancient things from their source. But if you just stop and think about it, you'll realize our language would have to predate the empire—otherwise, how did everyone talk to one another? Turns out it came from over there." He pointed across the open water. "We brought it with us when everyone fled the great flood."

"There was a flood?"

Esrahaddon stared at him and sighed.

"Hey . . . Jerish, is it? Don't worry about it," Niblick said. "The kid ain't as smart as he thinks he is. He wasn't pointing at ancient Marn just now—like he thinks he was—but in the direction of Calynia. No one knows it all. Everyone's got holes in their view of the world. The real problem comes in when folks try filling in the gaps with whatever's at hand. That's when gallimaufry happens, and the result is always walnuts."

"My uncle, the philosopher," Esrahaddon said.

"Now if you all don't mind, we got high tide here, so please come aboard 'cause I'd like to be on our way. I can't say I enjoy anchoring in the shadow of Borappathin."

The trip up the bay to Cryllion felt like it took no time at all and left Esrahaddon depressed.

True to his word, Niblick had broken out the good bog, and in the light of the setting sun, they all shared at least a taste. Jerish was shocked to discover he liked it. Elinya smiled and said nothing. Yolric wiped his beard clear and frowned, declaring his disappointment with the state of poor fermentation these days. They laughed beneath the stars as Mashie told them stories of life in the Gur Em, and Niblick taught them songs in his native Urgvarian tongue, which—while none of others knew it—were bawdy beyond belief.

"She's nice," Mashie told Esrahaddon when the two had gone for another bottle.

Esrahaddon looked back at Elinya sitting on the open deck between Jerish and Niblick, swaying side to side as they sang one of Niblick's more obscene shanties.

"Not much to look at," Mashie went on. "A little scrawny, but nice, you know?" He clapped Esrahaddon on the back with his good claw, staggering him.

"I think so. In fact, I'm going to ask her to marry me. What do you think of that?"

"Good for you." The big ghazel nodded. "You doing okay for yourself, then? They treating you all right back there in the big city?"

"Yeah, I'm doing okay."

"Good. 'Cause, you know, if they aren't—if they hurt you—I still got one claw." He raised it menacingly. "And I'll come down there. Don't think I won't."

That's when the depression settled in, and it remained with him the rest of that night and only intensified when Niblick ordered the sails reefed and the *Relentless Riva* slowed.

"This is as far as we can safely go, kid," Niblick explained as the two stood on the bow watching the morning sunrise. "Cryllion is only about a mile or two north. You need any supplies? Any coin? I got plenty. The rex set us up real good, and the riva left it all in the hold. Not sure why rats didn't eat it. There's always rats on ships, but maybe even they don't like being that close to Borappathin. I'll give you whatever you want. You can pay me when you get back."

"I'm fine. And, Niblick . . ." He couldn't bring himself to say it.

"Yeah, I know, kid. Knew it when I asked you." Niblick shrugged. "Probably shouldn't have. It was just a crazy idea. If we went off together, we'd turn into notorious pirates or something, maybe sail off the end of the world. No one wants that."

"So what will you do?"

Niblick clapped the rail. "I served on many ships in my life, but the *Great Excuse* was the first I could call mine. This one is like piloting a floating city. And talk about luxurious. Well, you saw the staterooms. The *Excuse* didn't even have rooms. I think I really will go exploring, check out the southern seas, maybe find a nice tropical island somewhere and call it home. Certainly can't return to the Old World or even Calynia. When a riva lends you a ship, he's gonna want it back."

Esrahaddon looked down at himself. "If you took this robe back with you—"

"Don't even think about it," Niblick snapped. "Your moth—" He stopped, looking angry with himself. "Hekkabah died to get you that robe. I don't know why and maybe she didn't, either, but I would be very disappointed if you ever gave it up. It'd be like you were saying her life meant nothing. Don't you ever do it."

He nodded. "But what about the crew? How are you going to keep them in line?"

Niblick smiled. "I still got Mashie. Even with just one claw, that Ankor is a monster. Besides, they like me now and aren't quite so keen on rivas no more. It's like anything. Change is hard, but once you get doing something, doing anything else becomes harder. As long as I don't make their lives too terrible, and if I can produce the goods, they'll be throwing rocks at effigies of the riva, and wondering where I've been all their lives. Don't worry about me, kid. Mashie and me are survivors. It's you that I . . ." He paused and coughed to clear his throat. "I mean, I don't think we're ever . . ." He stopped once more, this time turning away to face the end of the inlet.

"You all right?"

"Not really." Niblick sniffled, and he reached up and wiped his cheek. "See now . . . this here's the problem with taking in a stray cub. There always comes that time when you got to let them go back to the wild—that moment you know deep in your lousy heart that you're never gonna see them again. The moment you take them in, the instant you carry them home, you know freaking well that you're gonna have to say goodbye one day. And as the little furball starts purring and scratching you with his crazy needle claws, you also know when that time comes it's gonna rip your heart out." Niblick looked at him with a trembling chin. "And you know what? I need this heart. It's the only one I got. And you're killing me here. I didn't think it'd be so bad this time. I thought it was horrible when I had to leave you at the tree house to bury Hekkabah. I was sick with worry—physically ill—for a week after that. Now . . ." Niblick turned away and wiped his face again.

They stood in silence. Esrahaddon couldn't think of a single thing to say, and he was having his own trouble seeing through tears.

"But hey!" Niblick slapped the brass rail of the ship. "I got me one swell ship. The *Relentless* is a whole different world compared to that piece of crap, *Excuse*. Remember trying to fix that thing?"

"Yeah."

"We worked on that old scow for years, you and I."

"We did."

"Remember that day we went to the Klune camp? It was sunny. You brought up that wind, and I laid her over on her beam, making Hekkabah and Mashie hold on for dear life. That was a great day."

"It was."

"I swear I'd trade this floating palace in a heartbeat to get that old scow back if we could all be on her once more flying under a blue sky like that. I really would." He turned and took Esrahaddon by the shoulders. "I'm gonna miss you, kid, as if you were my own son. You know that, right?"

Esrahaddon couldn't talk anymore. He just nodded.

"And I'm freaking proud of you. I really am. And so is she. You know that too, right?"

Again he nodded as tears fell.

Then Niblick grabbed and held him tight. "Goodbye, my little tiger."

CHAPTER THIRTY-EIGHT

Visitors

THE RIVER NIDWALDEN, ERIVANIA

"Where have you been?" Deva asked just above a whisper, which was strange since they were in the middle of nowhere on the open road in a forest. Also strange was how exasperated she sounded when these were the first words between them in over a year.

"I missed you, too," Irawondona said. "And I was at home. You know that. I wouldn't have gotten your message otherwise. Why are you upset?"

With a frustrated glare, she took him by the arm, pulling him into the trees. He might have been concerned, or at least irritated, but Irawondona had known Deva since childhood. They grew up together, which was a rare thing in a society with so few births and such long lives. Being the grandson of Osla, Irawondona was a born celebrity, and Deva had always worshiped the ground he walked on. As a result, he wasn't concerned about her attitude, but it did surprise him.

"Deva, what are you doing? Where are we going?"

She refused to speak another word until they were deep in the brush and away from the road.

"Deva, what's going on?"

"Quiet," she shushed him.

Irawondona was quiet. The two stood perfectly still in the undergrowth, listening to the chittering of chipmunks and squirrels and the distant *caw* of a crow. The two had learned forest craft together. She had always been better at archery, tracking, foraging, and directions, and she could tell the difference between western and eastern meadowlarks simply by their song. Irawondona didn't even know the name of the forest they were in. In his mind it was simply *Three Days From Anywhere.*

"Are we listening for something?" he asked.

"Can't do it, can you? You can't just be silent for a single minute." Deva shook her head. "This is why you were so bad at forest craft."

"Sorry, but I'm a little tired. Been on the road for three days and two nights, and I—"

"What took you so long?"

"What do you mean? That's just how long it takes to get here from Estramnadon."

"Walking, yes."

"What did you want me to do, run? I missed you, of course, but running for three days would be . . . hold on, is that what this is about? Are you mad because I haven't visited? You haven't come to see me, either."

"I meant that you could have taken a horse. I said it was urgent. You'd have been here yesterday, maybe sooner. Now everyone's here."

"Everyone?" Irawondona looked around at the trees. "Are you referring to the squirrels and chipmunks? Or is it the crow that bothers you?"

"They're all at the river."

"Who is?"

"Salyndra."

Irawondona's eyes widened. "The Curator is here?"

"The whole of the Aquila is! How all of them managed to organize, pack, and make the journey with wagons and carriages and still arrive ahead of you is the mystery I can't fathom."

"I don't understand. We're in the middle of nowhere. The Nidwalden River is what? Only a few yards away, right? This is the end of the world. Why would the Curator and the Aquila—"

"Because there are people on the west bank."

"What? The *west* bank . . ." Irawondona thought a moment, and his mind went to the obvious conclusion twice, dismissing the idea both times as impossible.

But why else did Deva demand I drop everything and race to the banks of the Nidwalden? And why would the Curator of the Fhrey leave Estramnadon and make the same trip I did, and in less time? Why would Deva, normally so calm and serene, be shouting in whispers at me?

"Humans?"

Deva shook her head. "Doesn't look like it."

"But you *saw* them? With your own eyes?"

"Yes, they both still work." She blinked at him violently, then shook her head, took a breath, and continued. "There are three on the other side of the river. They all look Fhrey. Two in nice robes, one—a female—has a sword."

"Robes," he frowned. "Asicas?"

"Kinda looked that way."

"Western Miralyith." He shook his head. "That's all we need. Have they crossed?"

"Not yet. They have a little camp right down near the water, complete with a fire. They *want* to be seen."

"But they haven't extended a bridge? Haven't even gone to the tower?"

Deva shook her head.

"What's Salyndra doing?"

"Truth be told, she only just arrived. Beat you here by less than an hour or so."

Irawondona ran a hand through his hair, trying to absorb as much as he could. The world had fundamentally changed in the span of a few seconds, and he was struggling to regain his mental balance.

There are people on the west bank! "This is incredible. Do you think he's dead?"

She rolled her eyes, then snapped, "Why else would they be here?"

He held up his hands, as if to ward off an attack. "All right, okay, I get it. But Deva . . ." He sighed. "Deva, they won't give it to me. I'll be ignored just like before when they refused my petition to be Curator after Osla died."

"You were only eighty-seven then—a child. That was a hard sell for anyone."

"I'm still only five hundred and twenty. To most of them, I am still a child."

"Nyphron was also quite young—I don't think anyone knows how old—and Mawyndulë was what? *Thirty?* Not one hundred and thirty, just *thirty*, when the two of them fought for the throne."

"That was different. The Aquila didn't have a choice then. Now they do."

Deva took him by the hands and kissed his fingers. "Dona, you're the grandson of Osla. They might have passed you over for Curator, but they can't reject your bid for the Forest Throne. The time for caretakers is done. Erivan will have a fane again. And it needs to be you."

"Why? You've been saying this for years, and I've laughed at you because I've always thought it silly. But it's not so funny anymore. Tell me why, Deva? I'm no better than anyone else. I have no particular talents. You have more skill and ambition than I ever had. You're still out here keeping watch while I lounge in the Airenthenon's balcony listening to the Aquila debate whether or not to fix a broken paving stone in Florella Plaza. *You* should be fane instead of *me*."

"I'm nobody." She shook her head. "No—I'm less than nobody. They see all of us in the Asendwayr tribe as nothing but scouts and hunters, and let's not forget—my mother was a Gwydry, a lowly farmer. I'm lucky to be trusted with a bow. But you're the grandson of Osla, the last of the wartime councilors to the fane. That matters to a lot of people. For centuries, Imaly and Osla foretold this moment. As her descendant, you now have a loud voice."

"I don't see how that qualifies me to be a good ruler."

"You'll be a good ruler because you're a good person. I've known you all my life, Dona, and I would die for you. You're also Asendwayr, and we sorely need a hunter on the throne. Osla cut us no slack, and rightfully so, but she didn't *cut us*. Since Salyndra became Curator, the Umalyns see themselves as the last line of defense against anarchy. They think if people aren't reminded daily about Ferrol's Law, everyone will be killing everyone else just for the novelty. And they hate us most of all because we use weapons and spend time on the frontier. To them, we're the new Instarya. They celebrated when Osla died, you know."

Irawondona shook his head. "No, they didn't. They celebrated when Salyndra won the Curator's chair."

"Because the bad Asendwayr was gone, and the good Umalyn was in charge. The only ones they keep their heel on more is the Miralyith, but who can argue with that? We need you on the throne, or our tribe will be marginalized, left out, and perhaps sent, like the Instarya, to the western frontier once it's reopened. Dona, you must be a part of this." She pointed down the slope in the direction of the river and the roar of the falls.

"How? I wasn't invited to this thing. What am I going to do, walk up to the Curator and demand I be included in this historic moment because I'm the grandson of her predecessor? That will go over well, considering I don't think she especially likes me."

"Offer to talk to them."

"Who? The Aquila?"

Once more Deva displayed exasperation, this time with a drop of her shoulders accompanied by a synchronized frown. "No, the three on the far bank."

Irawondona looked through the trees but saw only leaves. "Are you joking?"

"No, someone must speak to them. Who's going to do that? Salyndra? Of course not. We don't know anything about them. They might be dangerous. So you will volunteer to be the brave one and see who they are and what they want. That will give you a place at the table. You will have done more than anyone else, proved your courage and dedication to your people. Nice qualities for a fane."

"What if they really *are* dangerous?"

"I doubt they traveled all this way to kill the first person they meet."

He continued to stare into the forest where the roar of the falls sounded like an angry beast.

"You need to do this, Dona," she said and hugged him. "And yes, I missed you, too."

Three wagons and two carriages were parked at the stone pier on the eastern bank that, once upon a time, formed the base of the bridge to the legendary tower of Avempartha. Irawondona had seen it before. Ever since the Rhunic War, the Asendwayr and Miralyith had shared patrol responsibilities along the riverbank, and everyone did their time trudging the sandy bank in what everyone had believed to be a pointless patrol. Nevertheless, the sight of that tower, balanced on the edge of that teeth-rattling waterfall, remained esteem-shattering. No one viewing such a thing could cling to any delusions that they were anything but insignificant. This did nothing but make Irawondona feel all the more foolish as he marched straight for the gathering of dignitaries surrounded by honor guards.

He knew each of them the way audiences were familiar with stage performers. Over the last couple of centuries, he had logged more and more time on the

Airenthenon balcony, observing the meetings of the Aquila. One of the things he'd been criticized for when applying for the position of Curator—aside from his young age and arrogance—was his utter lack of administrative experience. He knew nothing of how Erivan was governed. Irawondona hoped to learn by observation. Then he would go through the proper steps this time and request the junior councilor position for the Asendwayr. That way in a few hundred more years, he might land the role of full councilor. This would set him up to be Curator, or fane—should that ever truly happen.

And now it has, hundreds of years too soon. I'm not ready.

The members of the Aquila knew him, too. They spotted him in the balcony, easy to see since he was the only one there. On occasion they commented on this. "Can you please get to the point, Narda," Salyndra would say. "You're putting our audience to sleep." They never used his name, never spoke to him. Nevertheless, they knew him, and he knew them. Neither cared to do anything to bridge the distance between balcony and stage because this was the same general council who had unanimously rejected his request to be Curator.

Now Irawondona walked right up as if he had both the right and a purpose for being there. He approached with his back straight and his chin high, but inside he cringed. *This won't go well.*

"How many know?" Salyndra asked a group of five bank-workers. These were mostly Asendwayr who were charged with keeping watch, but Irawondona spotted a Miralyith with them—not unusual, but in this case unfortunate and likely the reason for the inquiry, which Salyndra made in a most miserable manner.

"I sent word to you alone," Haspin, one of Irawondona's distant cousins, replied. Haspin was a northerner from a remote village—a true backwoods Asendwayr who had likely gutted his first deer by the age of eight.

Salyndra looked at the Miralyith. "Does Krem know?"

The asica-adorned Artist shook his head. "Not from me, but I'm certain he soon will."

"So am I," Salyndra said, looking disgusted.

Turning, Salyndra spotted Irawondona and stared dumbfounded. Then she frowned and cast a sidelong glance at Haspin. "To me alone, you sent word. Or so you say?"

Haspin frowned and glared at Irawondona, as if he'd just wrung the neck of Haspin's pet bird.

"What are you doing here?" the Curator asked.

"I'm here to offer my services."

She narrowed her eyes. "We haven't a balcony here, child, and I don't need an audience today—don't want one, in fact." She said this more to Haspin, then looked back. "How did you find out?"

"I'm a prominent member of the tribe assigned to watch these banks. I am kept informed. Is that a problem? Is this a secret?"

"Obviously not." Salyndra looked as if she wanted to hit something or, more likely, someone.

"There's no telling how many know by now," Narda said. "So yes, it's safe to say Krem knows."

"Wonderful." Salyndra folded her arms in anger, then looked up as if expecting to see the gilarabrywn coming over the trees. She looked back at Irawondona, puzzled. "You can go now." She shooed him with her fingers.

"I'm here to help."

"You can't help. Go back to Estramnadon or go kill a bunny or something. You're distracting me."

"I'm your solution."

"To what problem?"

"You need someone to go over there and speak to them."

Salyndra looked across the water to where smoke rose from a distant campfire. "Even if that was needed, why would I send you?"

Irawondona had expected the question. Any idiot would have. He'd rehearsed the answer in his head a half dozen times on the walk there and just hoped it sounded as good coming out of his mouth. "We don't know what they want, or their intentions, so it is too dangerous for you or any member of the Aquila. Sending a member of the honor guard might be dangerous since a soldier could easily be seen as a threat. Historically, we know Nyphron hates Miralyith, and of those remaining candidates present, I at least have some experience in the workings of the council and as a result have some understanding of what your concerns might be. And last, but perhaps most importantly, this is potentially dangerous, and I am the most expendable."

"And first contact would be . . . how do the Asendwayr say it when you achieve status by killing your first game bird?"

"A feather in your cap," Haspin said.

"That's right. This would be quite the pretty feather for you, wouldn't it? Make you a name, right? Do you think it's a secret what you're doing? Why you attend the council meetings? We all know what you're after. This is a transparent attempt to gain the throne that is finally available."

"And that is exactly why you should send me. By the look of them, two appear to be Artists, and one seems to have a talent with a sword. Truth is, we know nothing. They might not even speak our language, and gestures with an Artist could get me killed. This might even be some kind of test. I go over there, they find me in violation of the law, and I'm killed on the spot. I honestly suspect I have just as much chance of dying as succeeding. Not good odds. Terrible odds for someone like you or even Haspin here, because neither of you has anything to gain. But as you pointed out, I do. This is a big risk, but as you say, it's also an opportunity to substantially improve my chance of becoming fane."

"At least the honesty is refreshing," Salyndra said.

"And one more thing . . . you've been here for more than an hour. Who else has volunteered?"

The other five members of the Aquila exchanged amused looks.

Salyndra frowned and huffed, then turned to the bank-watcher Miralyith. "Extend the bridge."

The Miralyith created a bridge across the Nidwalden using what they called the Art, and everyone else viewed as *magic*. His name was Mansa. Irawondona didn't know if he had a second name or a third. All Fhrey had at least two, except the Miralyith. The first fane's full name had been Gylindora Fane Nilyndd, composed of her given, family, and tribal names. But the Miralyith were different, as they weren't a hereditary group. Those who manifested talent for the Art were Miralyith, even if they were born to another tribe. Those who did not, even if they were children of two Artists, could not be a Miralyith. These sad few were designated *faquin* or *Artless*, which also carried the stigma of *tribeless*. At the very least, then, this fellow in the faded blue asica could be called Mansa Miralyith, but calling him that would be strange as no one used the tribe title except in exceptionally formal events. While this situation might be historic, it was far from formal, and he decided to go with the single name.

"Mansa, is this the first time since the Rhunic War that a bridge has been extended to the tower?" Irawondona shouted to be heard over the roar of the river as the two walked out across the disturbingly thin and narrow bridge, which the Miralyith had just formed by stretching out the stone on the bank as if it were taffy.

"I believe so. At least I have not heard of it happening previously."

Fascinated to be walking on extruded stone that a moment before appeared as feeble as dough and terrified to the point that he didn't dare look in any direction other than down at his feet, Irawondona noticed the color of the stone.

"Why is it blue? It was a dirty gray before."

Mansa looked down, as if unaware of the stone's color. "Oh, it's because of the dumortieritescence of its feldspar crystals."

"The what now?"

Mansa smiled. "This is granite, which is a conglomeration of minerals and rocks, primarily quartz, potassium feldspar, mica, amphiboles, and additional trace minerals. Dumortieritization is the peculiar reflection of the light from tiny planes oriented in one direction—rarely in two. The cause of this optical phenomenon is a phase exsolution lamellar structure, occurring in the gaps created by the unnatural stretching, resulting in the overall impression that the stone is blue."

"You could have just said it was magic. I would have been good with that."

Despite the roar, Irawondona could hear their footfalls making a hollow echo, the same as heels on floorboards. He looked over the side at the white water below. "I am correct in assuming this is safe, right? I only ask because we are right above the precipice of a thousand-foot waterfall."

"Technically, the waterfall drops more than two thousand feet."

"Is that a yes or a no?"

"You're perfectly safe, sir. Even if a wind blew you off, I could catch you."

"That's good. And, Mansa, my name is Irawondona—most call me Dona because the rest is a mouthful."

"I know, sir."

Irawondona chuckled. "I was suggesting that you call me Dona rather than sir because I hold no title or position of prestige."

"I know that, too, sir."

"Okay, you're not an idiot. Anyone who knows what in Ferrol's name dumortieritization is, clearly can't be stupid. So, can you explain what I'm missing here?"

"You have our support."

A moment ago, Irawondona had asked why the stone they walked on was blue and Mansa had lectured him on the aesthetics of rock types. Now he asked why he refused to speak to him like a normal person, and he responded with a mysterious four-word answer. At least Irawondona's confusion kept his mind off the fact that—*yes, the stone I'm walking on is so thin it's transparent. I am literally looking through stone. I can see the churning water below me. How thin does rock have to be to see through it?*

"What are you talking about?" Irawondona asked, as much to distract himself from the dizzying view than anything else.

"The Aquila will never allow another Miralyith to be fane. They will never grant us the opportunity to blow the horn in challenge. Our options are then Salyndra of the Umalyn, who despises the Miralyith more than anyone; Hon of the Gwydry, whom no sane person would ever nominate for the throne; Narda of the Eilywin, Salyndra's most ardent supporter; Faryntine of the Nilyndd, who suffers from having been born without a spine; and Gibbyn of the Asendwayr, who turns three thousand twenty-two this year. Aside from the members of the Aquila, only one other name stands out: the last surviving descendant of the last surviving member of the legendary leaders who saved Erivan from utter destruction in the Rhunic War. That would be you . . . sir."

"You're saying the Miralyith—your whole tribe—would support me as fane?"

"I'm saying, if we had our way, the Aquila would be disbanded, the Umalyn would be dissolved or restricted to their temples, and Krem would be fane right now."

"You mean Curator."

"I mean fane . . . and we'd be settling the west bank and reclaiming our strongholds in Avrlyn."

"That would be in defiance of the fane's edict."

"We have no fane."

"Nyphron is our fane."

"No one has seen him in two thousand years. Out of spite, he abandoned us and took the horn to intentionally cripple our entire civilization. I suspect he hoped that without an acting fane we would break down into civil war and destroy ourselves. We didn't. It is time we finished the war that was stolen from us. Too many died for it to have been in vain."

"But Krem is an outlaw."

Mansa stopped walking. He turned on Irawondona, speaking in an abruptly defensive tone. "Only because he refused to destroy the gilarabrywn he was ordered by Fane Lothian to make. He killed Indus, the love of his life, to do it. He was told the sacrifice was necessary to save his race because they needed the creatures to defend the homeland from the invading barbarians. The creature born from Indus's death waited on the riverbank to do its heroic duty. But no orders came. No barbarians arrived. Two weeks later, a spoiled child fought the leader of the barbarians, and, not surprisingly, Nyphron won. Krem was ordered by the new fane to forfeit the sacrifice he had made. He had killed her for nothing, and the new barbarian fane demanded he kill her again. Is it so hard to understand his decision to disobey?"

They were in the middle of the bridge, hovering over the water on a sheet of glass. Droplets of mist blew over Irawondona. He could see them giving a slippery sheen to the walkway. "Can we keep moving?"

"Sorry, sir." Mansa resumed their perilous trek and his respectful address. He even sounded a bit embarrassed as he offered, "To be honest, Krem scares many in the Miralyith as well. Having the only active gilarabrywn can do that."

"So why me?" Irawondona asked. "Is it just because I'm Osla's grandson?"

"Honestly, we like you. Anyone who demands to be considered for the Curatorship at the age of seventy has a sense of destiny that we like to see in our fane."

"I was eighty-seven."

"Same thing. Point is, the Asendwayr were the only other tribe to stand with us on this bank in the last days of the war, the only other tribe that fought them, and when Nyphron's term as fane ends, we want the war to resume, and we want a fane who will do that."

"And you think I will?"

"We don't know, but you're our only hope."

They reached the rock precipice upon which the tower was built. The profusion of white splatter on the ground announced in pitiable terms that only birds had visited Avempartha in centuries. The bridge ran to a pair of pillars—an ancient bridge dock. Across from this looked to be where a door into the tower ought to be, but all Irawondona saw was a wall.

"We'll go around, then I'll extend another bridge on the other side. After that, you'll be on your own."

Irawondona nodded. Too much was happening all at once. He'd just traveled halfway across Erivan, volunteered before the Aquila to make first contact with their western rulers, and was about to become the first—along with Mansa—to set foot on the Avempartha escarpment in two thousand years. In addition, a militant Miralyith—in obvious league with the outlaw Krem—was letting him know he had Miralyith support for the Forest Throne so long as he relaunched the Rhunic War. And he had yet to speak to the visitors from the west.

"Also, you don't need to be concerned about the robes," Mansa said. "None of those you're about to speak to are Artists."

"No? Are you sure? Because they look like they are."

"They wear what seem like asicas, but I don't feel any power. It's just for show. So if you get into trouble, run for the bridge. I'll do the rest."

"You seem awfully confident."

Mansa looked up. "There is a reason Fane Fenelyus created this tower here. She was the first Miralyith and knew the power that comes from standing in the middle of this cataract. To put it in Asendwayr terms, it's like I'm sitting here holding a huge bow and an endless supply of giant arrows. If I were able to actually enter the tower . . ." He looked up longingly. "This isn't just a building, sir. For Miralyith, it's an Artistic Focus and works much the same as how you can start fires with sunlight through a crystal."

"Why can't you go in?"

"Nyphron locked it, or more accurately, had it sealed. That's why you can't see the doors. They simply don't exist. All except one." He bent back and looked up. "See that tiny window way up there at the top? Jerydd left that one open."

"Why?"

Mansa shrugged. "Maybe it was too much trouble. Perhaps he was lazy and figured—rightly so—that no one could enter that high window unless they had wings. Or it could be that there was some spiritual meaning to it, like he expected his spirit would enter there or something. I don't know—don't think anyone does. But it is there, and you can see it—the only way in. Point is, sir, if you get into trouble, run for the bridge, and I'll take care of you."

"It's happening again," Hanis told Sadarshakar.

He didn't point—didn't need to. They were all looking across the river and watching as the second bridge extended out over the water, this one starting at the tower and stretching to their side of the river.

"Incredible," Sadarshakar replied, watching the stone lengthen and come directly at them like an impudent tongue.

"Someone is coming." Ulin stood up, strapping on her sword.

"He's coming alone," Hanis said.

"Unarmed," Ulin observed, sounding a tad disappointed.

"Miralyith, do you think?" Sadarshakar asked.

Hanis shook his head. "Wouldn't be my guess. He's dressed in leggings and boots: greens, browns, and yellow. Looks more Asendwayr, except for the long coat. Seems too formal for a hunter."

"Maybe he dressed up for us."

"Maybe he did! This is so exciting." Hanis grinned. The younger councilor shifted weight from one foot to the other, his hands clasped.

In an instant, all the miseries that comprised the previous week vanished. Even Sadarshakar felt foolish for his misgivings and doubt.

This is worth all of it.

The adventurers never did find any roads in the forest. Routes marked on the map they took from Marley's pack were useless. What trails they discovered were the routes of deer, which might have adhered to some ancient roadway, or maybe they merely followed some basic stag instinct. Realizing old pathways couldn't survive a two-thousand-year lack of traffic, it was Ulin who read the map while ignoring the marked routes. The river was east. This was obvious and unlikely to have changed. Determining directions proved more challenging. The forest's canopy choked undergrowth, making travel effortless, but reckoning east from west a quandary. Ulin proved to possess a fair amount of woodcraft and managed to keep their direction steadily toward the rising sun—even when there didn't appear to be one. They reached water quickly, but this was not the river. They were below it—a conclusion definitively confirmed by spotting the incredible Parthaloren Falls. The little band was forced to go back into the forest to search for a way up that avoided the sheer cliff.

What followed were three of the most grueling days in Sadarshakar's life. Trudging, climbing, struggling to advance, only to be stymied repeatedly by sheer stone. As they traveled on limited food and water, the days were long. Having jettisoned most of their gear back with the wagons, they slept on bare ground with only a blanket for cover. Yet the greatest torture came from his companions. It grated to hear Hanis complain with each step. He grumbled and wailed, as if he were lost in the forest alone. In contrast, Ulin was quiet, but it wasn't her silence that irked Sadarshakar. It was her attitude. Every time he glanced over, Ulin was smiling. None of it—not the thorn bushes, the sweat, the biting flies, soaked feet, saddle-soreness, or even Hanis's celebration of misery—bothered her. It was entirely possible she enjoyed the whole endeavor. He envied her, and in that awful jealousy, he found resentment. He knew it was wrong, and as a result found himself wallowing in self-loathing. This became her fault as well, and round and round the miserable wheel went.

Eventually, they discovered a route up and found Avempartha. Hard to mistake the massive tower that defied all known building technology, appearing as if a giant had dropped a rock into the river, and as the water splashed up, it had been frozen in place and turned to a bluish stone. The legendary fortress that had defied Nyphron frustrated them as well. The stronghold was in the middle of the river, built on a lone rock that jutted out over the waterfall's drop. The current in the area was insane. The blue-green water went white, then was utterly lost in the mist that rose from the sheer violence. The river lacked a bridge, and swimming was suicide. The trio camped on the riverbank for three nights, just staring at the tower and wondering if they had made the trip in vain. Then on the morning of the fourth day, they spotted movement on the far bank. Wagons arrived. Then the bridge was created.

"First contact in over two thousand years." Hanis had that look of delight Sadarshakar hadn't seen in a decade—the one originally stolen by the litter-bearers that first day in Percepliquis.

At long last, this is our dream.

"Look at his clothes and his hair. They wear it long, I guess. Is it white?"

"I think it's a very light blond," Sadarshakar replied. "But it could be dyed. Maybe that's the fashion now. Do you think we'll look silly to them?"

"Forgive my disrespect, councilmen," Ulin said. "I highly doubt it is our hair they will focus on."

The elf stopped the moment he stepped off the bridge. He was tall and trim, but not skinny, more athletic. This ambassador reminded Sadarshakar of his cousin who regularly won wrestling matches on Summersrule.

An awkward pause followed, as eyes exchanged indecipherable messages.

For all their dreams and all their planning, Sadarshakar hadn't put any thought into what exactly he might say. Such a thing felt presumptuous, even for two such audacious adventurers. Hanis was either in the same boat or he was waiting for Sadarshakar—the elder of the pair—to establish the lead.

Eventually, the Erivanian elf won the contest. He cleared his throat and said, "I am Irawondona of the Asendwayr, sent on behalf of the Aquila to speak with you."

I can understand him! This was Sadarshakar's first thought. The elf's accent was a dash unusual. He spoke more from the back of the throat, invoking a wider range of sounds, but also making it hard to instantly grasp every word. *But still, I can communicate with them!*

"I am Sadarshakar Sikaria, a member of the Imperial Council. This is Hanis Orphe, my associate."

Irawondona looked to Ulin, waiting.

"Oh yes. This is Ulin Myr Halcyon."

"Welcome," Irawondona said. "I presume you come bringing sad tidings."

Sadarshakar looked at Hanis, confused. "Not at all."

"No? Has the fane—what you call the *emperor*—has he not died?"

Sadarshakar laughed. "Of course not. The emperor is fine."

"Oh, I see. You're here to make preparations for when he does pass, which could be any day, I assume. You have the horn, no doubt. And you're in luck. The Aquila is here—just across the river."

Sadarshakar once more looked to Hanis, who frowned and shook his head, indicating he would be of absolutely no help. "Actually, no. I mean, the emperor is getting on in years, but we have no concerns about his dying." Sadarshakar caught himself, and wanting to appear courteous, he added, "But it is appreciated that you are so concerned over his welfare."

Irawondona seemed bewildered. "Then may I be so bold as to inquire why you are here?"

"Trade." Sadarshakar smiled.

CHAPTER THIRTY-NINE

A House Divided

ONE WEEK LATER . . .
IMPERIAL CAPITAL OF PERCEPLIQUIS, SPRING

Jerish was surprised to find the palace doors closed. In the nearly four years that he'd been tutoring the prince, they'd always been open.

Maybe it's because I'm early?

Usually he arrived well after sunrise, allowing the prince to wake up and have a full breakfast before training. No one got up before the sun, except in winter. Then with the days so short, the populace of the city relied on the tolling of bells. How the bell ringers kept track of time in the black of night was not something he'd ever understood but he'd often wondered about. This morning, however, was a special occasion. He, Esrahaddon, Elinya, and Yolric had returned only the night before, after having been away for close to three weeks. Yolric would provide the official report to the emperor later that day, which Jerish needed to attend. Not that he expected Yolric to lie, but Andreas Ranier and Gaylord Sire did. That's why they'd sent him, to act as a witness to any treason. Only there hadn't been any, which Jerish was anxious to report. He was certain that everyone could do with some good news for a change. This would cut his day short, so he wanted an early start to avoid cheating Nevrik out of his education.

At his approach, a palace guard stepped in his way, saying not a word.

"Excuse me, but I need to enter."

"Palace is closed." The words were short and aggressive, like quick, punching jabs.

"Closed? I don't understand."

"Are you feeble-minded? It means you can't go in."

"But I have business inside. I'm Jerish Grelad, tutor to Prince Nevrik. I come here every day."

The guard smirked. "You're a liar. I've never seen you."

The phrase *you're a liar* shocked him. In the guild, such an accusation was likely to result in someone's death. Yet Rawlings had taught him well. Jerish bit his tongue and swallowed his pride. "That's because you've never been here before."

"Been here nearly every day this week. Still never seen you."

"What's going on?" Esrahaddon, robe shimmering in the early morning light, trotted quickly up the steps toward them.

Jerish looked surprised. "You're early."

The Cenzar smiled. "All those days camping—I guess I got in the habit of rising with the sun. What's with Harold the Doorman?"

Jerish looked back at the imperial guard. The morning sun just clearing the Cenzarium's dome hit the man's silver helm, scintillating off the detailed gold ivy trimming. "I have no idea. Won't let me in."

"Name's not Harold," the guard said, his voice louder and far angrier than it needed to be. "And you two are trespassing. Best be on your way."

"Really?" Esrahaddon said.

"Yeah. You can either walk away or be dragged."

"No, I mean—it's just that you *really* look like a Harold. They call you Harry, maybe? Is that it? Kind of an unfortunate nickname, particularly when it appears"—he bent down to make a show of looking up under the guard's helm—"your hairline is in a definite retreat. In a few years, you'll be blinding the sun with that shiny cupola of yours, but people will still be calling you Harry. Kids can be so cruel."

"My name ain't Harold or Harry. And you two are getting on my nerves. Move along before I do something about it."

"What did I do?" Jerish asked the guard.

"You're with him."

"No, I'm not."

"Yes, he is," Esrahaddon said. "In fact, we're both tutors to the prince, we're late, and you're in our way. And I'd watch yourself because while Jerish here isn't wearing the armor, he is a Teshlor Knight and extremely dangerous."

The guard's face stiffened, and he gave a loud whistle.

"You're not helping," Jerish said to Esrahaddon.

"Sure I am. See? More guards are coming to welcome us back."

"I don't think they're coming to welcome us."

"Ah. You might be right." Then as the door guard drew his sword, Esrahaddon added, "Why *aren't* you wearing your armor?"

"I came to teach Nevrik, not fight palace guards. Why are you being so confrontational?"

"We'll discuss it later," the Cenzar said. "Remember, you're only Third Class. No hurting anyone."

"Third Class only means I can't *kill*."

"Whatever."

The door guard made a shockingly lethal stab at Jerish's heart, which Jerish deflected with his bare hand. "Harold, please. I don't want to fight you."

The guard swung again, this time at the Teshlor's neck. Jerish ducked.

"His name's not really Harold," Esrahaddon said. "You know that, right?"

Four additional guards responded to the whistle and charged with weapons drawn. Two came at Jerish, but two others ran up behind Esrahaddon. Jerish could tell the one in the lead planned to stab Esrahaddon in the back; the other intended a swing. Jerish was left with a heartbeat of hesitation until he saw the robe glow, and he knew the Cenzar wasn't being taken by surprise.

The guard—not actually named Harold—tried another stab. This time he put real effort into the attack, looking like he was attempting to thread a needle with a longsword as he stuck his tongue out for added concentration.

Jerish clapped the blade hard with both hands—one palm driving up, the other punching down. This broke the guard's weak grip and allowed Jerish to snatch the sword away, as if the imperial guard were a child. Just then, the two would-be Cenzar murderers slammed headlong into an invisible wall. The loud thumps followed by sharp cries suggested both had hurt themselves.

Seeing this and how easily Jerish had taken the sword from Harold—*there's simply no avoiding it now; the man's name will always be Harold to me*—the other two charging soldiers stopped, nearly running into one another in their effort not to be the first on the scene.

Jerish spun the blade he held and handed Harold's sword back to him in as polite and courteous a manner as he could. "We really do need to see the prince."

"Get help!" the guard shouted, with such force and volume that spit flew from his lips. His chest was heaving, likely from excitement or fear, as he hadn't exerted himself much. But then, the imperial guards weren't known for being in the best of shape. Nevertheless, he showed no further attempt to fight. He didn't even take his sword back.

The pair of guards ran off.

Jerish set Harold's sword down, then stepping past him, he pulled on the door's latch. True enough, it was locked.

"You bastards will never get in," Harold said. "It's bolted from the inside, and an army of soldiers will be here soon, and you'll be slaughtered like the traitorous dogs you are."

"Why are you being so unreasonable?" Jerish asked.

"That's right," Esrahaddon said. "Why would anyone slaughter dogs? That's just sick. They're man's best friend—bundles of love wrapped in fur."

"You had a dog?" Jerish asked, surprised. Esrahaddon had never struck him as a dog person.

"No, but I always wanted one. Excuse me, Harold." Esrahaddon stepped up to the door. Harold moved aside without argument. The Cenzar placed his palm against the imposing bronze metal. "There's a trick to these things," Esrahaddon explained. "Sometimes they get stuck, and you just need to"—he clapped the surface lightly—"jar them a little."

The entire twelve-foot door tilted over and fell inward, clanging loudly on the interior marble floor. "See?"

Harold's eyes went wide.

Jerish looked at his own feet, shaking his head in disbelief. "Now we are breaking and entering."

"It's okay," Esrahaddon said. "I'll fix it."

They stepped over the fallen door and entered the luxurious foyer.

"Hold up." Esrahaddon paused, and with a flick of his fingers, the door got up and slammed back into place, sealing them inside and Harold out. "Told you I'd fix it."

"Why are you being so . . . strange?" Jerish asked.

"It's the new fashion, or haven't you noticed?" Esrahaddon replaced the bolt, going to the effort of sliding it home by hand.

"What are you talking about?"

Esrahaddon peered at him carefully. "Let me guess. You went right to bed last night—didn't speak to anyone?"

"It was late. People were sleeping."

"Sure. And this morning you left extra early before anyone else was awake, correct?"

"Has something happened?"

"A few somethings, I think. None of them good." Esrahaddon looked around the empty reception room. "But now isn't the time to chat. You heard Harold. An army is on its way. We need to find Nevrik—now."

"Is he in danger?"

"Don't know. Maybe. You with me?"

"He'll be in his room." Jerish and Esrahaddon both ran.

Jerish had no idea what was happening and precious few clues. Locked palace doors, new guards, and the violent manner in which they reacted to learning he was a Teshlor Knight was concerning. Esrahaddon's overt belligerence in pushing a fight, combined with his concern for the prince, got him on edge. A month ago, he'd have challenged the Cenzar, suspecting the man was up to no good. But three weeks, a riva, and a quick trip to the bottom of the ocean had changed all that.

He half expected to find Nevrik dead in his bed, but arriving at the prince's chambers, he found the boy lacing up his dress jacket—hair still awaiting a comb.

He appeared frightened when they burst in unannounced. In a flash, the fear vanished, and in its place—joy. "You're back!"

Jerish scanned the room, not knowing what he looked for—assassins maybe. What he found was a cluttered mess. The fine canopy bed was big enough for three people and a couple of pets, but it was largely filled with rocks, blocks of wood, clay, and plaster. Chests took up much of the floor space, and the walls were lined with shelving. No books filled them. Instead, they were packed with figurines, some bas relief plaques done in bronze, and a handful of busts all carved from wood, plaster, or various types of stone. Many were beautiful works of art, but most were clearly unfinished projects. Other than the sculptures, Nevrik was alone.

Rushing forward, the boy hugged them both. Esrahaddon's face revealed he was just as surprised by the display of affection as Jerish was. They had never hugged before. "I started to wonder if either of you would ever return. How did it go?"

"No you don't." Esrahaddon shook his head. "Our tales of adventure can wait. What's going on?"

Nevrik hesitated and looked away. "What do you mean? Is something wrong?"

The Cenzar frowned and wagged a finger. "Don't play stupid. You're not good at it."

"Probably shouldn't stay here," Jerish said. "We told Harold we were here to tutor the prince. This will be the first place they look."

"Who's Harold?" Nevrik asked.

"You're right." Esrahaddon licked his lips in thought. "Luckily we have a secret hiding place."

The prince appeared bewildered. "Who's Harold?"

The Vault of Days looked exactly as it had the last time Jerish saw it—the exploded practice bags still hung like burlap corpses. Esrahaddon lit enough of the sconces to illuminate the room, but not so many as to blind. That chamber, lined with mirrors, didn't require much light.

"Now out with it," Esrahaddon demanded of Nevrik once Jerish had closed the stone door. "What happened while we were gone?"

Nevrik lowered his head, and just when it seemed the prince might refuse to talk, he said, "Gaylord Sire was murdered."

"What?" Jerish asked, but it was less a question and more an exclamation. From the lack of surprise on Esrahaddon's face, Jerish concluded the Cenzar already knew. "How?"

"He was . . . he was blown apart."

"*Blown* apart?"

"Exploded," the prince explained. "There were pieces of him found all over Imperial Plaza."

"Are they certain it was him?"

Nevrik nodded. "His head was found in one piece."

"So he was . . ." Jerish thought a moment. There was only one conclusion possible. The very thought was terrible, revolting yet strangely not unexpected. "He was killed by a Cenzar?"

"There are certainly many who think so."

"What do *you* think?" Esrahaddon asked. "And what does your father think?"

The stone door to the Vault of Days swung open.

"You didn't lock it?" Esrahaddon glared at Jerish.

Imperial guards poured in.

Harold was right about the army, Jerish thought, as more than a score of men passed through the door. He drew his swords and stepped in front of the prince.

Esrahaddon stepped in front of both of them. His robe flared to that dazzling, white-hot brilliance. Aided by the room's mirrors, it nearly blinded everyone. In a loud voice, the Cenzar declared, "Anyone who dares to advance on the prince will die." As if speaking in agreement, Jerish clapped his blades together.

Imperial soldiers did not wear the Orinfar like Teshlors did. Many flatly refused, believing the symbols were magic and that all magic was evil. If they had seen all that he had, Jerish was certain they'd be drawing the marks on right now. Glancing at the shredded burlap bags, Jerish knew what Esrahaddon would do when they attacked. Luckily, the light of the robe stopped them. They fanned out to either side of the entrance but did not advance. This was good. Maybe they knew better. Perhaps Harold had notified everyone that a Teshlor and a Cenzar were inside and not to do anything stupid. This was Jerish's hope. He didn't want to see the slaughter of imperial soldiers. The flood of men ended, and the three faced a wide wall of uniforms.

No one said a word.

More footsteps could be heard. From outside, the echoing claps approached at a casual pace. A moment later, Emperor Nareion stepped into the Vault of Days. He was dressed in silver armor with gold embossments. On its chest was the Imperial Dragon.

"Esrahaddon." He walked past his soldiers into the middle of the room. He raised a hand to shield his eyes from the brilliance of the robe and peered through his fingers. "Are you standing between me and my son?"

"I, ah . . ." The Cenzar looked stunned. Then the robe dimmed to a soft glow. "How did you find us?"

"He's my son. Did you think Nevrik didn't tell me you've been teaching him down here?"

The emperor looked over at Jerish. "And you—do you intend to cut me down where I stand?"

Jerish lowered his blades.

Lastly, Emperor Nareion focused on his son. "As for you . . ." He sighed, then frowned. "It would appear . . . you chose well."

A great grin flooded the prince's face. "You've decided!"

"I have." The emperor turned and addressed his soldiers. "Everyone out. Stand guard *outside* this door. No one is to enter without my permission—upon pain of death."

Jerish noticed that Nevrik was still smiling as the guards disappeared and the door closed. It made an ominous boom. Everything was happening so fast, or at least it felt like it. Questions had been added to questions until a pile of bewilderment stacked up. As of that moment, he wasn't at all certain what was happening.

"I didn't have anything to do with the death of Gaylord Sire," Esrahaddon declared. "We just returned last night."

Is that what all this is about? Jerish wondered. *They think we killed him?*

Like an exhale in a winter wind, the thought was dispersed nearly as fast as it formed, after Jerish saw the expression on Nareion's face. The emperor appeared amused.

"Relax, Esrahaddon. No one is accusing either of you of anything."

"Then I don't understand."

"That's two of us," Jerish added. He looked from the emperor to Nevrik and back.

The emperor began to walk around the vault, being drawn to the training gear. He touched the busted bags. "Has my son been a good student?"

"The best," Esrahaddon replied.

"Agreed," Jerish said.

"Do you think he will make a good emperor? And don't feel the need to flatter me, as his father, or spare his feelings merely because he's here. I command you to tell the truth."

Esrahaddon's robe lost all light. He looked at the boy with a critical eye. "He needs a few more years of formal education. Some travel wouldn't hurt. Be best if he saw some of the empire he'll control. But even if he were forced to assume the throne today, I can think of no other who would make a better ruler than your son. He is intelligent, empathetic, perhaps too idealistic as of yet, but most importantly, he is wise."

Nareion looked to Jerish.

"He is fair, kind, smart, and strong. I would die for him."

The emperor nodded and walked to the rack of wooden batons. He lifted one, swung it, then put it back. "I realize you only just returned, but I must insist that both of you leave with us today."

"Leave?" Esrahaddon asked. "Today?"

"You weren't the only ones to return recently from a historic trip. And congratulations on your success with the riva. I regret that I can't present a more formal recognition for your service, but a critical matter of state has arisen. Nevrik will be coming with me, and given the already substantial gap in his education posed by your absence, the two of you will be coming as well."

"Where are we going?"

Nareion picked up another baton and used it to point at them. "What I am about to tell you will not leave this room. If you breathe a word of it, you will be executed as traitors. Do I make myself clear?"

Esrahaddon and Jerish looked at each other, concerned, but both nodded.

The emperor swiped the air with the wooden sword, then laid it back down and turned to face them. "There is a conspiracy to bring down the House of Nyphron—has been for thousands of years. Over the centuries, this threat has claimed the lives of three emperors, threatened their children, the empire, and the very existence of mankind. Now the evil has struck again."

Jerish was surprised. He was all but certain that the accusations of his guild were misplaced. Now he looked at Esrahaddon, wondering how the Cenzar would react to learning the truth about his order.

"Does this have something to do with the death of Gaylord Sire?" Esrahaddon asked.

"I believe it does, and a great deal more. The empire is coming apart as if by some plan. I need to fix the growing rift between the Cenzarium and the Teshlor Guild that has recently shifted from suspicion to open hostility. Also, my family and I are in terrible danger, making this an awful time to travel. But thanks to a pair of foolish and ambitious Merredydd councilors, I have no choice but to leave. I will be gone no less than two weeks. I fear this is no coincidence, and my absence will grant ample time for sabotage.

"There's more to this story, which Nevrik can explain in detail once we are on the road, as he was the one who convinced me the two of you needed to know the truth. For now, however, allow me to reduce the plot to its bare bones. For over two thousand years, a Fhrey enemy named Mawyndulë has sought to wipe out the bloodline of Nyphron and obtain an ancient relic known as the Horn of Gylindora. He has tried to do this on at least three occasions so far. The first saw the death of Nyphron himself, the second killed Emperor Nurgya, the third ended the reign of Estermon II, and I believe what we are seeing now is his fourth attempt. Mawyndulë has learned from his former failures and grown more sophisticated in his approach. This time he has turned our greatest strengths against us—pitted the Cenzarium against the Teshlor Guild." Nareion shook his head. "A man cannot stand with two broken legs. I fought, but it's like trying to reason with water and convince it not to run downhill; that's the direction it has always wanted to go. Mawyndulë has only provided the opportunity. After years of building a pile of distrust and division, the death of Gaylord Sire becomes the spark to ignite all that carefully collected tinder."

He took a long breath then let it out as a miserable sigh.

Jerish stared, baffled. *What is he talking about?* He looked at Esrahaddon and saw a similar confusion.

"You're saying all this distrust and conflict between the Cenzarium and the Teshlor Guild has been manufactured?" Esrahaddon asked.

The emperor nodded. "Mawyndulë played on the ill will between the two, and we have suffered his curse. Teshlors have long blamed the Cenzars for Farilane's death." He walked toward the wall, most of which was lined in statues. The Vault of Days was a memorial to the honored dead. Most in that room were of women—the wives of emperors. Nareion made a point of facing Nolyn's wife, then walked to her father, and finally approached the statue of the lady many believed should have been empress. Dressed in the uniform of a legionnaire, she wore no weapon. In one hand, she clutched a book to her chest, in the other was a horn. "She was the goddess of the Teshlors; some even pray to her."

The emperor stopped at her feet. "In the past, we have always found heroes to fight Mawyndulë such as Sephryn, Tekchin, and of course, Princess Farilane. I fear we are all out of heroes. So this time, our enemy may well succeed."

"And what happens if he does?" Esrahaddon asked.

"If he kills Nevrik, Fanquila, and myself *and* obtains the Great Relic, the war with the elves will resume. And if we lose that, as we nearly did the first time, mankind might be erased from the face of Elan." He returned the baton to the rack. "Now get ready to leave. My son needs his tutors."

Esrahaddon had that look of thinking in his eyes. "May I ask where we are going?"

"A little tower on the edge of the elven frontier called Avempartha. Oh, and one more thing. As of this moment, Jerish, you are hereby recognized by the Imperial Throne and this emperor as a Teshlor Knight of the *First* Order."

"Thank you, Your Eminence."

"You aren't bringing a pair of tutors for your son," Esrahaddon said, working it out. "You're assigning him bodyguards."

"You're mistaken, Esrahaddon." The emperor opened the door. "It would be politically questionable if I suddenly assigned high-profile bodyguards to the crown prince. It might suggest I'm concerned about his safety. But who can object, or even find it suspicious, for Nevrik to be in the company of his tutors?"

As the emperor left, Jerish turned to Esrahaddon in desperation.

"What?" the Cenzar asked.

"Why did he swear us to silence? If all this is a lie, we should tell everyone. I ought to report to Andreas Ranier, and you to the Cenzarium, and we should explain what's really going on."

"And you think that would fix everything?"

"Why wouldn't it?"

Esrahaddon put his hands on Jerish's shoulders. "If the emperor told the Teshlors that everything they had believed in for generations—including the death of the First Emperor and that of Princess Farilane—is a lie made up by an elf, do you think they would nod, maybe slap their heads and think, 'Of course! It's so obvious. How could we all have been so stupid for thousands of years?'"

Jerish didn't like the way the question was being asked.

"I'm a Teshlor, and I believe the emperor. That's what knights do."

"No—that's what you do."

Jerish brushed off his hands. "Are you saying Teshlors are too stupid to—"

"Not at all. If I told the Cenzarium the same story, they wouldn't believe it, either. They would conclude I was young and naïve. They would agree this was a conspiracy, certainly, but of the Teshlors' making—a fanciful tale they convinced the emperor to accept as truth to take control. When a snowball rolls and grows this big, no one person can hope to just stand in front and stop it. The whole thing has a life of its own now, and mere words can't hope to kill it."

Jerish thought about that, and he didn't like where the thoughts led. *What will it take?*

CHAPTER FORTY

Preparing to Leave

The emperor had indicated they would be leaving before midday, and Esrahaddon had several stops to make. He returned to his room at the Cenzarium and grabbed his personal travel bag. He'd left it on the floor when he staggered in the night before. *I haven't even had time to unpack.* Esrahaddon was still mulling over whether this was a good or bad thing when Isilpor-Sond appeared in the doorway, blocking his exit.

"Gaylord Sire is dead." She dropped the news and watched him. When he had no reaction, she asked, "How did you do it?"

"You think I killed him?"

The little woman continued to stare, those old eyes examining his face, then running up and down his body until her glare felt indecent. Finally, she frowned. "Apparently not, but it is not news to you, either."

"How could it be? The entire city is practically humming the same tune. Why did you think I did it? I wasn't even here."

She waved her hand, shooing the comment away. "Because I asked everyone else. You were the last possibility."

"Couldn't someone have lied?"

She appeared entertained by the comment. "Of course not."

Isilpor-Sond had never impressed him as ridiculously naïve, so her reply gave him pause and left him a bit disturbed as to what had just happened—more than he thought, certainly.

She focused then on his bag. "Going somewhere so soon?"

"Yes, and I can't say I'm happy about it, but I wasn't given a choice."

"Where are you going?"

Esrahaddon hesitated. "I'm not certain I'm allowed to say."

This caused her brows to rise, but she didn't press. Instead, she shifted her inquiry. "Are you going alone?"

"No, and don't ask me any more questions. I can't answer them. I'm also in a hurry." He indicated her being in his way, which was mildly ironic, given her size.

"How did it happen?"

Esrahaddon was at a loss. "How did what happen?"

"How did Gaylord Sire die?"

"I heard he was, well . . ." Esrahaddon placed his fingertips together then quickly separated his hands and whispered the word *boom*. "It's not a hard thing to do, as I recently discovered."

"It is when your target has the Orinfar tattoo around his chest. All Teshlors have runes. The Art doesn't work on them. He was *pressure elapsed* in a violent manner. Nothing but the Art is capable of doing that, yet the Art couldn't have been used. So how could it have happened? How was it done?"

Esrahaddon felt stupid for not having thought of it sooner. He didn't have an answer but found the question dangerous. "Why are you asking me? I told you I didn't do it, and somehow you managed to determine I'm not lying, which is disturbing."

She shrugged. "We all have hidden talents. You, for example, are smarter than you let on, and at this moment, I'm desperate. Things are getting bad. The knights are angry. They want the emperor to punish the Cenzarium."

"He won't do that."

"No, he won't, but there's a rumor he's leaving town—going away for some time. Some suggest he's looking for a means to deny involvement."

"Involvement in what?"

"In whatever happens while he's gone. You know the old saying: While the cat's away the mice will foolishly seek vengeance on the innocent."

"Haven't heard that one."

"I fear you will."

"I need to go."

"You know more than you're telling me."

"Yes."

She frowned. "Fine, but think on it, Esrahaddon. Work it out. How did Gaylord Sire die? I don't think I'm exaggerating when I say the future of the empire might depend on answering that riddle."

Esrahaddon ran a risk in visiting Elinya. Evarburton's estate, where she both lived and worked, was a rambling villa just outside the urban density of the city, located on Mount Mari, which was really only a hill and mostly known for its grove of olive trees. Evarburton's wasn't the only estate on the hill, but it was the biggest and finest, and it was also nearly an hour away. He might be late getting back, but he couldn't leave without seeing her again.

Arriving late the night before, he'd seen her safely home and insisted on speaking to Ingram Evarburton himself. Esrahaddon made certain the textile king understood the reason for Elinya's absence, and the man would not penalize her. Hearing his household administrator had been on a special and dangerous mission for the emperor not only preempted any discipline, but it also granted her a newfound respect and gave Ingram something to brag about. What it hadn't done was give Esrahaddon much time for a proper goodbye.

The estate's staff, remembering Esrahaddon from the night before, waved him in with a plethora of welcoming gestures and an assortment of grandiose greetings. They assumed he was there to see the master of the house, but he corrected them and found Elinya in the courtyard, overseeing the planting of the spring garden. She was wearing new clothes, a stunning white gown with a wide gold necklace, her hair up in a cone made of a single braided coil.

"You look amazing." He greeted her with a hug. As always, she squeezed hard. "Should I be concerned about the intentions of your benefactor? Might I have competition?"

She smiled. "My benefactor is my employer, and he likes me to look smart and capable. He also knows that a Cenzar who tutors the emperor's son looks out for me. And of course, Cenzars are scarier than snakes, aren't they?"

"So, too, it would seem, are estate managers." He grinned at her.

She shook her head. "I no longer have the dagger. I am a toothless serpent now."

"You are the courageous slayer of evil. I wish I had been there."

"I'm glad you weren't."

He looked at her curiously.

"She would have killed you just as she did Ruby. I succeeded only because I'm nobody, and as such, invisible. I survived only because of Yolric."

"You"—he reached out and cupped her face—"are far from nobody." He considered saying it right then, but it didn't feel right, not when he was in such a hurry. "Elinya, I can't stay long. The emperor insists I go on another trip. I'll be gone two weeks, maybe a bit more, I'm not sure. I just came by so you wouldn't worry."

"I expect I'll worry more, now that I know you're going on another mission. Is it dangerous?"

"I don't think so. Nevrik is also going, so I can't imagine it being too perilous. What I meant was that I didn't want you to think I'd forgotten you."

"Oh." She looked pleasantly surprised. "That's . . ." Her eyelashes fluttered, and she looked down. "Thank you."

"Things are very hectic at this moment, but when they calm down, I'll want to take you out. We'll make a big day of it."

"Of what?"

He smiled. "I have a question I've been meaning to ask."

"You could ask it now."

He shook his head. "A question such as this deserves more fanfare, and so do you."

"So it won't be an inquiry about my favorite color?"

"No hints," he said sternly.

"Fine, just be safe."

"You, too. Things are . . . well, they're strange. Dangerously odd and, as you say, you no longer have your dagger." He looked around at the garden and the manor. "You know, I can't manage something as nice as this, but I think, if all goes well, I might arrange a pleasant little place for two. What do you think about living somewhere like Mehan? I hear it's a rapidly developing city, and the weather there is supposed to be wonderful. Or we could look into Rodencia if you prefer. They just finished a new sewer system, so it's bound to grow, and it's only a day's travel from the palace."

"Are you going to be there?"

He nodded.

"Then I don't care where this hovel is. I'll be happy to clean it for you."

"I don't think you understand the nature of the question I'll be asking."

"I could say the same of you."

For the second time in one month, Esrahaddon joined a party gathering for travel in the Imperial Plaza. This was nothing like the last; the emperor did not travel lightly. His entourage consisted of over a hundred servants, soldiers, artists, and scholars. Several wagons, a few carriages, and a multitude of horses—saddled and packed—waited in lines along either side of the plaza. In addition to a cohort of legionnaires, Esrahaddon spotted a detachment of Teshlor Knights. Jerish would not be alone. Esrahaddon would not be the only Cenzar, either, as Offman was dressed in traveling clothes—something Esrahaddon had never seen. *Who knew he had any?* The plaza felt oddly small and congested, finally explaining the need for such a large open space, which had always impressed him as wasteful.

"Cenzar Esrahaddon!" Bishop Venlin called out.

Esrahaddon, bag in hand, was directly in front of the church when the cleric spotted him.

"Morning, Bishop," he said respectfully and slowed his hurried march to a stop. Having believed himself horribly late, Esrahaddon was surprised to discover the imperial retinue far from ready to ride out.

"I'd like a word, but you seem in a hurry."

"I *was*," Esrahaddon replied with irritation. Relief that he was not late shifted to annoyance with the disarray of the still-gathering troops. The emperor was nowhere near ready. *I could have spent more time with Elinya.* "It seems I'm not in as great a rush as I thought."

The prince and his father wouldn't appear until minutes before departure. The idea of diving into the throng of fellow travelers and farewell wishers did not appeal to him.

"You're going with them, yes? Heading out with the emperor on your way to Avempartha."

Is this public now? What happened to 'pain of death?' "Yes. I am."

Venlin leaned against the pillar of his church and studied the crowd. The bishop dressed, as always, in the same simple white robe, which had an ugly stain along the tattered hem from grazing over filthy streets. This impressed Esrahaddon in the same way Venlin's arrangement of Elinya's employment had: The man eschewed appearance in favor of deeds—a rare thing.

"This is all so unfortunate," the bishop said.

"In what way?"

"Timing, mostly. The empire is coming apart, and the emperor takes a vacation." He shook his head slowly and folded his arms, revealing the frayed edges of his oversized sleeves. "The death of Gaylord Sire has the city on edge. Teshlors are convinced he was murdered by the Cenzarium—not an individual Cenzar, you understand, not a rogue incident, but an orchestrated conspiracy to eliminate their rivals. They see this as a first step, a test case to determine how Nareion will respond and what they can get away with. His leaving is a passive endorsement. Rather than punish the Cenzarium, the emperor is abdicating his responsibility by walking away. To them"—he gestured weakly at the Teshlor Guild—"this is evidence as to which side the emperor is on: proof of his intentions to betray them."

Venlin looked at Esrahaddon and smiled. "I see you don't agree. Why would you? None of that is true. I suspect you side with your Artist brethren in believing the emperor is intentionally abandoning all of you to the armor-plated, Orinfar-tattooed wolves. He could have made a public speech denouncing this gossip as dangerous rumor, called a special general meeting of both the Teshlor Guild and the Cenzarium to clear the air and vent the noxious vapors that build and threaten to poison the city. But no, the emperor goes on holiday."

"This trip is not a holiday and certainly far from a vacation."

"You needn't tell me. It's *they* who can't be convinced differently." He pointed out at the many citizens, soldiers, Teshlors, and Cenzars gathered in the shadows watching the assembly. "Words will not contradict what eyes witness. They saw the blood of Gaylord Sire, and now they see the emperor running away. Yet not one sees the truth, not even you. Emperor Nareion is not siding with the guild or the Cenzarium; he is not being manipulated by magic or fear of it; and he is not allying himself with the elves. Nareion is a good, honorable, and fair ruler, but he is also about to unwittingly destroy all of mankind."

Esrahaddon took a step back and eyed the bishop, carefully searching for signs of a smile, but the man wasn't joking.

"Don't look so surprised. I told you once, the success of the empire has been predicated on balance: Teshlor versus Cenzar. This system has served us well, but now that balance is falling apart. There was a time when the two sides respected each other, valued their rivals, but those days are history. Imbalance is here, and what we are seeing now is the result. But even you only see the obvious. At worst, I suspect you fear civil war." He shook his head. "Oh, how wrong you are."

"What are you talking about?"

"The war with the elves is about to resume, and you, my friend, will be on the front lines. Has the emperor told you why he is leaving at such a dangerous moment?" Venlin threw his hand up. "Don't bother answering. If he has, I'm certain you are sworn to secrecy. Allow *me* to tell *you*. Sadarshakar Sikaria and Hanis Orphe, imperial councilors from Merredydd, traveled to the forbidden Nidwalden River and met with members of the Erivan elves. They weren't authorized to do so and were not briefed on crucial facts. The two, I believe, may have disclosed a secret the empire has been hiding for centuries—one that will lead to a resumption of the Great War. Oh yes, they made quite a mess of things, those two. And this is why Nareion races to Avempartha, in a desperate attempt to throw water on a flame before it becomes an all-consuming fire. Either you know all this or you'll soon learn. But what you don't know, what you need to be aware of, is that Nareion is about to betray mankind—not on purpose, but just as *accidentally* as Sadarshakar and Hanis. He is going to Avempartha to give the elves the weapon they need to destroy us, and he will do it because he is a good and fair man."

The bishop sighed. "You've spent time with the Teshlors now. You must see how they are. Fine warriors, indeed, but all linked to the same creed of honor. If I called you a liar, you might stop talking to me, perhaps even curse me. But call one of them a liar, and they will kill you. Not out of anger, but because of tradition—a code of honor that demands such. They are mired in ancient rules that have long ago infiltrated their very sense of themselves, making stupid things like reputation important, while crucial necessities such as food and forgiveness are viewed as insignificant. Ignorance is what it is. As you have seen, men of brute force abstain from reading. They fail to build on the accumulated knowledge of generations and instead rely on doing what they have always done, assuming times will never inconveniently change. And for all his worldly wisdom, Nareion is, at heart, the descendant of Novron, a warrior."

"I guess I'm missing something. How is the emperor going to *accidentally* betray mankind? What weapon do you speak of?"

"It is called the Horn of Gylindora. Truth be told, it is not actually a weapon. In the hands of a human, it's utterly useless. Only a member of the Fhrey race can blow it, which speaks to the problem. If the horn remains in human hands, it's power is nullified, but because the horn belongs to the elves, the emperor plans to return it to them—an honorable but also misguided and horribly foolish act. Ages ago, the horn was stolen and given to Novron. This bit of thievery saved mankind from destruction. Now a false sense of justice will drive the virtuous emperor to return stolen property to the proper owners. In so doing, he will doom us all."

So much of what Venlin said teetered on the precipice of what Esrahaddon had come to recognize as religious crap, but two things kept him from a polite dismissal: He had grown to respect and even like the bishop, and there was the mention of the *horn*. The emperor had also named it in his summary of the Novron family curse. Nareion had neglected to say much about the Great Relic, but the fact that both the emperor and the bishop had focused on it suggested Venlin was telling at least some form of some truth. Anticipating that he would learn more about the nature of the cursed horn on the road, Esrahaddon considered an equally curious mystery.

"So what would you have me do, exactly?" Esrahaddon asked.

Venlin's eyes brightened a bit, and a hint of a smile turned the edges of his lips. "If you see Nareion intending to hand the horn over, then I strongly suggest you prevent it. Take possession of the horn."

"And how might I do that?"

"You are the only Cenzar going."

"Actually, Offman is coming as well. He'd likely object to me stealing from the emperor, and technically he outranks me."

Venlin smiled. "Between you, me, and this pillar I'm leaning on, Offman is no competition for the likes of you—neither is this entire entourage the emperor is assembling. If you decide to take possession of the horn, no one could stop you."

"They would try."

"And that would be their mistake, wouldn't it?"

"You're asking me to—what?—commit treason?"

"I'm asking you to save the human race. What is treason in comparison to that?"

Esrahaddon smiled at the reply the way he might at a well-played hand of cards. "Fine, but then I would be tracked down and executed. This horn would be taken from my dead hand and humanity would still be lost."

"I will make certain no such thing happens. If you return to me, I will protect you and hide the horn where no one will find it, securing the future of humanity."

"You have that sort of power, do you? You're capable of fending off the entire Cenzarium and the Teshlor Guild and all the legions and the imperial guard and the city guard and very likely the entire citizenry of the empire?"

"The church does."

Esrahaddon frowned, and Venlin threw his hands up. "Look, don't believe me, and for Novron's sake, don't trust me. I'm not asking for that. All I'm requesting is that while you are on this trip, keep your eyes and ears open. Judge for yourself the truth of my words. Then make your own decision." The bishop seesawed his head from side to side and grinned. "And don't worry, it's not a big deal—only the very existence of the human race is at stake."

Esrahaddon chuckled. "I need to go."

"Of course and I know you'll make the right choice. I'm an optimist that way, always hopeful. It's actually what Venlin means—*land of hope.*"

CHAPTER FORTY-ONE

The Secret

Jerish had expected to hear the rest of the story. From the growing frown on Esrahaddon's face, he could tell the Cenzar had expected it, too. The emperor had all but promised that Nevrik would provide the finer details about this mysterious *family curse* while they traveled, but they had been on the road for a full day, and neither had seen much of the prince.

The column that rode north up the imperial road toward Merredydd was easily more than a hundred, perhaps more than two hundred, in number. Officially, they were known as the emperor's company. Jerish wasn't certain if that included the advance, rear, and flanking guards, but he doubted it. The guards traveled at distances too far to see except for those rare times when the road ran through flat, open country. Then he could spot the ghostly figures on horseback all around. Usually, all he saw was their dust.

The emperor's company was composed of what Jerish thought was an odd assortment. Ten Teshlors, including Spencer and Kendell, traveled in staggered pairs around the outside of the column. There were cooks, grooms, and other servants, which were to be expected, but he also found men hauling canvas, artist brushes, and paint. One wagon was laden with dozens of massive squared-off logs, as if the emperor planned to build a cabin somewhere.

"And what's that?" Jerish asked Esrahaddon, who rode alongside. He gestured at a man with a queer metal device slung on his back.

"An astrolabe," the Cenzar replied. "Mapmakers use them along with quadrant, cross-staff, and sextant. And over there—in case you're curious—is a painter."

"Him, I figured out," Jerish said. "This is just such an odd group."

"It's a historic trip. Nareion wants to record it."

Jerish pointed at the three riding just ahead. The trio were Frhey. Two of them—the males—were well dressed, like imperial dignitaries. The lady was attired more like a man, in tunic and tight leggings, and displayed a formal dress sword: a fancy, delicate thing.

"Linguists, translators, I suppose," Esrahaddon guessed. "We're bound to need them."

"And the prince?" Jerish asked. "Is he still up there?"

Holding tight to the left front horn of his saddle, Esrahaddon leaned out to his right, nearly to the point where he might fall, then nodded. "Still in the front row."

"Do you think he forgot, or do they never plan to tell us any more?"

Esrahaddon shrugged. "Could simply mean that the one riding beside Nevrik is a pretty girl."

"I don't understand."

The Cenzar looked over. "Which word: *pretty* or *girl?*"

"I mean, how is that an answer to my question?"

Esrahaddon furrowed his brows. "I realize you're—" He stopped himself and Jerish knew why. Ever since returning from Alburnia, the Cenzar had been tripping over his normal inclinations, forcing himself not to say what he thought or to think twice before speaking. A month ago, the next word would have been *stupid* or perhaps more likely *uneducated*, but instead . . . "Surely you understand sexual attraction, and how a boy of a certain age might be distracted by a beautiful girl?"

Jerish frowned. "Yes, Grandfather, I know all about the birds and the bees."

"Birds and bees?" The Cenzar appeared bewildered.

Jerish was surprised. Esrahaddon knew, or at least acted as if he knew, everything. "Have you never heard the term?"

"In Calynia, we would say *bees and the flowers* if you were making a metaphor indicating the process of reproduction. But I fail to understand the relationship between birds and bees. They are different species. They don't mate."

"It just means all living things, even birds and bees are subject to the same rules. But how does flowers make any sense? They don't copulate at all."

"That's just the thing, they do—via bees."

Jerish peered at the Cenzar, then laughed. "I'm not *that* stupid, you know. Flowers grow from seeds."

"Yes, but—I didn't—" Esrahaddon sighed. "Never mind. I merely meant to say that anything might have distracted the boy because, after all, Nevrik *is* still a boy."

"And I," Jerish declared, "merely meant that he is also the prince and should put the interests of the empire and his people ahead of anything personal."

"I agree, but it is evident that reality does not concur. At least our narrow view of it. I suppose it is possible the lad is engaged in a vital debate of imperial security that neither of us can hear and therefore are ignorant of."

"You include yourself in that? In being ignorant?"

Esrahaddon sighed. "Jerish, I wasn't insulting you—wasn't making a joke at your expense . . . but perhaps I should take this opportunity to apologize for providing you with multiple reasons to suspect such. It's a little too easy sometimes to view one's strengths as the most important thing and see only deficiency in all others who lack that same talent. Arrogant and self-serving, really, and also sad because you fail to appreciate the value of others' gifts. Foolish, true, but oh so easy to do. Sorry."

Jerish nodded. "I suppose I'm just as guilty. Only the Teshlor Code prevents me from saying my thoughts out loud."

"Hold on," Esrahaddon said. "I'm completely wrong."

"What?" Jerish frowned. *Was all that a joke? Just when I'm starting to think—*

"The prince." The Cenzar, who had been looking ahead, faced Jerish. "He's coming back, and now I can clearly see the person who was riding to his left. It's not a beautiful girl or even a handsome man for that matter. It's Offman."

"That's what you were wrong about?" Jerish asked.

"You don't think that's a mistake?"

"Oh, absolutely—very wrong. One might even say—"

"Remember your Code."

Jerish grinned as Nevrik maneuvered his horse alongside them. Pure white, with pink skin and blue eyes, the prince's mount was one of the rare imperial

Alleyas. Bred without flaw, descended in a direct line from Novron's original Alon Rhist stock, the animals were reserved exclusively for the imperial family.

"You decided to finally join us and explain the rest of the story, did you?" Esrahaddon asked.

The prince looked puzzled.

"He did forget," Jerish said.

"Oh, that," Nevrik said. "No, I didn't forget. I'm still accumulating facts. And . . ." He looked awkward. "I'm actually not here to speak to you. I came to talk to them." He pointed at the Fhrey trio riding ahead.

Esrahaddon looked at Jerish. "I'm hurt. You raise them, give them the best years of your life—and for what?"

"Councilors?" Nevrik called and the two Fhrey turned as best they could on horseback. "I'm Prince Nevrik. I was hoping to speak with you."

"My apologies, Your Highness," the taller, older of the two males replied. "I didn't know—I didn't see you—"

"That's all right," Nevrik said. "I'm sneaky that way. You know, this is a good imperial road, and while not exactly the width of the Grand Marchway, I think there's enough room to ride four abreast."

It took only a moment for this to register, and the two councilors shifted right, granting the prince space to move up. Esrahaddon whispered to his horse, which hurried forward to follow Nevrik and wedge her way into the gap. Like seats at a wedding or holiday feast, rows in an imperial column were not filled at random. The more notable or higher ranks rode closer to the emperor. One couldn't fill in gaps without causing a political storm. The prince was either an exception or didn't care. Knowing Nevrik, it was both. The boy had always enjoyed breaking rules, and now *the boy* was nearly a man. Esrahaddon had taken advantage of the turmoil, which was his way as well. Jerish, however, was a creature of rules who believed in hierarchy, so he stayed put.

Alone in his row, he felt awkward and exposed until the female Fhrey reined her horse and dropped back. While the road might accommodate four comfortably, five was too much. She brought her horse into step alongside Jerish as the councilors, the prince, and Esrahaddon engaged in only a half-heard conversation.

"I'm Jerish Grelad," he introduced himself when he noticed the lady Fhrey staring.

She blinked and straightened up, as if awakened from a dream. "You're a Teshlor Knight."

"I am." He smiled. "And you might be . . . ?"

She looked aghast. "Oh, I'm horribly sorry. I am—I mean my name is, Ulin Myr Halcyon." There was a slight quaver in her voice.

"Are you all right?"

"Yes," she said and coughed, then straightened again, tugging at the bottom of her tunic, working to clear the folds and wrinkles.

"You also wear a crest." He pointed at the embroidered emblem of a blue-and-gold quartered shield divided by a huge tooth. "I'm not familiar."

She looked down, as if just noticing her own clothes. "Ah, yes, this is the emblem of House Tekchin. I am a member of the Order of the Fauyld."

"Oh yes, I think I do remember having—"

"No, I'm not. I'm sorry. I just lied. Forgive me. I can't—I can't lie to a Teshlor. This was my father's emblem. He was a member. I am not. They refused to accept me—not because I lacked ability, but because my family was banned because my father failed to save the dowager empress from assassination."

"Ah, okay."

"You're wondering why I wear it then. It's a matter of honor, you see. I'm trying to erase that stain upon our name, working to redeem our family's reputation."

"By falsely wearing a crest you didn't earn?"

"By making up for my father's failure, by achieving distinction and acclaim equal to or greater than the shame my father wrought." She spoke forcefully, as if pleading her case before a court.

"Well, then. I wish you good fortune and hope you manage it."

"Thank you, sir."

Jerish chuckled at that. "You don't have to—please don't call me sir."

"You're an imperial knight. Isn't it proper?"

Jerish dipped his head right and left. "Yes, but it makes me uncomfortable. I don't feel like a *sir*. I'm only twenty-three, and I haven't done anything that would earn such respect."

"You completed the guild training and were accepted and clapped by the emperor, weren't you?"

"Yes."

"Oh, I see," she said while looking at his chest. "Just because you are Third Order doesn't mean you don't deserve respect due a knight."

Jerish let his head droop, and muttered, "Actually, I'm First Order. The emperor conferred the title only hours ago. There wasn't time to get a new emblem."

Her eyes widened in what could only be awe. "You're a Knight of the First Order, but you don't think yourself worthy of being called . . . *sir?* You have the power of the emperor to make judgments and take lives without question. I should think anything below *lord* would be an insult."

"Look, could you just humor me? Call me Jerish. I'm comfortable with that."

"Given that you hold the power to execute me on a whim—okay. No honorifics. Duly noted. Anything else?"

"You could stop looking scared of me."

With that, her expression changed. Her eyes sharpened, and a smile threatened. "Oh, I'm not afraid. Impressed, certainly; excited and thrilled, sure—but not scared." Her sight drifted to his weapons. "I've always wondered—no, not wondered—*longed* to cross blades with a Teshlor. For so very long, I've tried to imagine what it would be like. Is it all a myth? Are the legends true? How would I fare in such a test?"

"You're good with a sword, then?"

She nodded, and that smile finally took hold. "Very."

"With that sword? It looks more like jewelry."

"Says the man with three. My father used to say one pricker should be good enough for any man."

"My father used to say there's wisdom in using the right tool for the job."

"Looks like we are both the products of our upbringing."

Jerish had never seen a lady in breeches, never spoken to a Fhrey, and while she made him feel self-conscious, like a man being watched while eating, he liked talking to her. The sound of her voice was musical in a way he couldn't put into thoughts but it soothed like running water. Her eyes were green and brilliant, not the dull, dark, dirty-brown of humans. And her face was so expressive that she told whole stories with but a lift of a single delicate, arching eyebrow. There had been few people in his life who had made him happy to be who he was, fewer still whom he could stare at for hours and begrudge himself even a single blink. "May I ask why it is you're here?"

"I'm not entirely sure." She smiled, as if this were some cosmic joke, an irony no one could fathom. "I live in Merredydd, but I doubt the emperor is seeing me home. Likely, having just returned from Avempartha has more to do with it. There aren't many road signs, and I found the way for the two councilors." She tilted her head toward the two Fhrey speaking to the prince. "So in a strange way, I suppose I'm a potential guide? Thing is, I haven't officially been informed of my purpose, merely told I was coming. Might just be that they're scared I'll talk."

"Talk?"

She nodded. "That's why the councilors insisted I return with them to Percepliquis. Concerned they may have made the blunder of the millennium, they're doing everything they can now to save their lives."

"I don't understand."

"Don't you know why we're traveling to Avempartha?"

"The prince was supposed to explain, but he hasn't gotten around to it, yet. At the moment, I haven't got a clue."

"They asked if the emperor was dead," Sadarshakar said with indignation worthy of having suffered an interrogation concerning his sexual history.

He was the senior councilor from Merredydd. Hanis Orphe, the sickly looking one who rode alongside, was the junior. This hadn't been explained. Nevrik appeared to already know and made no inquiry. Still, Esrahaddon had little trouble working out the dynamics from the story so far. The two—young by Fhrey standards, ancient by human—had asked permission to visit the forbidden province of Erivania. The emperor had denied it. They went anyway. *Why* was a bit murky so far, but hubris and aspirations of glory were unintentionally hinted at.

"Who asked, exactly?" Nevrik inquired. The prince was gentle yet direct, and Esrahaddon couldn't help but make comparisons. These councilors were both nearly or over a century old; Nevrik was but twelve, and still he appeared the adult in the mix.

"I believe her name was Salyndra. They referred to her as *Curator*, which is like an imperial governor, I suppose. She seemed to be in charge."

"And you replied . . . what?"

Sadarshakar made a nervous smile. "That's the lone flower in the weed field, isn't it?"

"Is it?"

Sadarshakar nodded in a pleading manner, as if begging Nevrik to agree. "I told them the emperor is still alive because *Emperor Nareion* is still alive. It never occurred to me they might mean Nyphron."

"That's Novron's Fhrey name," Hanis leaned in to explain, the junior councilor making the bad assumption that neither a graduate of the Cenzarium nor Novron's blood descendant would know this. Maybe because Nevrik looked so young Hanis expected ignorance. He was in for a shock.

"If I had understood," Sadarshakar went on, "if I hadn't been so obtuse from the beginning, things might be salvageable."

Nevrik gave Esrahaddon a scary look as if he felt things might already be in the unrecoverable realm. The gravity in those eyes didn't seem right—not for a boy so young.

"Then they asked about the horn," Sadarshakar said, once more with more drama than the words seemed to warrant. "They wanted to know if we brought it, saying they assumed the purpose of our arrival was to deliver the horn—to return it to the Aquila."

"That's the elven High Council," Hanis filled in, and this time Esrahaddon was grateful. He'd learned a great deal from the city library about the war and the elves, but much of it was spotty. He still didn't know the average lifespan of a pure-blooded Fhrey, and specific details concerning the end of the war were left oddly vague. "We learned the Aquila are the traditional gatekeepers of the horn. They decide who is allowed to use it."

"Yes"—Sadarshakar was nodding—"they expressed surprise when I said I didn't know anything about a horn."

The expression on Nevrik's face darkened, and his mouth squeezed, as if someone had punched him in the stomach.

Sadarshakar saw it and cringed. "They asked why we had come at all, and I explained that Hanis and I were hoping to establish proper diplomatic ties and open a lucrative trade route between Erivania and the west. I revealed our dream of renewed ties, open dialogue, and a sharing of culture. I thought they would be thrilled, but when I mentioned establishing a true governorship in Erivania"—he shook his head—"they said it was presumptuous to discuss an extension of the existing form of rule when the Uli Vermar was so close."

"You didn't ask what that was, did you?" Nevrik had a hand up to his mouth, fingers over his lips, as if he witnessed a horrible accident.

Sadarshakar gave a brisk shake of his head. "I would have, but they kept speaking, and I felt it was impolite to interrupt. Thank Ferrol I didn't because the next thing out of Salyndra's mouth was—and I will try to remember the exact words because your father insisted on that when we told him— 'Nyphron must be quite old by now. Almost everyone who took part in the war is dead. And when Nyphron dies, the horn must be blown to determine the new ruler.' I was stunned by this and said nothing more. Salyndra went on to explain that if the horn isn't blown, no one will be in control, no laws, no restrictions, no deterrents for anyone, and chaos will follow. 'This is why it is so important that the Aquila has the horn ahead of time,' she said. 'So that we can move quickly to pick the candidates and avoid this period of disorder and anarchy.' Then she added in a horrible tone of sympathy, 'And, I don't think it at all unreasonable to suggest that the next ruler will likely be an Erivan Fhrey. And as such, it will be we who consider the value of establishing a governorship in Alon Rhist . . . or whether such a thing will even be necessary.'"

"'Whether such a thing will even be necessary?'" Nevrik said, looking shaken.

"That's when I knew something was terribly wrong," Sadarshakar said. "And I refused to give direct answers to any more of their questions. They noticed and grew suspicious. Finally, they insisted on a meeting with Nyphron at Avempartha to be held at midday following the first night of the next full moon. They insisted I explain to the emperor—to Emperor Nyphron—that if he did not show up with the horn, they would come looking for him."

"That doesn't sound ominous at all," Esrahaddon said. "Nevrik, I—"

"Thank you, councilors, this was very enlightening," the prince said.

"Nevrik—"

"Can't talk now," the prince told Esrahaddon and sat back on his horse, then paused. "I'm sorry, I don't mean to be rude, but I do have to—look . . ." He pulled a little pouch from where it was looped on one of the saddle horns and handed it to Esrahaddon. "I found the stone yesterday morning when we broke camp. Thought you might like it."

Before Esrahaddon could open the pouch, the prince urged his Alleyas outside the column and trotted forward. Inside the little bag was a smoky quartz figurine of three people: a boy and two men, one dressed in armor, the other in a robe.

Two days later, they were in sight of Mount Mador, and still the prince hadn't made good on his father's promise. Jerish didn't press. Nevrik appeared haggard, worried to the point of sickness. Esrahaddon had filled Jerish in on what he learned in the conversation with the councilors. Both agreed much was missing. They speculated, but Esrahaddon cautioned that guessing was not only pointless but dangerous.

"He'll explain when he can," Esrahaddon had said. "If not, I'll beat the little brat until he does."

Jerish balked. "You're joking."

"Why do you say that?"

"One, he's the prince and hurting him is an imperial crime punishable by death; two, you love *that little brat*, and I think you'd make an oil spot out of anyone who *did* hurt him; and three, you might not be aware of it, but Nevrik is coming along in his lessons, and if you tried, you might find it harder than you think to beat him."

"Then I suppose we're forced to wait."

Jerish had accepted this, but he wasn't about to let Nevrik's lessons slide. It had been over a month since the prince's last training session. Such a hiatus, if left unchecked, would erode his advancement. More importantly, Jerish felt a little single-minded exercise would be good for the boy. Given his bowed posture and ashen face, some exercise could only help.

Nevrik was less than enthusiastic when Jerish insisted they leave the camp and practice in the field. His protests fell to mere grumbles when Jerish explained the sun would soon be down, so the lesson couldn't last long.

As far as practices were concerned, they couldn't have found a better place. They stood on a tabletop-level plain that went for miles. Being spring, the whole of it was carpeted with lawn-high grass and early-season flowers. As a backdrop, Mount Mador was lit by the golden glow of the setting sun, which made her snowy crown shine. Nevrik had graduated from wood batons to dull metal swords, and as they began warm-ups, the sun glinted brightly off the blades.

Life in camp had already become routine. The moment they began working through a review of basic moves, the sound of metal on metal rang, and people came out to watch. The first was one of the artists. He plopped himself on the ground and began sketching. The off-duty cooks, along with a few imperial soldiers, formed small clusters of spectators. Then Jerish spotted Spencer and Kendell. The two Teshlors stood shoulder to shoulder, watching, pointing, and whispering. The Teshlor Code prohibited making negative assumptions about otherwise honorable people, but Jerish couldn't help but suspect they were critical of his teaching methods. The next spectator was Ulin. She sat a few respectful sword lengths away.

Jerish focused on gauging Nevrik's skill erosion and what would need additional work, but he noticed that at some point, Ulin had moved closer and was speaking to Spencer and Kendell. She drew and handed her sword to Spencer. More was said, then it was returned.

What is she doing?

Jerish became so distracted that when Nevrik made an unexpected swipe, Jerish reacted not with thought but with reflex, disarming and nearly cutting the prince in the process.

"Master Ipstich would be proud." Spencer grinned.

"I think that's enough," Jerish said. "Light's starting to fade."

Nevrik nodded and wiped the sweat from his face.

"Feel any better?"

The prince looked confused, then smiled. "Yes, a little." He weighed the dull practice sword in his hand. "Thanks."

"Maybe you'll get around to telling me more about what's bothering you soon."

"I will." He made a point of looking Jerish in the eye as he said this. Then the prince walked back toward camp, and Jerish noticed the boy's back looked a dash straighter.

"The prince has good form," Kendell said as the three approached.

"He's out of practice and sloppy." Jerish dropped the prince's sword on the little pile of gear.

"You really are channeling Ipstich, aren't you?" Spencer said with a laugh.

Jerish gathered the pads and weapons and began stuffing them into a long canvas bag he'd borrowed from the guild's practice field.

"So are you making the prince into a Teshlor?" Ulin asked.

Jerish shook his head. "No, for that he'd need to eat and breathe combat. Nevrik has other studies. He's going to be emperor, not a knight."

"How far along is he? I didn't see anything surprising," she said.

"Surprising?" Jerish looked up to see both Kendell and Spencer also showing an interest in the comment.

"The moves and techniques. I saw nothing special, nothing I'm not familiar with. I expected, even at a basic level there would be a fundamentally different approach. The footwork, for example. I assumed it would be more complex. But if it was different at all, it was simpler," Ulin said.

"The Fauyld is based on the Tek'chin, the first of the original seven schools of the Tesh," Jerish explained. "It's the first discipline learned, as it teaches proper movement, patience, and blade control. I suppose that's what you're seeing."

"What I'm seeing is that it wasn't being performed correctly—by either of you. Which makes me wonder how much was lost in the transition."

"I'm getting the impression you'd like to cross swords," Kendell said with a grin.

"I very much would." She laid a hand on the pommel of her blade.

"No," Jerish said. His tone was harsh and commanding as if he had the authority to dictate the activities of two senior Teshlors and a law-abiding citizen of Merredydd. He abandoned the gear and stood.

They were all looking at him, even the artist and cook, but he focused only on Ulin. "You aren't going to fight Spencer or Kendell."

Her eyes showed suspicion, lots of irritation, perhaps even anger. This was her dream, he knew it, and he was knocking the cup away.

"Why is that?" she asked.

"Because there is a chance you might best them, and that would be harmful to the guild's honor."

This landed with impact. Surprise flooded every face and threatened to overflow into rebuttals. Kendell was in the process of opening his mouth when Jerish spoke over him. "If you're going to fight anyone, it will be me. I'm the best."

Whatever each of them was about to say was obliterated. Jerish focused on Spencer. "Do you disagree?"

His onetime senior classmate shook his head, then turning to Kendell, explained. "Jerish was never once defeated. He remained at the top of the leaderboard in his age group. The only one to achieve that since Gaylord Sire."

"*Will* you fight me?" Ulin asked and took a step forward. A hopeful longing filled her voice, wrenching Jerish's stomach.

If only she would ask something else of me.

Jerish glanced at Spencer and Kendell, knowing that if he refused, they would step in. "Yes, but I don't want to hurt you."

With those words, Ulin lit up brighter than the crest of Mount Mador. "You won't."

She threw off her cloak and drew that needle of a sword from its scabbard. She made a few practice swings before turning sideways. She pointed the toe of her front right foot at him.

Jerish took a breath and drew only his small sword.

"Just the one?" she asked. "Don't knights normally fight with two?"

"Sometimes."

"Why not this time?"

Jerish sighed and pulled his longer blade. As he did, she began to dance a bit, shuffling, moving in an arc around him, keeping the balls of her feet in contact with the ground. *Good form,* he thought. *She has skill.* Given how important this was to her, he knew she wouldn't rush, but they didn't have long. The sun was setting.

Jerish made a common jab. She knocked it aside but made no counter. He offered again. Once more she parried without response.

This is going to be a long fight at this rate.

In her eyes, he read her future. She was working conservatively. He was an unknown country to her, and she was hoping to tease out information. *I need to give her something to act on.* Given that she had insisted he pull both swords, Jerish drew from the basic school of Sebeka. It was a gamble. This would not be anything she'd seen before, and he hoped she could handle it.

He opened with a faint jab with the long sword.

Ulin blocked the attack, but guessing the ruse, she didn't commit.

Jerish followed on with the short—coming in underneath.

Ulin managed that difficult block by striking down with the elaborate guard of her sword—which was good. Most palace soldiers would have failed and died at this point.

Now came the real surprise.

Having forced her guard into the perfect position, Jerish trapped it with both weapons—something a single-blade-trained sword fighter might not anticipate.

Much to his delight, she performed a spectacular spin, freeing her sword and managing to give him a solid kick to the rump. Spencer and Kendell clapped, something he could have done without, but Jerish's declaration of being *the best* deserved it.

As planned, the victory stoked Ulin's confidence, and she finally attacked. The assault that came was fast—really fast. The needle blade moved quicker than eyesight. Instinct and something the masters referred to as memory magic saved him.

She is good, but now comes the hard part.

With exacting precision, Jerish forced himself to make a mistake. Like throwing a ball with the wrong hand or reading backward, it took effort and concentration. On top of that, he had to sell the move as genuine. The key was making the window of opportunity small enough that it didn't appear obvious but big enough to grant her the space to win without actually killing him. Jerish knew he'd succeeded when he saw the grin grow on her face. The result was adequately painful. She slammed the hilt into his face. Just a light kick to the back of his knee and he went flat on his back such that the air blew out of his lungs. He could have twisted, avoided the impact, but he needed to be believed.

This time applause did not follow. Spencer and Kendell just stared, confused.

Ulin stood over him, blade at his throat.

"I yield," Jerish declared loudly and clearly.

Esrahaddon rubbed his thumb over the little carved figurine as he watched Nevrik come off the field. The lad had a sheen of sweat on his face and that same conflict in his eyes. He looked like an old man being eaten up from the inside. *Cursed* was how Esrahaddon's father would have put it. Esrahaddon, who could drill a hole through water down to the ocean floor, didn't believe in curses. But something was eating that kid, and Esrahaddon was pretty sure he knew what it was and why Nevrik had avoided his teachers.

"That was short," Esrahaddon said as Nevrik walked past. "Are you washed up already? A has-been at twelve?"

"Lack of light," the prince replied, and after reaching one of the wash buckets, he splashed a bit of water on his face, rubbed it, then splashed again.

Esrahaddon handed him a towel from the rack, still astounded at the level of luxury the emperor enjoyed while on the road. Without the aid of magic, the emperor's company ate five-course meals, dined on linen, and covered the horses with quilted blankets—what Esrahaddon referred to jokingly as pajamas. Since no one else was familiar with the Calynian term, the humor garnered only puzzled looks. *Niblick would have loved it.*

"My prince," Offman called as he quickly marched up. He was in enough regalia—his robes adorned with silk panels and velvet cuffs—to suggest he was off on a date. His hair even appeared to have been brushed. "I'd like a word, if I may."

"Okay," Nevrik replied while setting the towel back.

Offman said nothing for a moment then his eyes settled on Esrahaddon. "Alone, if you please."

Esrahaddon peered at the Cenzar master. "No."

"Excuse me?" Offman asked, looking utterly baffled. He even glanced at Nevrik, as if he might supply clarity.

Esrahaddon decided to help him out. "You may not be alone with Nevrik. Until we return to the palace, I'm not taking my eyes off him."

Despite what Esrahaddon believed to have been a well-articulated, clearly stated explanation, Offman continued to display an expression of bewilderment. "What are you talking about? You haven't been with him at all. He's ridden beside me at the head of the line for two days."

"But never out of my sight."

"Are you suggesting the prince isn't safe with me?"

Esrahaddon shook his head. "I'm not *suggesting* anything. I'm stating flat out that he's not safe with you."

The master's eyes grew large, and his mouth gaped. This was meant to convey outrage, but like a harlot faking modestly, it was just for show. Esrahaddon hoped Offman would be happy with his display, and capable of realizing—if not with the Art, then at least by his tone of voice—that this wasn't a battle he would win.

Instead, Offman raised the bet. "You accuse me of treason, then?"

Esrahaddon sighed and shook his head. "No. Merely ineptitude. I don't think you're plotting to kill the prince, simply that you're incapable of protecting him from anyone who might. And for that reason, no, you can't have a word alone."

"Must I remind you that I am your senior in the ranks of the Cenzarium?"

"Must I remind *you* that there are *no* ranks in the Cenzarium? But if there were, I would be your superior. Your well is dry, sir. You're practically a faquin. Your only value to our institution is as a politician—a sad state of affairs for any man."

"How dare you!"

"With the knowledge and insight you obviously lack."

This time, the rigid body language and huffing breath weren't for show. Offman was genuinely angry. "Must I go to Nareion?"

"Won't do any good."

"You would defy the emperor?"

"In a heartbeat—if he ordered me not to protect his son."

Offman stood, breathing hard, his chest rising and falling like a child about to cry.

"Now, do you still want to speak to Nevrik," Esrahaddon asked, *"with* me here?"

Offman glared, then stomped away. His fancy ribbons fluttered in his wake as he fled back toward the tents.

"That was harsh," the prince said, his words apprehensive, unsure what to make of the evisceration he'd just witnessed.

Esrahaddon faced the boy straight on. "You've been lying to me."

Nevrik looked in the direction of Offman's retreating robes. "About what?"

"This." Esrahaddon held up the quartz figurine.

"What? You don't like it? I thought it was pretty good."

"It's beautiful and quite touching—a wonderful gift. How'd you make it?"

"I carved it. You know that. You've seen my room."

Esrahaddon nodded. "I did indeed. But you know what I didn't see in that room? Carving tools. No shavings, either. No chips, dust, nothing you'd expect as a by-product of scraping wood or stone. Might be that you're very neat, but your room was cluttered, bed unmade. If you were a stickler for tidiness, I don't think your chamber would be in such disarray. And would you care to show me the fine stone chisels and emery polish you brought with you that allowed for such a gorgeous creation in the matter of a day? Or demonstrate how you managed such fine detail while on horseback? Unless you care to produce these tools, perhaps you'd like to try again. How'd you make it?"

The boy didn't answer.

"At least you've given up lying to me. That's a step forward." Esrahaddon saw that Jerish was still out on the field. He was fighting that female Frhey. Why, he had no idea. But because everyone else was either watching the fight or lining up for the evening meal, Esrahaddon and the prince were alone beside the water barrel and the rack of towels. "I'm a bit embarrassed it took me so long to notice. The signs were all there. The way you picked us to be your tutors, how you tracked down Curtalus, the way you knew about Elinya and me. Does your father know?"

Nevrik shook his head, refusing to look him in the eye.

"You could have told me. Why didn't you?"

"It would be irresponsible—dangerous, wouldn't it?" the prince replied in a quiet voice. "If anyone knew, if anyone suspected that the son of the emperor . . ." He looked around cautiously. There was no one near, but still he never finished the thought.

"You're ashamed."

Nevrik's eyes came up. "No! No, not at all."

"Then why?"

"My father is the single pillar that holds up this entire civilization, and he stands with his feet supported by two foundations—that of the Cenzarium and the Teshlor Guild. This triangle, this trio is strong, or was, but now those two footholds are sliding apart. That makes it really hard to stand, especially when you're trying to hold up the weight of the world. You know, there's no tradition, no law that a crown prince has a Cenzar and a Teshlor tutor. I made that up. Although, I do believe such a tradition should exist. Now more than ever. So I asked my father to giftwrap me one of each so I could work an experiment. I wanted to see if I could bridge the gap. One day, I'll be emperor, and it will be my responsibility to work with the two halves. I want to find a means of healing, of uniting the empire's left and right hands, so they could work together again. But you two showed me how hard it is to change minds. Every day I told you of the other's virtues, and all I heard in return was animosity."

"I suspect you did better than you think."

"All evidence to the contrary." Nevrik frowned, then he, too, looked out at the field where Jerish was still sparring with the Fhrey. "Tell me, how do you suspect Jerish will react if you tell him my secret? Do you think he'll be happy? Or will he see the confirmation of all the rumors and conspiracies he's been fed since birth?"

"Maybe we should tell him and find out."

Nevrik chuckled without mirth.

"What I don't understand is how." Esrahaddon reached out and patted the neat stack of bleached white towels made of fine tree cotton imported from Wesbaden. "You're the crown prince. You've never been hurt, never wanted for anything in your life."

"And you have?"

"Oh yes."

Nevrik nodded. "You grew up in Calynia?"

"That's right."

Again Nevrik nodded. "Must have been nice."

Esrahaddon smiled. "It involved a lot of murder, terror, and bloodshed."

"Oh, I don't doubt that you suffered horribly. I meant that it must have been nice to *have a life*, even a hard one. You see, I haven't. I was born into captivity, made into a"—he pointed at Esrahaddon's clenched hand—"figurine. I was placed on a shelf and dusted twice a day so that I could be shown off. People were allowed to walk by my crib and marvel at the prince. Not much has changed for me since those days." He sighed and wiped his damp hands on his shirt. "Pain doesn't always come from suffering a terrible life; sometimes it comes from having no life at all and from the certainty you never will." He opened his arms and spread his hands. "What do you see before you? What else could you? I am a child who has everything. But honestly, I would trade places with just about anyone. For good or ill, I'll never know freedom, never be allowed to take a chance and experience accomplishment or failure. Never really know my own worth, or worthlessness. You know, never being allowed to fall down steals any gratification or confidence from standing up." The prince stared into Esrahaddon's eyes so that he could see the pain of envy. "I'll never go on a risky adventure where I"—he stopped and took a steadying breath—"where I save a pretty villager from a forest witch and then she falls in love with me. And I certainly won't go on to grind down a young prince's fragile sense of self-worth just because—"

"I yield." Esrahaddon said.

Nevrik wiped his eyes.

"And I'm sorry."

Nevrik shrugged. "It's your job. You're a grinder."

Esrahaddon nodded. "Yes, but I suppose I could use a slightly less coarse stone." Esrahaddon looked out across the field and saw Jerish lying on his back, the lady Fhrey holding the tip of her blade at his throat.

Nevrik saw it, too. "That's strange."

Ulin helped Jerish up as the artist and the guards on the sidelines applauded her accomplishment. They all appeared delighted at her victory. Jerish doubted they would have been so enthusiastic if he had won.

The Teshlors did not clap this time.

Ulin waved at her admirers. She nodded and smiled. Then as the last of the evening's light faded, everyone moved off in hopes of finding a meal.

Jerish picked up the few pads and two practice swords he'd brought out.

Ulin dropped her sword back in its scabbard, but aside from that she didn't move. Finally, when everyone had left, she asked. "Why did you do that?"

He didn't answer.

"On your honor as a Teshlor, tell me: Did I win this match?"

Jerish looked around at the empty, darkening field. "No."

Ulin's face sagged, and she struggled to swallow. "Could you have won?"

"Yes."

She gritted her teeth, causing her nostrils to flare as she took several deep breaths. "Why?"

"It would have been humiliating, and as I said, I didn't want to hurt you."

"But everyone expected you to win. Wasn't it more embarrassing for you to lose to me?"

He shrugged. "But I have nothing to prove."

"This proves nothing."

Jerish finished loading the bag and tied the mouth of it closed, then hauling it over his shoulder, he stood. "I'm not a philosopher, but I know that worth isn't found in a sword or the skill to wield it. Worthiness comes from the heart, from courage in the face of adversity, from fighting a battle you know you can't win with dignity." He looked at the pressed grass where he had fallen. "Sometimes you fight and lose because you must. Doing so is right and good and worth it. I learned that from Master Rawlings, the closest thing I had to a real father."

"How do you know it's worth it? How do you know what's right?"

"That comes from the heart, too, and it's for you to decide. But a good clue usually is that if what you're fighting for is what's best for *you*—then it's probably not the right thing."

She stared at him for a long time after that, neither saying a word nor making a move.

"Kendell and Spencer both know you let me win, don't they?"

He nodded. "They won't say anything. They're Teshlors."

Ulin made a sound like a laugh, but it also might have been the onset of tears. "You know, I never met my mother. She died in childbirth. All my life, I could never understand how my father could fall for a human. They live such short lives and aren't that pretty when compared to the Fhrey. At least not the ones I've seen. They lack grace, articulation, education, just about everything, really. It never made sense, so I just couldn't understand it." She looked up at him. "I'm finding it a little easier to understand now."

She walked back toward the brightening campfires.

CHAPTER FORTY-TWO

The Tower

THE RIVER NIDWALDEN, ERIVANIA

The emperor's company had been a week upon the road, running far behind schedule, and everything slowed that much more when they entered the forest. Esrahaddon knew the itinerary had been based on the previous trip made by the councilors and the lady Fhrey who'd put Jerish on his back, whose name he'd since learned was Ulin. But three individuals, even struggling through unfamiliar forest, had still made better time than a small army focused on the security and comfort of an emperor. Early estimates had to be changed, and for the last few days, the emperor had called for more haste. Hours in the saddle increased; conversations diminished; morale dropped. They set out before the sun rose and pitched camp by torchlight. The travelers did little more than ride, eat, and sleep, and on occasion, Esrahaddon was certain he did all three at once. Fatigue overwhelmed until time passed in a fog. Then on the night of the tenth day, when the moon came up full, they reached the Nidwalden River. Like magic, the wretched weariness vanished.

The first thing Esrahaddon noticed was the stars. He hadn't seen them since entering the Great Harwood days ago. Now they began to appear in a wedge shape that pointed at what Esrahaddon realized was the famous tower. Even at such a distance and without a campfire, torch, or so much as a single lighted window,

Avempartha still overwhelmed. The moonlight made it shine. The whole of the tower shimmered in silvery-blue, as if it did not belong on the ground at all but overhead with the rest of the stars. Taller than any construction Esrahaddon had ever seen, the lone pillar presented a delicate appearance, an upside-down icicle that any stiff wind would surely snap.

The entire caravan slowed to a stop, just to stare.

"Whoa," one of the cooks said.

"Will you look at that!" said another.

There were lights—not in the tower or on the tiny island upon which it perched, but across the river. On the far bank, a line of campfires twinkled. *Elves*, Esrahaddon thought. *Real elves.*

A thin, narrow bridge extended out from the trail they had been following. It led straight to the tower. From his position, Esrahaddon couldn't tell if there was another on the far side, but he guessed as much. And while he also couldn't see the river, he heard it. For some time, he had noticed a constant hum, which now had grown into a roar.

"So that's it?" Jerish asked Ulin.

The three had taken to riding together behind the councilors while Nevrik remained in the front row with his father, Offman, and one of the Teshlors. Esrahaddon wondered if Offman had ever told Nareion about their dispute. If he had, nothing had come of it, and he guessed the Cenzar master had kept quiet.

"Yes, that's Avempartha," Ulin replied, then asked, "What happens now?"

Jerish looked to Esrahaddon. "I'm not sure."

No one was.

The camp was set up on the west bank of the river, but doing so was far slower than usual. For once, the emperor's company had something to look at and talk about. Each face was bright and pale with the moonlight as it reflected off the tower. Esrahaddon watched the silhouette of a slender boy leaving the infant camp to walk along the riverbank. Handing his horse off to one of the grooms, Esrahaddon followed.

The farther upriver he went, the more placid the water became. Soon Esrahaddon could once again hear crickets and frogs and spotted the first lightning bugs of the season.

"It's sort of like looking at the entrance to a fairyland," Nevrik said as Esrahaddon approached. The prince had stopped walking and seated himself.

With his knees drawn up, his folded arms bridged the gap and supported his chin as he stared across the water at the distant lights. For the first time in days, Nevrik looked like the twelve-year-old he was, a boy enraptured by the mystery and excitement of an adventure. "They can see us, you know? The elves. Even at this distance. They are surprising like that. Better eyesight, hearing, balance. I suppose that's why humans are so quick to denounce them; when you rule the world, it is hard to concede you're not the best at everything."

Esrahaddon sat down beside him. The ground was damp with dew. The robe protected him, but Nevrik would likely end up with soaked pants. The boy didn't care—young boys never did. "That's the Old World over there," Esrahaddon said, peering across at the twinkling lights. "The start of it, at least. Estramnadon is supposed to be there somewhere deep in the forests. From what I read, they say it's their capital city, the onetime seat of their monarch."

"The fane," Nevrik said.

"So you know all this?"

"I know about the sacred grove where the first tree grows and is cared for by the Children of Ferrol."

"Someone's been doing their reading."

"I know more than that." Nevrik's eyes lost their innocence as the dark, cursed look returned.

"What do you know?"

Nevrik forced a smile. "Have you told Jerish—about me?"

Esrahaddon frowned but let it go. "No. It's not my place—not my secret."

"Thank you. I would prefer to tell him myself, but not yet. Things are so . . . strange right now. I don't feel I can risk it just yet." The prince looked over. "Will you teach me?"

"The Art? Yes. Someone has to. A rogue talent is dangerous. There are traps you can fall into. You must guard against indulgence. Too much will create a thirst. Quenching that thirst makes you drunk. Being drunk invites greater excess. Don't use the Art so much for yourself as for others, for the world in general. Keep in mind that happiness is the reward for struggle, and without struggle there can be no growth. What does not grow is dead—or should be. The Teshlor have codes to guide and restrict them from abuse, and all they are capable of is swinging swords. In theory, Artists can rearrange the stars and live forever. A power-hungry, selfish weaver can threaten the very existence of the world. Even trying to control one can wreak havoc. Placing constraints on us is challenging—some might say impossible. That's why they left Ruby Finn alone. But that doesn't work, either. Better to rely on self-policing. That's where education comes in. If you know right from wrong, if you understand the costs before you go too far, you most likely will find the willpower to resist."

"An evil emperor wizard would be a bit much, wouldn't it?"

"Scarier than snakes for sure." Esrahaddon replied.

"How's that?"

"Never mind. What have you managed to do, beyond exquisite sculptures?"

"Not much. I can't really practice or experiment. I closed a door once." He paused, and in a lower voice confessed, "And I killed a fly. I didn't even mean to. The buzzing, the constant batting at the window. It irritated me. Then the thing flew into my face. In my entire room, it ran into my face. I hardly even thought about it, practically a reflex. The fly just dropped to the floor. I felt bad. I don't know why. I've killed hundreds before with my slipper or even my bare hand, but this was different. It scared me. Not because I had killed a fly, but because . . ."

"It was so easy."

Nevrik nodded.

"Destruction always is. Living is a challenge because, it seems, death is a more natural state, the direction we all end up going. All things seek to return to dirt and dust. That's why life is so amazing, so powerful. It openly defies the rules. Light, water, wind, heat—these are the enemies of the void, of the cold darkness of nonexistence that seeks to reign. Life is made up of all four: warmth, water, breath—"

"Light?"

Esrahaddon pointed at the fireflies. "Where there is heat, there is often light. Some are brighter than others. You feel the river, don't you? The power in it?"

"Yes."

"Where it goes over the edge, that power explodes, becomes active like lightning. Collecting that strength is as effortless as scooping water. But you need to be careful. It's all too easy to become addicted to the rush, to the inflated sense of yourself, to the idea you're a god. You aren't, Nevrik. You need to remember that. The void is always there."

The boy nodded, but Esrahaddon doubted he really understood. *Emperor and Artist? What a toxic combination. He's going to need help, a steady hand, and a lot of patience. And he's going to need to trust me.*

"What else do you know, Nevrik?"

"I know I get tired after I do something complicated, like a big statue, and that—"

"No. Not about the Art. What is this curse?"

The prince bit his lip and once more looked across the black surface of the water. "It's a secret, an old one that only the emperor and his heirs are allowed to know."

He doesn't yet trust—

"But," Nevrik said, "I got permission to share it with you and Jerish. Wasn't easy, either. My father—he resisted, and for good reason. But I explained that the two of you had to know because I need advisors I can trust in case anything happens." Nevrik looked around the way a child does when fearful of being overheard. "You can't tell anyone." For a moment, he sounded like the quintessential twelve-year-old on the verge of admitting his crush. Then Nevrik added, "If you do, you'll be executed."

Nevrik didn't so much as smile or blink. This wasn't a joke.

So much for "I have a crush on my chambermaid."

"You know about the Great Relic, right?"

"You mean the—" Esrahaddon sensed the wave of fear rising in Nevrik and stopped. Instead, Esrahaddon simply put the end of his thumb to his lips and pretended to blow.

"Yes." The prince nodded as relief replaced alarm. Still, the boy was nervous.

What is this all about?

Nevrik moved closer. "Can you tell if anyone is around? Anyone who could be listening?"

Esrahaddon closed his eyes. He didn't need to, but it helped. Eyesight was such a powerful sense that it often overwhelmed the more subtle impressions given off by the Art, in the same way that looking toward the sun made it hard to see much else. With his eyes shut, hearing became the strongest sense, and he forced himself to block out the sounds of wind, water, insects, and frogs. Smells came next. He shut out the scent of dew on plants, worms, fish, and even the smoke of distant campfires. He accomplished all of this using the techniques taught in the

Cenzarium. He rarely ever had a need for most of what he had learned in his years beneath the dome. The bulk of it was stored in a mental junk drawer—left, but not forgotten because one day it might be needed. With his other senses chained, all that remained was Elan. She spoke to him of animals: chipmunks, moles, mice, a family of otters, a clan of beavers, several raccoons, three skunks, a multitude of bugs, worms, and dozens of rival ant colonies engaged in a horrific war of never-ending conquests to dominate the region. Fireflies created light patterns that only they understood. Fish played dangerously close to the edge of the falls, thrilled with the risk and curious about what lay on the other side. But as for men and elves—all of them were clustered at the camp or across the water.

Esrahaddon opened his eyes. "There's no one nearby who can understand language."

Nevrik nodded, then took several breaths, working himself up, as if preparing to dive into a scary lake. In a very faint, quiet voice, he said. "My father is not the emperor—not of the elves. You see, when an elven ruler dies, the horn must be blown. Usually this is done by someone challenging to be the new ruler. If it isn't, then there isn't a ruler. According to their law, they don't have to obey anymore."

"So why didn't your father blow the horn?"

"As I understand it, he can't. Being the eldest descendant, he's already in the running. Someone else of elven blood needs to blow it. And the elven Aquila is supposed to choose who that is."

"And, guessing they would pick one of their own, I assume your father would have to fight one of them. Winner takes all?"

"Winner takes all."

"But what if someone else—a local Frhey—blew it? Say, someone from Merredydd. Could that person just concede to Nareion without fighting him? Then nothing would have to change."

"Theoretically—I think so. But there's another problem. When that horn is sounded, *all the elves* hear it—no matter how far away they are. So they will know their ruler is dead and wonder why the horn wasn't presented to the Aquila."

"How is that possible? How could they know?"

Nevrik smiled. "You're a Cenzar. You can call down lightning and rain whenever you feel like it, yet you're baffled about how a horn can be heard from a great distance?"

"Fair enough."

"If they feel we have broken this sacred covenant by not presenting the horn, they'll likely restart the war, and we'll lose. But if we do present the horn, and don't win the challenge, we're doomed."

"Why?"

"Because the only reason we survived is because of that horn. If rule shifts to the Fhrey, it's not like we'll be forced to pay tribute or give up some land or something. I mean we will *all* die. They want to exterminate us from the face of Elan—at least they did, and I doubt that two thousand years of imprisonment has changed their minds."

"So, what are we doing here?"

"The councilors made a mess of things. The elven Aquila is suspicious. They expect to be meeting Nyphron tomorrow."

"And?"

"And my father hopes to fix it."

"How?"

Nevrik smiled. "By lying."

The morning after the first full moon began gray. Clouds filled the sky, and a fog rose from the river. The mystical quality of this undisturbed haze was enough to make Esrahaddon believe in gods, since a deity with a flair for the dramatic had to be the one decorating for the event. By midday, the mist had burned off, and the emperor assembled his retinue at the base of the bridge. The gathering was small. With no idea regarding how the meeting would go, Nareion would need protection, which explained the presence of all ten Teshlors. The knights were a safe bet. If he commanded them never to speak of what they witnessed, they'd be quiet. A few artists came in case the meeting would later be revealed and documented, but none of them spoke Fhrey. Offman came as well. The councilors were also included and an easy choice to round out the group as they already knew the secret and could act as translators.

"We're going, too," Nevrik informed Jerish and Esrahaddon, marching toward them up the little riverside path between the rows of tents, creating a commotion as everyone on either side knelt in respect. Dressed in his intricately patterned gold-

and-silver brocade tunic, Nevrik appeared wildly out of place on the riverbank. His jewel-encrusted slippers were already stained with mud, his legs wet with dew.

"We are?" Esrahaddon asked. "Is it safe to have both you and your father cast out on the same hook?"

"No," Nevrik replied, "but is it safe *not* to have *you* at my father's side? And would you prefer I wait here while you go?"

Esrahaddon frowned. "Are you sure you're twelve?"

"Almost thirteen," he replied. "You'll need to brace yourself for my rebellious teenage years. That's when I'll really be a handful."

Esrahaddon looked at Jerish. "I don't think we have that many hands."

"What about Ulin?" Jerish asked. The Fhrey had been busy wiping out her morning bowl of oats boiled in river water but had snapped to attention at the approach of the prince. "Can she come as well?"

Nevrik frowned, then eyed her critically. "You speak the elvish tongue, right?" Nevrik asked.

She nodded.

"Fine. Sadarshakar will be busy translating for my father, and Hanis for Offman. She can act as my interpreter. Be at the bridge in five minutes."

The prince walked away, forcing their neighbors back to their knees.

Esrahaddon had nothing to prepare, no clothes to change into. His readiness consisted of tossing his travel bag into the weak security of his canvas tent. Not that he was concerned about theft. He had nothing worth stealing, and who would dare rob *him?* After the ten-day trip, most everyone in the main party knew one another, or thought they did. Rumors circulated concerning his and Jerish's unusual trip to Alburnia. Curiosities had been piqued as to why The Tutors, as they were collectively known, had been sent on a secret mission for the emperor. Speculation ran the spectrum from sensible to absurd: from them being the most capable and skilled Cenzar and Teshlor in a generation to them being the illegitimate sons of Nareion. Either way, The Tutors were on a shelf by themselves—no one knelt, but no one approached, either.

Esrahaddon was ready to go, but Jerish and Ulin were both busy searching for Jerish's misplaced helmet. How he could lose such a thing was incomprehensible. The metal hat was huge and ostentatious, intended to resemble the head of an eagle with a great plume of feathers on top. Esrahaddon had always thought the helm looked like the creation of a maniacal taxidermist.

"Have you seen my helmet?" Jerish asked.

"Have you tried the river? Some sensible person likely threw it as far out in the current as they could, hoping it would wash over the falls."

"I found it," Ulin announced. She stepped out from Jerish's tent and held what Esrahaddon could only surmise was either a helmet or a dead bird mounted on a metal bucket.

"Oh, thank Novron," the Teshlor sighed.

Esrahaddon watched the Fhrey attempt to adjust one bent feather on the helmet. "What's with you and Ulin?"

"What?" Jerish replied. "Nothing, why?"

"The two of you seem . . . *friendly*."

"We are. Is that somehow mystifying?"

"Oh, not at all. That a contingent of elves is standing at the base of the tower waiting for us even though I don't see a bridge on their side of the river is *mystifying*. That you are friendly with Ulin is *wildly bizarre*."

The knight shifted his weight and the lay of his jaw, as if settling in for a confrontation he'd rather not face. "Why do you say that?"

"For one, she beat you in a fight, which looked painful. And for two, she's elvish—or hadn't you noticed?"

"Actually, she's a myr, but even if she were a full-blooded Fhrey, is there something wrong with being elvish?"

Esrahaddon laughed. "No, but there is certainly something borderline insane about *you* asking me *that* question. Since when are Teshlors accepting of elves?"

He frowned. "I'm more than a Teshlor, you know. You shouldn't make such broad judgments about groups of people, and . . ." He shrugged. "She's nice."

"I shouldn't . . . wait—nice?"

"Yes—unlike you."

"Are we going?" Ulin asked.

"Yes, we are," Jerish said, taking the helmet and putting the dead bird on his head. "How do I look?"

Esrahaddon opened his mouth, but Jerish raised a finger. "No—I wasn't asking you."

"You look wonderful," Ulin replied.

Esrahaddon laughed. "You're right. She is nice. And perhaps just a tad blind."

The trio caught up with the prince and joined the Imperial Court as the emperor began crossing the bridge. As far as walks went, this certainly ranked in

Esrahaddon's top five. His first steps into the Erbon Forest had likely been his most frightening; the forced stroll through the Field of Lions came in a close second; the wintry ride into the Forbidden Forest took the award for most atmospheric; and his entrance into the courtyard of Castell Blythium was the most disturbing. This, by far, was the grandest. The bridge was astoundingly straight and several stories above the water—at least on the left. In that direction, he could see a marvelous view of the broad river, displayed in all her beauty beneath a brilliant, climactic sun. On the right, there was nothing but mist and a sheer drop. The rising spray coated his cheeks and eyelashes. The overwhelming roar he felt as well as heard silenced conversation. With their approach, the tower appeared to grow larger and they, smaller. What at a distance suggested the impression of splendor was only a hint of the magnificence that was Avempartha. Up close, he could see this was a work of Art created by a master of the craft.

The elven assembly was smaller than their own. Only seven stood at the base of the tower. All fair and blond, each stood straight and still, with heads slightly bowed. Their clothes were simple elegance. Made of a shimmering cloth, void of complex patterns, they displayed only modest trim near the cuffs, collars, and hems. The septet stood in a chevron, three on either side of the foremost central figure, a middle-aged female with a determined expression.

"I am Salyndra," she declared, "daughter of Yolandrya, Curator of the Aquila and acting fane of the Erivan Frhey." Her voice was clear but cold. She remained motionless, hands clasped before her, the long sleeves of her gown hiding all but fingertips.

Ulin translated all this to the three of them as they stood toward the rear of the party, but Esrahaddon understood it on his own. Having a penchant for languages and using the city library, he'd taught himself a great deal of both Fhrey and the dwarven tongue known as Dromeian. All of it was easier than even he had expected, as Fhrey, Dromeian, and the Ba Ran dialects shared numerous words and syntax. Still, he hadn't had much opportunity to exercise his studies verbally, but for the last ten days, he'd ridden behind the councilors, who thought it prudent to speak mostly—but not entirely—in Fhrey. He had listened carefully. What he learned was that the two were preoccupied with punishment both from the emperor and their own families, whom he discovered were notable. More importantly, he improved his ability to connect his knowledge of the written word to the spoken. Now with Ulin, he was able to check his accuracy. So far, he was pleased.

Nareion stopped a prudent distance away—close enough to speak, far enough to be safe.

"I am Nareion, son of Nyphron."

This was translated by Sadarshakar.

An awkwardly long silence followed, and Sadarshakar frequently looked back and forth, waiting for the next word. For about a full minute, only the falls spoke. The raging roar and billowing clouds added a special level of tension, as if this meeting were taking place in a raging storm.

Confusion: Esrahaddon felt it radiating from the Frhey. The elves couldn't understand why the words of the fane's son were being translated.

Desperation: He could feel a great anticipation like a terrible hunger. They expected more—much more. This led to greater confusion when the emperor said nothing else.

For his part, Esrahaddon had no trouble understanding, as he knew silence was Nareion's most effective weapon. The less said, the more learned, and the least lost. They had insisted he come and needed to say why.

Incapable of waiting any longer, the elves folded first, asking the question, the answer to which they needed to know. "Where is Nyphron? Why hasn't he come?"

"Nyphron is not interested in meeting with you," Nareion replied. "I should think you'd understand that by now. Even if he were, your fane is no longer at an age where travel is comfortable."

Disbelief: That wasn't good. Esrahaddon needed to know more, but the Art wasn't giving that much detail. *What is it they don't accept? That Nareion is the son, or that Nyphron is alive? Or something else entirely?*

Another long pause, and one of those to the rear whispered in Salyndra's ear. She nodded.

"Forgive me, but you look remarkably human."

No pause—Nareion expected this. "My mother was human. Nyphron took a woman for his wife to unite his empire." He spoke with the confidence that honesty bestowed since both of these statements were entirely true.

"And the horn? Do you have it? Are you returning it?"

Esrahaddon held his breath as he studied the emperor.

"If you see Nareion intending to hand the horn over, then I strongly suggest you prevent it."

Esrahaddon sought a glimpse into Nareion's intentions, and body language wasn't going to cut it.

"Now a false sense of justice will drive the virtuous emperor to return stolen property to the proper owners. In so doing, he will doom us all."

It felt wrong, might even be illegal. At the very least, it was unethical and dangerous, but Esrahaddon couldn't afford a misjudgment—not if he were going to commit treason.

"Judge for yourself the truth of my words. Then make your own decision."

Employing the Art, Esrahaddon probed. Then he nearly gasped when, for the second time in one week, he found himself dumbfounded.

"Nyphron has the horn," Nareion declared. "And he will keep it."

"It belongs with the Aquila," Salyndra stated.

"It belongs wherever the fane says it belongs."

This was not received well. Salyndra's eyes hardened, and her jaw jutted out to form a disgruntled frown. "The Aquila has always kept the horn—since Gylindora Fane charged us with the duty to protect and preserve it and to decide who should be granted the privilege to sound it in challenge."

"And there was always an Instarya on the council," Nareion responded, "until Nyphron and his tribe were exiled and allowed no voice in the Aquila, no chance to challenge at all."

"The Aquila had no part in that act. Fane Lothian made that decision."

"And Fane Nyphron is making this one."

With teeth clenched and eyes wide, Salyndra glared, as if trying to burn a hole through him. Esrahaddon didn't need the Art to understand what was going through her mind. When she spoke again, her tone was less cordial, more abrasive. "You're *very* human, and it is quite possible you're lying."

The emperor showed no change. He neither looked away, blinked, nor revealed any hint of anger or concern, but his tone when he spoke was low, clear, and firm, carrying the weight of a hammer. "Be careful," Nareion told her. "It has been a long time, and I can understand some of your disappointment at being deprived of your fane, but there are far worse alternatives than two thousand years of isolated autonomous rule."

More silence filled with fog.

"I will require proof," Salyndra finally said.

"Proof?"

"Indisputable evidence that you are who you say you are. After so many years, it is likely Nyphron is dead, but the horn has not been blown, which suggests it's possible all the Fhrey on your side of the river are dead or imprisoned. The horn hasn't been sounded because there is no one capable. Only a Fhrey can blow it. So yes, I will need proof that you're truly the son of Nyphron and not merely some human who acquired power, who might even be Nyphron's murderer."

For the first time, Nareion looked unsure. He thought a moment, then shook his head. "I know of no means that could definitively convince you. Do you?"

Salyndra said nothing. She looked down for a moment, then off into the mist.

Frustration: It raged through her coupled closely with *helplessness* and, in the wings, *desperation* threatened.

"I know a way," said a member of Salyndra's group, who was farthest to the rear on her left-hand side. He was thin, taller and older-looking than all the other Fhrey, and dressed in a white wrap with no buttons or ties. "You could open the tower."

Esrahaddon felt considerable power emanating from the Fhrey, which he did nothing to hide—*Miralyith*.

"What are you talking about?" Salyndra snapped. Either she didn't like the interruption or the person, probably both.

The Miralyith showed no concern, no hint of tension at all as he stepped out of formation. "I suspect a surprising number of people, on both sides of this river—perhaps, even a few on this bridge—believe this tower to have been created during the war with the humans. They think it was made as a defensive fortress of some sort. But Avempartha was built centuries before Nyphron was born, before mankind or the moklins even appeared. Fane Fenelyus, the first and greatest Artist, created her masterpiece for one purpose: to increase the power and range of her Art. Its design harnesses the power of the Parthaloren Falls and focuses it so that even a weak Artist can perform wonders." The Miralyith moved forward, walking slowly over the wet stone.

At his approach, literally everyone in both groups stiffened, looking concerned.

This is unexpected, off script.

A threat? Esrahaddon received an ambivalent answer from Elan that put him on edge.

"At the end of the war," the Miralyith continued, "Nyphron didn't like the idea of a tower that could allow the Miralyith to perform devastating, long-range attacks, but he also knew that ordering its destruction would be politically dangerous. Instead, he commanded that Avempartha be sealed so that only he or his heirs could enter."

"How did he manage that?" Offman asked, and Sadarshakar translated.

The Miralyith peered at the Cenzar master just a little too much the way fire looks at paper. "Jerydd, the first and only kel of the tower, was more than willing to help. He pretended to be powerful, and he was, but only so long as he remained in Avempartha. Without the tower, Jerydd was weak as a faquin. This was the terrible secret he shared only with his beloved Avempartha. The kel was also close to death, and like any spiteful lover, he felt that if he could no longer have her, no one would. Now as I said, he was not powerful. But like all faquins, Jerydd was smart and devious. As such, he devised a complex lock, the combination to which is literally infinite. It's as if he wrapped the tower in an unfathomable amount of string. Then instead of tying it all in a knot, he tangled it beyond comprehension. No amount of power can force it open, and no Artist has a life span long enough to untangle all the knots that hold the tower shut. As we stand here, only Nyphron or his blood descendants have that ability." The Miralyith stopped when he stood alongside Salyndra and faced Nareion. "If you are he, then open it."

A trap? Esrahaddon queried the Grand Old Lady, but Elan said nothing.

The emperor looked at Offman, then at Esrahaddon. The same question was in his eyes. Finding no answers, he then faced the Miralyith. "I wasn't here when it was sealed. I don't know how to unlock it."

"Technically," the Miralyith said, "as far as you're concerned, it isn't locked at all. You can walk right in—if you are who you say you are."

Nareion looked at the tower. They all stood at its base. A short set of stone steps led up toward what appeared to be a solid wall. "I don't see a door."

"It's hidden. Your touch should reveal it."

"My touch?" Once more he looked back at his two Cenzars.

"I don't know about this," Offman finally said. "It doesn't seem right."

"Esrahaddon?" Nareion called. "What do you think?"

And the fate of the world is passed on to the new guy.

In a flash, Esrahaddon considered the possibilities. *The stone has been painted with some sort of contact poison; the steps or the landing are rigged to collapse or be crushed in some manner. Everything the Miralyith said was a lie and there is no door—never was. This is merely a way for him to claim, 'Impostor!' and justify the resumption of the war.* He ran each theory by Elan and got nothing. *No, not nothing—in this case, nothing is the answer.*

"It's safe," he replied and hoped the old lady wasn't about to have a laugh at his expense.

The emperor moved up the steps to the wall. He reached out tentatively and placed his palm on the stone. "Oh!" he gasped.

Two Teshlors shot to his side, but Nareion waved them off. "I'm fine—I'm just surprised it worked."

Everyone else witnessing the event was just as perplexed as Esrahaddon. As far as he could see, nothing had changed.

"What worked?" Salyndra asked, dragging out both words with toxic skepticism.

The emperor turned around puzzled. "The door." He gestured at the wall.

"Are you trying to pretend you can see a door?" she asked. This time her words were loaded to the brim with accusation.

"You can't see it?" he asked.

"Of course not," she said. "Because there is nothing—"

The emperor stepped forward and disappeared.

Everyone gasped.

A moment later, he reappeared. "I just entered that nonexistent door."

"Jerydd," the Miralyith said the name like a curse. "No one who isn't allowed in can even *see* an entrance."

"So none of you can see the door?" Nareion asked. "You can't go in?"

"Not without your permission," the Miralyith said. "That was the demand Nyphron made of the kel."

"Then I grant my permission."

The Miralyith laughed. "Try using your ancestor's language, and invite us by name. Mine is Krem."

The emperor began with Salyndra.

"Melentanaria, en venau aswen Salyndra, adona cuatron," Emperor Nareion said.

"I see a door," the Curator exclaimed, and fell to her knees to beg forgiveness.

Like the rest, Esrahaddon had walked into the tower after Nareion had granted him entry. Unlike the elves, however, he did not fall to his knees, genuflect, bow—or in the case of Krem—nod his head in respect to Nareion.

Light permeated the walls of Avempartha, seeping through the stone as if it were smoky glass. It made the interior an illuminated world of wondrous color and beauty. A large room opened before them that appeared to have no ceiling. Supports rose hundreds of feet high, where they spread out like a forest canopy. Intricate designs suggested branches and leaves, and through them they could see a series of stairs that went up tier after tier, leading to bridges that joined the spires.

"Welcome to the Entrance Hall," Krem addressed them.

"How do you know this place so well?" Offman asked.

"As a young Miralyith, I was stationed here during the war. I served under Jerydd. This is a magnificent structure. Allow me to give you a tour."

This brought a glare from Salyndra. She glared at people a lot, and this revealed far more about her than the Art was willing to explain. Esrahaddon had known others who glared, who bit their tongues but screamed with their eyes. Offman was a good example—so was Esrahaddon's Aunt Tadesha. They both were people who wanted to be in control, but weren't.

Silently screaming, Salyndra watched as the emperor nodded and Krem took control.

"Follow me," the Miralyith said and began walking backward like a practiced docent. "Legend says that Fane Fenelyus Mira used the Art to sculpt this tower over the course of three days while standing on a rock on the east bank. That stone is something of a shrine now, as it represents the birthplace of the greatest Artistic achievement ever created. Avempartha is a temple to the Art—the Miralyith's church, our holy place."

As he spoke, he led them through an archway into a series of chambers and then up the stairs, whose railings appeared to be curling tendrils of creeping vines. Nothing was without adornment, every inch imbued with beauty and care. They passed a giant statue of a magnificent swan taking flight and a bubbling fountain in the shape of a school of fish. There was a music to the place. The muted humming of the falls created a low, comforting pulse. The wind across the tips of the tower played as flutes—soft reassuring tones. The bubbling and trickling of fountains only added to the gentle rhythms.

"Allow me to show you the holiest of holies, the chamber of *Valentryne Layartren.*"

Artistic Vision.

Krem led them across a short but narrow bridge spanning a disturbingly deep gap to a tall arched doorway. Here the Miralyith stopped and sighed. He gestured at the blank outline. "Jerydd double-locked this. Would you be so kind?" he asked Nareion.

Once more, the emperor touched the wall, then granted permission to each.

Stepping inside was like walking into the interior of a hollow ball. Massive, smooth chamber walls showed no mark, crack, or seam. The only feature was a zigzagging stone staircase that rose from the floor to a platform that extended out from the steps and stood at the exact center of the sphere.

Just entering the space, Esrahaddon felt the power. It vibrated across the surface of his skin and raised the hair on his scalp.

"This is the heart and mind of Avempartha," Krem said. "From this focal point, the pinnacles above and the roots of the cliff combine with the flow of the water to grant an Artist unprecedented clarity of sight."

Esrahaddon sensed more. He could hear voices.

"Do you remember the Plesieantic Incantations I taught you, Arista?"

"Um . . . the, ah . . ."

"Do you or don't you?"

"I'm thinking."

"Think faster; this is no time for slow wits."

"Yes, I remember. Lord, but you've gotten testy."

The voices were faint, distant, and muffled, as if they came from outside and he was hearing them through the walls. The words were also strange, another dialect of some sort, and he struggled to work out their meaning.

"Are we the only ones in here?" Esrahaddon asked Krem, using his rudimentary Fhrey and hoping not to make a fool of himself. "I'm hearing voices."

"Voices?" Krem showed no trouble understanding him but seemed a dash surprised. Why, exactly, Esrahaddon wasn't able to determine. Maybe the comment about voices, or the fact he spoke Fhrey, or perhaps he sensed Esrahaddon's power despite his efforts to mask it.

"Who are you?" the Miralyith asked.

"He's the prince's tutor," Offman answered for him, offering his own glare.

"Oh, I see." Krem's voice suggested disappointment and disregard. "As I was saying, within these walls . . ."

Esrahaddon heard the voices again. They were coming from above. He needed to get closer.

As Krem continued to speak to the gathered group at the base of the stairs, Esrahaddon began to climb. With each step toward the platform, the words grew louder and clearer.

"I'll apologize later. Now, when we get up there, you are going to stand in the middle of the platform on the mark laid out on the floor as the apex. You will begin and maintain the Plesieantic Phrase. Start with the Gathering Incantation; when you do, you will likely feel a bit more of a jolt than you would normally because this place will amplify your power to gather resources. Don't be alarmed, don't stop the incantation, and whatever you do, don't scream."

"Esrahaddon?" the emperor called.

"Once you feel the power moving through your body, begin the Torsonic Chant. As you do, you will need to form the Crystal Matrix with your fingers, making certain you fold inward, not outward."

"So with my thumbs pointing out and the rest of my fingers pointing at me, right?"

"Yes. This is all basic formations, Arista."

"I know it, I know it—it's just been a while. I've been busy being Melengar's ambassador, not sitting in my tower practicing conjurations."

"Esrahaddon!"

He turned to discover he was nearly to the platform.

"We are leaving," the emperor said. "Please join us."

Esrahaddon was only three tiers from the center. *Who are they? Why can't anyone else hear?*

With a sigh, he turned around and returned to the group as Krem led them back out.

"What was that all about?" Jerish asked when Esrahaddon caught back up.

"Don't know. I was overhearing a distant conversation. You didn't hear anything?"

"No, but I'm not an Artist."

"What does that—oh . . . oh?" He considered this. "The tower sends and receives. I suppose I could have been overhearing anyone, then. If this place is as powerful as he says, then it could have been literally anyone, anywhere on the face of Elan."

"What were they saying?" Nevrik asked.

"They were discussing basic Artistic exercises. The odd thing was . . ." Esrahaddon reran the words in his head. "I think they were here. They were talking about standing on the platform."

"Maybe it was a sort of echo?" Nevrik suggested. "Maybe you were hearing voices from the past."

Would such a thing be possible? Esrahaddon shook his head. "No, that's not it. They weren't speaking elvish, and if that were the case, they would have to be."

Esrahaddon had another reason he didn't think it was an echo from the past or even from some faraway place. He was fairly certain one of the voices had been his own.

CHAPTER FORTY-THREE

As Light Fades

Krem continued his tour of the tower, taking them up a multitude of stairs and across open bridges that connected the spires. He paused to describe the various rooms and chambers, providing mysterious names such as a meeting room known as *Minith Dar Dane*, which Esrahaddon guessed might mean Explain What I Don't Know, a section of dormitories with a name that translated to Little Talwara, and the eating hall, simply called The Strawberry. The emperor made a joke that after so many stairs he wished The Strawberry were still operating. In response, Salyndra promptly drew one of her group aside and ordered him to fetch food and clean a space for eating. Though Nareion had shown no animosity since the door opened, the Curator displayed a fear of reprisal and a lust to survive.

Esrahaddon wondered what she'd think if she knew the truth. He also wondered what was going through Nareion's head. Had being ruler of the world for so many years made it easy to expect subservience from everyone? Had he expected nothing less? Or was he still sweating it? Did he just want to escape now that he'd put out the sparks—worried that every additional second provided another opportunity for someone, anyone, to make a mistake and ruin the whole thing? Esrahaddon didn't bother probing; he wouldn't find any answers.

Near the top, they entered a room that Krem referred to as a war memorial. Cordoned off by a delicate chain, a rack mounted to the wall held swords in ornate cases. A plaque on a pedestal stood before the rack. It read:

TO THE MEMORY OF THE BRAVE HEROES WHO SACRIFICED THEIR LIVES AND THEIR LOVED ONES IN DEFENSE OF THEIR HOMELAND.

All the swords appeared identical. Esrahaddon could see etchings clearly cut into each blade and notches hewn into the metal. Only one of them was unnotched.

"We call this the Hall of Regret," Krem told them as they gathered around to peer at the display. The artist, who had been sketching as he wandered, worked in earnest to capture the scene.

"Why regret?" Nareion asked.

"Each one of these swords was made when a Miralyith had to kill someone they loved. They did it to create a gilarabrywn." Seeing no understanding, he explained, "A creature formed by the Art from the intense power generated by both the loss of life and from the immeasurable, unimaginable pain an Artist feels in sacrificing the one they love. This was done, they were told, to save our people from obliteration. The gilarabrywns would be unstoppable, as no mortal weapon can harm them. Even the Art is useless. They would protect our homes from the coming hordes of Rhunes, I mean humans. Each sword has the incantation of the weave on one side of the blade. The name—the true name of the one sacrificed—gets impressed on the other by the spirit as it leaves. But . . ." Krem placed his hand on the case of the sword that was unnotched. "The gilarabrywns were never used. The war just ended.

"Nyphron blew the Horn of Gylindora, came here, fought Prince Mawyndulë, and won the war. It was over. We had lost. There was no bloodshed, no murderous rampage. Everyone just went home like nothing happened." He walked along the chain, touching the cases. "All these people, all these lovely Fhrey with so many centuries ahead of them, died for nothing. And then, just to rub salt into the wound, once Nyphron became fane, he ordered all the gilarabrywns destroyed. These swords were brought here to represent each creature. As they were slaughtered, each blade was notched. In every case, the one who created the gilarabrywn was also the one to destroy it. They had to be. How could they allow anyone else? But this forced them to relive that pain, with the added torture of knowing it had all been for nothing." He opened his arms toward the display. "We made this memorial the day before Jerydd sealed the tower."

"That sword doesn't have a notch," Nareion said.

Krem looked over. "No, it doesn't. The destruction of each gilarabrywn had to be witnessed by a human, who then made the notch. As you can expect, destroying the last remnant of the one you love was deeply personal. That sword was created by two young lovers who had only just found each other. They were at the start of their lives together. Full of hope and joy even in the midst of war, they were happy because they had each other. Then the order came down from Lothian and imposed by Jerydd. The sacrifice was horrible, but it was said to be for the greater good. Only, of course, it wasn't. So when the time came to sacrifice their loved one a second time, the idea of being gaped at by the enemy was too much to ask. This one wasn't notched because it wasn't witnessed."

The tour concluded on this somber note. The stairs continued up, and Esrahaddon expected the climax of the visit to be the view from the top, but Krem stopped there, and they all filed back down.

This was the first contact with a representative of the fane in two thousand years, and Salyndra insisted they discuss topics of great concern for both cultures. She suggested they enjoy a meal, then hold a discussion to speak about a broad spectrum of subjects. The emperor reluctantly agreed.

Concerns vanished and tensions faded as the terrible threat passed unrealized. For the first time in days, Nevrik once more smiled like a twelve-year-old boy.

As they descended the stairs toward The Strawberry and gained their first scents of cooking food, Esrahaddon found himself walking beside Krem. The Miralyith did not look terribly old. By human standards, he appeared to be in his late fifties, or he might be older and just wearing it well. The Fhrey in general did seem to age more gracefully.

"Did you actually see Mawyndulë?" Esrahaddon asked him.

Krem looked over as if surprised to discover someone there. "Ah, the tutor." He smiled. "Yes, I met him on more than one occasion."

"What was he like?"

"You want the truth or the legend?"

"Truth, please."

"He was an idiot, easily manipulated by a variety of people for their own personal interests. And when he realized this, he threw a tantrum. Left only to his own resources, which were minuscule, he was soundly beaten by the first person who didn't need him."

"Nyphron."

"Yes." Krem frowned. "Our fate was decided by a spoiled brat—one of the many absurdities of that time."

"He survived though, right?"

Krem nodded. "Nyphron scored points with the Miralyith by sparing the prince. We were all poised to launch an uprising the moment he killed Mawyndulë. Letting him live was the single smartest thing that Instarya ever did."

"How old would Mawyndulë be now?"

"Assuming he's still alive, which is doubtful—the kid didn't know enough to feed himself, and after his defeat, the brat was cast out, left to fend for himself. But if he did survive, I would guess him to be in his early two thousands."

"Is that old for a Fhrey?"

"It's not young, certainly, but I'm older."

"Any distinguishing features?"

Krem shrugged. "Not really. Why are you asking?"

"He's a fascinating historical figure, isn't he? Don't you wonder what became of him?"

"My hope is that he died from injuries inflicted by Nyphron after a few days of lingering misery. Although . . ." He paused just before the entrance to the eating hall. "There would be a certain satisfaction in him living to an old age."

"Why is that?"

"Would serve him right. He hated old people—always used to call them *dusty*. I don't think anyone ever knew why. That boy was just strange."

After eating, the emperor, Offman, and the others planned to sit down with the Aquila in one of the meeting rooms in the tower. Nevrik, Esrahaddon, Ulin, and Jerish didn't bother to stay for the meal. The moment the emperor excused them for the rest of the day, Nevrik begged to leave.

"The sun will be going down," the prince argued. "We only have a few more hours of light."

Esrahaddon was not surprised the emperor didn't insist on his son staying. What was to follow would be the long, dry acts of politics and diplomacy, and while it might be good for the prince to witness the process, this was a special situation. After that day, Esrahaddon guessed "that day" would be expunged from history. The fewer the witnesses, the easier the cleanup. The Teshlors remained, as did Offman. Councilors Sadarshakar and Hanis also stayed to continue their role as translators, but it was obvious they hoped to help shape the treaty to come. Esrahaddon didn't think there would be any treaty or official framework. The emperor had convinced the elves that Nyphron was still alive. The threat was averted, for now, at least. This was all theatrics, and soon the lid would be nailed down again, the problem locked back in the Vault, and the Imperial Province of Erivania quarantined once more.

Freed from obligation and parental oversight, Nevrik raced down the empty corridors. Eager to explore all the rooms and chambers, the prince ran far ahead, then slid on the dust-covered floors, leaving long streaks.

"With all this energy, we should use the remaining day's light to practice," Jerish called after him.

Esrahaddon doubted the boy even heard him. "Give it up, Jerish. There's no competing with all this. But I do wonder where he's getting the endurance from. We should go back to camp and get something to eat."

"They were going to serve us an entire meal," Ulin pointed out. "Why didn't you stay?"

"No one said we *had* to leave," Jerish said. "You could have eaten."

Esrahaddon shook his head. "I didn't see the rest of you looking to stay."

"Not a comfortable place to eat," Jerish said. "Tension and appetite don't mix."

"It's not like we're destitute or will suffer boiled cabbage round a dismal fire," Ulin said. "We travel with the imperial chef, remember? And it's getting late. He'll have something hot by now."

"Getting late?" Nevrik's head popped out from inside a little doorway. "We need to explore the waterfall before it gets dark!"

The prince raced off but still paused frequently to look at things and explore rooms.

"Careful on the stairs!" Esrahaddon yelled as Nevrik ran down them. "They're wet!"

"Practice your balance drills on the way down," Jerish called, then sighed. "At least he's normal again."

Esrahaddon felt strangely old, wishing for a handrail as he struggled to descend the stairs that the prince was jumping two at a time. "I don't think Nevrik could ever be called *normal*."

Nearing the bottom, the prince stopped and pointed up. "What are those?"

Massive sweeping banners hung overhead, held in place by long, braided cords with luxurious tassels. Easily five stories tall, and by far the largest textiles Esrahaddon had ever seen, they were adorned with only a single symbol each.

"They represent the elements of the Art," Esrahaddon replied. "At least, I think so."

"You don't know?" Nevrik asked with unaccustomed glee.

"We were on the same tour together, weren't we? How could I—" But the boy was off again.

He really is just a child—gifted and incredibly intelligent, but still a boy.

Esrahaddon and Jerish didn't catch up to the prince until they were outside. The last of the sun was just above the horizon, illuminating that side of the tower with a golden brilliance and casting the other in deep-blue shadow. Some Fhrey were outside, either unable to get in or just waiting. They spoke quietly among themselves, glancing up only briefly as the prince and his companions made their boisterous exit. Krem was among the gathered Fhrey and took more interest, staring at them a while. Offman was also outside. Standing far away from the Fhrey, he was sweaty and pale. He grimaced at Esrahaddon. "Elven food doesn't suit me." He placed a hand on his stomach.

"How bad?"

Offman looked toward the edge. "The cool mist from the falls is helping, but I keep thinking that jumping would help more." A hand went to his mouth as his eyes bulged. "Excuse me."

Nevrik had paused to study an assortment of wet elven garments lying on the stone and drying in the sun.

"What are these made out of?" the boy asked. "Not linen or wool. They shimmer."

Jerish looked expectantly at Esrahaddon.

"Elven history wasn't one of my interests." He faced Ulin and shrugged apologetically. "Sorry—just didn't seem important at the time."

She smiled back with understanding eyes. "I never had much interest in humans, either."

"This is fun," Nevrik said.

"What is?"

"You don't know any more than I do. Sort of levels the playing field between us, doesn't it?"

"No, not at all," Esrahaddon replied. "I'm still taller."

They moved to the front edge of the promontory rock, to the point where the prow became a true precipice, beyond which was nothing but a misty void.

"Nevrik," Esrahaddon said as fear caught hold of him.

There's nothing but a two-thousand-foot drop over that edge. If he slips, if he falls, he'll plummet like an eighty-five-pound rock. I doubt I could save him.

The prince walked right out to the point.

"NEVRIK!" Esrahaddon roared.

Jerish and even Ulin leaped forward, arms out, but the boy stopped and lay down on his belly to peer over the edge. The others slowly lowered their arms and took a breath. He was still out there, but this was better—not much, but some.

"We could just give him a shove, you know?" Esrahaddon told the others, as Nevrik waved his arms, claiming he was flying in a cloud. "Life would be so much easier."

"I heard that," the boy said.

"Oh? You didn't hear me calling, but you heard *that?*"

"No, I heard both."

"Brat."

"Commoner."

"Excuse me?" Esrahaddon added a parental tone.

"This time, maybe. And don't you mean *pardon me?*" Nevrik got up and turned around to show his grin. Then his eyes widened as he looked up over their heads. "Wow. Look at that." He pointed.

"Beautiful," Ulin said.

"A little rainbow. Maybe it's a sign," Jerish offered. "A portent of unity between the two races. You must admit this feels historic, doesn't it? Like everything is about to change."

Esrahaddon didn't look. He refused to take his eyes off the prince until Nevrik was off the precipice. He grabbed the boy's wrist and pulled him back from the edge.

"It's fading," Nevrik said as he was hauled forward.

"Sun's gone," Ulin explained.

"Yes, it is, and it's starting to get cold," Esrahaddon said. "And look at you." He stared at the prince. "No cloak and only a light tunic. You're getting soaked in this mist. We should—"

"What's that?" Nevrik pointed up in the sky again.

"We can't keep playing *what's that*," Esrahaddon said.

"But something flew into the window at the top of the tower."

"Probably a bird, or at this hour maybe a bat."

"Too big."

Esrahaddon looked up at the distant pinnacle that was now a black silhouette against a dark blue sky already displaying the first stars of evening. "How could you tell in this light? And at this distance, size would be difficult to pin down."

Nevrik continued to peer, squinting his eyes. "It also had a tail. We should go back in."

Esrahaddon had no intention of going back in, but he made the mistake of letting go of his charge's wrist. The prince sprang with the speed of a rabbit and disappeared through the still-open door.

"I blame you," Esrahaddon told Jerish, who looked back, stumped.

Reentering the tower, they spotted Nevrik only a few steps up the stairs. He'd stopped, his head tilted up.

"Nevrik," Esrahaddon called.

The boy held up a quieting hand as he continued to listen.

"What now?" Esrahaddon asked, but before the prince could answer, they all heard the screams.

Overhead, the cries and crash of metal cascaded down like torrential rain, which grew louder by the second. When they spotted the emperor racing down the stairs, all of them started to run up the steps toward him.

"Out!" he shouted at them. "Get Nevrik out!"

They each hesitated a moment, confused. Then they saw it—an enormous black-scaled lizard with wings of gray membrane and bone. It fought with the Teshlors, who were all that stood between it and the emperor. Muscular claws were armed with huge black talons that bashed as well as sliced at the Teshlors. Long sharp fangs protruded from beneath leathery lips, as did a row of frightening teeth that followed no visible scheme but seemed to mesh together like a wild fence of needles. Its ears lay back upon its head, and its vertical pupils didn't focus on the warriors before it. Instead, it stared at the emperor.

Jerish acted first. Grabbing Nevrik, he dragged the boy out.

Esrahaddon stood motionless, frozen by the sight of knights dying on the stairs. Then to his shock, he saw the elves—honor guards in blue armor and even the members of the Aquila. They came up from behind and attacked the monster in an attempt to stop it, or at least slow it down. As the men and elves died, the stairs and walls were painted with tears of blood.

Raising his hand, Esrahaddon began a weave. The space was tight. *Fire: too unwieldy. Lightning: too erratic.* Instead, he formed a spear of light that he could send with precision through the thing's eye into its head. He'd drop it where it was. Then as the creature killed another elf, tossing him aside like a doll, Esrahaddon shot his brilliant javelin. His aim was perfect, but upon impact the spear winked out. Nothing happened.

The creature's not real. It's the Art. The idea hit Esrahaddon like a return blow. *The Art manifested into corporeal form. I've never seen anything like it. The Art can't affect itself. It's . . . it's . . .*

"The gilarabrywns would be unstoppable, as no mortal weapon can harm them."

Esrahaddon gasped as he realized the full truth. *It's a gilarabrywn, but not just any one. This is the last beast, the one whose sword wasn't notched.*

Esrahaddon watched in horror as the emperor ran down the steps.

So high still, so many steps, so far to go.

He isn't going to make it.

"Save my son!" Nareion cried.

He knows it, too.

Only . . . Esrahaddon realized, *there's no way I can.*

Once the beast killed the emperor, once the gilarabrywn cleared the tower, the creature would circle on those terrible wings and snatch up Nevrik like a bunny in an open field.

"No mortal weapon can harm them, and even the Art is useless."

"I can't do anything to it," Esrahaddon cursed himself. "No one can, not even Yolric could—"

"Even if someone opens the doors to Castell Blythium, it won't matter—Mileva, her spirit—will not be able to escape . . . The enchantment is placed on the structure, not the prisoner."

"Thank you, Yolric!" Esrahaddon ran out, where he found Jerish still holding Nevrik. Ulin and Offman flanked them, all staring back, frightened. "Jerish! I need it slowed down. I need time or we'll all die!"

Jerish looked at the tower, then at the prince. That was all it took. No questions, no explanation. Without another word or a second passing, the man drew his swords and ran inside. Ulin followed.

"Offman! Watch Nevrik!" Esrahaddon barked. Then working as fast as he could, Esrahaddon struggled to recall the lesson Yolric had taught him.

What had been a novelty then, an entertaining bit of shop talk, was now life and death. Power was no problem. Standing on the edge of the falls, he had all he needed—like trying to spark a flame in a forest fire. The weave wasn't intricate, just unusual. It wasn't the sort of thing anyone ever did. He needed to drape the entire tower within a thin blanket of resistance. The weave was based on the same principle as the defensive shield, only this would be massive. While enveloping such a huge structure was a challenge, the hard part of the weave—the true genius that Yolric had showed him—was how to make the result *permanent*. Still, it took time, and Esrahaddon couldn't afford to get it wrong. He'd only have the one chance.

As he wove like a manic spider, Esrahaddon was only a few feet from the open door. With the loss of sunlight, the interior grew dark. It didn't matter; he closed his eyes anyway. He needed to concentrate. Still, he couldn't block out the sound of fighting. He heard the emperor once more beg for them to protect his son.

"Nareion! No!" Jerish shouted.

The beast roared.

Ulin cried out, "Jerish!"

That's when Esrahaddon made two fists. He folded one over the other and pulled them apart as if jerking tight an invisible knot. This was, in fact, exactly what he did, and not more than a heartbeat later, he heard a tremendous crash. Opening his eyes, he stood face to face with the monster.

The thing pressed itself hard up against the open space of the doorway as if it were a clear window. The beast slammed his head against the weave, then roared in frustration.

"It's trapped," Esrahaddon shouted. "Everyone out!"

The monster's huge eyes focused on Nevrik. Throwing its full body against the opening, it hit hard and bounced back, appearing hurt.

Esrahaddon smiled at it. "Welcome to your cage, my little bird," he said, then repeated it in Fhrey.

Hearing the words, the beast glared at him. It took a deep breath and breathed fire. The torrent of flames splashed against the exit, spraying in every direction except out. The Entrance Hall filled with fire and smoke, causing the creature itself to recoil and then retreat.

Esrahaddon felt sick as he realized that Jerish, Ulin, and Nareion were in that inferno. Whatever hope he had that they had survived the attack with healable wounds went up in those flames whose heat he couldn't even feel. Turning, he saw Nevrik standing before Offman, who hugged the boy. The prince had tears in his eyes as he clutched Offman's hand.

Entering the tower, Jerish saw the emperor coming down the last of the spiraling staircases. He was doing well for an old man—far more agile than he ever appeared sitting on that giant throne. Despite his unexpected athletics, he wasn't in the lead. Ahead of him were three Fhrey dressed in stained aprons—one still holding a two-pronged fork and a metal spatula and screaming like he was on fire. Behind Nareion, the two councilors, Sadarshakar and Hanis, looked as if they could pass the emperor, but neither did. Jerish couldn't figure out if it was loyalty or fear that kept them back. If loyalty, their bravery was impressive; if it was fear of imperial repercussions, they were an amazingly optimistic pair. Behind the councilors was a gap of several steps. Then came the monster.

The thing was huge, bigger by far than any animal Jerish had ever seen, with teeth and claws the size of long daggers. Reptilian in appearance, it nonetheless moved like a bird, racing down the stairs on two legs, using its wings for balance, not unlike a chicken. Its size ought to have slowed it down. Nothing that big could run so fast—but the wings helped. The space along the staircase was too small to afford a full deployment, but even a partial spread allowed the beast to take short jumps, gliding down two and three steps at a time.

Years of studying movement and spatial relationships gave Jerish the famous Teshlor precognition that granted him the ability to predict where and when a foot would fall or a sword would hit. It took only an instant for him to gauge the race for the exit as too tight to call. The doorway, however, was big. Even if the emperor won the race to the outside, the monster would catch him a step or two later. The only hope anyone had was that Esrahaddon could do something.

What that might be, he hadn't a clue. Jerish remembered the Miralyith saying the monster was immune to weapons and magic, which made an already daunting task nearly impossible. The only reason Jerish granted the proviso of *nearly* was because the Cenzar had amazed him several times before. As bad as Cenzars were supposed to be, there was no one he'd rather have backing him up at a time like this. Esrahaddon had asked for time; that's what Jerish aimed to provide.

He sprinted forward to the base of the stairs. Ulin was right behind, her footfalls lighter, quieter.

"There was a whole detachment of Teshlor Knights up there," she said in between breaths. "They couldn't stop it. What are we doing?"

"Slowing it down." Jerish ran up the steps, cutting the distance between him and the emperor. He didn't have to go far. Speed wasn't the problem. Timing was the challenge. Everyone would live or die based on a two- or three-second window of opportunity.

This is what I'm good at, he reminded himself, and hoped he was telling the truth.

The beast cleared the narrow stairwell and began descending the wide-open steps of the Entrance Hall: a large space graced with a high, vaulted ceiling. It slowed and paused for just a moment. Jerish read the muscles in its powerful legs as the creature fully extended its wings.

"Save my son!" The emperor cried out.

Nareion sees the future, too—of course he does. Not that hard to guess.

With room to fly, the monster would swoop down like a hawk over a parade of mice. Apparently, the emperor didn't wish to die a mouse. He stopped running, turned, and drew his sword.

"Nareion! No!" Jerish shouted.

The beast roared, seeing victory.

"Jerish!" Ulin cried out.

Jerish slashed at the ornate braided cords lashed to anchors mounted in the wall. The cords were as thick as ship mooring cables, but two sharp blades striking the same place in quick succession cut them clean.

The beast shoved off the steps, wings wide. Gaining lift, it flew forward and swooped down, then—

The massive banner fell on it. The sheer weight of that great drape folded the creature's wings, and the beast plummeted. To avoid being crushed, Nareion, the councilors, Jerish, and Ulin ran back up as the monster hit just below them and rolled down the remaining steps, further tangling itself in the banner and the attached cord. Hitting the bottom, the beast looked like a dog with a blanket wrapped around its head. The creature righted itself, shook, then roared.

The elven cooks, who had reached the main floor, also narrowly missed being crushed. One fell. The other two paused to help him up. Then they ran once more for the exit where Jerish could see Esrahaddon doing something Artistic with his hands.

Hurry! Jerish shouted at Esrahaddon in his head. *That's all the time I can buy!*

Having fallen past them, the beast was between everyone and the exit, so continuing down made no sense. Going back up made not much more. This left the emperor, his councilors, Jerish, and Ulin standing and watching as the dog threw off its blanket.

The creature spotted the cooks first, killing each with a swipe of its talons as they attempted to get by. Then seeing Esrahaddon standing in the open doorway, it charged.

Jerish held his breath as the creature slammed into an invisible wall.

"It's trapped!" Esrahaddon shouted. "Everyone out!"

Ulin, the emperor, Hanis, and Jerish all looked at one another with the same hopeless expression.

"Back up!" Sadarshakar whispered, pointing vaguely toward the upper story. "There's a window."

The monster threw itself against the doorway over and over as they climbed, trying to be just as silent as they were quick.

"Welcome to your cage, my little bird," Esrahaddon said. Then he spoke something else in Frhey.

A moment later, the room below became filled with fire.

CHAPTER FORTY-FOUR

Fallout

"*Open the tower!*"

Esrahaddon heard the words spoken in Fhrey and turned to see Krem marching over the wet clothes as if they were rugs. The Miralyith wore a nasty, irritated expression. But oddly, Krem wasn't addressing Esrahaddon. He was speaking to Offman, who continued to stand off to the side, his hands on Nevrik's shoulders such that Esrahaddon couldn't tell if he was protecting the boy or just using him to stay on his feet. The comment itself was bizarre but even more peculiar given that Offman didn't speak Fhrey.

"What?" Offman asked, bewildered.

"Release Indus immediately!" Krem demanded with a murderous glare in his eyes.

Offman looked to Esrahaddon for help. "What does he want?"

"Ah, the tutor. Wonderful," Krem said without looking. He kept his eyes on Offman, as if the Cenzar were a poisonous snake in the house and Krem needed Esrahaddon to hand him a rake. *"Tell him to open the tower. That is my beloved Indus he's trapped."*

Beloved Indus? That didn't sound right. Esrahaddon wasn't fluent in Fhrey. For all he knew, Krem might have said his slippers were stuck in the tower. There was more to it, though. *Didn't he see what happened? Maybe not. He was far from the door. But then how did he know the tower had been sealed? Maybe he saw me perform the weave? Then why is he accusing Offman? And if he knew that, why didn't he know the seal was a barrier only to the Art? He could walk straight in and get whatever he wanted, assuming he could avoid the giant, fire-breathing serpent.* All of it was far too much effort to work out, and Esrahaddon couldn't care less. He felt like his family had just died in a freak accident and some lunatic was yelling about losing his cat.

"He can't open it." Esrahaddon wiped a hand over his face as he watched the fire still burning inside the tower. *Too much smoke, too many shifting shadows, but I can see bodies—charred bodies.* Esrahaddon was numb, not because he couldn't feel but because he felt too many things at once. His mind was still sorting through the wreckage that had gone from a rainbow to a lethal inferno in only minutes. *"He didn't seal it. I did."*

"You?" Krem asked. *"How could—Oh . . . I see now. The tutor is also an Artist. You're shielding your power. Clever, but I don't care who did it. Undo it—now! Let her out."*

Some part of Esrahaddon, possibly even Elan herself, told him it wasn't healthy to keep looking inside. Dwelling on horror was never wise. It led to anguish, and anger—not a good direction for an Artist to wander when destruction was always so easy, so enticing. At moments like this, the average man might turn to drink—Artists had other, far worse intoxicants available.

Esrahaddon forced his eyes away from the flames and looked at Krem. *"Who are you talking about? Who is Indus?"*

"My beloved," he replied, shedding no light at all. Then he looked up at the top of the tower. *"It's a shame Nyphron himself didn't show. That would have been justice. But life, my little tutor, isn't fair. You'll learn that—learn it very soon."* He studied his own hands. *"I could have killed them myself, but how would that have helped? She needs to be the one. This is her victory, her reward. Don't you see? This was the reason for her sacrifice—she died for this."*

Indus is the . . . Esrahaddon glanced back at the fire. The beast was gone. It had left the doorway and retreated into the dark. *That sword. The one without the notch . . .*

With a grunt, Offman collapsed. Krem hadn't done anything. *Did Offman just faint?*

"I don't know what you did, but open the tower, tutor. She deserves it. She needs to be let out." He looked then at Nevrik, who had turned to help Offman. *"She's not done."*

Esrahaddon's eyes narrowed as finally at least part of the mystery cleared. *"You did this."* His numbness wore off as one emotion pushed to the front of the line.

Krem grew irritated. *"Did you hear m—"*

Esrahaddon's hand shot out, palm open, and Krem flew several feet through the air, slamming hard on his back just inches from the precipice.

That was an accident, Esrahaddon realized with real concern. He hadn't meant to do it. He'd just struck without thought. If he had paused to consider his actions, he never would have taken the chance that he might throw Krem off the falls. He didn't want that. Now that the picture was coming clearer, he didn't want it to end so soon.

Krem made the gilarabrywn. He had killed his lover, sacrificed her centuries ago, but refused to follow Nyphron's order to destroy his creation—his machine of war. Finding that the heirs of Nyphron had come to the tower, he sent the gilarabrywn in the open window. Krem had his hated mice trapped in a barrel, and like a cruel child, he dropped in a starving cat.

Nevrik bent over Offman, trying to help the old man sit up, but the Cenzar master appeared limp, his head swinging freely from his neck.

Esrahaddon gave Krem a moment to regain his breath and then the time to stand up. While he waited, in his mind Esrahaddon remembered a summer's day in the Imperial Palace.

"Jerish Grelad is one of our more accomplished graduates. Our only one this year."

"Him," the boy suddenly said.

"What's that?" The emperor looked down.

"I want him as well."

Krem stepped into his attack like a warrior and sent a blast of blue fire with one hand and a jagged bolt of lightning with the other. Esrahaddon didn't bother with a shield. He swatted both aside with counterforce. The blasts impacted on the tower, leaving black scorch marks.

"Why? Because he was late?" the emperor asked his son.

The boy shook his head. "No. He wasn't late."

The Miralyith had his shield up by then—a fine one: thick, sturdy, and strong. Esrahaddon opened his palm and poured out pure power. A broad beam of white light slammed against the shield, sparking along the surface, revealing the entirety of it.

"You can't beat me this way!" Krem declared, but there was a hint of concern in his voice. After all, the Miralyith wasn't an idiot—just a murderer. He saw the width of that beam, felt the shudder push him back closer to the edge. *"We both pull from the same source! We're at a stalemate."*

"No, we are not." Esrahaddon poured it on. The beam grew wider.

Krem dug in his heels but was being forced closer and closer to the drop. The Miralyith's eyes went wide as the light began to melt his shield, starting at the edges. And like an ice cube, the thing just kept getting smaller.

"I told him if he got into trouble, he shouldn't mention me. Well, he kept his word . . . And you still have no idea who I am, do you? . . . That's why."

Esrahaddon saw the terror on Krem's face as his shield was reduced to the size of a dinner plate. *"We aren't pulling from the same source,"* he explained. *"You're only using the falls."*

The shield disintegrated. The moment it fell, Esrahaddon stopped his attack, leaving Krem exhausted, shocked, and confused.

Esrahaddon was more than happy to enlighten him. After all, he was a tutor.

"You killed them all," he said. *"Everyone at the feast, and Ulin, but worst of all you killed my . . . you killed my friend—you killed Jerish—and I don't have a lot of friends."*

The Miralyith's eyes widened. *"You're like her!"* he said. *"You're like Suri, the girl at the river, the one Jerydd ordered me to kill. You're just like her!"*

"No, I'm not." Esrahaddon reached out with both hands, and with a word, he folded his fingers, then ran one fist over the other and drew them apart. The movement was similar to how he'd tied the knot on the tower, but this time he wasn't binding. As his fists crossed over each other, his arms stopped for just a moment as if his hands had caught on something. Krem cried, and when Esrahaddon pulled hard, the upper half of the Miralyith went one way and the lower went the other as slowly, horribly, Krem was ripped in half. "Right now, I'm more like Mashie."

Sadarshakar led them to a room two flights up. The chamber was small, meant perhaps as a cloak room or storage space. Being empty, its purpose was impossible to determine, but it did have a door and a window. Tall but narrow, the opening was further divided vertically by a single stone mullion. Still, Jerish felt they could all squeeze out—until he looked down.

"It's too far," he told them.

The emperor put his head out as well, and when he turned, he nodded. "Not only that, it's right on the edge of the falls. If we jump, there's just as much chance of hitting the water as the stone, and either will kill us."

"The rope," Ulin said, pointing back at the carefully closed and latched door—a mere wooden door. "The cord that Jerish cut!"

"Burned up," Hanis told her. The councilor looked like he was freezing as he held himself in a tight hug with his bony shoulders raised and his head down.

"There are more of them farther up. More banners." Ulin continued to point.

"That thing is still out there." Hanis spoke an octave higher than normal. He looked just a few breaths away from a scream, but for now he was still holding himself together.

"It might think we're dead," Jerish said as much to calm fears as to extend a plan. "If we wait—"

"It doesn't think we're dead," Ulin whispered.

Jerish didn't like the way she contradicted him even before he was finished. He expected better from her than from someone like Hanis. A trained fighter should be capable of handling stress. The odd thing was her sudden switch to whispering, which left him uneasy.

"No, it doesn't," Sadarshakar whispered back. "It's looking for us."

Jerish studied them both. "How do you know?"

Ulin tapped the side of her head. "Fhrey ears. We can hear it talking."

"Talking? It can talk? Who's it talking to?"

"Itself, I think," Emperor Nareion said. "Maybe us."

They all nodded, each looking terrified.

"It knows we're still here—still alive."

Jerish put his hand on the window sill. "We need to get you out of this window, Your Eminence." He looked at Ulin. "To do that, we need to get the cord that's holding up the next banner."

"Anyone going out there will draw its attention." Hanis said. "This room is too small for it to get in. Can't we just stay here?"

"Did you miss the part with the fire? It doesn't need to *get in*," Ulin replied.

"I'll go," Jerish said.

Ulin shook her head. "It's a two-person job. One to get the rope and bring it back, the other to distract the beast long enough for His Eminence to escape."

"Fine," Jerish said. "You get the rope. I'll get the monster's attention."

"No." Ulin took his hands in hers. "You can't."

"I'm pretty sure I—"

"Whoever distracts that thing won't be getting out, and you need to live," she told him. Her words were strangely soft and gentle, as if she were putting a child to bed. "You must save him." She nodded toward the emperor. "That's your job. You're a Teshlor. On the other hand, I'm nobody—not even a Fauyld. I'm just a lousy half-blooded myr from a dishonored house. That's who I really am. That's all I'll ever be."

"You're wrong," Nareion said. "You go out that door and you'll be more than that. If I live, I'll see to it. Believe me."

Ulin stared, stunned, tears welling in her eyes. "Thank you."

She stepped toward the door, then stopped and faced Jerish. "Are you ready?"

He didn't answer. He couldn't.

She nodded. "It's all right. It really is. This is all I ever wanted." She kissed him. Through the wet of her lips and the tear-slick cheek sliding on his, he felt her body shaking. Ulin drew back. She was struggling to breathe as she looked to the closed door and laid a hand on the latch. "What was it your father told you about worthiness?"

"Worthiness comes from the heart," Jerish said, finding it so much harder to repeat the principle now than before. "From courage in the face of adversity and fighting a battle with dignity even though you know you can't win. Sometimes you fight and lose because you must. Doing so is right and good and worth it."

"That's right," she said and pulled open the door.

Inside Avempartha, magical fire burned actual furniture and tapestries, producing real smoke and flames that leaked out the door. In the darkness that had finally enveloped the world, the fire burned brightly. Seeing it, people on the bank came running. Esrahaddon saw them moving in a group, a horde that headed for the bridge and came charging.

Nevrik wiped his face with one hand. His other lay on Offman's chest. "He's dead."

Too much is happening too fast, Esrahaddon thought.

Questions were piling into a heap, and he had a paltry handful of answers. Only one thing seemed clear. Nevrik had to be protected. How and from whom was still hazy. At that moment, Esrahaddon felt as if the two of them stood alone and exposed on an open battlefield. He quickly moved to the prince's side and pulled the boy up. "We need to get out of here.".

With the crowd coming at them across the only bridge, leaving wasn't going to be easy. Esrahaddon spotted imperial guards, several servants, the mapmaker, and even the artist who earlier that day had been on the tower tour. There were also several Fhrey. Common servants maybe, but Esrahaddon had no way of knowing. None looked familiar.

"Your robe is turning red again," Nevrik said, his voice shaking.

"Don't worry about it."

"It turned red just before you ripped Krem in half."

Esrahaddon pulled the boy closer. "I said, don't worry about it."

"I can't help it." Nevrik was fixated on the people running at them. "I keep thinking about the burlap bags in the Vault of Days." The prince started to cry. "My father is dead, isn't he?"

"Stay with me, Nevrik. I need you to be strong right now."

"What are you going to do?"

"That all depends on them." Esrahaddon rotated himself and the prince until they were fully facing the onrush of people, their backs to the tower, to the light and the fire.

"Who?"

"Right now?" Esrahaddon lowered his voice the way a dog might growl. "Any sonofabitch that so much as looks at you funny."

"You're going to burlap-bag them, aren't you?"

"Maybe you should just close your eyes."

But the crowd never got close. Instead, they slowed dramatically, then stopped altogether as each face became illuminated by the blood-red glow of his robe. Their eyes were on his, so maybe they saw their own death reflected, or perhaps it was the robe. *It's probably the robe.*

"Where is Nareion?" one of the soldiers found the voice to ask.

Esrahaddon had opened his mouth to answer when—

"I am here!"

Turning, Esrahaddon spotted Emperor Nareion walking up from near the tower. He looked haggard but healthy. With him were the two councilors from Merredydd, and bringing up the rear, Jerish.

Nevrik pulled away and rushed to hug his father. Esrahaddon didn't move. He stared at the four, bewildered. Part of him resisted joy, as stubborn disbelief refused to budge. This was too much to accept. *Life isn't this forgiving.* An invincible monster had attacked; Offman had dropped dead; and no one could have escaped that inferno and yet . . .

"Sorry I couldn't give you any more time," Jerish told him, his voice flat.

Esrahaddon thought he was kidding, making an unaccustomed—and as such—poorly delivered joke, but his face was ashen. Jerish's eyes lost their focus. He had been looking at Esrahaddon, then his stare just slid off. He went on staring, but now at nothing.

It didn't take a genius.

"Ulin—" Esrahaddon started, "she didn't . . . she's not with you."

"No," Jerish said. "She . . ." He swallowed and blinked but didn't look at Esrahaddon—didn't look at anything. Like a blind man, his eyes wandered aimlessly.

"Your Highness," said the foremost Fhrey in the band who had arrived with those from the bank encampment. He was tall, dressed in a damp tunic, leggings, and boots of greens, browns, and yellows. *"What happened?"*

The emperor looked to Sadarshakar.

"This is Irawondona, Your Eminence," the councilor said. "He's not part of the Aquila but was, in fact, the first contact we had here. A leader of some sort. He's asking what happened."

Nareion, still holding his son in a bear grip, raised his brows in surprise. "You tried to kill me, you bastard! And you did manage to murder a dozen good men!"

Irawondona took a step back and began shaking his hands feverishly even before Sadarshakar finished the translation: "No, not at all. The Erivan Nation had nothing to do with this. You must believe me."

"Believe you?" Nareion shouted. "Who else could have? We were attacked by a gilarabrywn! Do you expect me to believe that the Ba Ran Ghazel are making them now? And it wasn't just the flying lizard, either. My men were poisoned!

Everyone who ate with me fell ill and died soon after. My knights could barely stand when the beast attacked!"

Esrahaddon looked to where Offman lay, remembering what he had said, *"Elven food doesn't suit me."*

"Everyone was poisoned—everyone except the Fhrey and myself. So if it wasn't the Erivan Nation, who was it?"

"Krem," Esrahaddon said, drawing the emperor's attention. "The Miralyith was responsible."

"You know this?" Nareion asked.

Esrahaddon nodded. "He was in the Great War. He killed his lover to make a gilarabrywn that was never used. Heartbroken, he refused to destroy her when Nyphron commanded it. He's wanted revenge for nearly two thousand years. He sent the gilarabrywn—his creation, what he saw as his cheated lover—into the tower to do what she was made for: to kill the blood of Nyphron, whom he believed ruined their lives."

"And the poison?"

Esrahaddon thought a moment. "Knights of old—the original Teshlors—they had the Orinfar, yes?"

"Yes," Jerish said, his focus sharp, watching him. "They didn't tattoo it, but they did have it on their armor and weapons."

"Did the elves discover this?"

Emperor Nareion nodded. "They learned humans were using the Orinfar during the Battle of Grandford."

"Well, Krem served in the war, and being Miralyith, he would have likely known, too. He would have realized the flaw in his plan."

"What flaw?" Nareion asked.

"The Orinfar protects Teshlors from the Art, Your Eminence, and a gilarabrywn is the Art."

Sadarshakar was nodding. "I remember. All the cooks and Fhrey servants—they acted differently with him."

Hanis nodded. "I saw that, too. They made a lot of eye contact, as if Krem were the master of the house."

"And he didn't eat," Sadarshakar said. "Not a single bite, not a sip of anything."

"He wasn't taking chances." Hanis's tongue licked his lips, as if he tasted something bitter. "I ate. I was hungry. And I drank the wine."

"They didn't serve us the same thing," Sadarshakar said. "They . . . they couldn't—we're all Fhrey."

"But the gilarabrywn," Hanis replied. "It didn't adhere to the same rule. It would have killed everyone because it isn't Fhrey, and it has no soul to jeopardize. And Krem didn't need to order it to kill us. It was merely following ancient orders ordained by the previous fane."

"There is a secret militant sect among my people," Irawondona said. The Fhrey had likely figured out the drift of the conversation, based on the use of the name Krem, or some rudimentary grasp of the Marn language. It could also have been a blind guess, but it was a good one. *"They have long sought to restart the war. We have struggled to root them out, but many are Miralyith, and none of us has the power of a fane. It's very hard and dangerous to punish Miralyith without it."*

Sadarshakar translated all this, and the emperor gritted his teeth. "Where is Krem now?"

"You don't need to worry about him," Nevrik said. He was still holding onto his father's arm, as if afraid of losing him again. "Esrahaddon killed him."

Everyone stared, even Irawondona, but likely to see what everyone was looking at.

"What happened?" the emperor asked.

"I saw it look at me through the open doorway," the boy said. "I could see it. The thing hated me. It lunged. I cringed, thinking I was dead, but it slammed into Esrahaddon's barrier. Krem thought Cenzar Offman did it." Nevrik pointed at the dead Cenzar master lying on his back, eyes still open. "When Krem discovered it was Esrahaddon, the two fought. Wasn't much of a fight. Esrahaddon, he . . . Krem went . . ." He pointed toward the precipice.

Nareion looked toward the mist rising from the falls. "But being an Artist"—he looked at Esrahaddon—"could this Krem fellow have saved himself?"

Nevrik shook his head. "Krem went over the edge—"

"Yes, I know, Son, but being—"

"—both pieces."

The emperor looked at Nevrik. "I see." Appearing satisfied, his attention shifted to the tower. "Can it get out?"

"No," Esrahaddon replied. "Just as I can do nothing to it, it can do nothing to the barrier I've wrapped the tower in. It will remain in there forever."

"Can another Artist, another Miralyith, break your spell?"

"Possible, but unlikely. It's a strong and unusual weave. I learned it from Yolric. It would take a very skilled Artist to unravel."

The emperor once more nodded his approval. Then he spoke to Sadarshakar while pointing at Irawondona. "Explain to him what we've been saying."

The discussion between the emperor and the elven lords didn't last long. They were begging not to be killed, and Nareion just wanted to leave before something far worse happened. Esrahaddon's robe had lost its luminance, leaving them only the moonlight. Being full, the moon did just fine.

The councilors worked as translators, and Nevrik refused to budge from his father's side. Esrahaddon and Jerish sat a short distance away on the stone near the bridge. They listened to the falls and watched the moonlight make ghostly bright clouds out of the mist, but neither said a word to the other for a long time. Finally, Esrahaddon said, "I'm sorry. I liked her."

Jerish looked over and nodded. "I did, too."

"I guess you lost other friends as well? The Teshlors? You knew them, right?"

Jerish nodded. "I never had much to do with Kendell, but he was a good man. Spencer, I knew. We trained in the academy together, and I can honestly say he was the only boy there who I admired. I wanted to be like him." Jerish looked at the now-dark tower. "Poison is such a strange way for a knight to go. It feels so wrong, so senseless."

Esrahaddon nodded.

"How about you?" Jerish asked. "Offman must have been a father figure or something, right?"

Esrahaddon smiled. "Not even close. More like a disreputable friend of the family."

Jerish looked surprised.

Esrahaddon shrugged. "It's not like I'm happy he's dead. It's just that we were totally different people. I suppose he did what he felt was best. I think we all do. Even Krem."

Jerish raised a brow.

"If I had been him," Esrahaddon said, "if it had been Elinya, I might have done the same."

"I wouldn't have," Jerish muttered, lowering his head and studying the stone upon which he sat, tracing a finger across its surface. "And I think that's why knights have rules. They're a reminder. It isn't about us."

"What isn't?"

"Everything. We're just here for a moment—one drop of rain helping to fill a bucket. The bucket is what matters."

"Really?" Esrahaddon asked. "Why does the bucket matter?"

Jerish sighed. "That's just the thing, I'm not sure anyone really knows."

"But you have faith in this bucket even though you've no idea what it is or if it even exists?"

Jerish shook his head. "I'm pretty sure it exists, so I don't need faith in that. My trust is in the idea that somewhere there's someone who does know why the bucket matters, why it needs to be filled at such a terrible cost." He sighed, but it wasn't smooth or even, and his head dipped even lower. "She was Fhrey—not fully—but she sure looked like one," Jerish said, and Esrahaddon noticed he wasn't just randomly stroking the stone. He drew on it with the moisture of falling tears. "I never met anyone like that before, and I think . . . I don't know. We just met. I knew her for what? A week? A little more? I never felt like that about anyone, but it's not like I've lived a worldly life, so I don't know. How do you know?"

Esrahaddon didn't say anything. He wasn't certain whether it was a legitimate question or just an idea cast out into the void. It didn't matter. He didn't know the answer. In retrospect, Esrahaddon realized he had loved Elinya almost from the moment they met but didn't know it. The realization just sort of snuck up on him.

Jerish finished the outline he was making—a crude but glistening imitation of the Fauyld crest. "I should have gone. I should have been the one to distract the monster while she grabbed the rope. She told me I had to stay with Nareion because I was a Teshlor and that was my job. She was right, of course. That's one of the rules, maybe the most important: The emperor's safety always comes first, but . . . I had no idea that it couldn't hurt me. She didn't have to die. I was just too stupid to know."

"You're not stupid."

"No—no, you were right. I'm just an ignorant idiot—a brute with a stick."

"You're not."

"I am!"

"All right," Esrahaddon said. "*Now*, you're just being stupid."

Jerish looked up, surprised.

Esrahaddon frowned. "No one knows everything, and everyone makes mistakes," he said. "Even the gods, I suppose. And they ought to know better."

The meeting had broken up, and most of those on the island began crossing the bridge.

"Father wants to see you in his tent," Nevrik said to Esrahaddon. "Alone."

Esrahaddon looked to Jerish. "That doesn't sound ominous at all."

On the way to the emperor's tent, Esrahaddon pondered the possibilities. *Nareion might want to reward me for a job well done.* This thought nearly made him laugh. Dark humor was one of the many gifts Niblick had successfully bequeathed, along with sick humor, sarcasm, irony, and self-deprecation. His uncle was a veritable all-purpose comedian. *"When you're the orphan race of a deadbeat god,"* he'd said, *"laughter is one of your few steadfast allies."* More than likely, the emperor was unhappy with him. That was the tradition of private meetings; praise was for the masses. He probably was angry that Esrahaddon hadn't somehow saved Offman, though that was a stretch, as Esrahaddon didn't think emperors became one-on-one-meeting angry over the fate of others. This was personal. *Does he suspect I was involved? Responsible? Does he think this is part of the Mawyndulë conspiracy?*

The now-faded gold-and-blue imperial tent, cylindrical with a single central pole, was raised in the center of the camp. The senior staff and military chiefs encircled it, but they were also a respectful distance away. Esrahaddon passed Offman's canvas residence. The flap had blown open; nothing was inside.

Esrahaddon didn't know the protocol with official tents. *Can't really knock.*

Usually there was at least one Teshlor on duty outside the emperor's traveling palace, an intimidating brute clad in metal who was ready to question and announce any visitor's presence. That night the imperial entrance flap was as lonely as Offman's. With the exception of Jerish, all the Teshlors were gone. Still, Esrahaddon had expected a pair of soldiers. A displaced set of palatial guards ought to be staring him down. Instead, the doorway was deserted.

"Your Imperial Eminence?" Esrahaddon called.

"Come in," the emperor replied.

The interior was shockingly ordinary, downright austere. Esrahaddon had expected chaise lounges, a portable throne, an elaborate bed with insect netting, a staff of servants, and pillows—lots and lots of pillows. Instead, what he found was a small space, not much bigger than his own tent. There was a mattress, a desk, and a chair. A big carpet covered the dirt and grass near the bed. Another lay beneath the table and chair. A single burning brazier hung from the central pole, and there was a large traveling trunk set beneath the light. His Eminence was seated on the chair at the desk. He sat sideways, having turned to face Esrahaddon as he entered.

"Your guards are missing."

"I sent them away." Nareion's voice was neither warm nor cold.

Esrahaddon narrowed his eyes and pursed his lips. "Is that . . . *wise?* Given the circumstances, I mean?"

"Absolutely. You're simply not yet aware of the circumstances."

"Oh . . . kay." There was a pause within which the emperor shifted in his seat. "I don't like you standing over me, and I'm not getting up so sit on the bed."

"As you wish." Esrahaddon moved to the large rectangular sack. Each evening he'd seen servants gather grass, then fill and sew the mattress. Each morning they would rip the seams, empty the bag, and roll it up along with the tent. It looked better with the heavy quilt. Esrahaddon sat, feeling awkward. The mattress compressed, making an unpleasant crinkling sound.

The emperor leaned forward, placing his elbows on his knees. "Things are going to be fine with Erivania. The elves insist they knew nothing of the planned attack and have no idea where the gilarabrywn came from. Everyone knew that one gilarabrywn had been left unaccounted for after the wars, but they all assumed it had been destroyed. I believe you heard how they suggested a secret militant society—a growing movement within their realm seeking to rekindle conflict—might be to blame. They all apologized profusely and assured me they would investigate the matter fully."

"Do you think they will? Might they be lying?"

"I honestly don't care. I came here to prevent the Erivan elves from learning of Nyphron's current status. I've achieved that and even a bit more, I think. This incident should quell any immediate lust for revenge. In a thousand years when the Uli Vermar officially ends and no more excuses or lies will stave off the elves' violence, this problem will need to be dealt with in a more permanent manner, but for now, our little bandage should hold."

"Quite the inheritance you're giving Nevrik."

The emperor shook his head. "Our Fhrey blood is being thinned with each generation. My father didn't quite reach the age of four hundred. I'm starting to feel my years after only two and a quarter centuries. Nevrik will be lucky to see three hundred. No, the task will likely fall to his great-grandson, or possibly *his* grandson—Maribor willing."

Esrahaddon was intrigued that the emperor did not appear to partake in ancestry worship.

"Besides, I have more pressing issues to deal with at home. We won't stand a chance against the elves if I can't solve this schism between Teshlors and Cenzars. The two houses were never fond of each other, and they rarely agreed, but there was always respect—an appreciation that both were working for the good of the empire. Now both sides see the other as an enemy, as the *real* problem plaguing the realm. With the Ghazel at bay, the elves vanquished, and the Belgriclungreians annexed, our need for an enemy has turned inward. When something goes wrong—even when it's a random accident—if the result is a tragedy, someone must be held accountable. Someone must be punished. And that someone is always—*them*. I believe the sudden rise in this trend is likely caused by Mawyndulë's meddling. He's like a termite eating away the strength of the empire, and while much of the conflict might be resolved by finding him, he's only exploiting an existing defect. Somehow, I must solve the riddle and cure this disease, or when the time comes, the elves may be sorely disappointed to learn no war is needed."

Nareion folded then refolded his hands. "Today proved something to me: My fears are real, and I'm more vulnerable than I thought. The good news is this portion of the plan failed—in large part because of you. My son picked his tutors well. Don't ever repeat this to him, but I think Nevrik might be smarter than I am."

"This *portion* of the plan?" Esrahaddon asked.

"Yes, it won't end here. Mawyndulë has more arrows in his quiver, and I fear he's already got the next one nocked. I have no idea where he is, no means to attack, and precious little to defend with. On the other hand, I am a comparatively easy target. The only advantage I have is the horn. He needs it and doesn't know where it is. We must keep it that way. Whatever plan he has set up, I hope to foil it by denying him the ultimate prize. Mawyndulë has had years to determine its location, so it's time to shuffle the deck."

The emperor stood up and walked to the big trunk. He lifted the lid, dug a bit, then returned with a metal box. There was no lock, and he carefully lifted the lid. Inside was a ram's horn. It was plain, without gold, silver, gems, or velvet. The only adornment it possessed was a ring of numerous words around its surface.

"This is the Horn of Gylindora, perhaps the single most powerful relic in all the world."

"You brought this *here?*" Esrahaddon asked in a hissing whisper. "Why? Why would you do that?"

"Do you think it might have been safer left unguarded in the palace, with Mawyndulë closing in? And what would I have done if the Curator called my bluff, or if she somehow already knew that Nyphron was dead?"

"You were going to let them blow it and then fight the challenger."

The emperor nodded. "And pray to Maribor that I won." He closed the box. "If this falls into Mawyndulë's hands, it could destroy all of mankind, but since he can masquerade as anyone, it's impossible to be certain who to trust. You could be him, but since you just saved the heirs of Nyphron—something Mawyndulë would never do—I think not. And because you have proved yourself loyal, intelligent, and capable—and have won the trust of my son, who has a knack for picking winners . . ." Nareion held out the box. "Take it."

Esrahaddon accepted the thing like it was a serving tray balancing fine crystal. "What do you want me to do with it?"

"Whatever you think best. I don't want to influence your decision. Mawyndulë has anticipated every move . . . except maybe this one. Just keep it safe and away from Mawyndulë."

"Shouldn't we destroy it?"

"No. It must be presented to the elven lords before the Uli Vermar, the first day of the new year Three Thousand. If it is not, the Uli Vermar will officially end, and the elves will be free of any edict. Given what happened here today, I very much suspect they will take that opportunity to cross the Nidwalden and resume a war that we are ill-equipped to handle. Esrahaddon, our present—and the fate of future generations—are literally in your hands. Be very careful."

CHAPTER FORTY-FIVE

The Prince

ONE WEEK LATER . . .
IMPERIAL CAPITAL OF PERCEPLIQUIS

Patriarch.

Mawyndulë liked the sound of the word, so much more regal than *bishop*. Just that morning, he'd decided several bishops were necessary—one for each major city. *Yes, that will work nicely. They can function in the same way as imperial governors, except that they will report to me.* That meant Bishop Venlin needed a new title—something that would stand out. He'd considered several; *fane* even crossed his mind for a bit. That wouldn't do because he fully intended to acquire that title legitimately. It was important to get his plans in order because it wouldn't be long now.

Mawyndulë sat inside the church, looking out the window of his tiny room and watching the sun go down. Such a sad little place. He was tired of miserable rooms. His boyhood bedroom hadn't been much more than a prison. Then came that skin-crawling chamber in Borappathin. That wasn't small or sad—it was creepy. Trilos didn't seem to mind, and at the time Mawyndulë was in no position to argue or walk out. Even after recovering from the beating Nyphron delivered—which took forever—he had nowhere else to go. Then came the series of pathetic little rooms in Percepliquis, Maranonia, Calynia, and Dortha where he had hidden like a mole from hunting hawks. Someone actually had the misfortune of finding him—a Galantian named Tekchin. From prince to pauper, oh how far he had fallen. Yet sometimes a weak building must be torn to its foundation to be rebuilt properly.

Funny. I was patient to sit and bide my time for so long, but now . . .

He was tired of cowering in the dark. The closer the end came, the more anxious he grew.

How long has it been since I arrived here in Percepliquis? Eighteen? Nineteen? Twenty years? He wasn't certain. Time was such an inconsistent thing, moving like a rabbit one moment and other times like a . . . *like a rabbit with broken legs.* He wished he could break Time's legs. Time hadn't been much of a friend. *Come to think of it, I'd like to break a good many things—and I will.*

This time will be different.

While the emperors enjoyed their luxury, he'd been busy spinning his web. No corner of the empire was beyond his influence, and many of its citizens were more loyal to him than to Nareion. In the shadows, in the confines of those sad little rooms, he'd fashioned a second empire that was now more powerful than the first. Nareion controlled his subjects' minds and bodies, but Mawyndulë ruled their hearts and souls. They obeyed the emperor because they had to; they served Mawyndulë out of love. When the old empire collapsed, Mawyndulë's gossamer net would catch the pieces, and a new one would be born. He would sit at the center but continue ruling from the shadows—*but the rooms will be a whole lot nicer.*

The front door of the church burst open, then slammed shut, and the sudden noise startled him. He wasn't expecting anyone, and no one had ever barged into the church before. From outside his room came the sound of rapid steps—they were running toward him.

Oh no! You are kidding me! Not again!

Mawyndulë instinctively raised a shield, then sealed the door to his room with a powerful weave. His breathing quickened, his heart began to race, and as he waited for the inevitable, Mawyndulë ran through a list of possibilities, looking for any mistakes he might have made. *I inquired too often about the horn; someone saw through my disguise; they realized I was the one who killed Gaylord Sire—yes, that had to be it!*

Killing the Teshlor hero had been his biggest gamble. Up until then, he'd cleverly worked through other people, always maintaining a careful level of deniability. But the murder was something he'd been forced to do himself.

Someone saw me burst his dead body—of course they did. I blew him apart in the middle of Imperial Plaza! Anyone could have been there that night. Any pair of eyes peeping out a window would have witnessed it. I am so stupid!

Or maybe that pious prostitute who poisoned him for me talked before I managed to kill her. Could the devoted apothecary who prepared the poison have told anyone—written it down, maybe, before I burned him and his shop to ash? Someone might even have seen me mutilating the Orinfar tattoo on Gaylord's chest. What a sight that must have been! I shouldn't have done it at the way house. What was I thinking? There were people just downstairs! But no one came up, and the door was locked—I sealed it myself . . . didn't I?

Mawyndulë had come so close to attaining his goal on so many occasions. But now, once more, he was going to fail because of some stupid blunder, and he wasn't even sure how he'd messed up.

How can this keep happening? Maybe Yolric is right about this Invisible Hand always meddling, but that's the least of my worries now. They're coming for me. Who is it? Probably that miserable little troll, Isilpor-Sond. That means the rest of the Cenzarium are closing in from all sides.

He peered out the window at the plaza. People were there, but no robes—nothing obvious.

How many can I kill? How can I get out of this? What if I can't? Even a cat has only so many lives.

He wanted to scream in frustration and anger. He almost did.

Everything was going so perfectly; I was certain that this time it would be—

Someone knocked on his door.

Mawyndulë stared, stunned. *Murderers don't knock.*

"Your Grace?" Theopol called through the Art-reinforced wood.

Mawyndulë felt a wave of relief. He took a moment to breathe, then once more assumed the humble portrayal of Bishop Venlin and opened the door. Outside, his general secretary stood, a man who had gone decidedly gray, his face sagging with age. *Maybe it has been longer than twenty years?* Regardless, at that moment, Mawyndulë could have kissed him.

"The emperor has returned, Your Grace," Theopol said.

Mawyndulë's eyes brightened. "Alive?"

Theopol looked surprised by the question, but nodded. "The emperor's company just came through the plaza and entered the palace grounds."

Flying so quickly from terror to relief to excitement left Mawyndulë a bit nauseated. Still, a smile took hold that Theopol would, no doubt, interpret as joy that the emperor had come home safely. In truth, Mawyndulë's expression was born of one thought: *At long last . . . it's time.*

Mawyndulë's one regret was that with so many contacts, so many eyes and ears, he hadn't yet located the horn. He'd placed bait everywhere plausible and genuinely expected that someone would come forward and offer information concerning its whereabouts. No matter. He would find it. Easier to locate things when you're actively looking than just waiting for them to pop up. And soon he would wield the full power of the empire to aid in his search.

Yes, this time is going to be very different.

"Theopol, I need you to do something for me."

"Anything, Your Grace."

"Fetch the scribe. Tell her to bring chalk."

The moment one of the palace servants attempted to help Esrahaddon with his belongings, he knew he couldn't wait. Tired from the long day's travel, he wanted nothing more than to go home to his room at the Cenzarium and flop onto his bed. Aside from his obligatory visits to nature, he hadn't experienced the luxury of solitude or lain on a bed in two weeks. He would also relish reuniting with his old friend, Mister Hot Bath, one of the simple pleasures most easily enjoyed by Cenzars. But unlike the rest of the imperial entourage, Esrahaddon had one more task that demanded immediate attention.

It would be just my luck that Ruby Finn's prophecy about me comes true out of pure laziness.

A small army of servants had poured out of the palace to welcome the travelers home, and they immediately set to work unhitching animals and unloading carts. Several people dismounted, then waited in groups for their belongings to be unloaded. Esrahaddon had made the entire trip back with his travel bag slung over one shoulder or the other, never once setting it down, even when the muscles of his neck and back ached for relief. By now, he was certain he had abrasions on both sides, another incentive to finish his new assignment and to pay Mister Hot Bath a visit.

"Heading out already?" the prince asked, sounding disappointed as Esrahaddon waved goodbye. Nevrik and Jerish were among the many with their gear buried at the bottom. Knights and princes never traveled as light as a Cenzar.

"Leave him be," Jerish said in that somber, resigned tone he'd adopted ever since leaving Avempartha. Every word now sounded as if uttered with a dying breath. "He's served you long enough. The man has a woman to go to."

"Thanks," Esrahaddon told him, wondering if a single word of gratitude could still be a lie. After all, he did appreciate the support. He just wasn't going to see Elinya—at least not yet.

I have a delivery to make first.

He hoisted the bag's strap, searching for some imaginary comfortable place on his shoulder, and left the turmoil of the palace courtyard. He felt a twinge of concern when letting Nevrik out of his sight.

This is what a new mother must feel like the first time she leaves her baby in the care of a nurse.

Nevrik would be fine. He was back at the palace, where he'd been safe for twelve years—long before Esrahaddon had met him. *Of course he'll be fine,* Esrahaddon repeated in his head, but it sounded like another lie. After Avempartha, nothing felt safe.

Esrahaddon entered Imperial Plaza to witness the annual changing of the decorations. With the setting of the sun, workers were in the process of taking down the Day of Sorrow's black bunting that commemorated the death of Emperor Novron and replacing it with the garlands and streamers for Founder's Day. The twin observances always drew more people to the city than any other event. Part of the reason stemmed from the popularity of the fast-then-feast holidays, and some was from the ancient imperial edict requiring all governors, imperial magistrates, legion legates, ambassadors, Teshlor Knights, Cenzars, and other high-ranking officials to return to the city on that day. The idea had made more sense back when the empire was small and everyone could sit down at a table together. It likely promoted a sense of cohesion and provided the chance for everyone to be heard. To most people, the decorations heralded the coming end to abstinence and the overindulgence of the big feast to come. To Esrahaddon, they warned that tomorrow, the streets would be packed with people, the whole city one riotous state-sanctioned pandemonium. Just one more reason to hurry. He didn't want to do this in a congested, frenzied whirlwind of merrymakers, and he didn't feel at all comfortable carrying "The Thing" around. He also couldn't put it down or let it out of his sight. The relic was one more infant the emperor had asked him to babysit, a fragile child that needed looking after but whom no one could know about. Luckily, he knew just the place where it could be kept safe. He had the perfect midwife already waiting.

Esrahaddon reached the front doors of the Church of Nyphron just as the last of the sun's light left the plaza. An old gray-haired man in a loose tunic was just leaving, and Esrahaddon caught the door for him.

"Oh, thank you, sir," the elderly man said. He had a dull cloak over his arm and was struggling to determine the top from the bottom, presumably in anticipation of pulling it on.

"Is the bishop in?" Esrahaddon asked.

The man looked up from his clothing dilemma, as if caught by surprise. "Ah . . . yes, he is. But he's in his private chambers at the—"

"I know where his room is, thank you." Esrahaddon stepped inside and quickly—not to mention rudely—closed the door in the man's face. He waited a moment in the dark, cool interior of the church, watching the door to see if the man might open it and demand explanation. He didn't, and Esrahaddon marveled at his luck in having managed to enter without giving his name or providing explanations. *Best that I am a ghost in this mission.* Then he looked down at himself and sighed. The robe wasn't "on," not acting peculiar in any way, but it didn't need to. The material, color, cut, and style stood out as unique. *I might as well be wearing a sign with my name on it.*

Esrahaddon found that the inside of the church had lost none of its gloom. The lamps were unlit, leaving it darker than his last visit. *Feels like a cave,* he thought, *and also a bit like Mileva's home, in that the darkness seems deliberate. No,* he corrected himself, *they just can't afford it.* He guessed this to be true based solely on how the leader of the church dressed, the narrowness of his waistline, and the austerity of his room. He knew people gave money to the church—lots of it—but it didn't go into the bishop's pocket; that much was certain. Rumor was that donations went to the poor, and Esrahaddon was inclined to believe that. This purity of purpose and demonstration of selflessness, along with the bishop's neutrality and most especially his prior understanding of the situation, made Esrahaddon's decision easy. He needed someone to look after the horn—very possibly for longer than a human lifetime—and Bishop Venlin and his eternal church had already agreed to do just that.

"Theopol? Haven't you gone yet?" The bishop's voice reached him from the darkened interior.

"He has, Your Grace."

Venlin appeared out of the shadows like a ghost in his pale white smock and bare feet. "Esrahaddon?" He looked around, confused. "What brings you here?"

"We just returned, and I wanted to fill you in on how things turned out."

"Oh, wonderful!" The bishop gave a warm smile and rubbed his palms together as he padded forward on the cold stone like some destitute patient at the Imperial Hospitality House waiting to see a physician. "How was it?"

"Not good." Esrahaddon helped him out by cutting the distance between them, his heels making a loud echo. "There was an attempt on the emperor's life while at Avempartha."

"Oh dear!" Venlin stopped short and cast a hand to his face. "Is he all right?"

"He is."

"Who did it?"

"A Miralyith named Krem, who it seems had reason to hate Novron."

The bishop narrowed his eyes, raised an eyebrow, then asked in a near-sarcastic tone, "Did he know our Lord Novron no longer walks among us?"

Esrahaddon smiled at what he believed had been intended as a joke. The subject was, in fact, dangerously serious, but the bishop wouldn't know that.

"Actually, no, I don't think so, but he felt it was just as well to kill the First Emperor's descendants." Esrahaddon reached up and took hold of the strap on his shoulder. The metal box that contained the horn, combined with the rest of his gear, wasn't all that heavy, but it wasn't all that light, either. And the way it had sawed into his neck for the last week had become torture.

It's such a relief to finally be able to get rid of this.

"Ah yes," the bishop said, frowning and shaking his head in deep dismay. "Bitter are the dusty thoughts of the old and angry."

Esrahaddon paused with his thumbs under the strap. "Is that a saying or something? An adage of some sort?"

"Hmm? Oh, no," Venlin replied. "Just an observation. When people get old, they tire easily. Most find a comfortable place to sit themselves down. Then laziness takes over. Lack of use causes muscles to grow stiff and lose their flexibility. Same thing happens to the minds of the elderly. They grow, well, dusty from lack of use. Makes it hard to be flexible. And old grudges that can't be rectified make a person bitter, do they not?"

Esrahaddon didn't recall mentioning that Krem was old, but it was possible the bishop had deduced it. *I did say Krem had reasons to hate the First Emperor.* As even Esrahaddon didn't know the lifespan of an elf, maybe Venlin assumed such powerful hatred had to be the result of a contemporary conflict between the two individuals?

But there was another problem—a bigger problem. "Did you say *dusty?*"

Venlin smiled. "Oh yes." He gave a small chuckle. "It's an old habit from my youth, when I used to think anyone over the age of twenty was ancient. Quite childish. I mean, look at me now. Who am I to call anyone dusty?"

"I see," Esrahaddon replied, and meant it more than ever before.

He inhaled a calming breath and pushed out lightly with the Art. Like using naked fingers to explore a pitch-black cave where there might or might not be a poisonous snake, Esrahaddon felt around as delicately as possible. It took less than a second for him to perceive the faint aura. The modeling was near perfect. The edges of the illusion were tapered, folded, and blended just right, making the weave more than nearly imperceptible—it was elegant.

He's masking both his exterior and his power. How did I miss that?

The answer was easy. Not only was the deception exceptionally well done, but more than one illusion was in play. The first was woven with the Art, the second built out of the preconceived notions of human beings. Bishop Venlin was a product packaged and sold so well that many might have overlooked him even without the masking. Anyone searching for flaws found a pile of manufactured imperfections too deep to wade through. One need only look at the man to find fault. He was ugly, awkward, old—and he ignorantly believed in false gods and spewed divisive rhetoric. He was so pathetic that rather than generating ire the so-called cleric drew sympathy. His humble bumbling stoked that perception such that even Esrahaddon had overlooked the obvious.

Mawyndulë.

The name appeared in his head like smoke coalescing into form. This mythical idea assumed a physical shape, and now it had a face. Esrahaddon was standing an arm's length away from the Last Prince of the Fhrey. A notorious figure from legend was right there. Esrahaddon had read about him. He was the evil character from "The Battle of Grandford," Farilane's modern translation of the seminal epic poem by the equally mythic poet known by the single enigmatic name of Brin. No doubt about it, Esrahaddon was staring at an evil unicorn in the flesh. Here was the curse of the imperium and the murderer of the First Emperor, Novron the Great.

Esrahaddon held still, barely breathing, as if a wasp had landed on him.

Should I fight? the idea flashed. *I could end it all right here.*

But *here* was the lair of the enemy. He had accidentally stumbled in like some heroic oaf. That's how the tales always went bad. The champion, inadvertently discovering his enemy, doesn't bother to think. He fails to realize he's not prepared and that he's on ground familiar only to his opponent. He also never takes into account that he alone knows this crucial information, and if he's killed or locked up, disaster would result. Also, by sheer dumb luck, the hero of this story happens to be carrying the one thing the antagonist needs to destroy the world.

"What's in the bag?" the bishop asked.

"This?" Esrahaddon now pretended to merely adjust the strap to a more comfortable spot.

Stay calm. Breathe normally.

"This is just my traveling gear. I was on my way back to the Cenzarium when I thought I should stop by and let you know that everything is fine."

"And the horn?"

Esrahaddon forced himself to breathe, to take each inhale even and slow. He desperately wanted to raise a shield. He felt naked in the face of a blizzard. "It never came up."

"Are you certain?" The look on Venlin's face called him a liar.

He can't know. The Art is powerful, but it doesn't grant mind reading. Still, he can tell I'm agitated, hiding something. For gripe's sake, it wouldn't take an Artist to see that!

"Esra, you've never been very good at concealment."

Esrahaddon nodded. "It was all so upsetting—the attack, I mean, and, well . . ." He paused to suggest hesitancy and nervousness, which was more truth than lie. "I don't think I should be here telling you any of this. I doubt the emperor wants anyone to know. I really should be on my way. The longer I stay, the more likely someone will see, and—"

Venlin nodded sympathetically and placed a hand on Esrahaddon's shoulder—the shoulder with the strap. "I understand. Poor Nareion is under a lot of pressure. Growing a bit paranoid by now, and with good cause, obviously. But please, tell me what happened at that meeting. I promise not to breathe a word of it to anyone. And who knows, I might be of some assistance. You've seen for yourself how *helpful* I can be to those in need."

Esrahaddon nodded, hoping he had cast enough smoke to cloud the situation and to account for whatever the Art might be telling Mawyndulë. "So, I was there," he said, picking his words carefully, and feeling it necessary to explain that none of this was hearsay. "The emperor and the elven leaders went through a bunch of formalities, then the attack happened. After that, the Erivan elves were so embarrassed and—to be honest—terrified that they did nothing except seek to appease Nareion."

"And the horn was never brought up?"

Esrahaddon was careful not to speak a lie that the Art might reveal. "After the attack, I don't think the elves felt it sensible to bring up such a contentious subject."

The bishop stared at him a moment. Then appearing satisfied, he nodded. "And Krem? What became of him?"

"He died," Esrahaddon said. This time while looking directly into Mawyndulë's eyes, he added with a slight smile. "I killed him."

A moment of faint puzzlement revealed itself on the bishop's face. "Oh, well good for you," he said.

So much for Mister Hot Bath, Esrahaddon thought as he headed back to the palace. The tormenting bag continued to cut into his neck as Esrahaddon found himself with one more weight, one more secret, for his shoulders to bear.

I need to tell the emperor.

Looking out across Imperial Plaza, he saw the golden dome of the palace like the finish line in the last sprint of a long race. He wasn't even aware he was running. That grand rotunda had become the be-all and end-all goal of his life. He'd found the secret that everyone sought. This one act seemed so monumental, so world-changing, that getting there and safely delivering the news felt like all he ever need do. Afterward, the world would be forever transformed—but he still had to get there.

How stupid could I be?

Esrahaddon had imagined Mawyndulë—if he existed at all—to be living in the shadows, perhaps in some dark basement, the way all fantastical bogeymen were expected to. He never once thought he'd be the—*For gripe's sake! Bishop Venlin is involved in everything!* He had the ear of the Knights and the Cenzarium, playing one against the other. It was so obvious now, Esrahaddon couldn't understand why Isilpor-Sond or Offman hadn't seen through it. And what about Yolric? He seemed to know everything. Where was he?

This, coming from the man who was just seconds away from giving Mawyndulë the Horn of Gylindora. That thought chilled him like the aftereffect of a near-death realization. *What was I thinking?*

The same as everyone else—that Venlin is harmless.

He just needed to reach the emperor. If he did, everything could be saved. Both Nevrik and the horn would be safe. The division between the Cenzarium and the guild could be patched and healed. The empire could return to an era of renewed peace and prosperity. But already, in recrossing Imperial Plaza, he realized he'd made his first mistake.

I should have gone the other way. He's probably watching me. I told Venlin I was tired and that I was going to the Cenzarium. Now if he sees me beelining back to the palace, what's he going to think?

Ideas bounced in his head. His thoughts were moving too fast to be tied down.

Maybe he'll conclude I forgot something?

This made him feel better. There was no way the bishop could know the horn was in the sack or that Esrahaddon knew about Mawyndulë's habit of using the word *dusty*. Without those two facts, Venlin would have to conclude that Esrahaddon had forgotten something . . . *right?*

He can't know. If he knew I had the horn in the bag, he would have tried to take it.

Esrahaddon chanced a look back. He half expected to see the bishop charging at him with a rune-marked knife. All he saw were the new garlands, the festive streamers, and the handful of city workers putting them up. The bishop was nowhere in sight, and Esrahaddon managed to enter the palace courtyard unmolested.

The courtyard was quiet. Jerish and Nevrik were gone—so was nearly everyone else. Only a few workers remained, and they weren't doing much in the way of work as they stood beside the now-empty carts that lacked even their animals. A few looked up as he passed by, walking at top speed, just something short of a jog. Two scrambled out of the way, as if he were a runaway cart. No one stopped him. No one even tried. He marched straight through the front doors, not even needing to pause, because they were propped open to facilitate the carrying of boxes. Initially, he was relieved, then he became irritated by the lax security.

This all needs to change. Nothing is stopping Mawyndulë from walking in here and killing everyone. Esrahaddon continued unopposed through the palace. *We need guards in this place, and not just Knights. We need Cenzars.*

No sooner had he thought it than a new fear crept in. *What if the reason Offman and Isilpor-Sond never saw through the bishop's disguise was because they were in league with him? I nearly gave him the horn myself!*

So many of the knights had been poisoned by Mawyndulë's *innocent suggestions*, How arrogant was it to think none of the Cenzars had been equally seduced? How many bought into the idea that because the emperor occasionally sided with the guild, he was the problem? How many were convinced by the end-justifying-the-means argument that to save the empire they needed to kill the emperor?

"Think on it, Esrahaddon. Work it out. How did Gaylord Sire die? I don't think I'm exaggerating when I say the future of the empire might depend on answering that riddle."

Remembering Isilpor-Sond's words, Esrahaddon wondered what she had meant. Was it an honest question, the way he had first believed, or did she suspect someone? Did she know?

A body doesn't just explode. Only the Art can do that. Did she suspect a member of the Cenzarium? Several members? Or . . . Esrahaddon didn't like this last thought. *Was she in on it, too, and mentioning "the riddle" was her way of gauging which side he was on?*

"The peace must be maintained at all costs, my boy," he imagined Isilpor-Sond saying in her folksy eastern accent, comforting as a warm blanket on a winter's night, *"and if that means the emperor and his family must die, so be it. But tell me, how do you feel? Are you with us, or against us? Can we count on you, or do we need to take steps?"*

Esrahaddon felt a little sick as he headed toward the throne room.

They could all be in league, the entire Cenzarium.

He remembered so many of the late-night meetings. All were tinged with defensiveness, fear, and outrage—like people working themselves up to do something.

It's always so much easier to destroy than build.

Arriving at the throne room, Esrahaddon found the chamber empty.

Of course it is. Nareion is in the residence by now. The emperor is probably hugging his wife and daughter, happy to be safely home.

Esrahaddon left the throne room and returned to the corridor.

Dinner is likely being set for them. A shame that I'll need to interrupt. But better a delayed meal than—

Esrahaddon stopped. He stood in the Hall of Memory. A series of relief murals depicting all the imperial coronations that had taken place in Percepliquis ran along the walls. Esrahaddon had always found the images interesting for two reasons: They showed the various stages of growth and development of the city, and one face was repeated in each. The figure was a tall, thin man, always standing in the forefront. Esrahaddon assumed there was some symbolism going on—that perhaps the figure was intended to be Novron or Maribor. He also suspected commercialism and vanity, in that the visage might be the patron who financed the art or the artist himself. In the past, this mystery had been but a fleeting curiosity, but now he realized the face was familiar.

I've seen that person. He couldn't pin down who or where, only that he'd seen that face recently, or someone very similar. Esrahaddon was still pondering this as he climbed the stairs to the residence. He'd never been to the personal quarters of the emperor but guessed it was near Nevrik's bedroom.

Still no guards.

"What was it like?" Empress Amethes asked, her voice faint and muffled.

"Tall—very tall," Nareion replied, then he made a sound like he'd been struck. "Well, it was."

"Do they look different?" Princess Fanquila asked.

Esrahaddon moved down the corridor, passing doors, following the sound.

"Who, dear?"

"The elves. Do they look different from the ones here? Arabel says *real ones* glow."

"Real ones? Who is this Arabel?"

The voices came from behind the double doors at the end of the corridor.

If I were Mawyndulë, I could kill them all right now with a snap of my fingers, then walk away, whistling.

He felt terrified, the way he might feel when watching a five-year-old play on the edge of a cliff while the parents merrily laughed at the child's antics. Esrahaddon rapped loudly. He heard a commotion inside.

"Who is that?" the empress asked.

"It's Esrahaddon," he called. "I need to speak to the emperor. It's critical."

The door opened, revealing Nareion in a well-worn but comfortable-looking blue tunic. Behind him was a scene of such ordinary domestic life as to appear delightfully wholesome: a not-so-big room, a fire in the hearth, soft chairs and worn rugs; the little girl on the floor clutching a rag doll, her day skirt spread around her; the empress seated on a sofa, tugging on a pair of slippers; a big blond dog curled up by the flickering fire. They all looked up at him.

"What is it?" the emperor asked. His sight went to the bag, his face concerned.

"Mawyndulë," Esrahaddon said. "I've found him."

"Where?"

"He's been here all along. He's Bishop Venlin."

The emperor just stared, and Esrahaddon gave him a moment to process the news.

"You're sure?"

"Absolutely."

"Does he know you know?"

Esrahaddon shook his head. "Also, why are there no guards?"

"What?" Nareion began. "Oh, it's the Day of Sorrow. It's tradition to allow some of the staff the day off."

"You let *all* the guards go?"

"All the guards?" Nareion asked. "Of course not."

Esrahaddon opened his mouth to reply, then saw fear flash in Amethes's eyes.

"Esrahaddon," Nareion said, "give me a minute. Then meet me down in the throne room."

"As you wish."

Esrahaddon waited in the Center of the World, standing roughly on the Mystic Wood, with a toe in the East Bernum River. As he stared at the statues of the emperors, all of them appeared to be staring at him like he'd done something wrong—or at least someone had. The dread made no sense. Esrahaddon glared back at the reproving stone face of Novron.

It's just lingering anxiety from a near miss. I can't believe I nearly gave it to Mawyndulë! That must be it. But after all, I won.

Esrahaddon had succeeded at delivering the message. The world was safe—except it didn't feel that way.

Is this the jitters, or Elan? Do I need to calm down, or look deeper?

The sheer multitude of possibilities and utter lack of solid information left him feeling blind, deaf, and vulnerable, but he decided *something* was happening. Elan was communicating wildly in her typically vague manner. At that moment, it was a combination punch of a wretched dread and the condemning stares from stone statues as if all the emperors of old were watching and none of them was too pleased with his performance. A storm was coming, but when, what sort, how severe, and from what direction were all unknown. And just like the prelude to a terrible cloudburst, everything was so disturbingly quiet.

Hard heels on the polished floors announced the emperor's arrival. He wasn't alone. A second set of footfalls traveled with him. Who else had he invited? Nevrik? That would be good. Esrahaddon wanted to see him, needed to know he was safe. Might it also be Yolric? Nareion always seemed to favor his counsel. Esrahaddon wasn't certain how he felt about that. After Venlin, he had a hard time trusting anyone. Still, Yolric was a special case. The old man wasn't normal. Aside from being part genius and part senile, the Cenzar master remained indifferent to everything. He always seemed a casual spectator to life, as if he were only visiting. If Esrahaddon had to bet on anyone not being part of a conspiracy, it would be Yolric.

But reality had proved Esrahaddon a terrible guesser.

Nareion entered the throne room followed by . . . *a painter?*

He was one of the artists who had gone to Avempartha. He wore the same loose smock and carried the same two sacks, one over each shoulder, which prompted several questions: *Why is he still carrying his luggage from the trip?* This was easily erased since the painter could ask him the same question. *Fine*, Esrahaddon thought, *but why is he still here? Does he live at the palace? Everyone is apparently at home observing the holidays.* Both of these mysteries paled compared to the Grenmorian in the room—*Why is the emperor involving a palace painter in this? Does he want me to describe what Mawyndulë looks like? I told him it was the bishop.*

The two climbed the steps to the dais, where Nareion took his seat on the throne. The painter stopped beside Esrahaddon and offered him a cordial smile as he rocked back and forth on his feet as if he had places more important to be. Esrahaddon just stared, bewildered.

"Go on," the emperor said. "Tell me what happened. How did you come to this determination?"

Esrahaddon hesitated, looking at the painter. "May I ask why he's here?"

"Don't worry about him," Nareion said.

"At the moment, I worry about everyone. The bishop has manipulated so many people that at this point everyone is suspect."

The emperor's brows rose. "You can trust me, Esrahaddon, I'm the emperor—remember?" His voice had adopted that familiar ruler's tone, the one Esrahaddon remembered so well from their first meeting: *"I said we would relax the formalities. Don't presume that means we're best friends."*

"If I say he's fine, then he's fine. I don't have time to debate my decisions, and neither do you." Nareion took a breath, and when he spoke again, his words were softer. "Besides, he could likely answer the question I just posed to you, but I'd feel more comfortable hearing you say it."

Far from putting Esrahaddon at ease, this left him confused and more than a little concerned. As he had with Bishop Venlin, Esrahaddon called on the Art to study the painter. He expected hidden power but found none. Then he sought emotion: animosity, hate, hidden rage. Nothing. The painter was as he appeared, a normal, ordinary, entirely uninteresting man.

"Very well," Esrahaddon said, and he relayed how Krem had told him about Mawyndulë's habit of using the term *dusty*. He also explained that he had gone to the church to give the bishop the horn. He'd considered skipping that part, but at this point honesty was a rare and exceedingly crucial attribute. The emperor surprised him by not interrupting his story at that point, and Esrahaddon completed his report, including his concerns about the guild and the Cenzarium. But the emperor couldn't let it slide.

"You almost gave the horn to Mawyndulë. The relic I entrusted to you for the specific purpose of keeping it away from Mawyndulë."

"*Almost* is the important word in that sentence."

"But why the bishop?"

"The horn needs to be kept safe and secret for longer than my lifetime—for longer than any human's lifetime. The Church of Nyphron struck me as the ideal answer. It's existed for over two hundred years, at least. Members claim no love for elves, and Venlin demonstrated a greater understanding of the horn than I had."

"Being Mawyndulë, that's not surprising. You never suspected that?"

"Okay, so I admit to a blind spot. He did me a favor once—a good one. I suppose it made me *want* to trust him. It was certainly hard to believe he was a monster. And while we're on the subject, did *you* suspect Venlin?" Esrahaddon asked the emperor, then looked at the painter. "How about you?"

"Don't ask him questions," Nareion said in a suddenly sad and miserable tone.

"Why?"

"You won't like the answers he gives."

Esrahaddon stared at the painter, more puzzled than before.

"Tell me, Esrahaddon, can you make a gilarabrywn?" the emperor asked.

"Can I what? I don't understand."

"It's not a riddle. Do you know how one would go about making a gilarabrywn?"

"No, of course not."

"You were on the tour with us. You heard Krem talk about the process."

"Oh, well, yes, but I have no idea how such a weave would be done. It's . . . well, let's say it's not standard curriculum at the Cenzarium. If it were, I believe such a thing would be in the Dangerously Advanced section, right alongside raising the dead and immortality."

"What if you had one of the swords from the tower?"

"Those were just weapons."

"I meant what if you had the markings on the blade? Krem said the incantation—the weave—was written on each. Wouldn't that help?"

Esrahaddon thought a moment, then nodded. "I suppose. But why do you want to make a gilarabrywn?"

"I don't know that I do. I just want to know if it's possible. Is it?"

"Yes, but it would require a sacrifice. The spell demands that I kill someone I love—and before you ask—no, I won't do that. There are only a few people I love, and I'm not about to kill them to make a monster. You're the emperor, sure, but by now you must have guessed I don't take orders all that well. I respect you, so I do what you ask just as I would with anyone. This would be—well, let's just say demanding such a thing would make me not respect you anymore, and you don't have the power to compel me."

"I wasn't planning on asking you to kill anyone, Esrahaddon, because you're right. That's too much for anyone to ask someone else to do." Nareion looked solemn—a little too grave—and it frightened Esrahaddon.

What's he thinking?

Esrahaddon focused on the painter. "Your Eminence, I don't know what this guy is telling you, but now that we know who Mawyndulë is, we can solve this problem. Literally everyone is back for the holiday. I'll go to the Cenzarium and pick some people. Rappaport, and maybe Yolric—people I believe I can trust. We'll go to the church and end this."

"No," Nareion said, "I need you to take Nevrik out of the city."

"What? But I could be much more help against Mawyndulë. Who else will you send? Who else can you trust? Teshlors aren't going to get this job done. Mawyndulë has defeated them in the past. Only Cenzars have a chance. And honestly, outside of Yolric, I think I might be the only one who can stand against him."

"Esrahaddon"—Nareion leaned forward, speaking clearly and slowly, as if to a child—"Nevrik and I cannot be under the same roof. If we both die—if all of my family dies—that would end the bloodline of Nyphron. No matter how all this plays out—win or lose—in a thousand years, a descendant of Nevrik must fight for the Forest Throne. If there is no descendant, the elves will invade, the war will resume, and mankind stands a good chance of being wiped out. That is what's at stake. My life, even the continuance of the empire, is secondary."

Nareion sat, straightening his back. "Look, I will do my best to finally kill Mawyndulë, but not until I know Nevrik is safe. You and Jerish are my best hope for his survival. With the death of Gaylord, Kendell, and Spencer, Jerish may well be the world's preeminent warrior, and you have already admitted to your own abilities. What's more, both of you have demonstrated your love for my son. I know I can count on you to do whatever is necessary."

The emperor looked to the painter as if for approval.

The painter nodded.

Esrahaddon didn't like this silent conversation. He didn't like it at all.

Being dismissed, Esrahaddon left the throne room and walked down the corridor, feeling oddly betrayed. *I saved the emperor and Nevrik, and this is my reward? To be relegated to secondhand advisor behind the Imperial Painter? What is this guy telling Nareion? Is there blackmail involved?*

Whether there was or wasn't, Esrahaddon needed to find a place to hide the horn. Carrying it around was just stupid. He needed a place where it would be safe for centuries, a spot nearby where no one would ever look, a locale from which it could be retrieved when needed. The whole thing reminded him of something he'd read in the last adventure of Princess Farilane. And that's when it hit him—the perfect place.

"Ezra de Haddon."

Esrahaddon turned sharply to see the painter trotting to catch up with him. "What did you call me?"

The painter only smiled. He didn't come too close, stopping more than an arm's length away. "I wanted to talk to you."

"I want to talk to you, too. What are you telling the emperor?"

"I don't want to discuss that."

"I'm not much concerned about what you want."

The painter continued that dumb grin.

"All right, fine. How about you tell me who you are, how you got here, and what makes you so chummy with Nareion?"

Still smiling, the painter shook his head.

Esrahaddon glared. That scarier-than-a-snake look usually got him what he wanted, but the painter wasn't fazed. "Okay, what did *you* want to talk about?"

The man's expression slowly shifted. The smile left, and in its place, sadness flooded in. "I wanted to say that I'm sorry. I usually—I try to be there in a person's last hours as a sort of comfort. Although, if I'm honest with myself, these talks are always far more for me than anyone else. It helps with the guilt, I suppose. You see, everyone—well, almost everyone—gets their chance to make amends later. I never do, and I have far more amends to make. If I didn't visit—if I didn't apologize—I think the weight would eventually crush me. In your case, however, I'm not going to be able to be there when you die."

"When I—what are you talking about?"

"I'm saying that I need to do this now because I can't later. Going forward, things will happen quickly. And I just wanted you to know that I'm sorry."

"For what?"

"Everything, really. I can't be specific, but you'll understand later."

Esrahaddon was rapidly coming to the conclusion that the painter was not entirely sane, then he felt the robe move. The collar fluttered, and the hem whipped forward in the direction of the painter.

Esrahaddon stared down at himself. No wind, no draft. It felt like his clothes were alive. He pulled back on the collar and snapped the hem. "This is—it's never done this before."

The painter nodded. "It misses me."

Esrahaddon lifted his eyes and stared at the man in the dirty smock. "What?"

"It's been a long time."

"Who are you?" Esrahaddon asked.

"Me? I'm nobody."

"Whenever anyone says that, it's never true."

"Listen, I've placed a lot on your shoulders, and it only gets worse from here—a lot worse. I can't do anything about that—it's just the way it has to be. But keep this in mind. If I hadn't given you this task, you would have died in the forest three days after you were exiled. Thirst would have weakened you, then the lions would have done the rest. What a waste of a life that would have been. Just think about the good you've done by living," he said desperately as if Esrahaddon were arguing the point instead of standing there, dumbfounded. "Hal would have murdered more girls. Ruby Finn would have killed Elinya and gone on to become a full-fledged riva, inflicting a ridiculous amount of misery upon the world. Which, truthfully, is nothing compared to what Mileva would have done. And then of course, there's tomorrow."

"What happens then?"

"You're a smart fellow. You'll figure it out." He started to walk away, causing the robe to flutter again, and this time it lit up with a deep-blue glow. The painter saw it, looked back, and shook his head. "You stay with him. He'll need you a while longer."

The robe stopped fluttering, the light faded, and the painter began walking once more.

"Wait," Esrahaddon stopped him. "In Avempartha, I heard . . . in the Valentryne Layartren . . . there were voices—a conversation that I—well, it seemed as if one of the voices was my own. Do you know anything about what that means?"

"You were hearing the future. Some people sense things. I'm not talking about Artists. I mean everyone. They get an impression. Someplace they've never been feels familiar. In a way, it is Elan speaking, but it's more than that. The world—all of reality—is interconnected, like a web. Certain strands are secured to others. That's why wielding the Art is called weaving—it's because you're messing with the web of reality. So you were standing on a spot where you will be one day. It felt familiar even though you had never been there before. It is a significant node on the strand. That node just happens to be in the Valentryne Layartren, which amplified the impression such that you could actually hear the future. I honestly doubt Fenelyus has any idea just how powerful that tower truly is."

"So I will go back there? I'll know someone named Arista?"

The painter nodded. "Yes."

"What is it that I and this Arista person are doing in Avempartha?"

"Don't worry about it. That won't happen for a very long time—trust me. Right now, you have a job waiting."

"Who are you, really?"

"I'm exactly who you think I am." He pointed to the mural on the wall. "I am the ruler of the Realm of Awful Things." He reached into one of his bags and handed Esrahaddon a long blue-and-yellow feather. "Goodbye, Ezra de Haddon. Both of your mothers are most proud."

CHAPTER FORTY-SIX

The Night of Sorrow

LATER THAT EVENING . . .

"I miss her," Jerish told his armor.

He sat on his bed, wiping down Jerel's sword with an oil rag, a ritual he had performed every night for as long as the sword had been in his care. Jerish never once thought of the blade as *his*, any more than it had been Master Rawlings'.

Seven years before, immediately following Master Rawlings' death, the day Jerish forfeited the championship match to Darius Seret, the new Headmaster Lynch had asked to see him. They met in the Headmaster's office, what had previously always been Rawlings' room.

"Do you know what this is?" Master Lynch had asked, lifting the huge weapon off the mantle.

"Master Rawlings' great sword. Used to be Jerel DeMardefeld's ages ago."

"Yes. It is a spadone, believed to be the first ever of its design. It was crafted for one of the two founding fathers of the Teshlor Guild: Amicus Killian and Jerel DeMardefeld. The first was known for his martial skill, for having preserved the fighting disciplines originated during the Great War; the second for creating the Knightly Virtues—the code of honor that we teach here, which must go hand in hand with the skills to prevent Teshlors from becoming a force of evil in the world. This sword, Jerish, was Master Rawlings' most prized possession. If this guild burned to the ground, he would search through the ashes forever to find it—and it alone. You see, in his day, Morgan Rawlings was a great knight, but he wasn't like Gaylord Sire. His greatest feats weren't won with a sword. Rather, his victories were attained by virtue of his dedication to uncompromising ideals, personal integrity, and an unassailable reputation for honesty, fairness, and wisdom. It is for this reason the emperor honored him with DeMardefeld's sword. A most appropriate reward for a lifetime of impeccable service. Having finished his time on active duty, Master Rawlings could have done anything. He could have been a governor, a magistrate, taken a seat on the Imperial Council, or retired to a comfortable life in a luxurious villa in wine country. But instead, he chose to come here and teach hapless young boys how to swing sticks. I used to wonder about that, but I think I figured it out. You see, Master Rawlings never had a son. He married only once, and both his wife and their infant died in childbirth. So I think this post was a way for him to raise the sons he never had . . . except none of them ever lived up to his brutal standards. The day you faced Darius Seret in the corridor, the time he nearly killed you . . . I saw it then. You surprised him."

Lynch looked down at the sword he held. "Earlier today, you could have defeated Darius. You could have become the youngest and only undefeated champion this academy has ever produced, but you forfeited the match. Why?"

"I didn't need to win. The competition would only prove to everyone else what I already knew. When I saw the headmaster's chair was empty, when I learned that he . . . I realized I didn't need to win at all. To be honest, I didn't want to win if he wasn't there to see it."

Lynch nodded. "Giving up glory to honor the memory of a man is the very thing Morgan's hero, Jerel DeMardefeld, would have done."

"What will happen to the sword now?" Jerish asked. "Does it go back to the emperor?"

"No. Rawlings bequeathed the sword to his son."

"But I thought you said . . ."

"Turns out Morgan Rawlings had a son after all." Lynch held out the blade and placed the spadone in Jerish's hands. "A son he was very proud of."

The Sword of Jerel would outlive him, go on to a new owner, and then another, and more after that. Jerish was just a momentary caretaker of a sacred relic—one, that so far, he'd never used. Jerish was fine with that. He was a First Order now but hoped he would never need to take a life. In too many ways, he and the sword were brothers—both were finely crafted killing tools—yet the sword on his lap was far more experienced than he.

It hadn't taken long to unpack. The bulk of his gear was his suit of armor, and putting it away required only hanging all of it back up on the rack. Along with the plumed helm poised on top, the whole display looked like a militaristic scarecrow. Jerish called it Tucky after the boy he'd trained with in the guild because it sort of looked like him: at least it was about the same height. Tucky had been the perfect roommate. He never made any noise and never disagreed—just listened. Tucky was a very patient listener, and just then, Jerish really needed Tucky because he couldn't talk to anyone else—not about this.

"It makes no sense, really, no sense at all. Why her? Why was it that she made me feel so"—he struggled to put feelings into words—"happy to be me?" *Yes, that was it—that was exactly it.* "No one else ever did that. My whole life, people said I needed to change. I needed to be different—to be like them. It was a convincing argument, given how happy they appeared. They had friends, loved ones; they knew how to make jokes, dance, drink, laugh, smile—but not me." He paused to look up at the mannequin dressed for battle. "You're my best friend and only confidant, Tucky. That ought to tell you something right there." He stared at the place where a face ought to be, where he could imagine any expression he wanted, but only found a void. "The odd thing is that I never noticed before. I've never been lonely because I never knew, until now, what it's like not to be. Does that make any sense?"

He hung his head as the tears came.

"I only knew her for a few days!" he exclaimed and punched the bed with a fistful of oil rag. "How can that be? It's not fair. I was fine, Tucky. I didn't need anyone. Now I do. For the first time in my life, I need someone." He took a breath, wiped his eyes, and stared at the floor, his mouth forcing its way into a wretched frown that he had no control over. "I need her. I need her so much and . . . she's gone."

Jerish looked back up at the suit of armor, at that empty face. "You're absolutely no help, Tucky."

The door rattled as someone knocked.

"What?" he called out, not wanting to get up, not wanting to see anyone.

"You all right?" Asurkan asked.

"Yeah, sorry. Did I wake you or something?"

"The sun only set an hour ago. No one is sleeping."

"Oh, okay . . . ah . . ." Jerish didn't want to talk. He just wanted Asurkan to leave, so that he could continue his conversation with Tucky. Jerish had kept his feelings corked for a week and needed to relax that muscle, to spend one night freely wallowing in misery. Maybe then he could bury the sorrow deep in the hole inside himself where he jammed everything else. Jerish was pretty sure he could cram it between the loss of his mother and the death of Rawlings. There was still some space there, he thought.

"Jerish?"

Jerish got up and opened the door. "What is it?"

"A kid outside asked me to give you this." Asurkan held out an object smaller than a fist that was wrapped in brown parchment paper and tied with twine.

"A kid?"

"Yeah, said his name was Nary, and that he knew you. Said you bought this in a shop in the West Ebonydale Market."

Jerish took a moment and unwrapped what turned out to be a smoky quartz figurine, an exquisite statuette of three people. "Is he still outside?"

Asurkan shook his head. "No, he ran off. Probably in a hurry to steal something. He certainly looked the type. He did say that if you want anything else, the shop will be open for another hour."

Asurkan tried to get a look at the statuette in Jerish's hand. Jerish closed his fist over it.

"Strange," Asurkan said. "I never took you for a patron of the arts."

"You said the shop would only be open for another hour?"

"That's what the kid told me. Oh, and Andreas Ranier wants to see you."

"The Guild Lord wants to see *me?*"

"Is that a problem?"

"No, it's only that I just returned. Was hoping to relax a bit. I'll, ah—I'll head right down. Thanks, Ash."

Jerish closed the door and looked at the figurine of Nevrik, Esrahaddon, and himself. Then he looked up at the armor. "What's going on, Tucky?"

The city was quiet, as was usual the night before Founder's Day. Not that citizens were devout, as Jerish's mother once told him, but because the public houses were closed. That night he found the vacant thoroughfares eerie. In the moonlight, the stone looked slick and shiny. The narrow passageways trapped in shadow were impenetrably dark. Everywhere he heard sounds: clapping boards, metal clinking, footsteps, muffled voices—but so few people.

Never a fan of wandering city streets, his mental map was appalling. Even though he'd lived most of his life in Percepliquis, Jerish was usually forced to ask directions. He counted himself lucky to find a gray-haired woman dragging home two heavy sacks of vegetables and flour. He offered assistance in return for help. Getting her safely to her door, Jerish asked his question, and realized he'd picked the wrong lady. This one loved to talk.

"There's more than one market, you understand."

"I'm looking for Ebonydale Market."

She looked at him with a perturbed frown. "Ebonydale is a long street with a market on *both* ends of town. So there are two Ebonydale markets. The West Market is a crummy dung hole that caters more to rats than people. Filthy place full of flies and rotted produce that only sells three-day-old bread that's already going green. That's where I do my shopping 'cause the East Market is a haven for bloodsucking thieves, isn't it? Course you wouldn't know, would you? Well, let me tell you. They got better tomatoes and fresher bread, but the place has just as many rats—them being the two-legged sort that wear sandals and ride to market in private wagons. Henrietta Lambert shops there. Do you know her?"

Jerish shook his head, making the lady scowl, as if he'd just killed her cat.

"Well, she's so full of herself that if that old bag ate just a single sesame seed, she would explode. She wears her hem nearly up to her knees—her knees, I say—just to show off sandals she says she had custom made up in Farington. Well, I know for a fact that wrinkled old purse got them from Rodencia—and she got them cheap. That's the sort that goes to the East Market."

"I'm looking for the West Market," Jerish said.

"Why? All the shops are closed now."

"I really—could you just tell me, please?"

A frown joined the glare, and Jerish was certain he was about to be added to her pantheon of evil characters who inhabited the stories she would tell others—the sort that usually frequented East Market.

She pointed down the diagonal street, calling it Reglan Road, and told him all he needed to do was follow it. "No turns, no twists, goes right into West Market. Even you ought to be able to handle that."

He thanked her. She offered him a "Happy Founder's Day" and a wave, and he was off.

Jerish followed Reglan Road straight to the West Ebonydale Market, which was farther than he expected. He exited the Imperial District with its soaring marble columns, and he continued through residential areas of gradually decreasing affluence. On the corners, he passed several public houses. The doors were shut, lights off, just as his mother had said.

Jerish had no idea what was happening, but there was no mistaking the work of Nevrik. He'd carved that figurine and presumably hand-delivered it to the guildhall. Why, Jerish hadn't a clue. The prince had looked exhausted when they returned to the city and verbally dreamed of milk, cookies, a hot bath, and a soft bed. And if he had come visiting, why not just come up and see him, or at least wait outside?

"Said his name was Nary . . . Probably in a hurry to steal something. He certainly looked the type."

Something wasn't right. Esrahaddon had related the story of how the two had met in the Garment District. Nevrik had slipped out of the palace dressed like a pauper. *Is he doing that again? Is he in trouble?*

Jerish also wondered at the invitation to Andreas Ranier's office, which he had put off in favor of finding the prince. Ranier would want a report on what had happened. That could take more than an hour. While Jerish hadn't spoken to anyone since returning, he had felt a strange tension in the guildhall. In many ways, it reminded him of the academy on nights before the Summersrule games. Everyone was nervous, worried, and staying in their rooms. They tried to get a good night's sleep but were failing miserably. But there were no contests on Founder's Day. The biggest event was the parade. No one had a reason to be concerned about that.

Jerish entered a large open space where eight streets terminated at a square. The place was eerily empty. He spotted a dog sniffing around some barrels, and then—

Jerish saw a light blink. A white flash appeared for just an instant at the mouth of an alley. Then as he stared, it flickered again. *Only one person can do that.*

"Esrahaddon?"

Nevrik and Esrahaddon appeared out of the dark.

"What's—"

They waved him to silence and hauled him into the shadows of the alley. Moving down the constricted, trash-cluttered gap between a pottery store and a woodworker's shop, they slipped behind a crate of discarded wooden bits and sawdust. Then they waited a few seconds longer while occasionally looking back the way they'd come.

"Looks safe, right?" Nevrik said.

"We're clear," Esrahaddon replied. The Cenzar had the hood of his robe up. The whole garment appeared a dull, dark gray.

"What in the emperor's name is going on?" Jerish demanded, looking at a trio of rats eating the carcass of a cat.

"I found Mawyndulë," Esrahaddon explained. "The emperor is going to deal with him in the morning. We have orders to take little *Nary* here out of the city."

"Nary?"

"Don't you like it?" the prince asked. "Doesn't it just sound like the name of a clever street rascal?" Nevrik was dressed in patched trousers bound at the waist with a rope. Over his head, the limp hood of a tattered tunic had been pulled. Jerish couldn't begin to imagine where he had gotten the clothes. Even the most destitute palace servants dressed better than that.

"Our enemy is Bishop Venlin," Esrahaddon explained. "He has a lot of loyal followers, so the emperor wants his son to disappear for a while. Which is why we are babysitting Nary, the self-proclaimed urban rascal."

"The bishop?" Jerish knew he had heard the name correctly, but he couldn't square that with reality as he knew it. "That's not possible. Mawyndulë is an elf, the bishop is a man—a *good* man."

"I thought so, too," Esrahaddon replied. "A lot of people believe that, but it's not true. He's using the Art to disguise himself—doing an incredible job of it. Even up close and when looking for it, the façade is hard to see. He's been plotting this for generations, performing favors in return for services and friendships. And that church of his is everywhere now, filled with tens of thousands of people who will do whatever he wants, believe whatever he says."

"And you're certain of this?"

"I'm as shocked as you—maybe more—but yeah. Just think about it. Who else is positioned perfectly between your guild and my Cenzarium such that they could convincingly play both sides? I was so convinced of his virtues I—well, I nearly ruined everything. Just remembering how close I came still haunts me." Esrahaddon looked around, frowning. "But yeah, Venlin is Mawyndulë, and right now, we have no idea who we can trust and who might be involved. We can't go back to either the Cenzarium or the Teshlor Guildhall because while our colleagues are not bad people, they likely think, as we did, that Venlin can be trusted. The emperor will start sorting it all out tomorrow. In the meantime, we need a place to hole up, at least for tonight. I sort of thought we could go to Ingram Evarburton's villa. Elinya still works there. As Head of the House, she can provide us a place to sleep. Also, Evarburton sort of knows me. I don't think he'll interfere."

"You mean he's scared of you."

"More or less. Elinya will find us a place to spend the night, or maybe a couple of nights if we need it. But here's the thing. While he'll know who I am, I don't want anyone to know who you two are." Esrahaddon looked Jerish over. "You were smart to leave your armor and crest behind, but I'm surprised you brought the big sword. One of the little ones would have worked better. That big one stands out."

"None of this was intentional. I was in the middle of cleaning the blade. I just came out to see what was going on. Now that I know, I'll go back, get my gear, and meet you at the villa."

"No," Esrahaddon said, "you can't. I took a huge risk in letting Nary send you that figurine. I never would have done it if the emperor and this little rascal hadn't insisted on you coming. I still would have refused if I hadn't been able to maintain a line of sight on our little Nary, ready to bring down the moon and stars on anyone who so much as coughed near him. Mawyndulë would have focused most of his efforts on converting members of the Teshlor Guild, the Cenzarium, and palace staff. You got out clean. You can't go back."

"I'd feel better with my armor."

"Sorry. Now let's get moving. It's getting cold." Esrahaddon took a step, then stopped and held out his hand, palm up, to Jerish. "Where's the figurine? That was actually mine."

Jerish frowned. "I left it in my room. I hid it under my bed in case this wasn't just a princely prank. I didn't want anyone seeing it and making a good guess."

"I'm seriously impressed." Esrahaddon grinned. "Jerish, don't believe all those other people. You're smarter than you look."

"What other people?"

Evarburton's villa was just outside the city on a hill of olive trees, and Jerish thought it just might be the most beautiful place on Elan. By the time they arrived, the hour was late, but even by moonlight alone, Jerish felt he was walking into the most idyllic example of pastoral luxury he'd ever seen. Pale pastel clouds of silvery leaves hovered over thick gnarled trunks that gripped tightly to a vibrant green hillside. The air was filled with a sweet, flowery fragrance mixed with a rich woody aroma, and everywhere was the sound of nature. At night in the city, crickets and frogs performed in small bands, even occasionally as a solo act. Here, the world beneath the stars was loud with their grand symphony.

Built into this pristine slope was a cascading villa. As natural as exposed cliff rock, the home nevertheless stood out from the rolling green with its straight horizontal lines of red clay tiles and taupe walls. Out front, a wooden cart forgotten in a bed of lavender sat tongue up like a faithful dog awaiting its master. Here was a vision, the wish of every aging Teshlor. In a word: tranquility.

Esrahaddon told them to wait on the curving stone walk while he went to the door. The knocker made a loud, hollow sound that silenced the natural world for a moment. The night music resumed, and Esrahaddon had to knock twice more before the door opened. A bare-legged boy in a white tunic greeted Esrahaddon, then ran off. Soon Elinya appeared in the open doorway. Jerish heard a gasp, then the woman flung herself at Esrahaddon, the two embracing for a long moment.

"I guess she didn't know we got back today," Nevrik concluded.

"He should treat her better than he does," Jerish said. "You never know what's going to happen."

Nevrik took hold of his hand and squeezed in exactly the way Tucky never could.

After a few minutes, Esrahaddon pointed, and Elinya traced the gesture and spotted them. She looked aghast. Then she said something to Esrahaddon, shook her head, and waved for them to come up.

"Lady Elinya," Esrahaddon formally said, "this is Nary and, ah . . ." Esrahaddon hesitated, snapping his fingers as if he'd forgotten Jerish's name. "Gerald. Yes, I think that works. They're from . . . Rionillion."

"Indeed." Elinya smiled at each, nodding like a consummate actress. "I'm so pleased to meet you both."

"Gerald?" Jerish asked.

"It's only for one night," the Cenzar whispered. "You can be Gerald of Rionillion for one night."

"I actually am from Rionillion."

"Really?"

"Born near the docks."

"Oh. Well, that ought to make it easy then."

Elinya led them into the villa that managed to be both grand and homey. The simplicity appealed to Jerish. The ceilings weren't so high, the lines of the place straight and clean. There were plenty of windows, but not the tall, narrow sort that he was accustomed to. These were wide, offering stunning vistas of the valley below.

"Who is this, Elinya?" A gray-haired, tired-looking man wrapped in a thick shawl with gold trim stepped out of an open doorway into the corridor.

"Mister Evarburton," Elinya quickly said, "these are my cousins from Rionillion, Gerald and Nary. They are here for the holiday."

The old textile lord peered at them. "But why are they in my house?"

"I brought them," Esrahaddon said, dropping his hood.

Jerish saw the posture of Evarburton stiffen. He took a step back, as if finding a bear in his hallway.

"Cenzar Esrahaddon, what a pleasure it is to see you again." The man so obviously lied. It made Jerish uncomfortable.

Then like a cold drink on a hot day, Elinya poured into the conversation. "The good Cenzar here volunteered to help find a place in the city for my family to stay, but with the holiday, the city is full, every room occupied. We were hoping you wouldn't mind if they spent a night or two here. I'll find them space in the servants' house. I'll see they won't be a bother."

Evarburton stared at the Cenzar without breathing.

"Is that acceptable?" Esrahaddon asked in a normal tone, but the man cringed.

"Ah . . . yes, of course it is. Make your family comfortable, Elinya. You should have come to me right away. I would have sent a litter to carry them."

"Thank you, sir."

"The emperor and I have just this night returned from a long and harrowing journey," Esrahaddon said. "Given the hour, and the distance from the Cenzarium, I was hoping that I, too, might find a piece of floor to rest my head on."

"Floor?" Evarburton asked. "Oh no! Elinya, put new sheets on my bed. I will sleep in the visitor's apartment or out in the woodshed, if necessary."

"Neither is necessary."

"I'll find the Cenzar a comfortable bed, sir," Elinya assured him.

"See that you do. And Cenzar Esrahaddon—anything you want, you need but ask."

Elinya led them through the house into a central courtyard of flowers and fountains and then around to a smaller, humbler but still lovely building. Inside was a modest space with four beds, a table, and chairs. Work smocks were hung on wall pegs, and sandals sat near the door.

"Halivar and Casey can sleep elsewhere tonight," Elinya said, presumably to herself, as she moved around the space, frowning and gathering dropped garments.

"Sorry for the intrusion, Elinya," Esrahaddon apologized. "This was all unexpected."

"What is? What happened? Why do I now have relations from Rionillion, and why are we calling the crown prince *Nary?*"

"I can't really say, but it's the emperor's wish that—the boy here—be kept safe for a few days. It's therefore imperative that little Nary remains your destitute nephew from Rionillion."

"You mean my cousin?"

"Exactly."

She smiled. "Come on in. I'll get you all some food."

CHAPTER FORTY-SEVEN

Founder's Day

NEXT MORNING . . .
EVARBURTON ESTATE, PERCEPLIQUIS

The pounding on the door jolted Esrahaddon awake.

The little room had but one window. Not much light entered, and what did was the faint, sickly pale of predawn. Nevrik turned over with a groan, but Jerish was on his feet, that big sword in his hand. Neither he nor Esrahaddon said a word, but their eyes were loud with concern.

"Esra?" Elinya called from outside.

Esrahaddon threw the door open, and the damp chill of the courtyard and the song of unseen birds greeted him. Most everything remained covered in blankets of shadow, but there were lights in the main house.

Elinya stood outside, wrapped in a thick cloak that she held closed, as if she hadn't taken time to tie it. She had worried eyes. "Men have come from the city. One of the foremen from the shop I used to work at. There's been trouble."

Esrahaddon pulled her inside. "What sort of trouble?"

Jerish closed the door behind her, and Elinya bit her lip as she saw Nevrik sitting up and rubbing sleep from his eyes.

"Elinya?" Esrahaddon pressed.

"They said that . . ." She looked at the boy again, then at him.

"Yes?"

"They said the Cenzarium was destroyed."

Esrahaddon was at a loss. She could have made just as much sense if she told them the moon fell out of the sky and was rolling around Imperial Square. "What? How?"

"No one knows. Only that the dome has caved in, and some say they saw Teshlors coming out with blood on their weapons. Those same knights are now surrounding the palace."

Jerish's brows were pulled tight, his eyes squinting at her like she was the sun. "Teshlor Knights?"

"There's more," Elinya said in a way that made Esrahaddon wish there wasn't, The weight of those two words seemed equal to hauling a dead body. "The rumor is that the Cenzarium was destroyed . . . by Esrahaddon. That he is plotting to kill the imperial family."

Esrahaddon just stared, dumbfounded. There were no words for this.

"Did they give a reason?" Jerish asked.

"They did, but I didn't understand it. They're calling Esra *Mawyndulë*, as if that explains everything. I have no idea what that means. Not even sure I'm pronouncing it right."

Esrahaddon looked at Jerish, who stared back. The knight was still holding the naked blade as a terrible silence filled the room.

Excellent move, Bishop, Esrahaddon thought. *I just told Jerish, Nevrik, and the emperor that the evil elven Miralyith, Mawyndulë, was Venlin. A kindly, humble, Artless man known for his virtue and goodness. I said he used the Art to disguise himself and that he'd plotted this attack for generations. I accused the bishop while providing no evidence of the allegation because I have none. Now everything has switched. I could deny it, but so can Venlin. His word is as good—no, better—than mine. He could call on thousands as character witnesses who would willingly walk through fire for him. I could produce what? Three who sort of know me? One of whom is holding a sword right now trying to decide whether he should use it. The other is twelve and still wiping the sleep out of his eyes. Elinya would be the third, and she might have already turned me in if she understood the meaning of that word she'd pronounced just fine.*

The moment lasted for less than a minute, but it felt like an eternity. Esrahaddon couldn't read Jerish. The runes made that impossible. They also prevented him from affecting that giant, razor-sharp sword that the knight handled with the ease of a stick. He and Jerish had recently shared some good moments that made Esrahaddon think of him as an ally, as a friend.

Of course I never told him that. For some people, compliments and affirmations of appreciation come easily. Not me. Don't know why. I'd claim my upbringing, but Hekkabah was as warm and kindly as anyone. Even if I had said something, what good is a comment or two stacked up against years of disdain and ridicule? I made him the butt of jokes and belittled him in front of Nevrik from the day we met. This news will be welcomed by Jerish as confirmation that the world is just.

I can almost see the debate going on behind his eyes—like looking through windows at a domestic squabble that you know is going to turn violent. Only a matter of time before he swings or stabs. And then what?

Wasn't his fault. Jerish was a creature shaped by his environment, a warrior, a man of brute force. Esrahaddon's father, his brothers, Chief Elder Kenja and his sons, the warlord Banka and his thugs, Elinya's father, Hal, and the legionnaires who had pillaged Rochelle were all formed from the same clay, drawn from the same riverbank. Tigerwolves can't change their stripes.

I don't want to kill him, but I must save Nevrik, and if—

"He's not Mawyndulë," Nevrik said, his voice croaking with morning's first use. He coughed and swallowed. "Think about it. I'm only twelve, and maybe I lack the world experience of a centuries-old Mawyndulë, but if I was an Artist who could make myself look any way I wanted, and if it was important to blend in and gain the trust of as many people in Percepliquis as I could, I wouldn't choose to look like Esrahaddon. I wouldn't make myself appear as a foreigner, wear a flashy robe that changes color or build a reputation as a powerful Artist. That would be stupid. I'd make myself appear weak—unthreatening and disarming—unattractive to the point of eliciting sympathy. And I'd create a reputation for virtue and piety. Be the sort of man people would come to with news."

Jerish looked at the prince in disbelief, as if every word he said was insane.

Here it comes. Esrahaddon prepared himself.

"Of course he's not Mawyndulë." Jerish shook his head in disgust and frowned at the boy. "Did you really think I suspected him?" He looked at Esrahaddon and rolled his eyes as if to say, "Can you believe this kid?"

Esrahaddon didn't say a word.

"Magic can be very deceiving." Nevrik switched sides, defending the position no one argued.

"And if Esrahaddon were Mawyndulë, neither of us would have returned from Avempartha." Jerish put the sword away, symbolically declaring his victory.

Seeing this, and with Nevrik showing no sign of making a rebuttal, Esrahaddon couldn't help himself. "Technically, you're both wrong. Your evidence only proves that I wasn't Mawyndulë *before*. The real Esrahaddon could be dead, killed shortly after returning to the city. It's actually quite probable—and frighteningly clever—that I could have been murdered when I went to the church to speak to the bishop. Mawyndulë—formerly Bishop Venlin—might have stuffed my body under a bed or jammed me in a box or just obliterated my carcass into something that looks like raspberry jam, then assumed my appearance, knowing you would all trust me. Given that Bishop Venlin would no longer exist, I could blame everything on my former self, and through persuasion, I'd convince even a brilliant prince."

"But if that's true, why tell us?" Jerish asked.

Esrahaddon sighed. "Obviously, because it's *not* true. I *really am* Esrahaddon."

"Well, now I'm not so sure," Nevrik said. "That's an excellent argument."

"I was just pointing out that your logic was wrong."

Nevrik and Jerish looked at each other. "It's him."

"Are you all done?" Elinya asked. "Because the men that were in the main house—they know you're here. Ingram didn't even hesitate. He sent them back with orders to contact the Teshlor Guild or the palace and inform them of your whereabouts."

"We need to leave," Esrahaddon said.

"I'm so sorry." Elinya was near tears. "I tried—I wanted to . . ."

"It's not your fault. You did what I needed. Thank you." Esrahaddon caught himself as he felt a growing anxiety at his many failures to be honest with the ones most deserving of it. He cupped her face. "I love you, Elinya. Never doubt that. No matter what happens, believe it with your very soul. You've always been there for me when I needed you, but now you must stay here. You'll be safe. They're after me, not you. And when this is over, I'll return."

"What do we do?" Jerish asked.

Esrahaddon thought a moment and realized it was pointless. "It's all rumors. Everything we know is secondhand accounts of textile workers who might have seen, but more likely heard, from someone who said they saw *something*. We don't have any facts. Running off blindly might be just as dangerous as staying put. This is what we'll do. Jerish, you take Nary and make yourselves invisible by hiding in the holiday crowds. There'll be hundreds, maybe thousands of visitors jamming the city. Finding you will be like picking out a specific blade of grass from an overgrown meadow. Just stay away from the palace. I'll go to Imperial Square to see for myself what's happened. I'll try to speak to the emperor if I can."

"Be careful," Jerish told him. "You're now a wanted man, and you aren't as invincible as you think. If Mawyndulë destroyed the Cenzarium, he can kill you."

Esrahaddon nodded. "We'll meet in that same little alley in the Ebonydale West Market at midday. That alley runs north and south. This time of year when the sun is high, it should be devoid of shade. If I'm not back by the time shadows cover the whole of it, don't wait for me—run."

"And go where?" Jerish asked.

"I don't know," Esrahaddon replied. "If I don't make it back, things will be very wrong. You'll certainly need to flee the city, possibly the entire province of Rhenydd. You should go into hiding. And remember this, Nevrik needs to be kept safe. He must stay alive. His bloodline can't fail. You both understand me? In a thousand years, on the first day of the imperial year Three Thousand—the anniversary of Novron's defeat of Mawyndulë—his descendant *must* present the Horn of Gylindora to the elves at Avempartha. Then he must fight their chosen candidate for the survival of our race. If there is no heir of Novron, the elves will pick two candidates of their own. Then no matter what the outcome, mankind will be doomed."

Esrahaddon avoided the main streets, walking through the big warehouses of West End. He passed the Imperial Arena where the giant twin banners proclaimed

THE RED AND YELLOW CHARIOT TEAMS WILL
COMPETE FOR THE FOUNDER'S DAY CUP!

No one was there now. The stables, huge storehouses, and open yards filled with lumber and bins of raw wool felt frighteningly ominous. As a boy, during the first or second year living in the tree house, Esrahaddon had walked the coast and stumbled upon beached whales—two of them. This was years before Hekkabah revealed the Art in him, and back then he couldn't do anything but watch the enormous animals die. As best as he could figure, they were a pair, a mated couple. Maybe both accidentally got caught in the shallows, but Esrahaddon had the distinct impression that only one had. The other had intentionally joined its mate. Back then, Esrahaddon believed this sad fiction was all in his head, the morbid imagination of a child, but he cried anyway. Years later, he understood that Elan was speaking to him. That made it worse; that made it true. For weeks the whales were there, huge bodies slowly decaying. Animals ate some, but the whales were too big to consume in a single sitting and too heavy to drag. Esrahaddon avoided the beach. Walking past the giant lifeless bodies bothered him. That something so big, so powerful could be destroyed by little more than poor timing or simple distraction left him disturbed. Walking among the great but silent warehouses reminded Esrahaddon of those whales. He also remembered that after a nasty storm, the whales were both gone—washed away without a trace.

Esrahaddon paused and looked in every direction—not a single person visible.

It's as though a plague killed everyone in their beds.

He held his breath. *Could Mawyndulë have killed everyone while they slept?* The whole city might be filled with the decaying corpses of residents and visitors—too many to drag away.

It's always easier to destroy.

He shook his head. *It's a holiday and the sun is barely up. Why would anyone else be?*

Families were just rolling out of beds. Mothers would be taking extra time with breakfast and dressing children in their holiday best. The shops were a different issue. One of the most beautiful traditions of Founder's Day was how all shopkeepers opened their stores to the public. Anyone was welcome to go in and take whatever they liked. This was possible because as per the tradition, people were expected to take only what they needed and return what they took by sundown. Not everyone did, which was why the shopkeepers were slow to open and kept the really valuable stuff locked in their basements.

Esrahaddon made his way up Tope Street. To his relief, he spotted food cart vendors and beaded necklace sellers migrating with their wares toward Imperial

Square. Streamers, hung the night before, crisscrossed the streets, and tremble-wine stands were being erected and stocked.

If the world ended last night, a lot of people didn't get the news.

The closer he came to Imperial Square, the more people he encountered, and relief poured in—at least concerning a citywide massacre. Preoccupied with the rush to stake out the choice spots to set up their stands or to view the parade, few looked his way. Wouldn't have mattered if they did. All they would see was a man hidden by a dark robe and hood. The Gry Erlikon had gone black for the festive occasion. This left Esrahaddon wondering whether the robe understood his need for anonymity or if it knew something he didn't. Either way, Esrahaddon approved of the choice since he felt more and more like Death walking. If half the rumors proved true, he would be.

It's like I'm once more marching to Lord Banka's house. This made him think of Rappaport. *She'll be in the city. Was she in the Cenzarium? Was Yolric? Was Sond?*

As he entered Imperial Square, the sun was just clipping the face of the guildhall and slicing the palace's golden dome in the way Esrahaddon never saw except on those unusual days when he was forced out of bed at an early hour. This was one of those strange mornings filled with expectation and anxiety—the days he remembered best but cared for the least, as they were never comfortable. Trees along the Grand Marchway and in the plaza were in full bloom—the best in years. Pink petals filled the air and carpeted the streets. Blue and green flags were still being posted outside every door. A band was setting up near the fountain; one fellow had an old-fashioned lute. The plaza looked more like Ebonydale Market as it filled with colorful stands. Displays of cakes, nuts, baked treats, and of course, cups of tremble wine, were set out in neat rows in anticipation of the coming horde.

Not everything was holiday-normal. Two things stood out. A large number of soldiers, legionnaires, and Teshlor Knights were gathered around the palace. Most clustered near the doors, where they stood casually chatting, as if gathering in advance for the coming military parade. They appeared innocent until Esrahaddon noticed that some were stained with blood. The other obvious departure from normal was that the Cenzarium no longer had a dome. The rest of the building was fine. Only the top was missing. Few people noticed, or maybe they did but were in too great a hurry to gawk. A lack of debris outside the walls suggested that it had imploded. Some folks pointed, but that was all. What else could the average festival goer do when a building's roof appeared to collapse overnight?

Some gathered to talk near the Cenzarium, but they went on with their business as if the disappearance of the dome were no more shocking than a first snow.

Esrahaddon steered clear of the guildhall and skirted the fountain, wondering if anyone else had noticed on the square's paving stones the odd sets of bloody footprints that started at the Cenzarium and faded slowly as they traveled toward the palace. Guessing that the front door to the Cenzarium would be watched, he slipped around back.

That the Cenzarium could have been destroyed—that Cenzars could have lost a battle against Teshlors—had seemed unimaginable. His faith in this impossibility buoyed his confidence and fired enthusiasm to learn the truth. This truth he found written on the Cenzarium walls. In an unbroken circle, drawn in chalk, he saw Orinfar runes.

The realization stopped him. Shock stole air from his chest and strength from his legs such that he nearly fell. His hand went out to the wall for support. It felt cold. Maybe touching the wall triggered something, perhaps Elan was happy now to gossip, or most likely, Esrahaddon just put the easily connected pieces together. No matter the source, the story was a tragedy.

The Teshlors waited for the holiday, for all the Cenzars to be in the city, because even a single Artist would be dangerous. A holiday reunion was always held under the dome—the rotunda packed with every living Cenzar as they caught up with old friends and learned news from around the empire.

Mawyndulë had waited until everyone was inside. Then in the dark, the Teshlors drew the runes around the outside. Knights would have slowly encircled the building, and when the last rune was marked, the dome would have been smashed in.

Esrahaddon wasn't certain exactly who had done it. Mawyndulë was the obvious choice, but Esrahaddon was certain not all Cenzars had been inside. Venlin would have corrupted a few, at least. If not for being Nevrik's tutor, Esrahaddon would have been seduced by Venlin himself. The bishop's arguments so deftly mirrored what his victims already suspected and wanted so desperately to believe. He fed arrogance and fear alike; he slayed insecurity and inadequacy; he cast everyone as the hero of their story and in turn won affection and trust. Everyone knew he was on their side because he thought the way they did. And when the time came, how hard could it be to turn cats feral? The one positive in all this—if it could be seen as such—was that being labeled a traitor to the Cenzarium and the Imperial Family made Esrahaddon one of *them*. Venlin had, in effect, anointed him leader of *The Cause*, which, in theory, ought to provide him with some protection. It wasn't much, but given he didn't know who his enemies were, it could make the difference between life and death.

Then after the dome collapsed, the knights would have entered and slaughtered the helpless Cenzars.

Esrahaddon found the rear door closed but unlocked. He stepped inside, then recoiled at the rune-produced smothering sensation. Retreating, he defaced a rune, wiping away the chalk with his palm. This was all that was needed, but Esrahaddon wasn't about to stop with one. Forming a simple weave, he ran water down the walls, erasing the chalk. Reentering, Esrahaddon found the sensation of suffocation was gone, but breathing was still a challenge. The sight within made him sick.

Morning sun entered through the collapsed dome, revealing a massive pile of debris. Huge slabs of concrete and countless bricks covered dozens of robed bodies. Sick with dread, Esrahaddon approached, searching the faces. The first was only vaguely familiar. Then came an elderly woman. He sort of knew her, too. Most likely he'd only seen them at previous Founder's Day events. Might even have spoken briefly to one or both. He couldn't recall. Cenzars not only traveled far on continual circuits, but many, like Rappaport, had semi-permanent appointments to distant provinces and visited Percepliquis only on rare occasions—such as Founder's Day.

The next five bodies were of people Esrahaddon clearly remembered seeing before but didn't know well enough to recall their names. The first he could claim truly knowing was Pasiturn. The somewhat inept Artist who had once helped move Esrahaddon to his permanent room, and who was frequently accused of taking more than his fair share of baked goods from the Cenzarium commons, had been severed in half by a ceiling block that had landed edge first. Esrahaddon felt fairly certain the crumbled mound near the front door was Sebastian.

Taking only two steps toward him, Esrahaddon caught sight of a beautifully tailored long, yellow coat.

Esrahaddon hadn't seen Rappaport since the day she left him devastated on the steps of the library. She had come back, but he had always avoided her. So much had happened just that year that he hoped to finally wipe away that awkward past. This year he had planned to speak to her, to be gracious in the hope of renewing their friendship. He would meet her husband and introduce them to Elinya. They would talk of old times, of new clothing styles, of Wardley, Wesbaden, and wagons.

Rappaport lay mostly under a pile of concrete. Her face was visible, but most of her head was caved in. The one eye he could see was open, the glassiness dulled to a matte finish by collected dust. Next to her lay a well-dressed man. This, he guessed, was her husband the tailor. Clutched in his dead arms lay the lifeless body of an infant. It hadn't been crushed. The baby displayed a distinct stab wound.

"You should stay out of this."

Esrahaddon whirled to find Yolric standing between him and the exit.

Anger and rage welled up. "You? You did this?"

Yolric looked appalled. "Are you insane? Of course not." He looked at the wreckage, at the bodies, and Esrahaddon saw sadness. "It's strange. On one level, none of this matters, yet on another, this is *all* that matters. The nature of reality, in itself, is so—well, it's not tethered by any individual point of view or specific moment, which means all things exist at the same time, all with equal legitimacy and value. The individual mind, with its singular viewpoint and linear, anchored timeline, can't hope to understand the many perceived fragments. Instead, we just see them like shards of shattered glass reflecting fragments of truth, having no idea what that word even represents."

Esrahaddon was now confident Yolric had played no part in the attack, but he had no patience for another nonsensical rambling. "What happened here?"

"As you have no doubt deduced, the Cenzarium was ringed in Orinfar, then the dome came down. The Teshlor Knights finished anyone still breathing."

"Who did it?"

"Mawyndulë." He spoke the name easily, no stumbling over syllables. This was a word he knew well. "Today is his big day, the culmination of centuries of planning."

Esrahaddon took a steadying breath before asking his next question. "How did *you* survive?"

Yolric stepped over a jagged chunk of concrete, part of the old dome, one side gray, the other painted blue with puffy clouds—the sky that had fallen. "Mawyndulë warned me. Last night he explained that it would be best if I lodged elsewhere."

"You knew about him? Who he was? The danger he posed? And you did nothing?"

"I lodged elsewhere."

"He warned you of all this, and you didn't try to stop him? Are the two of you in league?"

"No, but we've known each other for some time."

Esrahaddon stared blankly. Yolric had always been an enigma, but in the past, he had seemed nothing more than an amusing puzzle. Nothing about this was amusing now. "I don't know what to make of you, Yolric."

"You're not alone," the old man said. "I suspect literally everyone feels exactly the same way."

"Is this a private party?" Mawyndulë, still in the guise of Bishop Venlin, stepped through the front door into the broken remains of the Cenzarium, lifting the hem of his smock to step over the body of Sebastian.

Esrahaddon raised a shield.

Mawyndulë made an act of looking about. "I always thought it was bigger in here. Really sort of small, isn't it? I don't feel so bad now."

Esrahaddon pulled power. Spring made it easy, the growing crowd outside made it easier, his heartbreak and hate was just overkill.

"You know, we missed you last night," Mawyndulë told Esrahaddon. "I thought you were heading back here to bed. Imagine my surprise to discover you weren't amid the rubble."

Esrahaddon raised his hands.

"Don't," Yolric barked.

The one word stopped him.

Yolric is taking his side. One in front, one behind, I can't fight both.

"Where were you last night?" Mawyndulë asked.

Esrahaddon looked from Mawyndulë to Yolric, trying to decide what to do.

"Don't," Yolric repeated softly.

"I suppose it doesn't matter. You're here now, aren't you?" Mawyndulë stepped around the broken concrete, dainty as a lady in a formal gown. Then he turned to look at Yolric. "I really should kill him now, you know."

"But you won't," Yolric replied.

Mawyndulë looked confused. "And why is that?"

"Because I said so."

Mawyndulë's puzzlement deepened. "You've never interfered with my anarchy before. In fact, you've always encouraged me. The greater the chaos, the better to see the Invisible Hand, right?"

Yolric nodded. "I think this is a development you might want to ponder."

Mawyndulë peered at the bearded Cenzar master for a long moment, then shrugged. "Doesn't matter, I suppose. Might actually be better. Esrahaddon, you provided me with the perfect scapegoat. I will assign all the blame for this day on you. The name Esrahaddon will become a synonym for evil, right up there with Uberlin himself. Maybe I can make you his son or something." He turned to Yolric again, pointing at Esrahaddon, and grinned. "The little fool is so easily read—he wants to kill me. He's only holding back because he doesn't think he can defeat both of us at the same time. Oh, the arrogance!" He looked at Esrahaddon. "If you had a hundred years to prepare, you couldn't kill either one of us."

"I wouldn't tease him if I were you," Yolric said. "Remember your humiliating defeat against Suri? He's a lot like her. If you read him as well as you say, you know that. And you have so much more to lose than he. Your very soul is on the line."

Mawyndulë peered at Yolric, his mouth partially open, his eyes baffled. "Why do I get the impression you're no longer on my side?"

Yolric smirked. "Mawyndulë, *no one* has *ever* been on your side. You're a loathsome creature who has been manipulated practically since birth. Everyone you've ever known has used you for their gain—including me. I would have thought you understood that by now."

Mawyndulë frowned, then stiffened.

Outside, someone began calling for the bishop.

"You'll excuse me," Mawyndulë said sharply. "I have a revolution to lead."

Esrahaddon and Yolric watched him struggle back out of the ruins, still employing that daintily raised-skirt technique. When he was gone, Esrahaddon faced Yolric, his shield still up.

Yolric waved nonchalantly. "Relax. I just saved your life."

"How so?"

Yolric smiled. "Because he's right. Mawyndulë would have killed you."

"You don't know that. And you told him I was a threat. Or were you lying?"

"I don't lie," he said with surprising conviction. "I've been known to issue hollow threats, but I don't lie. I predate that unpleasant convention. Yes, you're powerful. But can you make a strawberry?"

"Can I what?"

"Make a strawberry. Not an illusion, not a fake, a real honest-to-Elan strawberry. One that can be eaten and provide nourishment."

"That's creation." Esrahaddon shook his head. "No one can do that."

"He can." Yolric began walking out the back of the Cenzarium. "You're stronger than Mawyndulë. That's more than obvious. Your reservoir—your well of power—is far deeper. But there's more to fighting than strength. Jerish could explain it better than I. Knowledge is its own power. Understanding increases capability. Experience and practice does indeed make—well, nearly perfect."

Not yet done with his old master, Esrahaddon followed him out onto the little paved footpath that wove throughout the Cenzarium courtyard and gardens.

"What you don't know is that Mawyndulë has trained and studied for over a thousand years with the best tutor in the world."

"Who?"

"Me, of course." Yolric followed the footpath toward East Imperial Street. "That he knows as much as he does owes far more to my prowess as a teacher than his as a student. Although now, I'm starting to regret my success."

They made a right on East Imperial and headed south toward Ferry Street, where more people appeared. These were families carrying bags and blankets and pillows to aid in their comfort as they waited with children to watch the parade—all oblivious to the precarious state of the world.

Esrahaddon looked back to make sure no one followed. No one did.

This wasn't the first time the Cenzar master had alluded to being ancient. While Yolric was old, no man lived longer than a century. The way Yolric talked—the way he'd always talked—suggested the man was born at the start of the world. Alone on the back streets with Yolric, Esrahaddon was finally forced to consider the enigma. Was he an enemy or did Yolric consider Esrahaddon too inconsequential to bother with?

"If you're not in league with Mawyndulë, why didn't you stop him?"

"I can't," Yolric replied, still walking to who knew where.

"But you said you taught him. Surely that means you are more powerful."

Yolric smiled. "Fine. Yes, I misspoke. I *could* interfere, but I *shouldn't*. Saving you just now . . ." He shook his head. "I shouldn't have done that, either. I wouldn't have, except for that blasted robe you wear."

"What does my robe have to do with it?"

"It's not *your* robe. It's Turin's. He put that on you for a reason—several, if I know my brother. Walking around in it makes you stand out like a lone star on a moonless night—at least it does to those of us who remember. It screams, *"You're special!"* and marks you as his Anointed One."

"What does that mean?"

"Good question. I'm only guessing—that's all I can ever do. But it's obvious you're at the center of it all. If there were such a thing as fairies that danced on the head of a pin—you'd be that pin. You see, if you possessed a wider time perspective, it would be obvious that this moment we are living in—this very day, in fact—is a massively significant intersection of space and time. Moments like this are exceedingly rare. This just seems typical to you because this era is all you've ever known. And if you could observe your situation from outside, you'd see that each of the seemingly random events that have transpired over the last couple of decades are coalescing around you. Esrahaddon, you are the dust particle that creates the crystal that forms a snowflake. Through your actions today, the future will be formed, the direction of reality altered. And as amazing as that sounds, it's not all. I suspect something far greater is happening. Certainly, from my point of view. You see, I think there's a chance you are also being used as a messenger. I suspect my brother has chosen you as a conduit—the means for him and me to make first contact, after so very long. Through you, he's asking me a question. Now he's waiting for my answer."

"Which is?"

Yolric grinned. "I'm going to help you."

They ended up at the imperial library. At first, Esrahaddon wondered why, but only a few seconds were required before he realized that the Imperial Repository of Tomes and Knowledge would be the least popular location on Founder's Day. The place was so empty, even the reconstituted Oswald remained vacant.

"Is the emperor dead?" Esrahaddon asked once they were inside.

"No, Mawyndulë can't get inside the palace."

"Why not?"

"Because of Isilpor-Sond. She managed to escape. I suspect she felt the runes close and bolted for the door. She got halfway across Imperial Square before Mawyndulë killed her, but it was too late. She'd used her precious seconds to weave a protection over the palace. That little woman was powerful. No one can enter the grounds. Unfortunately, she's dead. And just like Ruby's unicorns, her weave will only last a few hours. Mawyndulë is waiting. Once the weave falls, he'll go in."

"Then I must stop him."

"You can't. As I said, Mawyndulë will beat you, and he's not alone. Not all the Cenzars were under the dome last night. Some sided with him, mostly those from the provinces where the church was most entrenched. And of course, there are all the Teshlors and the legions and most of the palace guards. You're outnumbered and underpowered. You don't stand a chance."

"So what do *you* think I should do?"

Yolric moved toward the hearth, and it caught fire. He rubbed his arms, appearing chilled. "I'm going to need to find a new home. These old bones are really starting to ache. You can only do so much. After a while, there's just no preventing the wear and tear of time."

Very slowly, Yolric took a seat on Oswald. He stretched out his legs with a sigh.

"Are you going to answer me?"

Yolric folded his arms. "The thing is, I really can't say or do *too* much to aid you. Just as with Mileva, it's dangerous. I don't expect you to understand, but just know that every action I take, every word I say, is potentially disruptive to Turin's plans. He has something set up, and—because he can't directly see me—the more I do, the greater the chance I will break things. Normally that's exactly what I try to do. This time is different. This time if I let things play out the way he wants, I suspect it will flag a truce and Turin will find me. I hope so. We need to talk—now more than ever. But then there's that robe, which I believe is a signal that I should play some part on your behalf. It's an invitation of sorts. Doing so will form the answer to his question. So that's what I'm going to do."

"You realize that nothing of what you just said makes any sense to me, starting with your needing to find a new home because your bones ache. To be clear, most of what you say is"—he waved his hands around haphazardly—"nonsense, really. You make ridiculous statements like being older than lies, or having trained Mawyndulë, who is obviously thousands of years older than you are. And you appear to claim that your brother is the god of—"

Esrahaddon paused as the ridiculous seemed somehow less so. "You aren't, are you? I mean . . . that would be absurd. Except, you knew Mileva, and just now Mawyndulë acted . . ."

Yolric smiled. "Just tell me what you plan on doing."

"I don't think I trust you enough to say."

Yolric frowned. "Which means you don't have one."

Esrahaddon opened his mouth to protest.

"I should point out that Mawyndulë was also right about you being easy to read. And while I'm setting things straight, allow me to point out that I'm very likely the most trustworthy person who has ever lived. Strange how no one seems to realize this. Brothers aren't always alike."

Esrahaddon thought a moment. Given his limited options, saying them aloud couldn't betray too much. "Well, at this point I need to see that the prince escapes the city and goes into hiding. I owe that to the emperor. Afterward, I'm not sure. I can either go with Nevrik as a protector or leave him with Jerish while I return to attempt to save the emperor, which I am inclined to do. Now, why don't you be a decent human being, or whatever you are, and tell me which option you think will succeed?"

"Neither."

Esrahaddon felt his whole body sink. "Care to explain?"

"If you fight, you'll die—simple as that. Then without your help, Mawyndulë will easily locate Nevrik and kill him. If you don't fight, you'll still lose. Keep in mind that once Emperor Nareion is dead, which at this point is a foregone conclusion, Mawyndulë—or rather, Bishop Venlin—will assume control. Not directly, I don't think. Mawyndulë can't stand responsibility or work, but he will be the one giving the orders. That means Mawyndulë will wield the power of the empire. Combined with his influence as bishop of the church, he will control the government, the military, the merchants, farmers, tradesmen, all the way down to the humblest parishioner. All of whom will be looking for you, since Esrahaddon will be labeled the emperor's murderer and kidnapper of the prince. *His* Cenzars will make sweeps, and in fairly short order, I imagine, they will locate and kill all of you."

"So there's no way to win?"

Yolric shook his head. "Mawyndulë finally got it right. This time he *will* succeed." A curious look came over Yolric. "Which makes me quite anxious to see what happens now."

"What do you mean?"

"The Invisible Hand—what will it do now? I have my suspicions, of course. But then I did once before, and now I see there's a good chance I was wrong. Only once before has the world spun this hard, so I believe we shall soon see a world-changing event. Someone—or something—will alter the present course, and the arrow between those two moments will point toward the secret."

"I still can't tell where you stand."

"There's a good reason for that," Yolric replied. "*I* don't know where I stand. A war is coming."

"With the elves, you mean?"

Yolric shook his head. "That conflict is a trifle by comparison. You see, there was a First War. My brother launched it—or at least was instrumental in doing so. He won, but I'm not certain *win* describes his situation. No, the war I'm speaking of now will be the Last War. When it comes, everyone will need to choose a side—everyone—because all of existence will be at risk. At this moment, I'm undecided, but how this day ends will most likely tip the scales."

How this day ends . . . Esrahaddon heard the words echo, bouncing inside his head, ricocheting off walls of frustration. He didn't know what to do. He wanted to scream, but didn't see how that would help. *If I run, we lose; if I fight, we lose; if I do nothing . . . we lose.*

Esrahaddon's head and shoulders drooped as his whole body felt heavy.

I'm being crushed on all sides.

Once more he saw the inscription on the wall:

MY PERSONAL COLLECTION WILL FORM THE SEEDS OF THIS BOOK GARDEN THAT WILL, I HOPE, FLOURISH AND GROW.

—PRINCESS FARILANE, FAREWELL ADDRESS, 1880.

He focused on the attribution—*Farewell Address*. The books never said much about her after 1880. He knew she passed away that year because her tomb in the Vault of Days had the same date, but there were no records of how she had died.

Did she face a similar no-win situation? I won't get a final address, Esrahaddon mused. *I won't see my words chiseled in*—

The Gry Erlikon began to brighten.

The robe had a mind of its own: changing colors, patterns, even textures, and being literally the Robe of Light, it frequently illuminated. Its actions weren't random or haphazard. It brightened when Esrahaddon needed light, turned red to frighten enemies, faded to a blending pattern to help him hide. Now it glowed with a simple white brilliance.

Does it think I'm having trouble reading the words on the wall? Is the robe—

"The robe," he said out loud as a new thought leaked into his brain in dribs and drabs. "It's all about the robe."

Until that moment, Esrahaddon had moved through life with blinders on, unwilling or unable to accept certain truths even as they stacked up around him. *What extravagant efforts I have gone through to ignore the obvious.* He respected Hekkabah's faith, struggles, and sacrifices because she had been his mother. Hekkabah believed, but he couldn't—not in some mythically absent god's vague demands. Ruby Finn's claims of chatting with the same omniscient god were clearly the ravings of a lunatic. Yolric's outlandish comments were nothing but the unfortunate results of old age.

Esrahaddon had not the slightest trouble believing in a riva or a raow or an ancient revenge-seeking Miralyith, as these things were horrific; and awful things were awfully easy to accept because . . . *it's always easier to destroy than to build.*

But the robe was real. The thing was light as a sheet but kept him warm in the coldest weather. It never got wet, always stayed clean, and of course, it moved.

"It misses me."

Esrahaddon had no explanation for that. Hadn't even tried to frame one. His encounter with *the painter* had simply been ignored, shoved to the back of his mind, and hastily covered up with *more pressing* issues. He hadn't wanted to look at it any more than he wanted to seriously consider the words of Hekkabah, Ruby, or Yolric. He was scared. Esrahaddon was terrified that his life hadn't been an accident.

"Listen, I've placed a lot on your shoulders, and it only gets worse from here—a lot worse. I can't do anything about that—it's just the way it has to be. But keep this in mind. If I hadn't given you this task, you would have died in the forest three days after you were exiled. Thirst would have weakened you, then the lions would have done the rest. What a waste of a life that would have been. Just think about the good you've done by living. Hal would have murdered more girls. Ruby Finn would have killed Elinya and gone on to become a full-fledged riva, inflicting a ridiculous amount of misery upon the world. Which, truthfully, is nothing compared to what Mileva would have done. And then of course, there's tomorrow."

"What happens then?"

"You're a smart fellow. You'll figure it out."

"What about the robe?" Yolric asked.

Esrahaddon's mind returned to the library: to the books, the walls, the fire, and the glowing robe that refused to be a normal thing. "You said it's important that I'm wearing it. This is Uberlin's, isn't it?"

Yolric nodded.

"Your brother, the one you call Turin is really Rex Uberlin, the First King?"

"Yes."

"So why do *I* have it? If, as you say, I am destined to fail, why for the neglect of the Missing God was I given . . ."

"I would prefer if you stopped using the Lord's name in vain the way you do."

"Seriously? Uberlin abandons us—his own people—and you—"

"He did not abandon us. He has a plan."

"Does that plan include allowing the empire to push the Ba Ran into the sea? Leaving us with no home?"

"An invasion is coming. Everyone is preparing for it."

"They always say that, but even if it's true, the empire with their Cenzars and Teshlors will just obliterate us again."

"Not this time."

"Why not?"

"Because Rex Uberlin did not forget his people."

The words, the faces, even the smell of the sea and feel of the warm sand between his toes rushed back vividly.

Then they were gone, and he was in a winter forest.

"What is this crime I'm expected to commit? The one you must kill me to prevent. Maybe I can just promise not to. What is it I'm supposedly going to do?"

"Destroy the world."

"And you're okay with me destroying the world?"

"I exaggerated. He didn't actually say that."

"What did *he say?"*

"He said you would destroy the empire."

Ruby Finn vanished, and Esrahaddon was in a cave, the smell of blood in his nostrils.

"Loss is gain . . . death is life . . . up is down."

"What are you talking about? I can—"

"No! Death is not something to be feared, Ezra. It is not some wrong to be fixed. Death is necessary, death is part of life. Fighting the end is the way of the riva, the way of the raow. This is my last lesson to you. Learn it well."

The sound of Hekkabah's words lingered as Esrahaddon was once more back in the library. He had no idea how long he'd stood between the fire and Oswald. Might have been a second or an hour. Such were the limits of time when the entire universe lined up.

Yolric was still there, still seated in the wingback chair. "You've discovered something. What?"

Esrahaddon faced him. "The less you know, the better, right?"

"The less I *do*, the better."

"Sure, but I'm guessing knowing less can only aid with that."

Yolric peered at him curiously. "So you have a plan now?"

"Yes." He nodded. "Yes, I think I do. And I would appreciate your help."

Yolric frowned, and started to speak.

"It's a simple matter," Esrahaddon stopped him. "Nothing world-changing at all. I just need you to teach me how to do something."

Yolric relaxed, his eyes squinting tighter than ever. "What?"

"I need you to show me how to enchant jewelry."

"Why?"

Esrahaddon hesitated.

"You need to tell me your intent, or I won't be able to properly assist you."

"Fine. I need to enchant a ring that Nevrik can wear that will hide him from any magical search."

"You don't need to enchant jewelry, just tattoo the Orinfar on him."

"No, that won't work. He must be able to take it off. And I also want this ring to allow me the ability to easily pinpoint his location even when he's wearing it—no matter where he goes."

Yolric pondered this. "Can't do it."

"Are you sure?"

"Not on a ring. That would be too small. What you need to do is create two concentric rings of symbols. On the inside will be the Orinfar runes, on the outside will be a specific signature, a signal that only you will know. And the length of the runes needed would not easily fit on a ring."

"So what are we talking about here? A belt?"

"Belt would have a separation point, so no, but there is a way to make a necklace and put the symbols on a medallion that hangs from it."

"Don't the runes need to circle the body?"

"Classic Orinfar runes certainly would. That's quite a rigid system—perfect for dwarfs, of course. I prefer a more flexible approach—say, one that blocks negative effects but accepts positive influences. To the unintelligent, it would almost appear like a good luck charm." Staring at the fire, he thought a moment more, then smiled. "There are trade-offs, of course. The boy will still be cut off from Elan while wearing it, and with flexibility, strength is sacrificed. A medallion won't be as powerful a shield as a ring of tattoos." He grimaced. "But then no sensible person would ever tattoo themselves with the Orinfar. That's like an archer cutting off his own fingers to avoid being called into the military. Teshlors live most of their lives utterly divorced from Elan, and that's a terrible way to exist."

"How much strength would be lost?"

Yolric tilted his head from side to side. "It will do what you want, certainly, and also stop the most direct assaults, but something really powerful like a focused strike from behind, or say one of those conjured creatures—"

"A gilarabrywn?"

Yolric frowned at the name and sighed. "I suppose, yes. An amulet can't hope to protect against something like that."

Esrahaddon nodded. "Odds of Nevrik running into one of those should be slim."

"All we need is some suitable metal to form the medallions out of."

Esrahaddon summoned two of the many silver candelabras that had always so poorly managed the task of illuminating the library. "How about these?"

"Perfect. Form something pretty, but leave two clear rings. I'll show you what to write on them."

"Can we make two?" Esrahaddon held up the candelabras.

"Sure."

"And can I make a different signal for both, so I can tell them apart?"

Yolric nodded.

"And how long will it take? How long do I have before Isilpor-Sond's shield fails?"

"The amulets can be done quickly enough. The shield will fail sometime after midday."

"So I have time, but just barely. Let's get started."

The plan would work. Esrahaddon no longer harbored doubts about that. The universe had lined up for him as if someone had painted arrows on the streets, and he had a pretty good idea who that painter was. The only variable remained Yolric himself. Admitting he held the power to flip the board and send all the playing pieces flying, a lot would depend on what he did. For the plan to work, all Esrahaddon required was for him to do nothing, which, so far, was what Yolric seemed best at.

Esrahaddon's great regret was Elinya. He wished he could have seen her one last time to explain, but the villa was too far. He didn't have the time. Instead, he wrote everything down in a letter while Yolric did his part on the medallions. Even so, Esrahaddon still didn't have the time to cover everything. He mostly wrote that he loved her, that he was sorry, that everything would turn out for the best, and that above all she needed to flee the city immediately. Esrahaddon had sent the message by courier whom he'd scared to death by casting a harmless weave that convinced the man he was about to turn into a human-sized rat if he didn't deliver the message as fast as possible.

Now Esrahaddon had one last stop to make. By the time the medallions were finished, it was nearing midday. He needed to reach the alley in West Market and deliver the bad news.

CHAPTER FORTY-EIGHT

Farewell

MIDDAY . . .
WEST EBONYDALE MARKET SQUARE, PERCEPLIQUIS

Jerish stared at the line of shadow as it crept across the alley's floor. Sunlight was already off the woodworker's trash crate. It had even cleared the last islands of sawdust that had spilled out of its many gaps. The dividing line between shadow and light was dead center. Time was running out.

Nevrik sat on the broken stool of an old pottery wheel that belonged to the House of Clay Pottery Emporium that did business across the alley from the woodworker. While All Things Wood had fallen into darkness, The House of Clay remained brilliant. Its whitewashed wall reflected the sun such that it was hard to look at. The prince absently turned the big stone kick wheel with his feet. This should have spun the wheel head, but the spindle was broken. The boy didn't look well as he stared at the ground—at the line of light that retreated. He looked pale, his mouth pulled tight in a miserable defense. Occasionally he bit his lower lip or tugged at his shirt collar or sleeve. He obviously didn't like the cheap clothes but hadn't said anything. Nevrik had been nearly silent since they left the villa. Didn't take a psychic to read his thoughts.

Jerish stood between the prince and the mouth of the alley. Anyone entering had to go through him first. The narrow gap between the buildings was both good and bad: constricted enough so that no more than two could approach at a time but also confined such that he couldn't swing Jerel's sword. He'd have to wield it like a quarter staff with his left hand near the flanges. He hadn't pulled it. The big sword lay against his back. Their best defense was invisibility, and so far, that had worked.

The city had come alive. Crowds moved through as shops opened. Music played, voices shouted, people laughed. Jerish watched them move past the alley opening. Most never even looked his way.

"Are we really going to leave if Grinder doesn't come back?" Nevrik asked, his words weak and a little desperate—a child's voice.

"Grinder?"

"It means *teacher* in Dromeian."

"Dromeian?"

"The dwarven language. I just thought we weren't using names, just in case."

The prince was smart. He talked fast and understood imperial trade management and resource development. He knew the names of all the High Council members, could play the lute, knew how to dance, spoke a little elvish and apparently Dromeian. All too often, Jerish forgot he was only twelve.

Nevrik was looking out the end of the alley at the square, at the people passing by. "Everything seems fine. People wouldn't be celebrating like this if something really bad had happened."

It did seem like any other Founder's Day, even better than normal because the weather was so fine—sunny and warm, but not too hot. And he was right. All the people passing wore smiles. They laughed, hummed, and whistled. Some even sang. Men carried little ones on their shoulders. Women bounced babies on hips. Those old enough ran with streamers on sticks.

"I mean, what will we do?" the boy asked, a pleading in his tone. "Where will we go?"

"I don't know," Jerish replied, realizing even before he said it that he shouldn't. *He's looking to me for reassurance, for guidance, for the hope that adults are supposed to provide.* "I suppose we would travel north to Rodencia, then maybe on to Rionillion. I know that city a little. I was born there. We might . . ." Jerish was about to suggest they seek help from Frewin Fassbinder and Deacon Kile at the Rionillion seminary but realized that was an awful idea, a dangerously terrible notion.

I'm not good at this.

"Except for Avempartha, I've never been anywhere, never done anything," Nevrik lamented. "I wanted to. I daydreamed of exploring, of seeing the world, even fighting in wars like Nolyn did before he ruled. He was the last warrior emperor. After him, we Nyphronians became civilized. I wanted to be like Nolyn: off on my own, spending my nights around a campfire, living by my wits and the edge of a sword. Only I really sort of got over the whole tent-and-campfire thing with the trip to Avempartha. And now—now, I don't want to go anywhere except back to my room." Nevrik kicked the wheel hard. "I want to see my family again. I want to watch the parade like we always used to, then sit down to eat in the big banquet hall and have my mother threaten me with marriage while Fanquila cheered her on."

The sunlit line reached the base of the pottery shop wall.

"Do we go when it touches, or wait until it climbs?" Nevrik asked.

Jerish swallowed. *Where are you, Esra?*

Truth was, Jerish had no answers. He knew how to fight, so he could teach combat, but that's all he knew. Esrahaddon was the thinker. What he didn't know, he figured out. The Cenzar had led the party to Borappathin, telling everyone else what to do, even though Yolric was his teacher and Ruby Finn more powerful.

"Basically, they're full of themselves—and a few other things, if you follow me," Spencer had once said about the Cenzars. *"They always assume they're the smartest in the room and see us as idiots."*

Jerish wondered if maybe they were.

Spencer was dead. Not his fault. Could have happened to anyone. The man was secretly poisoned. But even if he hadn't been, what could he have done? If not for Esrahaddon, if not for his magic and quick thinking, the emperor and the prince would be dead. And for that, the Teshlors had laughed and called Cenzars "bast-zards."

Spencer was a good man. Always decent, fair, kind, and considerate. And Esrahaddon—who really wasn't any of those things—could never hope to beat him in a sword fight or any physical contest, for that matter. But that didn't make Spencer a better man. Esrahaddon was a good man, too. *He's smart, creative, and just as brave, just as admirable—they're both heroes, both different, both flawed.*

All Jerish knew was that he didn't want to be the one to make the decisions about where to go and what to do. He wasn't good at that stuff, and no one liked being forced to do something they were bad at, especially when one wrong move could get both himself and the prince killed and all mankind erased. Should it come down to the three of them fleeing, Jerish didn't envy Esrahaddon's role. *Nothing like seeing the desolation on the other side of the dividing wall to make you sympathize with the competition.* Jerish made a mental note to be more supportive going forward. He'd do what he could to make Esrahaddon's leadership easier. If that meant being the butt of a joke now and then, he could handle that. Jerish only wanted one thing—not to be in charge.

Where are you, Esra?

Jerish nearly pulled the big sword when Esrahaddon darted into the alley looking like a demon, his robe ash-black, its hood up, the sleeves and skirt whipping behind in a strangely fluid manner. Something about the man was different. Jerish had always found him a bit intimidating—more than a bit, after Castell Blythium. But that afternoon the Cenzar appeared as if everything prior had been a rehearsal, and today was the premiere.

"Grinder," Nevrik said.

Esrahaddon smiled at him. "Nary."

"Were you followed?" Jerish asked, peering past him at the crowd.

Esrahaddon smirked.

"A Cenzar cannot be followed?"

"Not likely, except by another Cenzar, and I suspect those still alive believe I am loyal to their cause—or so the rumor goes." He drew in close so as to speak quietly. "We need to be quick. Here." He held out two necklaces, each a chain with a medallion. They were bright silver, not a hint of tarnish. Each was the width of two thumbs and etched with designs and markings. "This one is for you, Nary, and this is Jerish's."

Jerish studied the medallion. It had a pair of crossed swords and two concentric rings of runes, one that formed the outer edge, the other ring inside that. He couldn't read either of them, but at a glance the inner ring's markings looked familiar.

Nevrik slipped the chain over his head, then looked surprised, even frightened. He jerked the necklace off and glared at the Cenzar.

"Put them on and don't take them off," Esrahaddon said sternly. "Do you understand me? Never take them off. They will hide you from magical searches and protect you from enchantments while at the same time allow me to locate you when the time is safe—might even provide a bit of luck."

The prince examined the medallion skeptically then slipped it back on, grimacing as he did.

Jerish fixated on the words: *Allow me to find you when the time is safe,* which meant it wasn't safe now. Something *had* happened. Something bad. Worse, it appeared that Esrahaddon wanted them to leave, but wasn't coming along. "You intend to fight them?"

Esrahaddon nodded. "I will do what I can."

"Can you save Nareion?" Jerish asked.

He looked at Nevrik and saw the boy's lips tremble, his eyes begging.

"I will do my best, but first I must save what is dearest to him, his son and his empire. It may take time—a long time, perhaps—but I swear I will see the empire restored even if it kills me." Esrahaddon watched Jerish slip his amulet on. "Be sure to hide him well. Take Nary into the country, assume an ordinary life. Do nothing to draw attention and await my call."

Jerish looked down at the medallion. "Will these really protect us from . . . your *associates?*"

"I will have no associates after today." His words were hard, cold, even cruel. He spoke like a man with few options—resentful and angry.

Jerish was confused by this. *What's he planning?* "Even old Yolric?"

Esrahaddon hesitated, and Jerish thought he looked doubtful. "Yolric is very powerful but wise."

"If he is so wise, why is he with them?" Jerish asked. He didn't actually know which side Yolric was on, but Esrahaddon's expression suggested it wasn't theirs. "Isn't it better to preserve the empire and show loyalty to the emperor?"

"I am not certain Yolric is with them. He's always been an island. Yolric does as he wishes, and I don't know exactly what he'll do. I hope he does support me, but should he side with Venlin . . ." He shook his head sadly. "We must continue to hope."

Jerish nodded.

He didn't like it, but how much worse would it have been if Esrahaddon hadn't shown up at all? They had a plan—sort of. He and Nevrik would leave the city, find someplace to hide—a barn or something. Esrahaddon would see if he could save the emperor, then no matter how things washed out, he'd track them down using the medallions. *A good plan,* Jerish thought, *better than nothing.*

"It may take time—a long time, perhaps," Esrahaddon had said. Jerish assumed that meant they shouldn't be alarmed if night came and he didn't. Jerish hoped Esrahaddon was only suggesting a couple of days. He could handle that. Jerish had some money, not a lot but enough for food. A week might be pushing it.

"Okay," Jerish muttered, then louder said, "I trust you to watch our backs. I never thought I would ever say that—not to a Cenzar . . . not to you."

Esrahaddon smiled. "And I entrust you with the future of the empire and ultimately the fate of mankind. I certainly didn't expect to be saying that to you."

Jerish tore off his glove and held out his hand. "Goodbye, brother."

Esrahaddon took it and squeezed, then pulled Jerish into a hug.

"Goodbye, Nary," Esrahaddon then told the boy. At the sound of his voice, Nevrik rushed forward and threw his arms around him. Esrahaddon hugged him back.

"I'm scared," Nevrik said.

"Be brave. Remember, you are the son of Nareion, the emperor of the world, descendant of Novron, the savior of our race. And also remember that the time will come when the blood descendant of Novron must protect us again—*your* descendant. It may take years to finally wipe out all the evil that has risen today, so don't wait. If you find someone who makes your heart smile, make her your wife. Remember, Persephone was a mere farmer's daughter and she mothered a line of emperors. You must find a girl like that and have a family. Give your child your necklace and stay safe. Do what Jerish says. After this day, there will be no warrior greater than he. I will see to that as well." Esrahaddon then told Jerish, "It is necessary."

Jerish nodded. "What exactly do you intend to do?"

"Just make certain you are not in the city when I do it."

The young man reached the villa, panting and slick with sweat. "I need to see Lady Elinya!"

She heard this and came out of the kitchen, where she had been going through the motions of arranging for the household's midday feast. The big table was set with holiday fare, the wine was open and left to breathe, and guests were due any minute. Ingram Evarburton always held a legendary banquet on Founder's Day, just as he did on Wintertide. For Elinya, who acted as chief organizer—or First Primus, as one of the cooks often referred to her—these two separate holidays were always the worst times of her life. This one had already begun badly. The sound of the man at the door suggested things were going to get worse.

He held a folded and sealed parchment in his hand, his bare arm glistening with sweat. Jesup, the maid's son who worked the front door, was offering to take the note, but the messenger refused. "I *must* deliver this *directly* into the hands of *Lady Elinya!*" He sounded a bit deranged, and Jesup retreated.

"It's all right, Jesup. I'm here." She reached the porch. "I'm Elinya. What is it?"

"Here!" The messenger unceremoniously thrust the parchment into her hands then backed away. "There, I did it," he shouted to the sky. He waited as if listening. Then he sighed. "I hope it worked." He fingered his face, focusing mostly on his upper lip and then his ears. "I think it did."

"Who is this from?" she asked.

"A Cenzar," the messenger replied as he walked away. "A scary one. Said his name was Esrahaddon. Said it was important."

Elinya looked at the note. She broke the seal and stared at the markings inside.

Why would he—Understanding and dread flooded her, the second one coming on the heels of the first. *He doesn't know I can't read. He never asked, and I never told him. He must have just assumed.*

She continued to stand on the porch, staring at the page, at the indecipherable symbols. Not one did she understand.

What is he trying to tell me? She watched the messenger walk through the villa's gate. *Esrahaddon scared that poor fellow near to death to get him here. He ran all the way.* She looked back at the markings. *Mister Evarburton can read. I could ask him to*—

She recalled the exhausted messenger's insistence: *"I must deliver this directly into the hands of Lady Elinya!"*

He doesn't want anyone else to know what this says, and Evarburton isn't his friend anymore.

Ingram Evarburton never really was his friend; he was just scared of Esrahaddon. But now things had changed.

I can't let anyone see this.

Elinya reentered the villa and ignored questions thrown at her by the scullery crew and the linen troop. She walked as fast as she could to her room, where she always kept a lamp burning—Elinya was no good with the sparkers and tapers. She closed the door, took one last look at the letter, cursing herself for her ignorance, then caught the corner on fire.

The parchment burned fast. She let it fall. There wasn't much smoke, and flame consumed it until there was a near-perfect ash page. She stepped on it, crushing the message to dust. No one would ever know what he had written. Esrahaddon was safe.

She stared at the dark stain on the floor. *Why did he write this? Why did he send it with such urgency?*

She could only think of one possibility.

He needs help. He needs me.

Elinya cried, "I'm so stupid! I'm such an ignorant little fool. I can't even read. I can't understand when you ask for help!"

He's always been there for me. Always saved me, and the one time . . . the one time he asks . . .

She sobbed into her hands.

"Elinya?" Mister Evarburton tapped on the door. "Are you all right?"

She got up, wiping her eyes, and let him in.

"What's wrong? Is this about earlier? I told you I don't hold you responsible for anything that Cenzar did. How could I? I granted permission for him to stay. If you're guilty, I'm guilty, too."

Elinya shook her head. "It's not that. I . . . I must go."

"Go? Go where?"

"I need to go into the city. Someone needs my help. I'm sorry to leave you like this, and I understand if you dismiss me—throw me out. But I have to go. I have to go now."

Not bothering to so much as grab her wrap, Elinya rushed out the door and raced for the city.

CHAPTER FORTY-NINE

Fall the Wall

IMPERIAL CAPITAL OF PERCEPLIQUIS

As he rushed up the Grand Marchway toward the Imperial Palace, Esrahaddon prepared himself to kill. He hurried into Imperial Square, discovering he was late. Isilpor-Sond's shield was gone. So were the soldiers—inside, he guessed. The thought that he might not merely be late, but *too* late, both terrified and infuriated him. Those who noticed his approach moved away.

Esrahaddon entered the marbled hall, so cool, so elegant, and scented with incense that made him think of the umbra trees and abbra berries from the land of his birth—the smell so out of place here. He reached the long gallery, the arcade of storied columns, each topped with three lions looking down from their noble perch at all who passed that way.

Yolric was waiting for him. Seeing him there was frightening. *What does that mean? Did he betray me? Did he only pretend to help? Have Nevrik and Jerish already been captured?*

The old man leaned heavily on a staff. "So you have come," the master said. "But I knew you would. I knew someone would. I could have guessed it would be you. I did say you were the center of all this."

"All this is wrong," Esrahaddon protested. "You, of all people, should see that!"

Yolric shook his head. "Wrong, right—these words have no meaning except in the minds of men. They are but illusions. There is only what is and what isn't, what has been and what will be."

Esrahaddon was irritated that at a time like this Yolric continued to spout nonsense. "I am here to define that value for you."

"I know you are. I could have predicted it. My suspicions, it would seem, have weight. This is the second time now. I'm certain I must be right. It has taken so long to find, but there is a pattern to the world. Wobble it and it corrects, which should be impossible now. Chaos ought to beget chaos. There should be no spring, especially if my brother is still alive. Order should be an impossibility, and all life long gone. Eton's barrier should have fallen, Elan succumbed to darkness, and Chaos once more ruling all. There can be only one answer. There is another force at work—an *Invisible Hand*—and I think I now know who that is, and it isn't Turin. It's *her*, the Seed of the First Tree, my brother's daughter. Somehow, she remains immune to the disease that infected her parents. Even more miraculously, she appears to have cured Turin or is in the process of doing so. I'm all but certain now that my brother is acting on her behalf. If I'm right, the two are working together to keep the world alive, denying Chaos the meal it so desperately desires. That's what Mileva was doing, working toward providing that feast for her new master—one more riva attempting to destroy the world on behalf of nonexistence. You see, if they can't find a means to live forever, then the next best thing is to erase reality altogether because everyone hates being forced to leave a party before it's over. That's why you and Elinya and Ruby were sent. I was, too, so I could discover the truth—or at least what Turin wants me to believe is the truth. With him, it's always difficult to tell. Still, it's hard to argue with spring arriving in what ought to be winter."

"I don't have time to discuss this theory of yours again."

"Nor do I have need of you."

Esrahaddon stiffened. The sound of those words chilled him. *Is he about to—*

"As I said, I have finally worked it out. You see, the legends are true."

Is he toying with me? For gripe's sake! He bars my path but doesn't attack. He merely babbles on about theories. This is no time for metaphysical debates about the nature of existence, chaos versus order, or the values of good and evil. A storm rages. I need to get by!

In a fit of frustration, Esrahaddon demanded, "Do you side with Venlin or not?"

"Side with the bishop?" Yolric looked surprised. "Of course not."

Relief flooded in, and Esrahaddon felt the weight he carried lighten.

"Will you help me? Together we could stop him. Together we can save the emperor. Save the empire."

"I wouldn't need your help to do that."

"So you will let it happen?"

"Of course."

"Why?"

"I need the wobble. One does not a pattern make. I need to see if it will correct again and, perhaps, see how. I must find the fingerprint, the tracks that I can trace to the source. The legend of the witch is true. I know that now. And this time if everything is allowed to play out the way my brother wants, there is a good chance he will reveal himself to me, and through him I'll find her. So if he does reach out to me, if we talk, I suspect the world will change."

"I don't know what you are talking about!"

"I know you don't. You couldn't. You'd have to know the whole story for any of this to make sense. And I would tell you, but it's a long tale and you're in a hurry, aren't you?"

"Are you going to try to stop me or not?"

"The wobble, my boy. I must let it play out and not touch it once I have it going. Go on. Do what you must. I am only here to watch now. I need to see if I can finally prove the identity of the Invisible Hand."

Esrahaddon was confused, baffled by Yolric's fickleness and apathy. The man had intervened with Mawyndulë, assisted with the medallions, provided counsel. But now he stood aside, claiming to be but a spectator at the end of the world. *It doesn't matter*, Esrahaddon told himself. *He's not going to interfere, and that is all that's important.* Now it was just between him and Venlin—between Esrahaddon and Mawyndulë.

"I don't think we'll see each other again."

"No," the old master said, "we won't. I would wish you luck, but I do not believe it exists. Still, I suspect you have better than mere luck on your side—you have the Invisible Hand."

“Are you sure that’s not him?” Sadarshakar asked Hanis as the two reached the Yardley Bridge.

The span that traversed the West Bernum River was a choke point where the crowds of people coming into the city were jammed up. Everyone was heading into Percepliquis, rushing because they were late for the festival. Sadarshakar and Hanis were leaving.

“Why in the name of Ferrol would the prince be dressed up like an illegitimate son of a rat catcher and *leaving* the city on Founder’s Day?”

“I don’t know, but it sure looks like him. And isn’t that—yes, he’s with the young Teshlor who was trapped in the tower with us. What was his name?”

“Teshlor?” Hanis scoffed. “That’s a huntsman, or maybe a tree cutter.”

Sadarshakar laughed. “You think he uses that sword to fell trees, do you?”

Hanis stared at the pair awhile, his tongue pushing out on the inside of his cheek as he worked at solving the riddle. “It does look sort of like him.”

The pauper-dressed prince and the single-bladed Teshlor Knight were just ahead, the two likewise struggling to escape the vortex of the city. The knight had a tight hold on the prince’s hand as he forded the waves of incoming crowds. No one else took notice. This didn’t surprise Sadarshakar. The imperial family so rarely ever appeared in public, and Hanis was right: *What was the prince doing dressed like a beggar?* Even Sadarshakar continued to second-, third-, and fourth-guess himself.

“Banished?” Sadarshakar suggested as they pushed through a tight spot where some fool was attempting to pull a cart full of children, clogging traffic into a wad. All the kids were laughing and screaming with equal pleasure as if trapped in a thicket of sweaty bodies under a hot sun was the height of fine entertainment.

“Banished?” Hanis asked.

“Yes, could the prince have been, you know, disowned or something like that?”

“He’s the *crown prince*, Sadar. You don’t disown the heir apparent unless you want to invite succession disaster.”

“Hmm . . . I suppose.” Sadarshakar admitted that Hanis had a point. Nevrik was also quite young. Who would exile a child? “So what do you think, then?”

“I’m still not convinced it’s him. Might just look similar.”

"Spot on, if you ask me. But, okay, maybe he does merely bear an uncanny resemblance. Still, how do you explain the guy with him? One lookalike is possible, but two traveling together? What are the odds?"

Passing the midpoint of the bridge, traffic began to thin. Soon after, they cleared the causeway altogether and escaped the herd. They touched down on soil and into the joyous luxury of open space and fresh air. The cool breeze brushed Sadarshakar's sweat-coated skin with a lusciously refreshing kiss. He stopped walking, just to take a deep breath.

"They're going north," Hanis reported.

Sadarshakar cut his revelry short to look.

Unlike the busy southern road that came up along the riverbank from Vernes, the northern road to Merredydd was empty. No one came or went that direction except themselves—and the unlikely replicas of the prince and his knight.

"I still think it's him," Sadarshakar said. "Easy way to find out, I suppose." Hanis was still looking at him, confused, when Sadarshakar called out, "Prince Nevrik!"

The boy's head snapped around, and he instantly muttered a curse. The knight drew that big sword and advanced. Looking down its blade, facing that extended point, Sadarshakar thought it really could fell trees.

"Sorry," Sadarshakar held up his hands. "Didn't mean to, ah . . . I just thought I recognized you. I'm Sadarshakar, and this is Hanis Orphe. Do you remember us? We're the imperial councilors from Merredydd."

"The *former* imperial councilors from Merredydd," Hanis corrected bitterly.

The prince sighed. He looked to the knight. "Sorry, I should never have turned. I wasn't thinking."

"It's okay," the Teshlor said. "If they had called my name, I would have turned, too."

"What *is* your name?" Sadarshakar asked. "I mean, I remember *you*, of course, just don't recall if I ever heard your name."

The man frowned. "Jerish."

"Oh, that's right!" Sadarshakar bowed to the prince. "This is an honor, Your Highness."

The prince and the knight looked at each other miserably as if by spotting them Sadarshakar had ruined everything. "I'm getting the distinct impression you're not happy to be recognized."

"What was your first clue, Sadar?" Hanis asked.

"I'm sorry," Sadarshakar said. "We'll leave you alone. It's just, well, it's a long road to Merredydd, and it seemed silly not to . . . well, never mind. We'll not bother you anymore. Right, Hanis?"

"I wasn't going to bother them in the first place."

The prince frowned, scratched his head, and shifted his weight as he considered the two. "Why are you leaving on Founder's Day?" he asked. "And what do you mean, *former* councilors?"

"We were"—Sadarshakar took a moment to clear his throat—"recalled. Our families were disappointed to learn we had fallen out of favor with the emperor."

"That's what happens when you break a High Law and nearly destroy the empire," Hanis said, apparently feeling the need to highlight the warts—a personality feature that Sadarshakar had never cared for. "Honestly, I'm shocked to wake up this morning and still be breathing. I would have expected the emperor to have hanged us by now."

Stripping away polite genteelism was one thing, hyperbolic cynicism was too much. "I don't think he would hang us, Hanis. People of our station are usually beheaded."

"Oh, well, thank you for that load off my shoulders, Sadar."

"Funny," Sadarshakar replied with flat sarcasm.

The prince looked at Jerish and flashed him a brief raise of his eyebrows. The knight put his sword away and responded with a tilt of his head.

"I suppose we could travel together," Nevrik told them. "You two likely know the route better than we." He looked at Jerish, who nodded acceptance.

"Absolutely," Sadarshakar replied. "Are you actually going to Merredydd or somewhere else?"

Again the two exchanged looks.

"Not sure yet," Jerish answered.

"Oh, well, if you're not in a hurry, I'm certain I can offer you a welcome at my family's estate."

"We'd, ah . . ." Nevrik said. "We'd prefer not to be noticed." The boy indicated his clothes.

"You're not running away from home, are you?" Sadarshakar chuckled, then stopped when neither so much as smiled.

Two Teshlor Knights faced Esrahaddon as they stood guard before the magnificent golden doors. At his approach, each man reached for his sword. With a word, Esrahaddon commanded the doors to melt. The resulting wave of molten metal engulfed the two—their screams lost in the revelry of the city's celebration. An instant later, Esrahaddon walked over the solidified pool of gold where parts of two men protruded.

The reception hall and corridor were empty. They shouldn't have been. On that holiday, the palace ought to have been packed with celebrants and well-wishers. In that eerily silent vacuum, Esrahaddon's anger grew. The emperor was inside with his family. They would be hiding, and he knew where. At this point, with the universe lined up so neatly for him, such things were obvious. Maybe they always had been, and he never noticed. Esrahaddon was certain of one thing: This was his moment.

I'm done playing games. Esrahaddon flexed his fingers. He was free to act at last, free to take his revenge, free to show everyone, including himself, what he was truly capable of. All he needed was to find the emperor.

Hearing a pounding echo down the hallway, he made for it.

More knights appeared in the corridor. Over them, a two-ton block of stone fell from the ceiling, killing the lot. With a flick of Esrahaddon's finger, the block blew apart, leaving his way clear. Stepping around the crushed knights, he hit the stairs and went down. The pounding grew louder.

Esrahaddon followed the familiar course, the route he had walked nearly every day for four years, down the corridor as it bent sharply to the left. Along the walls, he once more saw the murals, ghostly depictions etched in the polished stone like burnished details on glass. The images told the story. Esrahaddon had seen them before, but this was the first time he truly recognized the man mysteriously repeated in each coronation picture.

He entered the records room with its vaulted ceiling and the huge statue of Novron at its center. Cubbyholes lined the walls and were stuffed with piles of rolled scrolls. On the far side was the stone door, closed tight.

Knights were busy pounding on the door trying to get in. At his approach they attacked. This time the floor opened and swallowed the group in a single bite. This left only the door. Esrahaddon had reached the Vault of Days. Inside, he could hear the emperor, his wife, and their daughter crying.

Esrahaddon placed a hand on the stone entryway and shook his head.

How had it come to this? How had it all gone so wrong?

Memories flooded him—a voice from the past. *"Killed his own mother . . . So vile, even a lion refused to eat him . . . Only a child but he's as evil as a new moon is dark."*

Esrahaddon felt the cool stone against his palm as he pushed the door open. As it swung in, the sound of the imperial family's sobs grew.

"This is all your fault, boy," his father's voice said out of the darkness of his past.

Yes, it is. All of it was my doing. I saved myself, you, and the lives of everyone in that pitiful village. Your weak, unfit son did what you were unable to do. That was my sin, and you couldn't live with that, and you certainly didn't want me to. You never deserved to have me as a son, but Hekkabah did. And it's for her that I'm here now—for her and on behalf of all the Magnificent Awful Things.

Esrahaddon entered the Vault of Days.

Elinya gasped when she saw the missing dome. The Cenzarium had been her best chance, and now she was at a loss.

She looked around Imperial Square, but it was hopeless. The place was packed with people. She squeezed her way toward the palace, dodging the elephants. The parade was on, the band coming, and she was beginning to panic.

How can I find him?

She entered the palace grounds. Thinking he might be inside, she sought to ask about him at the door, but no one was at the door.

"Elinya? You're not supposed to be here."

Master Yolric walked out of the palace, studying her with his furrowed and fuzzy white brows.

"I'm looking for Esrahaddon. Can you help me find him?"

"I could, but if I did, there's a good chance you'd die."

"I don't care. He sent me a message, but he doesn't know I can't read. He must be in trouble. He needs me. Please, help me find him."

Yolric smiled at her. "Elinya, you are a treasure."

"Will you help me, then?"

"Good day, Master Yolric," Bishop Venlin said as he approached from the turmoil of the square. "I see the palace is open for business once again." The bishop was wiping at his mouth, where what looked like leftover stains from a fruit-filled pastry lingered. "I trust no rats have escaped while I was eating."

"Not that I know of."

"Wonderful. And where is Esrahaddon? Has he fled, or is he going to play the foolish hero?"

"What he will or will not do is what I am waiting to find out."

"Ah, yes, you're on the hunt again. Do you think Turin will show up this time?"

"He's already here."

This appeared to shock the bishop, as if his question had been a joke. "Have you seen him?"

"No, but I think there's a good chance that I just might this time."

Venlin's eyes widened a bit, with a clearly false appearance of concern. "If that happens, doesn't time stop and life as we know it explode or something?"

"I don't know what will happen, but yes, I'm fairly certain the world will no longer be the same."

The bishop looked genuinely confused by this, even a bit irked. "Just don't interfere with me anymore. This is my time. Inside is my prize. With any luck, I'll find the horn in there and in three days, I'll be fane. Then I can order the slaught—" He paused as if just noticing Elinya was standing an arm's length away. "Who is this?"

"This is Elinya."

"Elinya . . . Elinya . . . how do I know that name?"

"You arranged a position for me at Mister Evarburton's household."

"I did? How wonderful of me." The bishop gestured at the woman with both hands. "Isn't that body too old for such recreations?"

Yolric grinned.

"Oh, I see. The body is weak, but the spirit is willing, eh?"

"We were just leaving," Yolric told him and took hold of Elinya's hand.

"But—" Elinya protested, pulling back. "Esrahaddon."

The bishop took interest once more. "What about Esrahaddon?"

"He's inside the palace," Yolric replied.

"And you're leaving? Oh, how wonderful." Venlin's eyes smiled. "This is truly a lovely day. You two have fun now. I have a few remaining chores to take care of." The bishop waved goodbye and entered the palace.

Elinya tried to follow. But Yolric held her tight. "I was there when he wrote the note, Elinya. He asked for you to leave the city: to drop everything and run."

"Why would he do that?"

"Because he doesn't want you to get hurt. I don't either, so I'm going to insist that you come with me."

Elinya stared at the palace entrance that the bishop had disappeared into.

"You can't help him. No one can now—no one but the Invisible Hand."

In the space left clear between Jerish's target dummies and Esrahaddon's table of books, the imperial family sat on the floor of the Vault of Days. Gigantic in the eyes of their subjects, the father, mother, and daughter appeared small, reduced by the vast grandeur of the hall and the humbling circumstances. A single dwindling candle left them isolated in near darkness. The moment he entered, Esrahaddon's robe filled the vast chamber with light—the illumination bright enough to make the streaks of tears shine on their cheeks and their eyes as brilliant as an opossum's caught by a light in the night.

Across the emperor's lap lay a sword.

Esrahaddon wasted no time. Without saying a word, he promptly closed the door, laid a hand against the stone, and ordered it to remain shut. In response, the door itself disappeared, becoming part of a continuous wall of rock that he doubted even Mawyndulë could breach. Nothing would enter until he allowed it.

"What is going on out there?" Nareion asked, one arm around his wife, the other hugging his daughter.

Seeing the little girl broke Esrahaddon's heart. She was a perfect porcelain cup about to be shattered; a lovely lullaby cut short.

"Not much at all, sir, even less now. Have you seen the bishop?"

The emperor shook his head.

"They're waiting, then. Keeping you trapped until Mawyndulë can arrive. He'll want to force you to reveal the whereabouts of the horn."

"I have no idea where it is anymore. Is it safe?"

"Yes." He looked at the sword in the emperor's lap, puzzled.

"You didn't know?" Nareion asked.

Esrahaddon's eyes went wide.

"He told me what needed to happen."

"You mean the painter?"

The emperor nodded.

"How long have you known?"

"About this?" Nareion handed him a parchment.

On it, Esrahaddon saw the same markings he'd seen on the sword blades in the memorial room of Avempartha, the ones used to make gilarabrywns. This was the weave in notation form.

"I've been aware of this for years. Of course, there's a difference between knowing and believing, and a whole gulf between believing and accepting." He looked at his family, kissed his wife's cheek, then the top of Fanquila's head. "They only learned today. I didn't see any reason for them to suffer longer than need be."

"We're going to die," the little girl said, her voice slushy with tears.

"I told you I wouldn't do this," Esrahaddon said defiantly.

"You don't have to. You just need to teach me how," said Nareion.

The idea was almost beyond understanding, and Esrahaddon stared openly at the emperor, both amazed at his courage and disgusted at his surrender. "You never tried to stop it?"

"You can't avoid fate."

"Is that what this is?"

"When the last living god visits you and paints a picture that reveals the divine truth of all things, including the future and the insignificant part you'll play in achieving it . . . yes."

"And you're absolutely certain he is a god?"

"He knew me better than I knew myself."

"You mean he knew how you and your son are Artists? Because I figured that out, too."

Nareion showed surprise. "Nevrik has the gift?"

"Guess the painter didn't feel you needed to know that." Esrahaddon nodded. "Fairly strong, too, I would guess."

"Usually it isn't hereditary, but I've long suspected Nyphron had it. The tattoos that saved his life in his battle against Mawyndulë weren't applied just prior to their fight. He likely added them because he didn't want to be a Miralyith. He refused the power and shut out the Gift of Elan. How much did that sacrifice cost him?" Nareion rubbed the metal of the blade. "And no, I wasn't told *everything*, but I was told *many* things—most before they happened, which convinced me. Like this moment now. He told me you would come and that you would show me how to do it."

"And you're certain that he's a god that can be trusted to do what is right?"

"When it comes to gods . . . is that really a consideration? And what is your point? Are you suggesting we simply thumb our collective noses at the divine and walk out of here hand in hand to a grand new dawn? Our options are a bit limited. We will both do what we must, and may I say that my limited future is better than what remains for you."

"Don't be cruel," Amethes told her husband. "Not now."

The emperor nodded. "You're right. I'm sorry. But in my own defense, I'm about to murder my beloved wife and daughter, then commit suicide, so I'm in an awful mood. I hope you can forgive me."

"You are more than forgiven, Your Eminence," Esrahaddon said, and for the first time, he wholeheartedly meant every word.

Mawyndulë whistled as he walked through the empty corridors of the palace, enjoying how the stone walls and polished floors made the sound rich and full, echoing back to him as if he weren't alone. He'd experienced numerous Founder's Day celebrations, which he knew to be the real day Nyphron had been killed and the reason he celebrated with the rest. This, however, was by far the very best. Thinking about it, he pondered whether it might be the best day of his entire life. It certainly beat the living crap out of the last two thousand years. The only other contenders for the top spot were the day he set out with Gryndal into Avrlyn, the Night Under the Bridge, and of course, the Day of Venlyn. But that wasn't a whole day, only a night really—the day itself had been rife with anxiety. The Night of Venlyn, then, was his last and best.

In two thousand, one hundred and forty-nine years, I've really only had a few hours of happiness.

Mawyndulë considered this and quickly concluded: *I deserved better.*

How horrific was it that he should be so cheated? Not only was he born Frhey—the greatest people to walk Elan—and a Miralyith—mortal gods in training—but he was also the prince. The Forest Throne was his by right. Mawyndulë, more than anyone, was entitled to have whatever he wished. His life ought to have been a nonstop spectacle of satisfaction, pleasure, and joy.

What I got was a few hours of happiness. Why?

The obvious answer came in the form of a parade of faces from his past: that hideous Rhune, Raithe; Arion; his so-called teachers, Jerydd and Vidar; and the whole of the Aquila, really. But most especially Imaly. She was the supreme architect of his lifelong misery. The old hag was certainly dead by now. All of them would have passed away centuries ago, yet here he was, more than twenty-one hundred years later—*how could I have lost track of the years?*—and still he had only his handful of pleasant hours?

Mawyndulë remembered the time he had spent recovering in Borappathin as one long nightmare. Then came the wandering and the failed attempts at revenge. The loathsome hiding that came with the years of being hunted by the likes of the last Galantian, Tekchin, and his brooding sidekick . . . *What was his name? Sikar? Yes, that was it, Sikar. Funny how Nolyn fell in with the Seventh Sikaria—more irritating than funny, really.*

He recalled the many indignities he had suffered and how the days had bled undefined from one to the next, becoming a wash of time with no hard edges. None of it—at least since he left Borappathin—was forced upon him. Certainly, his last millennium had been born of the choices he made. In review, beheld in total, the bulk of his life impressed him as . . . *pathetic.*

The honest assessment was so painful he not only stopped whistling, but he also stopped walking. Mawyndulë felt the horrible hand of self-doubt clutching at his throat. In an instant, he saw all the side paths, the ignored opportunities, starting with the night he and Makareta spent in the Airenthenon.

How different might my life have been if we had just run away together?

And there had been other chances, other people, other places wherein he might have found happiness. There was a pretty Fhrey in a small village north of Merredydd. She liked him. So did her family, who thought he possessed an Old-World charm, saying he had an authenticity about him that the other local Fhrey and myr only pretended at. The whole village suspected he was more than he seemed and fought for his attention. He might have stayed there and become a respected member of the community. He didn't. Mawyndulë was on a quest driven by the ache of emptiness in that place where once there had been a soul.

Has it all been my fault? Has my single-minded need for revenge against long-dead ghosts ruined me?

The question rocked him as he stood outside the throne room's door. As if to emphasize his own thoughts, he spotted the series of murals showing the passage of time in the form of Coronation Days. He saw each of the emperors, starting with Nolyn, receiving the crown and the growth of the city in the background.

"Mawyndulë, no one has ever been on your side. You're a loathsome creature who has been manipulated practically since birth. Everyone you've ever known has used you for their gain—including me. I would have thought you understood that by now."

There it was—the reason, the logic he sought. None of this was his fault. By his own admission, Trilos had said it plainly: *"Everyone you've ever known has used you for their gain—including me."* The world itself was set against him. All those who'd claimed to be his friends or insisted they were trying to help him were, in fact, plotting to milk him like a cow, and when the time was right, it was off to the slaughterhouse for the meat.

It's always been me alone against the world.

Except that one night in the Airenthenon when, for a few hours, it had been two.

It wasn't me who killed that dream. The world did that.

He spat on a mural, then as he watched his saliva run down the stone, he grinned.

Today I will learn if it was all worth it and see who wins—me or the world.

Somewhere in that awful building a small family cowered. A father, his wife, and their two children. He would begin by asking nicely where he might find the horn. When Nareion refused, he would begin torturing the wife, or maybe the children. He couldn't decide. Having had neither, Mawyndulë wasn't certain which would work best. *I'll begin with the children,* he concluded. *The wife would likely aid his cause by begging her husband to relent.* At some point, Mawyndulë would murder the children in some spectacularly gruesome and painful manner that only the Art could make possible. If Nareion still refused, he'd start on the wife.

It might take a few days, but the emperor would give in at some point. Then once he held the horn, Mawyndulë would kill them all, eliminating the line of

Nyphron and all remaining claims on the Forest Throne. He would then blow the horn and wait. In three days, he'd have his soul back and claim his long-lost inheritance by becoming the undisputed fane of the Fhrey people. This would grant him the power to erase the plague that was mankind. Everything would return to how it was always meant to be. He and the Fhrey would once more rule the world.

Then every day will be a Venlyn Day.

Looking back just once at the sad scene of the emperor crying over the loss of his family, Esrahaddon left the Vault of Days. He closed the door. Shortly after, he heard the cry from within. It was over, and Esrahaddon no longer rushed. Time was unimportant now. The emperor was dead, but Venlin had not killed him. He had missed his chance. Mawyndulë would win the battle but lose the war.

Slowly, casually, Esrahaddon climbed the stairs to the main floor and walked the corridor. He didn't get too far before he met the bishop coming up the corridor.

The bishop stopped.

Esrahaddon expected an attack. He was ready, but Mawyndulë showed no sign of assault.

Instead, the bishop frowned. "He's dead, then?"

Esrahaddon nodded.

The bishop shook his head slowly, frustration showing on his face. "And you're here to kill me?"

"Yes," Esrahaddon replied.

"You think you can? Such is the folly of youth. Even old Yolric is not so foolish as to challenge me. And you—you are the youngest of the Cenzarium, not even a member of the council, a pup—you dare bring your inexperience and meager knowledge of the Art against me? I *am* the Art—my family invented it. My brother taught Cenzlyor. The entire Cenzarium flows from the skills and knowledge of the Miralyith." Mawyndulë sighed. "You've caused me a lot of trouble. I really didn't expect it—not of you. Jerish was obvious. He has a built-in compass, that one. But you! You're a Cenzar—you want power! All of you do, right? And you hate the Teshlors—you, perhaps more than anyone. You can't stand their ignorant, brutish ways, right? Above all, I thought I could count on *your* support. You were going to bring me the horn last night, weren't you? I sensed it, or something like it. Got fuzzy quick, though. I had you in my pocket, I was certain."

"That was before Avempartha, before I discovered who you really are—Mawyndulë. You will not succeed."

"I already have. The emperor is dead. So is his . . ." Mawyndulë's face tightened, his eyes fixed on him with sudden urgency. "Nevrik isn't here! So it seems I have one loose end to tie up. Tell me, where is Nevrik?"

"I will die before telling you that."

"There are worse things than dying," Mawyndulë told him.

"I know," he said. "That's why I chose the easy way out. Death for me, death for you . . ." He looked down the corridor to where the sunlight was streaming in. He could still hear the parade marching past the cheering crowds. "Unfortunately, it has to be death for everyone. It ends here. Nevrik will return to his throne one day, but for now, it's time to bury the dead at last."

He looked out at the sun one more time and thought of Elinya, hoped she was clear of the city, then said, "Maribor take us both."

Esrahaddon began the weave.

As he did, he heard the thoughts of a young boy from another time and place: *"I'm one of the Awful Things. I should never have been born. I deserve to die, and now I will."*

Joining the child were others.

"He said you would destroy the empire."

"Still got that feather, do you?"

"He did not abandon us. He has a plan."

"They always say that, but even if it's true, the empire with their Cenzars and Teshlors will just obliterate us again."

"Not this time because Rex Uberlin didn't forget his people."

"Let Ezra decide."

"This, then, is the reason I traveled across the world to find you. Here is the Gift of Uberlin . . . The fruit of their sacrifice—the lives of seven good people—lies in your hands . . . Go now, and be the person Uberlin needs you to be."

Esrahaddon watched as Mawyndulë began his own weave. The Frhey must have seen what was coming. If he was half as capable as Yolric had said, Mawyndulë could decipher the movements of Esrahaddon's fingers like a scholar reading a giant signboard. Esrahaddon wanted to believe Mawyndulë was surprised, even shocked, at what he was witnessing. In contrast, Esrahaddon had no clue as to what Mawyndulë was doing. Not an attack that much was clear, but he'd never seen such a construct before. Concentrating on his own work, he couldn't afford to divert his attention. He couldn't stop his own weave. Not now.

"What do you think about living somewhere like Mehan. I hear it's a rapidly developing city, and the weather there is supposed to be wonderful. Or we could look into Rodencia if you prefer. They just finished a new sewer system, so it's bound to grow, and it's only a day's travel from the palace."

Esrahaddon pulled in more power than he'd ever dared as he sensed the hollow area beneath him, below the whole city—the ancient caves and caverns that led all the way to the sea.

"Are you going to be there?"

He nodded.

Esrahaddon reached deep within himself and the world of Elan and stretched out for the deep monolithic chords at the core of the world.

"Then I don't care where this hovel is. I'll be happy to clean it for you."

"I don't think you understand the nature of the question I'll be asking."

"I could say the same of you."

"Goodbye, Elinya. I'm so sorry."

Elan revealed to him the massive supports of existence that appeared like a primordial forest of impossibly tall trees, and the chords were the ancient roots—fingers that held in one tight fist all that was commonly known as reality.

Reaching out with all his might, Esrahaddon slammed the chords hard.

It's always easier to destroy.

That's when the robe burst out with a new light. This time the color was gold.

CHAPTER FIFTY

The Heir of Nyphron

INSTARYA PROVINCE NEAR YARDLEY BRIDGE

"In a way, I suppose we *are* running away from home," Nevrik replied to Sadarshakar. "But I'm hoping it'll be more like a short vacation."

Talking as they traveled, the four of them were now a fair way up the Merredydd Road, still in sight of the river, the bridge, and the city but high enough up the steep slope to see the first few pine trees. Jerish was no engineer but guessed the slope possessed some industry term like Maximum Cart Incline, as the road up from the river was a challenge for any ox or mule hauling a load. Being wide and smooth made up for the angle, and walking was easy. The empire had always excelled at making roads.

Looking back, Jerish was surprised by how high they were. He could blot out the entire bridge with his thumb held at arm's length. The traffic was still thick on the river road and the bridge. People crammed so tightly, they appeared like one great writhing mass of undulating movement.

"I wish *we* were on vacation," Hanis grumbled, adjusting his shoulder pack. "Feels like I'm marching to my execution." He looked at Sadarshakar. "You know my father is going to kill me."

"He won't. Hanis, he's only going to yell," Sadarshakar replied.

"He never raises his voice," Hanis said. "And somehow that makes it worse."

Jerish wasn't entirely pleased with the councilors joining them. He found it concerning that they just happened to be on the same road at the same time as he and the prince. He was likely being overly cautious, seeing danger in every shadow, but the look he'd seen in Esrahaddon's eyes had put him on edge.

"Something bad has happened, maybe something worse than bad."

Jerish had been handed a momentous responsibility and a dreadful burden. Shoved out into a world he hardly knew, one soon to be packed with enemies seeking to kill the boy, it was Jerish's duty to protect the heir to the throne. Being new to his role, it was understandable that he felt inadequate and jumpy. Jerish had looked forward to getting out of the city, away from people, where all he needed to worry about were bears and snakes. Now he had these two Fhrey to watch—these two imperial councilors who asked too many questions.

"I take it you don't want to discuss why you're sort of running away, my prince?" Sadarshakar asked.

"No, not really," Nevrik replied as he scrambled over a tree root that extended into the roadway. "And I'm not the prince."

"You're not?"

"This is Nary," Jerish explained. "He's my, ah . . ."

They all waited, but Jerish was at a loss as he ran the possibilities through his head, unsure which would be best.

"How old are you?" Nevrik asked Jerish.

"Twenty-three."

"So, eleven years older." The prince pondered this. "Okay, I could be your kid brother or your nephew—even a cousin, I suppose. Technically, I could also be your servant—but I'm not too thrilled with that one. I could also be an orphan. Maybe you killed my widower father in a duel and now feel obligated to take care of me. The poor old man, we were barely scraping by selling pocket lint to tailor shops when you came along and butchered him right in front of me. Mother long dead from a tragic seaside cliff fall, and all my brothers and sisters lost to the pox, what else was I to do? I had no choice but to obey my dear old dad's murderer, now suffering from the overwhelming guilt of slaughtering a defenseless man."

"I don't think *I'm* thrilled with being a murderer," Jerish said. "An older brother I could handle better."

"You don't look alike enough to be brothers," Sadarshakar pointed out.

"The prince would need to be your nephew—the son of your ten-years-older brother, who married a *myr*," Hanis said.

They all stared.

Hanis frowned. "Don't look at me. The features are on His Highness's face. Not pronounced enough to be the son of a Frhey, but obviously a watered-down version—a myr."

"Hanis!" Sadarshakar exclaimed in horror.

"No, no, he's right," Nevrik said. "We need to account for the Fhrey blood in me, so either my father or mother needs to be of Fhrey descent. Given my real mother is human and my father is the one with the Fhrey linage, it might be better to switch those. So I guess I'm Nary, Jerish's nephew—the product of his ten-years-older brother and sister-in-law who—"

They were passing beneath a small stand of birch trees when a host of sparrows burst into flight. Jerish assumed they had startled the flock, only to notice the sky filling with birds launching from trees all around.

"Look at that!" Nevrik said, his head tilted back, eyes following the feathered clouds as they darted in a sloppy unison.

Then they heard the barking and howls.

Dogs in the care of travelers heading across the bridge below fought their owners, pulling against leashes. The shocked shout of one man carried up the hillside, "He bit me! My old Remy bit me!"

A sudden crash from the nearby thickets caused Jerish to jump and once more grab the handle of his sword, only to see a trio of deer dart out of the trees a few yards ahead. A buck and two fawns joined them, all racing up the slope, hopping over hedgerows. Somewhere in the distance, Jerish heard the sound of sheep bleating.

"What's going on?" Nevrik asked.

They all exchanged mystified expressions and shrugged shoulders.

Then Jerish noticed something strange about the city below. The entirety of Percepliquis appeared to be engulfed in a strange fog. Only it wasn't fog. It might have been smoke, but it had appeared far too abruptly and was the color of dust. This filthy cloud rose, obliterating their view of even a single building.

Then the sound reached them. A powerful rumbling boom that would have embarrassed thunder shook the hillside.

"What is—" Hanis had started to say when a wave of wind raced up the hillside, slapping the tall grass flat. Trees were whipped, stripped of leaves, then entirely dismembered. Their remains blew with the wind. All that flying debris ripped across the landscape, shredding everything in its path. The water of the Bernum sloshed like a bumped glass of wine, slamming a massive wave against the eastern bank powerful enough to wash away the long line of travelers who had been trudging the river road. One second there, the next gone—hundreds vanished in the frothing water that churned like a boiling kettle.

Jerish had no time to think as the surge raced up the hillside, shattering the trunks of the older trees. Their cracking was loud enough to make him wince. Nevrik was screaming as Jerish threw him to the ground and then covered the boy with his own body.

The wave passed over them with a roar like the growl of a giant, angry beast. Jerish felt his clothes flutter and tug. He covered his face with his hands as stones, dirt, and twigs pelted hard enough to sting. Terrifying sounds were everywhere: cracks, booms, rips, and snaps. Some sounds were deep, others high and sharp.

Then it was over.

In the wake, twigs, leaves, and dirt rained. The air was filled with dust, and for several seconds, it was hard to breathe. Beneath him, Nevrik coughed, whimpered, and cried.

Jerish cautiously got up and peered about as an eerie silence filled the world.

Sadarshakar and Hanis had hit the dirt of the road as well and still lay prone. The birch trees closest to them remained standing, retaining some leaves. But they looked ravaged. Some branches had snapped. The bright blond of bristled wood appeared like gaping wounds. All the grass had been flattened into a strange green carpet. Down below, the bridge was gone, the entire span missing. The people were gone, too. Not one traveler, cart, or dog remained.

"Jerish?" The boy was on his feet, wiping his eyes and staring down the slope across the still-surging river that continued to slosh from side to side. "Jerish? Where's the city?"

The Teshlor moved around the wreckage of a fallen branch that was blocking his view and peered down at the valley across the river. Where once upon three hills had been gleaming domes and rooftops of buildings, shops and homes, spires and cupolas, walls and thoroughfares, avenues, fountains, markets, and the palace that was known as the Center of the World—there was now nothing but a vast crater filled with rubble.

The prince turned to look at him. The boy's face was a mix of horror, confusion, and disbelief. "Where's the city, Jerish? Where is it?" His lips trembled; new tears slipped. Then the boy's whole body began to shake. "Jerish? Where is the city, Jerish!"

The knight had no answers. He didn't know.

"All those people," Sadarshakar muttered. "There must have been . . . the last census . . . I think there were over a million."

Yes, all those people, Jerish thought, and as he did, he recalled Esrahaddon's last words, *"Just make certain you are not in the city when I do it."*

He did it, Jerish realized. It all made sense now, and he felt tears on his own cheeks.

The Cenzars, the Teshlors, the soldiers and the bishop—those who would seek to kill Nevrik, who would hunt us down—he took them all with him.

Esrahaddon, the haughty, irreverent, snide, intellectual easterner who had been so irritating for so many years.

"He lives for himself, Elinya, and doesn't understand sacrifice."

Jerish sought support and put his hand on the naked trunk of a nearby birch, for standing had become a challenge.

"I don't do friends very well."

Jerish stared at the desolation until the tears blinded him.

Hanis Orphe joined them in standing at the brink and looking down at the missing city. While the others remained at a loss, he summed everything up in five words. "The world is forever changed."

Seated on the road, on the southwestern side of the city, not far from Evarburton's estate, Elinya wept.

She'd seen it happen. The entire city destroyed and swallowed whole, sucked down into the bowels of Elan. Thousands upon thousands of people were dead: men, women, children all lost.

Bent over in grief, her stomach twisting and cramping, her lungs burning as her body involuntarily convulsed, rocked, and cried. As her fists tore up wads of grass that she squeezed as hard as she could, she thought she might be sick. Eventually she collapsed, burying her face in the sod and feeling her body rise and fall with each unwanted breath.

Somewhere behind her Cenzar Master Yolric waited.

He had dragged her out of the city—literally, at times. She'd fought him nearly the whole way. But for an ancient, white-bearded relic, Yolric was surprisingly strong. She had clawed him, dug her nails into his hand, might even have bitten him.

He saved my life.

Elinya would have preferred death.

The tears stopped, or just ran out. She imagined that, as with any spigot, it needed to refill. As she lay with her face in the grass, the world was silent. No bird song, no wind-rustling leaves. The world, it seemed, also wanted to be dead, or maybe it was just holding its breath . . . waiting.

Elinya had no idea what the world could be waiting for. She had no idea why she'd had such an odd thought in the first place. It had simply popped into her head. Yet upon its unexpected arrival, she knew it was true as if Elan herself had been the one to tell her.

Yes, she thought, *that's exactly what it's like. It's as if the world herself is so caught up in suspense, so devastatingly excited, that she can't contain it. Something huge is about to happen, and Elan is holding her breath in anticipation.*

While Elinya knew this to be true with every fiber of her being, mentally she didn't understand how it could be. Percepliquis had just been destroyed, perhaps the entire empire along with it. The event of the century—of the millennium—had just happened. What could be more momentous than that?

"I knew it," Yolric said, his voice hardly more than a whisper. "At long last, he comes."

She heard the Cenzar master stand up as someone approached.

Elinya turned over and looked up to see a tall, thin man wearing a simple smock-style tunic and carrying a bag over one shoulder. The bag appeared to weigh next to nothing, and when the man brushed it with his swinging arm, it looked to be filled with something soft—like a pillow.

"Elinya," the stranger said, smiling at her as he approached, "I'm so glad to see you're all right. I had hoped you would be." He glanced at Yolric. "For so many reasons."

Then the stranger faced Yolric, and the smile faded as the two studied each other. "Hello, brother."

THE END

Afterword

And there you have it! Hello all, Robin here, and thanks to the fantastic support from the backers of the Kickstarter (who reached a stretch goal to make this afterword a reality), I'm here to dish about the book and give you some behind-the-scenes information related to the creation process.

Let's start with the elephant in the room—the ending! If you are like me, you've been on pins and needles to see if Trilos/Yolric will ever catch up to his long-lost brother, Turin/Uberlin.

And now we know he does. But to steal from the musical Hamilton, I think we all "want to be in the room where it happened." Still, for those who have read the Riyria Revelations, we have the answers to some obvious questions, but I won't go into those spoilers here.

In my opinion, the best part about this ending is the door it leaves open. Many may already know that Michael has refused to write a "post-Riyria Revelations" tale because (a) he doesn't think he could top its ending and (b) he proclaimed to have tied up all his loose ends . . . except he didn't. A very long thread was left dangling, and it couldn't be tied down without A LOT of backstories, which we now have. Yes, it took nine books to get that required foundation, but now that it is laid, I think he'll want to build on it.

Now before I tempt Michael's wrath by saying that *Esrahaddon* might mean a post-Riyria set of books, I should mention a few things.

First, nothing is guaranteed, and no release dates will be mentioned. This is important because if Michael starts walking down that path, he'll have to get to the end to ensure everything works out as he had hoped. If things go badly, he will throw all of it into the trash, even if that means several years of lost time and hundreds of thousands of words down the drain.

Second, and this is the most important point, is that he will be attempting to write something more challenging than anything he's done before, and it must turn out exceptionally well for anyone beyond me to see what's been produced. The degree of difficulty is both a gift and a curse. The gift portion stems from Michael thriving on challenges; the curse exists because he has an extremely high bar, and there is a chance he won't be able to clear it. But hope springs eternal, and I'm a betting woman, and I think the odds are in my favor.

Okay, enough about what may or may not happen in the future. Let's return to this book as I'd like to share some of my favorite things. For me, the biggest surprise was the new piece in the puzzle about "The Invisible Hand." I'm sure I wasn't the only one who assumed it was Turin, so having that role attributed to Muriel (and all the new revelations about her) fascinated me. This proved that Michael can lie to us about events in the Legends of the First Empire as effortlessly as he did in Riyria. I loved all of it.

Speaking of things I love, I really enjoyed getting a peek into the world of the goblins; ah, sorry, I mean the ancient ones (I don't want to be demeaning toward them). Niblick was a hoot, and I was thrilled that we were reunited with him later in the book. I missed the little guy. Oh, and here's a behind-the-scenes thing. Years and years ago, I'm not sure how many, maybe ten or twelve, Michael and I were driving through a subdivision, and he took out his little notebook and started scribbling.

"What's that all about?" I asked.

He pointed at a sign. "These street names are great. They'll be perfect for a couple of characters I've been working on." And so Niblick and Mashie were born outside the Westwood Country Club in Vienna, Virginia. It wasn't until much later that we learned those were types of golf clubs, but by then, the names had solidified, and Michael didn't care if others were familiar with the terms they came from.

What else . . . oh yes. For those who have read the Riyria Chronicles, you might have been as excited as I was to see a bit about Castell Blythium and the evil that emanates from there. Michael has alluded to Royce and Hadrian's stay at that spooky castle by the ocean, so I think it's safe to say that *Drumindor* (probably releasing in 2024) won't be the last adventure of that nefarious pair. Oh, and I was thrilled to see more of Ruby Finn (whom we met in *Farilane*) and horrified to be introduced to Mileva. I hope to hear more about Falkirk, whom I've been interested in since *The Disappearance of Winter's Daughter* in the Riyria Chronicles. In my humble opinion, these "inter-series connections" are one of the best things about Michael's stories. For those who have only read the previous books once, it's worth going back and finding the multitude of cross-references. Each time I discover one, it brings a new perspective to the tale as a whole.

Okay, I wanted to save room for one other behind-the-scenes thing. While not widely known, I'll officially let the cat out of the bag here. A considerable portion of this book hit the cutting room floor. I don't recall the exact number of words, but it's probably around 40,000 - 45,000. That was primarily done by removing a lot of Jerish's backstory and, to a lesser degree, some additional detail involving the introduction of Sadarshakar and Hanis.

Why is it gone? Well, it wasn't done to shorten an already lengthy book. Michael wouldn't change his story for something as trivial as that. The truth is it had to go to improve the tale. You see, Michael always says that storytelling is like flying a plane. The most critical times are the takeoff and landing. In the version I received, the plane got off the ground, flew along at its cruising speed, and then the story rewound. We started back at square one with a different character. The same thing happened again with the pair of Fhrey from Merredydd. In other words, Michael launched three planes instead of one, and I felt (and he agreed) that this constant starting and stopping was distracting, unnecessary, and significantly hurt the book's pacing. We are making these cut scenes available through another stretch goal of the Kickstarter. If you've taken the time to read this afterword, you can have access as well. Just email **robin.sullivan.dc@gmail.com** with the subject "Esrahaddon Cut Scenes," and I'll send it to you. I should note, however, this is raw writing, and it's not been copyedited nor worked on to make it a standalone tale. I'm warning you about this because I want to set the appropriate expectations.

Okay, two last pieces of housekeeping duties, and then I'll be done. For me, starting this book was a little like watching *Titanic*. I mean, I came into the movie knowing the boat would sink. In the same way, I knew that Esrahaddon would destroy and bury Percepliquis. But just as in *Titanic*, the things we know are only a tiny part of the tale. That said, some may be curious about exactly what happens to Esrahaddon after the city collapses. Yes, we know he survives (as he heard a conversation with his "future self" while in the Valentryne Layartren), but what then? If you don't know, I'm going to guess you haven't read *Theft of Swords* because his fate is revealed in that book. Michael didn't see the need to rehash those details, so I'll refer you to that work if you want to discover more. And no, this isn't a ploy to sell more books. In fact, I'll send that portion of *Theft of Swords* for free to anyone who asks. Doing so won't violate our publishing agreement since we are allowed to share a certain percentage of the book independent of Orbit. Again write to me at **robin.sullivan.dc@gmail.com**, and this time put "Meeting Esrahaddon in Riyria" as the subject, and I'll send that to you.

Before I go, I want to formally apologize to my legion of beta readers. You see, *Esrahaddon* didn't go through my usual beta process, which is extensive and requires a long runway. While I'm always busy, the end of 2022 and the start of 2023 were unprecedented in my lack of time. I had hoped to hold the beta in January, but before I knew it, we were deep into March, and the recording date (set many years in advance) was barreling down on me. So there wasn't a "formal" beta. Instead, we picked a handful of people and gave them an incredibly short timeframe to provide feedback. I know that this disappointed many, and I'm sorry. It simply wasn't possible, and you have no one to blame but me. I'll try to do better for *Drumindor*, which as of March 2023, is now officially done!

I hope you enjoyed *Esrahaddon* as much as I did. We learned A LOT in this tale, and as I said, there's a good chance there will be more in the future. I want to especially thank those purchasing Michael's works through our Kickstarter or buying directly on our website. Retail purchases provide us a much smaller portion of the hard-earned money you pay. So if you'd rather put your dollars in the hands of those who create the stories rather than a bunch of middlemen, then please consider "buying direct," whether it be for Michael's stories or any tales by your favorite authors.

Robin Sullivan
March 2023

Riyria Sneak Peek

Have you read any of the Riyria novels? If not, you probably aren't aware that Esrahaddon is introduced in the Riyria Revelations (*Theft of Swords*, the first book in the series). Starting there would put you on the order-of-publication path, which is the author's recommendation. But for those who prefer to read chronologically, the next book after *Esrahaddon* is *The Crown Tower* (the first book of the Riyria Chronicles). Here is a sample from that story.

CHAPTER ONE
Pickles

Hadrian Blackwater hadn't gone more than five steps off the ship before being robbed.

The bag—his only one—was torn from his hand. He never even saw the thief. Hadrian couldn't see much of anything in the lantern-lit chaos surrounding the pier, just a mass of faces, people shoving to get away from the gangway or get nearer to the ship. Used to the rhythms of a pitching deck, he struggled to keep his feet on the stationary dock amidst the jostling scramble. The newly arrived moved hesitantly, causing congestion. Many onshore searched for friends and relatives, yelling, jumping, waving arms—chasing the attention of someone. Others were more professional, holding torches and shouting offers for lodging and jobs. One bald man with a voice like a war trumpet stood on a crate, promising that The Black Cat Tavern offered the strongest ale at the cheapest prices. Twenty feet away, his competition balanced on a wobbly barrel and proclaimed the bald man a liar. He further insisted The Lucky Hat was the only local tavern that didn't substitute dog meat for mutton. Hadrian didn't care. He wanted to get out of the crowd and find the thief who stole his bag. After only a few minutes, he realized that wasn't going to happen. He settled for protecting his purse and considered himself lucky. At least nothing of value was lost—just clothing, but given how cold Avryn was in autumn that might be a problem.

Hadrian followed the flow of bodies, not that he had much choice. Adrift in the strong current, he bobbed along with his head just above the surface. The dock creaked and moaned under the weight of escaping passengers who hurried away from what had been their cramped home for more than a month. Weeks breathing clean salt air had been replaced by the pungent smells of fish, smoke, and tar. Rising far above the dimly lit docks, the city's lights appeared as brighter points in a starlit world.

Hadrian followed four dark-skinned Calian men hauling crates packed with colorful birds, which squawked and rattled their cages. Behind him walked a poorly dressed man and woman. The man carried *two* bags, one over a shoulder and the other tucked under an arm. Apparently, no one was interested in *their* belongings. Hadrian realized he should have worn something else. His eastern attire was not only uselessly thin, but in a land of leather and wool, the bleached white linen thawb and the gold-trimmed cloak screamed *wealth*.

"Here! Over here!" The barely distinguishable voice was one more sound in the maelstrom of shouts, wagon wheels, bells, and whistles. "This way. Yes, you, come. Come!"

Reaching the end of the ramp and clearing most of the congestion, Hadrian spotted an adolescent boy. Dressed in tattered clothes, he waited beneath the fiery glow of a swaying lantern. The wiry youth held Hadrian's bag and beamed an enormous smile. "Yes, yes, you there. Please come. Right over here," he called, waving with his free hand.

"That's my bag!" Hadrian shouted, struggling to reach him and stymied by the remaining crowd blocking the narrow pier.

"Yes! Yes!" The lad grinned wider, his eyes bright with enthusiasm. "You are very lucky I took it from you or someone would have surely stolen it."

"*You* stole it!"

"No. No. Not at all. I have been faithfully protecting your most valued property." The youth straightened his willowy back such that Hadrian thought he might salute. "Someone like you should not be carrying your own bag."

Hadrian squeezed around three women who'd paused to comfort a crying child, only to be halted by an elderly man dragging an incredibly large trunk. The old guy, wraith thin with bright white hair, blocked the narrow isthmus already cluttered by the mountain of bags being recklessly thrown to the pier from the ship.

"What do you mean *someone like me?*" Hadrian shouted over the trunk as the old man struggled in front of him.

"You are a great knight, yes?"

"No, I'm not."

The boy pointed at him. "You must be. Look how big you are and you carry swords—three swords. And that one on your back is huge. Only a knight carries such things."

Hadrian sighed when the old man's trunk became wedged in the gap between the decking and the ramp. He reached down and lifted it free, receiving several vows of gratitude in an unfamiliar language.

"See," the boy said, "only a knight would help a stranger in need like that."

More bags crashed down on the pile beside him. One tumbled off, rolling into the harbor's dark water with a *plunk!* Hadrian pressed forward, both to avoid being hit from above and to retrieve his stolen property. "I'm not a knight. Now give me back my bag."

"I will carry it for you. My name is Pickles, but we must be going. Quickly now." The boy hugged Hadrian's bag and trotted off on dirty bare feet.

"Hey!"

"Quickly, quickly! We should not linger here."

"What's the rush? What are you talking about? And come back here with my bag!"

"You are very lucky to have me. I am an excellent guide. Anything you want, I know where to look. With me you can get the best of everything and all for the least amounts."

Hadrian finally caught up and grabbed his bag. He pulled and got the boy with it, his arms still tightly wrapped around the canvas.

"Ha! See?" The boy grinned. "No one is pulling your bag out of *my* hands!"

"Listen"—Hadrian took a moment to catch his breath—"I don't need a guide. I'm not staying here."

"Where are you going?"

"Up north. Way up north. A place called Sheridan."

"Ah! The university."

This surprised Hadrian. Pickles didn't look like the worldly type. The kid resembled an abandoned dog. The kind that might have once worn a collar but now possessed only fleas, visible ribs, and an overdeveloped sense for survival.

"You are studying to be a scholar? I should have known. My apologies for any insult. You are most smart—so, of course, you will make a great scholar. You should not tip me for making such a mistake. But that is even better. I know just where we must go. There is a barge that travels up the Bernum River. Yes, the barge will be perfect and one leaves tonight. There will not be another for days, and you do not want to stay in an awful city like this. We will be in Sheridan in no time."

"We?" Hadrian smirked.

"You will want me with you, yes? I am not just familiar with Vernes. I am an expert on all of Avryn—I have traveled far. I can help you, a steward who can see to your needs and watch your belongings to keep them safe from thieves while you study. A job I am most good at, yes?"

"I'm not a student, not going to be one, either. Just visiting someone, and I don't need a steward."

"Of course you do not need a steward—if you are not going to be a scholar—but as the son of a noble lord just back from the east, you definitely need a houseboy, and I will make a fine houseboy. I will make sure your chamber pot is always emptied, your fire well stoked in winter, and fan you in the summer to keep the flies away."

"Pickles," Hadrian said firmly. "I'm not a lord's son, and I don't need a servant. I—" He stopped after noticing the boy's attention had been drawn away, and his gleeful expression turned fearful. "What's wrong?"

"I told you we needed to hurry. We need to get away from the dock right now!"

Hadrian turned to see men with clubs marching up the pier, their heavy feet causing the dock to bounce.

"Press-gang," Pickles said. "They are always near when ships come in. Newcomers like you can get caught and wake up in the belly of a ship already at sea. Oh no!" Pickles gasped as one spotted them.

After a quick whistle and shoulder tap, four men headed their way. Pickles flinched. The boy's legs flexed, his weight shifting as if to bolt, but he looked at Hadrian, bit his lip, and didn't move.

The clubmen charged but slowed and came to a stop after spotting Hadrian's swords. The four could have been brothers. Each had almost-beards, oily hair, sunbaked skin, and angry faces. The expression must have been popular, as it left permanent creases in their brows.

They studied him for a second, puzzled. Then the foremost thug, wearing a stained tunic with one torn sleeve, asked, "You a knight?"

"No, I'm not a knight." Hadrian rolled his eyes.

Another laughed and gave the one with the torn sleeve a rough shove. "Daft fool—he's not much older than the boy next to him."

"Don't bleedin' shove me on this slimy dock, ya stupid sod." The man looked back at Hadrian. "He's not that young."

"It's possible," one of the others said. "Kings do stupid things. Heard one knighted his dog once. Sir Spot they called him."

The four laughed. Hadrian was tempted to join in, but he was sobered by the terrified look on Pickles's face.

The one with the torn sleeve took a step closer. "He's got to be at least a squire. Look at all that steel, for Maribor's sake. Where's yer master, boy? He around?"

"I'm not a squire either," Hadrian replied.

"No? What's with all the steel, then?"

"None of your business."

The men laughed. "Oh, you're a tough one, are ya?"

They spread out, taking firmer holds on their sticks. One had a strap of leather run through a hole in the handle and wrapped around his wrist. *Probably figured that was a good idea*, Hadrian thought.

"You better leave us alone," Pickles said, voice wavering. "Do you not know who this is?" He pointed at Hadrian. "He is a famous swordsman—a born killer."

Laughter. "Is that so?" the nearest said, and he paused to spit between yellow teeth.

"Oh yes!" Pickles insisted. "He's vicious—an animal—and very touchy, very dangerous."

"A young colt like him, eh?" The man gazed at Hadrian and pushed out his lips in judgment. "Big enough—I'll grant ya that—but it looks to me like he still has his mother's milk dripping down his chin." He focused on Pickles. "And *you're* no vicious killer, are ya, little lad? You're the dirty alley rat I saw yesterday under the alehouse boardwalks trying to catch crumbs. You, my boy, are about to embark on a new career at sea. Best thing for ya really. You'll get food and learn to work—work real hard. It'll make a man out of ya."

Pickles tried to dodge, but the thug grabbed him by the hair.

"Let him go," Hadrian said.

"How did ya put it?" The guy holding Pickles chuckled. *"None of your business?"*

"He's my squire," Hadrian declared.

The men laughed again. "You said you ain't a knight, remember?"

"He works for me—that's good enough."

"No, it ain't 'cause this one works for the maritime industry now." He threw a muscled arm around Pickles' neck and bent the boy over as another moved behind with a length of rope pulled from his belt.

"I said, let him go." Hadrian raised his voice.

"Hey!" the man with the torn sleeve barked. "Don't give us no orders, boy. We ain't taking you, 'cause you're somebody's property, someone who has you hauling three swords, someone who might miss you. That's problems we don't need, see? But don't push it. Push it and we'll break bones. Push us more and we'll drop you in a boat anyway. Push us too far, and you won't even get a boat."

"I really hate people like you," Hadrian said, shaking his head. "I just got here. I was at sea for a month—*a month!* That's how long I've traveled to get away from this kind of thing." He shook his head in disgust. "And here you are—you too." Hadrian pointed at Pickles as they worked at tying the boy's wrists behind his back. "I didn't ask for your help. I didn't ask for a guide, or a steward, or a houseboy. I was just fine on my own. But no, you had to take my bag and be so good-humored about everything. Worst of all, you didn't run. Maybe you're stupid—I don't know. But I can't help thinking you stuck around to help me."

"I'm sorry I didn't do a better job." Pickles looked up at him with sad eyes.

Hadrian sighed. "Damn it. There you go again." He looked back at the clubmen, already knowing how it would turn out—how it always turned out—but he would try anyway. "Look, I'm not a knight. I'm not a squire either, but these swords are mine, and while Pickles thought he was bluffing, I—"

"Oh, just shut up." The one with the torn sleeve took a step and thrust his club to shove Hadrian. On the slippery pier it was easy for Hadrian to put him off balance. He caught the man's arm, twisted the wrist and elbow around, and snapped the bone. The crack sounded like a walnut opening. He gave the screaming clubman a shove, which was followed by a splash as he went into the harbor.

Hadrian could have drawn his swords then—almost did out of reflex—but he'd promised himself things would be different. Besides, he stole the man's club before sending him over the side, a solid bit of hickory about an inch in diameter and a little longer than a foot. The grip had been polished smooth from years of use, the other end stained brown from blood that seeped into the wood grain.

The remaining men gave up trying to tie Pickles, but one continued to hold him in a headlock while the other two rushed Hadrian. He read their feet, noting their weight and momentum. Dodging his first attacker's swing, Hadrian tripped the second and struck him in the back of the head as he went down. The sound of club on skull made a hollow thud like slapping a pumpkin, and when the guy hit the deck, he stayed there. The other swung at him again. Hadrian parried with the hickory stick, striking fingers. The man cried out and lost his grip, the club left dangling from the leather strap around his wrist. Hadrian grabbed the weapon, twisted it tight, bent the man's arm back, and pulled hard. The bone didn't break, but the shoulder popped. The man's quivering legs signaled the fight had left him, and Hadrian sent him over the side to join his friend.

By the time Hadrian turned to face the last of the four, Pickles was standing alone and rubbing his neck. His would-be captor sprinted into the distance.

"Is he going to come back with friends, you think?" Hadrian asked.

Pickles didn't say anything. He just stared at Hadrian, his mouth open.

"No sense lingering to find out, I suppose," Hadrian answered himself. "So where's this barge you were talking about?"

Works by Michael J. Sullivan

THE LEGENDS OF THE FIRST EMPIRE

Age of Myth • *Age of Swords* • *Age of War*

Age of Legend • *Age of Death* • *Age of Empyre*

THE RISE AND FALL TRILOGY

Nolyn • *Farilane* • *Esrahaddon*

THE RIYRIA CHRONICLES

The Crown Tower • *The Rose and the Thorn*

The Death of Dulgath • *The Disappearance of Winter's Daughter*

Drumindor (release date pending)

THE RIYRIA REVELATIONS

Theft of Swords (*The Crown Conspiracy* • *Avempartha*)

Rise of Empire (*Nyphron Rising* • *The Emerald Storm*)

Heir of Novron (*Wintertide* • *Percepliquis*)

STANDALONE NOVEL

Hollow World (Sci-fi Thriller)

SHORT STORIES IN ANTHOLOGIES

When Swords Fall Silent: "May Luck Be With You" (Riyria Chronicles)

Heroes Wanted: "The Ashmoore Affair" (Riyria Chronicles)

Blackguards: "Professional Integrity" (Riyria Chronicles)

Unfettered: "The Jester" (Riyria Chronicles)

Unbound: "The Game" (Fantasy: LitRPG)

Unfettered II: "Little Wren and the Big Forest" (Legends of the First Empire)

The End: Visions of the Apocalypse: "Burning Alexandria" (Dystopian Sci-fi)

Triumph Over Tragedy: "Traditions" (Fantasy: Tales from Elan)

The Fantasy Faction Anthology: "Autumn Mist" (Fantasy: Contemporary)

Help Fund My Robot Army: "Be Careful What You Wish For" (Fantasy)

STANDALONE SHORT STORIES

"Pile of Bones" (Fantasy: The Legends of the First Empire)

About the Author

MICHAEL J. SULLIVAN is a New York Times, USA Today, and Washington Post bestselling author who has been nominated for nine Goodreads Choice Awards and has received six Amazon Editor's Picks. His first novel, The Crown Conspiracy was released by Aspirations Media Inc. in October of 2008. Michael has been published by the fantasy imprints of Penguin Random House (Del Rey) and Hachette Book Group (Orbit). He has also been a pioneer in the indie publishing movement. As of 2023, Michael has released twenty novels (nineteen set in his fictional world of Elan, and one standalone sci-fi thriller (Hollow World). His series include:

- The Riyria Revelations (6 books - released as three two-book omnibuses)
- The Riyria Chronicles (4 books)
- The Legends of the First Empire (6 books)
- The Rise and Fall (3 books)

Today, Michael has returned to his indie roots while still providing his novels through retail bookstores. Each novel is launched via Kickstarter (eleven books and counting), where his campaigns are among the most-backed and highest-funded fiction projects of all time. Doing so provides his most-ardent fans with unparalleled author access, deluxe limited-edition hardcovers, exclusive perks, and the ability to read the story months before its official release.

Michael always enjoyed hearing from readers, and you can email him at **michael@michael-j-sullivan.com.**